A Kingdom Forgotten
Book 1 of

By Charles W. McDonald Jr.

A Kingdom Forgotten © 2016 Book 1 of A Throne of Souls®© 2016 Copyright:
TXu 2-019-378
(www.copyright.gov)
ISBN 978-0-9981177-2-0 Print Edition

5th Edition featuring new maps, artwork, glossary content, additional proofreading and bug/error corrections.

Charles W. McDonald Jr.

Credits:

Very special thanks to the following for their feedback and contributions:

John Armond Howarth for the initial creation of Kellen, Goldenbow, Aaramus, Evanyil, Banthis, Rena Rectovich, and a few other characters important in the telling of this story. John helped awaken my creative thinking that further developed these—and other—characters, making the delivery of this work of fiction to you possible. With all my most sincere and best wishes, thank you, John.

The following Beta Reader(s):
Shawn Hudson
Brandy L. McDonald
Nathan Guice
Sabrina Plog
Charles McDonald Sr.
Patricia Anne McDonald

for their very honest and constructive criticism in reviewing early editions of this novel.

Story by: Charles W. McDonald Jr.
Written by: Charles W. McDonald Jr.
Edited by: Zora Alexandra Knauf
Proofread by: Kathy Russell and Jessamine Julian
Cover Art by: Anthony DiPaolo
Interior Art by: Anthony DiPaolo, Wes Rand, and Shady Curi
Interior Damon by: Jonathan Elliott and Larry Wilson
Cartography by: Charles W. McDonald Jr., Wes Rand and Shady Curi
e-Book Conversion by: Charles W. McDonald Jr.
Publication Artifacts by: Charles W. McDonald Jr.

Charles W. McDonald Jr.

Dedication:

Cauner Iain McDonald, my firstborn son;
May he be richly blessed wherever he goes. Dad loves you.

...and the Living Memory of:

Paul David McDonald (1945-1986)
Jo Ann Scott (formerly Jo Ann McDonald) (1955-2016)
Hoyt C. DeArmond (1934-1997)

Charles W. McDonald Jr.

When all that is left of great miracles are the waning memories of distant accounts, now questioned by Men, shall I come to you in the one, undeniable breath of God that your tattered faith be renewed. For in the final moments, shall you need it.

Charles W. McDonald Jr.

Preface: A Reader's Guide to A Throne of Souls

Don't be horrified that there's a bit of an instruction manual at the beginning of this novel. I can assure you there's a good reason for it.

The complexity of weaving the intricate plot lines and asynchronous timelines of this story required the breaking of a *lot* of rules to bring this product to you. Some of those rules involve unconventional capitalization, emphasis strategies, more modern word forms (home-world instead of home world), and intentional stylistic deviations from the Chicago Manual of Style. So, for example, there are many reserved words in this story (Humanity, Creation, Man, Mankind, Humanoid, God the Creator, etcetera). Those reserved words and phrases (such as titles of chapters or novels within this series) that will be consistently either capitalized and/or emphasized for this story and you might think *hey, that word shouldn't be capitalized or why is that phrase always in emphasis script*, but I assure you this is done with deliberate intent and should not be corrected to mainstream standards. This is not a mainstream story!

And I will tell you this for certain: if you want mainstream or establishment writing, look elsewhere. I'm going to give you bold and daring, hidden truths wrapped inside the most unconventional sci-fi, fantasy love story you have ever seen. My goal, at the end of your journey with me, is for you to say: 'I've never read anything like that in my life. And I want more....'

If you were to consider that different worlds might evolve differently, it might make sense that, from a many-worlds perspective, there could be a clash of old and new even when told in roughly the same timeline. And thus, stylistically, a writer must flex his/her style according to the technological level at play in a given scenario from a multi-world perspective. This is undoubtedly more complicated to pull off than most epic fantasy or sci-fi which is told either from a one-world perspective, or a uniform/homogenous technological level perspective such as *Dune*.

The bottom line is this: I'm not here to write like everyone else. I'm not here to placate the whims of the whore Gatekeepers of Deep State to win their phony, lauded praise from, at best, duplicitous and compromised people. I'm not here to rigidly adhere to boundaries established by others. I'm here to bring you something truly new and groundbreaking—but in *my* voice and *my* style. If that troubles you, perhaps you should find something more mainstream (or something with establishment's good housekeeping seal of approval) to read. But you're not going to find anything this thought-provoking written in the dark and intellectual void of the mainstream in the voice of the status quo. Groundbreaking content doesn't follow the status quo; else, it wouldn't be groundbreaking. George Lucas had to invent new special effects methods and new studio techniques to deliver the first Star Wars® trilogy because nothing like it had ever been attempted before. This is the space in which I find myself when writing the story of *A Throne of Souls* for you and for me.

It took twenty-one years for *A Throne of Souls* to reach escape velocity to find its way to you mostly because of my perfectionist standards. The novels that have followed *A Kingdom Forgotten* have required many hundreds of man hours of research and an enormous amount of effort has gone into artwork, iconography, character development, editing, proofreading, and so on. The point I'm making is this: NOTHING about the story that follows will fall into the category of conventional. I'm going to test and stretch, to the breaking point, the boundaries

Charles W. McDonald Jr.

and the very foundational pillars of your belief systems. I'm going to expose you to difficult and dangerous truths, for you to then go and research on your own.

I have written this entire series with the idea that eventually it would become a screenplay adaptation. As such, you'll see scene breaks that provide a 360-degree view of the unfolding events. This is especially true in battle vistas.

These unconventional scene breaks I've chosen to consistently handle in the follow manner:

*　　*　　*　　*

The four-star mark (above) will be used denote a scene break of a brief period of time without switching locations or switching locations (roughly the same time) but staying on the same planetary body.

The preceding flourish bracket will be used to denote a scene break of a large time difference and/or a planetary body shift in location.

A simple carriage return of white space will be used to denote a change in perspective within the same scene. For example, in a large battle sequence, it's important to understand the perspectives of multiple key players as they are engaged in the fight—to see the same event from multiple camera angles, if you will.

I want to be as assertive as possible here: ***please*** pay careful attention to the ***time and location markers when and where they are provided.*** It will greatly help you as the timelines begin to cross over one another asynchronously, and I promise it will contribute substantially to the whole story making perfect sense to you as the larger mosaic begins to paint itself. I'm not saying you *have* to take notes, nor have an eidetic memory. I'm just saying it will greatly help you deduce the clue drops and critical 'ah hah' moments I've woven into the story for those with ears to hear and eyes to see. And those who have gotten the most out of *A Throne of Souls* have had the trait in common of taking copious notes as they read the story. I've tried my best to standardize the following format for the time/location markers throughout:

(Specific Place, Planetary Body, Specific Time if Applicable)

If you look in the Glossary of Terms, I provide specifics on Time Stream examples and what they mean in this story. For example, I give a specific window of time for the terms 'Near Future,' or 'A Long Time Ago.' I cannot emphasize enough the importance of both the Glossary of Terms and the Glossary of Characters! I put them there for your benefit—not mine. There are so many unusual terms across so many different disciplines and subject domains, it's going to make your head spin if you don't use the Glossary of Terms, so please use it. For those who have read *The Wheel of Time by Robert Jordan*, this story has a comparable

Charles W. McDonald Jr.

number of characters in it. Thus, please use the Glossary of Characters whenever you get confused about who's who.

You would have figured out some, or most, of the above as you read the story, but I thought it would be nice not to exhaust your effort figuring out the mechanics of telling the story. Now, we can get to *A Throne of Souls*—Book 1....

This is the Fifth Edition of *A Kingdom Forgotten*. Why? With each new novel released in the series, I re-release the previous novels with updated maps, iconography, glossary content and so forth. I also use this opportunity for another glance at the content to ensure its integrity and delivery. This Fifth Edition includes all of the aforementioned updates and follows the release of *The Rise of Hope* (Book 4 of *A Throne of Souls*). It also includes another proofread pass from a seasoned editor with decades of experience, so I think that will address many, if not all, of the constructive comments in the reviews that I've seen. In essence, my goal was to get *A Kingdom Forgotten* up to my fourth-novel standards, which it now meets. We're getting very close to the end now, and the conclusion of *A Throne of Souls* will be everything I have promised ***and much more***....

Charles W. McDonald Jr.

Herein lay the first breath of God. Woe unto he that is unworthy.

The inscription read on the rough-hewn gold scroll case, housing the First Seal as discovered off the Isle of Fate, by the famous adventurer, Royvan Miral. His was the first expedition to the Bay of Wrath in more than a hundred years, yielding one of the greatest relics the world has ever known—The Scroll of Carnac.

Terrified by his thoughts, Royvan Miral began carefully, reverently running his weathered fingertips over the ominous warning in floating script on the gold outer casing—contemplating the disastrous. His senses coming about him, he brushed aside thoughts of just the slightest peek, slipping the relic into his leather satchel before casting the tent flap aside to exit. A stiff easterly breeze met him head-on as he faced the elements, whipping his long, brown locks against the sides of his chiseled, road-worn features. Time had come to leave, though he knew not where. *East*, he felt as he peered in that direction—his eyes seeing beyond the horizon, perhaps towards the oldest of the Nine Kingdoms.

Walking to his mount with his pack in tow, Royvan Miral never looked back at the words he had etched into the dirt floor with a wyrmwood branch....

Charles W. McDonald Jr.

Contents

Charles W. McDonald Jr.

Charles W. McDonald Jr.

This Edition's Last Modified Date:
March 26, 2021

Charles W. McDonald Jr.

Maps:

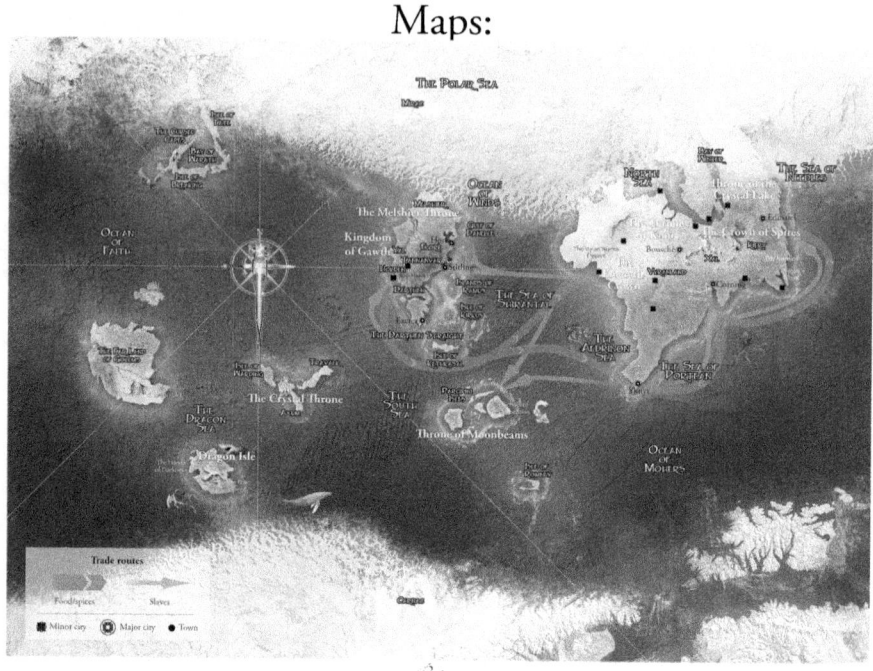

Charles W. McDonald Jr.

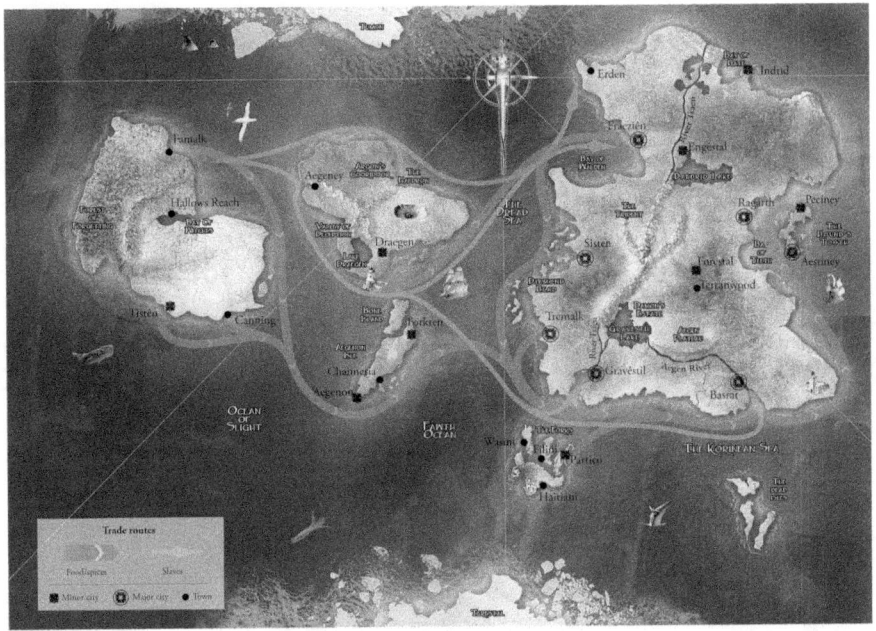

Kalewa

Charles W. McDonald Jr.

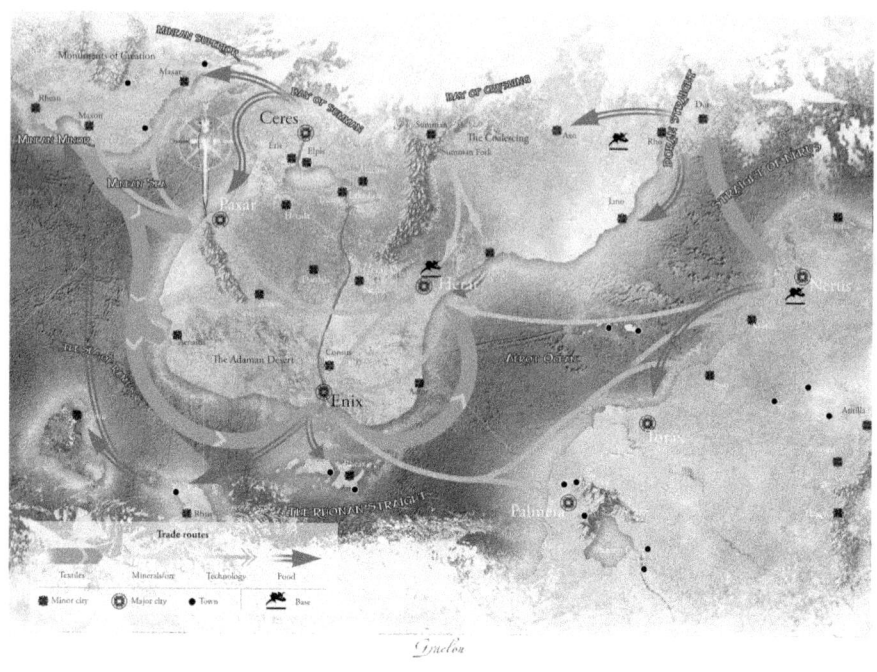

Charles W. McDonald Jr.

Eden

Charles W. McDonald Jr.

Pre-Flood Terran

Charles W. McDonald Jr.

Damon of Basrat - The Dark Knight of Magic

Damon the Banished - The Dark Knight of Magic

Charles W. McDonald Jr.

Prologue: The Unspeakable Memory

(Damon's Manor, Kaleion, A Long Time Ago)

A soft, transparent orb, floating just over his head and forward of his right brow, produced a pale but substantive candleless flame, seemingly burning inside its oxygenless environment, whilst he feverishly worked on something he truly feared successful. No pen nor inkwell adorned his desk, yet words and symbols appeared on the lambskin parchment before him as he gated his terrifying plot through his right index finger, now traversing the page left to right, down, then left to right again, and again—each fingernail like unto living, liquid gold dust. Each character seemed to burn itself into existence from nothing. Talented was not the right word for him. Unique. Dangerous. Ruthless. God-like. Those were all far more fitting descriptions for this...what one might call a man.

Charles W. McDonald Jr.

Damon sat shirtless at his desk; his muscular torso radiant from the Arcane light brought into existence by his own thought. Ever-so-faint scarring became visible about his chest, shoulders, and back as his *Light Orb* began traversing from his right brow to a spot just to the right of his face, responding to his will. His charcoal, herringbone silk pants clung more to his sweat than his lean, hard, caucasian body. Black bangs hung down across furrowed brow and the black irises of his eyes—*black mirrors of the soul.*

The scent of slow-burn sparkling cinnamon candles perfumed his nostrils that flared with purpose and malice of forethought. He knew he would pay a heavy toll for this but there was no abyssal bottom to the well of his revenge, for all things heinous and malevolent seemed justified at this point.

He recalled others telling of spells they had created—spells that had taken months, years, and even most of their adult lives to manifest. This was but night one, and it was nearly finished. One might call it inspired work, but only if they knew nothing of its intent or true impact. Far from inspirational, this was something that would reshape reality, making it in his own image. No smile, nor frown, crossed his face or lips—only a thin pressed, hard line of focus and most lethal gravity.

Now gating the last symbol into the parchment, Damon did something he had not done in hours—breathe. Sitting back in his chair, the *Light Orb* still hovered to give him light, yet did not move with him as he sunk into his chair seeking a level of comfort. Suddenly another symbol began burning itself into the paper, at the top of the spell; a symbol he knew far too well, but had not, himself, instantiated. Looking around his secret study, not expecting to find anyone or anything, he took another heavy breath. The symbol was more than calling card enough—the seal of Banthis. *Her acknowledgment perhaps*, thinking to himself. Now, even more certain it would work when he tested it tomorrow, Damon did fear that possibility—*no* that probability. Yet he wanted it too. His future with Banthis was worth risking everything now that the love of his life, and his purpose that thrived with her, lived no more. That thought—more than any other—justified the *hate* born in this spell.

Slowly tracing the name of the spell at the top of the page, then Banthis' seal, Damon contemplated the *fork of consequences* before him and where this would all lead.

It had all started with an enemy of course, as most things do. One couldn't walk through life without making a few here and there, unless one's life proved inconsequential. Chara had been a thorn, and an imminent threat in his life, for far too long. He had allowed the escalation of his war with her to cost him great treasure, blood, and toil. And the most precious cost of all in Dallia. It had to come to an end. And an end it would soon find.

Charles W. McDonald Jr.

*   *   *   *

Dawn came fast, even without sleep. Damon needed something for his test that wouldn't be available 'til morning—moreover, he needed *someone*. There, sitting on a pale stone bench just outside the citadel's walls bathed in the morning rays of the Kaleion sun. She might not yet have been ten years of age—*still prelude the age of innocence*, he believed. Beautifully delicate, curly golden bangs hiding the brightest green eyes, with full and radiant cheeks; she was so very full of life. She bore the hallmark of being well cared for—not royalty, but certainly not commoner either. She had eaten recently and eaten well. Her cream dress, with hearts of fire, passed her knees in elegant, pleated folds of childhood. Pulling her precious doll into her hands in a loving embrace, it quickly became the sole focus of her attention—and her distraction.

She's the one, Damon committed to himself, walking closer but non-threatening. Not close enough to harm, or so she must have thought—if even her innocence allowed her to think of threats at this age. Walking towards the gate of the great citadel of Basrat, the girl bearing slightly off to his left, he cast. Without a sound and just the slightest motion of his right hand, the beautiful little girl was gone, leaving only a small symbol of ash, in the shape of winged female, where her feet would have been—the seal of Banthis. He felt a sharp, pernicious crackle in the air all around him, traversing the ground with him as the terrain split under his feet with a small crack he knew would soon grow. The air hissed around him in faint but vile howls of the condemned. Gritty motes of dust in the Basrat air instantly became rancid with the cruelty of *Damon's Damnation*, creating an acrid taste upon his tongue that Damon played off as nothing.

Calmly walking through the gates of Basrat as if nothing had happened—certainly nothing of concern—Damon could hear the father's calls, off in the distance, for his beautiful little girl. She would never be seen again. Her sweet name, Lis, would fall ill-fated on the destiny she had just been robbed.

A familiar, sensual voice, carried on the wind, whispering in Damon's ear, confirmed the success of this monstrous spell. Banthis in receipt of the young child's soul no doubt. No smile crossed his face or lips—only that thin pressed, hard line. *Damon's Damnation* had worked on its first attempt. It was one thing to kill or to sacrifice a body, quite another entirely to permanently condemn a wholly innocent soul to the possession of anyone of his choosing— this one to Banthis. This was the very definition of perniciousness—malevolence most unfathomable. This was the start of it all—the first rock cast into the water of Life itself. This was the very first ripple in the pond of Creation undone. The forging of the very first *throne of souls* in the fire of Damon's *hate*.

His name was feared already, by almost everyone, long before this. Every living creature, on every world throughout Creation, would fear him now. He feared himself. And the ugly fate for himself he'd just made manifest. Already, those ripples cascaded toward oblivion, carrying Damon atop their waves of immeasurable destruction.

(Damon's Manor, Kaleion, Present Day)

Looking back through his many lifetimes as he contemplated his Master Plan, that was the one inerasable moment for Damon. Many moments stood out, of course, but none like that. He was a condemned man, caged in a prison of his own making. There was no saving him since that moment. *That unspeakable memory* and *that* banned spell had set him on an irrevocable path destined for a justice purpose built for *him*. *Damon's Damnation*, he contemplated all these lifetimes later. 'Twas a fitting name for that heinous spell, not for what it did to its victims as much as what it had already done to his own immortal soul.

Creation precariously balanced itself on the edge of a knife forged from the furnace of Damon's *hate*, and those waves from that pond he'd set in motion so very long ago, with the redirection of that little girl's soul, threatened to cast that knife into the Abyss allowing imbalance and chaos to rule. It was now or never. Damon had reached the tipping point of his very long life, and he had to commit one way or the other. His Master Plan, years in the making, would execute tactically the strategic outcome of his decision. Phase One of his Master Plan would start right here. Right now.

(Graelon Colonial Outpost, A Very Long Time Ago)

Just brought into the makeshift O.R. on a floating platform, the tall, brooding and handsome man of stark and straight raven hair, starry-bright-blue eyes, and chiseled features had a none-too-subtle look about his face as if to warn his medical staff to get on with it or suffer the intensity of his disappointment. Already incredibly powerful, this man sought to be the greatest of all time and if cybernetic enhancement was the path to achieving that end, then so be it.

Charles W. McDonald Jr.

Made of out of a decommissioned cargo ship, the hull door to the O.R. closed with a great and deep metal clang as the medical staff circled him—doing final staging and prep-work for his dangerous and unlawful operation.

"I'm going to put you out now," the aging, renegade neurosurgeon—well past his middle years—informed his wealthy and overly-talented patient, bringing the compressed airgun with a cartridge of anesthesia cocktail closer to the patient's carotid artery.

"Don't disappoint me, Doctor," the tall and serious patient warned, raising his right index finger causing the doctor's throat to constrict as if compressed by great and powerful unseen hands. "And don't even think about taking advantage of my unconscious body."

The neurosurgeon gasped trying to clear his airway as the patient finally released the doctor's throat after making his point quite clear. He wasn't sure how far-reaching this man's power was, but he didn't feel like testing it today. *Just get him done and get him out of here, before someone finds out.* Motioning for his medical staff to proceed, he drove the compressed airgun into the patient's neck, delivering the cocktail that knocked out the patient's body immediately so the delicate procedure could begin.

Moments later, a shaved cranium replaced the patient's long and perfect straight black hair as the amber light produced from a finger-length silver, metal instrument began cutting subcutaneously then through bone into the cerebral and pre-frontal cortex.

A male nurse in his forties with already graying stubble positioned the implant circuit board on a bare, stainless steel tray where it was delicately plucked into position by the fine-grain, robotic operating arm by the renegade surgeon.

A second robotic arm with fine-grain metal framework and attachments began reaching into the meat of the patient's cerebellum to retract the pre-frontal cortex for an exact placement of the implant held in position by the first robotic arm. Operating both robotic arms carefully, the doctor barely had time to react when the hull door was blown from its iron hinges into the makeshift O.R. smashing his male nurse against the far metal wall with a giant thud, blue-green blaster fire chasing the blown door into the room in a violent surge of the law.

Three great, tall, and menacing robots floated into the room single-file through the blow-open bulkhead doorway—their metal having the appearance of being anodized and war-ridden with deep blaster-fire scarring and pitted wounds that didn't faze their movement or abilities.

"WAIT," the doctor protested immediately dropping to his knees, then prostrating before them. "I BEG FOR MERCY! PLEASE...."

Charles W. McDonald Jr.

More blue-green blaster fire erupted from the lead metal Sentinel marred by the most scarring and pitting of its alloy—its weapon directly attached, seemingly fused—to its humanoid-shaped right-arm. It had legs too—sort of—and could walk when and where required, but they mostly floated via electrogravitic propulsion giving them great range, speed, and agility. A product of tens of thousands of years of evolution, it was vastly superior to Humanity in every measurable way.

Now, looking down at the burn wounds that went all the way through the doctor's eye sockets and out the back of his skull, *it* knew they had work to do. Dropping the implant from the robotic arm into its alloy left hand, the lead Sentinel crushed the microscopic implant to dust as the Sentinel behind it produced an even smaller implant from a storage unit hidden within its abdomen. Plucking the new implant circuitry with the robotic arm, the lead Sentinel began operating the retractor exposing the frontal cortex—not the pre-frontal—as it delicately inserted the *Instrument of Humanity's Hate* into the patient and quickly began the process of closing the patient.

(Isle of Romney, 100th day of The Great War, Perion, A Thousand Years Ago)

Pristine, yet menacing, stillness suppressed the inner corridors of the mighty keep—an atmosphere broken only by the movements of two powerful knights, brilliantly gleaming in silver armor with a crest of a golden, fiery sun, a silver moon eclipsing, and a red eagle crossing in front of the eclipse. The great golden crest and red eagle, accented by red and black tabards, marked them as Eldrac's Elite Guard. Pacing to the edge of the great hall, then back to the matte sheen onyx double doors, the two coolly scrutinized every particle within view. Their two counterparts remained stationary under a massive cathedral arch, just in front of the imposing onyx double doorway. The doorway itself bore no hint of any mechanism of entry—only emitting a deep-black hue glow around the doors' perimeter.

The blood-red and black tabards and gold fringe adorning the knights indicated they were of grand regard. Their beautifully embroidered tabards tousled this way and that beneath their two front waistguards as two of the knights continued their patrol—a tour that took them through a vastness of onyx and deep-blue marble that made up the spectral passages of Eldrac's stronghold.

Snowy-white fissures throughout the deep-blue marble tiles allied with elaborately-hued knife-oil paintings in a futile attempt to bring *hope* into the

Charles W. McDonald Jr.

heart of Eldrac's stone antechambers. Or perhaps it was an attempt at the taste and elegance expectant of his newfound position in life. Radiant colors flashed hither and thither reflecting off the knights' finely handcrafted armor as they neared the end of the corridor. Pausing at the edge of the hallway, breaking the unison of their pacing, one of the warriors suspiciously examined something only a few paces away. Raising his visor for a better look, a hushed creak of well-oiled metal shattered the silence. The great veteran soon dismissed his suspicions away as nothing, though the fire in his eyes only burned hotter as he slowly lowered his visor—its highly polished metal making a smooth, precise click as it met with its metallic mate. Again, they marched off together in unison—to their judgment.

Carefully working the mechanical components of the spell with his hands within his *Web of Mirrors*, the comely man of auburn hair and muscular build concentrated, and, with visible determination, cast. Needlelike shards of stone and fire exploding from hidden hands that had, only seconds ago, been turned palm-out at his sides, a look of regret briefly crossed his face as he brought down an anvil of his own condemnation upon Eldrac's men. A sentence previously unseen, yet nonetheless...*final*.

Only now resuming his watch, in sync with his partner and not even having enough time to turn to face the threat that instantly exploded in mid-air, Hollis was scorched alive by the blinding fire that ripped through his body. Horrific pain shot up his spine, setting every synapse in his body aflame, then...nothing. No trumpets. No standards. Just gone. All four great knights, brave and honorable in their own respect, were just another memory of war. Likely soon, not even remembered by any bard, nor sage, nor any written account of this siege.

Tiny metallic and organic residue quietly floated to the cold marble floors in motes of immutable mortality. Where there had been four of Eldrac's best, now there were only a few specs of blood and meager scraps of shredded bone and flesh. An absolute stillness quickly returned to the corridors of Eldrac's Keep as Talemar closed his eyes in a moment of contemplation, for there was much more killing to come.... Talemar's spell lasted only an instant yet left almost nothing that could be discerned as a corpse. It had to be that way. He could not afford the attention that would come from their ability to cry out in their final moments. Any announcement of their presence would

Charles W. McDonald Jr.

surely put their mission at risk.

Within the *Web of Mirrors*, Talemar, dressed in a regally embroidered grey and red shirt with grey wool pants covered in robes of charcoal-blue, visibly embedded their memory into the deepest chasm of his mind. Turning to look at Xaldran's silver pools—eyes that glimmered in the darkness beneath his hood—Talemar sought an end to all this destruction and *hate*. Now entering the dim light of the corridor, Xaldran swept back the hood of his purple robes for a better look around. A full hand shorter than Talemar and of a slender, fragile frame with thin graying hair, Xaldran returned his friend's look with one of respect and admiration, somewhat fighting the morbid and natural human urge to look upon the scant remains before them. He had seen enough death for several lifetimes, and this was only the beginning. Talemar's senior lamean, general, and advisor, Xaldran looked into the steel-blue eyes of his trusted friend wondering how much harder and colder Talemar would have to become. *What fate would their victory bring if all they knew was killing and hatred? Slay thine enemy.... Was it really so unmistakably righteous?* Nothing was ever so clearly murky.

Now a hundred days into this war betwixt *hate* and *hope*, this would be the first truly significant victory since the very first days of the war, which now raged beyond any measure of control, threatening an end to everything and everyone. The whole world knew of nothing but holocaust and misery of war. No, the war was just now under sail, powered by the winds of men's ferocity. There would be far more killing and destruction to come. Maybe even an end to all things. After all, this was the war prophesied to end Creation itself, or at least some had thought....

Talemar's eyes grew colder, harder, as he thought of battles past and those yet to come, while Xaldran considered the battle now raging within his young friend and would-be leader. War was hideous, putrid, and without glory or pageant. And in the struggle to win, the battle to keep one's heart pure, with Humanity intact, fell casualty—tainting each victory one by one.

Warring with his Humanity, Talemar turned his icy glare from Xaldran to each of his friends and Allies in turn, until his gaze fell upon the young woman they held captive—a woman Eldrac would most certainly torture to a slow and painful death if the full of her betrayal were known. At this moment, neither the woman nor anyone dared question his mettle to do what had to be done.

This long-awaited offensive, costly as it was, appeared to be going according to plan, but Talemar knew that would soon change. *Any plan for war was obsolete with the flight of the first arrow. War feeds itself and heeds no plan.* Thoughts he struggled with as an answer he sought kept returning to

Charles W. McDonald Jr.

him without change. *You cannot jeopardize everything for a woman you don't even know! She must die. NOW!* It was not well known what Eldrac *could* do to a Human—the kind of slave, the kind of spy, he could unwillingly make of you—but *he* knew, and that was enough to place the burden of responsibility for what would happen after these crucial moments squarely on his shoulders. *It was enough of a risk using her to get this far,* he reflected—visibly struggling with the decision, tormenting himself, he looked upon each of his friends— not for consensus but for understanding.

Seven others had come with Talemar this day—lameans all save one, who was a bard of great renown—Aeriel. Xaldran, Raghvin, Badril, Kiervan, Esaul, and Mirak the names of the others, and well known they were. He wanted to bring more, at least a few warriors with crossbows for close combat and protection of the lameans, but it would have complicated the mission. This was supposed to be a quick, lethal strike at the heart of their enemy—the world's enemy—Creation's enemy. There was a great deal more to it than just that, but the others did not know the full of Talemar's plans. Today he would bring enough firepower into the heart of the Wyrm to loose even Eldrac from the Dragon's grasp.

None of that would matter if today were only a partial victory. If Eldrac could sense what was happening, it would jeopardize everything. Out of desperation for the future, Talemar snatched the young woman from Raghvin's grasp, her shimmering amber evening robe now disheveled about her body, her long raven bangs concealing some of the cool glare she returned him. From amber to blue to midnight her robes shifted, then quickly back again. Talemar's grip tightened on her arm, cutting off her circulation.

"I have no choice. You understand that," Talemar stated flatly—emotionless—to the beautiful Mora. His stare seething with focus.

"Rid me of your conscience and be done with it," Mora chided, staring with her own judgment, back into his armor of numbness, through those beautiful black blades of her hair. It had already been a day of great judgment for others; *why not them…?*

Talemar's grip tightened again, nearly crushing her upper arm where she stood, channeling into her with trust and belief. And then she was gone. Precisely where, even Talemar could not say, but he knew she would most likely not survive, let alone return. And he knew what had to happen next.…

Aeriel stepped to the front, checking for traps as he moved carefully to the doors. There was no telling what kind of trap a man of Eldrac's power could leave behind, but he soon found out as, with visible frustration and confusion, he looked at the seam of great doors, moving his hands at a half-pace distance up and down the seam of the thick and heavy onyx. Kneeling at the base of the massive doors, his soft brown leather pants provided no warmth from the coolness of the deep-blue marble tiles. Sighing, he reached into the interior pocket of his road-worn, grey jerkin, pulling out a leather-wrapped object. Unrolling the leather, revealing its compartments, he removed a pair of his longest picks. Since there was no visible lock or discernible handle of any kind, he would need something long enough and fine enough to make adjustments in the physical traps between the doors. "This is a bad idea," he whispered to himself as he began to work the traps in series after determining their sequence of fire. The comment was really only intended for himself, but Talemar, Xaldran, and Raghvin exchanged concerned glances from their camouflaged position still within the *Web of Mirrors*.

Both heavy onyx doors slowly pushed outward toward Aeriel, sliding in unison as if on unseen rails, at the collapse of the last lock. Quickly repositioning himself, and the others in turn with him, Aeriel moved out of the path of doors that surely must have been carved and instilled with magic. The threshold was marked with a circular seal made of several runes, shifting and dancing with life inside the marble floor. Inside was what could only be discerned as a vast expanse into nothingness—the edge of the world—infinity itself. Yet only a few cubits into the midst of the expanse and off to the right, appeared a shimmering, ethereal curtain wall, taller than a Titan, flanked by twin, round mural towers with archer arsenal slits. Spectral as it was, it did appear first having a gated entrance, nearly seamless from point of entry to curtain wall, though a great jagged fissure slashed downward at an angle, making that seam more pronounced—as if scars of a great former siege. The curtain wall shimmered into, and then out of, existence.

Talemar stepped under the arch, to the edge of the runes, peering into a darkness that reflected his hard-facial features, drawing him further into the blackness. Even with Xaldran and Raghvin, the most powerful of the lameans, close at his heels, he felt no comfort here, but he knew this was the right place. He could feel it. Eldrac was here.

Feeling the presence of something—or *someone*—else significant, Talemar turned to face the others; someone else was out there—someone he knew. "He's here. Prepare yourselves," Talemar instructed, though he doubted any level of protection would suffice. With more than a residue of trepidation, Talemar stepped over the threshold but found—and felt—himself thrust several steps beyond where he should have been. His black soft leather boots made only a slight echo on what could barely be considered a floor—its transparency revealing deep shifting hues broken by knifelike blades of brilliance—like diamonds moving about a dimmed light.

Now inside the room between ethereal gate and threshold, his senses became confused by the cacophony of mixed sounds and by the scent of something strange—something ancient. It was as if he had just walked into a sanctuary from the cradle of Creation, the sounds being all the souls that had come before him. He turned to face Raghvin, who was following inside, but they were gone. For an instant, he panicked, like a bird captured in a cage. His thoughts must have been exposed by the expressions on his face, for when he blinked his friends looked back with visible concern—the threshold open again. "Are you—?" Raghvin barely got the words out, before Talemar cut him off, "I'm fine," he replied, motioning with his hands to proceed.

"He is here," Mirak confirmed as he crossed the threshold into the darkness. His steps not taking him nearly the distance Talemar had traveled with one step.

The curtain wall shimmered out of existence—this time for a prolonged absence.

"What do you think it is?" Raghvin questioned, looking at Talemar, though half expecting the all-knowing, all-curious Xaldran to answer.

"A dimensional portal," Xaldran answered as if on cue.

"What makes you say that?" Talemar clearly wasn't seeing what Xaldran was, and he wondered what his inexperience was masking from plain view.

"This whole expanse wasn't just created from nothingness; its space was stolen, and I think wherever the space was taken from wants it back." Xaldran's stroking of his chin in contemplation made his words and postulations more weighty as he exchanged glances with the rest of the team.

It was an intriguing hypothesis Talemar allowed to roll through his thoughts. However, sometimes you cut to the truth a lot faster if you assess the man versus the action, and Eldrac was entirely about power and possessions. So, whatever this was, it was either a trap or a path to one or both of those goals. He still wasn't sure why Xaldran's explanation meant it had to be a dimensional portal, but he trusted Xaldran more than anyone, mostly because he'd never known Xaldran to be wrong.

Abruptly coming to a halt as he crossed the seal entering the expanse, Kiervan's red robes whirled about him due to his momentum, slowly coming to rest on his body only a couple steps beyond the runes. Following close behind Kiervan, Badril dared only take two more carefully measured steps, bringing him to the edge of the runes. As Badril peered inside, his hands moved, reaching for a small leather pouch along the thin leather beltline that held his color-shifting robes, indicating his dedication to the practice of time. Channeling, Badril saw ethereal light from beyond the threshold revealing an older black man with short black hair and sharp brown eyes, who bore the mark of seven small runes about his face and neck amidst a landscape of festering moles—disfigured by the weight of his own decisions. Gathering the components needed from his pouch, Badril continued to channel, beginning a chant—unintelligible to even those in his presence.

Talemar had seen him too, as had the others—the old man appearing like a knowing face about a field of stars. What did *he* know that *they* did not?

Xaldran, Talemar, and Raghvin exchanged curious glances among themselves and back into the darkness, when instantly, as quickly as it had disappeared, the shimmering wall was back, this time much less ethereal than before. Louder and louder the level of noise rose, pounding into their heads. At first, the noise was meaningless—like a background of adjoined voices. Then, individual voices that had been concatenated into a cacophony of darkness began breaking away from the group, revealing themselves one by one. Talemar, Raghvin, and Xaldran all exchanged concerned glances as they started to disseminate their distinct messages. Until the last, Aeriel, stepped over the seal of runes, and suddenly the voices ceased. The curtain wall, now completely solid, failed to waiver and shone only with the polish on the face of the stone from which it was made.

The jagged and slashed fissure was now much more defined, chasing down the wall diagonally, splintering off in three directions at the bottom, bordered by the strange blackness that appeared to form the barriers of a room. *A room designed for what,* Talemar calculated, rubbing his chin in contemplation as the others gathered round him.

"I can't quite recall where, but I'm certain I've run across such a thing somewhere in my readings," Xaldran stated, examining the wall at an even closer distance than Talemar, running his hand along the fissure only a cubit from the surface of the stone. It did not appear a splinter of stone up close, more like a cut from something incredibly sharp. "Hmmm," he thought aloud. "Yes, I'm certain of it. I have read of such a thing."

Brilliant, inescapable, pure-white radiance was all Talemar could see... and a voice of immeasurable power coming from the other side of a great lake of crystal. Then, in an instant, he was back before the wall. *Another waking dream,* he thought to himself—*and always the same one.* Talemar blinked, trying to recall Xaldran's last comment without appearing weakened or troubled, but as Talemar regarded the cut in the wall before him, he was troubled.

"Xaldran exaggerates," Raghvin quipped with a half-mocking gesture of his right hand, tousling the grand cuff of his earth brown robes. Not the youngest of them, Raghvin was no child to magic for certain, but he lacked the appreciation and fine countenance that came with Xaldran's experience.

Charles W. McDonald Jr.

The rough edges of his magic found themselves only bested by the coarse edges of his words. With unremarkable hazel eyes and short brown hair, he was, at best, handsome, though he had captured many women's hearts with that beguiling smile he now displayed as he looked to the wall, though speaking to his side. "He's run across everything in his readings at one time or another." He didn't have to look to see the expression of contempt on Xaldran's leathered face. He could feel it.

Chuckling, Talemar pushed his concerns away for the moment, knowing they would undoubtedly come back to him. Xaldran simply frowned at the both of them, shaking his head and mumbling something to himself, or at least something he had not intended for others to hear entirely.

A sudden draft of ice-cold, stale air, enough to raise everyone's hackles, drew all eyes to the wall as Talemar took one step closer to the curtain wall. Again, he convulsed in the midst of the blinding white light and booming voice that relentlessly confronted him in this persistent waking dream of his. And, just as quickly as it had come, it was again gone, but this time, it had left Talemar beyond the great, fissured curtain wall, facing his friends on the other side who now pounded on the wall at his disappearance. It was as if the stone were transparent from his side, watching his friends and vaguely hearing Xaldran and Raghvin argue over what had just happened. Talemar pounded his fist against the stone with a booming thud of energy that only seemed to travel away from the wall, not through it.

Now banging with both fists, Talemar pulled his dagger and thrust hard against the stone, his muscles flexing as the finest metal known broke off at the tip. Allowing his muscles to relax, he released the hilt of the blade, letting it fall to what could barely be called a floor where it landed with a small, muted thud. He could see his friends on the other side, but from their expressions, it did not appear that they could see him. The best he could hope for was that the others would come—and be allowed to pass through into whatever—or wherever—this was. Perhaps this was Eldrac's trap, getting him here alone—wherever *here* was. If that was what Eldrac wanted, so be it. Eldrac's presence was unmistakable now. *Perhaps this was best, after all*, Talemar supposed, steeling himself. Best they did not follow.

Looking around, searching for any place that might yield some advantage, all he could see was vast emptiness—certainly nothing he could leverage. There was no point in staying; his advantage had been lost. It was forward into the void or futile inaction. Barely a choice. He turned, for the first time really examining where it was this journey had brought him. Before him lay an even greater expanse of this blackness that seemed to form its own barriers. With stale air perfumed with the stench of darkened fate and timeless morass,

Charles W. McDonald Jr.

his nose flared at the threat of this strange place. The lack of color made it difficult to perceive distance, direction, and time. He surely could not discern time if he could not tell how far it was that he had walked, or if he could not tell how much further he had to go. *Impossible*, he reasoned. *How am I ever going to find my way? How can I possibly know the straightest course? Straightest course to what*, was the foremost question in his mind. Whatever lay out there in-waiting for him, he would come. Whether he wanted to or not, his feet began carrying him away from his friends, hoping they would find him. Hoping he would find Eldrac before Eldrac found him, or his friends.

Wherever he was, Talemar's experience told him he was very likely no longer on Perion. After walking what must have seemed several turns of the sand, Talemar finally sat, encountering nothing thus far, though he had heard the voices again, this time with unmistakable clarity. They were the cries of his friends, and a voice he did not recognize, "You *will* die here," the strange male voice intoned. *A man could go mad here*, he thought. It seemed futile—neither running to engage the enemy nor running from the enemy—just running.

Hairs on his arms and on the back of his neck abruptly stood on end—sensing movement. Someone was here. Rising, turning to face the threat and preparing to cast, Talemar sought out the threat he knew was about him, yet there was no one. *Blast this place; I'm losing my mind already.* He thought it was safe to sit back down; perhaps sitting would calm him. He could still feel his heart racing, the Arcane coursing through his veins as he held on to as much as he dare for precaution. It was not so easy a weapon to sheathe, nor bare, as a sword, but then sometimes, neither was a sword. He stood there for a few moments, staring into the blackness, attempting to calm himself and regain his senses before continuing. *Continuing toward what*, he contemplated. *What is so important about this place? Surely it is a trap, though like none I've ever seen.*

As if in an attempt to answer, he heard something off in the distance, though it felt close by—unnervingly close. Again, he turned, looking around for the source, noticing a trail of fog leading off into the darkness, or was it leading to him? Stepping back a few paces, Talemar put some distance between himself and the fog that crept across the surface of whatever this darkness was. *Damn this void!*

"You don't have to worry about going in the wrong direction here,"

Charles W. McDonald Jr.

that same strange male voice intoned from not quite behind and to the left of Talemar, still at some distance away.

Talemar turned on the ready, Arcane scorching through his veins—stretching him to his limits. "Who are you?" Talemar challenged, facing the man he could not entirely make out, the hood of his dark, aged, grey robes still unyielding of the stranger's features.

"A name is a powerful thing, and I care not answer such a question given in such disrespectful tone, child." His voice grew colder with each word, impatient and agitated with the final insult 'child.' It was the voice of many men and of none—of many cultures spanning a great vastness of time. That accent was…reminiscent, yet difficult to place.

Talemar collected and assembled all the senses from the stranger's words, paying attention to every detail of tone, nationality, age, experience and implied intent, this time using both patience and respect in his reply. "Fine then. Can you at least tell me why I'm here?" The words came out in an even, fair-minded tone, yielding at least some of what the stranger sought—respect. What features were not shrouded by the man's hood and robes appeared cloaked by the darkness forming the barriers of their existence as if the space borrowed to make this place held a vested interest in his veil of starless-night, though Talemar could begin to make out the weathered creases of the man's face.

"Better," the stranger replied in a flat tone as he stepped closer, motioning with open arms, his vast cuffs all but swallowing the features of the man's hands and arms. "Sometimes you cannot skip directly to the end. If I told you my name, *I* would be at a disadvantage. You see, names hold great worth. They are not mere words to be thrown about," the stranger smirked at that, taking another step closer, delighting in the fact he had not answered either question. Talemar could now make out a chain around the man's neck, which held a heavy wrought iron key in the shape of a dragon unlike anything he'd ever seen before hanging down the center of his chest, resting against the grey folds of wool that made up his aged robes. "So, if I told you my name, what would *I* gain from it? What would you give *me* in return?"

"My name," Talemar stated matter-of-factly. He couldn't help staring at the strangeness of that metallic key around the man's neck. It looked…ancient—like unto a dragon whose teeth formed the tangs of the key itself.

"Your name I already have…." The strange man smirked; apparently the failure to invoke the young man's name was not an oversight, nor of as great importance as having his own name raised.

"How do you…. WHO ARE YOU?" Talemar snapped, feeling his anger well up inside him from his abdomen.

Charles W. McDonald Jr.

"Ah. Ah." The man visibly tsk'd with his right index finger outstretched toward Talemar. "I told you already, names are powerful, and you shan't have mine until you have *earned* it. What would you give me in return that I do not already possess?" Again, the stranger smirked, taunting...toying. He was having fun at Talemar's expense.

With barely a partial motion of the stranger's right hand, they were instantly standing at the center of a ring of nine crumbled Rune Stones, the empty blackness that defined this world, wherever it was, somewhat replaced with verdant green grass and beachside rolling hills that appeared only half in existence. The center three Rune Stones bore both a mark and a shaft as if accepting a mated key, though the very center of the nine bore a shaft looking to accept more of a rod than a key. It appeared an illusion, yet there was so much more to it than that—as if world upon world layered the appearance around them and centered themselves upon this one place. Only a lamean of unfathomable power and experience could deduce what had just been done with a mere thought.

"Do you know this place?"

"I do," Talemar toned with certainty.

The strange mage smiled openly this time, his features now more apparent with some of the expanse's darkness replaced with the color and light of his divination. His graying, aged skin matched the hue of his robes with their loose threads, cuts, and tatters. His eyes glowed red and gold with a seething hatred and contempt of Man. The silver of his hair was a streaming mass of seemingly sweaty, wet curls, and gnarled braids. His skin was like unto the dead—dry, tough, and creased close to the bone with the blade of his own anguish. Yet, this man was not unkempt. He held the look of a once-great and careful lamean, no longer interested in his appearance as if what he'd seen had proven such things irrelevant. "This thing—this key—you seek is a *powerful* relic," the strange man proclaimed, still not answering any of Talemar's real questions. Only generating more questions for a mind already teetering on the brink in this menacing place.

It was the first time he had made mention of the key or the Crown—their reason for bringing the fight directly to Eldrac in the first place. Trying to think of a way to kill the man to take it, Talemar's eyes darted to the object around the man's neck, contemplating a better approach. *No, he could not attack the man now, but perhaps....* No. Talemar locked his jaw tight, clenching his fist hard at his side, his fingernails nearly cutting into the palm of his hand. He had to exercise restraint with this thing posing as a man. Patience.... There was no telling what this thing was capable of, and he was certain the stranger had the resolve to do whatever he deemed necessary.

Charles W. McDonald Jr.

The stranger continued, moving about the projections of the flat stones that surrounded them, fastidiously brushing his robes, careful—very careful—not to touch the ethereal representation of the stones appearing among them. "It was only meant to be used twice throughout all times, you know?"

Finally, some answers, Talemar thought, but he was taking his sweet time about it. It was time to press him for more…. "Why are *you* telling *me* this? Why now?"

Smiling, and obviously amused, the clever mage replied, thoughtfully, "In time, you will come to know more than you wished. In time, you will come to know me and a great many others as well. But, **only** in time…and that time has yet to come, *Youngling*." Stopping abruptly, the strange man smiled vilely at the last word of contempt—another insult. *Youngling* was a word from his day and time—a time long since passed—often used in reference to an apprentice.

The man turned and began walking away, his vision of stones and hillside already yielding to the returning darkness. "You shall not have Eldrac today," the strange man called back to him. "This day, and this victory is his and his alone. His rudder is steady. His course set. His sails filled with the winds of his *hate*. And you shall not catch him, but *there is always more time*." The stranger chuckled at that last and most apropos quip given their location, disappearing from sight in silvery, ethereal tendrils that licked and hissed at the matted and muted blackened surface of the void around them, chasing his exit.

Perhaps it was the retreat of the vision of stones and grass playing lighting tricks with his eyes. Perhaps it had been there all along, but where the strange man had walked away and disappeared out of site appeared a structure. He could only make out minor details at this distance, but it was gigantic, whatever it was.

Talemar paused a moment, thinking and looking around in all directions. The now too familiar darkness was the only thing staring back. The lack of blue sky, white clouds, and green grass was confusing and frustrating at best. Given the circumstances, and the fact he could no longer tell which way would lead him back whence he came, it seemed the obvious choice was forward to whatever the structure was in the distance. Yet he could not help but think of those he left behind and the danger they might have to face without him. Just the same, Talemar set out in the direction of the structure, hoping and believing for those he left behind, recalling the strange man's words, "There is no wrong direction in this place…."

Charles W. McDonald Jr.

*   *   *   *

Painfully the time passed. Or his perception of it at least.... The idea of turning back was like a constant knife in his thoughts. The structure seemed no closer now than it had seemingly hours ago, but at least he could make out that it appeared to be a keep or great hall of some sort. Laid out more lengthwise than depth in his facing of it. At least now he could see the ethereal, luminescent tendrils that appeared to hold the massive gothic structure hostage amidst the backdrop of endless night. It was not a comforting site in the least, but it did not appear monstrous either; *ancient and powerful* was his first impression of the structure from this distance.

Kneeling on one knee, Talemar let out a long, slow sigh, looking down at the nothingness that made up the ground, the sky: everything here. *Strength and persistence*, he considered. Strength and persistence got him this far. *Yeah, strength and persistence got you HERE!* It was hard to maintain focus. It was getting harder, by the minute, not letting this black void get to him in his exhausted mental state.

With increasing trepidation, Talemar's first consideration was *forward. You can never go in the wrong direction HERE. You can NEVER go in the wrong direction HERE!!!* Thinking of the curtain wall, he *did* think of a way back.

"No Love, that is not the place."

Eyes scanning for the voice his heart knew so very well, Talemar turned to see the wall only a few paces away, appearing just the way it had looked when he turned to walk away from his friends, before beginning his journey through the endless night. He could see his friends on the other side, appearing exactly as they had the instant he walked away. Xaldran, Raghvin, and Aeriel still visibly arguing with one another, trying to get through to find him.

"No Love. Please no." Again, the voice called out to him.

Panting, desperate to find her, Talemar turned in the direction of the voice, screaming at the tops of his lungs, "WHERE ARE YOU??? Please.... Where?" The last came as a whisper. Looking up, and truly looking for the first time in hours, Talemar could see the Keep lit only by the luminescent tendrils of fog surrounding it, appearing like a beacon against the backdrop of abyssal night. He may not have known how or why yet, but he *did* know *where.*

The voices were gone, save the one of his conscience. In the first moment of true clarity since this day had begun, he knew what had to be done. Just at that moment, he felt Eldrac's presence stronger than ever, causing him to turn back to the wall; spells at the ready. Through the smoky transparent stone, which composed the strange wall that crossed the plains, he could see

Charles W. McDonald Jr.

the battle before him. Xaldran, Raghvin, Badril, Mirak, Esaul, and Kiervan channeled with all their might amidst a castle in ruins against Eldrac and three other unknown lameans—two female, one male. Amidst them fought a host of swordsmen, archers, and heavy guard. Eldrac's trap had been sprung.

Huge sections of Eldrac's castle were blown apart—obliterated. Wood, drapes, paintings, and furniture still smoldered, ablaze across the landscape. Talemar could no longer tell whether the room that had obviously been created with magic, housing the portal to this plane, still existed or if the others could even see the curtain wall anymore. He wasn't sure if he could even get through, or if his spells could either, but he had to do something. Even with the voice of his love pleading with him otherwise in his thoughts, he cast. *BLAST, he had to try!*

Summoning all the power he could muster, which felt immeasurably stronger here, Talemar cast *Blistering Iron,* sending shards of metal, fire, and acid racing toward Eldrac. If he could just get his attention for an instant, maybe it would be enough to give them the chance they needed. Growing to immense proportions by the time they slammed into the curtain wall portal, Talemar thought it might just work, only to see all that energy absorbed by the portal in the form of the backside of the curtain wall, which brought him to this place.

Again, the voice of his love called out to him, "You cannot help them, My Love."

Helplessly, Talemar watched as his friends were picked apart one by one. He wanted to turn and walk away, but he couldn't. He just couldn't. It was wrong but watching wasn't doing any good either. Eldrac was winning.

Two great swordsmen, Rémy and Garin, battled with Aeriel. Rémy was thought the best swordsman anyone had ever seen, though his morals were always of question, as were his motives, save the one you could always count on—money. Garin was his protégé of late. It was rumored for many years Rémy went through them with great regularity, though Garin appeared different. It was rumored he had been with Rémy longer than any other, four turnings of the seasons. Maybe there was something there to be used to serve him, but he would have to escape here first, and it would be for naught if any of his friends were lost in this battle. He could afford no more losses.

Talemar was sure Aeriel knew them both well and knew that he was far outmatched. The sword was not even his mastery but blow for blow Aeriel matched the two on him, while two of the lameans, Kiervan and Raghvin, battled with the mortals, leaving Badril and Esaul to deal with Eldrac's allied lameans and Xaldran to deal with Eldrac himself. Great smoldering craters, wider than the girth of a dozen men, and man-sized chunks of stone were all that was left of Eldrac's keep. On opposite sides of the rubble, the lameans dueled, leaving Rémy, Garin, and Aeriel to clash amidst the center of the rubble, dancing about the broken masonry in search of the best footing for the stance that would lend them the best advantage.

A quick blow to Aeriel's shoulder from Rémy left Aeriel staggering sideways over crushed stone and metal. Garin quickly took the opportunity, leaping forward, thrusting hard into Aeriel's side. Talemar could almost feel the gash in Aeriel's side watching Aeriel's grimaced expression. Leaving Aeriel for dead, Rémy and Garin moved quickly toward Xaldran.

Desperately seeking more and more power, more and more spells, Badril and Esaul began to look to Xaldran, exchanging frantic glances. The panic was setting in. The tide was turning—the momentum eroding away at them like unto the torrent of a powerful river carrying them to the falls of their unmaking.

Xaldran quickly found Eldrac alone. Just standing there would have been challenge enough as lightning, fire, ice, thunderclaps, and shards of something glass-like streaked from the sky all around Xaldran. Great, writhing, squid-like, poisonous tendrils erupted from the ground all round Kiervan and Mirak—leftovers from Eldrac. *You shall not have him. Not this day!* Talemar recalled the strange man's comments. Eldrac was well prepared for them and he berated himself for allowing himself to lead his friends into such a horrific trap. Perhaps the woman he had imprisoned to places unknown had betrayed more than just Eldrac. *What could I have done differently?* Perhaps he could have swayed the balance, if but on the other side of the curtain wall. Maybe it would have just got him killed along with everyone else. For a moment, the morbid idea was welcome. Death would be a welcome end, but that was exactly the kind of thinking they would want of him—exactly the sort of thinking that could end everything. *No*, there would be NO surrender for Talemar. He had to live. He had to fight. *Perseverance had to count for something. It had to.*

Something was happening. Rémy and Garin surrounded Xaldran, blades ready to strike. A blinding stroke of lightning blistered the dusk hours, and an unheard thunderclap shook the ground, knocking nearly everyone to the ground, save Eldrac, who continued the weaving of his spell. Shifting rubble all but buried Aeriel alive, while crushing Garin and throwing Rémy and Xaldran, headfirst, into a nearby crater—the result of a heated exchange of spells. Heavy dirt and pebbles cast airborne fell back to the ground all round Eldrac as he completed his spell. For a moment, all was still. Talemar could see some movement among the rubble, Kiervan and Mirak trying to get up. Then something caught Talemar's eye. Perhaps it was the sudden shift in

Charles W. McDonald Jr.

the sky where dusk became the short arbiter 'twixt day and night. Looking through the curtain wall to the sky above, Talemar witnessed the white clouds retreat and the formation of something unnatural in the clouds. Like unto a great, dark firestorm in the sky, a massive swirling vortex of fire picked up debris from the ground as it came down upon the remnants of Eldrac's Keep. Suddenly Eldrac was gone, and his Allies with him, save Garin and Rémy. Stone columns, great oak beams, and mortar launched into the air, hurling around the exterior wall of the fiery vortex as it began its methodic, remote sweep of the rubble, threatening to obliterate anyone in its path. Then, only an instant after it began, it was gone, throwing its debris back to the ground below, crushing anything beneath it. Scanning the rubble from where he stood beyond the ethereal gate, Talemar failed to find any of his friends. All were gone, save the broken body of Aeriel. Part of his torso and battered face were slightly visible. A large stone slab lay diagonal across his body, and several smaller stones surrounded his head and neck, revealing only a portion of his soot and ash-covered face to view. He stood there awhile. Aeriel's mouth barely moved, twisting silently—perhaps it was a prayer or coming to terms of sort. Talemar looked around the rest of the battlefield, via the curtain wall, for a few moments, ensuring he burned this scene of horrors into his mind before he would allow himself to move on.

Turning away from the curtain wall and staring back into the darkness of the strange world in which he had found himself, Talemar pressed forward toward the great structure in the distance, thinking of his friends and that one might have been able to survive if he was where he should have been. Another memory of war he would have to carry the rest of his life—however long that was meant to be. That made the keep in the distance even more important than ever before. There he had better find what he had come for. He had to find something to justify this day's loss.

Some places still smoldered now; it had been some time since Xaldran had fled the battlefield in retreat. Now walking among the ruins, Xaldran was careful not to disturb remains he may yet uncover. Garin's face, cracked and still bleeding, stared up at him with lifeless eyes from in between the chunks of stone and marble. Xaldran's face twisting at the sight of him as he continued to look for Aeriel. His thoughts still relentlessly tormented him for fleeing the scene after falling into the crater with Rémy, yet he knew the others would retreat as well. Retreat or die. Though, if there was even a chance for Aeriel, he

Charles W. McDonald Jr.

had to come back for him. Even now, he felt the unseen eyes that must have been watching him, as he quickened his pace, moving to Aeriel's last known position.

"Aeriel," he called out, fearing the attention he may draw. Xaldran's eyes darted piercingly in every direction as he called out again, "Aeriel, I've come back for you. Please, man, speak now."

Soft, muffled coughing seemed to come from different directions, though it was the first place he looked where he found his companion, buried in rubble of Eldrac's keep. Rushing over, then cautiously moving around the top of Aeriel's head so as not to crush his body further with the debris, Xaldran quickly began to cast, hurling the heavy man-sized stone chunks that lay across Aeriel's body, hundreds of paces away where they burst in mid-air. With Aeriel's body partially cleared, he could now see the crushing wounds of the slab, and the piercing injury from Garin's blade. Pools of blood hemorrhaged out of his body from everywhere, staining rock, dirt, and clothes. "You'll be all right," he muttered hopefully, lifting his friend's head to cradle it in his arms as Xaldran knelt in the rubble.

Aeriel lay quiet but still breathing in Xaldran's arms, though his strength evaporated. He could feel the weaves of Aeriel's spirit losing their claim to the flesh of his mortal coil. "I'm sorry," the only words that could come to his mind. *What more could he say*, to explain his actions—his flight for his own life? *How could he have left that way?* The visual tormented him— what Aeriel must have thought as he lay here abandoned and alone to die. His teeth ground in the frustration of his own inaction. The thin hard line his mouth formed demonstrated a resolve to move forward less his excuses.

This war had taken more than its toll in blood and emotions, but now it seemed to be leaching away at his dignity, his very essence of decency, blurring right from wrong. Perhaps that was what they wanted—to demoralize them. Perhaps that was an even bigger victory than trapping them like they had today. Break the righteous into selfish, undignified, and petulant beings. If that was their goal, victory for the enemy was at hand. Somehow, they now had to find their way without Talemar. Even though they were on the brink of disaster, they could not become what it was they were meant to defeat.

Tear-laden eyes leaving cleansing streaks down his soot-covered leathery skin, Xaldran searched the deepest corners of his mind for the one spell that might save his friend, and the rare components he would have to seek out. It would take even more than that—perhaps even finding the one place where his magic soared like the rays of the morning. He had to try, and if putting himself at that much risk was what it would take, then so be it. Damn his very soul, he would do what he must!

Charles W. McDonald Jr.

(The World Below and Between, Time Neutral)

Moss and fungi-laden trees, with a girth the size of a Titan, were all that Mora could see—however far that was. It was so dark, she was lucky to see her hand in front of her face at times, yet the glow of the moss on the tops of the trees gave off a subtle glimmer so that she could at least make out some obstacles down here—wherever here was. She had heard Eldrac speak of such a place before, and those had not been his fondest of tales. Though, she was uncertain if he had ever had any memories one could call fond. During her time with Eldrac, she had witnessed unspeakable events. Perhaps this dark, damp, and sinister place could be a highlight in her petulant adolescence.

Wading through the shin-deep, murky water, Mora brushed back the black blades of her bangs, trying to make some progress in any direction. She just wished she had some small stones, or anything really, that she could use to mark where she had been. She thought of tearing off a bit of her clothing, but quickly dismissed that, given the sheer material of her robe—fearing rape far worse than being lost. It was bad enough being transported to this moldy, damp Hell. The last thing she wanted was to find herself forever lost down here.

Even though it was not cold, she felt more than inadequately dressed for such a journey. She had been in her bath when they had found her—Talemar and the others. Damn them all! Straightening the robe to cover her lush, soft bosom, Mora pressed onward, thinking of how she might get out, thinking Eldrac would come for her as soon as he realized she had been taken. *Or…, perhaps not.*

(Valley of Power, Perion, A Thousand Years Ago)

Turning to walk down the mountain, shivering slightly, Xaldran tried to orient himself after *Gating* far from his mark. It had to be done that way here. *Portals* were not allowed in the Valley of Power, and even *Gates* proved pretty inaccurate. Trying to materialize with precision in the valley below was suicidal at best, regardless of what spell you used. It was frigid, as the *Gate* had placed him very high in elevation. He knew precisely where he was, though he had only been here a few times before.

Charles W. McDonald Jr.

It was mid-spring here, yet he was knee-deep in snow. Jagged rock formations stabbed outwardly from the side of the mountain, while boulders threatened to relieve themselves from their precarious stations above. Peeking out from behind a tall, snow-laden fir, a young doe stood, motionless, looking into his soul from a short distance away. Fearless, it came closer as he reached out a hand to greet his new friend. Its fur was soft and innocent—its eyes forgiving. Looking around, Xaldran counted six other snow-capped mountains within his sight as he gently petted the doe. Four broader peaks, with only remnants of the last snowfall upon them, stood imposing against the skyline. This place was always so beautiful to him, with its majestic mountain peaks and virgin wilderness. It seemed the most unmolested of all places. In a very unnerving way, it had become home to him.

Moving through the snow with difficulty in his soft leather boots and purple robes, Xaldran let his staff aid him as much as his age would allow. His thoughts raced from Aeriel to Talemar to the task at hand, then back through all of his friends, one by one, as if recounting and reconciling life before death. His journey becoming increasingly more difficult with each passing moment as the blame rose out of the snow first claiming and anchoring his feet, then his legs and chest, then his conscience in perpetuity. There was so much more that had to be done and so few left to do it, if it could be done at all now. Now, more than ever, he needed to count on *hope* to carry him—to carry them all. *Yes, hope it would have to be.*

Hearing the crunch of a branch behind him, Xaldran turned to see the doe he had left now following him down the mountainside. Petting it one last time, he turned back to continue trudging perilously down the face of the mountain, but the doe continued to follow.

(Axum, Perion, Tens of Thousands of Years Ago)

The FTL gravity warp drive of their tactical starship had brought them thousands of light years from home. It was time for them to settle this virgin world. They would be left behind to fend for themselves—without technology, without weapons, even without food. That was the deal. They were prisoners after all—hardened criminals in a society that no longer believed in the death penalty and he had already served as much time as his captives felt they could contain him. This was their lasting punishment—banishment on a world where they might be able to survive, but only through the hardest of toil and sweat. *Purificatio via cruciabilitas.* Translated, 'Purification via the crucible of torment.'

His banishment callously carried out by the alloy Sentinels who had brought him here via orders from *The Eye*, Alexelio didn't fight back as their rigid alloy arms shoved him, handcuffed, into the transporter.

The surface of the virgin planet below appeared to only have animal and plant life as Alexelio materialized next to the white sand beaches with the sea actively lapping at the fertile green coastline. Beautiful, lush green grass rolled over the hillsides of the island before him, creating a sense of new life and new home on a world he hoped would prove a new opportunity.

Alexelio's fine, nanite metallic jumpsuit finally settled on a mirror-reflective forest green tint, blending him into the lush and fertile grass as he surveyed his new home. His grey, satin-finish field-displacement handcuffs clicked smoothly before falling to his feet, freeing him—sort of. Looking like a head sticking out of the air, completely unsupported by his human form, Alexelio tossed the hood of his jump-suit forward over his head, disappearing into the countryside for precaution. He knew not the threats that might be lurking about.

Now freed of his cuffs, for the first time in a very long time, Alexelio cast, reaching out across the island with his mind's eye in search of something he knew would last the sands of time until coming upon a quarry of dark granite sarsen stone. "*Ibi*," he thought aloud. 'There.'

He couldn't recall the last time he'd cast, but it felt...wondrous here. This planet was rich with so much living organic matter to source the energy he needed. His power felt immeasurably stronger here. He'd be able to create a marvelous monument here, and this was the perfect place, but food and shelter were the first order of business as the rest of his family materialized not far from him on the lush green grass of a place he would call Axum. Using his natural abilities in *Telekinesis*, he floated toward his family, closing the distance between them.

Magic was forbidden tech on his homeworld. It didn't matter your intentions or usage. Forbidden meant forbidden, and that law, above all others, was very unforgiving. That was there, and this was *his* world—his and those banished here with him. Magic would *not* be forbidden here. Here it would become a vital tool as it was meant to be.

(Axum, Perion, Present Day)

From ground level, the dew appeared like heavy raindrops on blades

Charles W. McDonald Jr.

of verdant green grass, causing each blade to careen under its weight. Brilliant sunlight, casting prismatic rays through the crystalline drops, threatened to evaporate every cloud in the sky with radiant amber trumpets of light, heralding the arrival of the morning. Wave-crashing sounds of the South Sea lapped at the virgin white sand beaches of the Nine Towers. Amid the drifts of fertile green grass, nine massive blue-grey granite sarsens, some broken into pieces, marched about a three-quarter staggered circle, flanked by massive white marble Humanoid statues, half-buried by weather and time. The statues, further flanked by nine quartz-like obelisks, shot up out of the ground at a slight angle, as if leaning on their backs. Each ring marching three-quarter way around like unto a king's crown. The white-capped waves battered the solemn shores of the Nine Towers, accompanied by the wind whipping across the tall grassy fields of sarsen rubble Rune Stones. The entire site had a feeling of ageless royalty like unto a forever king.

In the grassy field, the three center stones, of nine total, bore markings: runes—one on each stone. On each of those three, just above each rune lay a slender opening: a shaft. The center of the three bore snowy-white fissures that leapt and danced with life anew in the early morning light as if rejoicing in the coming of the morning—its shaft looked to be the mate of a rod. The two Rune Stones flanking the center bore shafts more reminiscent of mating to a key. The sacred and holy ground of the Rune Stones lay silent, waiting for the summons from the one voice that would call out across the chasm of the ages. And so, it begins....

Charles W. McDonald Jr.

Part 1: The Sword of Kings

Charles W. McDonald Jr.

Chapter 1: The Fatal Wound

(Dover Castle, England, Earth, Early Spring, Near Future)

The stiff breeze off of the English Channel was much colder than the norm for this time of year; even the seagulls appeared to know something was wrong as they scattered to the four winds, away from the cliffs in great, undulating mass as if frightened by gunfire. Overlooking the famed Cliffs of Dover out toward Calais, the water-laden North Atlantic wind chilled Michael Anthony Day to the core, frosting his well-kept, short and scruffy dirty blond—almost brown—hair. His leather armor jerkin over ringlet vest, with his coat of arms about a quadrant crest of brilliant red, blue and white panels, an anachronism nearly fourteen centuries out of time, made him stand out like an imperial standard amidst the chalk cliffs of Dover. The golden-bronze, heavily-textured scabbard at his side, adorned with simple runes, housed a uniquely longer Roman short sword, made even more unique with its wider guard, hand-and-a-half hilt, and a beautifully hammered hexagonal pommel about two inches in diameter—reminiscent of an English longsword. It looked almost the perfect evolutionary step between sixth-century and renaissance craftsmanship with just a hint of something…more.

Slightly broad and hard in the face though in perfect symmetry and proportion to his broad shoulders, Michael watched the great swells and Atlantic white caps batter *his* coastline—*his* homeland. Even in the early spring, with the clouds threatening to rain nearly every day, it was still the most beautiful place on Earth for Michael Anthony Day.

He loved coming here at this time, to watch the ships from afar, the gulls, and pelicans. Yet as his gaze fell upon a site much further away than merely the Channel his thoughts drifted….

God be praised. We have our king. Those words shouted not too long ago echoed in his thoughts as he recalled the brilliant white light all around him, and a fiery god-like presence unlike anything, or anyone, he had ever felt

Charles W. McDonald Jr.

before. A fire at the crucible of Creation akin to his waking dreams that still destabilized his consciousness from time to time. That moment not so long ago had authenticated him as the one, true king. Not only of Britain, but so very much more....

There had been many others around him and a great sea of glass, like unto crystal, with the booming voice on the other side. It was some kind of ceremony, though not like any of the pomp he had seen since taking his station. He could recall only a few words—the command really, and he shivered at the image of what was to come. Knowing *this* future 'twas not a blessing but a curse. It was an increasingly iron burden, knowing this certainty—an anvil thrown about his neck. If others knew.... *No!* He could not think that. *That could not happen!* Yet others did know. That was, again, prophecy fulfilling itself. *Is there any truth to prophecy?* All things were possible. He was only a man, though king to some; even he could not stand in the way of *this* fate— whether prophecy-driven or not. He was but a reed in the winds of the magic of the gods, and those winds began to blow, cold and merciless.

"Your majesty?" The familiar, middle-aged and rugged voice scattered his thoughts, like the gulls off the cliffs only moments before. Visibly gathering himself, Michael turned to face his father, wearing a stately charcoal bespoke wool suit befitting his station as both Lord of the Realm and Father of the King. Its fabric held a deep herringbone, satin sheen and texture, providing just the right contrast to the shimmer of his well-kept, silvery-white hair and beard. He looked very much the part of Father, and of Lord, yet the frame of his body and his chiseled features spoke more of his years as a field agent and naval commander. Not many sons, in the history of all nations, ruled while their father still breathed. Yet not many who ever ruled did so through means other than their blood or nobility. Michael didn't see himself as devinely chosen to lead because he was a 'better' man. He loathed this burden but carried it because it was *his* to carry. He only knew that mistakes at his level had dire consequences and people could lose their lives at just the slightest of his missteps.

"I've told you repeatedly to stop calling me that." Michael paused, facing his namesake, realizing his tone was disrespectful. Recanting, "I've asked, Dad. Please...."

Smiling as he burst with pride, Michael Sr. replied only with a forgiving look. "It's time, you should be going," he offered, placing his hand on his son's shoulder as he led his son away from the cliffs. "You were thinking of something," he continued as they began their walk back to the immense grey stone castle in the background. "I interrupted. Do you want to tell me about it?"

Charles W. McDonald Jr.

"Just thinking, 'He that leadeth into captivity, shall go into captivity; he that doth kill with the sword must be killed with the sword. Here is the patience and faith of the saints.'"

"Are you questioning its meaning, or trying to tell me something?" He paused, knowing his son and the way his mind worked—tirelessly and at warp speed. "...Or trying to convince yourself of a course not desired but necessary?"

"Dad, only a fool would say, with certainty, that he knew anything like this, but I guess that makes me a fool for telling you because I believe I do know." Michael paused, looking into his father's eyes for something, anything that would lead him to the truth, if there was such a thing. "As King, I cannot allow the events that are about to happen to unfold. My God, the things I have seen, Dad. If you only knew.... I mean, it's one thing for us to talk about it in private, but it's entirely something else to see it in your thoughts every time you close your eyes, or even in your waking moments."

Sighing in frustration, his father paused, "I believe in you, my Son, and I know our time is short, but know this: do what you believe you must do and I will be there, by your side. I held you every night when you were a baby. I taught you through the years, and I think I know you better than anyone, so if you say a thing must be done, then we shall go do it together."

Michael tried to steady the emotional torrent just underneath the surface of his doubt, "Then let's go."

Hand still on his son's shoulder, Michael Sr. led his son as they finished the long walk back up the hillside toward Dover Castle and the silver Rolls Royce® limousine waiting to drive them away.

*   *   *   *

(London, England, Earth, Hours Later, Dusk)

"Your majesty, are you quite sure about this?" Lord Quincy Arthur Billings, commander of White Hall, hesitantly asked while making nervous downward curling strokes at the ends of his graying mustache. It was pretty much all he had left to stroke—more than a decade as the head of White Hall had left him with barely his sideburns and nothing much to speak of up top. Billing's bespoke pinstripe suit, somewhere between copper and rustic gold, accompanied by his handcrafted walking cane and Rolex® watch, spoke to his wealth and power, but none of it appeared to work on *this* man. Michael was stubborn long before his abrupt ascension to the throne. *Now he was impossible!* He supposed he did have a faint glimmer of *hope* while they were still in the limousine, but he could plainly see it was as hopeless as asking a woman to reconsider once she had made up her mind to do anything. "I mean, it's not like there's any bloody going back after *this*, you know. The whole country will find you mad. Christ—the whole *world* for that matter. You won't survive this politically, Michael. You simply *cannot* do this."

Glaring sidelong and pretending to only half-hear his friend's concern, Michael did seriously contemplate what he was about to do. *None* of his actions were ever taken lightly. Billings was a longtime friend and ally; brave, honest, and a tough, weathered bastard—and a sharp man above all other things. If Billings felt there was reason to be this concerned after all they had been through together, then there was certainly plenty that could go wrong. He first suspected Billings was merely nervous at the idea of getting ready to denounce the one who 'gave' him his title. Or rather abdicated and cleared the way for his title. He supposed his nervousness was just, but he knew there was much more to it than that. Billings was never as shallow as his posturing. Billings knew, as he supposed they all did by now, that the old ways were returning. Great machines, computers, robots, cybernetics, and artificial intelligence could do nothing to stop what they were about to set in motion. Faith would have to carry their standard now. They were all mad. All of them.

Oddly, but not surprisingly to Michael, there had been little to no traffic. He had worked with political leadership ensuring capital would be under curfew for the next several days due to matters of national security. The limousine carried them to the front security gates of the palace, but there was no one to be found. No guards. No cars. No service personnel. The gate was swung open wide—the normally busy intersection empty. Not a single person could be found on the streets and not a shop was left open. Everyone was sheltering in place as if the end was upon them. Everything had been boarded up with plywood as if expecting.... Downtown London looked as if it were Miami preparing for a category-five hurricane, or the end of all things....

Michael could feel the electricity in the air; the feeling one gets on the edge of a brewing storm. It was enough to make the hair stand on the back of his neck as the limousine came to a stop at the gate of the most famous address in all of England: London SW1A 1AA, England. Michael's father opened his door, getting out first, scanning the abandoned streets for hidden threats and finding none. A cold evening breeze whipped at the tops of his short-cut silvery-white hair, knocking most of it out of place as he held the door open for his son. Michael stepped out, sheathed sword in hand, tightening the two-inch-wide leather belt that held it on his left side as he began his stride toward the palace, not waiting for the others. Billings stepped out, frowning at the both of them, nearly having to chase Michael down, while Michael's father brought up the rear—expecting the unexpected.

"Now you're not going to tell us some foolish nonsense about having to do this alone." It was a command really, at least that's the way Billings had intended it. He still wasn't used to having to take commands from Michael, for so long it had been the other way around, but this was a time of great change. And great upheaval. They all knew it. Everyone intentionally not on the streets of London tonight knew it. Even the gathering storm knew. Dark clouds coalesced overhead, threatening neither wind nor rain nor sleet, but threatening nonetheless.

Again, Michael returned a sidelong glance to Billings to which Billings had become all too accustomed.

"Right then," Billings proclaimed with a wave of his hands in the air and an obvious vast reserve of sarcasm-in-waiting, "A bloody hero you think you've become. Well, I'll have you know that *thing* on your side can't protect you from *everything.*"

"I know," Michael replied flatly, sounding a lot like a man trying to convince himself of the sort. It was only a tool—as was he. *For who and what* were the biggest questions in his thoughts; he assumed he knew the *why.*

Sighing and frowning deeply, Billings resigned himself, following Michael and his father into the unguarded and open palace.

Now inside the famed place of gold gild and pearl, it was easy to see where he needed to go. The whole interior lay in darkness, save the dim reflection of candlelight off the extravagant gold leaf of the palace walls.

"This way," Michael suggested, gesturing with a directional nod. He caught himself reaching into his jerkin for the weapon he used to carry—his custom .40 caliber Sig Sauer® P226. Old habit, he supposed, dismissing the thought that his Sig Sauer® would prove any use against *this* foe. Frowning at the thought, his right hand fell upon the hilt of a weapon ancient beyond imagination. Built at the cradle of Creation. Candlelight danced first off his coat of arms, then his eyes, as he felt the warmth and energy of the immortal weapon in his grip as it glowed and hummed for him even sheathed.

Michael wore neither of the traditional coat of arms of an English and Scottish Monarch. He had refused to wear the traditional heraldic beast and the Red Dragon of his enemy. When asked, he would never say why. Instead, he had chosen a simple cup from the house of his wife, Elise, and a pewter Celtic cross for his own. His Celtic cross was embroidered in pewter against diagonally opposing white background panels while the cup of his wife's sigil was embroidered in burnished rust and gold against diagonally opposing patriot-blue and blood-red background panels. Many had questioned his decision to dress in such attire, and more had questioned the need for a sword, but they did *not* question his ascension to the throne. Michael appeared to have all the necessary support from all over the realm—politically and militarily. No one had even heard from the old ruling house, save the letter relinquishing the throne to Michael's unique and historic challenge. Old royalty had gone into seclusion and no one, not even the media, nor his staff, knew precisely where they had all gone. Though many toxic rumors floated about their pending 'day of reckoning.'

The candlelight ahead flickered with increasing urgency as Michael felt his breathing slow, his heart race, as his awareness of Billings and even his father fade. He had to focus on what mattered.

Shadows of candlelight, like tall waves off the Atlantic, lapped at them from gilded walls as they approached the inner chambers of the throne room. The flames themselves tilted as if influenced by an unseen hand, toward Michael, from all directions. Hackles stood erect on every portion of their bodies as they crossed the great circular seal of a serpentine Dragon in the floor at the threshold of the entryway into the old king's throne room. The double doors were left agape, facing inward, as if guests were expected. There sat, on a great throne of gold, about a wide dais of white inlaid tiles, a young man, not so much older than Michael. Though dressed in simple brown slacks and a white long-sleeve executive shirt, his aristocratic gaze and well-kept features echoed his noble rearing. Dozens of candles of every shape and color littered the two scribe tables on either side of the room, as well as the white tiled floor, every other tile inlaid with a red dragon or a gold heraldic beast. The flickering light barely shown on the chest the former monarch revealed with a few buttons left open at the top, nor did it reveal the depth of his brown eyes, nor the storm raging beneath them.

An unabated, seething sensation of evil and contempt swept over them, not evil like that of being in the same room with a serial killer, nor contempt like that of a rapist, but something unattainable by mortals. Michael only thought he knew what evil was and having met this man some years earlier; he couldn't believe the transformation into...*whoever* or *whatever* this creature was now before him. This was much different, much more than something or someone he could control with the rule of law. This was immeasurable hatred—an ancient and unsettled debt between Creation and the Fallen or the *Watchers*.

Smoothly moving about the gilded throne with heraldic beasts about the feet and crown, the former monarch sent Billings and Michael Sr. flailing up against the wall outside his chamber, slamming the doors shut behind them with but a slight gesture of his hand.

Deliberately closing the distance between them, Harold hissed in an icy and guttural voice not his own, "I suppose it's up to us now."

Though it had been years since they had met, Michael had never heard him speak like that before. He wanted to parley. To hash things out, but it would be a wasted effort since this *was not* Harold. Merely being in the presence of this...*thing* was overwhelming, and the only thought running through his mind was to *strike*. Strike while he still could—while he still breathed. Throbbing at his side, the immortal weapon of Creation threatened to sear its Gordon Russell-designed scabbard out of existence. The pommel pulsed in the palm of his right hand, threatening to brand him with its ancient inscription from time immemorial.

"It was always going to come down to us." Michael's struggle to hide his fear amused the former monarch—a kind of sweet justice if Harold could only savor it.

Laughing boldly, Harold paced about Michael, never staying in one place to let the terror settle or subside. Michael was *his*, and he would make the arrogant young fool pay for his lack of vision. His inability to sense and see the inescapable truth.... That *he* would rule this Earth for a thousand years. "What could you have hoped to accomplish by coming here?!! If you knew enough to bring *that*," he stared at Michael's side, eyes focusing on the Sword of Kings, "...you must know you are already too late; you cannot kill me now."

"I came," Michael chided, mustering every shred of his emotional strength and determination, "...to do what I must. And, you should already know that." Slowly, Michael began to move in sync with the former monarch about the glimmering white inlaid tiles of Harold's throne room. His right hand begged to release his mighty weapon from its prison, wanting to hear its ancient song unleashed for all the worlds to hear. Tapping his fingers rhythmically on its hilt and grip as he countered the former monarchs moves about the white tiles, Michael occasionally glanced down at the golden heraldic beasts, recalling portions of the prophecy: The body of a leopard, the feet of a bear, the mouth of a lion, and the dragon who gave him *his* power, *his* seat, and *his* great authority.

Suddenly Harold stopped his pacing, rather choosing to walk back to his throne where he took his seat luxuriously, as if to ignore or defuse the threat Michael posed. Tilting his head and gazing past Michael, the former monarch laughed. "You know, it's funny...," he sighed softly in an old familiar voice more *his* than **its**, taking a deep breath, then slowly letting it back out as if taking a drag from a favorite cigarette, "...when I first realized it, I was angry." A slight pause and subtle laugh as he continued, "Why me? I thought to myself. I guess you could say I became madder than Hell about it."

Charles W. McDonald Jr.

Michael swallowed at the not-so-cute pun made in incredibly bad taste.

"But it isn't so bad I suppose. You know the power is quite intoxicating. I've never felt so…," Harold paused again, looking pitifully at Michael as if he just personally realized a great injustice. "Well, I suppose *you'll never know*."

Trying to see beyond the *veil of white* and into the heart of someone he once knew, Michael wanted another way out than what was immenently before them, "It's never too late, at least not for yourself. You're a child of fate, but I believe we all have a choice. We always have our free will. You *do* have a choice." Michael recalled his research into metaphysics and his own personal realization about what was meant by the philisophical idiom that free will was the *first* distortion of the *Law of One*.

"I did." It was a simple resignation, though nonetheless complete. A last moment—and in it, the death of all things Harold once loved.

The way he said that…. There could be no more doubt! Calling on his years of experience and killer instincts, Michael drew his immortal weapon without hesitating the cruelty required to perform what must be done. Its song released, and the voices of all the true kings and gods before him, speaking to his heart, giving him the strength to do what he must. A sudden rush of wind blew out all the candles and all their light as the Sword of Kings shone like a white-hot molten star in the darkness of the void just created. Michael rushed up the dais to where he last saw Harold before the candlelight was extinguished—the Sword of Kings now lighting his way.

Just as the light of his sword shone on Harold's face, he felt crystal, heavy silver, and gilded candle holders from all around the chamber bashing about his back, neck, shoulders and skull as he tried to reposition himself without losing sight of Harold. Now bleeding about the neck and shoulders from his wounds, Michael cleared his thoughts, using his field experience to douse the pain like water to fire.

Rushing Harold in the darkness of his throne room, Michael felt the blunt force of unseen hands trying to drive him backward. Thrusting the Sword of Kings forward, it cut through those dark and unseen principalities and entities, allowing him to close the distance between himself and Harold—close enough for him to strike at last as he spun about the former monarch, shifting his sword's position from his right hand to his left.

Splitting Harold's skull with surgical precision, cleaving off the back third, Michael watched the severed third roll violently about the bloodstained inlaid tiles as Harold's body slumped to the floor in a rancid, dying heap.

Erupting with guttural, beastly howls, the chamber's foundation split at the epicenter of the dais in a great quake that rocked the palace. Tiles violently burst and splintered, falling into a great deep fissure now forming in the floor of the throne room. A hint of something vile made Michael's stomach involuntarily roll inside his abdomen as Harold's lifeless body gravitated to the forming crack in the floor at the base of the dais, while every hair on Michael's body stood on end—electrified! The taste of sulphur-perfumed air bitter and gritty upon Michael's tongue. A hellish abyss unleashed.

Blood slowly ran down the fuller of Michael's blade; its ancient magic succumbing to the thick, dark blood of the most vile, as its metal grew cold and its light flickered and winked out of existence. For a brief moment, Michael stared at the runes running down the length of the unearthly metal; runes that once danced with a magical life of their own now lay static and faded as if the blood was corrosive enough to permanently tarnish even the Sword of Creation.

Sheathing his bloody blade, Michael quickly turned back to the double doors that burst open just as he neared. Pivoting back to Harold for a final look, Michael wanted to be certain his stroke had hit home. Harold's body still lay in a lifeless heap, gravitating into the open fissure. Turning back again to the double doors, Michael gathered Billings and his father, pausing only to briefly check their pulse, then throwing his father over his shoulder like a great sack, while dragging Billings indignantly behind by the collar of his €3,000 suit. From his peripheral vision he felt as if he'd seen someone else in the chamber kneeling over Harold's body—a beautifully forged female silhouette with long, flowing platinum hair, buxom—and with wings.

Outside, everywhere there was fire and destruction. Michael's limousine lay upside down in a burning heap of twisted metal—his driver's body in bloody pieces strewn about the car's interior and the pavement. Even though Michael had seen terrible things from his experiences in the field, he still had to close his eyes and look away from the gruesome sight before him.

Gotta get out of here while we still can! Scanning the immediate area, Michael's eyes fell on an abandoned, faded red Audi® A4 that must have been fifteen years or more out of good favor, stretched across another fissure in the road, its front tires resting on the curb. Someone must have left it where it was, choosing instead to run from the devastating quake that appeared to decapitate at least some of downtown London. The fissure wasn't yet wide enough to prevent the car from being able to traverse its otherwise precarious position. Turning his back to the driver's door and bursting the glass with a powerful backstroke of his elbow, Michael hastily thrust Billings and his father into the back seat of the Audi®. Frowning, he realized a problem—no keys. Kneeling at the foot of the driver's seat, he called on his experience as a field agent and operative in the Special Reconnaissance Regiment to hot-wire the abandoned vehicle as its engine roared to life a moment later. Hammering the gas pedal nearly through the floorboard and leaving tread marks all over the pavement, Michael sped through the broken and empty streets of London as the skies began to darken even more—the Sun blackening the sky as it set on the western horizon. The storm had only just begun—unleashed by the Sword of Creation and the fatal wound he had dealt.

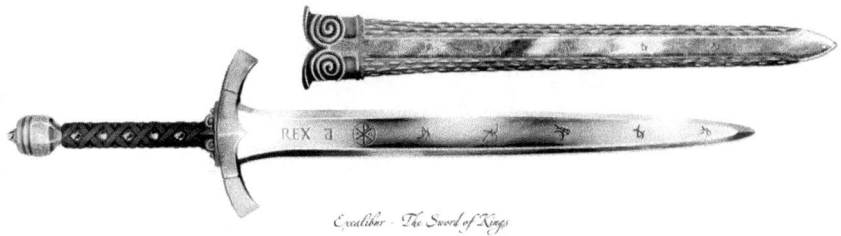

Excalibur - The Sword of Kings

Charles W. McDonald Jr.

Part 2: The Master Plan Invoked

Charles W. McDonald Jr.

Chapter 2: The Void

(The Void, Time Neutral)

Time was held stationless here, void of both pattern and sequence. An endless black abyss provided the backdrop for the asteroids floating through the Never. Here were the remnants of something—someplace—broken to dust a long time ago. Not quite like unto space, not *all* of the laws of physics applied *here*. The hollow light cast into the midst seemed to come from nowhere and everywhere, providing barely enough light to see the immense rocky bodies as they drifted close. Here, in the vacuum, there should have been no sound, yet there were the stark haunting echoes of the spirits lost here between what is, what was, and what should be. These tormented souls were condemned to this place, but it was *their* domain after-all. There were no living things here; no lifeform most beings would comprehend. Such was the veiled place of today's most important gathering.

A barely noticeable ripple in the void appeared over one of the larger rocks, forming a clear dome just large enough for a couple of tall men to move unhindered. Another ripple pumped fresh air inside the newly formed atmospheric bubble, accompanied by a brilliant flash of the silvery-blue light of a *Portal* just as Damon arrived first. Strikingly young and handsome with rough-cut planes of a symmetrical, multi-cultural face, bold and confident, yet even he seemed a little uneasy at first; a little uncertain, as if…. Yet, only an

Charles W. McDonald Jr.

instant later, a look of complete clarity settled in his veteran black pools, vanquishing all doubt. Damon knew. His shoulder-length raven hair flowed like his smoky, herringbone, charcoal-blue mage regalia of silver piping. Damon threw back his hood, running his fingers through his hair, knowing the precise moment—if time were even relevant here. His old acquaintance was somewhere about. After ages of dealing with the man, he could almost sense his presence and the terror that followed.

(Kaleion, Present Day)

The slender and unnaturally handsome man of just over average height with graying beard in fluidic grey robes of gold and silver embroidery with blood-red sashes visibly tsked his majesty with his right index finger only inches from the king's face. Royalty or not; beautifully gilded crown or not, Kellen had the king right where he wanted him. His army, his castle, and his life in ruins at the hands of Kellen the Destroyer, all he could do was....

"I surrender," King Argon pleaded, praying internally, but knowing Kellen's reputation of no quarter better than that.

"*Where is it,*" Kellen asked angrily, shaking his fist in the king's face, causing his grey robes to ripple in response to his *hate.*

King Argon knew the only thing that would bring someone like Kellen here looking for him and he swore he'd die before giving it up, but now that the moment was here, he'd changed his mind...in a hurry. His wife had been the only one to ever use it in the last thousand years, but she lay dead and bleeding on his cream marble floors, split in half by a massive lightning bolt made from Kellen's unique brand of magic.

"I'll take you to it," The king offered, carefully getting up with his hands raised above his head in a surrendering position, examining Kellen's watchful gaze that never faltered away from him.

King Argon didn't move *too* quickly, not wanting to feel or experience Kellen's unique magic any further. Walking through his magic-blistered corridors, avoiding rubble along the way, he showed Kellen to his suite. Walking over to a dark-stained bookcase that seemed attached to the stone wall, he pushed at the left side of the bookcase revealing a secret swivel-door leading to a hidden room on the other side of the stone wall. Inside Kellen found all four walls lined with bookshelves filled with books from floor to ceiling—many of them ancient, dating back to the rule of Durial. Taking Kellen to the far-right side of the bookshelf, deep in the northwest corner of the room, the king showed Kellen a small plain silver rod with no markings of any kind, and a pair of handcuffs with digital readouts. "I don't know how they work," the king stammered, "...but my wife did. I found them next to this." The king pointed to a book in a language he'd never before seen, but as soon as Kellen saw the structure of the text, he knew.... Latin in root at least. Kellen was familiar with Earth's variant as well as his own homeworld's variant, but this was different. He flipped through the pages to the index, "Hmmm," Kellen groaned. "You get to live *today*, your majesty," Kellen reviled while withdrawing with what he'd come for.

Blasting a massive hole through the wall with a ball of lightning, Kellen the Destroyer stepped through the collapsing hole of debris, his spherical shield protecting him as the debris sealed off the room where the king remained. He had said the king would get live for today, and it would take about twenty-six hours before the king would run out of oxygen, so it technically wasn't a lie. Damon's influence upon his conscience becoming more prescient in his old age he supposed.

Tossing another volley of massive lightning balls behind him as he walked out, Kellen ensured no one would be saving the king as the king's inner keep began collapsing in all around the royal bloodline.

Tossing his newfound treasure into a small black velvet bag, seemingly far too small to accommodate any of the three items alone, let alone together, Kellen formed a *Portal* with a thought just in front of him walking through to the Void on the other side.

(The Void, Time Neutral)

Damon turned to face the brilliant sunburst of a disturbance in the air that quickly became Kellen. The two handsome and lethal archmages stood toe-to-toe before one another once again, for the first time in years, and every kingdom shook to their core. Damon's charcoal-blue sleeves, in silver elegant scrollwork and seams, danced about his wrists and arms as he began to cast something shrewd, crafty, and powerful. Black and silver stoles embossed in invocation runes ran down the length of his formal mage regalia, shifting with Damon's motions as he masterfully wove the many complex components together with his precise monotone chants, creating a swirling, shifting mass of webs overhead, producing a dome which encompassed the atmospheric bubble and them with it. The new darkened, web-like dome pulsed with a life of its own, shifting from matte black to a brilliant gold, to blood-red. It appeared, from the inside, like a giant web with the colors moving through the pattern itself.

Kellen deliberately lowered his hood as he spoke first in a certain voice of a madman in an accent seemingly from nowhere and everywhere, "Once again, Damon, you impress me with new spells." Kellen's green eyes sparkled like dark emeralds against the backdrop of the dimly lit distorted shell. His voice was timeless—a myriad of places and periods in time. Though, Kellen wasn't *really* impressed. He could prove diplomatic when the occasion called for it and his relationship with Damon was...*complicated.* Given the many years in absentia between them, he thought it prudent to show caution when dealing with this most dangerous man of Basrat.

"Good to see you again, Kellen." Damon's voice was that of a seasoned and far too dangerous young man, dedicated to an agenda—not necessarily of his own making. Damon observed his old friend carefully, examining him. *For what?* Damon did not know, but it *did* bother him.

Physically, Damon was superior to Kellen—larger and more muscular even, but in their field that was largely irrelevant. He knew it mattered to Damon for some odd reason. Damon was always strange that way—always concerned about the physical. Yet this incessant observation on Damon's part was beginning to rattle—even unnerve—Kellen. He needed to say or do something to get Damon's eyes off him.

"Where did you learn this one?" Kellen pointed upward to Damon's *Distorting Web.* He was intrigued by Damon's new spell, which meant it was time to trade. Kellen was often a source of ancient and unpublished spells for Damon. Damon, on the other hand, was the source of new, original, and risky spells for Kellen. Some, Kellen never dared to cast, and Kellen was thought by many to be without any restraint whatsoever. He was, after all, the mage who destroyed an entire city by casting the same spell fifty times, delayed such that all fifty went off simultaneously; obliterating most of an ancient seaport citadel on their homeworld. A highly unconventional and risky method of casting, but it proved utterly destructive in the conflagration that followed. Thousands died at the hands of Kellen the Destroyer that day, but the reputation it afforded him going forward was...*useful.* Earning him a new title as an outcome: The Midnight Morning.

Damon smirked, whether or not it was from knowing how much discomfort he had just caused Kellen was uncertain. Damon's voice was careful and calculated as he answered his old friend, "Her name is Kylyn. She's a cave elf. It is called, '*The Distorting Web.*' It's designed to both scramble and encrypt conversations as well as keep out prying eyes. Our conversation is safe." Damon smiled again as if there was something he was intentionally omitting.

Charles W. McDonald Jr.

Kellen pretended not to notice, "Oh, a new one. The girl, of course. You have not had an elf since Dallia. Why have I not heard about this one?"

Kellen had made too much of a show of the girl and the *Distorting Web*. Kellen was afraid, and Damon was picking up on those fears ever observantly. Damon was finally beginning to learn how to play Kellen, though it had taken centuries.

"I'm afraid we don't have much time for pleasantries," Damon cut to the chase in a matter-of-fact tone, "Evanyil's plans and mine are now in sync with one another, and we've begun to coordinate on them."

"I want to meet with Evanyil. I think hearing her plans from her lips will help me understand a great deal." Kellen failed to even mention Damon's plans, because he felt like he already knew it. Kellen's ambiguity was intended to test Damon's reaction. Kellen could, after all, play Damon just as well.

"You don't trust me...?" It wasn't really a question from Damon, though Damon's eyes walked over every inch of his old ally as if to discourage a private meeting between Kellen and Evanyil.

"It's not that, Damon, and you know it," Kellen scolded—if carefully so. "As *I* understand her plans, it puts us all at risk of a fate far worse than death. If I'm going to take those kinds of risks, I want to hear it directly from the horse's mouth—so to speak."

Damon frowned, thinking of all the times he'd come to save Kellen, and all the times Kellen had done so in return. He thought they were beyond all this gamesmanship. Trust was fragile between them, though their friendship wasn't.

"Fine," Damon yielded, knowing it damn well wasn't. One-word responses from Damon were almost never a good thing. *Would Kellen be able to piece it together*, Damon wondered. *That could be dangerous*. He needed to keep his plans close to the vest—compartmentalized for everyone's safety. Especially his. "At least do me the favor of verifying what she tells you with me. I wouldn't want her playing us against one another and believe me she'd do it if it served her."

"Agreed." That's what he truly appreciated about Damon. He wasn't an unreasonable person to deal with. You just had to show a measure of respect and latitude with him. Allow him the space and time to come to you and your way of thinking. Some measure of rationale always worked with him, because, for the most part, Damon was a rational actor. If you disrespected Damon or put him up against the wall, the results could be...*bad*.

Snapping out of his momentary thoughts, Kellen continued, "When do we move on Evanyil's problem?"

"Soon," Damon smirked. "Very soon."

Charles W. McDonald Jr.

"We will go in small numbers," Kellen added, burnishing his hands, one against the other, with the glee of a child opening presents. "But the power contained in those few...," Kellen mused, remembering, "...I might be getting senile in my old age, but I think I have not seen this much fun since the Halls of Aaramus." His smile broadened with that reference, as it did for Damon as well. Kellen paused, observing him again in much the way Damon had observed him moments before. It was good to see him set aside his agenda long enough to smile. Damon always took things *so* seriously that he often forgot to have fun.

"I must go now. There are many old acquaintances that I must visit," Kellen offered as he began walking away from Damon but suddenly turned back to his old friend with a broad smile, adding, "Do you think they will remember me, Day?" With that and a sadistic laugh, he vanished with a brilliant shaft of white-hot light. A few bolts of electricity crackled on the surface of the rock where he just stood. Tiny shards of lightning remained active for a short while, dancing to and fro, chasing Kellen's exit.

Damon sat upon the ancient rock floating in the void, pondering Kellen's words. A few lonely moments passed; moments that seemed like hours as the only thing to accompany him were the odd noises inside the *Distorting Web* and the souls captured in the purgatory of The Void.

Notes of cinnamon and jasmine perfumed the void around Damon just before he felt the silky tenderness of a woman's hand running through his shoulder-length, straight raven hair. Damon wasn't startled, nor surprised, by her silent and sudden appearance behind him, even though she was 'the enemy.' "It's been a long time," the soft but throaty tone in his voice expressed a calmed concern in the presence of one of his oldest Allies of a sort: Illirian Starfire.

"Yes, it has. Am I on time?" Illirian's voice was sweet, sexy and sensual—her scent intoxicating and her beauty lethal. Damon could not help but immediately take notice of her as she sexily walked around him, *or around for him*, in a scandalously short white summer dress. Erotically, it revealed creamy thighs and so very much more as her right leg pushed open the deep slit running down the right center of the dress's scandalous pleats, only stopped by a delicate and very loosely tied gold-gild sash just below her navel. Made from some enchanted diaphanous white silk, the material scintillated as it revealed perfect, seductive and soft womanly curves everywhere. Red-gold hair spilled down her white backless dress in semi-liquid waves, glittering magically when caught by the lighting of the webbed shell. She was never anything short of stunning and Damon's *black mirrors of the soul* could not help but follow her every little move.

Charles W. McDonald Jr.

"You were always right on time." He felt her settle down behind him, lovingly caressing his hair and the back of his neck with delicate to-and-fro strokes of the back of her fingertips that made his eyelids involuntarily close in his imagination of her doing so much more.

"How can I help you, Darling? Your message left quite a bit to the imagination. It sounded almost like…an invitation."

"I think I'm in trouble this time."

She fell in love with his throaty voice centuries ago, though she'd never, ever admit such a thing. However, the way her eyes gazed upon Damon and the way he could feel her eyes upon him from behind said plenty. "Well, that's certainly nothing new," Illirian laughed, only half mocking. "You were born for trouble."

"You know about my plans with Kellen?"

Illirian answered with silence, rising to sensually walk around to face him—feeling his eyes wantonly lingering on her shapely legs and taut ass revealed by scandalous pleats that swayed with her movements. Her smile was dangerous and erotic. A grand master at a most dangerous game. He was helpless. Any man would have been. It did not help that his weakness for women was as legendary as his adventures, but this woman could break any man's will. Then again, she was no mere woman.

Damon watched her every movement, her diaphanous dress barely clinging to the edges of her supple breasts, revealing silken inner thighs as she lowered herself to sit within the palpable warmth of his breath upon hers and hers upon his. Straddling his lap, she playfully teased and rocked her body against his with her lips within a wanton kiss's breadth of his, proving herself as unpredictable as he. It was hard to focus when all he could think about at the moment was sex and looking down at a dress that barely covered only the tiniest portions of her breasts did little to help free himself from the prison of his very intimate thoughts of Illirian Starfire.

Illirian was very dangerous, even without considering her extraordinary powers. For several minutes, they stared at each other's bodies and into each other's eyes, wondering, until the moment came that signified their desperate need to kiss one another. Casting his hesitation to the void all around them, Damon leaned into her, caressing her through her sensual dress as he gently touched her moist lips with his own, softly tasting her for the first time in forever. Half expecting the end of Creation at their act—he *knew* their feelings were forbidden—but he could not stop wanting her nor thinking of her. It was a very dangerous game they played. Each time it went just a little further, both fearing where it would finish. Yet the fear was, as the passionate foreplay, exhilarating! It drove them recklessly into forbidden regions with haste and abandon as their kissing intensified to the point of boiling over into something uncontrollable.

He could not help but wonder if she were the only truly good thing he desired, though certainly didn't deserve.

"You know what their reaction will be?" He could barely force the words out past the distractions of her hot and sensual caress of him with her slowly rocking back and forth upon him in his lap.

"Yes...," she softly moaned into his left earlobe, feeling his fingertips gently caressing the inside of her thighs—feeling her bare flesh grow warmer and warmer under the excitement of his touch.

"Do you have any sage words of advice?"

"Don't do it," she recommended as her eyes shifted in that sweet and innocent way that she always used with him. For an instant, he couldn't tell if 'don't do it' applied to his physical intentions with her or his Master Plan. The look in her eyes seemed inappropriate given the fact that the only thoughts going through her mind, at this moment, were anything *but* innocent.

"I have made promises that must be kept," he whispered sensually in her left ear just as his lips touched a most sensitive part of her beautiful flesh right in between her neck and clavicle. His left hand kneading her right breast as he teased and rolled her very erect nipple in between his thumb and forefinger, pushing the fabric of her naughty little dress out of his way.

"Oh God, Damon," she moaned into his ear again, feeling her body start to surrender to him in ways that could not be undone.

And then, a moment of sobriety washed over her from head to toe as she began to contemplate the bigger picture.... Her body pulling back from his very sexual arousing caress of her, while still remaining in Damon's lap. "How do you get yourself into these situations?" She seemed almost resigned in her efforts to keep him out of trouble. After all, she had to. Damon was far too important to the bigger equation. She had to do everything possible, but discreetly so, to ensure he met his destiny and she hers. She was playing God, but then that was nothing new. Damon was certainly no child to be watched over; he could take care of himself with even the most dangerous of enemies. Only twice in their past did she truly *have* to intervene, for which he was appreciative only after venting about his masculinity being violated by her incessant *meddling*. In the end, though, she supposed she was accepted as an ally of a sort. That only left the question: was she an ally, or was she merely trying to clear her conscience by thinking of herself in such a way? She knew his fate, as well as the others', but still she did more than merely pull him from the fire; she had made certain he had power—*lots* of power. And, even at times, she wished she had not, but what was done was done. *Spilled milk*, she thought to

Charles W. McDonald Jr.

herself. *No turning back now.*

"I'm serious. I need your advice," Damon paused for an instant, wondering what was going on in that pretty little head of hers. Rare were the moments where Illirian appeared weak in thought. "What I'm planning will not be received well."

"That depends on who you ask," she whispered into his ear again. "The game must go on, but I have to go now. I don't know if I can stop myself if I stay any longer." With that, she returned his soft kiss and vanished before him. No lightning. No thunderclap. Simple elegance was always more her style. Only her scent remained and the impression of her body in his lap, along with his burning and palpable need for her.

(Paradise, Time Neutral)

Illirian appeared on the outskirts of the Crystal Keep, as usual. She hated materializing close to this place; to say that it was dangerous was a huge understatement, but old habits died hard. She realized her fortune not to have materialized inside of a wall, or staircase, or worse. Set on a vast white marble floor as far as the eye could see, the Crystal Keep was a miracle of architectural character—a brilliantly faceted crystal and sapphire gem eight times the size of the Colosseum set on a sea of white, magnificently crafted from diamond-embossed crystal and extraordinarily rare blue ivory. Yet dread still welled in her every time she was summoned here. Illirian supposed she *could* risk casting to get to the front of the castle, but it was simply best not to cast until you were ready to leave. Besides, they could stand to wait on *her* for a change. Grudgingly adjusting the regal white, grey, and gold robes of her station, she pressed toward the Crystal Keep, ignoring the near whiteout conditions to focus her thoughts on the war that would deliver her message.

* * * *

Stark, mastercrafted columns of blue ivory sprung outward from the chamber's façade, rising some forty cubits, spanning the length of the huge chamber, forming elegant, cathedral archways, low and high, while crisscrossing the immense vaulted ceiling akin to the cavities in between a spider's web. A mastercrafted, inlaid oak table span nearly the entire length of the room—nearly one hundred cubits in all. Hundreds of candelabras flooded the room with wick-and-wax-perfumed light, as did the whiteout conditions visible through the stained glass, cathedral windows that spanned the length and height of the outer wall in stacked pairs. There stood as many chairs as one would care to take the time to count, but only eight were occupied at one end of the table—a huge hearth raged red and orange flames behind them. The old, white-bearded man at the end spoke out in a voice of harnessed thunder, "Once again, Illirian's credibility comes into doubt." His voice boomed through the chamber from floor to ceiling, but the bright aura about him masked most of his features making them hard to discern—save that of his immeasurable age.

Others around the table were openly visible, and all beautiful to behold. In all, there were four men and three women, plus the one gentleman at the end—the Chairman. The men sat to one side, their backs to the cathedral windows, the women to the opposing side. Each dressed in differing attire befitting their station: some white and gold, some grey and red, and some black and silver. Yet all appeared stately, prominent people of wealth and power. It held the character of a council and the morass of bureaucracy with the only certainty a complicated and quite possibly, duplicitous, outcome.

"Illirian's credibility is not at issue. She is merely influenced by him because you have ordered her to watch him so closely—to guide him to his 'natural' entropy as you instructed. She cannot operate in such proximity to him without her influencing him and him her. Damon has proven over the years to be a very influential man. He has learned well the art of manipulation, and now he seeks to use it on the very woman who taught it to him," the seemingly ageless woman, closest to the fire scolded the Chairman—if carefully so. Her eyes sequentially darted from one council member to the next as if to gauge her own performance. Though some in the room were uncertain the target of her incense. The woman's radiant hair and brilliant eyes were like unto liquified gold, shimmering in the awe-inspiring light. Age was a difficult attribute to measure amongst people of obvious ability to unnaturally extend their own lifespan. Though, she appeared the youngest and most beautiful of the women in attendance, examining each of the others closely after her statement, ready to pounce on those who dare offer a dissenting opinion.

"I did not order her," The Chairman countered. *A lie? Perhaps....* *Strongly persuaded* might be a more apt description but such details were not necessary in *this* company and *this* forum, where *his* word ruled. "I chose her because she was the *only* choice to be made. ***That*** man trusts no one—certainly none of us. But Illirian, he trusts for reasons *you* do not understand, Youngling."

"However you choose to word it, you forced Illirian to make friends

Charles W. McDonald Jr.

with the enemy then complained about how close she is to him. It sounds to me that Illirian has done precisely as you asked, to a fair degree of excellence, rather than failing miserably as you would have us believe through your spin on the facts." This time, the others watched intently—some with hushed whispers and downward, disapproving glares—expecting judgment upon her to be swift. Yet, a few tense moments passed in uncomfortable silence. He knew it useless—arguing the failure of a woman with another woman.

*   *   *   *

A longer walk than usual, this time, Illirian noticed. She stood at the foot of the enormous, studded oak doors of the Chairman's audience hall within the Crystal Keep. The main doors themselves spanned some forty cubits into the air with massively thick header beams that were an extension of headers supported by the blue ivory columns, colonnade and cathedral archways that offered the most pronounced feature of the chamber's interior façade. That lengthwise part of the chamber which faced the interior of the wider Crystal Keep. It seemed odd—the massive, studded doors leading to a chamber seemingly accessible via the open-air archways, but then not everything was as it seemed.

The colossal oak doors smoothly and fluidically opened for her as if on cue, making very little noise as she was greeted by a myriad of lights, created by more stained glass, candelabras, and a single gatehouse-sized fireplace at the Chairman's end of the room. Everyone was clearly visible, save the Chairman at the end, who spoke first, "What news do you bring us, Illirian Starfire: Ruler of Rod of the Nine, Watcher of the Runes of Fate, and Guardian of *Durial's Eye?*"

Illirian paused only for a moment then offered, "I believe *Damon the Banished* to be on the verge of what we feared was not possible."

Muttering erupted from both sides of the table. Illirian couldn't quite make any of it out, but she knew what they were thinking; that it would not be long now.

"Be silent," the Chairman's thunderous voice commanded in deafening and fateful, throaty tones. After the echoes of his command had chased the separate conversations from his audience hall, the chamber fell silent again. Tense and uneasy they all sat. Breathlessly anticipating Illirian's next report.

Even without being able to see all of his features, one could tell the Chairman was deep in thought. Suddenly he broke the silence voicing his own internal deliberation, "We have known this moment would come and have

Charles W. McDonald Jr.

prepared for it. The mortals must learn to fight for themselves. There is no prophecy to guide us along a path never before charted, yet we have planned for this and must not find ourselves in panic," he paused briefly, looking at the others and then back at Illirian. "Illirian. Hear me! You will stay away from Damon henceforth. His path is set—his destruction certain—his justice purpose-built. You will perish, and the remainder of your immortality will be spent in torment if you continue your little personal tête-à-tête with this man. He is lost! Do not let him influence you any further. I fear you are...." He hesitated to say it, but he didn't have to. He had already said enough to make Illirian's blood boil. Station or not, a line had been crossed that was...unacceptable!

Shock marred Illirian's lovely face; her self-control vanquished, "You *arrogant, self-important, pompous bastard!* How dare *you* speak to **me** like.... I was a member of this council when you were but lost in the wilderness. You will not dare to speak to me in such a manner ever again! Do you understand me?!" Outrage consumed her, but caution began to creep in as well. This was the Chairman, and there was a chain of command—even for her! She'd made her point quite ferociously. Her body flooded with Arcane and much more as she prepared herself—for what, she didn't know. "Oh, it doesn't surprise me, coming from you, but just to set the record straight: **I** can handle him! I **will** handle him! Nevertheless, we should have better things to do than argue amongst ourselves." Icy-fingered silence crept in, again. Illirian loved getting the upper hand on the council, and she could feel it palpably within her grasp as the silence held everyone captive in introspection. She knew she had given him a satisfactory thrashing and hoped he would not snap back at her from his seat of *great* authority. She would have to show herself more mature than they. "I will, of course, do as you suggest," Illirian lied, noting to herself he hadn't suggested. "But isn't he—as you said—*too* valuable?" She had no intention of doing such a thing, of course. She could not and would not allow Damon to walk his course alone. Doing so had consequences beyond measure, and with her own immortality at risk, she wasn't about to let fate guide Damon unaided. *Better to fail through action than inaction,* she accepted internally. Damon needed subtle guidance to go where he must, but guidance **only** from her. One had to be delicate with Damon. If you ever tried to force him to do anything or back him into a corner, he was impossible to deal with from that moment onward. No one else could ever handle or guide him the way *she* could. She had spent far too much time building the bridges between them to simply let them fall to ashes, while Damon wandered around aimlessly and the future of Creation itself hung on the edge of ruin. No, she would have to work more subtly than ever before, but work she would, and no one could ever convince her otherwise. Ever.

"You *may* go now, Illirian. May the Light forever shelter you from darkness and illuminate your path," the Chairman waved her off with the back of his hand, dismissing her as if she were a small child. Illirian smoldered; her eyes burned hot akin well-stoked coals, but she bowed nonetheless, though a bit shallow while shifting her heated eyes slightly to the left and back to the right as she measured the temperature of the room before departing. Turning slowly, Illirian walked away, as a myriad of distinct conversations welled back up before she even made it to the door.

(Perion, Present Day)

The crashing sound of steel on steel resonated throughout as the men wielded their lethal weapons of battle against one another. Their screams and cries permeated the air.

Breathing laboriously under the protection of his steel helmet, a young man, desperate to find out what had just happened, quickly flashed his blue-grey eyes in search of answers. Desperate to keep his head about his neck, he quickly found himself ducking a hard brute of a swing from a man as thick and as tall as two, using his boot heels thrust into the side of his Grey to spur his mount and thunder hard up the battlefield hillside. Pausing momentarily to spin around and change positions, he headed for higher ground via another path less likely to be blocked before finding himself the target of the next warrior.

Not knowing where he was, nor the men he fought, he struggled to understand. *How did I get here?* The symbol of a lightning bolt on their breastplates bustled in the back of his mind, as did the voice he heard calling out over the roar of the fighting. Turning his horse to see where the voice came from and spotting a much better place from which to look if he could only get there, Radin sought out the source of the familiar voice.

"My Lord? My Lord? I'm trying to get to you. Hold on. I'm coming." The voice came from nearby. Radin spotted the tall, middle-aged hulk of man, who had lost his helmet—or shunned it for being able to more accurately see where he swung his blade. What was left of his short hair was not all grey and was either cut or worn very close to his skin, much like it had been shaven recently. His full beard, with streaks of grey, was now matted with blood about his face. Blood upon his shield, armor, and horse, as well as careening down the fuller of his long blade, spoke long tales of his deadly acts. Strik-

Charles W. McDonald Jr.

ing his attacker bluntly against his breastplate with his blade, then running it across his body as he spurred his horse onward, the middle-aged man nearly took his combatant's head with one blow as his sword collected another toll. Wildly he thrashed his horse side-to-side, swinging his longsword, taking out the enemy wherever they crossed his path, like a moving wall of iron between himself and Radin. "I'm coming, my Lord. Hold on! Hold on!"

The older man's efforts did not go unnoticed, and the huge brute of a man was soon swarmed before he could get to Radin. That may have very well been the intent of the man, to get enough of them off of Radin so that he could escape. Seizing the opportunity, Radin again spurred his heels into his mount's firm side, bolting to higher ground. He hoped the middle-aged man would be okay and felt almost shameful for leaving him behind as if he were a friend or an old ally he could not remember, but there was little time to worry about him now. He could not help but feel angry, even tormented by his battlefield decision to flee. Radin felt like he should be by his side, helping him, fighting alongside him.

Radin's feelings subsided somewhat as he neared the top of the hill, looking back down on the grassy field of crumbled Rune Stones to see the middle-aged man beating down his attackers in retreat. His regret began to fade, as he surveyed the devastation amidst the beachside Rune Stones of a place he felt…familiar and profound.

Suddenly, the air before him rippled like waves on a pond whisking through an unseen veil, as flashes of lightning chased Radin and his mount through the disturbance with a deafening thunderclap. Abruptly, he found himself lost yet again—his mount gone. He found himself standing amidst a hall of staggered blue and white tiles, every other tile midnight blue and in regal decor with a golden crown. Huge paintings—masterworks all—adorned the walls, while rotund marble columns supported a grand arched cathedral ceiling, which resonated his every labored breath. Dazed and confused, he scanned about, not wanting to question his arrival nor the power at work. Something about the place tingled in his thoughts as if it should mean something, similar to the thoughts he had had earlier about the brave man who fought to help him. He knew there was a war raging somewhere just beyond the horizon of his consciousness, but for now, his memory was at war with his current thoughts and awareness.

Turning towards what appeared to be a home library or great study, Radin slowly removed his helmet and gauntlets, revealing shoulder-length auburn hair, blue-grey eyes, and a young, handsome face of hard-cut planes and a multi-cultural countenance beyond his years. His flesh and muscles were chiseled, but the harsh stubble and worrisome look about his face added another generation to his appearance. Making note of his specific location, Radin could not help but be in awe of the majesty and power of this place as he began his journey through the keep. Opposite the great library, and much further away, was what appeared to be a formal dining hall—though it was hard to be certain at such a great distance. A thought struck him as he peered down the great hallway, noticing the even and smooth lighting appearing to come from underneath moldings, cabinetry, and from other hidden places, not at all like the flicker of candlelight one might expect. Everywhere the indirect lighting was smooth and bright like daylight—not the least bit like flames and without the scent of wick or burning wax or oil. *A grand place*, he thought to himself, heading to the entrance. Careful not to become distracted or lost, Radin explored in the direction of the great library. The feeling of an answer in some unknown form nurtured his confidence in his actions as he pressed forward. *There has to be an explanation around here, somewhere*, he reassured himself as he listened to the echo of his boots upon the great marble flooring.

Just inside the library, a strong sense of impending danger beat at the doors of his consciousness, warning him. *Where was this place? And what?*

Now inside the library, the colossal, beautifully stained, rich-grain, built-in bookshelves intimidated and impressed. It was odd being able to see the stars outside through such an enormous ceiling above. *How did they shape the glass so, and use it for a ceiling?* He certainly had never seen anything like that before. *Wherever this place was, whatever the palace, it must belong to a great lord or king*, he considered. The murals, the tapestries, the thousands of leather and gold gilded books, and the castle itself must have taken more wealth than he could ever imagine. *So, where am I?* That question he wanted to know more than any other as he spotted another much smaller chamber toward the back of the library, deciding it as good a place as any to start.

This chamber appeared to be a smaller and more private study, adorned with richly mastercrafted woodwork, area rugs, paintings, and a very large, brooding desk. Some kind of painted blue orb with tan and black markings, suspended on a pedestal at an angle, sat in the far corner of the room looking akin to a map. Some strange board with opposing dark and light squares—similar to the floor in the foyer—and ornately carved pieces sat on another smaller end table, under yet another strange lamp that failed to flicker as it burned smooth and bright. Curiously, he picked up one of the small wooden pieces off the board, examining it, then placing it back on the board, but on a different square. The piece looked like a knight mounted upon a horse, and it was originally placed next to a piece that looked something like a round turret.

Behind the desk sat a burgundy leather chair, studded with gold rivets, its back to the wall. Two smaller matching wingback chairs sat in front of the desk on a handsome oval rug that felt rich in texture. A painting of two lovely, young children—babes really—hung behind the desk. On the desk itself, sat a portrait of a kind he had never seen before—a likeness of a beautiful strawberry-blonde young woman—though definitely not a painting. The likeness of the beautiful young woman sat inside a burnt gold frame embroidered with tiny globes, each made of celestial circles, which enclosed an even smaller orb—seemingly suspended midway between the circles. Radin leaned over the front of the desk, losing himself in the innocence of the young woman's likeness. She must have been. *What's this…?* He looked closer and found his thoughts drifting….

> *Dimly lit by the chemical reactions given off by the strange underground vegetation, the interior of the city seemed darker, more dangerous, than the outer that butted up against the native plant life of the massive caverns. He paid little attention. This place was very dangerous, especially for a new mage of little experience and power, but he felt the advantage still belonged to him. If someone wanted a fight, he would give them all they* **couldn't** *handle.*
>
> *Sitting on the steps of the temple, he watched others go by— elves and trollocs alike, even the occasional human, though that was much less common down here. Turning his attention temporarily back to the temple's entrance, he could see a figure moving in the shadows—definitely female—unquestionably beautiful. Just as quickly as she had appeared, she was gone—perhaps inside. He couldn't tell.*
>
> *Sighing, he turned back to face the street, regretting his decision to wait here for Evanyil. What am I doing? I don't need her, or her even more unstable sister. I'd be better off on my own.*
>
> *"I think so too." As if Evanyil was reading Damon's most personal and intimate thoughts like a diary at her whim. The sultry voice of Evanyil was more than enough to make him jump out of his skin right there on the spot. Spinning around, rising to his feet before he knew it, Damon found himself confronted by the most beautiful woman in all Creation. Her satin, yet shimmering, black skin was perfection as was her ageless youth. Her perfect symmetry, glowing violet eyes, shimmering platinum hair to the small of her back, and her stunning breasts turned every head—man, woman, elf—everyone. She seemingly appeared not even twenty summers of age. They say first impressions are everything. Damon's first impression of Evanyil in the flesh was…. WOW!*

(Stirling, Perion, Present Day)

Charles W. McDonald Jr.

Shaking his sweat-laden head as he eerily came out of another increasingly troubling dream of late and gripping his sweat-soaked sheets balled up in between his tight, white knuckles, Radin d'Aguillon inhaled deeply—his chest still heaving. The dreams, if one could call them that, that had come to him at the turning of his eighteenth birthday had already scarred him in ways he might never understand. Opening his eyes to other realms and people that begged for answers and connections he felt were just beyond his reach. For now.... He barely dared open his eyes for fear of again finding himself someplace other than his own room. Inside he knew those answers and connections wouldn't wait for whether he was ready or not. As the raven-haired, black-eyed tall man burned himself into the pathways of Radin's consciousness, he felt the tether between them forming and knew it would never be allowed to break.

Charles W. McDonald Jr.

Chapter 3: Decapitated

(Mediterranean Sea, 25 miles off the coastline of Syria, Earth, Present Day)

Maintaining that knifed edge he'd come to know over many down-range missions, Michael Anthony Day sought the calm, focused, and committed singularity of mind as he busied himself with inverted pushups with his feet up against the triple bunk bed compartment of his special ops accommodations aboard USS Virginia, stealthily operating in international waters. The Operational Orders (OPORD) had already come down. The Delta Force and NAVY SEAL Team leads were finalizing the tactical and operational plans in the Intelligence Summary (INTSUM) from the Other Government Agency (OGA) in the next room astern. Colonel Terry Goodwin of the British Special Reconnaissance Regiment casually walked in with lieutenants Thomas Hanson and Acres Manifort trailing behind. Being Terry's right-hand man, and second in command of his unit, Michael *should* have been in that meeting, but Terry knew he was trying to keep his killer instincts honed and icy. Terry had worked with him long enough to know Michael's routine, so he made nothing of it, slapping the tactical satellite imagery maps down on the floor where Michael could view them as he continued his inverted pushups.

"This," Terry pointed to a pile of rubble that could barely pass for a four-storey building, "…is where we expect him to be." The target, highlighted inside a red kill-box, surrounded other buildings in various states of ruin and roads that now barely qualified as goat trails. What else would one expect in the southeastern parts of Raqqa, Syria? The whole country had been ravaged by years of civil war, Arab Spring, plus being blasted to bits by pseudo-allied forces of highly questionable armament and funding. Squeezed between the bastard Assad, ISIS, Russia, and the United States, there wasn't much of anything left standing. The incompetence and neglect of the Syrian Government allowed bad and even duplicitous U.S. and Western policies to seed, then grow a legion of monsters in the so called, "Islamic State." Throw in some good old-fashioned Russian and U.S. interventionism—uncoordinated of course—and you had yourself a real shitstorm of unintended consequences. But at least now there was reliable intel—allegedly—and just maybe they could do something with it.

"What's the probability they're giving us he'll actually be there," Michael asked, never breaking from his workout routine, knowing the CIA's resources to be competent but their agenda almost entirely corrupt from the head down. So, there was always that....

"They're saying between forty-five and seventy-five percent," Terry replied, adding, "...but when I probed about how they got the intel, they wouldn't tell me shit. That's Americans for you, but I suppose if it were one of our human assets, we'd probably do the same."

"HELO entry," Michael presumed, already knowing. There was no way to storm Raqqa from the coastline with it being so far inland. Not unless you brought in D-Day-like forces. They'd get cut to pieces and decapitated before they made it halfway there, special ops units or not.

"Transfer to USS Kidd Destroyer in forty-five minutes for HELO transport."

"I'm guessing we're not telling the Syrians we're coming," Michael righted himself, stopping his pushup routine as he stood before his friend and Team Lead.

"Would you?"

"FUCK NO!" Michael offered Terry a sweaty but sincere smile, acknowledging his brethren SRR team members with a nod though his blood was still chilling in his veins as his heart rate found a happy medium between elevated and nominal. There was still a night of heavy killing in front of them. It was 2000 hours local and normally these kinds of ops went down in the pre-dawn hours, but the time of the meeting dictated the assault window this time.

"Back into the sandbox," Terry smiled at his friend-in-brotherhood, with a reassuring hand on Michael's shoulder. "Team briefing in 30 and we'll get some chow once we're on the Kidd."

"Roger that," Michael didn't smile, because he didn't find this as *fun* as Terry did—not quite as gung ho. His brothers-in-arms all said he was too damn serious like that, but Michael was being Michael. Nonetheless, it was his third time operating in the sandbox; each time the stakes got higher.

A pat on Michael's shoulders from Terry, as he, Acres, and Thomas gave the room to Michael to finish his prep. They knew he liked to get his mind and body right—alone if possible. And when Michael was right, the team was right. Michael was the straw that stirred the team's drink. They needed all that shit locked down tight because they needed each other at one-hundred percent.

As they left, Michael finished organizing his gear, throwing his PLUG-GER into his pack. Next on the list was meditating and praying.

*   *   *   *

(Just outside Raqqa, Syria, Earth, 2345 hours local Syria time, Present Day)

The whipping, thrashing, and chopping sound of the Blackhawk chopper blades felt comfortable against the internal thump of his own heartbeat, and not nearly as loud as what he was used to. They were using the latest stealth variants, used in the Osama bin Laden raids. Modified since then actually.... Hopefully, they'd have better luck with these than the SEALs had with theirs that fateful May night in 2011, though that whole scene had never sat right with Michael and he knew there was more to it than the official narrative. There *always* was....

Geared up in body armor, night vision goggles, and his favorite MP5, Michael was in the kill zone, mentally. Physically, they were less than a mile out from the LZ.

The hard part about this was landing far enough out so no one in the meeting, or aware of the meeting, would hear or see the choppers or warn those ahead. But they still had to be close enough to secure the kill box without having to go through any more *very* unfriendly territory than necessary.

The Blackhawk blade's rotated and thumped even more as it squatted just over the GPS coordinates of the LZ allowing Colonel Terry Goodwin to sling repelling ropes for his men and the Delta Force that were with his team. The SEALs were in the lead chopper, already deploying and fanning out over the goat trails beneath them. Slinging his custom MP5 over his dominant side shoulder, Michael quickly hit the repel ropes, going down first. Twenty-two men in all, including the eight from his unit, Michael gave an acknowledging nod to SEAL Team II Lead Commander Roger Penniston as they fanned out in standard two-by-two formation doing the very dangerous work of progressing deep into the heart of the Islamic State in the dead of night, on foot. It had become increasingly difficult for Michael not to chuckle internally every time he looked at Penniston now, recalling Mars referring to Commander Penniston as Washington's Driver. Seeing Penniston's graying sideburns and designer stubble marked him a man easily in his upper forties.

Quickly checking his Blue Force Tracker (BFT), identifying his location in relation to the hostiles being reported in real-time from the Globalhawk-streaming telemetry from overhead, Michael stowed the vital field electronics, making note of the two SAWs, one Delta Force—Conan and one SEAL Team Operator—Ace, now fanning out left and right down the goat trails, according to the plan.

It was difficult—here—telling the difference between city and village because everywhere they looked was nothing but bombed-out rubble. It reminded Michael of pictures of Fallujah he'd seen on the Internet just after Bush 43 sent in the Americans and invoked that bloody insurgency that had both born and paved the ruin-laden path to this moment. As they surrounded and squeezed the kill box, it looked way worse than anything he'd ever seen from photos of Fallujah. This was Hell on Earth, and Michael wondered how anyone could live here.

The tap and squeeze on his left shoulder said Terry was right on him, right where he was supposed to be, as they cleared another block of the rubble that was Raqqa, Syria. The designated kill box was in sight, and he could see the sequentially parked white Toyota trucks they expected to see. Five plain, non-descript, same year, make and model—all looking like clones of one another. *Tradecraft*, Michael confirmed internally. If he weren't here, Michael would be very surprised. One didn't waste tradecraft like that on just anybody.

Squatting in place beside Terry, they awaited the 'go' order from Commander Penniston. Observing the kill box and the area outward about one hundred yards in all directions, Michael counted some fifty-odd mujahideen with AK-47s. There had to be at least that many inside the building where the meeting was taking place. That was another good sign, at least in his mind. Twenty-two-to-one-hundred odds—he'd take that any day of the week, especially given the skills and experience in the twenty-one brothers with him. Looking into Terry's combat-focused eyes, Michael hand-signaled the four on the right he wanted. Terry hand-signaled he'd push forward and left to a spot where he could take out another four on the left while putting himself in a safe position to cover Michael if needed.

Over the comm-link in his ear, Michael heard the order come down from Commander Penniston with his men now in position, "I have the count: Three. Two. One. EXECUTE!" The execute command came simultaneously with a closed fist signal Commander Penniston made with his right hand held high in the air.

Immediately thereafter, ISIS fighters started dropping like flies to the soft whish of silenced M-4s and MP5s who quickly began returning fire as they hid behind rubble wherever they could find cover. The hostiles couldn't see the Operator's muzzle flashes and didn't have night vision, so the ISIS militia was at a severe disadvantage as they continued dwindling in numbers until support came from within the building.

"I've got three Squirters, including a PKM and an RPG, heading into the building to the northwest. Copy?" Michael radioed in the threat.

THWACK! A silenced Barrett® .50 cal sniper rifle nearly split the ISIS fighter, and associated RPG, in half as he tried to take up a high-ground position on the fourth floor of the building to the northwest of the kill box.

"Roger that, Scout." Overwatch was doing his job, though it was a near miss from the SEAL's Overwatch perspective, not to be repeated as he would make adjustments for the wind to get the headshots he sought thereafter. THWACK! Another .50 cal Overwatch sniper round turned another Squirter's head into a misty cloud of blood and cranial gore—his PKM falling to the rubble in a metallic clatter.

ISIS fighters returned fire from un-silenced AK-47s and hand grenades exploding in the night, announcing their location to an unwelcoming public. Their love of death proved useful in their unabashed, unprotected, and un-shielded return fire—making allied forces' headshots an easier task.

Enough of this playing footsie with these assholes, Michael determined, tossing a grenade some twenty yards forward and to his right, ducking behind the safety of a large piece of rubble. **BOOM!** Rubble splintering everywhere as he advanced, firing simultaneously at where his targets *had* been with his silenced MP5. Catching one that the grenade missed, Michael scanned for other targets. *Got three, missed one.* **ACK! ACK! ACK! ACK!** The AK-47 rounds whizzed past Michael, chipping off pieces of rubble just inches from his face. Tossing another grenade to where the rounds came from, Michael barely ducked this time. **BOOM!** Advancing again, almost simultaneous with the explosion of his grenade, Michael pivoted left and right as he searched for the target. A slight movement in the settling dust and he fired, not sure if it was his target or not. The ISIS fighter slumped dead against the rubble, bleeding out. *Never hesitate*, Michael affirmed in his own mind. He detested shooting at a target he could barely see, but if he hesitated at all either he, or one of his teammates, wouldn't be making it home tonight.

The buzzing sound of the twin M249 SAWs, coming from four-storey cross-fire positions, lit up the night sky in straight amber lines of molten kinetic rounds, obliterating ISIS fighters trying to charge Penniston's advancing forces.

The kill ratio was good—at least as good as expected, but the ISIS fighters coming out of the building were Hell-bent on killing the forces of the Great Satan, charging with knives, pistols, and machine-guns—whatever weapon they could most easily get. THWACK! Another silenced .50 cal sniper round decapitated an ISIS fighter charging Michael and Terry's position as Michael looked up to the Overwatch, giving a thumb's up as he recognized the man coming out of the building with an AK-47, starting to fire on his position in a Death Blossom. *He* was their target. Michael rushed forward to a large chunk of rubble thirty feet in front of the HVT (High-Value Target) and what *had* been a building, ducking just as rounds chipped at the rubble directly in front of him. Letting some twenty rounds click off right at his position, Michael pivoted just as the rounds stopped, watching Commander Penniston and one of his SEAL Team members, as well as what looked like another ISIS fighter behind the middle-aged cleric, jump all over the HVT just as his clip had emptied.

Scanning right then left, Michael caught another target on the third level, through his night vision—firing. That target fell forward through obliterated outer walls of a building that once was, splitting his head open as he landed head-first into the rubble below.

"CLEAR," Michael called out.

"CLEAR," Terry called out similarly. A chorus of "CLEAR" followed from other Operators.

Michael and Terry rushed forward with Mason, Acres and Thomas, hearing Commander Penniston shouting at the man they'd knocked to the ground and disarmed. "NAME," Penniston yelled at the middle-aged man in Arabic. "NAME," Penniston yelled again at him in English this time.

The last remaining ISIS fighter, who had jumped on top of the HVT, looking to be maybe mid-thirties, rose to his feet.

Quickly aiming his muzzle straight at the mid-thirties ISIS fighter, about twelve feet away from him and to his left, Michael had his finger on the trigger—waiting for him to make the move that would end his life.

In perfect, unbroken English the middle-aged, grey-streak-bearded cleric finally responded, "I am Abu Bakr al-Baghdadi. I surrender."

Commander Penniston seemingly satisfied at the target's response, seeing his features matched that of their intended HVT, motioned Michael to keep his muzzle trained on the last remaining ISIS fighter.

"Eric Clapton. Jeff Beck." Commander Penniston provided the prescribed challenge code to the surviving ISIS Fighter, clearly expecting a coded reply.

"Jimmy Page. The Yardbirds," the mid-thirties ISIS fighter replied, never taking his eyes of Michael.

"Roger that Trojan. Glad to see you alive," Commander Penniston offered his hand to what was obviously the mole in al-Baghdadi's organization. Motioning Michael to muzzle down, Penniston called out over the comm-link, "Overlord, this is Spear actual. Come in."

Charles W. McDonald Jr.

"This is Overlord actual, go ahead with your sitrep Spear," Joint Special Operations Command (JSOC) replied, awaiting a mission status report.

"Body Snatch. Body Snatch. We have the package and Trojan in UP status, incurred three wounded, one K.I.A. Mars is down." Commander Penniston provided the status report, visually scanning around for threats through his night vision.

DAMN, Michael hadn't even noticed Mars' lifeless body was being held up by 8Ball. Mars had given Michael his SEAL call-sign—Scout—like he needed another anyway. SRR members named him 'Tincup' for his love of golf. He didn't even know how he earned the name Scout. Most likely it was a derogatory term of endearment, knowing the Americans. Regardless, he liked Mars—enough to know he earned the call sign because his wife's favorite book: *MEN are from MARS, WOMEN are from VENUS, by John Gray.*

"Confirmed Spear, we have you EXFIL WITH Package. Total plus two. Proceed to waypoint Charlie. Globalhawk has eyes on. Move with all possible speed. We can see at least forty hostiles enroute to your position from points Hotel and India."

"LET'S MOVE!" Penniston ordered.

Michael had already moved to 8Ball offering in a tone weighted in the shade of combat, "I got Mars."

"Sure thing," 8Ball acknowledged, releasing Mars into Michael's hands as Michael tossed the two-hundred pound, high-and-tight-cut, KIA Mars over his right shoulder for EXFIL. Terry coming up on Michael's right side, Mason on his left in standard echelon formation as they started moving out of the heart of the Islamic State.

ISIS leadership now decapitated; the War on Terror would enter a new phase as the Allies would need to focus on defeating the radicalized ideology of 'The Narrative' rather than trying to kill their way out of it, for there were not enough bullets and bombs on Earth to do so.

(Perion, Present Day)

Radiant, rainbow-backlit birds of late spring chirped and fluttered amidst the blooming jasmine and wildflowers dotting the lush green hillsides. Elms, maples, pecans, bradford pears, cherry blossoms, and dogwoods swayed gently with the will of the wind as warmth finally returned to northern lands of the oldest of the Nine Kingdoms. The wind swept its way across the landscape, just stiff enough to disturb the crested banners that draped over the sides and chest of the majestic Grey. Adorning the mount, the crest displayed a king's crown inside an oval ring, caught between two griffins struggling to capture the power of the crown. In the foreground of the crown sat two angels amidst an array of broken arrows and olive branches. In the background, and standing over the crown, was a fiery phoenix, wings spread wide, engulfing the warring griffins. A handsomely crafted hilt of gold stuck out from the well-worn silver scabbard, nestled against the white and red banner. The exterior of the scabbard was embossed with a few unintelligible runes while a leather strap and clip ran across the sword's guard, holding it in place at the beast's side. A travel-worn saddle straddled the faithful mount as he began to graze in his master's absence.

A standard, far older than most, mounted on a sleek metal pole had been driven into the hillside and now rippled wild and free, though not yet tattered, in the stiff breeze. Upon the standard, a gold phoenix on a blue background seemed ready to take flight under the power of the wind that held it aloft.

The old mount began to tire, swaying slightly side-to-side, as the dusk brilliantly tinted clouds, leaves, and verdant grass in beautiful reds, magentas and orange bursts of sunset. It had been days already and would be much longer still. Yet the Grey stayed.

The birds sang through the moments of dusk. Only a few feet away from the banner and the faithful Grey stood an oval *Portal* in the background, shrinking ever so slightly as time and magic ran to an end. On the other side of the man-sized *Portal* was the heart of absolute darkness. Waiting with worry-laden eyes, the faithful mount looked down the hill, back to the *Portal* where Iain Longbow had entered some days back. He would wait as long as it took.

*　　*　　*　　*

(Florè Castle, Perion, Present Day)

Just outside the castle walls, Ethan Marshall walked a well-worn dirt path to meet up with friends before heading to work inside Florè Castle. It would be nice to take a break from the hammer and anvil for a while and get back to some time spent with good friends.

Passing a merchant carriage that appeared to be stopping at a makeshift tent set up for selling wares, Ethan continued towards the straw-roofed tavern with long, weathered wooden planked siding that marked the first major protected structure in Florè, though still not inside the castle walls. It was

Charles W. McDonald Jr.

protected because it was the best food in, or outside, the castle walls. Several times the Steward of Florè had tried to recruit the cook to work inside the castle, though never successfully so. His stomach growled, turning over inside at the smell of fresh buttered bread, potatoes, eggs, and ham.

Opening the door to the establishment, Ethan quickly scanned inside, not seeing his friend and he would have classified as an easy-to-spot sort.

A crushing hand landed on his left shoulder, "Ethan, glad to see you away from the smithy for a change!"

How could such a hulking man sneak about like that? Ethan hadn't heard him approach at all. *Damn, I need to have my hearing checked!*

"Brigance," Ethan offered in a slightly exasperated reply. It wasn't the first time Brigance Fireheart had made a fool of him and likely wouldn't be the last. But it was good to have friends that could rip an average man in half with their bare hands. "So, what's the job? You know I don't like leaving the family with raiders roaming the open countryside."

"It's good pay, easy work, and you get to stay within walking distance of your place. Fair enough," Brigance posed to his blacksmith friend of many years. Smithing was usually the sort of thing you found the biggest of men doing for a living, but Ethan was just slightly above average, yet his craftsmanship was the best Brigance had ever seen. The massive broadsword Brigance carried on his left side was Ethan's work, and he loved it. The weight and balance were perfect, and he could cut an armored man in half with it with one blow and had already done so several times in the past. "Let's get you some breakfast and head on up to the castle to talk with the Steward. I'll fill you in on the way."

"Sounds good, I'm starving," Ethan accepted, carefully side-stepping the large, intimidating white wolf just inside the open front door.

(Damon's Manor, Kaleion, Present Day)

He was equally tall as Damon and even more muscular, with bushy blonde hair—short-cropped to make for easier maintenance in the field where he no longer spent as much time as he used to. His stark blue eyes were an intense contrast to the black mirrors of Damon, while the contrast between his near chaotic attitude and Damon's logic proved even bigger. Yet they were the best of friends for longer than either could remember—brothers really. More so than Kellen and Damon. Kellen was always just beyond the horizon of Damon's complete trust, whereas Goldenbow was squarely inside, and always had

Charles W. McDonald Jr.

been. Goldenbow lazily kicked his left leg to and fro as he sat on the edge of Damon's desk in his private study—a place Damon allowed almost no one but his innermost circle.

Goldenbow's palette of colors swung through the entire spectrum of neutral, from the incredibly dull greys of his pants to the soft tans of his belt, to the pale forest green of his vest covering the slightly dirty off-white of his long-sleeve shirt. If you didn't know better, your eyes would walk over him a hundred times before noticing anything remarkable about him, despite his youthful and rugged good looks. Goldenbow liked it that way. It was an absolute necessity for an assassin of his caliber—probably the greatest assassin Damon had ever seen. Goldenbow was a legitimate living legend, and while many would never get a good enough look at his face to ever remember it; his name—whether real or not—was synonymous with a guaranteed kill. Damon had known him for many lifetimes and never knew, or had ever asked, his real name. Everyone only knew him for the golden shortbow spiked with living poisonous thorns he carried everywhere without fail. It was a pure extension of his arm—completely inseparable from Goldenbow, the man.

"So, when's all this going down, Day?" Goldenbow inquired in a friendly tone, still lazily swinging his leg as he relaxed with a bottle of Damon's best red wine. Nothing but the best for Goldenbow—ever.

"I wish I could tell you."

"That's pretty non-committal for you, Day."

"Sorry, not a matter of trust," he smiled at his longtime friend. "More a matter of not really knowing how these next few critical steps are going to play out. When I get past Phase One, I'll check back with you."

"And you're not going to tell me what's involved with Phase One I suppose...." It came out like a question, but Damon knew otherwise.

"The less you know, the better." Damon paused, genuinely wanting to tell his friend more of his Master Plan but surviving the Master Plan was more important than bragging about it or sharing it. "For both of our safety."

"Not like you to worry about your safety, our ours, for that matter," Goldenbow began his line of thinking aloud, "I mean you've been pretty damn cavalier for the last hundred years or more. What makes you so cautious now?"

"Stakes have been raised," Damon sketched a sword, unlike any either had ever seen, on the paper on his desk before them. "Are you sure you don't want to stay for dinner? You're welcome anytime, you know."

"And listen to more of this hidden-meaning banter all night? No thanks."

"Very well," Damon countered, putting down the pen as he paused his sketch-in-progress. "You're the most lethal person I know, and when I need you, I need you to be prepared to come fast. I need you to come prepared for the biggest threat you or I have ever faced. How's that?"

"Boy, I love a challenge!" Goldenbow's million-watt smile was enough to chase away even the menacing aura of the *Staff of the Invoker* as he jumped off the desk, pivoting back toward Damon. "You've still got one of my arrow-heads, right?"

"Of course!"

"Might be a good idea to start carrying that thing on you at all times."

"Consider it done. I'll signal you when I'm ready, or at the end of Phase One, whichever comes first."

"Cool, Day. You want to…." he didn't have to ask when Goldenbow started getting within touch range, Damon knew. A touch of Damon's left index finger and Goldenbow was gone without a trace.

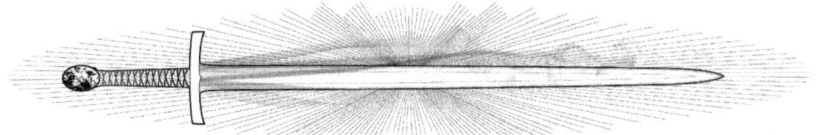

Chapter 4: A Crucible of Will

(Damon's Manor, Kaleion, Present Day)

While preferring to do most work in his secret, fourth-floor study, today's work required a great deal of space for Damon to perform the laborious task at hand. He could, of course, manufacture the space required out of nothing, but it was just easier to work within the spacious caverns Dallia had carved out of the bedrock under the foundation of his manor so many centuries ago. This was the largest of all the cavern chambers, measuring some four-hundred cubits by nearly a thousand. From the cavern ceiling, Damon appeared merely a dot on the landscape below as he worked shirtless with a series of smithy hammers. A great anvil and a blacksmith's fire, burning with stoked amber coals, lay before him.

Invoking *Distorting Web* to mask and encrypt his work from prying eyes, Damon used long tong heavy iron clamps to maneuver a large, enchanted ingot of metal, heating it in the fire. This heavy task and all the ones leading up to it were taking their toll on Damon's significant constitution. Exhaustion came rare to him, but he was certainly testing his endurance with this artifact. *A challenge finally*, he acidly realized, twisting the molten ingot again to heat treat it evenly. He was no master blacksmith, but this task was one he had done many dozens of times before, though never with such a complicated artifact as the one he was making now. No doubt with its intended and ultimate use, this *weapon of unmaking* needed to be far different than all the other artifacts that came before. Twisting the enchanted, molten ingot again, he assured smooth distributed heating—all its surfaces a beautifully hot amber-gold.

Pulling it from the fire, he placed the glowing ingot on the anvil and with firm, but careful blows, began to form what would become a longsword blade. Hours he worked—stretching then folding the metal back on itself again and again, then flattening it again each time, Damon forged into the piece the strength, durability and flexibility for the blade to perform its singular function. Pinched in between a vice to hold it steady, he struck a deep gouge down the length of the blade on both sides that would become the fuller that terminated at the tapered center ridge about one-third from the blade's tip.

The warm glow from the forge highlighted ever-so-faint scars of a tormented childhood about his chest, back, neck, and shoulders. The result of his *cauldron of hate*.

The captured masses, which he had spent the last month accumulating—now exactly one hundred of the most pristine souls he could find in this world and many others—watched him work tirelessly through the night. Some found a way to sleep on the cavern floor. Others looked at the *Distorting Web* in awe as it encapsulated the entire massive cavern chamber all the way to the ceiling. All had stopped their attempts to escape the swirling transparent blue field, which imprisoned them here, below his keep. Women, children, and men of all ages huddled in terror at what lay directly beside them. It had been asleep for hours, but still, no one dared speak or utter even a word for fear of waking it.

                    *   *   *   *

(Some hours later....)

Surely, it's morning by now, Damon wondered, now well past exhaustion. However, the blade was formed: fuller, tang, and all. He was ready to quench. Using his natural *Telekinesis* to elevate the blade into the air just in front of its man-sized teeth, Damon cleared his throat loudly to get *its* attention. "Now if you would be so kind, please," Damon glanced sidelong at Hadron—the great golden beast he'd captured solely for this purpose. Though, captured might not have been the best description since their relationship went *way* back. To owed debts....

With a scowl, it raised to its feet, standing some eighty cubits tall. Taking a deep breath, it exhaled a very accurate directional burst of white-hot fire through its enormous, razor sharp teeth at the blade, suspended in mid-air before it by Damon's *Telekinesis*. Only an instant was required, and the blade glowed a perfect molten amber-gold as he guided it down into the oil, ensuring the entire blade was straight and pointed at a perfect magnetic north, so as not to warp the blade as it quenched for strength, scattering and spitting forth plumes of sparks and smoke.

Moments later, lifting the blade with *Telekinesis*, using one of his floating *Light Orbs* to examine the blade for defects, Damon sighed with relief, finding none. *Well, that was the easy part. Must rest now.*

Damon collapsed to the cavern floor right where he stood, only a

Charles W. McDonald Jr.

couple of cubits from the massive, diamond-hard teeth of the Gold Dragon that had helped him. Snorting puffs of smoke through its nostrils to clear its airways, *it* chose sleep as well. The huddled masses, still held captive, were left to sit and ponder their fate a while longer. The blade hung in the air only a moment longer, clanging loudly as it landed squarely on the anvil waiting for Damon, obeying his unconscious thoughts.

* * * *

Damon wasn't sure what day it was when he woke, or even what week. Not even bothering to check on his captives, or where Hadron might have gone, he opened a *Portal* to his kitchen stepping through. *Fuck, I'm starving!*

* * * *

After the necessities of his mortal coil had been satisfied, he wanted to return to the cavern, but he needed something from his private, fourth-floor study first. Knowing exactly where to look and having an organized library helped. He quickly snatched the required spell and blank parchment, opening and walking through a *Portal* to the cavern below. Acknowledging his captives for the first time in forever, he could see they were all still alive, but looked starved and exceptionally weak. Damon knew he didn't have much time until he'd have to start feeding them to keep them alive until he could finish. He unrolled *Damon's Damnation*, setting it on the floor to his left, then set the blank parchment immediately right of it and began gating his thoughts, his imagination, his vision and his controlled emotions into characters and runes on the blank parchment. He had been building this spell in his mind for months. It need only to be documented to be made manifest for what *had* to come next.

Lifting the blade off the anvil back into the air with his *Telekinesis*, it slowly twisted next to the *Light Orb* he had used to examine it days before. Flooding his entire body with the energy he sourced from Arcane, Damon held up his right hand, casting first into the prison and dispelled the shield that had held his captives. When nothing appeared to happen, save the dispelling of the shield, he raised his left hand, causing a white-hot stream to burst into existence from nothingness, shooting its energetic stream, about the width of his forearm, directly into the center of the blade as it continued to twist in the air. A look to his right confirmed all one hundred living souls were gone with not a trace left. No ashes. No symbols on the ground where they *had* been as one might expect from *Damnation*. Nothing. Only the slowly turning blade remained, now gleaming with an exceptionally hard edge, sharpened by the souls it now housed. *A Crucible of Will*, Damon admired his work while the blade's mirror finish threw the *Orb's* light into every corner of the chamber, vanquishing the darkness of Dallia's cavern. It still needed a grip, guard, pommel, and an appropriate scabbard, but now the hard part was done. He also needed a place to hide it from prying eyes until the moment it would be needed. But, for this moment, within his Master Plan, he could truly rest.

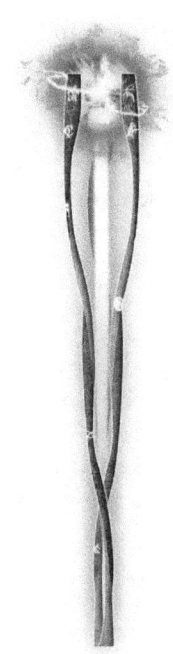

Chapter 5: Broken

(Damon's Manor, Kaleion, Present Day)

Rolling her muscular, nude body toward Damon, letting her scarlet hair spill down over his face in waves of seduction, Victoria knew he was not sleeping, though his eyes were closed and his breathing relaxed.

"What are you thinking, my Love? Tired so soon…?" Nothing jabbed so well as a shot to the ego.

Only one eye opening in playful response, Damon's forehead furrowed—that one eye closing again in mild rebuke.

Frustrated, furrowing herself, Victoria thought he might need some reminding, "Lest you forget so soon, I AM stronger than even you."

That statement proved worthy enough for a rebuke from both eyes. "What would you have me say to that? You should not tell such big lies when smaller ones are much more believable."

"And what would you know about telling lies? I thought you and your *code* would not allow that." She knew him too well after being with him for so

Charles W. McDonald Jr.

long—well, long according to her lifespan, not his. "What's been bothering you so much lately? I know I'm not one of your typical women, but you've always been able to at least make some conversation with me."

He understood her concern and agreed, though there were some thoughts he simply couldn't share. He knew there were things, that if she fully knew, she would not understand. There was simply too much history that didn't include her and too much future that *couldn't*.

A decidedly thoughtful look seemed his best defense. He swore successfully navigating a relationship with a woman a thousand times the feat of his greatest magic. Sometimes he regretted his promise to himself that he would never use magic to maintain the love of a relationship. A brief inward, reflective moment pointed out the obvious flaw to his 'conscience.' "If you knew the full of my thoughts, you'd run."

Sitting straight up, she threatened to get up from the bed in complete frustration, though it was evident in the squinting of her beautiful green eyes and her tone that she didn't *really* want to leave him, "I may not know all your thoughts, but I know you."

Reaching up, caressing her long sun-red strands, slowly letting his fingers touch her cheeks as he dragged them along the way to her lips, he felt his internal struggle whether to encourage her to go or pull her back into his lethal orbit. "I know. Kellen always warns me about keeping people, especially you, close to me when secrecy becomes of greater need. I should listen to him more often. He's right." Pulling her down, gently kissing her, softly caressing her tongue with his, he wanted to tell her everything. He needed a confidante. Colors whirled in his thoughts as they formed into a magnificent lush—though much shorter—body in a seductive dress with flowing brunette hair with starry-blue eyes—*Mira*, he thought before dismissing her with an old but powerful sense of loss. Some voids were not meant to ever be filled again. He wanted to be free to tell someone everything, but his secrets had a way of killing the unintended as well as the intended. *Everyone may perish still*—'twas a comforting thought.

"You know I can't tell you everything," he whispered, resting his head back on the pillows. "There's just a lot happening, and it takes all the concentration I have to keep the planning straight."

A brief glimmer of a memory threatened to drag away her attention, "Were you always like this?"

Cocking his head inquisitively, he blinked at the question. "What do mean?"

"Soooo deliberate. I can just tell; you were not always that way—I mean before we ever met. Were you ever a free spirit?"

Charles W. McDonald Jr.

Though smiling outwardly and apparently taken by the detail with which she tried to know him, inside he wanted to hide from her. It was as if she wanted to live inside of him at times. But, to truly know Damon was... perilous at best...unimaginable horror at worst. "No," he suggested not wanting to elaborate on that—instead he resumed slowly caressing her hair. "There were...many *memorable* times.... Perhaps someday, I will tell you of how Evanyil and I 'met.'"

"You keep promising," she quipped, gently stroking and caressing his body.

"Well," he defended, "It's a rather long story, you see." Squinting, piercing him with her eyes, Victoria begged him to continue with her delicious smile and seductive strokes of his thighs. "I'm certain it is."

"Once I was even less predictable—some might have incorrectly presumed chaotic. I've only managed to keep *that* reputation by becoming excellent at keeping my plans complicated, and in seclusion, such that the execution of my plan appears random. Let's just say that guts only get you so far, and then they'll get you dead. It took me a while to learn that lesson, but I only had to learn it once. What seems many lifetimes ago...."

"You're talking about Banthis, aren't you...?"

It was not quite a look of death, but certainly an icy one. Working his mouth, Damon snapped his head, turning from her, taking some of the covers with him.

Uncomfortable silence crept in as Victoria rose from the bed, covering some of her enticing curves with bedding. "I'm sorry," she murmured, walking out of the bedroom to his darkened study.

It was too late, the memory had been well dredged like preparing the soil for a foundation; much had been uncovered that he thought had been buried a lifetime ago. "Chara," it was only a thought, a memory, but he could not stop himself from muttering that...name! The bitterness of it tainted his lips. Decades, she had been a thorn in his side, so much so, he dedicated every resource, every man, every spell, every coin, every thought—WHATEVER it took to annihilate that woman! An obsession like none before, and there had been none quite so severe since, though his current situation with the Master Plan could be called nothing less than an obsession. So determined was he; she warranted the creation of spells just for her. Banned or not, damned or not, he would destroy her utterly and completely, leaving not even her ash to revive.

Turning toward the study, seeing her curves in the darkened shadows, wanting to tell her, he exhaled, mentally exhausted—tormented. Quietly he whispered into the darkness, "If you only knew all the thoughts racing through my mind, you would run as far away, and as fast, as you could. There are, in everyone's life, lasting implications. Like festered wounds that ever scab and bleed and scab yet again. Partners throughout life, whose only purpose is to cause pain, to prick and discomfort, and eventually, cause your end. It was in that moment; I knew I had sealed my future and all those around me. I've become a black hole of consequences. Do not come too close to the event horizon that circles my singularity of death." He thought for a moment about what would come of his next words, closing his eyes at the words as they quickly escaped his lips for fear of not escaping at all, "*Run*, Victoria. *Run* while you still can." Quietly he sank back into the comfort of his bed.

The comforter only slightly covering his magnificently black-jeweled eyes, his silken black bangs razor-like across his irises, but his face showed his thoughts, drifting. Memories were terrible creations, especially this one....

(Kaleion, A Long Time Ago)

Two giant hemispheres, one of elemental fire, the other of concentrated lightning bolts, like two immense bowls turned upside down and overlapping in half their diameter, exploded with incredible violence where **she** had stood only an instant before. Headstone rubble, dirt, rock, and ash erupted outwardly in all directions away from the blast area—some as far as 150 cubits away. The blast area itself was some ninety cubits across in all, though he couldn't be certain it had yielded a direct hit. Chara was entirely too crafty for her own good. "Show yourself Chara! I *have* something for you," Damon taunted just as barbed and flaming arrows struck at his chest only to deflect off of an invisible force into the ground and into the air instead of piercing their intended target. *The church rooftop*, he thought as his vision registered a brief glimmer of darkened-cloud-penetrating moonlight off metal, likely a nocked arrowhead. Weaving another custom crafted spell, a pebble-sized ball of lightning raced forth from his upward-facing right palm, piercing the church window—completely shattering it. Only an instant later dirt, foundation, plaster, stained glass, and roof exploded, taking more than half the church structure in one enormous blast that yielded a mushrooming debris cloud overhead, drifting back in Damon's direction on a bitter, chilled, evening breeze. A brief satisfactory smile appeared on the hard planes of his face as his eyes caught sight of feathers, from the attempted assassins' quiver, drifting on the breeze toward him. Satisfaction at his obliteration of both the assassin and the church was short lived as he felt something tugging at his legs and waist—threatening to tear his legs from his body. *Ironic*, he thought. *Would she kill him with one of his favorites?* This spell he knew quite well, and he would surely die horrifically if he didn't act quickly. The squid-like writhing tendrils, piercing the ground beneath him in between himself and his protective shield, had wrapped around almost all of his lower body. Their lanced stingers finding flesh through his herringbone charcoal-blue robes slashed with silver and gold seams. His stoles running the length down his robes embossed in silver with five invocation runes and his symbol were rapidly being ripped apart about his flesh. He could already feel their poison taking hold—his vision starting to shift and blur under its influence—only an instant left before he would no longer have the concentration to channel. He had only one hope remaining as he collapsed against the headstone rubble, his mortal shell starting to break under the tendril's iron grip. Already he could smell his own bile from his broken body and the acrid taste of it upon his lips and parched tongue just as the air around him became perfumed with sulfur and the howls of all things unholy and rebuked.

It clearly wasn't safe to show **her** face to him, but she wanted to be sure Damon saw that it was her who had beaten him before his torn entrails were strewn all over the sanctified graveyard. *Fitting*, she thought; *I'll bury the wretch in holy ground.* Her fire-red hair whirled around the gorgeous features of her face while her dead eyes burned like icy coals—a shark rolling back its eyelids before sinking its teeth into a meal of flesh. Chara's flowing red dress— quite simple for her standing yet slit high enough to expose her fair skin— whipped around her sultry legs as she continued to step ever closer, cursing under her breath as she had to right herself, stepping over battlefield rubble and burned, broken bodies. "Damon, Honey, I do hope you're still alive," she jeered, wanting him to live *only* long enough for her face to be the last thing he ever glimpsed.

But just as she got close, powerful gusts accelerated more and more as she neared his broken body; his chest still heaved as he gulped for air that wispily seeped through open wounds of his lungs. Her dress nearly being blown off her lush, silken body, Chara turned to see what was causing the disturbance in the debris-laden, chilled, evening air. *Had he managed to summon a storm?* Oddly there was no storm visible in the distance, yet birds suddenly scattered in all directions—fleeing! Only a few crows remained about the headstone debris Damon now leaned against—his familiars no doubt. She began to see clouds being pushed outwardly in all directions, *but from where and what?* Chance favored she look directly overhead, and what she witnessed made the hackles on her lifeless flesh stand on end as her core chilled enough to make her vomit her most-recent blood meal upon the shattered headstone

Charles W. McDonald Jr.

where Damon's body still clung to life.

Damon's Hellgate caused clouds to abscond and the moon to give way as the sky whirlpooled inward on itself from above; dim light, like unto a molten volcano's heart, was visible right before they started to fall through. Landing with thunderous herald, the ground erupted in all directions as creatures of abyssal imagination began to fall through the rift everywhere throughout the Hellish landscape.

Run! Chara's last distinct thought before being slashed through her center with a long, curved katana blade—its ancient rune alive and blazing in the blade's center as it was pulled from her torso before she was blasted the tens of cubits away from Damon by unseen hands. Placing a hand over her wound as it had already begun healing itself, she couldn't help looking back to see who or what had dealt the blow. She knew running was the only smart thing to do, but there would be time to kill what had struck at her later! If she survived the night....

Kneeling over Damon's broken body, only barely visible to her now from the leathery, ribbed wings some twenty cubits in width, her blade still blazed with a fiery, molten haze. She must have been no taller than Chara—certainly not much more beautiful—though with a hard body seemingly more forged than formed, her firm curves shone in shimmering golden and red tones in the blade's firelight. With hair of golden silk and abyssal eyes, she laid her left hand upon Damon's forehead, muttering something that made the ground under him thrust his body upward slightly as the tendrils sunk into the ground and his chest heaved, further anchoring Damon to life in this world. All in what seemed less than an instant, as time appeared to still itself, the seemingly forged, golden-haired creature started toward Chara at a frightening speed. Rounding Chara with a body and quickness that seemed to defy even Chara's imagination of her own abilities, the creature seemed content to strike at her with her sword. Sword versus magic, Chara thought, for all her speed I'll still have time to kill her before fleeing the rest of whatever Damon summoned. Banthis' first katana strike came across Chara at neck height from her left and recovered gracefully into her next strike that swiped at Chara's chest, cutting off the front of her dress at just below her breasts. As Chara countered with nearly equal speed, causing Banthis to back away with some measure of caution, a white-hot, explosive blast directly in front of Banthis caused Banthis to temporarily lose sight. Regaining her faculties fast, but her vision still slightly fuzzy, Banthis nearly ran through Chara, taking one smooth, quick motion to her left at what would have been Chara's middle had she not shifted with all possible speed, still managing to again slice open her flesh, even if not as deep as the last. Grimacing, Chara realized there may be more to this underworldling than she first thought.

Silvery-blue slashes in mid-air rent the Hellish evening in a rectangular doorway to another place before them as Chara ran toward the *Portal* before it had even finished forming.

Leaping after her with all possible speed, knowing she had but an instant, Banthis used her powerful wing muscles to fly her to the *Portal*. Slumping to the ground with an unceremonious thud, Banthis' body—what remained—lay lifeless as the *Portal* collapsed on her, cutting her forged body in half. Banthis corpse still searing on the ground, Hell breaking loose around them as Damon's abyssal summoned creatures tore through the graveyard killing anything that moved and desecrating what didn't, Damon tried to sit up; looking to where the *Portal* had been and where his Banthis now lay dead. His mouth worked at muttering something while his black eyes burned like well-stoked coals. Through the hot amber-gold glow around the black irises of his eyes, the tears of yet more loss came as Damon slumped against the severed headstone where Chara had *again* broken him in ways he would never heal.

Charles W. McDonald Jr.

Chapter 6: The Fork of Consequences

(Kaleion, A Long Time Ago, Continuation….)

Slowly descending via *Damon's Hellgate* into what had been consecrated ground only moments before, *it* walked slowly amidst the broken and destroyed granite headstones, ensuring the desecration of *each* and *every* one, stepping atop each grave in disrespect and loathing. A massive, pernicious, leathery-winged beast left Humanoid footprints in the soil, with the talons of its six-digit feet, in its wake as it closed the distance between *it* and Damon. Its shape changed from dragon, to beast, to man, to woman as it approached Damon, who was still slumped half unconscious against a large piece of headstone debris; breathing still, but unaware of its presence. Finalizing on its instantiation to converse with this particular disciple, *it* had settled on a brunette with large breasts and a slender waist,

Charles W. McDonald Jr.

legs, and frame, just more than a hand shorter than Damon and wearing what he would know to be Roman robes, revealing her absolutely perfect flesh everywhere Damon desired. Fitting she thought—the Roman aspect of it. She reached down to his slumped masculine frame, running *her* fingers through his raven hair as Damon suddenly gasped for air—waking to her touch.

"Damon. I've meant to come visit, and my apologies for the timing. If only I'd come sooner…." She trailed off, looking to Banthis' broken body, severed in half by Chara's *Portal*, destroying her only *real immortal* shell.

It was hard for Damon to speak. The words came out slow and measured as he looked down at her, or rather *its*, golden heels that were actually part of *its* feet. "I…know…you."

"Of course, you do. I'd be disappointed if you didn't." She…*it*…still slowly caressed his hair. He did not pull back. He didn't appear, or feel, repulsed by her, or rather *its*, presence. It had made a good choice in choosing this representation of itself. Or maybe it was because he was even more broken than Banthis, that the warmth of her hand on his head was…needed. *Hmmm*, *it* could leverage that. Her, *its*, caress became more tender, more nurturing—close to motherly, but still eerily, creepily seductive.

"I am truly sorry for Banthis. She was one of my favorites, just as she was yours." She paused, thinking—rather *knowing* in its omnipotence—how Damon would react to the next. "I know what you sent her," she, *it*, whispered in hush tones only a breath away from his earlobe.

Looking directly into her eyes now so she could see the fire in his black mirrors of the soul, he replied, "Of course, you do. I'd be disappointed if you didn't." Damon's wit perilously dangled his own soul before her, before *it*. He no longer cared. What was there left for him to lose?

The irises of her eyes were two amber flames in response as it continued to lovingly stroke and caress Damon's raven locks. He knew who he was talking to, and yet this wasn't disrespect. This was either his challenge or him showing his backbone. Either way, she could crush him with it or *use* him. "My point is that I don't have a problem with what you've done. Only that I wish to share in its rewards. Would you think that a possibility?" Her, *its*, true purpose now finally shining through as *it* decided on how best to use Damon. **Souls were power, and power was useful.** If she scaled in power even a little, it could keep the gap between her and Banthis manageable.

"*Damnation* was made for one intended target and one intended destination. Both are gone now."

"Oh, Chara's very much alive, and I can tell you where she's hiding. And Banthis…." She, *it*, paused again. "I know where the other half of her immortal shell is, and I can bring her back fully and completely. She'll be your

Charles W. McDonald Jr.

wife again—whole. Haven't you suffered enough, Damon? Besides, Banthis wasn't meant to die this way, nor at this time. Chara has tampered with what was to be. So, helping you to set things right works for both of us. Doesn't it?" A lie was most convincing when hidden between two or more truths— such was her, or **its**, modus operandi.

"I won't send you more than I do to her, nor even equal shares. That won't happen—ever." It was a take it or leave it offer from Damon, or rather a take it or destroy me now offer. Either way, he didn't care. Living or dying without Banthis wasn't an acceptable outcome from his perspective at this temporal branch of his life, but he knew her well enough to know she'd take his offer. The **only** thing she, **it**, wanted was more power, and **he** was the **only** one who could, or would, deliver it.

It gave him one, and one only, accepting nod. Then **it** was suddenly gone with a stiff breeze. No sound or theatrics accompanied the Dragon's departure. Damon surveyed the hellish landscape ensuring the planular rift he had summoned had now fully closed. *No more surprises*, he assured himself cautiously. Turning back to look over to Banthis, he saw her beautiful and whole again and starting to breathe where Chara's *Portal* had severed her immortal shell moments before. As he got up to walk to her, he felt himself whole again without a scratch nor bruise, having his full mobility restored. And…. He noticed a place planted in his thoughts—a place where he could find Chara. Wasting not another instant, he opened a *Portal* where he stood with his right index finger walking through to his private fourth-floor study where he needed to gather a couple of scrolls and his second surprise for Chara before using the information he was just given to face her, but this time on *his* terms and with *both* his surprises at the ready.

*   *   *   *

She'd only been breathing again for a few brief moments, face down in the dirt. Now fully aware of her own death and rebirth, she felt herself with her left hand where she'd been severed in half by the *Portal*. Feeling no scar, wound, or pain, she started to upright herself with her right hand still holding her katana, leveraging it to help her to her feet. It wasn't that she was still wounded, but just…. Something felt very different about her and everything around her. Neither new nor old. Gathering her bearings, pushing those thoughts she hadn't the time to afford to the back of her mind, she looked around for Damon. Searching beyond this place for her tether to him to pinpoint his location. *What have you done,* Banthis rebuked her brilliantly mad and wayward husband.

(Damon's Manor, Kaleion, Present Day)

Hard breath pushed at the comforter to let him feel the illusion of his freedom while his memory of Chara, Banthis, and that *thing*, reflected in his *black mirrors of the soul.* His face now ice, his body stiff, as he remembered.... The image of Victoria's body surprisingly still standing in his doorway reflected in the glass of the master bedroom windows as he began bringing himself back—thankfully. Memories were a vile creation. If he only had the courage to wipe them forever from his mind, he would have done so long ago.

The die had been cast. His Master Plan now set. His mind made up. Damon was arguably the most powerful mage on the planet, and yet his power was a nit in comparison to what he would need to execute his plans. He needed to think. He needed to research new power sources he could use for his magic where living matter and belief in magic were not required, and he knew those answers would *not* be found on his homeworld.

Charles W. McDonald Jr.

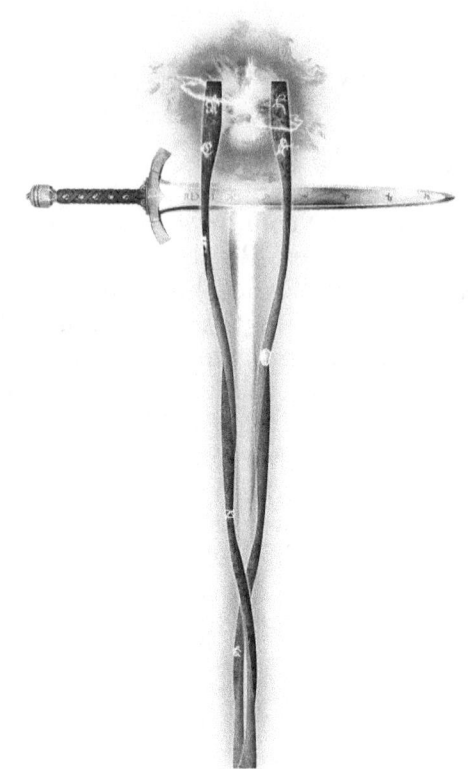

Chapter 7: Forgiveness Sought

(Stirling, Perion, Present Day)

The bustling and often perfidious marketplace of Stirling was among the busiest of places to be found. A morning no different than most others for Radin d'Aguillon. He had a full day's work ahead of him: preparing rooms, fixing a couple of fussy doorknobs that only wanted to work if certain celestial bodies were in complete alignment, tending to not only *their* own horses, but those of their guests as well—the usual. Father had given him four days' work to complete in four hours—yet he would get it all done, as he did on a daily basis. Rowarc could always count on his son, though Radin did begin to wonder if his father was merely trying to challenge him, or just taking advantage of his inherited work ethic and free labor.

Charles W. McDonald Jr.

Formerly a tracker of some notoriety, Rowarc led by example as his workday would be just as full. Radin believed his father a great man—a hero to him always. *Who has time for heroes*, Radin thought sardonically, heading out the front door of his father's inn to accomplish today's to-do list, while his father cursed, removing stubborn door hardware from room number four just above the main dining area.

*   *   *   *

Adjusting his off-white, weathered cavalier shirt and puffing it away from his chest for ventilation, Radin noticed how much warmer it had been this spring compared to last, given how relatively far north they were. *This'll only make the marketplace more charming*, he thought bitterly as he made flirtatious eye contact with a beautiful, buxom, curly-haired redhead in a pretty lily-colored handmaid's dress who winked back at him before giggling something into the ear of a plump girl who walked alongside her. *More chores*, he thought as he continued to run through his to-do list in his head. *Guests have to eat I suppose*, he smiled at another passing young beauty, turning his head to get a second and third glance as she passed. *Blondes*, he chided internally. *Trouble!*

You would have thought every breathing soul within two hundred leagues was here, attempting to buy or sell something. Then there were those who had no intention to *buy* anything—those were always the least appreciated. Thievery carried with it a very stiff penalty in most of the northern countries, but especially in the Kingdom of Gawth, where King Aaron, Keeper of the Wind, took his duties as judge and ruler very seriously. Punishment here was notorious—legendary even. Yet it did not always stop the desperate, nor the experienced professional.

Thought to be the oldest of Kingdoms, the ruling house of Gawth held the title Keeper of the Wind long before the object that made the title known around the rim of the world. Built in the center of the oldest parts of the city, near the plateau of the king's palace, stood a colossal effort of human ingenuity, strength of will, and cooperation with the world of magic. At the time of the great war, it was supposed to be the last line of defense, the last gasp of a world under siege by darkness. A doomsday weapon.

Soaring three hundred cubits into the air, before arching outward to sea like half of a great crystal rainbow, the watchtower held only one occupant for nearly a thousand years: a beautiful, womanly figure of crystal and gold with her sword pointed out to sea—The Lady of the Wind. Standing four times the size of a human female—her sword proportionate to her—it was a remarkable feat of architecture. No one knew if it ever worked, nor if it was ever used, only that it was built mostly with the old magic, and that it could never be destroyed.

It was the sole object of obsession for the young and ambitious ruler. If it could do half of what was claimed, and no one outside a very tight circle even knew what had been claimed, the power of the magic required to make such a creation would have to have been beyond imagination. So fascinated was the reigning monarch that he commissioned the building of a new expansion to the king's castle, building alongside the immense artifact so that he could sleep closer to it, under the sphere of its influence.

Monarchs before King Aaron had given the Lady of the Wind credit due, but paid it no real attention, thinking it was nonsensical to mess with its power, *if* it had any at all. They all continued the research, but not until King Aaron did any ruler show interest in unlocking its powers. In his obsession, King Aaron more than tripled the manpower and intellect on the task, recruiting the best minds from as far as a message could carry, investing vast amounts of the kingdom's wealth and resources in a project some saw as futile, while others saw it for what it really was: dangerous. New streets went unfinished, and new building construction slowed to a crawl to satisfy the king's whims and obsessions.

In a roundabout way, that's what all of this was about: making Stirling the center of attention. The king offered a reward of five hundred gold crowns to the champion of a tournament that would be held on the royal grounds south of the palace. The competition would include several rounds with the best that could be found abroad facing the king's best men in the final rounds. There was some talk of the winner also leading an expedition to seek out some great relic—it was never really said *what* exactly, but the king made it all sound necessary to the growth and security of Stirling. *Necessary enough to levy more taxes!* Radin clenched his jaw at that thought.

Oh well, he had work to do: supper ingredients and a few trinkets to spruce up the inn. Tradition suggested he haggle the merchant down at least once for each purchase. Rowarc d'Aguillon already owned one of the more respected and profitable inns. It had been exceptionally profitable of late, but Rowarc always took pride in making it better at every opportunity. Reinvesting his money back into his labor of love. He had made it his passion since his wife's passing. Everything had changed since then. At least Radin felt so when he and his father were alone. He felt they should have grown closer. Instead, he could feel the gap widening with each passing week. The chasm of awkward silence between them was doing untold damage and he didn't have a solution for it. Different generations he supposed. What did he really have in common with his legendary father other than blood?

Shoving those thoughts away and trying to remain cautious of who was around him, Radin fought his way through streets thronged with sweaty masses. After six different booths, finding nothing but worthless junk on sale for ten times its worth, he finally spotted a booth that might have something of genuine value. A merchant tent, much larger than most, with room in the aisles for people to peruse. Even so, it was filled to capacity and mostly with young men. The reason for that became evident as he ducked into the tent, crossing a line of paying customers. An alluring young woman, with eyes of emeralds, flesh of silk, and strawberry-blonde locks stood behind a small table with a large wooden lock box, taking care of the sales. She appeared to be taking over for someone else, an older gentleman walking out of the back with sack lunch in hand. *Maybe a father or uncle*, he considered as he started to look around.

A quick glance down the line of customers and he could see each of the young men staring with virile eyes back past him at the young woman. Smiling, shaking his head slightly at his own thoughts of the strawberry-blonde-haired beauty, he pressed toward the back of the tent where he thought he could look around at what they had to sell. He found a little bit of everything, ranging from cryptic staves and ornate canes to small statues and trinkets of every nature. Everything was very nice and moderately priced.

"Apologies, Master," the words from a seemingly genderless voice coming from a slender patron covered in tattered grey woolen rags that must have been stifling hot on such a warm day. More than a bit late too as he had already been shoved into one of the shelves. Radin barely maintained his balance, dropping to his knees as he braced himself with his balled-up fists to keep from falling flat on the canvas. Whoever it was, he must have been in a big hurry. By the time he looked up, whoever it had been was long gone. Frowning, he began pulling himself up, noticing something on one of the lower shelves that caught his eye.

Very small and nestled toward the back of shelf was a sculpture portraying a ring of weathered stones set upon a grassy plane—somewhere. Picking it up, he quickly began to lose himself in the intricacies of the artifact—the tiny pits in the battered stone's surface, causing his thoughts and memories to flash in his mind's eye.

Was it humming, he wondered as he sat it back down on the shelf, stepping away from it as his senses of the here and now returned to him. He wasn't sure if his ears were ringing, or perhaps it had been playing tricks on him. Such extraordinary detail for something so small, as if witnessed firsthand and captured in thought and clay on site. His father had warned him about such things before, but those were just tales. *Two silver pence,* he noticed looking at the bottom of it. Reaching into his pockets to see if he had enough of his own coin, he decided to pay for it with his own money, realizing his father would be furious with him if he knew.

Approaching the lovely young woman, he noted she couldn't have been much older than himself or any of his friends. Trying to project confidence—however manufactured—he managed to look into her emerald eyes. Then it hit him. His dream from a few nights ago—the portrait that wasn't a portrait on that desk. *It was her!*

Much more than just beautiful, she was elegant—regal even, and now making the connection to his dream, it made sense. Even in a wool sackcloth, he could have picked her out of a mass of thousands, with her head held strong—prideful, with hot burning eyes. Her wavy, strawberry-blonde hair cascaded off her shoulders in radiant strands of silk. From what he could see of her profile as he walked up to her, she had a slim, taut waist with a firm, fair bosom, and healthy, medium hips. It was a difficult choice picking out her best feature—everywhere he looked, he liked. She wasn't a hard, forged girl. She was a soft curves, shapely girl. With the eyes and look of a woman.

He decided not to ask if her father had made these works, thinking that might very well be a horribly embarrassing miscalculation if he were wrong. He knew he would thrash himself mentally, and otherwise, if he passed up an opportunity with someone like her. Though, he wondered if his dream of her meant she was spoken for or not—if the dream was even accurate or had any purpose at all. Dream or not, she felt so out of reach for him, but, mustering his confidence, he took a deep breath. A quick brush of his right hand through his shoulder-length auburn hair, maybe just enough to feather it for her.

"Afternoon. Are you new to Stirling, or just here for the Shirantal," he asked through a disarming smile, hoping it would be enough to charm, even if only for a bit.

She twisted the small artifact at eye level in her left hand, feigning to look at it while actually returning his smile with a radiant one of her own. *Did she actually swoon for him,* he hoped. *Does that mean what I think it does?*

"Do you like it," she asked, regarding the artifact as she handed it back to him, letting the back of her hand delicately touch his palm as she passed the object.

Could I be that lucky? Something was working, whether his charm or not did not matter at the moment. Trying to calm down and not think of how incredible the lady before him was, his heart began to race, swallowed and

Charles W. McDonald Jr.

exhilarated by her seductive charms at work. "It's so detailed for something so small. Did you make it?"

He thought the radiant glow from her smile could be seen from outside the booth. "How did you know? Everyone always assumes that all of these are the work of my Pa, or uncle, grandpa, or some such other relative. Is it so inconceivable that it could be mine?"

"Not if they pay attention to you, no," Radin reasoned with a smile. "Truthfully, I thought the same thing until I got a closer look at you."

"Really? So, what is there in a closer look at me that gave it away?"

"Everything," he advocated quietly, softly, leaning in over the counter towards her. The coy look and dangerous smile she returned him held promise and excitement. She was not a scared little girl. Not easily intimidated nor impressed. He was in unprecedented territory with her and that suited him just fine. "My name is Radin," he offered, pausing in hopes she would fill the void with the beauty of her name.

"Elise."

"So, Elise, will you be here long?"

"Not sure. I'll go where I go."

Radin raised an eyebrow at that, wondering how such a beautiful woman could be so free, wondering what it would be like if he were able to do whatever he wanted—go wherever he dared. That thought carried with it punishment. Nevertheless, he could *not* go back home without at least asking, "So, where will you be going when you close up tonight?"

Elise smiled knowingly, obviously enjoying this to-and-fro banter far more than she should. It wasn't as if he were the first to ask. Everywhere they had gone she was asked, but already this was different—*he* was different. She sensed something special about him—something old, like one of the places she had been to over the years. Something behind his pretty, grey-blue eyes sang familiar songs to her soul. The features of his face looked…oddly familiar in a way. A dangerous way. Still, she liked what she sensed in him, and felt confident in its meaning. Her instincts about him were all saying good and noble things. Even now, as she examined him, with his auburn eyebrows cutely furrowed expectantly at her, he touched her in ways she liked without touching her at all. "Well, I suppose I'll be going somewhere with you."

Radin swallowed hard, trying to gather his words, not wanting to suddenly become the babbling idiot after doing so well thus far. He managed a genuine smile while his words came to him, "Well, then I guess I'll stop by at dusk to help you close up shop."

"Well, I guess I'll see you then, Radin."

"What about th—" he was cut off by her as he held up the carving.

Charles W. McDonald Jr.

"Don't worry about it, Radin. Consider it a gift."

He didn't know what to say. *She was giving him things already. Wow! Whatever I just did, I need to write it down and sell it. Who would have thought? Perhaps, I should use the money I was going to spend to find her something. Good idea.* There had to be something amidst all these merchant tents *she* might like. He needed to check out some of the other booths anyway to see if there would be anything to bring back for his father's inn. He couldn't go back empty handed, or there would be more questions than he cared answer.

Pushing the tent flap out of his way as he left, Radin began his diligent search for something she might like—something to make her swoon for him again—he liked that very much. And for what he had been sent as well. *Priorities*, he thought exuberantly, knowing it wouldn't be his father's items he first attended!

With the hundreds of booths and permanent shops in the city, surely there would be something that a woman might fancy, alas.... Resigning to this deceivingly difficult task of picking out something for a woman, Radin started walking back to one of the tents he had run across earlier, earmarking it as a possibility for his father's needs. Then he remembered her, pulling out the tiny sculpture she had given him. *What about something like this? Not bad,* he thought, *but where, besides her booth, would I find something like this?* He put the sculpture back into his pocket, scanning around the marketplace, searching for anyplace that might have some decent woodwork. His eyes caught a brute of a middle-aged man and his son coming out of a large white tent that advertised his goods with a sign carved out of singed wyrmwood. Carrying a small wooden practice sword and brandishing it in play, the son kept himself busy just outside the tent's entrance. *Maybe there,* he considered as he set out to cross the sea of people that stood between him and the merchant tent.

The air was thick with the sweat of the masses, threatening to suffocate him before he ever reached the carpenter's tent. Suddenly someone ran into him, nearly knocking him to the ground.

"Hey!" Searching for his balance before he went all the way to the ground, Radin jumped back up, shaking his fist in the air, trying to see who had knocked him down so rudely. Only catching a glimpse of a torn grey beggar's cloak, nothing more. *Was that the same person from before?* Whoever it was had managed to vanish among the multitude. Radin snarled, checking himself over. "If that was a thief, I'm gonna ki...," he blurted. Unable to find the gift Elise had given him, he started to panic. Again, he shook his fist furiously in the air in the direction of the fleeing peasant.

People were turning to look at him. Realizing how ridiculous he must have looked, Radin shrugged, turning away from them, trying to make

Charles W. McDonald Jr.

himself appear smaller and draw less attention. He didn't want anyone who might have known him to spot him like that. In his effort to shrink in place, he couldn't help but notice it now—the beautiful piece of jewelry laying at his feet alongside his missing carving. Leaning over, conscious of everyone around him this time, he picked up both, shoving the gleaming jewelry into the right-side pocket of his dark brown pants and Elise's carving into his left. If anyone saw him with that, they would think him the thief, and there would be no explaining his way out of it. He'd be hung in hours—if not minutes.

Radin looked around once more, trying to find the person who had nearly knocked him to the ground, but it was as if they just vanished—scattering into the hot, stale air. Spotting a secluded alley where he could take a better look at the jewelry without the prying eyes of the masses watching over him, Radin tried to calm himself enough to walk there without causing more suspicion.

Pulling it out of his pants once he reached the back of the alley, near a small fence used to separate the property lines, he saw that it appeared to be designed like an amulet, and certainly was pretty for a fake. *It can't be real.* Barely filling his palm, and seemingly made of gold, its emerald-cut ruby set in the center was edged with dozens of small round glass stones. Etched into the gold circumference and extending from the Ruby itself were five navigational arrows with unintelligible runes at each point. Each rune, at each of the five points, set inside a small star sapphire stone. He could not imagine anyone possessing such a thing if it were real, not unless they were royalty. Radin paused in thought 'til he could nearly feel his own heartbeat beginning to race. *No. No. NO!*

*   *   *   *

Gleaming silver eyes stared back at the boy from underneath the hood of her matted and tattered grey cloak—a cloak that did not befit the woman wearing it, nor of her beautiful features. Youthfully middle-aged with straight platinum hair, she would not have been able to pass for simply anyone were it not for the tattered cloak of a commoner. A burdened smile crossed the very soft skin of her face as she watched him from a safe distance. A solitary tear streaked down her cheek as she forced herself to turn away. He would find happiness soon. She could see it in his eyes, and in the girl he fancied. He was becoming a man. Her only desire was to turn back for a final look, but…. *Forgive me*, she begged of him in her thoughts from afar, forcing herself to walk away without that last, needed glimpse. *Please forgive me.* Each of her

Charles W. McDonald Jr.

burdened footsteps away from where she wanted to be brought the weight of another tear hitting her soft, dusty and weathered, leather boots.

Radin with the Amulet of the Five Gates

Charles W. McDonald Jr.

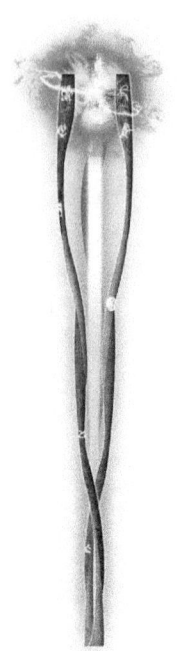

Chapter 8: Die Glocke

(Charleston, SC, Earth, Present Day)

A brilliant, vertical shaft of silvery-blue light split the now highly charged air particles just outside the manor of Wolf Dietrich in the suburbs of Charleston, South Carolina. It was sweltering hot, and Damon was grateful that he wasn't wearing his full mage regalia, though he had to be judicious in his use of magic. He didn't want to leave traces of his skills beyond the transportation required to come and go as his *Portal* whooshed to a close behind him in transparent waves like unto a rock thrown into a pond, but inverted and transparent.

Dressed only in his UNTUCKit® navy short-sleeve, button-down, collared shirt and Levi's® 501 jeans, he did his best to adapt to the cultures and norms of his host world in this time period, for this was not his first time on Earth. He'd been here many, many times before…. Throughout the centuries and epochs of this world.

Carrying a .45 ACP Glock® in the small of his back, covered by his shirt, he pulled out a 5.5" Android Smartphone and began texting Wolf, letting him know he had arrived for their pre-arranged meeting. Casually walking up to the ten-foot double-doors and brushing his long straight black bangs out of his face, Damon smiled for the security camera, no doubt recording his entrance as he rang the doorbell. *He would have to take care of **that** before he left*, as he considered the possibility of his *Portal* being recorded, again smiling one more time for the camera. He could sense someone approaching from the other side of the door. All his precautionary spells were still working here; that was a good sign. Magic wasn't entirely dead here. Yet.

A healthy, but weathered old gentleman answered the door in shorts and a button-down short-sleeve grey shirt similar to Damon's.

"Dr. Dietrich, I presume," Damon proclaimed extending his right hand for a firm and cordial handshake in the customary exchange of pleasantries. "I want to thank you for making time to meet with me. I was so glad when you accepted my invitation. I'm a huge fan of your work," Damon offered, coming precariously close to a bold-faced lie, which would have been grotesquely out of the norm for him. Still, appearances had to be maintained. For now.

Damon could lie when lying was called for, but he preferred the operational standards of truth because truth made it easier to buttress your flanks upon solid foundations. Truth made it easier to build and maintain Allies, while simultaneously making it harder for your enemies to undermine your work.

"Oh, no need for all that flattery, son. I'm well past the need for that at my age. Won't you come inside and tell me why you've come so far? You mentioned you came from Austin—that's quite a long trip. You must be tired from that drive."

"Oh, it wasn't quite so bad," Damon smirked—not making much effort to hide it either.

"Well, we can have our meeting in my study if you want. That way we have my books close by if we need them for our conversation." His English was quite good and without much of an accent for his German heritage. Some of the Germans had adapted well to living in the states. Some had deep German accents to this very day—if they still lived at all. WW-II was a long time ago, considering these Earth Humans and their very short lifespans, so he counted himself fortunate to even be able to have this meeting. First-hand information and accounts were always better than reading from a book, so he needed to seize this opportunity with this Paperclip scientist.

Wolf started to lead the way to his study while Damon followed behind him and to his right. "You studied physics at the University of Texas is that right?"

Charles W. McDonald Jr.

"Yes, that's right," Damon replied nonchalantly. "I just wanted to talk to an authority on Die Glocke. Really needed someone that was part archeologist, scientist, and historian. Your name was the only one that kept coming up again and again. So, I'm very pleased we could finally talk."

"Yes, yes. Like I said, my Son, all the pleasantries are not necessary," Wolf mildly protested, taking his seat just a couple of feet away from his executive desk—his back up against one of three walls dedicated to floor-to-ceiling built-in bookshelves. This man liked his books; Damon could relate. Pointing to the diamond patterned, pleated, coffee-colored wingback opposite his own, Wolf motioned for Damon to take a seat. "Tell me, how can I help?" Wolf began sipping on a steaming cup of tea that had been resting upon an oval, mahogany coffee table with inlaid maple scrollwork as his feet rested upon the warmth of the area rug beneath the table and chairs.

Damon pulled out a single gold coin sitting it on the coffee table between them. "For your time, Sir. I just want to make sure you understand I'm not here to take up your time for free. I imagine you get bothered all the time, and I'm not the bothering type." Damon smiled disarmingly as his eyes never bothered to look at the ancient and weathered gold coin he'd offered. Priceless in age and rarity—regardless of its weight. Damon could be exceedingly disarming when necessary. Kellen always said, 'Damon's best weapon was how close he could get to you before you knew how close to death you were.'

"Oh…. Well." Wolf cleared his throat, examining the coin from a distance, not wanting to be so gauche as to pick it up while talking to his guest. He had never seen one quite like it. *Perhaps it was Roman.* "How can I help?"

"Let's talk about toroidal field energy. I'm very interested in finding out what you know from Die Glocke experiments and observations about how the Nazi's tapped into this energy field, or at least found a way to measure it."

*   *   *   *

(A few hours later….)

The clock was ticking, but Damon took the necessary time to find the safe room where the security camera feeds recorded in one centralized location. He needed to be sure he took care of any recordings before continuing his search through the house to see if anyone else needed to be erased. Taking care of Dietrich only required his bare hands, but still, he had to remove any trace of his presence. The four flat panels, each with four independent camera feeds and a series of low-voltage wires chasing down a flexible conduit, assured him that he was in the right place. The house was loaded with CCTV cameras.

Charles W. McDonald Jr.

Looking around, he noticed some lower cabinets with blinking lights shining from in between the door seams. Looking inside the cabinets, he saw what he knew to be two computers. Ripping out their power cords and stealing their hard-drives should take care of the problem. Just to be sure, he searched the upper cabinets too. "Good thing you looked," he breathed aloud as he found a NAS drive, most likely the persistent destination of the digital video, and he smashed it to the floor, putting a bullet through all four drives in the NAS and two more in each of the other drives he took from the computers. *Gotta move fast now. So loud,* he admonished internally as he holstered the .45 ACP back into the small of his back. Another ninety seconds and he had searched the vast majority of the rest of the manor, not finding anyone else he needed to neutralize as he walked out the front door with a few advanced physics books under his left arm. *The Zero-Point Field, Einstein's cosmological constant, Dark Energy, Thermodynamics, and Garrett Lisi's Unification Theory* would keep Damon busy for some time as he went back into his concentrated development mode. With a mere wave of his right hand, a fissure of energy split and superheated the air in front of him as he found himself back home—worlds and many lightyears away. Damon was grateful his *Portal* spell still worked on a world now so devoid of magic. Even if barely so.

Part 3: The Rapture

Charles W. McDonald Jr.

I long to be both raptured and caged
by your love immortal;
To feel the threads of time intertwine between us
'Til there is only eternal bliss,
And all my memories, both near and far,
Are of you, My Darling Love.

Charles W. McDonald Jr.

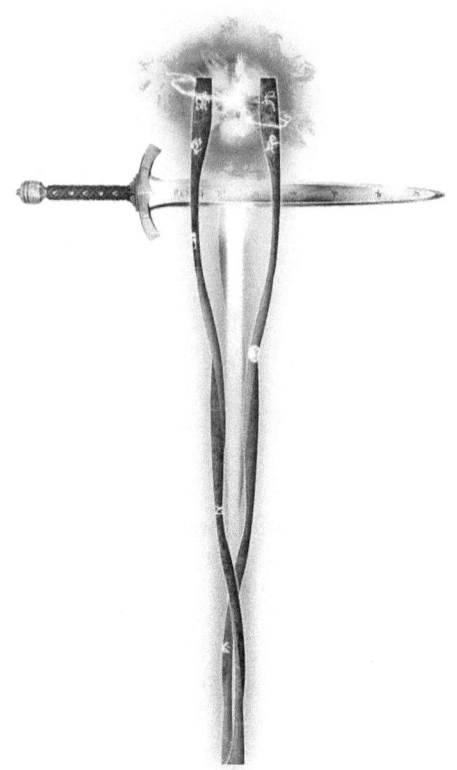

Chapter 9: Surrender

(Stirling, Perion, Present Day)

Still hard at work, Rowarc d'Aguillon was about his typical day, trying to do ten things at the same time—normal for this time of year. This would be a very busy, and hopefully profitable, next couple of weeks for him during the annual festivities. The inn had been filled to capacity the past several nights, requiring him to hire extra help in the pub downstairs. He hoped the two new girls would work well for him. They certainly cost enough. Brushing back his short black hair now graying at the sides, he began repairs on a chair broken nearly to splinters by some fat lummox who couldn't handle his ale any better than a little schoolgirl.

Hopefully, with the addition of the new help, Radin could hold things together until he could get back. It was a lousy time for him take on extra work, but this tracking job was too big of an opportunity—beyond just the extra coin. It was a chance to get out and do something he sorely missed, perhaps even to find his own way again now that Arella was gone. With all the money these men were offering he could finally afford to make major additions and improvements to his inn, or perhaps.... *Hmm*, he thought, *with Arella gone and Radin grown....* Rowarc quickly shook off those thoughts before they unleashed a wave of guilt and betrayal he did not need to deal with right now. That was no way for a boy to grow up. Besides, it was only a temporary arrangement. There was no room in his life of responsibilities for traipsing about the world anymore. That time had come and gone....

One concern still bothered him as he went about his repairs: in this city alone, there had to be at least twenty experienced trackers of at least some renown, many of them much younger and still in their prime. So, *why did they want him? Ah*, he thought, *You're making more out of this than there is. If you look for dirt in an alley, you're bound to find plenty!* Not that these men were of untrustworthy backgrounds, but something was definitely going on that they were not sharing. He felt their treachery afoot and had learned to trust his instincts. After years of retirement, his senses may have been rusty, but they were not dead. He could smell it, but in this line of business, there was always something that neglected to be mentioned. Some trades just revolved around trouble—such was a major reason he retired from it. It was a rare man, an honorable man, who showed you his true intent right from the start. That was just the nature of the business. You just didn't hire a professional tracker if you didn't have something you wanted to keep from the local authorities.

Oh well. If they want Rowarc d'Aguillon to come out of retirement to find some wealthy noble's stray little girl, so be it. Besides, shouldn't take long to find a stray woman, he thought sarcastically, just stick my head outside and look in any direction. This was going to be like finding a particular needle in a stack of needles, but nothing he hadn't done before. He just hoped the trail wasn't ice by now. The urgency to start about her trail gnawed at him in the back of his mind.

Frowning, and wondering where that boy of his was, Rowarc tied a string around the chair to hold the pieces in place giving the glue time to set. *Where is that boy?*

Rowarc's brown eyes nearly tripped over their sockets as he beheld the sight that walked through the front door, only to be followed in by his very late and wayward son, who had hold of her *by the hand.* Rowarc harrumphed boisterously, searching for the right words as he fumbled to get the glue off his hands. It was not the first time Radin had brought home someone special for him to meet, but they usually didn't leave him a stammering idiot. *Is there a*

Charles W. McDonald Jr.

right thing to say? Oh well. "Radin," he said with a long pause followed by, "My Lady." *Was she a lady?* She looked between a lady and a girl…. With an air of aristocracy. Appearing more nervous, his eyes kept shifting from the girl to Radin, then back to the strawberry-blonde girl, apparently in an attempt to get the greetings out of the way before he stumbled all over himself.

Noticing his father's discomfort and not wanting to prolong it too terribly long, Radin motioned to Elise, "Father, this is Elise." Elise curtsied for him, while Radin beamed with studded pride.

"Don't suppose you found anything in that flea-infested place Stirling calls a market, did you?" Pausing while he placed the repaired chair upside down on top of a table to dry, "I swear that place is full of nothing but thieves stealing from crooks."

Not exactly the greeting he was hoping for from his father…. Radin visibly cringed looking to Elise, wishing his father had asked where they had met before making that comment. Who knew what his father would say next, but whatever it was, he knew the odds were pretty strong that it would be even more embarrassing than the last. *That has to be the primary role of a parent*, he realized, *to completely embarrass their offspring.* Radin looked to his father as if trying to tell him to shut up with his eyes, then back to Elise, finding her trying to hold herself together instead of cracking up—deciding instead to just drop it.

Apparently, she found the omission of how they met *both* adorable *and* priceless. She seemed content to let Rowarc dig a deeper hole for himself.

"I swear if there is but one honest, reputable merchant amongst the whole lot of them, I'll bend over buck naked in the center of the street," Rowarc proclaimed with a flourish that caused both hands to land perfectly on the cheeks of his butt.

Radin couldn't stop his hand from involuntarily moving to cover his face from the horror of it all. Elise burst out laughing, nearly splitting her side despite her desperate efforts to muffle her reaction.

"Okay, Dad, we're gonna be going now!"

"But…. But…," Rowarc protested with his hands apologetically outstretched.

"Radin, don't forget about the things you bought," Elise offered in a sweetly innocent tone that was anything but. Radin wasn't sure if Elise had brought that up to prolong his suffering, or if she was genuinely trying to be polite. *No*, he was sure now, she was definitely *not* being polite! Gruffly running his fingers through his long auburn hair in much the way his father had done only a moment before, Radin tried to shake off the uncomfortable feeling of being this close to his father with a beautiful woman that he desperately needed to impress rather than scare her off with his father's rapier wit.

"Oh, yeah...," Radin paused, giving Elise a look of certain reprisal which she merely welcomed with a wink, "I guess I forgot. What, in all the excitement and everything...," again pausing—glaring, "Elise helped me pick out some really nice things. Here," he mentioned, placing a bag full of ornaments, trinkets, sculptures, and nick-knacks on the countertop in front of him. Rowarc appeared satisfied—even a little impressed as he rifled through the bag, making note of what they had picked out, all apparently very nice choices. "And there was a little a left over," Radin remarked, handing over the change.

Rowarc was obviously stunned, but never without comment, "And, you got these things from *Stirling's* Marketplace?" Rowarc thumbed through the change, more than forty silver pence in all. Shocking.

Radin sighed. This was too much. His father had to know he was tormenting him by now. Intentionally. Surely, he was not that blind. Maybe he just didn't care. *Yes,* that had to be it. Elise couldn't help but chuckle again. *That was it. It was a conspiracy. It had to be! They were **both** having fun at his expense.*

Radin simmered as he looked to Elise, examining her—watching for anything that might give her away. Seeing the expression of doubt and inquisition on his face, she knew she had caused enough damage to his ego for now. "Well, it was nice meeting you, Mr. d'Aguillon," Elise proffered as she pulled Radin along by the hand. Leading him just outside the inn, and hopefully out of earshot of Radin's father, "I'm sorry...."

"Sure, you are...." Scruffily running his fingertips through his hair again.

"That was just too priceless to pass up. You understand, don't you?" Her eyes sought forgiveness and seemed quite genuine. Just as he was about to say, 'yes,' he was caught in the most awkward of all moments as her face drew nearer to his. Her hands pulled him closer. His throat became dry in an instant that seemed to last forever, as her soft lips enveloped and tasted his bottom lip and tongue. His heart raced then stopped as he tasted her back. Closing his eyes, he let her lips tenderly drape across his in a move indicative of her having more experience than him; blood surging through him with new life. Inside, he felt it. Something beyond the physical.... At that moment, he felt the gentle caress of her immortal soul. Something magical had just happened. Slowly, and with great tenderness, he began kissing her back, caressing the side of her beautiful face with the backs his fingertips. *Had something indescribable been captured or caged between them?*

Physically his heart was pounding and his blood surging, making everything more vivid and sensitive to her touch. With his eyes closed, his consciousness felt the caress of her energy and her light that seemed in search of something inside him.

Still inexperienced at all this, he opened his eyes to see she was looking right through him. He stopped for just a second, still caressing her face. Her mood had completely changed in that instant. Her countenance was one of seriousness, knowing, and something else his limited experience couldn't quantify. "What is it? Is something wrong," he brooded, trying to commit himself fully to the moment. Previous girls had told him he wasn't 'in the moment' enough when he was 'with them.' He didn't understand how he could be with a girl and 'not be with her,' but *such was the logic of girls*, he thought. *She might look like a girl in some ways, but she kissed like a woman.*

"I…. It's nothing. Nothing…," she lied.

Her reassurances were not at all convincing. She had completely changed from a young lady of wit, humor, and confidence to one of…. She was afraid—terrified. *Had he done something wrong?* With her now shaking in his arms, Radin pulled her closer, holding her tight as he caressed her back. Still, she shook as if nothing he could do could calm her. "Hey. Hey. It's all right. It's gonna be all right."

"What if it already is?" Her expression, her mood, and everything about her changed again in an instant, as she kissed him deeply once more.

He didn't know what to do but hold on. It had taken her only an instant to work her way into his heart, and already he prayed it would take the rest of eternity for her to work her way out.

A blinding, waking vision of white light upon a great lake of crystal with a booming voice from beyond rocked Radin as the combination of Elise, and the waking vision, appeared almost too much for him to hang on to the reality around him, causing him to briefly lose his stance and stumble sideways.

Pulling away from her and the seductive and perfumed, feminine scent of her long strawberry-blonde hair, he felt the passion and excitement she had invoked coursing through his veins bringing him back to a reality still electrified by all things Elise. The intoxication of sensual success weaving its tapestry of confusion on a young man's mind. It was perhaps more potent a spell than anything manmade in the way it could completely annihilate all male reasoning. Smiling, Radin pulled the amulet he had found from his pocket, holding it out for her. Her breath immediately caught in its magnificence; her eyes sparkling in fascination and curiosity at the sight of its beauty. *What is it with girls and jewelry? They would have to pick the most expensive things. Oh well, at least she could be impressed with a fake.* "Here," he offered, placing it into her hands, closing her soft fingers around the artifact. "It probably isn't real, but

Charles W. McDonald Jr.

it's pretty and I want you to have it."

She loved his rich and throaty voice for such a young man—a myriad of places and cultures but with a strong common-tongue accent, speaking of his whole life raised in the area. "But, but…. Radin are you sure it's…?"

"What?"

Elise couldn't help but smile. She opened her hand to take a closer look at it without appearing to examine it in front of him—she would wait 'til later for that. But she was already fairly certain…. "Where did you get this? It's incredible!"

"I found it on the ground when I was looking for a gift for you. Somebody bumped into me, and I guess they dropped it." Radin appeared guilty for a moment. "Maybe we should turn it in. I wouldn't want to get us in trouble."

"Turn it in to who? Who would we be in trouble with?"

"Don't know. Either it's real and belongs to some royal family or some such thing. Or maybe a very wealthy merchant, but like I said I'm pretty sure it's a fake so there's really no telling. I can't imagine anyone being careless enough to drop something like that if it were real." *And, not have paid me a special visit by now,* he caustically mused to himself, briefly turning to look down the alley as if that were not such a far-fetched idea.

Elise smirked. "Well, you know that if it is part of the crown jewels, we can look it up and find out. Surely there would be some writings about such things here locally."

Radin nodded knowingly, though he had not considered that before. Smiling, he offered, "Well, I don't want to give it up unless we have to. So, let's hope that we can keep it. And, if so, it's yours. Let's just hope the thing doesn't cause us more trouble than it's worth." His managed smile seemed fragile at the possibility that it just might be.

Smiling a half-smile, Elise held him, quietly putting the pieces together in the secrecy of her own thoughts. The way he kissed, his voice, his gift, and the stranger who 'dropped it,' all mocked her from the void of her very long journey here. *Who was Radin d'Aguillon, really?*

Charles W. McDonald Jr.

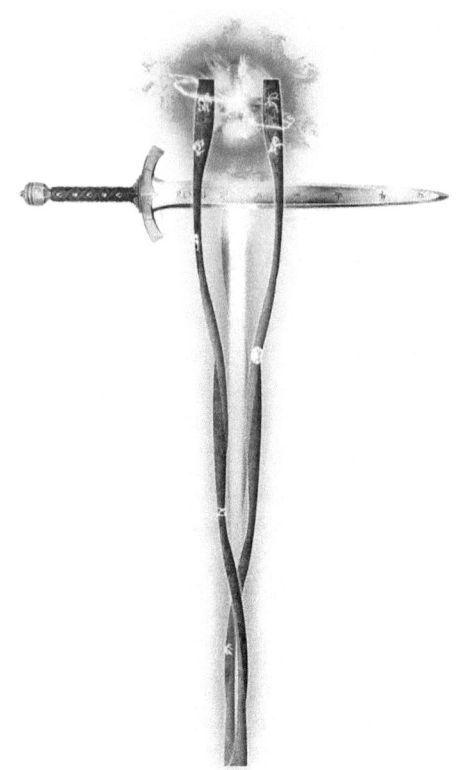

Chapter 10: Heartstrings and Moonbeams

(Stirling, Perion, Present Day)

The warmth and soft comfort of Radin's bed had been welcome after the long and eventful preceding day, not to mention the steady schedule of traveling from one town to the next in her tireless search. Standing at the bedroom window, watching the street below for Radin's return, Elise slowly, nervously, fingered the jewels of the beautiful amulet while she waited. He had only been gone a short while, but already she missed him—thoughts of him racing incessantly through her mind. *Ridiculous*, she chided internally. *Already swooning over him.... A little caution might be best at times like this, rather than tripping over heartstrings and moonbeams.*

Frowning while mentally shooing the last thought away, Elise set the

Charles W. McDonald Jr.

sparkling amulet down on the bed, smoothing the soft, cream pleats of her summer dress. No longer able to resist the urge, Elise began to wear her way through the floorboards, pacing to and from the edge of Radin's room; only to find herself back by the bed's edge and the mysterious amulet after satisfactorily releasing enough of her pensive thoughts. Appearing to stare back up at her from the soft quilt bedding on each of her return trips, the amulet quietly screamed at her for her attention. *Probably a fake*, she cynically considered. The amulet gleamed, faceted rays dancing in the morning light from its gilded and enchanted surfaces. Elise merely scowled back it warily. She'd seen enough significant artifacts across many worlds in her time to know better.

Sitting back down on the bed, cautiously picking up the amulet, Elise felt it for the first time—a powerful and ominous presence. It seemed to possess.... Taking it to the mirror, carefully, slowly placing it around her neck, the confirmation slammed home with urgent immediacy. Elise ripped the amulet from her neck, as if it were a deadly viper, yet held it with the greatest reverence. Placing it down on the dresser and checking to make sure Radin had not returned, Elise reached for something she had kept hidden around her neck. Hidden between large, supple breasts, she pulled out a pewter Celtic cross, supported by a necklace of exquisitely elegant and delicate, beveled links. Not something a merchant might possess but a gift of undying love. Something of obvious far greater value and sentiment as tears came to her eyes just looking at it.

"Thank you," she whispered to the old and familiar cross, closing her fingers and thoughts around it and the profound memories it invoked.

She thought she knew when she kissed him for the first time, yet there was still much doubt. *How could such a thing be? This place, this young man, and there was something else....* Something she had not expected, but perhaps held at least some, if not all, of the answers. *Could her prayers have been answered so completely? Could her love have traveled this far? Would it have transcended even the coils of mortality?*

Elise fought tears of joy as she carefully placed the beautiful amulet around her neck, tucking it and her Celtic cross in between her bosom. Prickling at her soul like a crown of thorns about her head, she had no idea what it was—only that it did not belong to any king or monarch. It was meant for them—or people *like* them. Now the only questions were: *why them, and what powers did it possess?*

The door to Radin's room opened abruptly, catching Elise by surprise as she straightened the cleavage of her dress. Radin was as surprised as she, by the look on his face. His whole world had just changed in but a day, and he would never be the same. He did wonder how all this happened. It wasn't like

Charles W. McDonald Jr.

this was his first experience with a woman, but none had come close to the level of power and influence she held over him already. He feared what influence a more prolonged exposure to her would have over him.

"Everything okay," he asked from the doorway as she settled down on the bed after quickly comporting herself.

"M'hum," she lied smoothly as if practiced at it while shaking her head innocently, though leveraging her beautiful eyes to help hide her obfuscation.

"I didn't interrupt you, did I…? I mean, I can leave if you need some privacy."

Laying back down on his bed in anything but an innocent manner, she wrapped his thoughts in strands of seduction with the subtle moves of her body. A seemingly innocent enough brush of a thigh with her fingertips, followed by a nonchalant and completely unnecessary adjustment of the pleats of her dress, only to let them reveal a tad more for him than they had before. Her breasts pinched together by seemingly innocent inward motions of her elbows enough to cause a little more cleavage to show for him as the strands holding summer dress together around her chest strained.

How do they do that, Radin wondered, forgetting what he had just said—and everything else for that matter. It began to dawn on him that he was standing in the doorway—motionless—staring at her body moving seductively about his bed. And when his eyes did drift over her flesh, to her hemline, as she slowly moved her legs for him, to her flat stomach and soft breasts to her beautiful face, he found her smiling at him. Knowingly. He could feel his face and neckline blush and could only manage a gulp as he struggled to force his legs to move his body toward her. One foot in front of the other. The danger bells in his mind had shattered from ringing so hard for her seduction was all-consuming. Testing himself, he tried to recall the face of any other girl he had been with before, drawing a blank. *Hmmm,* he knew, *that's bad.*

Staring at her for a very long moment, which he was sure had been her intent, Radin slowly left the plate of food he'd prepared downstairs on the dresser at the end of his room, sitting down beside her, letting his right hand rest on the inside of her bare thigh just below the delicate hem of her dress.

"What are you doing to me," he asked, slowly caressing the inside of her thigh as he looked into her wide, aroused eyes glowing with misbehaving and mischievous intent.

Taking Radin's hand with hers and moving it just above her hemline, pushing up her dress so he could feel her warmth and wetness, she offered, "I could ask the same question." Now sitting up beside him on the edge of his bed, she let her pretty eyes linger into his as her neck and breasts flushed with surging blood for him, completely electrified and aroused to his every touch.

Charles W. McDonald Jr.

Her chest heaved as she inhaled his breath and felt his intimate caress, her lips right next to his as they gazed into one another.

A hard and lingering, sensuous kiss formed between them as they met in the middle, both advancing toward the other simultaneously. Her experience showed through in the soft probing of her tongue against his. His physicality pulsated against the delicate caress of her fingertips settled in his lap, enticingly working on him through his pants as he twitched and ached against her touch. Feeling the outline of his very swollen head twitch against her lingering touch and the bead of wetness she'd encouraged at its tip, she knew there was only one place this could now lead as his tongue licked hers and she arched her back for him, yielding her very sensitive and flushed neck and clavicle for him to devour.

She knew she was on fire for him.... She could feel the way she was responding to his touch as her summer dress crumpled all around her for him. The slightest of tugs here. The most innocent of brush there and her tiny, little shoulder straps fell by the wayside, fully exposing her supple breasts to his lips as his index and middle finger found her center and liquescing seam.

Her experience easily had undone the knot that held his pants taut, letting his throbbing length spill into her waiting caress. She could feel every profoundly raised vein along his excitement for her as she teased him only mere moments before helping him find her velvety vulva and loving, teasing caress.

She couldn't be certain it was *him*, but certainty was often casualty to lust.

$*$ $*$ $*$ $*$

"I should probably be going," Elise suggested sheepishly, brushing breadcrumbs off her and the quilt comforter as she got up. Her eyes and body language not comporting to her words in the least.

What was it with women anyway? Do they practice stabbing men verbally? Glaring at her and seeing more than just her words, Radin thought he would take a chance on her real feelings and of his own.

"Where will you go? Do you have a place to stay tonight?"

"No, not yet."

"Don't think so," he ordered in a voice beyond his years, shaking his head in protest. He smiled disarmingly as if preparing to force the issue without being too overbearing. Whatever she may or may not have been accustomed to, he was not about to let her stay outside the city walls. He had not just met the woman of his dreams to watch her get killed, or worse, with her carelessness or free spirit as he was certain she saw it. *She needs your protection, you dolt.*

She could see the wheels of his thoughts turning as she continued looking into his beautiful blue-grey eyes and could see what was to come. Right about now, he would be thinking of a reason to make her stay. "I was just kidding. I'd like to stay with you if that's okay. I really don't have any place that I would *rather* be."

Straightening his stance and cocking his head, perplexed, he was trying to figure out what exactly just happened. The warning bells had definitely shattered in his thoughts.

Relaxing—very nearly letting go, he took her hand in his, pulling her back down to the bed atop him, gently kissing her. Laying her head back down in his arms, Elise felt the relaxation from comfort and safety wash over her, *though she wasn't the damsel in distress he thought she was.* The road *had* been hard on her, and her body needed the rest. And sex…. She hadn't realized how much her body had longed for such things until she'd felt it once again. Yes, she needed sex. *Was that such a horrible thing?*

Feeling Elise fall asleep in the protection of his arms, sleep did not come so easily for Radin. His mind raced with thoughts of Elise all night, as it had the night before, and now with her back in his arms, the thoughts and feelings only became stronger—like an uncontrollable torrent.

Hours passed…listening to the scuttle of guests checking in and out. He wanted to get up and help. He knew his father would be angry at his absence, but, at the same time, *would Rowarc really understand he was starting to grow into a man and having a man's needs?*

Time continued to pass in the torment from sleep being just out of reach, but in the confirmation of knowing happiness, and of the wonder of what may come of them. *Would it disappear as quickly as it had been found? Was it as fleeting as his father had often spoke of?* His father used to say, *leave it up to a woman to turn your world upside down in the time it took for the fleeting moments of dusk to pass before your eyes. Truer words never spoken*, he mused, shuffling his pillows in search of a comfort that might allow sleep. Radin wasn't sure if his last thought was a comforting one or not but could feel the haze of sleep forming over him—his eyelids becoming heavy. Not entirely sure whether in dream or not, Radin caught the glimmer of something inside her amulet as he finally drifted off. Dreaming of a foreign landscape in dusky repose and the glow of a molten star—seemingly on or very close to the ground—that would not be denied.

Charles W. McDonald Jr.

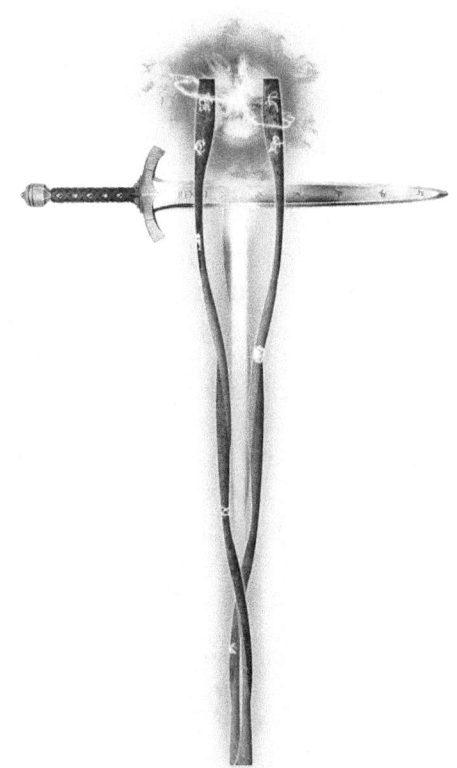

Chapter 11: Manifested Signs

(Stirling, Perion, Present Day)

waking to a beautiful woman rustling in his arms and gradually recalling the events of the past hours, Radin looked around, not knowing the time—seeing only the waning tawny rays of their star from the window. *Surely, we didn't sleep long enough for it to be morning again.* His father would have switched him already if that had been the case. Frowning and realizing he had neglected *all* his responsibilities, Radin wondered why his father had not come for him. *I'll need to thank him for the unexpected privacy.*

Looking around the room, wondering how he would get up without waking her, Radin recalled the mysterious amulet and his last thoughts before he drifted off to an elusive sleep. He wondered who it must have belonged to, and where they might find that sort of information without drawing attention to themselves. The last thing he wanted was for either of them to get in trouble for having that blasted thing. *It might not be worth the trouble if it's real....* But, if it *was* real, and they could find who it belonged to, *perhaps there could be a reward in it for them. Perhaps even enough to start out on a life of his own, maybe even a life with Elise. Where would they go? What would they do? Would she go with him?* It was all too much to think about right now, but there it was regardless. The prevailing idea of independence and romance made it hard to think of anything else. He was becoming a man.

Again, she jostled her head in his arms, not that he could feel his arm anymore. It had gone to sleep a long time ago. Frowning, he thought, *how can she sleep so much? It must have been a long journey for her to Stirling—a journey from where? Where was she born? What was her heritage? Her background? Her culture?* There was so much about her he did not know, but the mystery and task of getting to know her was welcome in its newness. Thoughts of Elise and what she must be like continued to race through his head alongside his new waking dreams that hadn't bothered him of late and his dreams that had. He knew it would take time to truly understand her, and those dreams, if he ever did....

The thud of a closing dresser drawer brought him out of his thoughts. At this hour, the only one likely to be moving about was his father. Realizing this was the day his father had mentioned he may have to leave for a while, he carefully moved Elise's body off of him, so that he could at least say goodbye. He did not know, with things the way they were between them, if his father would leave without saying goodbye or not, but he wasn't going to take that chance. Sneaking out of bed without disturbing Elise was a challenge, but worth it to see her sleeping alone in his bed, with her strawberry-golden hair cascading off of his cream, pleated pillowcases and bedding. *By the Creator, he had surely made not many more beautiful.* Her body seemed so delicate and feminine in its slender, nude repose. So soft in its lush curves that formed her breasts that kissed his sheets laying on their side as she lay in a fetal position next to where he was an instant before. He could almost feel her relaxed breath peacefully exhaled in the space of his absence, wondering if this was as good as it gets....

Sighing, he closed the door behind him as he walked towards his father's room.

Pushing open his door just slightly and knocking on the door frame, he could see his father packing an old duffel with riding clothes, maps, and a thin black box, his father had always called his 'tools.'

"I wondered if I would see you again. You're obsessed with her already.

Abandoning your work," Rowarc both chided and coached from beyond the doorway, packing for his trip.

"I wanted to make sure I got to say goodbye before you left," Radin meekly replied in a tone that recognized his deserved admonition, standing in the doorway.

"So, is the inn still going to be standing when I get back, or did you plan to just let it fall into anyone's hands, abandoning it?"

"You're upset with me. I get that. I deserve that." Pausing. Thinking. "I'm sorry."

Rowarc turned, placing a few last shirts in his pack, trying to seem busy in an obviously awkward moment between them. "You have a good head on your shoulders when you choose to use it. I'm hoping you decide to use it, more than not, while I'm gone."

"That's fair, Dad." Thinking about how much he should share, Radin added, "I don't know exactly what to do about Elise, but I don't want to let her out of my sight. I might ask her to stay with me, and I don't know what she'll say to that." He thought about asking if that were alright with him, but best to simply do, rather than ask, where Elise was concerned. That's what he felt his father would have done. "I'm also planning on doing some research with her as soon as time allows, but I won't let that interfere with work. I promise."

"Mhmm," Rowarc nodded knowingly, recognizing his son becoming a man. Making his own decisions now, making plans, but *could Radin do all those things and still remain the responsible son he had raised?* That was somewhat still in doubt. *Women often got in the way of a man's responsibilities,* he scorned internally. "She's a sweet girl. I'm happy for you, Son." Just a few words of recognition but it made Radin beam with pride. He actually got a genuine compliment from his father—the first in a very long time.

"I'm glad you approve. Are you gonna tell me where you're going?"

Rowarc tried to appear too busy to answer his son's question, bustling around the room in search of nothing and everything.

"What if I need to find you?" Radin wasn't giving up just yet. He felt as if he and his father were on the verge of a breakthrough between them and he wasn't ready to let that elusive aim out of his sight.

"Look," Rowarc barked, "…you're going to have to trust me. Okay? I'll be alright, I know what I'm doing. And I'll be back before you know I'm gone. This shouldn't take that long. So, you just make sure that everything runs smooth while I'm away. I don't want to come back and find everything out of control. Understand?"

The words he had wanted to say for a long time seemed lost in the harsh words of his father, but still, his heart was heavy. Something felt wrong,

Charles W. McDonald Jr.

really wrong. It was as if there was this pent-up tension between them and he was trying his best to bring them together so that the tension didn't break their relationship, but.... "I...," he stuttered, "...I'm sorry. I didn't mean to.... I love you, Dad."

There they were—the words for which there was no defense. No parent could remain hard-edged when faced with the love of their child nor the memory of their child's laughter at play. There was only shame in the way he had treated Radin of late. Shame in the words he could *not* say. Taking a seat at the edge of his bed, Rowarc had to stop. He had to think for a minute about what he was doing and what he needed to say to keep it all together. His son was all he had left, and he loved him more than spoken words could describe, but he couldn't fix everything in just this one moment. *Too much broken and not enough time for.... Ah, I don't have time for this,* Rowarc chastised himself. No, he needed more time, but something felt wrong. It all felt wrong. *Who was this guy? And why did he want him—specifically him?* Rowarc picked up his things and headed for the door. He stopped in front of his son, wanting to say something—anything that would help not leave too many things unsaid, but Rowarc's words failed him. Rowarc's chin moved, that way it always did when he was emotional, but he said nothing, preferring instead to pat his son on the shoulder on his way out the door, perhaps in a feign attempt to convey through touch what could not be spoken—at least not now. Different people spoke in different ways and not everyone was gifted with words. Rowarc was a man of action, deeds, and senses that paid attention to his surroundings. It was part of what made him a great ranger, if not a good father.

Radin turned, watching his father descend the staircase, disappearing out the front door. That nagging feeling from a few moments ago now screamed throughout every corner of his mind.

*   *   *   *

Passing by the first alley past his inn, the clop of his boot heels on the cobblestone streets provided the solemn atmosphere Rowarc needed to be alone with his thoughts. Just maybe, it would provide the answers he desperately sought—answers that had little to do with a stray girl. His foremost thoughts and hopes were that Radin would understand and grow into a stronger, kinder man than him. A more complete man, capable of properly raising his own children better than he had done with his own son. Losing Arella had brought him to his knees. A beautiful, loving mate and traveling companion for years on end. She had been his guiding force. He still remembered that day and would never be able to let it go. Losing Radin would surely kill him if he didn't end it all first, himself.

Watching the wooden signs of the local establishments sway in the early morning breeze on his way to the edge of town, Rowarc retraced the once familiar path to find an old friend he would need once more. Gripping the hilt of another trusted friend, Rowarc suppressed the thoughts of his son, recalling the skills and memories of vast experience he would need to stay alive.

*　　*　　*　　*

Dawn broke a while back, casting brilliant beams over the lush green land that was the Kingdom of Gawth. Radin sipped on hot tea, breaking off another piece of bread as he sat at the table next to one of the downstairs windows while a singular memory of his mom kept stirring in his thoughts. Radin was tiny at the time and had been very sick. He recalled waking in her arms as she rocked him slowly while she sang to him. It was his first memory of looking into her golden eyes, and some years had passed before he understood the significance of that. Some professions manifested signs in different ways just as surnames tagged a smithy. Some signs were best kept hidden.

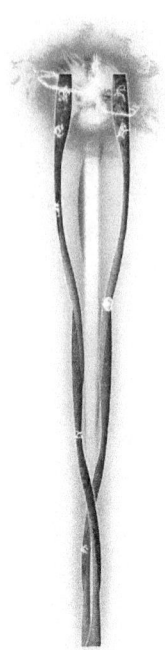

Chapter 12: Banthis

(Southlake, TX, Earth, Present Day)

Southlake Town Center, Southlake, Texas was *always* busy. You could barely find a parking space anywhere on the weekend, and forget about getting a table at The Cheesecake Factory® after 7:00 p.m. The two-storey, brick-and-mortar bookstore next door bustled with millennials, in their coolest frump gear, man buns, untucked shirts, and designer facial hair—all jamming on the Wi-Fi while pretending to read; in reality, people-watching or searching for that certain someone. The bookstore staff sneered knowingly, but what could you do? They were customers—sort of. Leslie fluffed long fingers through her long and beautiful, blonde wavy hair, wondering how many times she'd get hit on tonight. Even her husband's purchase of an even obsessively bigger ring, which could nearly be seen by satellite, didn't deter them. She pushed the book cart through the aisles, restocking shelves, answering the dumbest questions every five minutes—and *yes* there was such a thing as a *stupid* question. Of that, she was most certain!

    She wondered if she was pushing it a tad too far with the black, satin mini-skirt, white button-down blouse and three-inch black and red heels, but *what the Hell?!* She was only twenty-one, still in college, and she needed to feel sexy every now and then. In the back of her mind, she really didn't mind being hit on if they were cute. Not like it was ever going to go anywhere or anything. *Oh well, back to work,* sighing as she climbed the step stool, replenishing some stock on the top shelf.

"Shit," she barely got the word out as the ground rushed up to meet her from her sudden fall.

"Careful," unseen hands catching her mid-air like comforting and safe cushions of warm air pushing back against the left side of her ribcage, slowing and softening her fall until she could right herself.

*Where did **he** come from?* His right hand on her right scapula from behind as his left found the small of her back, helping her regain her balance by kicking the step stool out of her way. "Seriously, how did you do that? I didn't see you anywhere near me when I climbed on that stool."

"That...." He smiled at her as she pivoted to face him for the first time. *Oh my,* she thought, *OMG that gruff smile and those rugged good looks.* She was in trouble now.... *Was he Native American? Greek? Central American?* He had features of many cultures and of none with those hard, faceted planes about his face.

"That was nothing," letting the back of his fingertips graze and caress the small of her back while his right hand pulled wired earbuds from his ears, blasting *Led Zeppelin's Kashmir* as loud as his Android® phone would allow.

Those jet-black eyes and perfectly sculpted straight, though almost wind-swept, raven hair with those chiseled and tanned good looks. *Oh my, indeed.* He had this...dangerous look almost akin to Cherokee with those deep-set black gems of his. Her heart pounded as worry and apprehension crept into her thoughts.

"Leslie, you really should be more careful."

Okay, he was positively caressing the small of her back, and *was he checking her out too? Oh, crap!* "Hey, how do you know my name?"

His fingers went from the small of her back to her breasts. *Oh shit, did he have his hand on her breast—HERE??!!* He tapped her name tag with his index finger just over her left breast, and she felt as dumb as the dude in the man bun asking where to find the self-help books. At least that dude was in the right section of the store for him. *SERIOUSLY, woman get your crap together!* She berated herself even though he *still* had his hand on her breast.

"I'm Damon. Pleased to meet you." His hand moved to shake hers as she delicately offered hers to him. "Well, if you're okay and promise not to get on that stool without taking off your heels, I'll let you go."

Charles W. McDonald Jr.

"And if I don't?" *Wow, that was flirtatious. Holy crap, what's gotten into you?*

"Then I might just have to punish you!" A grin crept across Damon's hard-planed face as his eyes overtly and wantonly walked over every single inch of Leslie's hot and very married body.

Did he just say he was going to punish me? Doing a double-take in her mind, she considered his seriousness. *Holy shit! And I bet he meant it too,* she examined those black eyes with her sapphire eyes. *God, he's hot!* Taking just a moment to take him in. He dressed somewhere between a collegiate senior and tech God—like one of those venture capitalists who made their first billion in their early twenties, but **way** hotter and a lot taller!

He smiled again, knowingly, wondering if he'd need to use magic to seduce her or not. She was far too beautiful to be working *here*. She needed to be with *him*. She should have been a model, but looking at that wedding ring, she obviously had a husband that was either super jealous or super insecure—most likely both. She definitely had the figure for the mini-skirt, but *he* envisioned her in something far more daring. He was such a sucker for a small waist with big breasts, blonde hair, beautiful facial symmetry, and blue eyes. He definitely had a type but preferred not to discriminate. All women were fair game in his eyes—married or not. Besides, the most beautiful women were always taken or spoken for in one way or another, so he certainly wasn't going to let a little detail like her marital status get in the way.

"So, what are you doing here?" She paused, *wait, that didn't come out right.* "…I mean; what are you here looking for?" *Shit, pull it together.* "I mean; can I help you find something?"

"What I'm looking for should be on the second floor according to your inventory management system," he held up his Android® knowingly, pointing to the reference location on the store map.

Boy, did *she* feel stupid?! She exhaled, looking down at her heels, noting the right one had snapped off during her fall. "Great," she thought aloud, exasperated at her own stupidity.

"It *is* a great app. Very helpful." He smiled again and suddenly she couldn't help but smile back.

What the hell was he doing to her?

"Leslie," he snapped his fingers a few inches in front of her face, bringing her back to planet Earth, causing her to beam for him again and sway towards him so he could brush up against her again. "…You can help me."

"Yeah?" Leslie beamed an even broader smile for him again.

"I'm in room 312, about two hundred feet that way," Damon proclaimed, pointing toward the Hilton® just outside and to the right from their

Charles W. McDonald Jr.

southwestern-facing location. "I'll see you at 10:00 p.m. in *my* room for *our* date." Before she could even protest, about to hold up her wedding ring, he pulled her to him with his left hand nestled once more in the small of her back, kissing her, casting *Seduction.*

Leslie wilted completely and immediately in his arms, becoming hot everywhere throughout her body inside, and out. Tingling electrically from the tips of her toes all the way to her forehead as her eyes nearly glazed over in lust. Feverishly kissing him back in front of God, co-workers, customers, and everyone. Not caring. Her only thoughts of Damon. She couldn't even remember her husband's name as Damon's fingertips delicately caressed her beautiful face while his tongue caressed hers.

Breaking his kiss and pulling away, knowing she needed more, Damon was setting the tone for their date. She tried, in vain, to pull him back to her, but he was an order of magnitude stronger than her. He wasn't budging. "Leslie."

"Yes." She paused right at the edge of panting as she looked into his beautiful black eyes—helpless. The sweet, salty and sensual taste of him on her lips and tongue had already aroused her enough to flush her cheeks as she felt a tingling ripple upward from her solar plexus all the way up to her brow. "Damon." She loved his name; it was unique. He certainly was too. Very! Something about his age and accent was just so mysterious. He *had* to be much older than he looked.

"You are far too beautiful," he paused as she beamed for him again. "... to dress like that for our date. I want you in *next to nothing* when you knock on my hotel room door tonight, and I *don't want you to disappoint me*, or I definitely *will* punish you when you come to me."

Wow, she thought, *just WOW.* He was seriously giving her a command that he expected her to follow.

Damon walked away, leaving her to a slow simmer on his orders for her date attire, heading upstairs for the book on M-Theory he sought—his original purpose for coming to this particular store. It was an obscure book by a cosmologist who died shortly after writing it. Too bad. Damon would love to have picked his brain the way he had Dr. Dietrich. The book was only available in print, and this was the only brick and mortar bookstore in North America with that book in stock, and only one copy apparently left according to their inventory system. He needed to act fast.

He could have *Portal'd* in and right back out, but he didn't want to risk it. And he was in the general area anyway, so why not...? While there was plenty of living organic matter to support the use of Arcane, the belief in magic was so limited, the accessing of Arcane as an energy source here barely

Charles W. McDonald Jr.

worked. It was a much different place the last time he was on Earth so many centuries before. Back then he could cast so much more freely—almost akin to his homeworld. Hopefully, his research, and subsequent work, would prove fruitful in making belief in magic an unnecessary requirement for his spells to work the way they were intended.

Smoldering as she watched Damon ascend the ascending half of the twin set of escalators, Leslie balked internally. *Did he just walk away from me? From ME? Holy shit! Who does **HE** think **he** is? Giving **me** orders and expecting **me** to follow them.* Crap, she looked down at her wedding ring. *What was she going to tell her husband so he wouldn't be looking for her after 10:00 p.m. tonight?* She needed an excuse to give her a few hours alone with Damon, and she had to go shopping—like now. Damon expected her in *next to nothing*. *Hmmm*, she thought deviously, her naughty side seemingly now in total control of her body ever since Damon. *WOW!* That was seriously the only word for it—for him. *Just WOW in every way.* And she knew she was going to give herself to him completely tonight. In every possible way. She knew she couldn't say no to him and had no intention of even trying. Her body tingled everywhere at the thought of giving herself to him. And she couldn't wait!

Using her broken heels as an excuse, she went up to her boss and got the rest of the night off. Fortunately, working in a high-end shopping center had its perks. You could find pretty much anything you needed in walking distance—even with a broken heel. More pressingly, she was flushed and in desperate need of some strong *bourbon*!

*   *   *   *

Barefoot in only his Levi's®, Damon started walking to the door before the first rap of Leslie's knuckles hit the outside of his hotel door, letting her knock before opening it so as not to raise too much suspicion. Leslie had long since fixed the heel issue, stepping into ones a little longer than those she broke a couple of hours ago. His eyes drifted up her long, slender, shapely legs as she stood there in nothing but a very transparent white babydoll, revealing perfect young flesh everywhere he looked. It plunged in a deep V-neck over her ample, tear-drop breasts, cut so most of her nipples were bare, and what was covered, might as well not have been. The hem of the babydoll had ten two-inch slits equidistant all the way around her waistline, and it was very obvious she had left her panties somewhere else.

Visibly licking his lips in lustful thoughts of devouring her before pulling her to him, Damon saturated her lips with his own. She had this delectable taste of cinnamon and honey on her lips and tongue as Damon began to devour her.

Leslie immediately felt hot all over, wilting again in this exotic man's arms as she caressed the outline of his ardor for her through his jeans, melting for him, willingly letting his hands roam everywhere he wished in his claim over her body. Everywhere he caressed and kissed she tingled with little eletric shocks that sent shockwaves of lust throughout her center. She was his.

The door to Damon's room thudded against the interior doorstop as he dragged Leslie into his room with both his hands gripped upon her wrists hard enough to leave marks. Shoving her lush curves against the wall where her back smacked against the sheetrock and cream wainscoting hard enough to knock some of the air out of her lungs, Damon rushed forward into her where his right knee wedged in between her legs—opening them as the front of his thigh throbbed and chaffed against her naked center. As his lips again devoured her beautiful neck and clavicle in trailed, sensual kisses that led from shoulder to just under her ear lobe, Damon stopped to inhale, smelling her scent of lilac and cinnamon that perfumed his room along with her powerful and fully awakened pheromones that had him aching for her against the inside of her thigh.

His right hand found her heart through the tepid fabric that barely made an attempt to cover hither and thither. And with his hand nestled in between her heavy breasts, their lips met again in sensual, sideways draping motions one against the other as he felt her heart pounding against his touch in anticipation of the inevitable.

It was all happening so fast, she didn't know quite how to register the brilliant golden flash of his black eyes before his teeth suckled upon the perfectly flush flesh of her neck, completely consuming her and leaving little love bites everywhere he desired.

*   *   *   *

Laying nude on the room's king bed, Leslie stirred, shaking her head, wondering what time it was. She felt very hungover, but she'd only had those two bourbon-on-the-rocks at Brio's® before heading over to Damon's room. *Surely that wasn't.... Hey, wait. What the Hell?* A woman that could only be described as beyond stunning suddenly lay nude next to and just slightly atop her such that her large breasts fit in between her own. The woman's fingertips electrified every part of Leslie's flesh, wherever she touched. "What's happening?" Leslie asked her, looking around for Damon, then looking into the color-shifting and deeply magnetic eyes of this magnificent woman lying atop her. Her hair cascading waves of blonde, then brunette, then auburn, then jet black. "What the Hell?"

"Interesting expression," Banthis mused as her fingertips teased Leslie's fully erect nipples in tender milking motions between thumb and forefinger. "I just wanted to see if you were having fun with my husband."

"*Banthis*!" Damon's tone somewhere between exasperated and pissed, he practically leapt out of the bathroom where he'd been cleaning up, now wearing nothing but a towel. "Your timing sucks!!"

"I'm hurt," Banthis feigned offense while her wandering fingertips probed Leslie's center in ways that made even Damon raise his eyebrows.

Leslie was clearly in the middle of something she wished she wasn't, causing her to look between them, while biting her lower lip, trying to figure this one out. When she could look at all. Banthis had her *so very* distracted she could barely focus her eyes on anything at all.

Pointing his right index finger at Banthis accusingly, Damon chided, "…you know if you came to see me more than twice a year, I wouldn't need to go…" trailing off with that one while looking at a profoundly aroused Leslie. *Damn she was hot while being caressed by a nude Banthis like that!* But the wheels of his mind quickly started deducing the hidden agenda at work. Knowing Banthis the way he did, he didn't like where this was going.

"Darling, for you and I to be together more often, it would require you being dead, and you're *clearly* not done living…." Banthis motioned toward Leslie's nude torso with her left hand as her right hand found Leslie's most sensitive spots before allowing her left hand to return to sensually petting Leslie's beautiful body, exciting Leslie beyond words. Leslie's eyes rolling into the back of her head as her body climaxed again and again at Banthis' every touch. Her form now solidified, auburn-brunette hair down to her butt with bright green eyes—a reflection of Leslie's previously unknown and untapped sexual desires. "I think I'm going to have lots of fun with this one."

"Wait! Banthis!" Damon paused knowing what was coming next, trying to think of a way to…. "What if I told you I liked this one?"

"Darling, of course, you like her. You just got her pregnant. And she's totally in love with you. And how's that going to work out with her *husband*? Are you going to take her back with you, away from her husband, and raise your child? I think not." The top of the mattress opened up beneath Leslie as hot amber tentacles pulled her down into a chasm appearing from nothingness. Two seconds later, Leslie was gone; the bed and mattress looked as if nothing had happened. Banthis acted as if nothing had happened, batting her beautifully long eyelashes at her adulterous husband as she pat the pillow next to her, motioning for Damon to lay down beside her.

"That wasn't necessary." Grudgingly, he complied, laying down so his legs entangled with hers, looking into her now beautiful sapphire eyes, her hair now the platinum blonde, and her breasts now slightly larger than Leslie's. This was Damon's preferred instantiation of Banthis and the one he married so many centuries before.

"Darling Love, you've got hundreds of hot, young girls out there you need to impregnate. You're literally not done sowing your seed. You're not ready to spend the rest of eternity with your wife. *Not yet*. Besides, I was just doing what I do best." The wicked smile upon Banthis' face spoke of unspeakable things she would do to—and with—Leslie for time immemorial.

"Ha. Ha." The situation wasn't at all funny, but she was being truthful. Damon sniffed, considering his wife's powerful and potent abilities to seduce and consume souls, however necessary. Climbing a ladder of naked ambition common to all underworldlings but with uncommon success and tenacity where Banthis was concerned.

"Although, *she's* been giving me a lot more responsibility. Thanks to all the presents you've been sending me." She warmed her hands against Damon's bare chest, feeling him pulse with heat and energy underneath his towel that twitched upward against her wrists and forearms in anticipation of her every loving touch. Sometimes she wished she were alive. How mortals felt and how sensitive their bodies could be....

"Keep your enemies closer," he thought aloud, smiling at his wife.

"Precisely." Batting her eyelashes knowingly at her husband. "Oh, *she* knows. You didn't believe that you could hide it from *her*, did you?"

"Of course not. Her level of omnipotence has its advantages, but she doesn't know everything. There *are* gaps in her knowledge. She only knows the why and the who." *More than dangerous enough*, he thought to himself—especially if their plans failed. He already knew he wouldn't have the full element of surprise, but there are many accounts throughout the history of many worlds where overwhelming force, accompanied with the right tools and the right plan, didn't require the element of surprise to achieve victory. Still, he knew and felt a very persuasive conversation coming from their soon-to-be target and he wondered how he would handle it when that conversation inevitably came....

(Physical Cave Entrance to The World Below and Between, Kaleion, Recent

Charles W. McDonald Jr.

History)

Dawn still a couple of hours away, they stood and talked, continuing their conversation from inside—where they first met *so many* centuries before. He was still in awe of *her* every time they met—her dark elven skin perfection incarnate. She was quite literally the definition of a living goddess.

Lithe, dark, and beyond beautiful, Evanyil stood there basking in full moonlight with her radiant platinum hair and unique violet eyes, batting them at the doer of all doers. No one—not in all her lifetimes—could compare to Damon's ability to get things done. That made him the only possible candidate for *this* task—the only one she could trust to get the job done right the first time and with no loose ends. And with this task, *there would be no second chances.* They would either all succeed and reap the benefits, or they would all suffer a fate far worse than any death imaginable. It was a zero-sum game of eternal death versus life immortal and unmolested.

Damon stood there in his full, charcoal-blue mage regalia, letting Evanyil caress, or rather pet, the top of his right hand as she peered into his beautiful *black mirrors of the soul.* They were so amazing lit up in that cool smoky aura, backlit by the perfect moonlight. He was an amazing specimen. She did love him—truly so. It wasn't just physical love, or lust, between them. It was a love of trust, a love of reliability, a love of dependability, a love of so very much history together, and the love of rescuing one another more times than either could count. They had been a powerful team from the very first moment they met. They knew each other's thoughts and could complete each other's sentences, and they were just opposite enough to attract without driving each other insane. *Well,* Evanyil *would* fit the definition of insane already—with, or without, Damon. Even *that* he loved about her. She was just sane enough to be surprisingly lucid at times, and just crazy enough to come up with the most brilliant and unconventional thinking that frequently dovetailed perfectly with his structure and order.

The vines and dogwood masked the entrance entirely to the untrained eye, but they had been here so many times, they knew right where they were going—physically and otherwise.

"Sweetie, I'm not saying it has to be now-now. I'm saying I know it takes time to plot something of this magnitude, and I'd like to start the planning now." So unusual coming from *her*—the realization of planning something like this. Evanyil was the act first, solve problems-on-the-fly personality. But, if she, of all people, was realizing the need to plan something like this, then she truly *did* have an understanding of the consequences.

He was trying to keep his thoughts focused and ordered as she continued lovingly stroking his hand, leaning her perfect body into his as she blinked at him with those magnificent violet eyes of hers. He knew he wasn't being used—not really at least. *Was he?* It was the briefest of thoughts crossing across his consciousness as he replied, "Look, I'm just saying my biggest concern has always been about what happens after. I mean, we're going to bring enough to this fight, I'm pretty confident we'll win. The question is, in the massive power vacuum that follows, who gets what, when, how, where, and why are all extremely important questions that need to be asked and answered before the first spell is cast in this war we're about to start. There has to be a viable path to a lasting equilibrium. That's all I'm saying. And forgive me for saying this, but you're not the 'share my toys' type."

Evanyil feigned insult pouting, but she knew where Damon was coming from. He had a valid point—he always did. "You're suggesting a meeting between myself and your wifey."

"I am."

A huff of derision at *that* thought from Evanyil. She didn't *hate* Banthis. They had largely stayed out of one another's way all this time, but Banthis took Damon away from her. It wasn't a jealousy thing between Evanyil and Banthis. More like, Damon and Evanyil were best friends, teammates, traveling companions 'til the end, and then one day Dallia came in and changed all that. And shortly after Dallia, there was Banthis and even more change came, driving an even bigger wedge between her and Damon. She detested the change that came with Banthis in Damon's life more than she detested Banthis herself. Evanyil knew she wasn't the marrying type, and neither was Damon and yet he'd done it—more than once already. Their relationship had been violently hot, then cold, then hot, then unbearably distant, then ethereal, then…. Like two great binary stars orbiting one another elliptically only to cause spatial chaos every century or two they came close. The one constant between them was that they could count on one another, particularly when commitments were given.

He could see the wheels of chaos turning in that half-psychotic mind of hers and thought better to interrupt her train of thought before someone got killed—or worse. "Look, you two need to figure out who gets what when this goes down. I've known you a lot longer than I've known her but don't ask me to choose between you two. That won't be good for any of us."

"And what if I *am* asking you to choose me?"

"Evanyil, please don't. Please."

A batted eyelash, then a look down at the lush grass beneath them bathed in perfect moonlight as her spiders stood sentry around them, made Evanyil consider her options if it came down to it. "I miss *the old us.*"

Charles W. McDonald Jr.

A broad smile from Damon—she loved his smile—caused Damon to reminisce. Thoughts of their first meeting flooded his mind…then their first time together in combat…then all the years she spent with him at his manor. They covered a lot of ground together—shared tremendous history with one another. Cupping her magnificent face, he kissed her—really kissed her—like their lives depended on it. *Was that because it did*, he wondered. "If this works, we'll have all the freedom to be whoever we want, to forge or reforge whatever state of relationship we desire. And, for the record, I miss the old us too. You mean…," he paused thinking as a lump formed in his throat, searching for the words that came slowly in her awesome presence, "…more to me than words can describe. You're my last real living link to the past—at least that part of my past I remember with fondness. I adore you, Evanyil. Please don't ever change."

It was a strange, and rare moment, seeing a silvery, starlit tear streaking down the cheek of a living goddess, but she had what she wanted—for now at least. She had Damon's commitment to execute the plan that would set them both free. Though, here with him tonight, in this perfect moonlit night, she wanted more…. She wanted a future *with* Damon…*without* Banthis.

Charles W. McDonald Jr.

Part 4: Nonlinearity

Charles W. McDonald Jr.

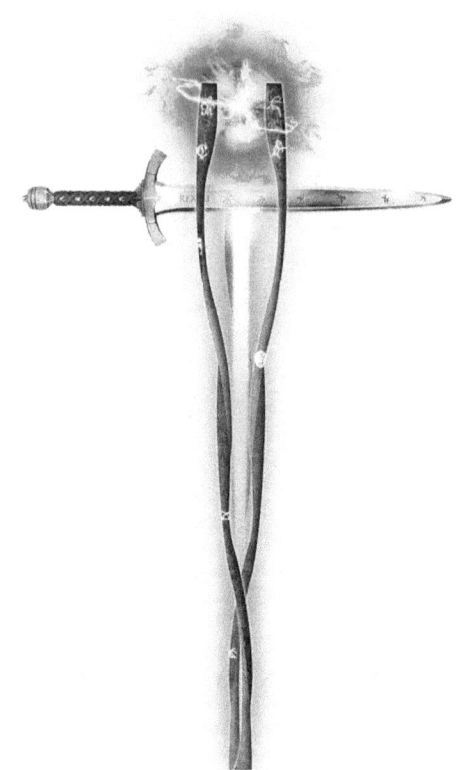

Chapter 13: The Sojourn Begins

(Perion, Present Day)

A sudden start and Radin was sweeping his glass off the table with an involuntary reflex, reaching to his left side for something that was not there—his eyes full, alertly focusing on something in the distance, just beyond the waking world. Letting out a dubious sigh of relief and a quiet, worrisome laugh, he looked down to see the amulet he had unknowingly thrown to the floor, watching it gleam even in the midst of the bar-cast shadow. It had not been easy getting it off Elise for a closer examination. Quietly he studied it while it lay in darkness. His chin worked much like his father's had earlier in the morning. "Where do you belong," he thought aloud. "…And to whom?"

Charles W. McDonald Jr.

*   *   *   *

Lit only by sunrays scintillating through the striking stained-glass, cathedral-arched windows, making motes of dust that hung in the air shimmer like enchanted stardust and sprites, the grand hall seemed none-to-ready to reveal its secrets. There was, instead, a singularly foreboding sense—something much larger than the three of them. It was enough to send chills up Elise's spine as she took in the huge silver candelabras, barely visible through the thick, dankly-scented and aged blankets of web and dust. It was a magnificent place—hewn from the hearts of the devoted. Even its state of decay added to its mystery—the power of its presence.

Enormous shelves, most three spans high and carefully placed throughout the north and south wings of the very old library, intimidated those who would dare to disturb this forgotten and forsaken place of secrets. Striding from one end of the library to the other, trying to decide where to start, they could not help but think of the vast array of knowledge held silent here all these centuries and the great care that must have gone into managing all this at one time in the ancient past. To see the state of things now buried in dust, as thick as a man's hand in some places, brought the perspective of time as a predator to Radin's thoughts. *Without time, death has no teeth*, Radin recalled. Something his father had said long ago that never really registered with him until now. Looking around at the work of decay, clearly, time and death still had their teeth.

Endless webs draped shelf to shelf as if only spiders and locust had been left to feed upon the leather-bound skin of the extensive writings. It was as if all their work and knowledge had been intentionally condemned to a silent and slow death. That was it...the only thing Radin could compare it to as he stopped cold, now in the belly of the library. *Death. A great tomb. Condemned!* Even the air was stale and *old* like an ancient catacomb, like something out of one of his father's stories, leaving a parched and rancid taste on his lips and tongue. It was...*exciting?*

After combing through countless ancient works, scrolls, and tablets alike, Elise had found little-to-nothing of the amulet. There were simply too many works to sift through. *Too much information!* Knowing where to start was a far bigger problem than anticipated.

The old caretakers, long since gone with only their ashes left to speak for them, used some cryptic method of indexing their works making it perplexing, if not impossible, for anyone else to find anything. Most likely intentional, though no less frustrating.

As intense as his feelings were for Elise already, Radin did not want her

Charles W. McDonald Jr.

here with him, especially not alone. He could not watch over her and search all this at the same time, and she would surely venture off on her own to 'help.' *This place was too dangerous for her.* Everyone knew the stories. You could not grow up east of the river Haden without knowing at least enough of the history of Tannanvar to know to stay away. Over the years, his father had told him how dangerous this place was, and that the king had even issued an edict declaring the entire grounds off limits—to everyone. It was highly unlikely that they would be able to find information about the amulet—if real—in just any library. If it were as special as he believed it could be, it would require specialized resources for answers. *Unique problems required unique solutions.* Something else his father taught him over the years. *Where was his father now, and how was he faring?* He could only hope for the best from afar. His father was right. Whatever it was, he was sure it was nothing his father had not already done a thousand times before, but that didn't make him feel much better about it. His father was brave, intelligent and talented, but more than a bit past his prime. *No. His father would be okay. He had to be....*

Radin had not yet told Elise of his suspicions about the amulet but hoped they could discover at least something before it revealed more of itself in a dangerous fashion. He knew it to have some power, and he hoped it benign. The more time he spent around it, the probability of it being a fake was seemingly more and more remote. Radin just wished he could have come alone. Now he had put his friends at risk. *Caution in no small measure*, recalling his father's words.

Holding the massive manuscript open against his stomach, Radin looked across the room to his childhood friend Kerrich and Elise, wanting to say something. His mouth worked like there were many thoughts he wished he could speak aloud. Instead, he buried his head again in the ancient work, continuing his search—hoping.

Standing guard by the central staircase leading into the vaulted chambers of the library, Kerrich Walsh now sat on the edge of one of the larger study tables, lazily swinging his right leg in boredom. Not so tall as Radin, but with similar eyes of a somewhat deeper blue and hair more brown than anything else, Kerrich wore a leather front-laced doublet over a wine-colored tunic with worn grey pants. Its fit was less than complimentary of his frame, appearing to have belonged to an older and larger brother at one time or another.

Bored from doodling on crumbling empty scrolls of unknown worth, Kerrich took a piece of wood from his soft grey wool pants and began whittling. Kerrich's talent for art was broad but shallow, as with most other things. *Jack of all trades, master of none.* Instead, he fancied himself a somewhat renowned ranger—thus his closeness with father d'Aguillon and son alike. Though it did seem to him, entirely natural that there was at least a little artist in us all, and to have some need to tap into it from time to time.

Not completely neglect in his watch duties, Kerrich checked in on the both of them from time to time, seeming to grow more and more nervous as time passed. He didn't like this place—none of them did. Something felt very wrong as if something horrific had happened here and been masked by time or by someone.

None knew what to expect, except that, hopefully, Radin could find some useful information here. He didn't understand why they didn't just drop the blasted thing off somewhere if it scared them so much. He certainly doubted it was a genuine relic of some kind, though he'd never known Radin to lie. There must have been some reason for his concern, and his not telling Kerrich any of the details. Turning to check again, Kerrich looked upon his friend with suspicious eyes, as Radin busily flipped through the pages of yet another huge dusty, leather volume. *What are we doing here*, Kerrich thought to himself, *and what could he possibly hope to find?* Coming up here is, by far, the craziest thing Radin had ever asked of him, *and for what...?* Kerrich looked around the room again, trying not to let it get to him. It's not as if he had a vast well of experience to draw from, so he didn't know exactly what to look for; it was all...creepy.

Wiping the sweat from her brow as she shut another volume, Elise noted how the sound echoed throughout the vastness of the tall chamber. Looking over to Radin and hoping he was having better luck, she was getting frustrated as her pensive expression revealed. There was just too much to look through, most of it in some unintelligible language and useless. What she could understand had been a fascinating history lesson, indeed worthy of risking another trip. Yet, still, she wondered if they were not wasting time—as if the answers were not yet meant to come to them. However, they would never find any information if they just gave up.

Sighing, she resumed reading the great leather-bound volume she had set aside moments before. Having already scanned through it once before, she knew it clung tightly to its secrets using vague inferences and half-truths. It appeared to have been written, consistently, in the same handwriting—like unto a personal journal more than anything else, its mysteries woven in the same enigmatic writing style. Whoever the author, the truth he sought to ex-

Charles W. McDonald Jr.

pose caused him to fear for his life in so doing. Painfully frustrating to read, it had to go with her. Its magnitude was all too evident to loosen her clutch upon it. *It would yield answers soon!*

There was one particularly interesting half-torn page, with a portrait of a beautiful woman with shoulder-length, platinum hair, clad in a pale, simple dress of a period long since passed. Her forlorn expression burned into the page—possibly a foreshadowing of some event. Several times she had passed it, paying more attention to the words now. Painted with light, sketch-like brush strokes and dull hues so as not to draw attention to it, she'd found the amulet. And, in the paragraph below the illustration, a reference to another work....

Rising with new reserve, Elise began her search for the referenced scroll, wondering if authored by the same man. Looking to Kerrich then quickly to Radin, she wondered where this would all lead. Starting where she had found the first book, and searching around its previous location, Elise quickly found the referenced work inside a bent metallic scroll case, buried in a stack of other scrolls on the wood floor. All of them had apparently been tipped out of their cabinet housing on the shelves, having the appearance of being disturbed more recently than surrounding works. *Someone's been here recently*, she thought, picking up the scroll case, emptying its contents...*but who? She felt she could wager on the why!*

This scroll pertaining exclusively to enchanted artifacts, Elise's eyes shimmered like diamond pools with wonder as she scanned the document for amulets matching the description of the one she now held in a small leather pouch at her side after having retrieved it again from Radin. Carefully, reverently, she rolled the scroll back up, placing it in the satchel they would be taking with them. So, this little fake of theirs had a name—*The Amulet of the Five Gates*—whatever that had meant. She had to tell Radin.

Appearing from behind the musty shelves, trying to cling to her innocent role a bit longer, Elise looked at Kerrich and Radin, feeling more and more of her suspicions rising to the surface. She believed in a reason for everything—a belief co-created in the light of love of a prior relationship. God the Creator did not work in random acts, or so she had developed good reason to believe. His hand held in it purpose...and a plan beyond the comprehension of mortals. The Creator would leave nothing of significance to chance— if there was such a thing at all. And anyone that has ever known or felt that magical glimmer of light that flashes across the periphery of one's mind from within knows that such genius inspiration could only come from a higher intelligence—darting into our thoughts like an arrow tipped with the poisonous fire of fate. Once before had she been struck with that arrow, and now experience told her what she already knew. Fate would guide her again if it wasn't already.

There were still far too many questions to be answered to be certain, but her instincts were working once again. Like a favored old quilt, she could feel the warmth of its assuredness guiding her in the right direction as surely as she could feel the beat of her own heart. It had been far too long since she had trusted her feelings and instincts, and now it felt...wondrous.

Quietly walking back to the book that had referenced the scroll she now kept on her, trying not to draw attention to herself as she tried piecing it together, Elise noticed something: a brilliant, radiant blue flash out of the corner of her eye—something entirely recognizable to *her*. Turning to the splendid, huge, cathedral windows—beyond the great study tables—broken untold years before, there appeared to be nothing but overgrown moss and vines draping the simple, yet elegant, frame and glass. Yet she was certain. She was positive of what she had seen, and she knew....

A chilling, indescribable feeling crept over Elise coating her arms and neck in goosebumps as she opted to take a different position, facing the windowsill while she took up her reading again. *Calm down,* she thought. Yet her better senses told her to at least go outside and verify. This was Tannanvar, and that alone was reason enough to show extra caution. Perhaps....

The instincts that had driven her thoughts only moments before now howled as she felt someone's eyes upon her.

"Kerrich," she called out in a tone weighty in its own anxiety. Briefly glancing around, looking for Radin, not seeing him anywhere. Perhaps he had gone to the other wing of the library. Wherever he had gone, she needed him—now!

Kerrich leapt from the table, sword in hand, tossing aside his modest carving, now partially shaped into a cup—not some grand construction of gild, but something far meeker. "What's wrong," he challenged, closing the distance between himself and Elise.

"I'm not sure, but could you come *here*?" Getting up, Elise backed away from the table, the great book, *and* the cathedral window. The moss, the vines, the sea—everything about and on the window appeared to hold an aura about it, like a halo of fear. Someone was here.

Kerrich was quickly next to her, taking her arm and glancing to the window. "What is it? You look like you've just seen the dead." Though stressed with apprehension, Kerrich's voice was young and vibrant, not yet rich and throaty as a gentleman or even as much so as Radin's; it was that of a boy not too long since transformed into a man. But his voice still boomed in the vast space.

Charles W. McDonald Jr.

Elise gripped his arm tightly in return, pushing Kerrich away from the window. Even now, he could feel the urgency in her grasp and in her eyes as she ordered him, "Find Radin. NOW!" His mouth worked as if to question, but his instincts were telling him to run. Not even taking time to sheath his sword, perhaps in the thought that it might soon be needed, Kerrich darted away, skidding on dusty hardwood planks, to the place where he last saw Radin, on the other side of the hall.

"Get away from the window!" A new voice yelled out from the staircase where Kerrich had stood watch—a voice rich, aged and throaty, that of a gentleman.

An arrow narrowly missing Elise took part of her strawberry-gold locks with it sticking into the far wall after streaking through the old broken window-frame.

Both of them now ducking, Elise and Kerrich stared back at the old man who motioned for them to stay down. None of them knowing exactly what was happening or why, it was evident in all their eyes that something was about to explode. Just as another arrow screeched through the open window-frame narrowly missing the old man in a seemingly last-instant, diverted, sure-head-shot to stick into the far wall opposite the first arrow aimed at Elise, a shimmering transparent shield now sealed off the broken cathedral window with a wave of the old man's right hand.

Unphased, and in soft, travel-worn, dark brown robes over a white shirt and rustic pants, the man who'd just seemingly invoked the cathedral window shield, appearing in his sixties as tall as Radin, and in sharp health, motioned for them to come to him as he worked his cane furiously against the hardwood floors to get to the staircase. "Well," he prompted as he rounded the dust-covered, ornate oak rail and magnificently turned spindles, "Are you just going to stand there, or do you want to live?!!"

Another moment of hesitation quickly expired and then, "You might not understand what's going on, my Son," the old man looking Kerrich in the eye from afar, "…but just ask the girl when I get you out of here. I'm certain she can tell you enough that you should learn to trust me. There is not time to earn trust at this moment. You have but an instant to decide whether or not you want to believe me." The old man wasn't stopping, instead breaking his glare with Kerrich to head upstairs in search of the boy he'd come to protect. It was lead, follow or get out of the way decision time for Kerrich.

Glancing to the window where the arrows had come, now blocked by the old man's shimmering shield, Kerrich was certain he'd seen movement in the last few seconds and visibly worked his jaw in anticipation, realizing the old man was right. Gripping his sword a bit tighter, Kerrich made a dash for the staircase to follow the old man, dragging Elise with his left hand.

The old man's cane worked furiously on the old wood floor leaving a staggered trail of small circles where he'd disturbed generations of dust and webs. Seemingly delicate in design with its heavily carved façade and heavy gold Pendragon tip, his aged cane easily held up to the task of aiding the old man's mobility. Whoever he was, he had money even if he tried to disguise it. "Right then, let's go find the boy and be none too long about it!" It was his first time mentioning Radin, causing both Kerrich and Elise to look at one another wondering what was happening and how he knew they needed help.

Had Rowarc asked him to follow them? It was only a brief thought as Kerrich's grip tightened upon Elise's wrists enough to leave marks, practically dragging Elise with him.

Worried exchanged glances between her and Kerrich said she was just as lost in all this as Kerrich. *Funny he should look to me for guidance*, she considered briefly as she tried to keep up with Kerrich's furious pace that far outpaced the old man as Kerrich was already rounding the top baluster.

"Radin!" Kerrich called out for his friend, striding to the exact spot where he had last seen Radin as he dragged Elise in tow. Kerrich watched the old man intently, waiting to see what he would do next as he finally caught up with them at the top of the stairs. Kerrich's grip on his hand-and-a-half longsword unconsciously becoming tighter as the situation grew more tense, though he hadn't seen any more arrows flying and that made him more nervous than if they had been under constant assault. The whole thing was quiet—too quiet.

Usually an excellent judge of character, Kerrich was unable to read anything from the old man. And while normally that would have increased his level of discomfort. In this old man, there was...trust. He could not place the feeling, but it was there nonetheless—like an aura of Humanity compelling him to believe, if only for this instant. And the old man was...commanding. There was just something about those golden eyes of his that read as honest.

Abruptly, the old man drew his cane upward, pointing its tip out in front of Kerrich and Elise, drawing it downward in a smooth stroke, closing his eyes as he cast. Superheated air in front of them split by silvery-blue fissures of light began opening a space in front of them, streaking outward about ten paces, opening a *Portal* rift to a grassy field where the sun had already long since set.

"GO NOW," exclaimed the old man with short graying hair and irises of gold that now burned and flowed as if they were molten metal. "GO! You will find a cabin on the other side of the hill. I'll locate the boy and meet you there."

Charles W. McDonald Jr.

"Hey!" Elise protested, turning back to the old man. Before she could get her body fully turned, both she and Kerrich found themselves shoved through Ykstherin's *Portal* by unseen hands pushing on every part of their bodies, tossing them to the ground. They were through; the *Portal* leading back to Radin and Tannanvar winked out of existence behind them.

*   *   *   *

(Somewhere West of Bouschè, Perion, Present Day)

"Wait," Kerrich shouted, "You can't do this." He was up in a flash and back at the spot where the old man's *Portal* had just whooshed to a spiraling close, grasping at the air like trying to cage a puff of smoke.

"I think he just did," she realized aloud, accepting Kerrich's hand up as she dusted herself off with the other, looking around to see where they were. Roughly-hewn logs fenced the property as far as the eye could see, pinning in livestock and hens that strewn and roamed the landscape. The land revealed no cabin in sight, but amidst the still darkening sky and duskily hewed wisps of clouds, Elise could see billows of smoke rising from just over the horizon. Sighing, she looked to Kerrich, though for comfort or grateful companionship, Kerrich could not say. He merely returned the glance with his own visible frustration, grimacing as he scanned the horizon in every direction—though seeming to look even beyond the horizon with his thoughts.

"What are your thoughts," she asked. She had to get to know this young man, and if Radin had trusted him, then she needed to get to know him a little better. She didn't know where their travels would take them next nor when they'd meet up with Radin again.

"My thoughts," he sniffed into the cuffs of his shirt. "You want to tell me how he just did that? My thoughts are of that, and of Radin—how we just abandoned him. We have to go back!" Kerrich's words sprang accusingly from his lips before he had time to think of their results, causing his eyes to turn downward at the soil at his accusational tone. But blast...he didn't know this girl. Didn't know why Radin trusted her other than she was beautiful, and they were likely.... Well, there was certainly that!

Elise felt the cut of his words, knowing their source mistrust, but that was expected. She would feel the same in his position. Time, and shared experience, was the best maker of friends and enemies alike. Feigning a confused look, she knew it only a matter of time before he would ask more pointed questions. "You know, as well as I, we didn't abandon him and what makes you think I would know what just happened to us," Elise lied through straight face and glaring eyes that she tried to keep calm in the face of a situation a bit outside her control. She hadn't meant for it to go this way, but she wasn't quite ready to hold more sway over events, preferring instead to let them evolve organically. "Besides, I don't think going back is an option. Take a look around. It's dark here, and where we left the sun had not yet reached its peak. We're nearly a quarter way around the world to the east from where we were."

Kerrich sniffed, looking not so dubious anymore. It was time for answers. That's what the whole day had been about: finding answers to their questions about that stupid amulet and such. Well, now *he* had questions and *he* wanted some answers! And if she wasn't going to provide answers to them, then maybe the old man was right after all. Maybe the answers could be found at the source of those smoky ringlet plumes just over the hillside. Thoughtfully patting Elise on the back, he started to follow the worn dirt path that marked the road to Bouschè and the plume of smoke just over the hill before them.

Glaring at him sidelong and raising her eyebrows a bit, Elise didn't know the source of his comforting touch, but it was there nonetheless. Perhaps there was more to Kerrich than met the eye.

Kerrich's touch *had* been soothing. He would do well with time and experience. They all would. For now, she was still fuming watching Kerrich leave her behind. His words had all but implied her as root-cause, and perhaps that wasn't too far off the mark. Her heels kicked up dust as she began chasing down Kerrich with thoughts of what might come next and how much she could reveal—and when.

"Wait, Kerrich. You think me a witch then." Her words halted him in his tracks just slightly before her hand arrested his arm. She knew her words too harsh and instigative the instant they left her lips as she relaxed her grip upon his wrist. *They were together, and that was that. No sense creating a pit of snakes between them.* "I'm sorry, that wasn't fair. You never said anything like that."

Elise had to turn away from his eyes, vainly focusing on the smoke plume in the distance, gathering her thoughts. Kerrich's silence spoke for him as his thoughts stormed with tales of the past. He recalled stories passed down from his father, grandfather, grandmother and even Rowarc of great feats performed with magic. Internally, he invoked the lamean of the Lady of the Wind in his mind's eye as he tried to reign in his thoughts. "Your words were not all that unfair, Elise. It *did* cross my mind." Kerrich wanted to run but sighing seemed more appropriate. *Witchery!*

Elise sighed alongside him, "I don't think that even together we could explain everything that has happened or get Radin back. What's say we just go to the cabin like the old man said and just wait. What else would you suggest?"

Kerrich scowled, but not at her. *She was right!* He scowled at the singular option which seemed completely out of his control. *Radin, be safe, my friend.* "I suppose we'll be safer together than apart, don't you?"

Elise smiled, "Together then. Let's go." Just then her thoughts turned to who might be waiting for them. *Did they know the old man? Would they welcome them?* Half of her wanted to wait right here for Radin and the old man, but they would likely freeze if they waited here much longer. It was already getting harshly cold as her breath visibly warned. She had to force herself to stop looking back as they pressed forward. Eventually, they crested the hill, and their past path was no longer visible—only the cabin and their future. Whoever was stoking their fire over the horizon was about to receive company.

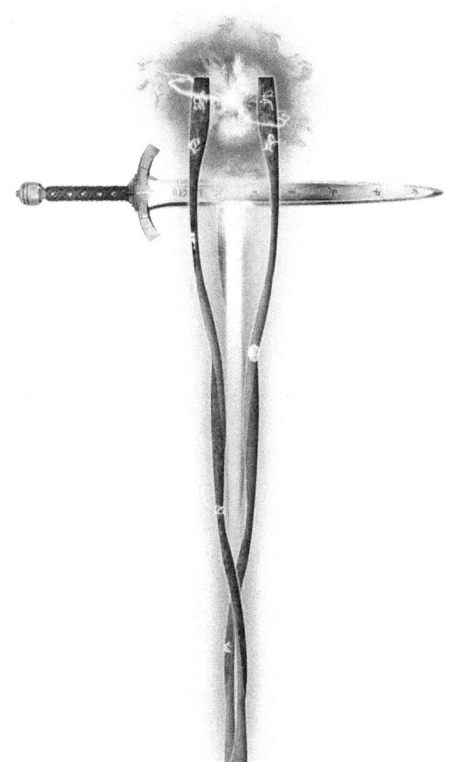

Chapter 14: Raphael

(West of Bouschè, Perion, Present Day)

uietly, Luke Armstead read by a raging hearth of roughly honed blue and white quarry stone, while fire and snow reflected off the windows of his family cabin—an heirloom of many generations to come, he hoped. A sheathed sword rested, slightly inclined, against a glass-enclosed, built-in cabinet, while Luke enjoyed the warmth of home and hearth underneath a family quilt as he slowly rocked to and fro. The dreamy reflections and quiet atmosphere helped his thoughts drift with fading hues of dusk-become-night and a thinly clouded and chilled starlit sky.

He had built the family cabin with his two grandsons some years back. It was straightforward and functional in every way, nothing fancy—just solid carpentry, one of the many skills he had passed along to his boys. All they had was each other now. Luke's only son was killed some years back; they never found the murderer. His son's wife just took off one day last winter, disappearing into the woods never to be seen again. His own wife passed away so many years back; there were times when he could barely remember her appearance and that failure of his memory shamed him. He could never forgive himself for that, no matter how long it had been. Yet time was rarely helpful to his memory nor his failing body. It was hard to recall anything more than a day or two back. Only a few powerful, long-term memories still echoed through his thoughts. There couldn't be much more time left for him. That much he knew. He longed to share the last of his truly great memories before it was too late. He supposed that time was at his doorstep. Luke could hear Gareth working in the kitchen, cleaning up after the evening meal.

Being the oldest, Gareth vowed to take care of their grandfather, while Pern, eight years younger, left in search of something his grandfather would never share with him. He did not even know where Luke had sent him, only that it was somewhere far away, across the Sea of Shirantal. He was not aware if he would ever see his brother again, only that his brother would never see Luke again, not alive anyway. His cough was getting worse by the hour now. Even now, more blood stained Luke's handkerchief as he heard Luke struggling with another bout.

"Grandpa?" Gareth's concern was tinged by his knowledge of the imminent. There was no hiding his knowing of what was to come. Hopelessness tainted his tone and his spirit.

Clearing his throat and coughing up more blood, Luke gathered himself, starting to rock his chair again. "I'm fine. Fine...." Luke deflected, trailing off as he mumbled something not entirely to himself, still clearing his throat.

"Gareth come here. There will be time for your chores later."

A strikingly vibrant young man walked into the reading room from the kitchen. Arms, chest, shoulders—all chiseled in the personification of strength. Years of tending to the family property had honed Gareth into a rock-hard man. Gareth saw himself in the hollowed and pale eye sockets of his grandfather. The white hair and wrinkled skin could not snuff the fiery spirit inside, and that was what Gareth chose to see in his grandfather, his best friend, and his surrogate father. Seeing Luke as anything else would deny him the dignity he had so richly deserved and labored for all his life.

The coming starry night and dogwood blossoms reflected off every shiny surface in the room, but the welling tears in Luke's eyes outshone them all—partly from the fire a few feet away, though mostly with the brilliance of a soul crescendoing toward its supernova back to the source. It was almost impossible to look him in the eyes anymore. The knowing was painful. Gareth almost wished for the end to take him and end his grandfather's suffering. *Great Creator, I'm a monster for wanting such a thing.* But Gareth did wish it. *Come for him soon. Please.*

He paused to take his grandfather's hand, holding the frail thing as gently as he could manage. There was little left but pallor, wrinkled skin and bones so delicate he feared snapping them in two just holding his grandfather's hand for comfort. "I fear what the world shall become without your presence among us, and I know I will fall to my knees when you go. I am afraid it will break me." Gareth fought with all his might, but this powerful man was losing the fight. Gareth's words had unleashed emotions he had buried for years— whether for sake of convenience or his own inability to deal with them until the moment he could no longer deny had come.

Smiling, Luke lifted his hand to his grandson's cheek and wiped away a tear. Something he had done with great frequency when Gareth was but a small boy, but somehow now it held much more weight than ever before. He supposed living so long had its merits after all. There were reasons. He knew there had to be. Of that much, he was certain.

"The words I am about to speak, you shall not repeat until you're my age. Understand?!" It was a question of fact, but a command in spirit. A serious one at that. Nodding, Gareth leaned forward.

Luke worked his mouth and mandible laboriously, searching for the strength or the words. "Some lives are not entirely our own. You see…? Like the seed that becometh the dogwood," Luke clenched his mouth at the words, looking specifically at the dogwood reflection upon hearth and window, rather than the dogwood visible through the window, hoping he could pass on the spirit of the message without violating it. Hoping Gareth would understand. Gareth sat quietly, working his mouth slightly, but remaining silent.

"Your Father, my only Son," Luke paused looking into Gareth's welling eyes, "…until you. Was such a life, and…." He did not want to say it. It felt wrong to say it about himself like that. Instead, Luke took his own hand and trembling he brought it to his own chest with one finger slightly extended to himself. His eyes said the rest. Gareth understood much of what was being said, but what did it mean, *what was this secret?*

Luke's head bobbed agedly as he looked into his grandson's eyes. "You have it too," Luke whispered. He had seen it before in other men too. A long time ago, almost in a different time entirely. "Your brother." Luke shook his head knowingly, confirming some of the unspoken but known suspicions Gareth had of Pern. "Yes…." Luke muttered. "Yes." Luke labored with his mouth again, continuing, "You're wondering why I sent him away, for what

Charles W. McDonald Jr.

purpose." A long pause. "Your father was very special for a reason. And when he met his death, that cause did not die with him. It kindled anew. It was… **reborn**." The last word came out with nearly all the strength he could muster, enough to make Gareth nearly retreat, his eyes growing wide.

Minutes seemed to pass before Luke would—or could—speak again, merely glaring into Gareth's eyes the whole time. "And when I…," Again he shakily pointed a finger towards the metallic object leaning against the cabinet across the room. "You take that sword when my time is over. Don't ever lose it. Treat it with respect. Treat it with *honor*." Another long pause. "…And I **will** be there with you—always." It was not an afterthought, but something he wanted to place great emphasis on, "…My Son."

"People are coming," Luke continued, causing Gareth to nearly get up and look outside, but surprising strength still housed inside his grandfather pulled him back down in his chair. "People that will need you and your strength."

"But, Grandpa, I can't…. I must stay here and—"

"Listen to me. **You will**…." Rarely did he ever cut Gareth off in such a manner, but time was not on his side anymore. The words had been spoken. His time was short. "*You will* leave me, my Son. Over your life, your father and I have taught you the difference between right and wrong. You will follow your heart and your soul and *do what is right*, and it **will** lead you to your brother in his greatest hour of need. I have seen it." Luke worked his mouth quietly, letting his words sink in.

"Now, I have also seen these people. Yes, my old friend will be with them. And *you will* go with them. Now, remember what I've told you. Help me to my bed and say your goodbyes, my Son, my beloved boy who shall become a *great* man. A **great** man!"

Gareth rose as commanded. Gathering his emotional strength was impossible, but he did manage to look into his grandfather's eyes as he followed Luke's final wishes.

As Gareth helped his grandfather into bed, Luke offered his last secret and gift for his boys and his legacy, "Death is not the end and I am ready. Leave me and be the great man you were born to be…."

Closing the door to Luke's bedroom behind him, Gareth turned to walk away, stopping short of the main cabin entrance and looking back, not at the door to his grandfather's room, but at Luke's sword, at the far end of the room.

*   *   *   *

Charles W. McDonald Jr.

Laboring to pull his legs up onto the bed and pull the covers over his frail body, Luke would face this moment without resentment or fear. He had not lived such a long and fruitful life to let it end in fear or frailty. It had been a happy and meaningful life, filled with moments of great joy and sadness and everything in between. Others should be so lucky to have lived so long and so well. The family name would live on, but more importantly, so would the power—the magic—and the knowledge and character imparted.

Luke lay with eyes closed, then opening them one last time as the room filled with a warm, blazing light.

"I knew it would be you," he breathed aloud with his eyes glowing even more wildly than before. "I've been waiting for so long. Thank you for coming."

"*It is done*." The three words came as thunderbolts inside the small cabin, threatening to blast it from its foundation.

And Luke's noble soul was taken with but a kiss....

* * * *

Glaring shafts of pure-white light blistered through the doorjamb and seams of the bedroom door, flooding the interior living area of the cabin. Turning to face the hot rays of light filtering through the door, Gareth shielded his eyes just as the cabin was rocked by a thunderous voice in some unintelligible language, hurling objects from the kitchen into the reading room, and vice versa. Paintings throughout the cabin, leapt from the walls as if thrown, crashing to the floor in broken rhythm.

If there had been any doubt, it was gone even before the thunderous voice stopped resonating throughout every object in the cabin, save one. Turning back to the object of his first attention, Gareth quickly moved to his grandfather's sword, slowing as he drew near to pick it up. Rust, scrapes, gashes, and gouges marred the folded steel. It had seen many days of harsh, relentless combat, yet it remained unbroken and still shone with burnished luster. As the rays disappeared from beyond the door, a small epicenter, precisely in the middle of the old blade, began to grow white-hot as the whole of the sword quickly began to resonate with heat and energy and it began to gleam anew again in the hands of a new master.

(Austin, TX, North of the Main Campus, Earth, 11:00 p.m., Present Day)

Charles W. McDonald Jr.

If he was going to operate from here for a while, he needed a place of his own, and this was as good as any. The climate most closely matched his homeworld and being close to the university would have its advantages. He checked out the diverse housing styles in the lighting afforded by the street-lights down Duval St.

"Get your hands off me, asshole!" A young brunette woman in a tight black miniskirt looked as if she might have been coming out of a house party a couple of doors down the street. Two men, each of them Damon's size, followed her down the front stairs of the two-storey structure. One of two yanking her lithe body back towards him with his grip like a vice on her forearm.

"You're not going anywhere, bitch! Get back here!" The one gripping her arm looked about college age in a grotesque orange football T-shirt and jeans with what Damon had learned was a 'high and tight' military haircut. His friend wore a black leather jacket, absurd in this heat, over a white T-shirt with greased black hair; he was even more muscular than Damon. "She wants it. They all want it," the leather-jacketed man mocked, grabbing her waist from behind as the two began putting their hands wherever they liked.

"GET OFF ME," she shouted, kicking the leather-jacketed man in his shin, then his balls, causing his hands to instinctively protect himself as he backed away, surrendering her to his friend.

Nice shot, Damon thought, admiring her spunk. But this wasn't right. Even Damon had standards for picking up women, and this wasn't in his book of okay. A brief thought from Damon sent a small trail of fire, like unto a cigarette lighter leaking lighter-fluid, racing from Damon right between the legs of the orange shirt man holding the young brunette, up the telephone pole right behind them. *That should get their attention.*

"Keep walking asshole," Football T-shirt warned, pulling out a six-inch switchblade that reflected the yellowing streetlight from the poles on either side of Duval Street.

"You're right, I am an asshole," Damon mocked, causing Football T to stare and frown, obviously not expecting the admission. "I'm the last asshole you're ever going to see."

Everything instantly stilled—only the sound of crickets could be heard as the escalating situation mutated the faces of the young men holding the girl into a snarl of testosterone-driven rage.

All three of them looked at the Led Zeppelin Swansong® Label T-shirt and Levi's® 501 clad Damon, not knowing exactly what to make of the tall, chiseled, black-eyed man of many cultures and none. He had turned the situation sideways in an instant, but the leather-jacketed man changed the entire dynamic when he pulled out from the small of his back what Damon knew to

Charles W. McDonald Jr.

be a .40 cal Sig Sauer®.

"Oh, now why'd you have to do that," Damon tsk'd with his right index finger, causing the gun to glow red-hot, searing its grip into the man's hand. Holding his burned right hand with his left, the leather-jacketed man cried out in agony, dropping to his knees on the spot as his balls still ached from being kicked in.

With his switchblade drawn, Football T rushed Damon, barely making it a couple of steps before Damon's *Telekinesis* threw the high-and-tight up against the telephone pole behind them so hard it broke his body in half around the pole, causing him to bleed dark-red blood and gore from broken entrails and a gaping wound below his ribcage before Damon and the young brunette.

"May I walk you home," he asked, brushing the tears from her cheeks with the backs of his fingertips, as she leaned her body into her dark-haired savior.

"Hey, fuckhead!" Leather-jacket yelled at them, causing Damon to make a smooth motion of his right index finger that sheared off a branch from the neighbors Elm and drove it straight through Leather-jacket's chest. Blood, gore and bones piercing Leather-jacket's torn flesh, ruined the leather jacket and left the man's face twisted on the ground in agony.

"Why don't you tell me where you live," Damon asked the brunette, gently caressing her palms with his fingertips to calm her.

"How did you—" she didn't get to finish her question before Damon put his finger to her lips. "They got what they deserved," Damon paused, reassuring her, "I don't want to see you get hurt by anyone else. Let's get you home, and no more dating assholes okay…?" Damon's rich and multi-cultural smile was disarming and yet another lethal weapon in his arsenal.

"Just down the street a ways—the blue and white house on the left up the hill," she didn't know him, but she knew enough that he was a better choice than either of the other two.

"Good, now…*Forget*," Damon commanded as she collapsed against him unconscious.

Charles W. McDonald Jr.

Chapter 15: Many Worlds

(Perion, Present Day)

he old gentleman's voice echoed throughout the antechamber as he called out for the young boy-becoming-man, "RADIN?!!!" Cascading from hewn columns to web-enclosed arched domes to dust laden floors and beyond, the old man's voice sought out the one he'd come to save. By the Creator's own grace had he saved the others, but there was still one left and his task wasn't complete without him. And while his companions had put themselves in harm's way, sending them to his old friend could not reverse what had been summoned.

     Deafening silence…. *Why is the boy not responding? Surely, he can hear me.* With that thought, he pulled the smallest sample of root and powder from a pocket lining inside his vest. Carefully unwrapping the components,

Charles W. McDonald Jr.

each wrapped in white linen, the old man concentrated, praying it was not too late. Closing his eyes so that he might see, he began to cast, searching—believing! In mere seconds, he scanned the entire vastness of the forbidden realm around him. Seeking this level, then the one above, then the one above that, finding the boy on the third level in a monk's private chambers—unconscious on the floor, scroll in hand.

"Good then. At least he's alive." Working his finely-scrolled cane against the floor, he began climbing the stairs to the boy's location. Throwing open the door to find Radin on the floor just as his divination spell had shown, Ykstherin held the boy's head against his lap as he knelt to the floor with creaking, arthretic knees. Reaching for the still-rolled-up scroll in Radin's right hand and seeing its seal now broken, Ykstherin made an unintelligible noise noting the significance and old familiarity of the seal. A pentangle, inside an opposing pentagram, inside a pentagon, inside a circle.

(Damon's Manor, Kaleion, Present Day)

Three massive crystal chandeliers, each of which cost more than most people make in a lifetime, hung from a twenty-cubit high ceiling of the foyer in which Radin now found himself. The ceiling looked to be the same throughout the entire first floor—at least what was visible to him from this vantage point. They threw out a stable and consistent white light without the use of candles and had wires running through the center of the chains suspending them from the ceiling. *Strange*, he thought, scanning. Four double-wide doorways were visible from where he stood, assuming it was the front of the manor. Even his soft leather shoes echoed with each step he took on the two-by-two exotic tan and white marble tiles laid on the diagonal. At first, he tried to step softly but then realized whoever had summoned him here must have already known his location and been alerted to his presence. He wondered if this was another dream like the one before, or if there was more powerful magic afoot. Yes, he could sense and feel this was magic at work…. However tepid his feet may have stepped upon the foreign tiles, he knew to his core this was magic.

As he walked under the first of the three chandeliers, he noticed a good bit of height from the top of his head to the bottom of the light fixture—maybe putting the bottom of them at ten cubits or thereabouts. As he probed a bit to his left, he noticed a long rectangular room with what appeared to be some kind of gaming table perhaps, with cards and coins stacked in the center.

At the end of the room was a huge marble mantle and fireplace hearth large enough for two grown men to stand inside. The foyer was shaped in an upside down 'T,' so that the near left corner of the large rectangular room on his left formed one of the right angles of the upside down 'T.' Radin noticed only one doorway to the rectangular chamber, and as he passed it, expecting to see a connecting door to what must have been another room between the rectangular game room and the front of the manor, but he saw none; nor did the game room continue into that space.

"Hmmm," he thought aloud, "well that's one hidden room." He continued walking down the foyer, assuming the long rectangular room to the right was a formal dining room from the large oak dining table with twenty-six chairs by his count. It looked as if the far end if the right side of the upside-down 'T' was a butler's kitchen or a staging area for food, as he could see small staircases both up and down, making him assume that was servant's access for food prep—likely leading to a main kitchen below.

Now passing under the second of three chandeliers, he noticed a massive circular staircase on his left, only going up. Now he could see another couple of doorways to the right making a total of six on the first floor—at least six visible. He could clearly see parts of a large kitchen over to his right, wondering if it extended all the way back to the front on the level below where the butler's kitchen staircase might have come out. *Hmmm…. Who needs a two-storey kitchen?*

He decided to go to his left, up the massive circular staircase, since *up* seemed to be what his gut was telling him. He didn't know what magic had brought him here, or where here *was*, but he trusted his instincts just as his father had always told him.

The second floor appeared to be mostly guest bedrooms, washrooms, a massive library where the foyer would have been below, a room that might have passed for a den, and another staircase on the right side of the manor, as he had walked all the way through the second floor via the U-shaped hallway with murals on the walls and hard oak parquet floors flowing throughout each room. Everywhere a consistent white light poured out from niches in the walls, recessed ceiling fixtures, wall sconces, and yet not a single candle in sight anywhere and no scent of them burning either. The only scent he picked up on was the smell of fresh flowers as he passed certain rooms.

He could either go up this smaller staircase or go back to the one he just left, but down wasn't an option on this wing of the manor. He assumed down to still be an option should he go back to the massive circular staircase, but he wasn't willing to bet on that. This place seemed to be constructed—either in part—or in whole, by magic. Nonetheless he was here, and he was

Charles W. McDonald Jr.

known to be here, so he might as well go up. He began ascending the small staircase with access only to the third floor.

This floor appeared to be arranged very similarly to the floor below—with a U-shaped hallway, more murals and paintings, and more parquet hardwood flooring throughout. At first glance, the murals seemed innocuous: grassy fields, walled cities, buildings that looked like they might be schools of some kind, majestic snow-capped mountains, and beautiful women in all manner of garb—some more scandalous than others and some obviously elvish. He knew there was more to it than that, and half expected to see whoever brought him here portrayed. "Hmmm." Another thought Radin permitted aloud.

Walking in the opposite direction this time, back toward what should be the massive circular staircase, Radin noticed more guest bedrooms, and other bedrooms obviously personalized, yet no one occupying them at the moment. Then, where the library would have been below, was an enormous rectangular room with double-wide onyx doors, now closed. The double-doors were toward the front of the manor, just over what would be the first foyer chandelier below, the doors inset in an upside-down U-shaped recess. Opposite the recessed double-doors was an upright U-shaped niche with another recessed mural wall flanked by paintings of a man he recognized from his dreams—paintings of that very man in varying stages of conquest.

Cautiously, he moved to the ten-cubit by four-cubit double onyx doors, opening them with little-to-no effort. They operated so smoothly he felt he could have opened them with one finger despite their obvious size, weight, and thickness. Once inside, the room could only be described as a blank—an entirely black canvas. Nothing on the walls, floors, or ceiling—each of them matte black with a satin-like sheen and the material was not anything he recognized though it was smooth to the touch and his mind felt a hum as his fingers drew near each surface. It did appear much larger than possible from the inside unless the manor was more than ten times the size of the first floor on this level.

"Hmmm, I'm not sure if this is good or bad," Radin allowed himself the luxury of having a conversation with himself since whoever brought him here appeared in no hurry to seek him out.

"My apologies for being late." The tall and obviously powerful man from the paintings—and his dreams—walked into the room dressed in the strangest attire. He was wearing light blue seemingly rugged pants with white fissures of thread throughout, tight against his body, some kind of grey button-down shirt—though none like anything he'd ever seen before with a collar that also had its own buttons, and a white undershirt. And his shoes.... He

Charles W. McDonald Jr.

had nothing to compare them to, but they appeared to be rather...*comfortable*. Primarily made of a charcoal weave with medium-blue and black accents with a white sole, he didn't know quite what to think about them, except that he'd never seen materials like that before.

Appearing slightly taller and not too much older than Radin, the man had raven hair and black eyes with a healthy tan glow about his skin and his features were...difficult to place. Multi-cultural was the best way to describe him. Broad-shouldered with long, straight hair that shimmered the smooth, even lighting that filtered in from nowhere and everywhere at the same time.

"I wasn't aware we were to meet," Radin questioned, hoping for some level of clarification. He didn't fear this other man, though everything about him was imposing and intimidating. And old. Instead, he felt something opposing about him. Like two great bodies orbiting one another, one playing off the energy and momentum of the other.

"No, I suppose not, at least not from your perspective," Damon paused. He wanted to give the boy plenty of room so as not to appear too threatening. Keeping his disarming smile intact at all times, "You must have found one of my scrolls, Radin. It brought you to me and summoned me simultaneously. I'm Damon."

"So, you're a lamean then," it wasn't really a question of Radin's—more stating the obvious. He wasn't going to bother asking how Damon knew his name. He was quite certain Damon knew a great deal more about him than just his name.

"Sure, on your world I guess that's what one might call my profession." Pausing and realizing he'd just shattered the boy's reality with two words. "Oh, I suppose I should start with saying, there are other worlds you know? When you look at the sky at night and see all those shiny dots, what did you think they were?"

Radin just shook his head, assuming Damon would tell him regardless. Everything his instincts was telling him was that his dreams were some vision or divination of these 'other worlds.'

"So, those are suns, and there are hundreds of billions of them in just about every galaxy with hundreds of billions of galaxies in our known universe." From his right hand, Damon produced a holographic map the size of the room, stretching from wall to wall, of the known universe and its cosmic web filaments connecting each galaxy and clusters of galaxies. He intentionally kept the edges of the hologram from touching any part of the floor, walls, or ceiling so as not to allow the room's unique construction to dispel the entire universal map. With his left hand, he produced a small, flashing, yellow arrow. "You are here—this is my homeworld—Kaleion." Another flashing little arrow

Charles W. M{c}Donald Jr.

in green, "This is your homeworld—Perion." Taking note of the distance, the map displayed between the two worlds was about as far as he was in height. Damon could see him trying to make sense of what he was seeing, "You're trying to figure out the real distance in scale. Let's see…it's about ten thousand light-years, which means light would take approximately ten thousand years to traverse that distance. So, when you look at my star—Kaleion's star—the light you would see took ten thousand years to arrive at your homeworld, so you are seeing my world and my star as it appeared ten thousand years ago. The speed of light is the fastest natural known phenomenon."

"Who *are* you?"

"You're having a hard time adjusting to this. I get it."

"How do you?" Pausing, "No I'm not going to waste your time asking you the obvious." That made Damon smile. The boy was smart. "Why did you bring me here, Damon?"

"Well, as I said, you did that when you opened the scroll, but to be entirely fair, not just anyone who opened that would have been brought here. Most would have been destroyed outright." Closing a bit of the distance while letting the map collapse into nothingness, Damon managed his sincerest tone, "I didn't bring you here to hurt you, kill you, or damage you in any way. You just recently turned eighteen, right?" Damon knew his birthdate but wanted to allow Radin some latitude.

"Yes, some weeks ago, but I don't think this is a belated birthday present."

"No, it's not, and you're right to be suspicious. Trust your instincts." Damon sat on the floor wanting to diffuse any tension or threat Radin may have perceived. "We can go to one of my studies or the library if you'd like a comfortable seat, Radin."

"I'm fine standing." Radin had already made note of Damon's echoing of his father's advice to 'trust his own instincts,' and apparently sound advice from both. Though, his instincts didn't have a solid read on the mysterious conqueror before him.

"Good. So, when you opened the scroll and looked at it, what did you see exactly?"

"Runes perhaps. They were moving, dancing back and forth on the parchment."

"Yes, that's Arcane—the language of the magi, or *lamean*—if you prefer—on your world. We go by other names as well. Depends on the world. Some worlds have no magic at all. On others, like the one I just came from…," Damon paused, making a sweeping motion of his right hand over his strange attire as if it referred to something or some place. "…There, magic is dying. Has been dying for thousands of years, and barely works enough to safely visit and return." He paused letting Radin take it all in. "Are you sure I can't get you something to eat or drink?"

"I'm fine."

"Good then. When you looked at the Arcane, did it speak to you?"

"Pardon me?"

"Did it make sense to you in some way you couldn't quite quantify or perceive?" Damon produced a few symbols between them with more holograms. They danced to and fro. "Nothing," Damon asked.

A very sudden and piercing headache originated from the front of Radin's brain, right behind the nasal cavity, as the symbols seared into his memory. Putting his right hand to his forehead, trying to balance himself with his left. Damon quickly dissipated the hologram. "Sorry," Damon appeared genuine in not wanting to cause Radin harm. "It doesn't come easily to everyone, even those with tremendous capabilities. It takes time, dedication, research, and a very open mind. It takes the…." He paused as he searched for the right word, "…resources of a powerful consciousness."

"And a teacher," Radin assumed.

"Oh, not I." Damon appeared firm on that. Waving his hand dismissively at the idea. "You don't want me to teach you." Damon rose to his feet, "That would be…bad, as they would say."

"As who would say?"

"Oh, never mind." Pausing as he looked Radin directly in the eyes, "I won't teach you. I can't. However, I never actually answered your question as to why I 'brought' you here, so I can do *that* for you."

Radin nodded, acknowledging the fairness and intent of the man. His piercing headache had mostly subsided by now, though every corner of his mind tingled with newly-excited energy as Damon continued to stir his every waking thought with a spoon of his own inquisitiveness, "So I make it my business to know important people, no matter where they are, who they are, what side they're on, their point of view, their skill level, their experiences, etcetera. You…," Damon proffered, referring to Radin as he extended his left hand out towards Radin, "…are such a person. A person I wanted to know. A person who I felt should know me."

"So, if you don't want to teach me, why the lesson with the map?"

"Well, your eyes were closed. Because you were asleep…. I just opened them a little."

"But why?"

"Because others are going to kill you if you don't wake up. Immediately."

Charles W. McDonald Jr.

"Why? What have I done?"

"Nothing. Yet."

"I don't get it." He didn't. Radin scratched his furrowed brow before scratching his chin. "You want to know me, and you want me to know certain things, but you refuse to teach me...."

"I told you, I can't teach you. I'm sorry. I can help open your eyes. I can show you a few things here and there when your mind is ready to accept them, but right now you're not far enough along and my teaching you might kill you, or at the very least.... It might get you murdered by association."

"What does *that* mean?"

"I'm *not* a nice man, Radin. I'm what some might call a monster."

He didn't need to search his feelings to know the forthrightness of the man. He was a plainspoken person—one both he and his father might respect. One could respect one's enemies he supposed, but was Damon *his* enemy? Or just the enemy of a great many others?

"I'm not going to call you a monster, Damon. I'll just call you Damon, if that's okay?"

Damon smiled, acknowledging the respect. "That would be fine. You may call me Damon." He paused again, raising his right index finger in the air, "...but you might want to be careful how, where, and with whom you use my name. I am..." searching for the right word. "...*infamous.*"

Radin nodded in agreement. "You have many friends, don't you?"

He was sharp. Very sharp. He was already putting pieces together. "Yes."

"I can see that in you."

"So..., we already understand each other a bit. In some ways at least," Damon replied, acknowledging the success of their first meeting. He had set the path. And now Damon would give Radin a bit more light with which to see it. "Time is not just linear."

"Come again?"

"You need to go now. However, take that scroll with you everywhere you go. If you need me, break the seal again. It will bring you here. You're more than welcome to explore while you wait for me. It will summon me right away, but I might be in the middle of something, and it might take me a bit of time to come home if I'm away. I take it you've seen the kitchen, and there is a complete staff available if you need anything."

Radin was about to protest, then felt his lifeforce crash back down into his physical body as he awoke with his head in the lap of an elderly gentleman back in the monastery outside Tannanvar.

Charles W. McDonald Jr.

*   *   *   *

Radin caught his breath as if surfacing from being trapped underwater for however long he was away. On another world. So many new words jumped to the front of his consciousness, 'many worlds,' 'universes,' and 'galaxies.' 'Twas a task just to gain his senses. Who was this man who now held his head in his lap as if he were his grandfather? Radin started to move, as the old man protested.

"I don't think we need to start jumping about just yet."

The old man's voice was rich and notable in its lack of accent. Or its blending of many accents.... "I'm all right," Radin protested as well, pushing himself upright against the dusty hardwood floor. He noticed the man examining the scroll in his hands. "Can I have that back please?" Radin asked, extending his hand towards the old man, furrowing his brow.

"Your friends are safe. I sent them somewhere far away to be protected by the most trustworthy people possible. I'm sure you'll have lots of questions, but would you like to go to them?" Using his walking cane, the old man helped Radin to his feet after situating himself first. "I might be able to help you find some answers. That is why you were here, correct? To find answers to certain, formidable questions...?"

Shaking his head, in neither the affirmative nor negative, merely trying to gain his bearings, Radin responded, "Forgive me. I simply don't know you yet."

"Fair enough. My name is Ykstherin." He extended his hand to shake Radin's, hoping the threat he felt here would allow for enough pleasantries for Ykstherin to leverage some level of trust to quickly get them out of harm's way.

Radin shook the old man's hand, but apprehensively so. Yes, he appeared old, but appearances can be *very* deceiving. Of that much he was certain. "Sent them where exactly?"

"Close to Bouschè."

"You sent them halfway around the world? Why?" Finding it odd, he didn't even question how.

But after seeing what he had already seen, that was probably nothing. Except for the fact it meant he was dealing with another *lamean*. His second of the day and the day was still young.

"People I've trusted far longer than you've been alive, my Son. People worthy of trust."

He certainly didn't fully trust this man, but clearly, he knew more than he was telling. Perhaps that was because time was short. His instincts didn't alarm as if this man were intentionally hiding something. Taking the scroll from the old man and putting it into his satchel, Radin could see the concern building in Ykstherin by the way his eyes darted this way and that, back whence he'd already come.

"What is it you're here to protect us from, Ykstherin? And how did you find us?"

"I'm sorry to disappoint you. The answer isn't as nefarious as you might have thought. Your father asked me to look after you." That met with a furrowed brow from Radin as he paused, circling the old man.

"Okay then. I'm guessing you know about the item we found...? The kind of attention that it might draw—the kind of attention that makes us all unsafe?"

"You're starting to think like a responsible adult. Rowarc would be proud. I can take us both to the others where we can regroup if it's what you want, but I'm not going to force you into that decision." He paused for a minute knowing Radin had left his responsibilities already. "Your father had made preparations for others to watch the business just in case. His primary concern is you—not his business. That I can assure you."

"Fine then. Let's go, and you can tell me how you know my father." He observed the old man's behavior and while his eyes searched for threats, his body language felt comfortable and in command of his faculties as if he wasn't about to panic even if Radin did. Though, he didn't feel panicked, it actually felt like a capitulation to weight of the moment before him, but wherever he'd sent Elise, that's where he needed to be. Period.

Bringing his cane up, then in a smooth downward stroke with his right hand, Ykstherin formed a *Portal* revealing a far-away snowy hillside field with snow-capped sharp mountain peaks in the distant background. Radin assumed somewhere close to Bouschè. He didn't think twice about what he was seeing—just assumed there was much more forthcoming as he stepped through to the chilled and hard soil on the other side.

(Stonehenge, England, Earth, Near Future, Moments Before Dawn)

The same isometric characteristics at the other Monuments of Creation were not present here. Damon walked the outside of the outer ring, his consciousness probing the ground beneath him for the same features he'd found at the others. Yet, still, there was no doubt.... They had been made for the same purpose. Canaanite, stone sacrificial alter aside, the feeling of the land itself confirmed that. There was a charge here—an energetic feeling—that ebbed and flowed with the land. He could see why the occurrences of crop circles here was more prevalent than any other part of Earth.

He hadn't been here in a long time and didn't have a pre-cleansing baseline reading of the energy here to draw from, but the energy he felt here now was powerful. The hairs on his arms stood on end increasingly so with his proximity to the sarsen stones themselves.

This wasn't his first time here, of course.... He'd been here a thousand years before, and a few times since, though none recent. But, in comparison to the recent other visits, this was his first—each time seeing it in a new light. A new morning—freer than the one before—was now dawning after their slaughter of thousands of interlopers, here to subjugate the Human race, as the god(s) of old, playing their deity-like tricks of meddling and influencing for nobody's gain but theirs. He'd had enough. Seen enough of that. The absolute termination of that was at the core of the Master Plan, and he was more determined than ever now to see it through. As he felt his new powers, from his greatly increased *Throne of Souls*, surge through his chest, he knew his senses more finely tuned to the act of Creation itself.

If DNA were the universal currency between species, then souls, consciousness, and light bodies were the resulting download, and each powerful soul he trapped for his own sake gave away profound mysteries not only of what might lay beyond the veil but how we got here....

At just over 21Hz, he tuned his consciousness, which tuned his nervous system, which opened pathways—especially here.

His mind saw and felt and heard the past as clear as the present before him now, watching the making of the great Stonehenge akin to watching a 3D holographic movie play out before him, but more importantly it showed why it had come to such an abrupt conclusion. The reality hit home that the Stonehenge before him *was an unfinished Monument of Creation.*

Closing his eyes to matter, Damon opened his thoughts to the quantum probabilities, envisioning each one of them in detail; the when, the where, the how, the why, and the what.... Isolating the one that made the most sense, Damon reached into his consciousness as he now sat down in the very center of Stonehenge, pressing his hands towards the Earth and letting the morning dew upon the verdant green grass meet his palms.

Feeling the Earth's newly increased frequency upwardly flow through him in a spiral akin to negative laminar flow, he mated his frequency to that of the Earth, fueling his isolated probability selected from a moment before, and allowed his heart to broadcast the summation of thought wrapped in energy, hearing the altar stone before him split open.

The distinct sound of stone cracking hadn't been unexpected, but it was still loud enough—abrupt enough—to cause Damon's body to flinch in between his shoulder blades as he fully exhaled his breath, and with it his thought, and with that his own reality now shared by all....

Opening his eyes to close the loop, he rose from his position to see what he knew would be there that was not before. Three shafts correlating to three runes or glyphs that did not dance as the others...until he came closer.... Just as his hand reached into the center shaft, that rune danced in the morning light of the Sol star just now cresting over his shoulder. Feeling the inside of the center shaft, he felt the familiar contours, in negative relief, of the mighty *Staff of the Invoker*, again confirming his role in the unmaking of *A Throne of Souls* correlating to the unmaking of Man. He hadn't manifested this part—merely finishing the connection that they hadn't had time to complete. The one—or really, three—thing(s) that connected all the Monuments of Creation...to make possible the greatest of all unmakings....

He thought about that again, as he had often these last few years as his adventures had carried him to the far reaches of this galaxy and beyond. To other planes and other times.... And now, other realities. Always and forever, he contemplated the unmaking of Creation not being the end of all things, but the beginning. He was more certain of that than ever and he hoped it wasn't a self-affirming reality. That, instead, he'd done the proper homework, and had it reviewed by others to make sure he was right, because there could be no going back to what was before. They were fully and totally committed. Forward and nothing else....

This would be the end of one story of Man (one cycle of Man) to beget another. The caterpillar must die so the butterfly could be born.

Quickly examining the other two shafts, to see their runes too come to life as his hand neared, their purpose too became clear: *The Sword of Creation* and *The Key to the Abyss*.

A hard line of renewed determination formed across Damon's face as he considered Kellen and Michael's roles in this end to the first story of Man, even if, on this world, there had already been three prior cycles of Man and now a fourth. Those were akin to acts in a play, whereas what would follow after their work was done would be an entirely new play.

Fireworks from nearby communities no doubt learning of last night's many successes burst, boomed, and sparkled overhead at the dawning of Earth's first true freedom, as those people also learned of a reality they never knew but somehow, on some unconscious level, felt existed. Disclosure after disclosure after disclosure had obliterated the lies of the Deep State in one fateful moment, making way for the dawn of a new day where birth certificates were no longer sold on the open market in the making of chattel from people.

Charles W. McDonald Jr.

Where countries were sovereign nations again and no longer corporate entities ruled under maritime laws. Where debt slavery gave way to everyone working towards the common good of Man as a star-faring race.

Not even centuries of experience could have prepared Damon for the deafening explosion bursting overhead.... Fireworks in the distant background were immediately dwarfed by the seeming thermonuclear blast in the upper ionosphere radiating concentric rings of blue-green concussive waves throughout the atmosphere—so massive in scale as to be seen by at least half the Earth, if not more. From Damon's perspective it sounded like a hundred tons of TNT exploding two hundred yards overhead as the air felt far more superheated than it would if he'd created a thousand *Portals* right where he stood. The ground reverberated and felt more liquid than solid for a brief instant as the crust manifested tiny blot echoes underneath him.

Shielding his hearing in much the way he did when he battled Eldrac, Damon collapsed to his knees with both palms covering his ears as he looked up to the sky—his nostrils filled with the scent of imminent danger and transformation in the air. The explosions of the last few fireworks tangentially overlapped with the concussive waves forcing clouds from the sky to make room for the ominous and deafening silence that rained down seconds later. Birds whirled uncontrollably to the Earth, barely finding enough just-in-time lift mere feet above the ground to prevent crashing to their death.

The Earth stood still—halting its rotation about its axis—as the poles immediately finished their race to shift positions as they had dozens of times before throughout Earth's catastrophe cycle. What had taken decades for the poles to traverse hundreds of miles concluded in seconds as the dawning atmosphere transitioned from bluish-orange and red to luminescent green. Still kneeling and shielding his hearing on the ground, Damon's body shook violently and felt aflame inside as if every synapse and every nerve ending throughout his entire form was suddenly awake as if it never had been before. 'Til now....

Charles W. McDonald Jr.

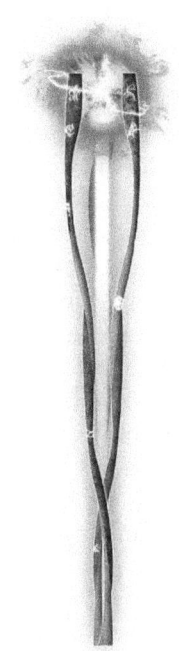

Chapter 16: A Present

(Damon's Manor, Kaleion, A Long Time Ago)

The nearly man-sized hammer struck the white-hot, adamantine-steel ingot just so, preparing it for yet another fold to add strength and character to the would-be rod. Again, he pulled the massive hammer up, wielding it with ease, striking down with expert precision to form the long, superheated metal rod on the giant anvil's surface. The ingot was massive, becoming more so with each strike of the Titan's hammer. Again and again, he struck 'til the rod was ten cubits in length. Precisely. Satisfied with his hard labor, Kasrael folded the metal back on itself, shoving it back into his immense forge where it would reheat for the next step.

A twelve-cubit-long wooden trough, sealed so it would hold liquids, held a light quenching oil, flanked the massive anvil and another wooden barrel nearly filled to the brim with water. A worktable, some twenty-five-cubits by forty cubits by twelve cubits deep, helped complete the immense subterranean workspace, carved out of the bedrock underneath the foundation of Damon's manor with Dallia's magic, purpose-built for the making of this one

Charles W. McDonald Jr.

first-anniversary gift for the husband who already had everything.

Another series of lengthening, then folding the first of the three ten-cubit-long rods, was re-heated and being pushed through a triangular die at the far end of the giant anvil via a large screw Kasrael turned slowly and consistently, forcing the first of the trio of rods through the triangular die at an even pace. With the stem of the press fully extended, and the rod nearly all the way through the triangular die, Kasrael grabbed the now triangular rod on the other side of the die, pulling it the rest of the way through. He didn't want to quench, for hardening, until he was done rough-shaping it. Right now, it was nearly a ten-cubit-long triangular rod, though without its necessary revolutions. This staff was architected in three's: three triangular rods, twisted in exactly three revolutions each, in a triple helix assembly. Laboring on his massive anvil, shirtless, Kasrael put the now triangular rod into the forge to heat-treat it to a molten-amber glow, preparing to put the three revolutions of twists into it.

The sound of Dallia's soft footsteps descending into the subterranean cavern and the flowered scent of her perfume caused Kasrael to look up from his massive forge. Completely dwarfed by him as she neared and barely coming to his chest, Dallia was as lovely as she was talented. An archmage in her own right, and Damon's wife, she struggled for her own identity against the backdrop of such an accomplished conqueror as her husband—though her specialty had always eluded most others, even Damon. 'Twas always a rare art, fast becoming a lost one—specializing in the enchantment of relics.

"How's it going?" Dallia's voice was even more soft and beautiful than the flesh she revealed with the deep V-neck in her powder blue robes, as she pulled down her hood trying to lessen the heat wafting off of Kasrael's forge. As the pleats of her hood nestled around her neck and clavicle, Dallia's golden curls and half-elven flesh shone and shimmered in the firelight of Kasrael's mighty forge.

Titans often didn't speak. You were lucky if you could get a single word out of them. Kasrael said plenty with grunts and his mannerisms, though she received a gruff, "Fine," from Kasrael this time, as he motioned to the now triangular rod reheating in the forge.

Pulling the glowing white-amber heated triangular rod from the forge, Kasrael set the bottom end into a triangular foot form, anchored to the cavern floor with rivets hot shot into the cavern rock, he would use to hold it in place. Grabbing the top of the ten-cubit-length rod with a heavy-duty, custom-made wrench, Kasrael began twisting in a counterclockwise manner. Casting to further stabilize the rod as soon as Kasrael began twisting, Dallia's magic ensured Kasrael's revolutions were perfectly smooth and symmetrical, and the triangu-

Charles W. McDonald Jr.

lar rod stayed true during the final shaping process.

"Mhmm," bellowed from Kasrael, pulling the first of the triangular twisted rods out of the anchored foot form, taking it back over to his forge for the final heat-treat. Another moment later and his tongs pulled the first perfected, molten helical rod of what would become the mighty *Staff of the Invoker* to quench it in his light oil trough. Ensuring its top end pointed due magnetic north, he smoothly lowered the twisted rod into the quenching oil with a pair of heavy blacksmith tongs. It hissed in the oil, causing the liquid to bubble for a moment as he left it momentarily submerged, quickly pulling it after it had soaked for a precise moment.

"NOW," Kasrael's voice boomed in the cavern, deep in the belly of the manor, as he held the twisted rod with his tongs over his massive anvil. Several footsteps rumbled alongside the distinct sound of rattling chains. Acrid black, almost-ethereal acidic flames engulfed the twisted rod, anvil, hammer, and the Titan's hand still holding the rod. "ENOUGH," Kasrael barked loudly and in anger and pain, quickly setting the rod against the worktable and shaking off his smoking hand to dip it into the barrel of water. Kasrael snarled, turning to scowl at the beast now snorting puffs of black smoke through its nostrils— its fiery-edged black scales glinted in the darkness. Pulling his hand from the water, Kasrael looked concerned as his skin continued to deteriorate before his eyes; the water should have subdued the fire completely, but not the acid unique to the flames of *this* dragon: Cauldron. An ancient and angry *beast....*

Acting on the rod first to save it before it was totally ruined by the etching of the dragon's breath, Dallia blasted the rod with enough cool air so as to remove the acidic part of Cauldron's breath, allowing the other components of his breath to do their work on the twisted helical rod. Dallia moved quickly from the rod to Kasrael as she took his arm into her delicate, healing hands.

It was difficult not to be enamored with Dallia's soft feminine features; Kasrael's giant ears twitched at her touch. Looking at her elven ears and beautiful high cheekbones, he'd do anything to help Dallia. He just loved being near her. Just being around her.

"Don't touch it," Dallia recommended, looking over at Cauldron, "You need to be very careful when working with this one. I'm sure you've crafted many a weapon before, even with the aid of a dragon, but you must not get careless with Cauldron. Making this will require the greatest of care and your very best craftsmanship, my friend."

Her words worked a magical sonnet in his tufty ears, causing him nearly to sway against her side. Slowly, she caressed his injured hand, running her fingertips over him hypnotically—new skin forming beneath her touch. "There," she murmured. "Go lie down until you feel the tingling in your hand subside. Then you can begin your work again."

Dallia examined what would become part of her anniversary present to her husband if all went well. She had made many relics before, but never anything close to the power of this one, and she was certain no one else had ever attempted anything like it before—at least not in recorded history. Picking it up with tongs and dropping it into the water, it hissed and popped with a power *most* promising. Pulling the twisted rod from the water, standing it beside her with a fair amount of effort due to its weight, its charcoal-blue, acid-etched surface shone with an aura capturing glimmers of her powder blue and silver robes, twisting them in subdued and blackened reflections, gnarled and coiled around the helical revolutions Kasrael had formed so masterfully. Twisted like a giant metal helix, it was only a third of the puzzle as it began to glow with an ominous charcoal-blue aura, imbued with the power of Cauldron's breath.

The rod's three precise revolutions—no more, no less—were not merely ornamental but served the purpose of strengthening the metal and providing more material with which to hold Dallia's powerful enchantment. Most were made from wood, specifically, high mountain ash, making them light yet durable. Yet high mountain ash could not hold the level of enchantment she required—no, *this staff would be like none before. Worthy of its one and only master.*

Dallia smiled, watching the reflection of her smile twist around the rod's perimeter. "Cauldron," she called out to the dragon, pointing the tip of the in-progress staff toward the darkness. "I want you to be careful not to harm Kasrael when working together."

Thunderous footsteps accompanied the beast from out of the darkness as it stretched the limits of its chains to place itself directly in front of her. Snorting, billowing poisonous gas and smoke out of its nostrils before her, its teeth individually dwarfed her lithe, half-elven silhouette. Its tail, curling around and covering half the incredible distance which made up the main body of the beast, was as thick at its tip as a full-grown man was tall.

Spreading his wings, which made his massive central body seem modest in comparison, Cauldron cupped them around Dallia, completely surrounding the powerful archmage in his webbed and ribbed darkness. Only his man-sized teeth and the glimmer of gold surrounding the black irises of his eyes were visible now as he bore his teeth only a few paces from her seemingly delicate flesh.

Dallia tried not to flinch, but she was quaking inside. It must have been at least ten times older than even her. *How clever and cunning could a dragon become in that much time?* Even she had to show caution and respect,

Charles W. McDonald Jr.

with a healthy measure of confidence, before Cauldron. Even now, she could still see her magic suppressing many of its abilities. She had been the one to capture it in the first place, but it had been very...*painful* the first time. Just that memory alone was enough to torment her dreams for weeks, but it must show her some respect. *It must!*

"This," she shook the helical rod before Cauldron's glimmering, razor sharp teeth, "...is a present for my husband, so enough of your playing around." Slamming the rod back down on the anvil so hard its echo was sufficient to shatter glass, Dallia paced around the perimeter of Cauldron's wingspan to get around the beast, heading back to the staircase leading back up to the main levels of Damon's manor. She had hoped Damon did not even know about this new place she had carved out of the bedrock below his manor specifically for this purpose. Hopefully, it would all be a grand surprise if Cauldron didn't mess it all up first.

"Blasted, worthless dragon may not fear me, but if Damon found out and came down here, I bet it would fear *him*," mumbling to herself as she ascended the bedrock staircase out of the bowels of her powerful husband's manor.

Dallia's gift lay on the anvil, its metal core still coursing as it slowly released the resonating energy Dallia had primed it with by slamming it down. No longer watching her body climb the stairs, Cauldron breathed more acrid fiery acid upon the anvil, engulfing the first of the helical rods of what would become the mighty *Staff of the Invoker* 'til he could breathe no more. The enchanted metal shone black molten throughout but remained intact. The acid etched and deeply textured the metal even more, burnishing it, but stopped quickly on its own as the metal was becoming indestructible. Cauldron billowed more smoke and poisonous gas from his nostrils in disgust; the rod had already grown too powerful for even *him* to destroy and would only become stronger with his every breath poured upon it.

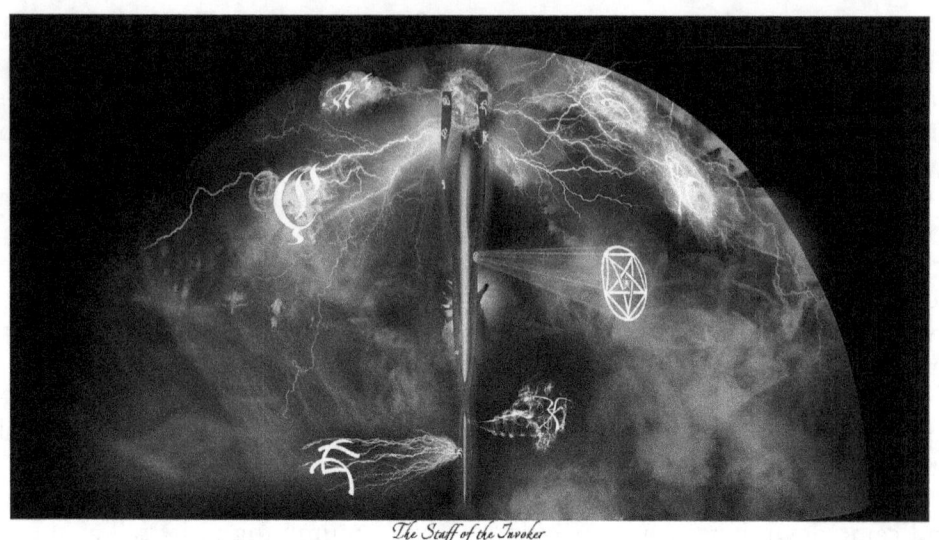

The Staff of the Invoker

Charles W. McDonald Jr.

Chapter 17: The Bitter End

(Damon's Manor, Kaleion, Present Day)

eflections of flames hazily flickering on the walls hinted at the room's unique composition to the experienced eye. Arcane components of invocation, golden-hewn in their magical fire, danced and surged barely within Damon's consciousness—so wild, yet so familiar and welcome. Acute and astute, fixing his eyes on a point in the corner of his spell test room, Damon ripped the components from that familiar, yet physically unexplored place where magic ran like raging rivers. Leaping from his palm, multiplying over and over, a seemingly harmless solitary flame transformed into one tremendous fiery explosion after another. Fifty eruptions in all, starting at one corner of the test area, spanning nearly a hundred cubits to the extreme end of the treated and enclosed area, it was an impressive site— enough to bring a smile, if a bit measured, to Damon's face. In all his years, he had only seen one that could create more havoc and unleash more destruction than himself, and Damon hadn't finished advancing his skills. Yet.... Timing the second phase of this custom spell an instant behind the first, plumes of dust raised by each fiery explosion slowly descended to the floor as each particle became more and more heavy with the chaos Damon had invoked at its core. Gas turning to liquid, then to acid. Almost nothing that could be imagined could harm the enchantment he'd put on the onyx material construction of his spell test room, though the sizzling acidic bubbles exploding on the

Charles W. McDonald Jr.

walls and floors were evidence enough of the spell's destructive capability. This one, called *Damon's Unrelenting Hate*, as many of his custom spells, was purpose built—a ranged weapon designed for the destruction of multiple armored targets. He estimated each blast easily powerful enough to turn sand to glass where the fiery sphere overlapped ground.

A sudden and unexpected flash of light—an explosion of unimaginable proportion, unlike any Damon had experienced in recent memory—sent him flailing across the entire length of the test chamber. The closed double-door entrance bringing him to an abrupt stop with a bone-crushing thud. The white-hot heat from the explosion was enough to set his robes aflame as Damon slid down the wall unconscious and unresponsive.

The air on the far side of the room, away from Damon, became superheated with silvery-blue flashes of light that rent the atmosphere in a lightning-bordered vertical seam—a *Portal*—enabling ingress of a slender, black-bearded man of determined facial planes, not quite as young nor tall as Damon, in magnificent charcoal-grey robes with hints of silver gild and red piping here and there with swept raven hair slightly shorter than Damon's. It was not supposed to happen that way. Ingress and egress to and from the spell test room via magic was not allowed by the enchantments built into the construction materials of the room itself. The only way in or out was *supposed* to be physically through the double-door entrance. Nonetheless, there Kellen stood before his old friend and ally as dozens of little lightning shards crackled upon the test room's floor—a residue of the unique brand of magic of Kellen the Destroyer, The Midnight Morning. Kellen frowned at the sight of an unconscious Damon. So many times Damon had come so very close to death. *Why did he flirt with it so?* It was coming for him soon enough, organically. Kellen saw no need to artificially hurry the process along.

"I guess nothing is foolproof," Kellen jibed, cocking his head and scratching his facial stubble curiously as he examined Damon's near-death state. "Ah well," he breathed in resignation, "Hmmm." Seemingly not in any hurry, whatsoever, to render aid, Kellen slowly closed the distance between them, casually looking around the room, noticing the acid still trying to etch the floor's treated surface, nodding along the way—seemingly impressed at the destructive capabilities of Damon's failed spell.

Kneeling down beside his 'friend,' Kellen unceremoniously grabbed a clump of Damon's long raven hair, tilting Damon's head back to better take in his condition. Nodding and grunting to himself knowingly, Kellen determined the appropriate *Healing* technique and began searching through a small, silver-laced, black bag he pulled from underneath the belt and blood-red sash of his garments. Frowning, he pulled a moderately sized ampoule, very nearly larger than the bag from which it came, removing the cap as he took in the heinous aroma of the concoction.

"You better appreciate this," he breathed just loud enough that Damon might later remember. "This *is* my last one." Nearly ripping Damon's mouth apart while opening it, Kellen poured the yellow sulfuric-like fluid from the ampoule down Damon's throat as he massaged Damon's throat to force the substance down. Damon's left eye half opening signaled the *Healing* taking root as Kellen seriously contemplated leaving. Damon could be a *very* violent man when coming to after being knocked out. He still remembered Damon's reaction the last time he'd saved him!

"Day...?"

Damon's other eye opened, slightly more than the other, his pupils still unable to focus. Again, he considered leaving! Frowning, Kellen slowly increased the distance between the two, backing *away*....

"Uh, Day???"

Bottomless groan..., "What??? **WHO**?!!" Focus and consciousness came in small doses, bad for Damon—*good* for Kellen!

"Uh, Day, I think your little project blew up. I mean, I was getting ready to drop in, and was just kinda checking, ya know, then...." Kellen was searching for the right word, settling on using Damon's favorite: "BOOM!"

"Blew up?" Frowning, furious, and more than a little confused, Damon recounted the spell in what memories of the event he could unscramble. "No. No, can't be."

"Hey, it happens to the best of us. You think you're immune? I mean you're really good and all. Some would say even great, but..." Kellen's backhanded compliments were the worst kind of insults.

Standing suddenly, enough to cause Kellen to back up again, Damon gathered himself—his black irises, now focused and alert, through those long raven bangs, upon his old ally. Kellen's best response was a priceless look, composed mostly of only half-feigned fear, curiosity, and...mischief. Dastardly was a word that frequently came to Damon when looking upon his old friend.

"What did you need to see me about?" Damon asked, gingerly exiting the spell test room into a hall of large, elaborate paintings and rugs, paying little attention whether Kellen followed or not. The paintings depicted significant victories and extremely close battles Damon had survived in the past. He had commissioned another old friend, a thief, and a somewhat renowned artist, to paint them.

Charles W. MᶜDonald Jr.

"What is it this time? More women???" Damon continued, gesturing as he descended the circular main staircase down to the first floor, heading toward the dining area, his favorite meeting place of late—ever since Goldenbow at least! "As if you needed any more! Or perhaps another of my custom spells? I'd be happy to give you the one you just saw in the test room if I could convince myself that it would *blast* you into the Nether!"

"Day, I'm hurt!" Damon still wasn't paying any attention to Kellen as he followed a few paces behind Damon with an expression that could only be described as mischievous.

"I wish I could convince myself of that." Shooting a sidelong glare, Damon pushed open the double doors of his formal dining area, exposing air with a myriad of diffused hues from rays of sunlight through stained glass behind them. Blues, reds, violets, and yellows, resting on the polished surface of the elaborately carved, dark oak dining table, spanning nearly the entire length of the dining hall. Four great cathedral windows countered four thick archways leading to the cooking areas, while two massive fireplaces, apparently one intended for reheating meals, burned at each of the long ends of the hall. Diffuse, but even, white light poured from every light fixture without the presence of candles or lamp oils, dancing off the surface of beautiful black marble tile flooring throughout.

"So, tell me then…," Damon paused as he took his seat at the end of the table, gesturing for Kellen to take the seat beside him. Damon knew it had to be good if the mighty Kellen the Destroyer was coming to him, and that was worrisome.

"The Scroll of Carnac has been discovered," Kellen proclaimed flatly, adjusting his thick charcoal-grey robes as he sat at the side of his only 'friend.'

His chest more visible now that the robes had parted slightly, Damon could see Kellen was dressed in his full traveling garb, apparently ready to go anywhere—not entirely unusual but interesting nonetheless. More than a few times Kellen had come on the spur of the moment to start some grand adventure to save this or annihilate that. Both were men of action—doers—perhaps that was part of their bond. Only scattered thoughts rambling through Damon's mind as he focused on the problem at hand, "You think I don't know," he chided, adding, "You think I don't have my own sources?!!!"

Raising his eyebrows at Damon's verbal joust, "A little irritable, are we?"

Furrowing his brow, realizing his tone, his manner, and his company, Damon paused, thoughtful, "Have you ever thought about us, I mean really thought about it?"

"Where is this going Day? You're really starting to worry me. Are you

Charles W. McDonald Jr.

sure you feel okay; I mean after that ex—"

Waving off the obvious in protest, Damon was going to drag Kellen into this one. He wanted a real answer to a real question. Kellen could barely relate to their friendship, and never spoke of it aloud, though Damon was persistent enough to talk about anything. "What if it.... We've been through a lot, you and I."

Nodding, the ever-stony Kellen visibly held back the desire to needlessly fidget with his robes and accouterments.

"What if, when it all came to an end, one of us really needed the other, and the help might require the ultimate sacrifice. I mean that isn't all that inconceivable, is it? It **could** happen."

Gesturing his right hand in feigned concern, Kellen tried waving off his friend's erroneous distress, "You really are not well, Day. I mean we've already been down that road together.... MANY times."

"Not like this we haven't."

"What are you talking about?"

"The reason you're here—the scroll."

"Yes, well—THAT. This Royvan Miral, apparently an adventurer of some regard, at least *there*, he did find *that—that thing!* Prophecy says that it will eventually find itself in the hands of the *One*."

"Prophecy, yes...," Damon paused, somewhat trailing off deep in thought, smiling in only slight disdain, "...has a nasty way of proving itself accurate in ways no one could ever have foreseen." Suddenly the glossy, but somewhat distressed, stain on top of the table began to shimmer, gleaming to life as Damon slowly moved his hands over the surface, concentrating as he peered through the ages. A fire came into focus, soon distinguishing itself as a campfire, the horizon fast approaching sunset, with horses tied to makeshift corrals and tents strewn about the frozen plains landscape giving no apparent indication of the party's location, yet Damon knew. The window through the worlds, about the gleaming tabletop, shifted abruptly, centering itself on a brown leather traveling satchel. "Prophecy," Damon thought aloud. "Everything comes to an end.... Some more abruptly than others. What if these prophecies are dead wrong?"

"Come again? I'm not a believer in that sort of thing. You know that." Kellen traced imaginary ringlets with the index finger of his left hand upon the surface of Damon's dining room table as he often did in moments of deep contemplation. "Yet, I believe there are those we trust that can verify the authenticity of these findings and that would prove worthy of some level of concern that there might also be validity in the prophecies themselves."

"A fine, fulsome, and educated answer, my friend, and I would expect nothing less. And yet, I am not convinced. In fact, I've never come across a serious and significant prophecy delivered in the way in which it was described. So, call me skeptical." Damon's mind seemed to be operating on a different frequency than Kellen's, but that was the purpose of this conversation.... To find out for sure.

Not quite sure whether he should nod in affirmation or not, Kellen smoothed the sides of his robes, unable to hold back the fidgeting that came so rarely to a man of such apparent power and confidence. *Damon was getting weird in his old age.*

"Do we need the seals to do what they claim they do," Kellen asked, thinking he already knew the answer, but he wanted to hear Damon's thoughts on the matter.

"Only the last one," Damon answered with finality and certainty as if he'd already seen the wrath of his future with his own eyes.

Pausing, Kellen visibly pondered his friend's suggestions and concerns. He did not want to stonewall. Kellen really wanted to give Damon an answer he could count on, a word—a promise to address his original question. Kellen knew that was the kind of man he was dealing with but didn't know if he was that kind of man himself...yet. "So, seals aside, you want to know if I'll save your skin.... Even if it meant there was someone else out there—some-where—whom neither of us has met, yet could easily kill us both," he asked his clarifying question while looking Damon eye to eye.

Glaring directly into the cold eyes of one of the most powerful arch-mages he had ever known, Damon set the record straight, "What I want to know, Kellen, is are you with me *to the bitter end...?*"

Kellen's answer came in the hot blaze, sitting in place of once cool iris-es, and in the brilliant fiery aura of pure and ancient Arcane emanating from Kellen the Destroyer's flesh.

(The Ice Bridge Between the Cursed Capes and the Isle of Fate, Perion, Present Day)

Throwing his leather sack over his broad shoulders, trying not to think about its contents and the consequences it might bring, Royvan Miral strode to his horse, his companion for more than a decade—Essean. Petting the Grey comfortingly as he untied Essean from the post, Royvan mounted, swinging Essean around. Hazy rings of amber, the hues of a glorious sunset, met him head-on painting an ethereal sheen around them, cascading in ocher waves off his long brown locks, casting a shadowy void behind them to the east. Royvan Miral watched the sun wink out of existence over the frozen ocean horizon they would now leave behind. A multitude of concerns could be seen passing one-by-one across Royvan's smoke-hued eyes, as they made their way home through the Valley of Power.

Chapter 18: In the Thunder's Wake

(Holden, Perion, Present Day)

Rain and thunder battered at the grounds and grey stone keep of the old Lockhart Manor. Lightning strokes, nearly on the keep's grounds, invoked smoky motes of crimson mist, barely visible against the storm-woven tapestry of the night air. The wind rustled through chimes strewn about the grounds, swinging the old iron gate this way and that ever since the latch had broken long ago. The chime intonations concatenated with the moaning and metal gnashing of the gate into frightening howls carried on the night air. Between the thunder strokes, porch oil lamps hung from overhead just inside the main gate, noisily swung to and fro, tossing their light in schizophrenic patterns on the porch and in the weather-beaten courtyard.

Inside, burning purple, red, black, and white candles of every size and shape rendered a sinister backdrop against virgin white Elian and lace window treatments.

Slamming the heavily embossed door behind her with a deafening quake that shook the entire manor to its foundation, Michelle stormed her way up the spiral staircase in the main foyer, ripping her silken dress from her body as she made her way to the master chambers. Lamenting over the loss of her beautiful clothes, she stepped out of the dress and her underwear as she entered their bedroom, scanning the room for a towel to dry her long, wavy-blonde hair.

"Shelle? Is that you? What took you so long?" A familiar and beloved female voice rang out from the adjacent suite, crawling its way across the ceiling and around the elaborate, three-stage crown moulding toward her from the spacious bath, on the other end of the opposing room.

Charles W. McDonald Jr.

"Yeah.... It's me alright," Michelle vamped in disgust, toweling herself off as icy water still dripped from her naked curves onto the finely crafted area rugs. Walking toward the opposing chamber, she wrapped her cold, wet hair up in the towel.

"For what it's worth, I think I might have something...finally," Michelle offered, taking a seat on the edge of the bed, shoving Lawna's nightgown aside. Sighing heavily as she propped up her cheek with her arm on her knee. "God, I swear, we've been stuck here forever."

"Patience," Lawna coached, "You can't solve *everything* in a day. I mean, besides, we've only been here what...not even a couple weeks yet?" It had barely been enough time for them to adjust to the common tongue much akin to a romance language evolved from a similar root of Latin. They frequently had taken to using it instead of English to talk to one another to stay in practice.

Frowning, Michelle let out the knot in her towel, her hair spilling down her back and shoulder in moist, golden hues. Running her fingers through her hair, she pulled it back over her shoulder so she could work through it in sight, leaving the rest of her mane to lay against her curvy chest. Soft, lush, and beautiful in almost any setting, even Michelle looked...distressed. Becoming an incessant worrier of late did not fit her, but there seemed much to worry about. "Yeah well, it feels like forever," Michelle continued her line of thought.

Slender, lean, hard, and muscular, Lawna worked more soap into the sponge, running it down each leg, one at a time as she continued to bathe. Lawna, herself, was attractive enough in her own right, though being around Michelle challenged her self-esteem. "Relax, Shelle. You're going to start developing lines if you don't relax a little. Why don't you tell me what you found?"

Managing a smile, trying not to think of all they had left behind—*who* they'd left behind, Michelle recounted, "Well, there are several people I'm working to find out more information on, not the least of which is the incredible woman I was reading about. Her name was Arella. Apparently, she was killed a few years back." As she had done all day every day since she'd been here, she tried not to think about her daughters. The pain of missing her three little girls festered in her every waking moment, but it would have to be set aside now. What hurt the most was that she could no longer feel her tether to them in her thoughts.... *Too far away*, she assumed.

"What do you make of it?" Lawna's silky voice neither here nor there; difficult to place even though Michelle knew it was coming from not more than thirty feet away. One of Lawna's many gifts....

Charles W. McDonald Jr.

"I can't say just yet. Not enough information. It's like a jigsaw puzzle or even a great mosaic. There are all of these really huge pieces, and you just think there's no way they're going to fit together. Individually they look like something you may recognize. Then you begin to see all the smaller fragments that make it possible, but only if those larger pieces were nothing like you originally assumed."

"Assumptions are for assholes," Lawna chided, knowing Michelle would take it in the manner intended: fucking with her.

"You would know," Michelle quipped, though softly so.

"I heard that." Lawna squeezed more warm soap out of the sponge upon left leg.

"Damn." The smile on Michelle's face could only be described as… *wicked.* "…Anyway, that's what I've been working on; not only identifying the big pieces but the little ones that make it fit together. What about you? How has your work been going?"

"Well, I wasn't unfortunate enough to stay out as long as you," Lawna mocked, producing a scowl from Michelle. "In fact, I spent most of the day going through what I could find in this old place. They had quite an extensive library here."

"Tough job…not even leaving the house. Can we switch?" Genuinely smiling now, at least Michelle felt herself getting in a better mood as she grabbed her hair in groups of strands, running her towel through her tangled muss of her hair.

"It *was* tough," Lawna defended, climbing from the tub, reaching for her towel. "You have any idea how many pages I read today? I mean, My GOD," she exclaimed, toweling off her straight, shoulder-length, dirty-blonde hair. "I'm gonna need glasses after this is over," Lawna glowered, moving to the stately mirrored dresser, squinting in its reflection.

Pouting for love, Michelle mockingly rubbed her thumb and forefinger together in a back-and-forth motion directly in Lawna's inverted line-of-sight via the dresser mirror, feigning bow-like motions across a microscopic-sized violin.

Furrowing her brow sharply in the mirror's reflection, Lawna turned walking to the bed, reaching over Michelle and snatching up her nightgown. "No, seriously, you wouldn't believe the collection this Lady Morella had amassed before she died. I mean there's quite a bit here, at least about their history, previous wars, ancient legends, and all kinds of stuff. Apparently, she was into all that. She's got this particular book on Creation, *Viri Vastator.* I really think it's like their equivalent of the Apocrypha. You need to take a look at it. It's…. Well, you'll see…."

Charles W. McDonald Jr.

Raising her eyebrows, Michelle got up, walking to her chambers for clothes. "Show it to me. I want to see it."

"Shelle, wait up. What's the rush? What's going on," Lawna chased after Michelle, trying to understand the urgency.

"'*Viri Vastator*,' translated literally, means the 'The Destroyer of Men.'" Linguistics was one of Michelle's many talents, and some of Perion's root languages closely resembled Latin.

Looking into Lawna's eyes as they walked the halls of Lockhart Manor, Michelle wondered what perils Rena had gotten them into and for how long they would be gone. They had left very big problems at home, and their girls needed them both. She could not fight the thoughts creeping into her mind that they were being used. *The question was by who. And why? And what did Rena know she'd never shared with them before sending them on this mission?*

Charles W. McDonald Jr.

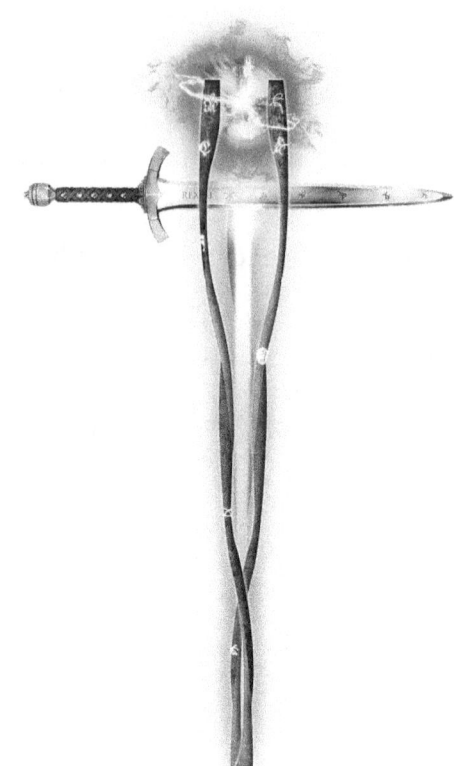

Chapter 19: Between Hope and Ruin

(Xal, Perion, A long time ago)

The consequences of an auburn and purple dusky twilight howled through the secret places of his ardent, secluded study, firmly reminding him of the dangers that lay just outside his sanctuary. Time did not allow for a thorough accounting; only the most necessary could be saved. Continuing his feverish preparations, desperately trying not to look at the fading hues of sunset, Xaldran quickly tried to accurately inventory everything he would need for his flight from those that would have him destroyed, now with the Great Talemar no more. It was much more than just dangerous, being *here…now*, at least without the protections he once enjoyed. With Talemar and most of their Allies gone, Xaldran's options for sanctuary were rapidly dwindling as fast as the coming nightfall of terror. He

Charles W. McDonald Jr.

had to think about his own survival now—and the survival of a knowledge left specifically in *his* care.

This time of day was more dangerous than any other, and especially for *who* and *what* he was. Adena!!! That witch! How dare she do this to him! *Oh, Adena; you will pay dearly for this*, he smoldered as he tried to recount his most prized volumes, scrolls, writing materials, and other artifacts of his ancient profession. "Only the necessities," he hurried himself aloud. Surely whatever he left behind would be forever lost to *her*. Probably to be taken back to Corning and the broken towers. *ADENA!!! If he only could live just long enough to see her hang!*

A crashing sound accompanying shards of thick oak blasting inward from the front entrance of one of Xaldran's many homes brought to a screeching halt any further dawdling; only time to grab one last thing. Quickly he knelt where he was, casting to expose a hidden opening in the wood flooring as he reached for a large brown, seemingly unnamed leather-bound volume.

Already through the splintered remnants of the front door, Xaldran was within its grasp. Another casting, thinking of where he could escape, the only place in the world left for him to hide, and by the breath of wind, his form disintegrated into a fine red dust blown across the room's flooring into nothingness.

The undead life behind the lifeless form shrouded in tattered rags walked to the empty hole in the floor where the Tome of Power had been. Its dead eyes came to life in a burnt-red-orange glow as it gruffly wielded its bones and tattered shards of decayed flesh back toward the splintered doorway. Adena would not be pleased. *At least there was little more she could do to him.* That prospect brought a twisted sneer to what remained of his mangled face.

(The Needles, Perion, Present Day)

It was odd seeing his old homeland like this, almost nothing still recognizable from so long before. *Had he been gone so long?* He would have to find some landmark still standing to gain his bearings. Hope was hard to find in moments of well-founded panic, even his age and experience could not deny his feelings, but if he were right, *hope* was never far.

It seemed he'd been flying forever, from west of Xal, until at last…. From the air it was utterly unmistakable; even time had been incapable of erasing the sharp barrier reefs clustering the waters below. *The Needles*, he remembered, causing his heartrate to increase as his pulse pounded. The air felt…

Charles W. McDonald Jr.

familiar and welcome, coursing aerodynamically over his enormous wingspan, more so now that he had his bearings, recalling a place that should still be…if anything at all was still left of what once was.

A swift snap of his wings with a directional arch of his massive neck and tail, and he was changing course, descending in altitude as he expertly banked through the clouds over crisp northern air flows. If indeed *it* still was, then he *must* be close. *Would he still be able to….* YES! The only place left standing, old enough for him to recognize. 'Edinaiel,' by its oldest name….

From the air, it was still enigmatic, beautiful—camouflaged among the forest below, only recognizable from the air, until one was close enough to see not everything standing was trees. A series of twelve granite and crystalline towers, a virtual manmade forest amidst the towering spruce, redwood, and fir of the valley below. Each tower wider at the base, angling toward the planet's crust in sharply faceted granite planes, while slimming to a spire of enchanted lead crystal that seemingly stretched to the heavens without end. Twice each tower changed angles, reaching toward its spire's peak, the first steepened sharply upward, growing the tower almost purely vertical, the second angled back—almost flattening at the pinnacle. At the lower angle change—precisely one-third the way up the tower—six symmetrically placed elegant buttresses arched downward in beautiful blue-crystal arcs. At the second angular shift— two-thirds of the way up each tower—were elaborate diaphanous causeways made of diamond-shaped tiles interconnecting one tower to the next, ascending incrementally from the two forward towers outward in both directions as the towers formed an enormous circle with the tallest tower at the center rear position. Approaching from the air, it looked like the most beautiful crystal crown of all. The Crown of Spires had been intended to intimidate and humble as the seat of *great* authority. It did.

Each of the sheer causeways allowed for a stunning view of grounds and strategically-placed moats below, with the back of the crown completely surrounded by crystal blue waters, thought to hold magical powers of both protection and defense of the towers as well as the great longevity of their people.

Shimmering in prismatic rays off the diamond-shaped crystal diaphanous tiles, the morning accompanied his arrival. If he were not welcome, he would surely die, but living this long liberated him of his fear of death. It was said that if one had the power, one could see any place in the world at any time, by looking into the crystal tiles where he now walked after transforming, giving the appearance of walking on top of the world from a *lofty* position as one walked the divination causeways of the Crown of Spires. Even now the divination causeways and the winds of the future displayed uncertain visions

Charles W. McDonald Jr.

of Adena in her long-held seat of great power. Disgusted at the lack of change *here,* when so much around him had changed so drastically, he ignored the visions focusing instead on what he'd come for.

Everywhere the towers bustled with early morning activities. He tried to blend in with the few male workers—the 'drones' as they were once called. Women of every nationality and principality walked about the inner crystalline structure, dressed in varying garments and sash, some in seductive and even scandalous dress, revealing forbidden flesh peeking through diaphanous materials. Some more respectably clothed in striking long dresses of rose-silk, lace, and Elian. Though most so attired had seen more than thirty turnings of the seasons, making it appear to be a rite of passage to be so elegantly styled.

Flying buttressed vaulted ceilings of gold and silver leaf, murals, and cathedral corridors refracted the beautiful morning throughout, a sight rarely short of breathtaking. A matriarchal community, seemingly built on harmony and cooperation of the grandest scale, but in actuality, built on the backs of a broken people, driven by the relentless perfectionist vision of an entirely self-centered society. For now, at least, *that* past had been forgotten—at least by most. A great and ancient tree sicked from the top branch down....

*   *   *   *

Somewhere in an alcove among hidden corridors, where even the brilliant shafts of dawn could not penetrate, other things had been left forgotten. Vertically positioned in dozens of massive man-sized nooks hewn out of whole slabs of blue-grey granite, lining both sides, Adena's secret army lay motionless—quiet. Appearing androgynous yet holding most of the appearance of a large male, with very long straight brown hair, slender arms, and fingertips looking to belong to something other than a human, its eyes lay closed to the outside world—asleep. No movement underneath its placid eyelids could have warned. No heaving of its chest to preamble. Everything tranquil, until abruptly it slept no more. In its first breath, it knew why, as the crystal shell protecting it all these years fissured, shattering in all directions to the granite below in tinging sounds that echoed down the corridor and beyond.

*   *   *   *

Not much time he thought, racing out of Adena's treasury, trying not to draw too much attention to himself, Toblain, still in Human form, needed to find a place to transform so he could escape by air. *I will have my revenge,*

Charles W. McDonald Jr.

Toblain plotted, finding a foliage-shielded place to transform beneath the causeways.

Chapter 20: A Dying Wish

(Kellen's Manor, Kaleion, Present Day Evening)

mber light danced in enigmatic elegance off the singular cornea burning in his brazier. Its black iris expanded to its fullest extent, frozen in the horror of the last moments of the victim from which it came. It burned quickly in the flames, which licked at it from the heart of the brazier. It, alongside a piece of small intestine, burned equally fast, leaving an acrid and distasteful odor in the air. It was not like Kellen to resort to such witchcraft as this, but he needed to see what it was Damon could not.

Witchcraft was a distasteful art and witches were meddling bunch for that matter. Damon often found uses for them, most they would never have approved of if only they knew. They had sold themselves to their god, whoever it might be, to attain their power, and therefore were beneath contempt—unworthy of existence. Yet their involvement, their practices, had become undeniably intertwined into his affairs, and that made their 'art' his business.

Sitting underneath the small round worktable, Camille clinched her fists in well-founded fear as she carefully watched the components burn to the desired state. She wondered in the back of her mind what would have her master resorting to such odd spells of late. *Perhaps he was in trouble. Perhaps she could…no*, she could not begin to think such things. Her elation would become uncontrollable and impossible for her to mask from *him. Mustn't*

Charles W. McDonald Jr.

think that, she tried to maintain control of her thoughts.   It wasn't like her to even take any concern of her master's actions, but he had been acting even stranger of late. *What is he doing? What is he involved in?*

*   *   *   *

Now in his favorite chair, alone in one of the many purpose-built libraries in his estate, Kellen opened the large, black, leather-bound manuscript to a place bookmarked near the end. He began to read from the ancient spell, preparing himself as the nearby hearth burst into flames of seductive hues from a mere thought. He could not read this incantation without the warmth, and presence, of fire.

"Master?" Camille must have crawled in on the floor quietly so as not to disturb him. He had not heard her movement. Naked and shackled so that she could not go far, she bore a collar around her neck with a small tag dangling from the collar—her name, beautifully inscribed on a pure silver dog tag. Beautiful and seductive, she came closer, her bruises from previous beatings now easily visible along her ribcage. Her knees red and swollen from crawling on hardwood floors did nothing to phase her outwardly, nor did the internal shiver that always came when she was this close to him. She had learned better. It had been a very painful lesson. *Must not*, she reprimanded, *I can't*. Walking was permitted only when he gave permission, and he had not. Her shimmering raven hair and bright-blue eyes sparkled in the light of the fire, but their own internal brilliance of spirit had been broken when she had been captured. It was only a memory now—freedom—a distant memory at that. She was kept immaculate by the other girls, after all, *she* was his favorite.

"Yes," Kellen replied with a stern and unforgiving look.

Camille shrugged away slightly, "I think it's ready now, Master. I watched until they had burned away almost to ash, just as you said." She hoped her justification for her interruption would prevent her from another beating.

Please, she prayed silently as he rose threateningly from his chair, gliding past her, the trailing edges of his robe cascading off of her bare flesh in disturbing, bone-chilling waves. Mastering her shattered emotions, she waited until he had left the room before her whole body shivered in fear and *revulsion*. Showing fear was not allowed. They had all been taught restraint. They did not understand why, but they did know the penalties.

Walking into the next room, carrying his book with him, Kellen observed the still smoldering brazier. The odor was almost more than he could tolerate. *Getting soft in your old age*, he thought to himself. *Soft and pampered.*

Camille had served him well. He would have to reward her with some time permitted walking. *Just in time*, he commended himself. Walking to the small circular table set up beside the brazier, opening his large manuscript back to the designated page he had been studying before, he began to recite the spell's many detailed stages.

Noticing the sunrise just out of his peripheral vision, he tried to remain focused on the enchantment. "Wait a minute."

(West of Bouschè, Perion, Present Day)

The knock came as a surprise only in its timing. Luke was never wrong when it came to his foreseeings. They were rare, but he was never wrong. Not long until dawn, his bloodshot eyes were heavy, but there would be little sleep.

Who were these people coming to see his grandfather? He could only guess at their motives. Many had come in search of his grandfather over the years for varying reasons, some less respectable than others—his grandfather never turning any of them away, only ensuring his help furthered the cause of justice over hate. Gareth was beginning to understand. *But where was the help for his grandfather?* It was hard not to be bitter. Another knock brought Gareth out of his thoughts. Still on his knees, leaning forward against his grandfather's sword, he had not moved since coming out of his grandfather's room. Rising to his feet, Gareth walked to the door, not knowing if he was ready to meet those of his grandfather's dying wish.

Opening the door, a blast of cold mountain air rushed inside, blowing his short, dark hair out of place, his bangs now nearly in his way of seeing the two frozen kids before him. He couldn't call them adults. The girl barely looked old enough to take a husband, and the boy barely old enough to know what a husband was. Neither were dressed for the extreme cold and snow that could swoop down from the mountains and swallow the unprepared. "Well," he barked with an expectant look. "Get inside before you both freeze to death."

Not waiting for anyone or anything, Elise practically leapt into the cabin, not stopping until she was in front of the raging fireplace several paces from the cabin's front door. Still standing just outside the door, Kerrich looked into Gareth's eyes, shivering—teeth nearly chattering.

"Come in," Gareth assured, gesturing with his right hand, "I need to close the door; I think the girl's half frozen."

Charles W. McDonald Jr.

Giving Gareth a full, precautionary berth, Kerrich entered, turning and walking backward to the fire to keep Gareth to his front.

Walking to the girl, not paying too much attention to Kerrich, Gareth picked up a quilt his grandfather had been using to keep warm by the fire, offering it to the girl and offering her his grandfather's chair. Shivering as he wrapped the quilt around her body, Elise paced before the fireplace a couple of times before walking to the chair, carefully watching the building intensity between the two 'boys.' She hoped she would not have to get in between them.

Kerrich watched as Elise took the chair, taking his turn at pacing in front of the fireplace.

"Do you always take just anyone into your home?" Kerrich asked.

"In a way, when it was my grandfather's, I suppose you could say, 'yes.' True it is that I do not know you, but company I *was* expecting."

"How?" Kerrich tried not to shiver himself, but he was chilled to the core. It had gotten so cold, so quickly. He would have to remember that when they left, wherever their travels might take them. His first thoughts had been that they would start for home once Radin caught up with them, but the more he deliberated it, the more he doubted he would see home anytime soon. His mind tried to comprehend the possibilities as he edged closer to the fire while trying not to close too much of the distance between himself and Gareth.

"I was hoping you might know more about that. I mean you came here for help, right? What made you think help could be found here?"

"We were told to come."

"Well, there you have it. I would think that the person who told you to come would be able to help us all understand a little bit more. Please sit, my name is Gareth. We can talk for a bit—get to know each other, and maybe then it will become clearer how we might be able to help each other. What do you say?" Gareth motioned Kerrich to his chair, opposite his grandfather's and symmetrically angled toward the fireplace. When it seemed Kerrich was satisfied enough to sit, Gareth took a seat on the rug in front of the fire, between the two chairs. With his back to the fire, he looked between the two, cursing himself internally for not offering them something warm to eat and drink. "Forgive my manners," he apologized, "I can get you both something warm to drink; perhaps some food. Are you hungry? Surely you didn't travel far, dressed like that!"

*   *   *   *

(Tannanvar, Perion, Present Day)

The match burned hot and fast as soon as it was struck, but it was more than enough time to light the tobacco in his pipe. A smirk was evident as he watched the young boy and the old man disappear into the *Portal*—he wasn't sure, but he didn't recognize the exact hillside. The mountains were pretty, obviously belonging to Bouschè. Well, it was a start. That would make following them a bit more complicated, but nothing that couldn't be worked out with the right amount of coin in front of the right sort.

Just as the match had all but burned away in between his fingertips, the flickering light revealed a slight scar on the young man's face. The spent matchstick dropped from his fingers, bouncing on the hardwood floors before it had a chance to burn flesh. Puffing lightly on the pipe, getting the tobacco to smolder just right, he started on his way, disappearing into the night, knowing he'd need help before he could follow any further.

Charles W. McDonald Jr.

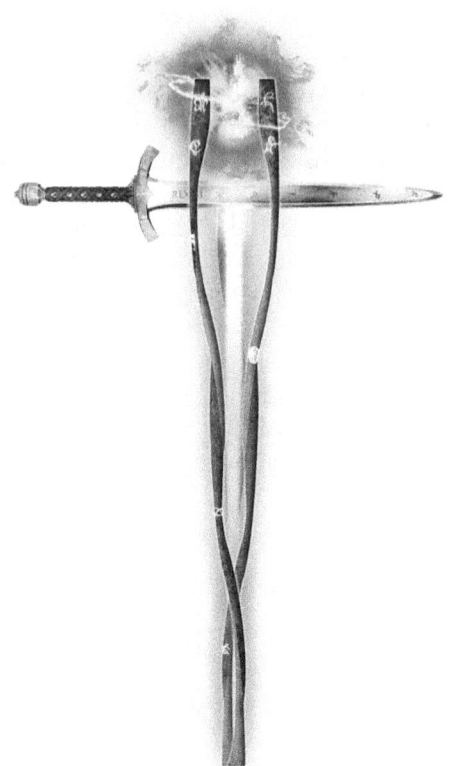

Chapter 21: Breadcrumbs

(Kingdom of Gawth, Almeron Castle, Perion, Present Day)

orning had come and gone quickly. He despised the morning. Evenings were always more pleasant—especially in candlelight. Almeron Castle was an excellent beginning for the new young statesman, but that name.... *Yes, that name would have to go soon,* he contemplated behind the commanding old oak desk. Now, Phaestos was a name he much fancied. *Yes,* he gleefully burnished his hands one against the other. "Castle Phaestos," he proclaimed with a grandiose sweeping gesture of his arms as the words echoed through the adjacent hall.

Jeremy was barely on time with the afternoon refreshments. He dare not say anything after seeing what had happened to his former master—only what must be said. "Will there be anything else, My Lord," he asked, mono-

Charles W. McDonald Jr.

tone, as he sat the tray of pure engraved silver, laden with food and tea, onto a small end table next to the desk. "No, Jeremy, I don't believe so," stated the young man as he set down his pipe and picked up a morsel of fresh, warm bread, spreading some butter and sweet preserves over it. No sooner had he brought the food to his lips than an echoing knock came to the double doors of the main entryway.

"Ah, something for you to do.... Be a good man and fetch that."

"Yes, My Lord." No hesitation needed, yes, the word 'fetch' left a nasty, bitter taste in his thoughts, but at least he was still alive to have thoughts.

"And...," he interjected with his index finger pointed threateningly toward the young boy with a morsel nearly at his mouth. "Do try to smile," the youthful man offered as a final slight.

The young boy did his best imitation of a smile while silently praying it would be enough to satisfy the madman who now sat behind his old master's desk. "Yes. Of course, sir," replying meekly, as he traversed the ornate marble foyer flooring to the main entryway.

Swinging the double doors wide, while making a grand welcoming gesture by bowing deeply for the middle-aged man before him. Their new guest was somewhat tall and still in decent shape for his age with short black but graying hair and brown eyes.

"Ah," the young Lord stated, getting up from behind the desk to greet his guest. "Good afternoon to you, Mr. d'Aguillon. I trust your journey set well with you."

"Fine," Rowarc d'Aguillon responded in business-like tone. He had to get used to his new, or rather old, role. Being a hired tracker was rather different from running his own inn. Just working for someone else was the biggest difference. He missed being his own boss already, even if it didn't pay half as well. Yet it was something he *had* been good at, and, like his father would tell him, 'best if you stick to what you're good at and learn to love it.' He managed to make quite a name for himself over the years, perhaps his time had come again. "You would be Lord Almeron then?"

Thoughtfully stroking his chin, the seemingly youthful Asamel began sizing up the man he would *use*—though never answering Rowarc's question. As if to selectively pick and choose the information he would share. Though, his choice of tracker had not been so random after all. "So," Asamel swiveled his high-back chair behind the desk. "It seems you were intrigued by my offer after all."

"That depends," Rowarc's caution was evident, as were his senses which warned of something he could not place. "It was my understanding the offer came from a Lord Almeron. I don't know anything about you, and I never work with someone I **don't** know." Rowarc pulled out and unfolded the letter which held the seal found on Almeron's manor, showing it to the young man behind the desk. Whoever in the hell he was....

"I speak for Lord Almeron," Asamel lied, continuing, "The request came from me. My name is Asamel. I'm an aide to Lord Almeron." Asamel smiled, looking Rowarc in the eye. "Would you like to hear more about the job?"

Rowarc approached ever slower as Asamel began sketching something for him on a piece of paper he pulled from his desk drawers. Rowarc's better senses had not stopped ringing in his thoughts; he just wanted to get on with it and get back on the road. He almost didn't care where now, so long as he was out of this man's presence. Asamel's eyes held the look of someone who enjoyed lying for a living and someone who fancied himself good at it, whether he was or not. That look one developed with a dead darkness surrounding their pupils. He knew that look from experience and he'd have to weigh that against the risk and the up-front pay.

The features upon Asamel's sketch were becoming clearer—lovely and elegant as his pencil stroked this way and that. Asamel drew with some level of expertise, though Rowarc didn't think it was his primary profession. Perhaps more of a hobby, like Kerrich's whittling.

"She looks to me like no girl—rather a full woman—young and beautiful perhaps, but certainly not the little one you led me to believe. What are you really after?" Senses that had been ringing were now all but screaming in Rowarc's thoughts as his desire for leaving grew more and more palpable with each passing moment. Rowarc's hand slipped to the hilt of his familiar companion, gripping it taut as the handle leveraged forward under the pressure he was now steadily applying. He hated wealth and the wealthy even more. They were all up to no good as far as he was concerned—this one especially so. All they ever wanted was *more*.

"Rowarc.... My apologies, I should have asked...may I call you Rowarc?"

At least he was playing at being nice for a Lord or whatever he was. Rowarc nodded for the young Lord Asamel to continue.

"Can you find her for me, Rowarc?" Asamel raised an eyebrow in a pleading manner along with a carefully managed smile for his would-be ranger of dubious tasking.

Asamel's question was...aristocratic, even delegating, but serious and attempting at legitimacy, while Rowarc carefully eyed Asamel's sketch upon the great study desk.

Twisting the drawing, pushing it right-side-up toward Rowarc, Asamel

Charles W. McDonald Jr.

pulled another rendering out of the top right drawer of his desk, placing it beside the features of the lovely woman in her middle prime with long, wavy hair and eyes that tried to hide and burn at the same time. This other rendering was a map. Suddenly all the adventures before came stirring up violently in Rowarc's head. He knew it would not be easy, or they would have taken care of it with their own people, but there it was before him—the map of the lands across the Ocean of Winds where nations collided and formed the highest mountains known. "This woman you want...," Rowarc started, but then reconsidered how he would ask this, "I mean, it's not my business what you want her for, just that I won't break the law in what I do for you. Just clarifying.... So, you don't expect me to break the law—just find her?"

"No, I wouldn't have you kill her or anything as nefarious as all that," Asamel smiled disarmingly. "I just want you to bring her to me. That is not against the law."

"It is if it is by force."

"You won't be able to force this woman to do anything, Rowarc. You will have to get...creative. You will have to sway her."

Rowarc frowned. *You won't be able to force this woman to do anything*, he frowned internally. Well, that said a lot, and where he would be going said even more. A lamean, and a deadly one at that, was what—or rather who—he was tracking.

"With a man of your experience, I'm certain the answers will come to you in time. I'm certain you'll adapt well to the situation. You are well in the mind, Rowarc d'Aguillon. Your reputation, experience, past relationships, and knowledge make you the right man for this job and will see you to success where this," Asamel placed a small black bag, slightly bigger than his own palm, on the desk before him, "...will be given over tenfold. I believe this should more than cover your expenses to get you started."

Taking a deep breath, Rowarc took the bag of silver pieces, the map, and the sketch of the woman, placing them into his brown, leather traveling pack before slinging it back over his shoulder. "This might take some time," Rowarc offered flatly in setting proper expectations as he strode toward the door.

"I'm not without patience for the right results," Asamel touted, watching his hired ranger trek for the exit. "...And with my reward, Mr. d'Aguillon, I think you'll be able to do whatever you like for most of the rest of your life, don't you think?"

As his weathered boots crossed the threshold of Almeron Manor, he couldn't help but feel as if he needed to bathe Asamel's ilk from his body. He hated money—truly so. Though it made life easier, and it might even help

Charles W. McDonald Jr.

him find himself, as would his adventures across the sea, for if he didn't find himself and his senses quickly, he would not survive the journey to Xal.

*   *   *   *

(West of Bouschè, Perion, Present Day)

"The old man you're describing sounds a lot like Ykstherin," Gareth stoked the fire from where he sat on the floor. "My grandfather's known him all his life. And…," he paused swallowing hard, "…he just passed from old age. So that gives you some idea about Ykstherin."

"I'm sorry. What was your grandfather's name?" Kerrich might not show any concern for the broad man on the floor between them, clearly hurting, but Elise genuinely cared, and her concern was evident in her tone.

"Luke. He was…simply the best of us." Burning motes of spent and freshly-stirred wood struck and seared the air around Gareth, reflecting off the cornea of his weary eyes.

Kerrich had taken back to whittling. It was better than fidgeting and gave him something to pass the time. "What do *you* know about Ykstherin," Kerrich interrupted, though continuing his carving on the piece of ash he found from the firewood pile outside the cabin.

"He's old! Really old. Really experienced. Powerful." Gareth paused, half smirking, "…and don't buy that frail cane business of his." Gareth got up to start pacing between the kitchen and the fireplace. He always thought better on his feet, and the floor wasn't comfortable. "However, his intentions I've never known to be anything but true. If my grandfather trusted him, that tells me everything I need to know about the man—or whatever he is."

"What's that supposed to mean?" Kerrich sat up straight, setting down his carving that was beginning to take the shape of an eagle.

Abrupt knocking on the front cabin door got Kerrich all the way out of his seat—sword drawn, and his back to the fireplace—as Gareth walked to the door, sword in hand. It must have been close to midnight, and the air outside was bitter cold when Gareth opened the door to see the very man they'd been discussing.

"Ykstherin, come in. We have some of your new friends here I believe," motioning towards the fireplace, letting the tall young, auburn-haired man of Kerrich's age, shuffle in first as he cleaned the new snow off his shoes before making his way inside.

"Radin," he offered, extending his hand toward Gareth introducing himself as he inspected his boots to make sure he wasn't tracking in fresh snow into the man's cabin.

"Gareth," a firm handshake was supposed to show you carried no weapon, so Gareth sheathed his sword before shaking Radin's hand. He could feel the chilled blood coursing through Radin's hand as he shook it, but the auburn-haired boy didn't display any obvious signs of hypothermia. *Must not have traveled far*, Gareth presumed as he considered Ykstherin's abilities at work. "You should make yourself comfortable by the fireplace. Elise, can you go in the back room over there and bring out some more chairs while I fetch some food? I think we'll all be up for a while." He swung back to the door, ushering Ykstherin in, "Luke's gone. He passed a few hours back."

Ykstherin froze, not for the cold, but for the news. His mouth worked though no words came out at first as his eyes scanned the interior of the cabin for the friend he once knew for so long. He knew Luke's condition and his frailty in his old age but hearing of one's passing from the mortal coils of reality was never less than a cold and stark reminder of how fleeting life could be. "My boy, I'm so sorry. He was...a beautiful example of a man." Ykstherin's words were welcome, genuine, and disarming. More than that, to Gareth, they were needed.

The fire blazed in front of Radin as he took the amulet from Elise holding it in his hands in front of the fire, watching the runes dance to and fro in the hot amber firelight of the blaze. Their swaying reflection in his eyes spoke of the newly kindled fire inside Radin.

Charles W. McDonald Jr.

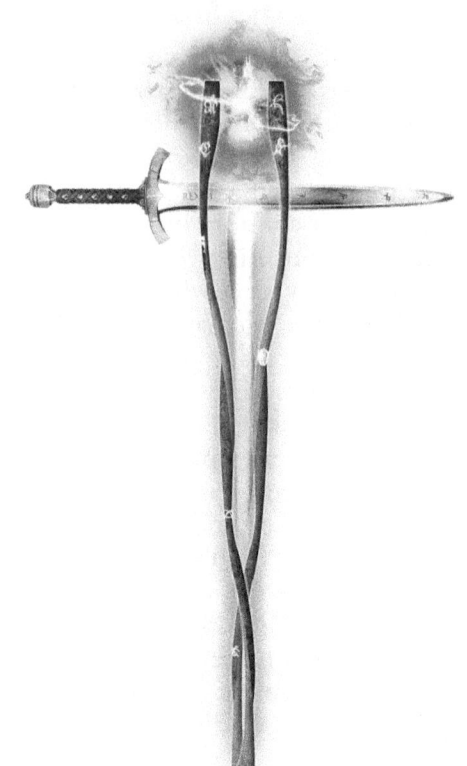

<u>Chapter 22: The Path Not Chosen</u>

(Bouschè, Perion, Present Day)

he Twin Moons was the name on the swinging, singed oak placard. A painting on the hung sign of one full moon and one crescent moon in a night sky looked to be the work of an amateur, but it seemed like a nice place. Elise had stopped several folks along the way, asking them about the most reputable place to stay for a night. The majority of them seemed to agree on this place, which was not so deep into the inner city, making it less of a ride for them. That undoubtedly influenced their thinking at this point with Elise nearly faltering as she dismounted Sissy, catching herself on the tie-down railing while giving Kerrich a threatening look that quashed any idea he might have had making some chauvinist comment about her riding skills. Kerrich merely smirked, opening the door for her

Charles W. McDonald Jr.

though she paid him no attention or regard, just examining the bustling interior as her feet welcomed solid footing. Radin and Gareth looked both ways down the street for threats, while Ykstherin followed Elise inside. Nodding to each other, apparently satisfied they were not being followed, Radin and Gareth tried to appear casual as they too followed Kerrich and Ykstherin inside.

The interior of the Twin Moons was pleasant and amiable if a bit stoic in nature. The formal area was neat and sterile with polished brass plates here and there, with odd, but cute trinkets spread about with the occasional portrait or imported area rug. Elise allowed her eyes to drift over the whole of the interior before they finally rested on the middle-aged woman behind the bar of the downstairs pub, which was connected to the formal area through an archway into sunken floor on the other side. The bar was larger than Rowarc's, with chairs and tables for at least fifty and a separate staircase leading upstairs and connecting to the other staircase coming up from the formal area.

"Excuse me, miss," Elise proffered, clearing her throat to get the woman's attention. Kerrich was just about to say something, but saw that Elise was in one of those independent, 'I'm a woman and don't need a man's help' kind of moods. He figured it best to just let her go at it. Besides, maybe she could get them a better rate.

"Yes, child," the woman replied in the motherliest of tones. It was enough to make Kerrich squirm, wondering if she had a switch hiding under the bar.

"We'll be needing three rooms. Two if three is too much of an imposition." Elise tried her best to appear innocent, but she could quickly see that it wasn't going to fly. Pushing three silver coins across the counter to the middle-aged woman, she asked, "Would this be enough for three rooms maybe for two nights?"

"I think we can make that work, and I'll make sure you get plenty of fresh linens," pushing old, heavy, iron keys towards Elise.

Elise turned around to Radin, handing him keys to distribute. Radin gave one key to Ykstherin the other to Kerrich, "Why don't we meet in my room in a few?" Nodding in agreement, Kerrich, Gareth, and Ykstherin all headed to their respective rooms. Elise, sneaking up behind him softly, took Radin's elbow, feeling him tense up as he furrowed his brow at her.

"I wish you weren't so good at sneaking up on me...." Still very tense, his normally youthful voice seemed laced in overtones of worry and undertones of thoughts that kept him awake last night and most likely tonight as well.

Something was going on with him as her caress upon his back—normally soothing—had the opposite effect of causing the space between his shoulder blades to flex in a tight constraint, as he still refused to discuss whatever happened to him at the library. "Come on. We can all use some sleep." Her hands moving from his back to Radin's arm and wrist, Elise practically had to drag him upstairs before he'd had a chance to completely vet the first floor to his satisfaction.

*   *   *   *

A knock on Radin's door jolted his eyes open from a fleeting and somewhat forced respite. The disruptions spaced just enough apart so as to keep him from any decent amount of deep sleep. Already up, Elise paced to the door, opening it to find Gareth, Ykstherin, and Kerrich waiting to come in.

"There's a lot you've not been telling me, and now would be a good time before we get ourselves further into this, and someone gets killed," Gareth's tone was serious and naturally concerned.

Sitting up on the edge of his bed while the others took seats, Radin rubbed his bloodshot eyes, while mulling over what he could and couldn't share as Gareth picked a spot by the window to stand, half keeping an eye out as the sun began to set on Bouschè. Radin tried to recall his encounter for them…. "Assume everything we do and say is being watched and heard at all times," Radin didn't bat an eyelash at how strange that might have sounded coming from him as his tone met the moment of the weight of his words. Radin's view of the world had been shaken to its core, and there was no more pretending or going back to what could only be regarded now as blissful ignorance. Ykstherin cast something. He couldn't tell what, but he knew it really didn't matter, "And that won't stop it either. This *man* is powerful beyond imagination. Beyond anything any of us has ever seen or heard of."

"Who is *he*?" The last comment had Gareth's full attention as he was fully engaged now. No longer allowing even a glance outside, Gareth's sole focus was on every word coming out of Radin's mouth.

"Someone who's taken an acute interest in me. Enough to whisk me away to another world so we could 'talk.'" He paused, realizing he hadn't fully answered the question, "He told me his name was Damon." Radin gauged the response of Elise whose eyes grew slightly at his use of the words 'other world,' and while the visible goose bumps on her flesh said she was concerned, her scent had not changed from that of her perfume. He didn't smell or sense fear in her and that was telling from his perspective.

"What do you mean another world? Is he a threat to us? Do we know what he wants?" Kerrich wanted so desperately to whittle, but inside he was shaking. *Other worlds*, Kerrich considered thoughtfully—pensively—as he nervously stroked his chin.

Elise looked to Radin, then in turn to each of the others examining their reactions very carefully. She wanted to say something but her lack of re-action to the 'another world' comment said plenty to the careful observer.

"I don't know what he wants," Radin began in a sincere and carefully managed tone. "...But I know if he wanted us dead, we'd be dead already. He came across to me as a very serious, very dedicated, very knowledgeable man. His place was unlike anything I'd ever seen. Smooth and consistent lighting without candles or daylight. Sounds coming out of the walls—I think it was some form of music. Rooms apparently built from space that didn't exist. Just from what he showed me in a brief time, he knows more than any person or lamean I've ever heard of. He regularly travels to other worlds to gain more and more knowledge. But to what end, I can't say."

Kerrich and Gareth both gulped nearly simultaneously though Elise and Ykstherin appeared to take the news much more in-stride.

"This man," Ykstherin's statesman-like tone commanded everyone's at-tention, "I don't know him personally, but I do know of some of his spells. I've seen them—the banned ones at least. He's despicable if his work is any indica-tion of the man."

"I think even he would agree with you." That earned an incredulous glare from just about everyone except Elise, who was beginning to appear more and more nervous as she fidgeted with the pleats of her summer dress at the edge of his bed. He needed to buy her something more appropriate for the climate they now found themselves forced into. "So, I asked him, sort of, if he would teach me? His response was: 'that would be very bad.'"

"Teach you *what*?" Kerrich practically leapt out of his chair facing Ra-din down from across the room.

Radin could have tried to describe it, but instead pointed his right in-dex finger at Elise, and her hair began to lift off of her shoulders as she spun herself completely off the bed, looking at Radin, knowing it was him who had just used *Telekinesis* on her.

Clearing his throat with a noticeable harrumph, "Well, doesn't that just change everything?" Ykstherin might have been stating the obvious, but it was the last thing that was said for a long time as an uncomfortable silence fell upon the room like a thick, black oil.

Radin tried not to let the Arcane sear him from the inside out. It flowed from everywhere and nowhere simultaneously as he reached out to it—feeling and sensing its power. He hadn't needed Arcane to perform the demonstration—only his natural abilities in *Telekinesis*. Yet without studying,

Charles W. McDonald Jr.

mentoring, or teaching of any kind, his body sang and resonated at the frequency of life as he reached out to touch the source of living matter, he knew to be Arcane. His head pounded with a force he could barely comprehend. Even as it threatened to rip him apart, he drew more, trying not to move, or draw more attention with uncontrolled results.

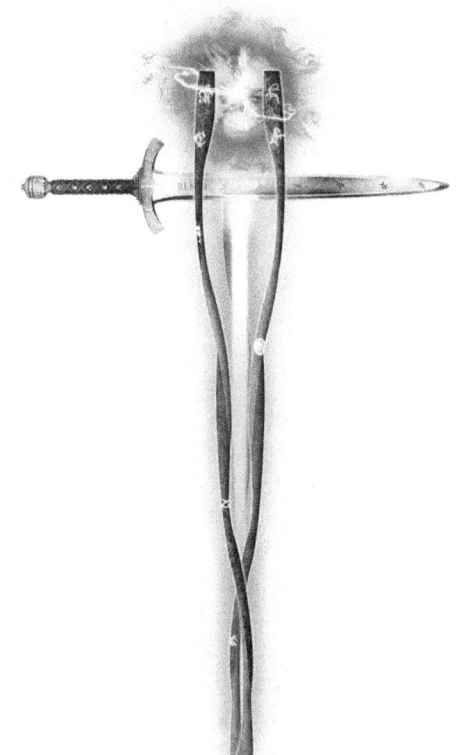

Chapter 23: The Destroyer of Men

(The Crown of Spires, Perion, Present Day)

The cold and sterile inner sanctum of Edinaiel was both sparse and elegant, while vast and commanding. Made inside the executive skywalk, in between the spired towers with segments that arched this way and that, the chamber spanned a hundred paces or more in depth by nearly three hundred paces in length. The ceiling sloped downward from the base of a three-planed crystal tower built directly over the solid ivory dais. The inner tower was more than a hundred cubits tall, while the rest of the ceiling sloped downward from the tower's base of fifty cubits. The floor was made of the same, strange diamond-shaped tiles as the divination causeways, providing a euphoric sense of being in the clouds, watching over all that transpired below—and the future that might be.

Charles W. McDonald Jr.

The High Seat of Thane, Edinaiel, the High Seat, and the Office of the Talon were all commanding and noble titles describing the famed Crown of Spires, but it had known only one name—one *Keeper*—in its entire existence.

She sat regally to one side of her oversized throne, holding a large and ancient book in her lap with paper so frail one could only safely turn the pages with magic—or, in her case, witchcraft. Her long and radiant gold hair and sapphire eyes befitted her slender and seductive youthful frame. Her gentle, loving face, as well as her cloud white, full-length dress with sleeve openings that hung to the floor, were a woefully inaccurate telling of what lay beneath. Everything about her was deceiving, especially her delicate and tender appearance. The art of deception, more than anything else, she had mastered over millennia of feudal interference with local lords, stewards, and even sovereign Kings. Where *nothing* was as it seemed....

She smirked at the artist's impressions of herself, on canvas, from long ago that she kept close by as a reminder. He had performed great acts of treachery by defacing her nobility and station in such a manner and paid dearly for his offenses. She smiled as she recalled his sentencing, handed down nearly nine-hundred years' past. And *no one* had dared such a betrayal hence. In death, he had served her *far better* than in life.

She stirred her tea briskly, making a tinging sound as the spoon hit the sides of the gold-brimmed, pearl-white cup. The tea had become cold from sitting at her side far too long, but that didn't seem to matter—the act of stirring it more out of habit, than of function. She had no intent of actually drinking *that* particular cup but merely kept it at her side to give her something to stir. She would have to summon a servant to fetch her a fresh cup when she became truly ready for her morning tea. The bowl of fruit beside the cold cup of tea on an elegant, embossed silver platter had barely been touched, as had her morning meal of toast, butter, and jam. A beautiful long-stemmed white rose stood in an ivory vase in between the fruit and tea. Next to the fruit and vase, a message lay rolled up on its side—its seal broken.

The news had been neither good nor bad—merely expected. She had called for the old Chronicle once she read the three words, hastily written onto the parchment, '*The boy casts.*' The message bore no signature, for she knew the source of it well—Desindra. Yes, she would have to call her back to the Crystal Towers soon. She had been free from her far-too-long leash for far too long. It was time for her to come back, where she could keep a better watch over her and her dangerous words. Desindra had always been far too careless with what she wrote. The written word, after all, was a very powerful thing. That kind of thing simply would not do very much longer. The game was getting dangerous and complicated now. The margin for error was getting smaller

Charles W. McDonald Jr.

and smaller with each passing event. *Resha—The Destroyer of Men*—had been loosed upon the world of Men.

She sighed as she recalled the news that Sabine had brought to her earlier in the morning. It seemed someone had broken into the ancient vault and taken a relic of grave importance from her treasury. She supposed it was as much her fault as any other, although she had already put the guards to their death for their treacherous and gross negligence. Perhaps, if she had visited the vault more often than once a year, this might not have happened. She pondered over who might do such a thing and could come to no logical conclusion, save the fact that there was a new player amongst them whom the tiles would reveal in due time. This, unfortunately, allowed for even less of a margin for error. This was not good news for Desindra, who had persistently been a moral thorn in her side. *Yes*, she accepted with a heavy sigh, as she let go of the spoon with which she had used to swirl the tea, *I suppose Desindra's usefulness has come to an end.* Adena cocked her head regally, watching with the greatest of fascination as the spoon continued to swirl about the tea for a moment before coming to rest. Adena sighed heavily again as she turned her whimsical and frivolous attention back to the Chronicle.

Adena found amusement in everything, and yet nothing. She was quite mad, of course. Her craft may have kept her young and beautiful, but it could not hold together the already delicate strings of her sanity. A millennia of games and torment had wrecked the fragile balance within her mind. Even immortality had its drawbacks.

*   *   *   *

Desindra tried not to think about her divided loyalties, but Adena was becoming too big of a liability for her and her kind to tolerate any further. The meeting with Asamel hadn't gone entirely to plan, and he couldn't be trusted any more than Adena—if even that much—but this boy, and what he would become, represented far too big of a threat to Mankind than Adena could alone manage. That was as plain to see as the soft and elegant cream Elian fabric cascading off her delicate wrists in waves as she took notes watching the boy through a viewing window before her, while perched from the balcony of her room at the inn across from the Twin Moons where she kept an eye on him *and* his companions. Ykstherin she knew, but the others were unknown—at least to her. The one he called Elise bothered Desindra the most, not because of her beauty—she couldn't compare to Desindra of course. No, Elise bothered her primarily because Elise was hiding a very big secret and peo-

Charles W. McDonald Jr.

ple hiding a secret that big did so only for one of a handful of reasons—most problematic to her cause of managing the boy's wake of destruction.

Watching the strange buxom blonde with blue eyes in a full-length silk dress, obviously not from around here, skulking about the exterior of the Twin Moons, Desindra knew she and Asamel were not the only ones watching the boy. Understandable, but it only made her curious what the other parties knew that they were not sharing. Something about the way this woman stealthily skulked about made Desindra nervous. Furrowing her brow as the reflection of the blonde's features appeared in her viewing window, Desindra began thinking to herself aloud. "Who are you, My Pretty? You're not from around here, are you...?"

Elise might not have caused Desindra self-esteem issues, but this woman did. Beautiful in her own right with long, silky sandy brown hair and hazel eyes, she'd used her skills to halt her aging process in much the way Adena had, but she'd been given better natural assets to work with. Still, this strange and beautiful, buxom blonde was becoming a thorn in her thoughts by the moment. Perhaps she should tell Adena.

Watching the strange blonde disappear in a blur, unable to relocate her, Desindra contemplated otherwise. Perhaps she wouldn't put this in her next status to Adena after all.

*   *   *   *

(Stirling, Perion, Present Day)

Rowarc didn't like the look of things as soon as he walked through the door. One of the new girls he had hired, Lilly, was at the front desk, and Mary Danvers was behind the bar with her father, learning how to serve customers. Rowarc sighed, nodding to Lilly, then walked straight into the pub.

Edwin nodded to Rowarc, acknowledging him as he came into the room. Edwin appeared a bit surprised at Rowarc returning so quickly, brushing his workman-like hands one against the other, closing the distance between him and his old friend. Edwin could plainly see the expression on Rowarc's face was not one of pleasantries and smiles, but one of serious business.

Not so tall as Rowarc, and a tad older, Edwin fidgeted with how his white long-sleeve shirt wasn't quite fitting into his tan linen pants the way it used to. He'd apparently been helping in the kitchen as Rowarc could see morsels of various ingredients here and there about his clothing.

"We had not expected you back so soon, Rowarc," Edwin noted, putting a hand on his daughter's back. "Why don't you go have your mother bring us out some refreshments so Rowarc and I can be alone for a few minutes."

"Yes, Father," Mary replied, briefly glancing between them. She apparently wanted to stay and hear what was going on, but her better instincts said to mind her own business for now and sneak about later when the sneaking was easier.

"Where is he?" Rowarc rarely beat around the bush where Radin was concerned. They were the only words Edwin had expected to come out of his mouth, given the situation. Edwin was sure that he was the last person Rowarc expected to see caring for his business in Rowarc's absence.

"Well, Rowarc. I was kind of hoping you could tell me. Why don't you sit down," Edwin invited, motioning to a round table, large enough for four, behind him. Edwin came around the bar and pulled up a chair next to him, turning it around and sitting in it backward with his arms resting on the back. "You see Radin, that new girl of his, and Kerrich, all said they were going to that old forbidden monastery outside the city walls. That was two days ago. We haven't seen them since. Was hoping you could tell us where they might be."

Frowning deeply, Rowarc didn't need his tracking senses to tell where the rest of this was going. Yet, he let Edwin continue, wanting to hear the whole lot of it before he tore the place down.

"Now I'm not one to condemn your boy, Rowarc. You and Arella did an excellent job of raising him, and he turned out to be a good one. And the Creator knows that's a miracle enough these days, but I think he went off half-cocked by leaving on his own. And I fear he's got himself into trouble as well. He said he might be gone for a day, maybe two, but I don't know. I don't think he's a coming back. I heard you was coming out of retirement. Maybe you best hold off on whatever job you got and go find your boy. We'll watch things here 'til you come back. I can put together a search party and we'll handle it…."

Rowarc clinched his fist, pounding the table so hard it nearly cracked, and just in time as Mary came back with two cold mugs, some bread, and cheeses.

"I hope this is all right with you, Father. Mother sent me out instead. She said she had to take care of something in the kitchen."

Edwin frowned, wondering what his wife was doing that she could not do as he asked. "Yes, that just fine," he redirected to get her out of their conversation. "Now, you go on back to the kitchen. We're not through with our parley."

"Yes, Father." *I wonder if he knows about Kerrich. Maybe that's what*

Charles W. McDonald Jr.

Mr. d'Aguillon was so upset about. Maybe he knows. Mary turned and walked away, looking back at the pair twice on her way back to the kitchen.

The wheels were turning inside Rowarc's head. A girl was who he was initially hired to find, then this Elise shows up out of nowhere and takes his boy off Creator-only-knows-where. Both of them were in the marketplace during the time in question. *Hmmm,* he thought. "Did Radin say anything about where they might be going or what they were looking for? Did he say anything specific about this new girl he's with?" Rowarc didn't know enough to accuse Elise of anything, and she seemed sweet enough, but the sweeter the girl, the bigger the lie she was hiding—at least in his experience.

Edwin just shook his head in resignation. "The only other thing he mentioned besides what I told you, was that he was worried about you coming out of retirement."

"Kerrich didn't come back either?" Rowarc interjected, clarifying.

"No, and when you find the lot of 'em, you send that Kerrich young fella to me."

Rowarc stroked his beard in consideration, mildly making note of the Kerrich comment. That boy was always getting in trouble with parents of pretty girls. That was certainly nothing new. Edwin probably wanted to force the issue of marriage or some such nonsense. Either way, it was none of his concern. Edwin could do what he wanted with Kerrich, so long as he found out what was going on with Radin and this girl.

"Yes, of course," Rowarc proffered. "I'll be sure and send Kerrich to you once I find them."

"Mhmm. You do that," Edwin jibed flatly.

Not knowing quite how to take that comment, Rowarc stroked his chin thinking someone had to have seen them all together. If they'd returned from Tannanvar in one piece, someone near the city walls would have seen them. One person slipping by—no big deal, but three young and attractive kids like that all traveling together. *Someone should have seen something. Where was Ykstherin and why hadn't he reported back?*

Maybe someone near the inner bailey could tell him something, and surely he would have better luck at that than he'd had in the marketplace. This was, after all, his own son he was looking for. Rowarc sighed heavily, getting up from the table, knowing the day's work was only beginning. *What had Radin got himself into, and what was his boy about to drag him into? What a mess. And all for this madness of love.* Feeling the sketch of the woman through his jacket, Rowarc considered his options, quickly deciding on finding the woman as fast as possible then getting back here fast to track down his wayward boy. His boy had a good head on his shoulders and good skills. He'd gone out on his own before a couple of nights at a time, so he wasn't fiercely concerned yet. Still, he needed to be quick about his business and get back here to take care of things closer to home.

"Well," Rowarc offered after a moment of consideration, extending a hand to his old friend. "In case my son comes back, and I am not here, tell him that I am looking for him, and he needs to stay put. I will check back with you in a couple of days to see if he's come back. If you can put the word out to a few of our men and just ask them to keep an eye out and report back anything that might make sense of this, that'd be better than putting together a search party. I don't think we need to take it that far just yet. Meanwhile, I'm going to do some looking around locally while I'm out working on this new job. If we don't have them back where we can lay eyes on them in a few days, I'm going to have to find some old friends to help sort this out."

Edwin nodded, taking note of Rowarc's wishes. "I wish you luck, Rowarc. I'm sorry about your boy, but maybe he's just anxious to get out on his own or something. You know what crazy things love does to a young man's thinking."

"Yep," Rowarc agreed knowingly while shaking his head. "I certainly do." Rowarc turned and walked away, frowning deeply again by the time he reached the front door. *Radin, where are you, my Son?*

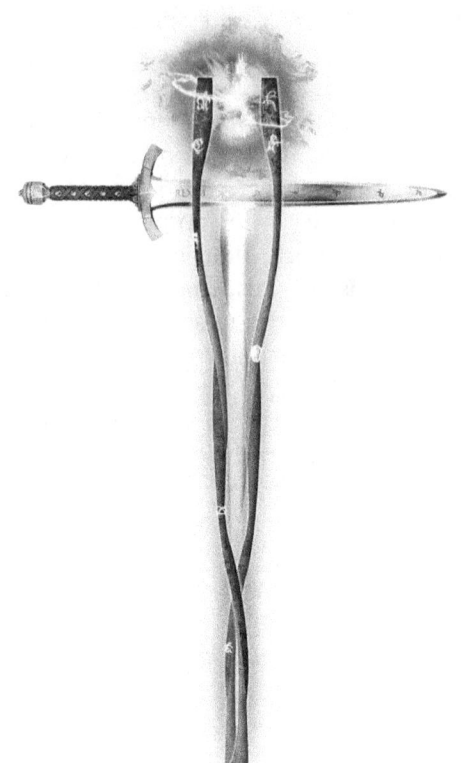

Chapter 24: A Confluence of Events

(South China Sea, Earth, Near Future)

The trimaran USS Independence littoral combat frigate, the very latest of her design, cruised sea-side abreast the USS CVN Ronald Reagan just astern the Arleigh Burke-class Destroyer, the USS Michael Murphy. The Reagan's battlegroup contained some eight ships in all, including the two submarines: the USS North Dakota and the prototype USS Seawolf. Congress loved the Virginia Class submarines, but the Navy loved the Seawolf; as did the new President, who immediately ordered it back into service. The Independence was forced to cruise all ahead two-thirds while the rest of the Carrier Battle Group cruised all ahead standard just so she didn't leave the group behind.

The Chinese man-made island—one of many—housed a massive military installation about a thousand yards off the port bow. They were in international waters—sort of—depending on your perspective.

Captain Harry Chastain didn't know what to make of the politics of it, but he knew this was going to piss off the Chinese. Sure, technically they were in International Waters since they were more than the designated twenty-five miles from China's mainland to qualify as such, but he supposed if the Chinese didn't want this level of push-back, then maybe they shouldn't have built their man-made base more than thirty miles off-shore. Such thinking was above his paygrade. He had plenty to worry about as he called out commands from the Captain's chair on the bridge housing the latest and greatest of American ingenuity, "TAO, keep that RAM warm," the Captain's reference to the RIM-116 Rolling Airframe Missile (RAM) not going unnoticed as he garnered concerned looks from around the bridge.

"Aye, sir." Tactical Action Officer (TAO) Lieutenant Agatha Mac-Donald confirmed, keeping close observation on her Aegis-com-synchronized threat matrix, her long red hair, a reflection of her Scottish and Irish heritage, pinned and stuffed to perfect regulation specifications under her cap. Just like everyone else, she felt the tension reverberating across the bridge too, but she had a job to do.

"XO, you're with me," Captain Chastain ordered his Executive Officer (XO) Dallas Kent, motioning for Kent to leave the bridge with him. "Officer of the Deck, you have the Conn." The Captain's matter-of-fact tonality was a direct reflection of their intensely hostile surroundings and the professionalism the crew trained at round-the-clock.

"Aye, sir, OOD has the Conn." Officer of the Deck (OOD) Larry Zummwalt, a surname synonymous with generations of Navy heritage, proudly puffed out his chest, looking out over the bow of their gleaming new ship through the slim-profiled and stealthy conning tower.

Quickly opening the door to his Captain's quarters, seeing the 6'4" intruder with shoulder-length black hair and black eyes, wearing jeans and a Led Zeppelin T-Shirt, Captain Chastain didn't have time to call for help before unseen hands silently dragged him and the XO into the Captain's quarters—the door slamming shut behind them. Both felt themselves being gagged by something they couldn't see, feel or touch; yet it was there, in their throats, silencing them immediately and suppressing their tongue like a giant weight in their mouths. Circling the two broad-shouldered Navy line officers, the tall, dark, and chiseled man of many nations and of none spoke to them with his thoughts—his lips never moving.

I'm not here to hurt you, the thoughts telepathically forced their way into the Captain's and the XO's mind. *If I wanted you dead, I would have killed you already.*

Casting *Suggestion*, Damon wormed his way into the deepest recesses of their minds, probing for exactly the right place to plant his suggestion. His right hand over their forehead in succession, starting with the Captain, Damon leered as he probed, finding just the right place and right moment for the implant. The seed of hate and doubt would propagate like a tidal wave internally, providing just the right level of justification for his needs. And just like that, it was done…. Casting *Forget*, they both collapsed to the floor. He needed to wake them up, but remotely so.

From the far side of the *Portal*, in his living room in Austin, Damon used *Telekinesis* to slap the two line officers awake, closing the *Portal* with a whoosh as they were coming to. *The rest should take care of itself.*

Captain Chastain didn't remember how he had gotten to his quarters, nor why his XO was with him. The last clear memory he had was being on the bridge, watching and waiting for the damn Chinese to make their move. *Can't trust any of them*, he thought to himself, memories of his father, killed by the Chinese Triad mafia, flooding all of his conscious thoughts. "Come on," Captain Chastain ordered, hastening his pace back to the Conn—XO in tow.

"TAO, what targets are you painting?" The Captain asked, bristling as he walked back into the Conn.

"Painting, sir?" TAO MacDonald didn't understand. She hadn't been asked to *paint* any 'targets.' She had a pair of Chinese J-31's barely showing on the scope, somewhat impressed by the very limited footprint of their stealth signature, but she sure as Hell wasn't about to start 'painting' them without a good goddamn reason. "I have two J-31's broadcasting on international frequencies, warning us about approaching too close to their base. Would you like us to respond?" Typically, the Admiral of the Battle Group, aboard the Carrier or his flagship, replied on behalf of the Carrier Battle Group. She knew that. So did the Captain.

"Yes, I would," Captain Chastain replied, climbing into the Captain's Chair. "Paint them with the RAM."

"Sir?!"

"You heard me, TAO."

"Aye, sir," TAO MacDonald looked between the hot scowl of the XO and the outright glower of the Captain, wondering, *What the Hell is going on?* "Painting now, sir." With precision and care, she placed the target finder on the lead J-31 while the Admiral responded over the comm, "Chinese Fighters. Chinese Fighters. This is Admiral Deed, aboard the USS Ronald Reagan. Our Battle Group is cruising through International Waters with no intention of conflict. Please confirm your intent."

Charles W. McDonald Jr.

*   *   *   *

The conflicting messages of being painted by the U.S. frigate combined with the benign message of Admiral Deed caused Captain Xiang Min indescribable concern. This could go sideways at a moment's notice, then there would be war. Motioning to his wingman to check his Attack Control Systems, he wanted to get confirmation they were being painted. He wanted *someone else* to make this decision.

*   *   *   *

"Do you have him yet?" Captain Chastain hastened his TAO, practically standing over her even while seated some sixteen feet away in his Captain's chair.

WTF? "Sir, I have him painted as ordered."

"Weapons Free, TAO."

"WHAT?!" Realizing how inappropriate and derelict her tone was, Agatha MacDonald quickly regrouped internally, recalling her training, "Sir, rules of engagement state—"

"You heard me, TAO! You are Weapons Free! Shoot that bastard out of the sky! RIGHT GODDAMN NOW!"

Before she could protest, the XO practically ripped her from her chair with one powerful arm, squeezing the trigger on the black plastic joystick with the other, releasing the RIM-116 Rolling Airframe Missile for a clean kill only two seconds later.

A moment later the lookout could see aircraft parts dropping from the sky through his tactical binoculars as the remaining Chinese J-31 could be heard calling home, reporting the shootdown, asking for further instructions. Suddenly his message was cut off mid-sentence, as the USS Independence registered another clean and confirmed shootdown.

*   *   *   *

(G8 Summit, London, Earth, Near Future)

The beautiful but sterile environment of the hotel's ballroom may have made for a place of neutrality, but that didn't necessarily facilitate neutral conversation among the G-8 participants. People were still people. Some you gelled with, and others you didn't. The title of President, or Prime Minister, or even King, didn't matter when it came to getting along with someone. Either you knew how to make friends and influence people, or you didn't. It wasn't really a skill you *learned*—at least not from Michael's perspective. Michael's dad had always taught him that there would be those who intended him harm no matter what he did or said, and with those people you just needed to give them enough rope to let them hang themselves. *Don't bother trying to please everyone. Just be yourself,* Michael's father told him frequently. *You'll cock everything up trying to be something and someone you're not.*

He wasn't even really supposed to be here. This was the Prime Minister's dog and pony show—not his. However, everyone had been asking about the new king, but more wanted to see *his sword* than meet him. He couldn't blame them. How could *he* ever compare to the *Sword of King's* fame? It was fine really. He wore it practically everywhere he went now. It was like a worldwide accepted anachronism. He'd been on mercy missions to Africa with it and attended far too many memorials of terrorist events throughout Europe and the United States where they all wanted to see the famed *Sword of Kings.* He was used to it now. Even now it hung on his left hip like an old familiar friend within its textured gold, pewter and sterling silver scabbard embossed with five runes running down its length. He had no idea what they meant— the scabbard had been a gift from his wife, Elise. She had commissioned Gordon Russell to custom make it for her wedding present to him but hadn't said what the Hell those runes meant, other than they were a reflection of the runes upon the blade itself. Supposedly made in the fires of Creation.... The scabbard was far heavier than *the sword itself,* but he'd gotten used to it over time, and it went well with Michael's proper earth-tone bespoke suit.

Michael was grateful for the badly needed break. Things had been droning on for half the day already, and he was getting a migraine from the lack of doing anything really tactically useful. The focus of this G8 was terrorism in our world today and modifying the role of NATO to deal with it. Yet, there had been so much talk, so little action, and non-existent details. Generic grandiose talk.... He wondered how anyone got things done with such nebulous speak. Such were the circles he ran in these days—not like walking around with a .40 cal Sig Sauer® on you with a license to kill. *That was how you got things done,* he cynically believed.

Walking the perimeter of the royal-mahogany stained walnut round table with trim of natural maple, which in and of itself he found humorous given the relic at his left side, Michael wanted to go shake the hand of the new American President—whatever his reputation.

"Mr. President," Michael began, addressing the American President, acknowledging the Secret Service within arm's reach as their eyes went directly to the *Sword of Kings* at his side.

Charles W. McDonald Jr.

"Your Majesty," The President half-bowed, uncertain of the formality of royalty decorum.

"Oh please," Michael protested, "…none of that business. We're all equals here." The last causing a broad smile across the American President's face. He figured he could relate better to this particular President, given the newness of their ascension to power and having that in common, but you never knew.

"I've heard such great things about you and that fancy sword. I'm surprised they let you in here with that thing." The President was ribbing of course, but Michael always worried about perception. It could be a dangerous thing, especially when unchecked by real and genuine familiarity with the person. That was his *real* reason for coming over.

"Don't believe everything you hear, Mr. President," Michael rebuffed with a broad smile, looking to address the Secret Service Agent directly behind the President, motioning to his scabbard on his left side. "Is it okay if I show it to him?"

The job of the Secret Service was to stay out of the picture and blend into the background like a chameleon, but obviously the man appreciated the gesture of asking as he provided Michael a smile and an affirmative nod, though never took his eyes off Michael or his hands as they went to retrieve the sheathed sword that was not a sword.

"It's magnificent," The President breathed aloud in awe, as Michael unsheathed the *Sword of Kings*, showing him the Latin inscriptions down one side of the fuller and five runes down the other. "I heard the story about how you found it under water. That's just astonishing. It really makes you wonder." The President's eyes glimmered in the soft glow of the immortal weapon that ceased as soon as Michael handed it over to the President for closer examination.

It still felt magnificent and warm in the President's hands, like nothing he'd ever felt. It coursed with energy yet felt lighter than his favorite driver. It felt perfect. Its balance was perfect. "Well, you have to come for a State Visit at the White House," The President insisted, still holding the *Sword of Kings* lengthwise across both hands—not like one would hold a sword, more like one would hold something precious he was presenting as a gift.

"Of course," Michael agreed. "Elise and I would be honored. I have to check with her on travel, due to her pregnancy." Michael beamed, being the ever-so-proud father-to-be, patting the President on the shoulder who still held the *Sword of Kings*, unable to take his eyes off it.

Watching the middle-aged brunette female he knew to be the President's chief of staff weaving her way through the crowd to get to the President,

Charles W. McDonald Jr.

Michael wondered how sideways this impromptu parley with the President was about to go. The chief of staff never interrupted a State meeting like this unless it was bad—really bad.

Whispering into his left ear, she barely came up to the President's shoulders, but apparently, he heard her loud and clear; as the President's eyes tried not to give away the seriousness of the moment and failed.

"ALLAHU AKBAR!!!" The shout coming from a young man's voice on the far side of the room, immediately followed by large caliber, live gunfire.

Michael didn't even think, shoving the American President to the floor just as the Secret Service jumped into place shielding them both simultaneously. "I'll need that back, Mr. President," Michael jibed with a half-smile, trying to keep everyone calm as he grabbed the *Sword of Kings* from the American President's hands.

A soft glow erupted into a white-hot star in the middle of the ballroom as Michael jumped a few feet in front of the Secret Service, throwing his sword's intense white and piercing hemispherical aura of light right into the eyes of the terrorist, leaving the backside of its aura pale and modest for the Secret Service to more easily see and return fire. *How had they gotten guns this close to such a secure event*, Michael questioned internally as he continued directing his sword's light into the gunman's eyes, blinding him while the Secret Service returned fire with an almighty salvo of .40 cal fury.

Just as fast as it had begun, the gunfire coming at them stopped as one-by-one the Secret Service ceased their return fire—realizing the termination of their target. Michael turned to look behind him, seeing the American President long since gone. *Probably executing their exfiltration plan for POTUS*, Michael estimated, as the rest of the Executive Protection Unit charged the assailant, guns drawn.

Feeling a set of hands on his shoulders that he didn't recognize, didn't make them any less capable of dragging him out of the ballroom-converted conference hall just as an explosion and tinging of exploded glass could be heard from an adjacent corridor where refreshments had been served moments ago. *Holy shit! This guy is strong*, he thought, finding himself outside, quickly being escorted to a Cadillac limousine resembling "The Beast" as it was known. *Can't be. The President would have long since been removed from the scene.* The massive bullet and blast-proof door to "The Beast" was opened by Secret Service as he felt his head being pushed down as he was practically thrown into the limousine to land on plush, black leather. Suddenly Michael's Android phone buzzed and rang out in emergency tones from his interior jacket pocket.

"No way was I going to let them leave you behind," The new American President offered in a serious and controlled tone, motioning to his chief of staff as Michael retrieved his Android phone to read the message on the locked screen. 'Excalibur is UP.' Michael frowned at the government encoded message, knowing its meaning as soon as he read it.

"Your Majesty," she offered in a somber yet focused tone, "Your Prime Minister is reported to be fatally shot in the attack. There were multiple gunmen. You and the Secret Service got one of them. There was another in the break hall who assassinated your Prime Minister. I'm sorry, Your Majesty. But the United States of America thanks you for your bravery today." Her report confirming the government emergency broadcast he'd just received.

"I thank you," The President offered flatly, scrolling through incoming urgent messages on his own secured phone. "Go ahead," The President ordered his chief of staff, "Tell him."

"Your Majesty, we have a situation in the South China Sea. An incident." Her mouth worked, trying not to get choked up, but she was terrified. That was perfectly clear from her cracked voice to her still-shaking hands.

Sideways, Michael mulled internally. *Properly sideways.*

"We'll help however we can, Mr. President. You know that," Michael reassured POTUS, wondering about the exact nature of the commitment he'd just made. But this was an important moment where tough decisions had to be made and relationships would be tested, and their relationship with the United States was not up for negotiations. It had to remain intact.

(Stirling, Perion, Present Day)

The streets of Stirling's Marketplace almost never wound down, especially during this time of the year. Rowarc had spent most of the day sleeping, preferring to take on the Marketplace at night. He had already done some asking around about Radin and Elise and gotten nowhere. Perhaps, the evening sort as he worked his way towards the inner bailey would be of more help, but he had to be more cautious as well. Not only was it more dangerous for a person to be out alone, but the sort he would be dealing with would be likely to tell him anything for the right price. And disinformation was of little value in finding his wayward son. Or the 'girl' he was supposed to find.

He was just glad that he was being paid enough to afford the cost of a *Portal*—assuming he could find a lamean powerful enough to help him. The ones who could form *Portals* tended to keep to themselves these days—what with the mad king and all. Thinking about lameans just made Rowarc long for the company of his beloved wife. *Arella*.

Charles W. McDonald Jr.

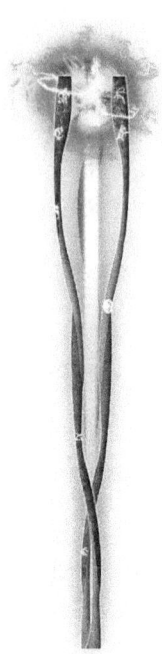

Chapter 25: The Burden of Grief

(Graelon Colonial Outpost, Present Day)

The inner chamber was even darker and more unwelcoming than he remembered all those centuries ago. The two man-sized cylindrical prisons were empty, their prisoners released by Damon and Mira long, long ago. The center pedestal stood barren; its precious artifact blown to dust in but an instant. He hadn't come specifically to destroy it and often thought of how things would be different if he hadn't. This was the one place where everything in his life changed in the blink of an eye. His powers would rival that of the gods after his adventure here, but it wasn't enough to save his beloved Mira. Mira's powers had also increased some threefold after coming here with Damon. She had solved the most formidable of the three challenges granting them access to the inner chamber where he now stood, alone, tracing a feminine handprint depression with the tips of his fingers. To this day, Damon had not recovered from the loss of Mira.

Slamming his fist down on the center console of the pedestal, nearly shattering it to dust as he had the artifact so long ago with new fractures now

Charles W. McDonald Jr.

appearing in the console where his hand had just struck. "Just do what you came to do and get out of here," Damon chastised himself aloud. He had never grieved properly for Mira, only missing her every waking hour in much the same way he missed Dallia but for very different reasons. They were both very different loves of his all-too-long life.

Once, just once, if you are very lucky, do you find a mate so perfect for you that it leaves no doubt in your mind that they were placed into existence solely for you. Not Dallia, nor Banthis, nor Victoria, nor Sijil, nor Kylin had intertwined their being with his, the way Mira had without even trying. Sharing something in common with your mate—especially something you love more than anything else, does not come about more than once in a hundred lifetimes. This place, more than any other, proved that.

It had been his last great joint venture—everything else after, he had accomplished solo. The Hall of Aaramus was more involved, and required much more help, but this experience changed him more than any other. Only Forkettès could walk these halls and set foot in this chamber. Specifically, only one male Forkettè and one female Forkettè—no others were allowed. On the pedestal once stood a very unique model of a college that existed here eons ago. The whole outpost had been ravaged by the kinds of lameans produced from it, torn apart by their destructive capabilities in elemental spells or so he came to believe through his research. So torn apart was this world that when he first came here, he saw something the likes of which he had never seen. Every last breathing man and beast had allied themselves against the Forkettès of this school. Now, there was nothing left but memory. The world outside barren, desolate, and burned beyond recognition.

Damon fought his longing for Mira as he did what he had come to do, sweeping every last, precious grain of dust from the pedestal and floor into a particular golden container, marked by a single rune. He needed to be quick about this and get out. This was no place for someone to be alone, not even someone of his power. He was just thankful that he did not have to go through the traps again. Once in a lifetime had proven enough. He still remembered them with great anxiety, making him sweep up the last of the dust with his *Telekinesis* even faster. What really bothered him was the fact that you could not *Portal*, or materialize, in or out of any part of this complex. You had to physically walk in or out. You had to be at least at the maw of the cave entrance before *Portals* would work.

Damon finished gathering the last of the artifact dust, snapping the lid shut on the small container, shoving it unceremoniously into his ever-present black velvet bag attached to the belt about his waist and robes. He turned to walk out of the cylindrical chamber but then turned back now just under the

Charles W. McDonald Jr.

stone archway. Hoping beyond hope this would be the last time he would ever set foot in this place, Damon couldn't take the risk of coming back a third time. Twice was pushing it. He was only immortal to an extent, and he had seen that limit reached with Mira, Dallia, and others he loved. He could *never* come back.

"Goodbye Mira," he whispered to the empty chamber as if Mira's spirit was still here with him. Still listening—still watching over him—as if he could somehow *feel* her presence. His voice reverberated throughout the chamber as he turned to walk away. His head drooped from the weight of his aching for her as he passed down the dangerous and secret corridors of what little remained of a total war so very long ago. Gripping only one of triangular, metal, helical rods, comprising the *Staff of the Invoker*, Damon walked with confidence and purpose, but he could no longer hold back the tears and longing anymore as they flowed relentlessly down the stony planes of a face hardened by memories and trials that could not be shared *with* or understood *by* just anyone. The burden of his grief finally shattered the floor of his soul—freeing him at last of *his* Mira. Streaming down his face in anguish, they appeared uncharacteristic on such a powerful man, and yet they seemed just. His tears may have helped to bring Banthis back, but he knew it was far too much to ask for such a thing to happen again for Mira. These tears came without the *hope* of ever seeing Mira alive again—tears of Damon's final goodbye.

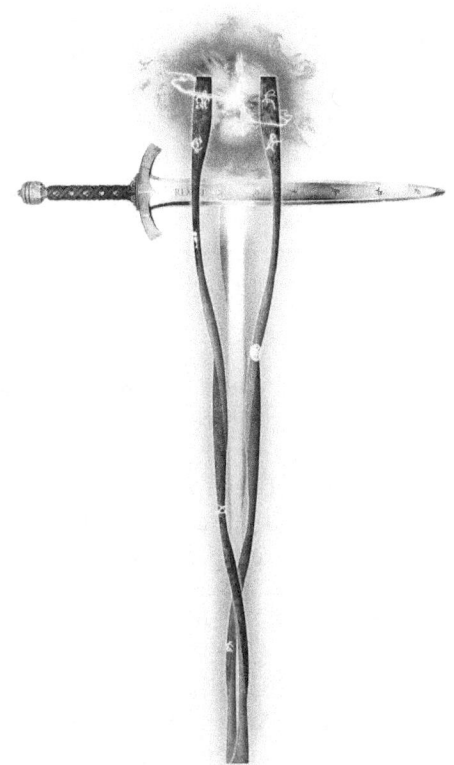

Chapter 26: Free

(Perion, Present Day)

He watched the children play from a distance on a park bench of his own making. They were only a short distance away, but none had seemed to notice him yet. *How innocent*, he morbidly contemplated. *Innocent and naive.* He wondered if he could have ever been so as a child, though his childhood he could not recall. It had been too long ago, but there were many other reasons for the loss of childhood memories. Dark magic had a way of forging new pathways in one's mind while eradicating others that might become stumbling blocks for the things that must be done. The trappings of humanity and encumbrance of its conscience were useless luxuries of others, long left behind by Eldrac even before being in the awesome presence of the Dragon of Darkness.

Charles W. McDonald Jr.

Scratching his short-cropped, scruffy platinum hair, goatee and mustache, Eldrac savored the pleasant sensation of the strands of his own hair against the compression of his thumb and index finger. So much had changed while he was gone and yet much remained the same. Released once again upon the world to perform a specific task not his own this time, but with potential rewards beyond measure, Eldrac gazed upon the new lens of the old world with vivid and newfound purpose and drive. An ambition, not felt in forever, roiled inside him at the thought of the promises dangled before him, causing his gold eyes to flame anew, bringing a youthful pyre to his lean and weathered, middle-aged face.

"Mr.?"

A small girl had managed to sneak up from behind him. She had not been one of the others playing down on the field, but probably a sister or relative of one of the others, shunned from play because she was too young. She was very young and precious, with her red-gold hair, still in curls, and her lovely green eyes. Her freckles were still large and dark, not having time enough yet to have subdued on her flesh as aging would allow. He estimated that she could not have been more than five or six.

"Mr.? Can you fix my bear?" Her pretty eyes batted at him in anticipation.

The young girl handed him the shabby teddy bear that had probably already belonged to an older sibling at one time; having nearly been loved to tatters. He could immediately see that it had started to come apart at the arms and legs, now only hanging on by a few loose threads. The man, dressed in robes of a dark forest green, smiled, taking the bear and placing a hand on its chest. He mumbled something unintelligible to the girl, and the bear was like new again. Giving the newly repaired bear back to the little girl, the stranger smiled in delight.

Hopping into his lap, the little girl smoothed her cream wool dress on her tiny legs. "My name is Amanda. Thank you soooo much for fixing Mr. Robins. He says, 'thank you' too."

She was truly precious, not like the others who had already learned how to be cruel to one another. This one had not yet learned to be cruel to anything, nor anyone. She had been shown mostly, or only, love and knew nothing else of Human potential. She was perfect.

"Mr. What's your name," Amanda innocently asked in the sweet voice of a child never before knowing harm.

"My name is Eldrac," he offered, all-too-easily managing, or obfuscating, an honest smile with his right hand over his heart. "And it was a pleasure fixing Mr. Robins for you," Eldrac feigned. "...I think he feels much better

Charles W. M{c}Donald Jr.

now." His smile morphed into wickedness, only briefly, but it was enough to make the girl frown for a second. She hopped down from his lap, saying, "My Pa is gonna switch me if I don't get back in time for dinner, so I better go. Would you like to have dinner with me and my Pa?"

"It would be my honor," Eldrac beamed for the precious little girl, standing as he made a sweeping bow to her as if she were royalty. He couldn't help thinking how easy it all was.

Eldrac watched with fiery eyes as the young girl skipped away, up the hillside. Her back was turned to him. He couldn't resist. It only took a flick of his wrist, a small component, and one word to cause her to burst into ash with her very next stride. The bear flew out of her hands, and she was gone with but one tiny yelp.

"Ah, one more for you," he whispered, seemingly to himself, as he began walking to her ashen remains spread all over the grass in a symbol of his master.

Eldrac felt so much better—words couldn't describe it. He walked with newfound rejuvenation as he gleefully went to see the remains of the girl—a slight pile of ash, and, of course, the bear a few cubits away. As he leaned over to pick up the bear, a small and distant thunderclap sounded behind him. He turned and looked up into the cloudless sky behind him, furrowing his brow.

It had not been enough to kill the small child. As he looked at the ash that signified the condemnation of her soul via *Damon's Damnation*, he could not help but smile, for he knew another had been swallowed by the ancient *throne of souls*.

Eldrac held the small bear loosely between his fingertips, smelling the scent of the innocent girl mingled with the components of the spell that had obliterated her and consigned her very soul to a place not destined for her. He smiled with a satisfaction he had not felt in a thousand years and began to slowly walk up the hillside. He had, after all, been invited to dinner, and a thousand years was enough to make any man famished. Eldrac unceremoniously dropped the bear to the ground, casting as he walked away. A wall of fire raced down the hill, mercilessly consuming all the other children at play.

*   *   *   *

Toblain was not sure of what he was dealing with until he picked up the bear, looking back down the hillside where the grass had been completely charred to the dirt. His bright gold hair flurried in the breeze and spilled

Charles W. McDonald Jr.

down the back of his cowl and soft cream, woolen robes. A tear came to one of his golden eyes as he looked back up the hill—knowing it was done. The bear gave him the confirmation he needed. Toblain could smell the old devil on the fabric of the bear.

He opened his robes, pulling out a small black bag just far enough to drop the bear inside. "So, Eldrac," he declared to the wind. "'Tis time to war with you once more." Toblain looked back down the hillside one last time, making note of the remains he could see from here. Then he turned to walk up the hill, hunting Eldrac.

*   *   *   *

(Xal, Perion, Present Day)

Rowarc d'Aguillon was having a tough time, trying to make some kind of headway. Those who, at first, appeared to know something always ended up stringing him along for as long as they could. He used to be pretty good at spotting those kinds of people, but retirement had dulled certain senses not used in decades. He seemed to be getting back some of his old instincts, for he surely caught the last couple of buggers in lies as thick as winter molasses. Catching someone in a bold-faced lie would have made for priceless fun if this job and his missing son wasn't so serious.

Then there were those who just knew nothing and were genuine about it. And then, of course, there were those who would simply say nothing, only because he looked the part of a tracker. And *most people don't want to be found*. It was an old truism, but that didn't make it any less true. It had cost him a fair piece to get half-way-round the world, near the land of Xal. At least people here didn't know him nor his old reputation. That was often better— working on virgin turf. Reputations could be dangerous.

Charles W. McDonald Jr.

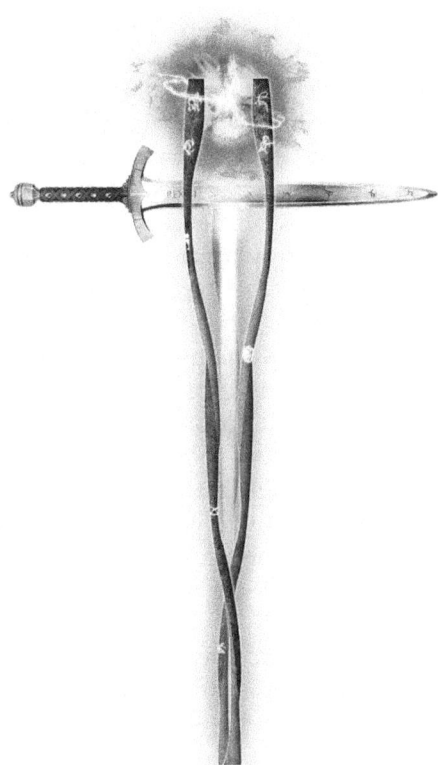

Chapter 27: Two Fronts

(Almeron Castle, Perion, Present Day)

alls accented in gold leaf reflected his thin goatee and long mustache as he brought the rotund glass of aged brandy to his lips. He had not tasted the fruits of wealth in so long, he had forgotten what it was like to be pampered—to have your every whim satisfied in an instant, but then he had forgotten so many things over the millennia that it would take another lifetime to recount them all. Good thing for him.

Eldrac walked through the pristine halls of Almeron Castle, making note of the late impressionist artwork of Phalar, a native Saer artist of great renown and little talent. Saer was one of the oldest parts of the Kingdom of Gawth in the north of the Kingdom—almost in Melshier. Eldrac smirked arrogantly at Phalar's alleged greatest masterpiece—a recounting of one of the

Charles W. McDonald Jr.

first kings of Gawth, and his rather sordid escapades in and about the royal palace. The painting did make him chuckle, but as much from its poor artistic value as much as the attempt at the content.

"You find something amusing, Eldrac of Dragon's Point?" The voice came from only a few spans away. The handsome young man would have made a fine tracker with such stealthy skills. Twice someone had snuck up on him since his freedom. Perhaps his hearing was not what used to be, or in need of *Healing*. Maybe he had grown arrogant over a thousand years in the arms of the Dragon. Of course, it never seemed that long really. Time was so different there. A thousand years, a thousand moments—'twas all the same. Age crept by in fluidic torrents; a minute here, a millennium there. Unless one held an artifact powerful enough to anchor oneself in time, but those were rare and hard to come by, but he'd have to look into that. An anchor might prove useful....

Eldrac turned to face Asamel, making note of the scar about his left cheek. "My," he whispered ominously. "Wherever did you get that," he asked, motioning to the scar with his glass of brandy.

"Long story...." Asamel pivoted away from Eldrac, turning his scar away from Eldrac's gaze.

That was all the clarity Eldrac was going to get on that. It must have been a point of embarrassment for Asamel. Asamel never dealt with reality very well.

"Doesn't matter. You summoned me for a reason, Asamel. What is it?"

"I wanted to understand the terms of your freedom." Scratching an insatiable itch amidst the short-cropped black hair just under his right temple, Asamel never mixed words with him. With others, he was an intolerable enigma.

"We are fighting a two-front war for all time. For everything. For balance." Eldrac's eyes danced with the possibilities. "We haven't time to waste for games anymore, Asamel. My terms of freedom are to help maintain balance on the edge of the knife. I need Vosh and what she possesses to do that. Do we know where she is?"

"Not exactly; not yet," Asamel admitted, almost cringing inside. Eldrac wasn't the *most* unpredictable dangerous man he knew, but he was the most unstable. Understandable given his circumstances and his *travels* of late. "But I am working the problem."

Eldrac's grip tightened around his brandy glass, crushing it in his hand. Eldrac growled, throwing what remained up against the wall. The brandy ran down the wall and over the inept painting—though one couldn't say *he* had

Charles W. McDonald Jr.

ruined it. *Appropriate that he added some color and life to it*, he thought.

Asamel didn't want to push it with Eldrac, but he did nonetheless. "Are you sure she even has it?"

Baring his teeth through his growl, Eldrac replied in the thin wisps of what remained of his sanity, "You don't want to question the *source* of *this* information."

Asamel didn't trust Eldrac any further than he could physically throw him, but he *did* believe Eldrac—this time. Their relationship was old—ancient really—and Eldrac had given him no reason to doubt the credibility of the source of his information. He just didn't want to waste any more resources trying to find Vosh if she didn't have it.

"And," Eldrac interjected as if reading Asamel's thoughts, "…if she doesn't have it, I know *who* does."

Visibly disturbed by Eldrac's reading of his own private thoughts, Asamel busied focus looking into his brandy glass.

Eldrac had started to march, in disgust, down the hallway to the main doors, but stopped in his tracks—turning back to Asamel. The possibilities raced through his mind, one after the other, as he calculated his forthcoming victory and their promised rewards. The fire returned in his eyes as the answer came to him. "Keep searching," he commanded, flatly pausing to deliver his final point with deadly emphasis. "And Asamel, have a better answer for me next time I see you." He hadn't given any indication of when he might come to Asamel again for answers, and that had been entirely intentional. *Better to light an unconditional fire under him*, Eldrac considered storming off to deal with the other front of this war.

*   *   *   *

(Xal, Perion, Present Day)

It was his seventh little village in as many days. There were no major cities left in Xal, only ruins and little fiefdoms. Even the villages and hamlets could barely justify being called such. For such a huge swath of land, the population was more sparse than just about anywhere else he'd ever traveled. The wind brushed through the grey-streaked beard he'd accumulated over the last several days of travel. It was now past the point of new growth where it bothered him incessantly. *Creator*, it was violently cold here, trapped by mountains on all sides! *A place where armies came to die*, Rowarc thought to himself as he gathered the sketch from the Hillman. They aged much slower than anyone else he'd ever seen and did so without magic. No one understood how they did it, but it had something to do with their skin being darker than most; most having solid white hair. 'Twas a striking contrast against their dark skin.

There had not been that many people to talk to and even fewer willing to talk to him once he showed them the sketch. Reading their reactions, he figured the ones who recognized her said the least. Those willing to have a legitimate conversation didn't know squat. It was frustrating. Whoever she was, the cone of silence around her was protecting her from being found.

Shoving her sketch into the vest covering his long-sleeve tunic, Rowarc turned his Grey toward the trio of peaks in the Valley of Xal that marked the heart of the valley. Only Rary's Corridor, to the east of the valley, marked the only other way in or out. Otherwise, it was a perfect trap for an army—*almost purpose built*, he wondered. Even Rary's Corridor was fraught with disaster for any army intending to get in or out of the Valley of Xal. The continental divide made passage by horse practically impossible as the crust of one continent forced the other skyward in plateaus over a hundred paces high in most places. The only comforting thought was that magic wasn't supposed to work inside the interior of the valley or anywhere between the trio of peaks and the surrounding snow-capped mountains that formed the perimeter of the valley. He questioned that as fact, only because he'd never personally tested it, but for now, it was an assumption he was betting his life on. Another stiff, blistering breeze announced dusk's arrival. It would get miserably cold fast. He needed to make shelter soon if he wasn't going to stay in this village. Spurring his Grey forward while hoping to gain some ground before making camp, Rowarc ran fingers of his free left hand through the icy thicket forming in his beard while his right hand held his mount on path. There was a good-sized crop of fir trees on the horizon he knew he could make if he hurried. *Best get there and stop dawdling.*

A last look back, Rowarc's senses were screaming at him that he was being followed. If he'd learned anything in all his years of working in this profession, it was to trust his instincts. It wasn't the question of *if* he was being followed that bothered him. He expected that, given the nature of who'd sent him. He had a bad feeling about that man from the very beginning. What bothered him was the question of *who* was following him and why.

Charles W. McDonald Jr.

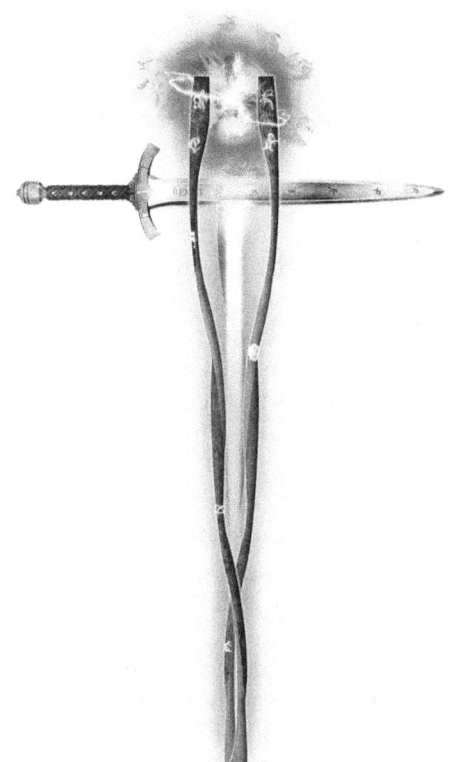

Chapter 28: A Debt

(Xal, Perion, Present Day)

is fire crackled and popped against the blue stones he used to contain it, as Rowarc stretched his blanket taut, building his lean-to shelter. It made a much bigger smoke footprint than he desired, but it was so cold he didn't care. He wasn't twenty anymore, and this wasn't as fun as it used to be. His more-than-middle-aged joints didn't really care for it either. *Besides, whoever might be after him could probably smell him before they caught sight of him.* That consideration brought a smirk to his face as he tried to remember the last time he'd bathed.

Lean-to now tethered, he moved back to the fire to warm his joints, pulling another blanket over himself as he leaned his back against the base of a fir, hundreds of years old and eight times as round as he, facing the most likely

Charles W. McDonald Jr.

approach route. *Best sleep with your back protected.*

His eyelids heavy, his grip on his sword relaxing, Rowarc started to drift.

"You're drawing *entirely* too much attention to me," the soft female voice proposed flatly, suddenly standing right in front of Rowarc without so much as making a sound. Or so he assumed. He was so tired, there's no telling how long she'd been standing there. She could have taken her sweet time creeping up on him, and he might not have even noticed.

She was beautiful for nearly being a youthful middle-age, with soft and long blonde wavy hair tucked under her full-length white wool coat of grey accents and piping. Her hood tried to hide some of her features, but her high cheekbones, firm milk-skin, and shiny silver eyes gave her away. The sketch hadn't done her justice at all.

"It wasn't my intention to draw attention to you," Rowarc slapped his cheeks, trying to force himself awake while not looking directly at her. He wasn't sure if he felt guilty for finding her or not, but it had crossed his mind more than once—what he would say and do *when* he found her—or *she* found him....

"Intentions are useless, and almost never relevant to the outcome." A cold reply for a colder night delivering her harsh words on breezes bitter and ill-suited for the all-too pleasant sound of her voice.

"The man who paid me to find you. His name is Asamel," he had to earn her trust if this was going to work. No sense in hiding anything from her. She'd find the truth as quickly as she snuck up on him. Apparently, she held the advantage.

"Yes, that doesn't surprise me. You are not the first he's sent." She paused knowingly, but not really wanting to terrify the man who seemed genuine enough at a glance. "You're just the first I haven't killed."

Rowarc cleared his throat, half coughing, "Well, let me first thank you for that," smoothing his vest and sitting up against the tree a bit straighter now. "Would you happen to know why he picked me? You see that's been bothering me all the way from Stirling."

"My guess is your son. I gave him something in Stirling—something very valuable." He was being forthright with her. She would do the same.

"Yeah, the amulet. I saw it. They tried to sneak it past me, but I still caught a glimpse of it. I heard them debating whether it was a fake or real. I'm guessing it wasn't a fake after all."

"Hardly," she scoffed.

Charles W. McDonald Jr.

"Want to tell me why?" He wanted to stand, but he didn't want to make any threatening moves either.

"Because we're about to fall off the edge of the knife—you, and I, and everyone, and everything."

An arrow streaked past the both of them, clipping the white and grey hood of Vosh's coat, sticking into a fir directly behind her, but not before putting another scar on Asamel's cheek opposite the other scar already on his face. Wincing in pain, Asamel spun around the tree, putting it between him and the expert archer he still couldn't see. He hadn't even seen any movement in the brush. Whoever it was, they were good. Touching his finger to his new wound, Asamel cursed, snarling. That one would be worse than the other side. Pulling out his poisoned daggers, he threw a volley at the two he could see, Vosh and Rowarc, watching them bury into the opposing fir. It wasn't his intention to hit either of them—that would not have been good for his well-being. He just needed some cover to get away. Three-to-one odds didn't favor him now that his advantage of surprise had been lost.

With three daggers whizzing past him, close enough to cut some of his hair, Rowarc lost Asamel in the woods behind them. *Fast. Probably won't be collecting the rest of that bounty now*, he rebuked himself internally. No longer worrying about startling the woman, he fully uprighted himself, his back still to the tree as he carefully moved around it, looking for the archer that had just saved their lives. He didn't see anything until the woman made a motion with her left hand, clearing out the underbrush to reveal a very tall, balding middle-aged man built like a granite keep. Iain Longbow wore a camouflaging cloak of varying shades of green and brown over his crimson and white house colors and family crest: A king's crown inside an oval ring caught between two griffins struggling to capture the power of the crown. In the foreground of the crown sat two angels amidst an array of broken arrows and olive branches. In the background, and standing over the crown, was a fiery phoenix, wings spread wide, engulfing the warring griffins. It had been decades, but the man was unmistakable in any generation.

"You!" Rowarc tried not to appear too stunned, but the fact that so many had snuck up on him made him question his acumen for the job. *Had he already lost so much of his edge?*

"Yes, me!" Iain stood in the clearing created by Vosh, wondering how she was able to cast here at all. "You know you're lot easier to find in your retirement," Iain quipped, moving toward them.... Carefully. Never taking his eyes off Vosh. She was beautiful, but so were most deadly things.

"You didn't see him following you from two villages past?" Her words cut far deeper than intended, but Vosh didn't seem to be the type to care who her brutal honesty injured.

Now he was really questioning his mettle for the job. *Shouldn't have come out of retirement. You're just going to embarrass yourself or get yourself killed,* Rowarc sullenly realized.

"Iain Longbow," Rowarc extended his left hand to the woman, lowering his bow in his right.

"Vosh," she took Iain's hand fearlessly, but this man was dangerous— even for her. She was certain of it.

"Well," Iain offered, turning back to his old traveling companion, "I owed you." He paused looking back and forth between them as he now positioned himself between them. "I heard you were coming out of retirement and knew that couldn't be good. I was sorry to hear about your wife."

"Well apparently…," Rowarc thought aloud, brushing his fingers through his short-cropped hair, realizing how much he must have stunk from weeks without bathing. "I was more in need of help than I realized. Must have…," he didn't want to finish that thought aloud. "Won't be collecting my bounty now, because I'm certainly not going to try and convince her to meet with this man who clearly can't be trusted."

"That was your plan?" Vosh seemed dubious to the idea.

"Well, forcing you wasn't going to be an option. Even if I could, I wouldn't. I made that clear to him. He suggested convincing you, but I doubt he planned on getting caught." Thinking aloud again, "So why do you think he wanted me to bring you to him? He made it clear I wasn't to hurt you in any way."

"Whatever that man tells you, he can't be trusted. He works for someone named Eldrac. And, Eldrac, whether or not his motives are aligned with yours, is as dangerous as they come. Totally mad!"

Vosh tended to talk with her hands. Not that this was unusual, but for a lamean to be moving their hands about was unsettling nonetheless. It was more than enough hand gestures to keep Rowarc on edge.

"If Asamel wants me, that means Eldrac wants me." Something she had known for some time which is why she'd ditched the amulet, but if Radin wasn't being careful with it, she might have put him in more danger by giving it to him.

"And why would Eldrac want you?" Iain studied her carefully. She was hard on the inside, and he wondered how she'd become so.

"Besides the amulet, I would assume he intends to recruit me."

Chapter 29: Pulling Back the Curtain

(Bouschè, Perion, Present Day)

After days on end with her sixth sense pegged at maximum, Michelle's head pounded relentlessly: forcing her to act against her own will and better judgment at this point. Working in the shadows, as if she was trying to observe some grand Prime Directive or something, hadn't changed a thing and clearly wasn't doing any good either. Lawna would be furious with her, but a different approach was required. She watched from her chair in the corner of Radin's room as he and his 'girlfriend' started to wake. If she was going to leave unnoticed, it was now or never. *Was she ready to pull back the curtain already?*

Too late. Radin eyes popped open as he looked her dead in the eyes, giving Elise a good shove to make sure she woke fully with one good push. "Hey," she exclaimed, pulling the covers to her face then noticing what, or who, Radin was staring at in the corner.

"Don't scream...." Michelle cursed herself internally. Bad choice of words. She sounded like *Dexter*, or worse. *You can do better than that.* "I mean, I'm not here to hurt you." She offered in the most genuine tone she could muster, "I thought you could use my help."

"And you couldn't just knock on the door?" Elise ripped the sheets off Radin, unintentionally leaving him naked on the bed in front of this 'woman,' wrapping the sheet around her body as she unceremoniously walked to the dresser for her clothes.

"Fair point, but you're in more danger than you can possibly imagine at all hours of the day and night, and you needed surveillance." She visibly cringed at the use of that word. *Bad Michelle,* she chastised herself, trying not to look at the naked young man before her while he reached down feeling

Charles W. McDonald Jr.

around for his clothes on the floor—never taking his eyes off the intruder still seated in the outside corner of the room.

Elise immediately took notice of the use of *that* word—*surveillance*—pivoting from where she was about to open the top drawer of the dresser, now staring the beautiful buxom blonde dead in the eyes.

"I mean you needed someone to watch over you—especially throughout the night." *Not good. This isn't going according to plan. Maybe she should have listened to Lawna after all.* "My name is Michelle, and I'm here to help." She paused again. "I'm at your service." She actually stood and curtsied to a nude Radin who still fumbled for his clothes.

Elise practically choked as she struggled against the vomit threatening to come up right then and there.

Radin looked between the two beautiful blondes, though Elise was more strawberry-blonde. They could have been sisters. Roughly the same age. Similar features. Both having soft curves, but Michelle had a hard edge and an aura that hinted at her physical ability to take matters into her own hands. At least they couldn't intimidate each other with their looks, as women so often did to one another. He swore, he'd never understand women! "Are you two related?" He had to ask. He just had to!

"WHAT?!" It was a simultaneous reply from both of them as they both pivoted to glare at him.

Great, they were at each other's throats. Now they're both at yours! Women! Silence was the best response. They did gradually return to face each other instead of him, but it took a moment, and the silence was insufferable.

"So, Michelle, you said," Elise was going to go there, and Michelle's brow had already furrowed, preemptively warning. "My, that's an unusual name. Wherever did you get such a name?"

"From my parents." *Too smartass*, Michelle considered.

"And what lands might they be from?" There it was.

"Far, far away." *Suitably smartass* from Michelle, enough to cause a smile to adorn her beautiful face.

She's magnificent, Radin reflected. "I don't think that's all that important right now." He was trying to refocus the discussion on what mattered—the threat at hand. "Why do you feel I'm in so much danger? And it's not as if I doubt you. I don't. I believe you're right about the threat. I've seen it...," he offered as he paused to slip his tunic over his head. "In one manner or another. I'm just curious if you might know a little more about the *why.*"

"Because this affects more than just your world." There it was. She watched as Elise's jaw practically dropped to the floor. *Worth the price of admission*, Michelle chuckled internally.

Charles W. McDonald Jr.

"You have my undivided attention..." Radin immediately stopped what he was doing to listen intently to the information Michelle had to offer. "...Michelle, is it?"

"You're not supposed to be less shocked than her," Michelle noticed aloud. That was it. The final uppercut to Elise's disguise, causing Radin to pivot to her...slowly.

"Care to explain?" It was only three words from Radin, but Elise just got painted into a corner for which she hadn't yet prepared herself. Radin recalled when he'd brought up the many worlds comment from Damon and her lack of reaction to that comment. There was more there there that needed to be uncovered. Now.

Elise's lips worked, trying to find the words. She always knew she'd have to tell him at some point, but this was all too soon. The best-laid plans, she thought. "When my husband died, I followed the trail here."

"What trail?" His heart sank, "What husband?"

"Not important, but powerful magic, like what was being used to traverse between worlds leaves a trail—a wake." She looked to Michelle, knowing she must have done something similar that led her here. "On worlds where magic is dying, powerful magic leaves a visible trail and one that can be followed if you know how to look *and* what you're looking for."

"Damon mentioned such a place," Radin recalled his conversation and the map with the great spiral arm of stars.

"Yes, well, Damon left quite a trail between this world and mine as if he had traversed it *many* times." Elise looked to Michelle, "I'm sure you sensed it as well."

Michelle nodded, slowly rocking back and forth in her chair in the corner of the room, as she offered up a bit more. "I was sent here..." Michelle paused, thinking *might as well rip the whole band-aid off.* "...and I wasn't sent alone. I brought help."

Raised eyebrows from both Elise and Radin met Michelle's flat stare. "How much help?" Radin was becoming more and more practical by the minute—youth, innocence and ignorant bliss mercilessly shed along the way.

"Significant help!" Michelle leaned forward, and before the blink of an eye, she was standing at the front door to the room leaving a gust in her wake that shifted clothes from the top of the dresser all the way to the floor and halfway across the room, chasing Michelle to the door. Again, Elise's jaw dropped. Again, *priceless.* Michelle just stood at the door smiling at them, tapping her right foot. "Right then, so you'll accept my help...?" It wasn't really a question.

Radin merely nodded. Elise worked to shut her jaw though it required some effort.

Part 5: The Distorted Continuum

Charles W. McDonald Jr.

Chapter 30: Welcome to New York

(Utica, New York, Earth, Late Spring, 1930 Hundred Hours Eastern, Near Future)

The placid chirping of birds and rustling of wind through the hackberry, white ash, and silver maple trees was slowly consumed by the sound of advancing armor. In a matter of moments, huge tread marks marred the beautiful green spring grass and rolling hillsides of upstate New York as the Chinese VT-4 tanks—a more modern variant of the Type-99A—pressed further south, onward to their imminent clash with the Allies.

*   *   *   *

(A few miles to the south....)

There were a few larger houses scattered over the rolling hills, mostly new mansions and expensive housing developments, but this was the best place to make a stand. It was the only place, really. The Chinese Armor proved much more reliable and accurate than the Allies had thought possible, forcing them to move up any plans they may have had of stopping them before they made Maryland. Even the British Challenger II and the M1 Abrams had their hands full against the full-scale invasion of the Chinese ground forces backed and reinforced by the DPRK. The U.S. had been carved up, quick and neat, by the multi-prong attack of the Chinese. Their terrorist approach at eliminating several key military bases in both Russia and the U.S. proved to be genius and unexpected. The Chinese now controlled more than enough long-range ICBM's to be a lethal nuclear threat to any major city in the U.S., but the Russians swore up and down there was no possibility of the Chinese cracking their launch codes. Still, that was a gamble, and you never bet on the Russian Government, especially when they start making assurances. It was a deadly game, on equal footing, now. Neither side wanted to push the button that would end the world. No, it would have to be a conventional war from this point.

The only real piece of good news, to this stage, was that Chinese appeared to have bitten off a lot more than they could chew with the U.S. Navy and her thirteen active-duty Carrier Battle Groups—now reduced down to ten with the loss of the Stennis, Enterprise and Eisenhower. There were a few carrier groups assigned to U.S. protection, but there were several battling the Chinese Navy and firebombing their major cities to ash. The USS Gerald R. Ford (CVN 78), and the John F. Kennedy (CVN 79) were both rushed into service, and what was left of the defense industry was booming, trying to keep up with demands for WW-III. Air cover for today's series of battles would be provided by Reserve F-15 E's, A-10 Warthogs, Apaches and Blackhawks from Massachusetts, and the usual F-14 SuperTomcat/F-18 Hornet/JSF F-35 combination from the Ronald Reagan (CVN 76) carrier group, currently thirty nautical miles off the coast. The Chinese, however, were not without air cover and satellite DEW (Directed Energy Weapons) of their own. They would most likely be receiving support from the captured airfields in New Hampshire and Vermont as their own advanced air support equipment puddle-jumped to the newly-captured FOB (Forward Operating Bases).

The Chinese had to know invading a country where there's more than one firearm for every breathing person wasn't going to work out too well for them. Nonetheless, they came in force, learning a whole new appreciation for America's Second Amendment.

Now it was just up to the U.S. Army 3rd Battalion Armor. Everything was set. Sixty of their M1-Abram tanks, lined up in two separate V-formations, were scattered all over the hillsides and among the housing developments. Their engines idled ominously, in unison, as they waited for the precise moment. HIMARS and M777 155mm howitzer artillery would back them up from behind their fortified lines, and the Apache/AH-64's would spear the attack along with the M1-A2 Abrams mainline battle tanks. Major Mitchell Grady watched the Chinese advance over the hillside, just now coming into range of their main guns.

"Can you see 'em, Major?" Staff Sergeant Ronald Stencowsky anxiously manned the main gun, putting in his foam ear protection just before putting on his headset. Both he and the Major had served together in the Gulf recently. You got to know each other pretty well, serving in the confines of an M1-A2 mainline battle tank. You might say you got to know one another a bit *too* well. Ron was now looking up at the Major's legs, waiting for the signal that would blister the coming night.

Charles W. McDonald Jr.

The Major suddenly descended into the tank; his eyes still distant. "The E2s from the Washington said to expect at least three hundred. I counted over two-hundred-and-fifty myself, Ronnie," he proclaimed with a grave sound in his voice, as he hurriedly strapped himself into the tank commander's seat. *Damn*, he thought, *Why are they gonna sacrifice us like this?* He could only hope that the reason was not intentional—that perhaps they thought their enemy numbers would not be so high, and that they could not get any more armor up to their location in time. Maybe they were so proud of their kill ratio, they thought five-to-one odds wasn't so bad. He knew that all resources were spread pretty thin. He could always hope, but *hope* was always a shitty strategy at best. He really had no other choice, because there was a battle to be fought here. Right now!

Ron stared blankly back at him, his eyes blinking far less than normal, but he knew what had to be done. "That's OK Major, because I got a 120mm of sabot lovin' ready and awaiting your command," Ronnie suggested as he slammed the shell home, closing the breach. "One 'Silver Bullet' in the pipe, sir!"

"Very well," the major acknowledged, sending out the command to advance and engage to the rest of his spear. Tanks to east, under Major Grady's command, began their advance first, with the tanks to the west, under the leadership of the battalion commander, Col. Rich Walters, following an instant later. The Major's group was to assault the Chinese straight on, while the Col.'s tanks would slam the back door. A lot to ask when you're outnumbered five-to-one. The numbers looked bad—real bad, but it would depend on the accuracy of the tanks and the performance of the crews, among many other things. There were so many variables, so many possibilities. From terrain to weather to human error; fate would carry the day. Even so, the odds were *not* good.

Night was just beginning to fall as the armor from both sides clashed in the first battle for New York, in a war most were certain was Armageddon. The beginning of the End Times. The M1-A2 Abrams were fast and accurate, proving their worth on the battlefield, but the Chinese air cover was much stronger than anticipated, and their armor deadlier than previously thought. Their VT-4's came in huge numbers, well over three hundred in all. Third Battalion reduced that number by more than a third before the night was over, and the combination air assault claimed another forty-to-fifty more, but it was not enough.

The full moon shone bright in a night sky just starting to cloud up as the battlefield roasted in the aftermath of the Battle of Utica. Burning tanks and mechanized units littered the previously picturesque landscape, while

Charles W. McDonald Jr.

large, noble houses of the surrounding developments lit up the night sky in a giant conflagration, crumbling into the ash of their own footprint. The only other sounds were the hum of Chinese Armor, advancing ever southward—to Warwick.

*   *   *   *

(Warwick, New York, Earth, Late Spring, 2220 Hundred Hours Eastern, Same Evening, Near Future)

Col. Quincy Arthur Billings struck a match upon the metal frame of Michael's tank to light his pipe. The hot flame against the crisp night air briefly revealed both his and Michael's faces. Their stern flame-revealed looks a haunting sign of the news that came to them barely an hour earlier. The news had not been good, but it had been expected. The night grew cold and hard among the camp of the British 1st Armored Division, the famed 7th Infantry Brigade. *The Desert Rats* as they were infamously known around the world—created around the Napoleonic Wars—awaited the inevitable armored clash that was soon forthcoming. Everything was quiet now, but that would soon change.

"Bloody damn shame, what happened to those yanks up north." Sir Col. Quincy Arthur Billings II slapped the silver cap of his lighter shut after he had managed to light his pipe in a stiff breeze that raced between their tanks. Leaning against the treads of Michael's tank, he puffed slowly and deliberately on his pipe, wondering what was going through the mind of his old friend. He knew why Michael felt like he had to be out here with the rest of them, but it was still too damn dangerous, and he just wanted to make sure Michael didn't shut him out as Michael could do in his moments of steeling himself for combat.

"I know what you mean…," Michael Anthony Day offered with a contemplating pause, sighing heavily as he clenched his right hand into a hard fist. "Time for revenge draws nearer. You'll soon have your chance to express the intensity of your displeasure in person." His Majesty came over to his old acquaintance, sitting down on the ground beside him against the treads of his Challenger II mainline battle tank. There was no mistaking the king amongst his army, as he dressed, for nostalgia's sake, in a pseudo-period correct sixth-century leather surcoat somewhere between satin, copper, and pewter, with his coat of arms about a quartered shield crest on his chest. His Celtic cross was embroidered in pewter against diagonally opposing white backgrounds while the cup of his wife's sigil was embroidered in burnished rust and gold against diagonally opposing patriot-blue and blood-red backgrounds. The short-sleeve surcoat, with ringlet armor cascading down his left arm while very full and textured, was still tailored against his body chiseled by years in the field with his SRR unit, but it went well with his brown pants and soft leather boots of the same color as his surcoat but with a glossier sheen.

Many had quipped that he had seen the 80's version of *Excalibur* one too many times, but he took it in stride, laughing at himself with them. Everything Michael did was deliberate. His uniform, centuries out of place, was an intentional embrace of a time gone by, but not forgotten, enabling him to invoke the full power of the immortal weapon at his side. He had even offered it up to scientists for empirical analysis. The best they could come up with to describe its metal compound was, "not of this Earth." Some confided that Michael's being here had been a real morale boost for the men in both the U.S. and British camps. That news seemed to make him smile, for that was its real intent. They needed something to make them smile, for this war was going to be a bloody one and it was just beginning.

"You'll need to gather the lads to speak to them." Billings deflected, talking about 'the men' while he struggled to find the right words—the words that needed to be spoken between them. "They'll be wanting to hear you."

"Yeah," Michael sighed, wondering what was going through his friend's thoughts, "You're right. It's getting to be that time." Michael looked to Billings, smiling at him, putting a comforting hand on his shoulder. There was a long pause, and then Michael began to shake his head knowingly. "Gather the men," he commanded in a tone of finality, causing Billings to put out his pipe, walking off to assemble the men.

Abruptly Billings stopped, pivoting back to Michael, "You know you don't have to do this."

Michael closed the distance between them both physically and emotionally, "I feel like it is my responsibility to lead my men into battle. To lead by example." He paused for a second, wanting his old friend to understand that there was much more at stake than he knew, "If I were not qualified to do this, then I would not. I would never risk the lives of any of my troops just so I could say that I led my men into battle. However, I am imminently and professionally qualified for this task, and I will lead my subjects into battle this night, as is my duty to do so. This is as much a part of my title as is the castle, or the crown. I must do this, my friend. We will do this *together*." Michael's smile, however bright and genuine it carried his message on the crisp air of hate-in-waiting, didn't mask the realization in his eyes. The knowing....

Billings, in a rare moment, was speechless, trying to work his mouth

Charles W. McDonald Jr.

into words his emotions would not allow. When Michael was right, he was right. He was qualified for this task, and he had both the right and the authority to be here. It was just so damn dangerous, though.

Billings stared at the king, not wanting to question him on this subject anymore, but he just had to mention two other things, or else he would most surely be neglect in his duties, both as a friend and as a Knight of the Realm. "What about Elise, your Majesty? And what are your orders for the country should they survive you this night?"

Michael didn't bat an eyelash at the question. As king, he had responsibilities beyond just this battle. "If I am killed or incapacitated, then you are to instruct that my last wishes were for the crown to fall to Elise, then to my son, Alexander, when he emancipates. At Dover Castle, you'll find instructions in my private study, on my desk, below the portrait of my children." Michael looked around at the enlisted personnel scurrying about, ensuring there were several witnesses to his instructions.

"As you wish, Your Majesty."

"Billings," Michael furrowed his brow, "GO!"

Finally, alone in profound thought, Michael walked over to and leaned over the back of his tank, looking out over the moonlit landscape of Warwick. How appropriate that this battle should be fought at a place, named after his favorite castle. He had always loved going to visit Warwick Castle as a child. It was the epitome of everything a castle should be—strong, intimidating, foreboding, handsome, functional, masculine, and warlike. Yes, Warwick was a proper choice to make a stand.

Michael leaned on the tank for several minutes, waiting for Arthur's return. His thoughts were mostly of Elise and his family. "Dear God, *am* I doing the right thing," he asked the Creator aloud. He seemed so certain only a moment ago. Was his own certainty a product of his own propaganda, used on Billings only moments ago? His eyes watered, now praying to the Creator, "God, please help me. Don't let any of them die because of my foolishness. Help us all to be strong in our hearts and sound in our minds as we do this terrible thing we must do. Let there be, in this battle…, in this war, a moment of mercy for us all." And as he began to open his eyes, he saw a brief flash of light within his mind. It was gone in but an instant, but he was certain of what he saw—blinding white light everywhere and a large figure holding out a familiar sword extended out toward him and that booming voice he'd come to know through so many waking dreams before. When he opened his eyes, he saw one of his own men, looking at him. It was one of the Bagpipe Corps, James McPherson. He bore a look of concern, but it quickly went away as he drew himself up proud and stiff, throwing a solid British salute. The king smiled, offering, "Play those pipes with as much pride as you threw that salute, and we'll have no morale problems tonight."

James McPherson's smile was as broad and genuine as anyone he had ever seen. "Sir," James responded resoundingly as he snapped a perfect ninety-degree turn and marched off into the darkness. The king was once again alone with his thoughts the only thing to keep him company. And, somewhere in the cold of the night, he thought he heard the warmth of Elise's voice telling him how much she loved him and needed him to come home. He could have sworn he heard her weeping from thousands of kilometers away.

*   *   *   *

Ron Stencowsky's eyes were wide and chalked with blood. The look of sanity had vanished from them from the moment their tank had been hit in the side with some new kind of round that their reactive armor did not like. Shrapnel from the blast had killed the Major, wounding both himself and the driver. He couldn't feel the pain in his right leg anymore and had decided to leave the shrapnel in for now. It felt like it was buried far too deep for him, or even a medic, to remove safely. He supposed that there was a chance that he could survive this night and receive proper medical attention, but he soon began to laugh at that thought. *No, there would most likely be no surviving this night. Best take as many bastards with him as he could before calling it a night.*

The tank limped along the best it could, tossing Stencowsky and the driver about the tank like two kids riding shotgun in the back of pickup doing ninety-to-nothing down an old country road. The best speed that they had been able to manage was about thirty-five miles per hour, but that was still almost as fast as the Chinese tanks. It felt like one of the treads wasn't responding quite right, and they had to borrow fuel from other tanks just to make it this far. The Chinese had forced the supply lines to fall back to positions south of Warwick, so they were on their own. That was okay with Ron, but his determination bordered on the psychotic at the moment. Nothing short of the tank's obliteration was going to stop them from chasing the Chinese all the way into *Hell.*

Ron stared blankly into the green backlit night vision target finder, knowing how many rounds he had left. He wasn't really thinking anything, just passing time by losing what was left of his mind. Blood began to run down from his ears again. He could feel it even through his numbness. They were caked with blood, and he thought they had stopped bleeding, but he nevertheless felt the unmistakable feeling of warm blood running down the side of

Charles W. McDonald Jr.

his neck. Ron smiled slightly, starting to laugh as his nose took in the unmistakable smell of spent JP-4 fuel and burned gunpowder and high explosives. If the driver could still hear, he surely would have turned around, but there was no one left with any functional hearing in this tank. Ron questioned the luck of his still being alive as he stared into the scope, trying to get in range of another bastard to send straight to *Hell*. Five sabot rounds wouldn't last long. Stencowsky smiled wickedly again and began to chuckle as another Chinese VT-4 came into range.

*   *   *   *

Michael tried to think of what he would say as he climbed atop his British Challenger II mainline battle tank. There were no speech writers for this. This needed to come from the heart, and his was threatening to burst out of his chest at the moment. Atop his Challenger II tank, he could now see out over the entire encampment from the vantage point as well as the Chinese VT-4's now apexing a hill not far away—Middletown burning in the background. His men were arranged in loose formation around his tank. A full battery of American HIMARS readied itself close-by while more of his men poured out of a nearby Foxhound to hear Michael speak. It was an impressive display of both manpower and equipment. Even a few of the command staff from the American encampment came to hear him speak, standing in solidarity by Michael's tank. All of his men stood at attention, waiting. A few of the Americans scurried about making preparations by their HUM-V, but Michael didn't mind. It was really *his* men to whom he was speaking.

"Tonight…" Michael's voice boomed without the need of a microphone, carried on the cold of the night by powers older than Man. Michael felt the stiff, cool breeze hit the back of his neck running through his dirty-blonde—almost brown, forward-swept hair. *How appropriate that this night should turn cold,* he thought. "…we're going to break the back of the Chinese advance!" He paused briefly, "They're going to bring everything they have against us. Some of you already have news of the Battle of Utica, and if you look north you can see Middletown burning." He could see the faces of acknowledgment everywhere among his men, and with it faces of pensive doubt and worry. "The Chinese Armor outnumbered them five to one. They were tough and they destroyed our forces there, continuing to press southward with nearly two-hundred VT-4's. They will be here momentarily and are bringing with them some ten thousand infantry as well as heavy artillery and air support. So, even with the Americans, this will be no cakewalk. You are going to have to *want* this victory! So, when you have to kill—KILL!" Michael took note of the intense agreement in his lad's faces, but he wondered if they would agree with the rest of it: "And, for God's sake, when you have the chance to be merciful—be merciful," he solemnly commanded. Their mood swings had changed with his, from pride to doubt, from intensity to now a feeling of Humanity. Now, they were where he wanted them. Now, they were where they needed to be for him to rouse their spirits. "And so, when you are dismissed remember the purpose for which you are here. We are here not as disciples of death! We are not here to *take* anything! We are here to help our friends take back what is theirs—*to defend*! And so, anyone here who likens himself to be a defender, rather than a killer, may call himself my brother. For, we are all brothers here. Tonight, I am not here as your King, but as a man whose heart is bursting with pride just to be here with you. As I look out over this field of Desert Rats and Americans alike, I'm honored to fight alongside you if you'll fight alongside me; to fight *for* you if you'll fight *for* me. Tonight, I see here before me the very best of Humanity assembled to do what must be done." Taking hold of the hand-and-a-half grip of the immortal weapon at his side, Michael witnessed the honor, pride, selflessness, conviction, and courage, all combined in the souls of his men, radiating an aura of righteousness around the encampment. A single tear rolled down Michael's cheek as he looked out over the land, seeing the fires burning in the distance and knowing what would soon be coming over that hillside. Looking back to his men, he had but one more thing to say.

"*To Arms*," Michael unleashed the magnificent and immortal blade of kings before him, holding it high and perfectly vertical over his head as he invoked the ancient summoning with all the majesty and power of his station, and the heroes of ages gone by. Witnessing the king's sword glowing like unto a star in the dead of night, a mighty pride swelled in his men, while a pure-white starburst-like aura engulfed the king, his tank, and the American leadership. Lumps began forming in their throats, and fires burst to life in their hearts as their beloved king worked his ancient magic on their souls, causing many to break protocol in their cheers and fists held high.

Michael looked out upon his men now with eyes of blue fire, and with his flesh basked in the glow of The *Sword of Kings* he completed the ancient summons, "*To Arms*! Your *Brother* calls you to Arms!" Even the wind answered his mighty summons, carrying his booming voice and his noble command, swiftly and surreally throughout the entire camp. His voice resonated out over the still of his army, carried on the crisp night air in every direction, just as two American Blackhawk helicopters whirled by overhead; the heavy chopping of their blades a cutting reality violently snapping everyone back to the task before them as they carried more men and equipment to the front lines.

"FIRE," the American HIMARS commander shouted, firing the first salvo as the giant GMLRS lit up the night right beside Michael, bursting forth from the launch canister with a forward fire-plume shooting some fifty-feet into the air, chasing the GMLRS projectile out of the launcher as the canister backplate dislodged from the back of the launcher allowing a massive fire plume to escape out the back.

An Apache made the northward turn right over their heads, picking up intel telemetry streaming in real-time from the drone launched some moments earlier just before Michael started talking to his men.

Michael could already hear heavy artillery prepping to follow leading shots from the HIMARS and Apache as he started to climb down from his tank.

"DISMISSED," Col. Billings belted out to the men in his command voice. "BATTLE STATIONS and God be with you!" His command cascaded down the ranks, echoed by tank commanders in the dark of the night.

Michael's army dispersed and organized in mere moments, rushing to get to their appointed stations. Michael's crew scrambled into his tank just as he was coming down to speak to Billings.

U.S. Army Colonel Max Bridges walked over to him as he was coming down, offering his hand to help him down. His subordinate officers stood slightly behind the colonel, as if what he was about to say came from all of them. A middle-aged man, the colonel was just beginning to bald on top, showing softened signs of graying among his short blond hair. He seemed fit and fairly handsome for a man his age, even if his nose was a bit too large for his face. His hazel eyes sparkled in the battle-lit night as he approached the king, bearing genuine friendship, even though they had never met. "You have already received the thanks of my government for your help," Colonel Bridges offered, "but allow me to thank you, personally, just for being here." The colonel smiled broadly, continuing, "We've heard a great deal about you, and didn't know quite what to think—until *now*! You've given us all something to tell our families about. And…," he tried to continue after a pause to gather his thoughts and emotions, a bit choked up, "You've helped me find something I thought I had lost." The colonel extending his hand for Michael to shake it, which Michael did heartily, if a bit questioningly. "By your leave, your Majesty…" Col. Bridges managed a smile, feeling an indescribable sensation coursing through his veins as the *Sword of Kings* continued to glow in Michael's left hand.

"You have it, noble Colonel," the king thoughtfully granted. Michael couldn't quite let go of something the colonel had said. "Colonel Bridges,"

Michael called out to him as he was just about to leave, causing the colonel pivot back to him. "You never said what it was that I helped you find."

"No…," the colonel countered with a smirk, "…I didn't, but perhaps I'll tell you the next time I see you." With that, he and his subordinates turned to get in his HUM-V, heading for their stations.

Michael turned to his old friend, who now stood by the treads of the king's tank, smiling. "God be with you, your Majesty," Billings offered a stiff, proper salute. "And with you, Arthur." Michael gave him a quick pat on the back. With that, Billings disappeared into the night, tending to his station as Michael hopped back up onto his Challenger II tank, climbing inside. The time approached 23-hundred hours, and the mechanized sound of Chinese advancing armor could now be heard in the distance. The Allies and the Chinese were about to clash for New York for the second time in just the last few hours.

*　　*　　*　　*

Stencowsky hoped their luck would last just a little bit longer as their M1-A2 rolled into the trailing edge of this epic land battle. All around him, he could see Chinese infantry and armor engaging the Allies, meeting their every move with powerful countermoves. He thought he'd have to be deaf by now, but they were close enough he could *feel* the Chinese heavy artillery positions in their slow creep behind the fast pace of the Armor. He could feel their shells leaving—some of them air burst heavy shrapnel, some traditional high-explosive. It would be a long, bloody battle, and he just hoped his tank would limp along enough for him to get to use his last four shells. The fifth was a beauty!

Trailing most of the Chinese advance, going largely unnoticed as a flanking threat since it was really just them, their tank was only beginning to drive into the thick of the fray when they encountered small arms fire all around them. It wasn't a huge threat, but he did see them readying something that was. It looked to him like a variant of their own TOW missile. Stencowsky grunted something, then moved to the 20mm, promptly mowing down every living thing wearing a Chinese uniform. Stencowsky chuckled and smiled psychotically as he resumed his search for the one that got away from them moments before—the one with all the pretty little Chinese flags all over it. The one that had put the shrapnel in his leg and killed the major. *That One, he was going to make go boom.*

A massive trailing fireball erupted from the end of their 120mm main

Charles W. McDonald Jr.

gun, producing a deafening thunderclap inside the tank, as Stencowsky could barely be heard over the cacophony of war, "YEAH!!! Come get you some of that! Suck on my boomstick, motherfucker." Thick grey smoke filled the interior of the tank as Stencowsky again cleared the breach and loaded his next sabot round, doggedly hunting Pretty Flags. He chuckled to himself madly, taking pride in the devastation he'd wrought on one of the few T-90's the Chinese had brought with them. Still, lifeless, and burning with its top tilted and blown half off, was all that remained of his previous target and *that* had *not* gone unnoticed. Pretty Flags was pivoting back to him now.

It passed by the edge of his scope—what had to be the command tank. Another VT-4, but this one looked like it had more reactive armor around its belly. Whatever it was, it was big. The main gun had to be at least a 130mm, and there were three pretty little Chinese flags all over it. Stencowsky licked his lips, checking his armed status to make sure his sabot round was ready. He wasn't getting a confirmation status from the damaged fire control, but he didn't care. Either it would blow up in the breach, killing him and the driver, or it would send Pretty Flags straight to *Hell*.

"Come to Daddy," Ron madly whispered, taking aim. He had time— maybe. Quickly, he opened the breach with the live sabot round still in it, sharpied a few appropriate words on the round's metal casing and slammed the breach shut again: *Welcome to New York*! Verifying their target's position one last time before firing, Ron pulled the trigger just at the exact moment he saw Pretty Flags fire on one of the British Challenger II tanks. He was close enough, and the round hit Pretty Flags with such force, it completely severed the top of the tank causing it to flip upside down as it crashed to the ground in a burning heap. Body parts, blood, ash, fire, and soot had redecorated Pretty Flags into something more akin to Ron Stencowsky's liking.

*   *   *   *

Michael went about finding them another target as soon as they confirmed their tenth kill. They had done well so far but were beginning to draw some attention and some additional heat. Just then, he saw a flash lighting up the periphery of his scope. *It appeared it might have come from beh....*

Fire everywhere! Michael could barely remember the last thing that had happened. He remembered being thrown from his seat as the turret jerked to one side then recoiled back. He found himself on the floor of his burning tank, his safety straps had been severed by shrapnel, and he could feel himself bleeding from several places. Michael looked around, assessing the best possibilities of survival for his crew. He could see the driver slumped completely forward against the controls; most of his neck had been blown away by the mass of shrapnel that must have been introduced from the rear part of the turret. If he had been a little further forward, that would have been him. He could see the gunner, Jimmy, still moving his legs a bit on the floor as he groaned in agony and the fog of war. Michael couldn't see his own wounds, but reached out to Jimmy, in a raspy voice, "Jimmy, come on. We've gotta get outta here." Michael heard Jimmy groan in some kind of recognition, but he was just on the periphery of lucid thought. Michael managed to prop himself up with his right hand reaching for the ladder when he suddenly felt horrendous pain shooting through his chest and his entire right side. He could feel the blood coming out in rivers but could not see the wound when he looked down. Only the massive amount of what he knew to be his own blood all over his boots. The shrapnel must have come in through his back. He had to get them out of there, or they were as good as dead. They were a sitting duck in a burning tank. The smell of burning JP-4 fuel, gunpowder, and high explosives permeated the air—especially inside the tank. Perhaps it was best that Michael could not see the large piece of shrapnel buried deep into his right flank, and the blood gushing from around its edges.

Even though stretching his right side caused him immense pain, Michael managed to catch hold of the ladder with his right hand, while stretching out to grab Jimmy with his left. A powerful man, easily capable of bench pressing 100 kilograms, Michael thought he could manage but his wounds had broken his body. It was a hard enough fight just to survive. He had never felt more weakened in his whole life as he did while trying to lift himself and Jimmy out of his burning tank.

Outside the view appeared twisted and distorted, everything around them was on fire. Everywhere, particles from fuel, explosives, debris and body parts floated on the air like hot embers of death. They were in *Hell*. He couldn't tell whether he was losing his senses, or if the tank had really been blown onto its side. He could see a significant portion of the turret had been blown away, and it appeared somewhat severed from the main body of the tank, but his senses were rapidly fading as he fell gracelessly from the tank hatch, taking Jimmy with him in a gnarled heap. Michael's vision shifted and blurred when he hit the ground, feeling a sharp and hard twinge in and around his heart as that muscle spasmed uncontrollably. The blaring sounds of the raging battle faded to almost nothing, and he could feel himself gasping for air as his consciousness slipped ever closer to the brink. In a last remaining instant, he thought of Elise and of his children. He was very vaguely aware of someone grabbing him as Michael took one last breath, *I'm sorry, Elise. I love*

Charles W. McDonald Jr.

you, Sweetheart.

*   *   *   *

Corporal Geoffrey Robins put down his MP5 rifle, pulling Michael to him, holding him close to his chest, "Please don't leave us, your Majesty. You have to stay with us. You have to." The Corporal paused, looking skyward praying aloud for Michael, "Please, if there's a God in Heaven, please bring him back." The bagpipes could barely be heard over all of the fury of gunfire and artillery, but one pipe could be heard over all the others, for it played at Michael's feet. James played his pipes somberly to the tune of *Battle on the Tyne.* He knew it to be one of the king's favorites. And, as the music played mournfully, Corporal Geoffrey Robins felt Michael's body begin to go limp in his arms, but he refused to let go. Instead, holding his beloved king even closer to his chest as he began to weep openly. Just as Michael Anthony Day took his last breath on Earth, the soft glow of Excalibur, visible through its gold scabbard, winked out of existence as Michael's lifeforce left his bloodied and broken body. "Oh, Dear God," Corporal Robbins beckoned the Creator as another of his tears fell upon Michael's blood-and-soot-laden face.

Charles W. McDonald Jr.

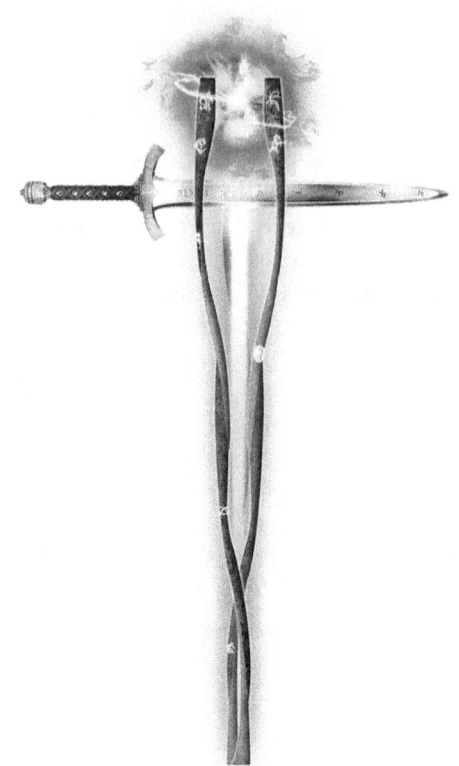

<u>Chapter 31: Six</u>

(Holden, Perion, Present Day)

Michelle, Lawna, Radin, Elise, Ykstherin, Kerrich, and Gareth all gathered in the Holden formal dining room where they had enough seating in the manor that Michelle and Lawna had taken as their own since their arrival. Lawna *still* did not look pleased. It had been hours since Michelle had told her and hours more getting the rest up to speed, but now it was all out in the open. Now, they could start to focus on what mattered…the next steps.

"So, have you thought about using his scroll," Michelle paused briefly, "his invitation…to go back to him now that you're armed with so much more knowledge? I mean, it might be useful to hear from him again. We still don't have any idea what he's planning. Only that what he's planning is significant enough to affect us all."

"It's a fair question, and yes, I have thought about it," Radin considered aloud, while sipping on his tea. "I have two major concerns about that. One, I don't want to abuse his invitation. Two, he was very explicit about not being a teacher or mentor to me, and I believe him when he says, 'that would be bad.'" Radin again sipped at his tea, letting his left hand rest on Elise's thigh comfortably. She had shared so much about her slain husband over the last few hours, bringing her to tears so many times her eye sockets were almost sunken, red and aged from the torment of her loss and the tears they invoked. Now, more than ever, he was convinced Elise was not ready to love again; regardless of her protests and what she told him of her feelings for him.

"Maybe it's enough to just have a conversation with him," Michelle reasoned. "From what you've described of him, he's not going to hurt you, and it's entirely possible he might even enjoy being in the company of the 'enemy' so long as you let him control the situation. Don't do anything brave or rash. Just have a conversation with him." She paused a minute, "...and maybe 'the enemy' thing isn't really accurate. Just because he isn't the nicest guy doesn't necessarily make him your enemy. You don't know until you build some trust between you—if that's possible."

"I'm not saying 'no' to the idea. I'm saying let's see if we can figure out what our next steps should be without Damon before we go down that path," Radin rebutted, trying to find his own internal compass of how to proceed.

That was probably the most reasonable thing said in the last several hours, Lawna thought, fidgeting with her dress, though wondering why she even bothered with the charade. She missed her jeans. Besides, Michelle had already broken every mission protocol already. *Why the continued need of her in a dress....*

Ykstherin cleared his throat, setting down his tea as he looked to Lawna and Michelle, offering with a flourish of his right hand, "Where you come from, you say this great battle has been raging for some time, right?"

"It would be a few years now," Lawna had been quiet until now, but she wasn't really the silent type. "Some call it World War III, but most call it what it really is," she paused looking to Michelle, "Armageddon. The Last Battle between good and evil. And the evil we speak of isn't Damon. At least not to my knowledge. It's an ancient evil that has lived on Earth for thousands of years."

"Hmmm," Ykstherin stroked his mustache in curls, "Last Battle indeed, and this was a prophecy?"

"Yes," Michelle answered flatly. "In virtually every religion on the planet. All recorded history from every corner of our world has commonality to it, describing a savior and an End Times prophecy, as well as many other common data points as well." Again, Michelle internally shrugged at her use of modern lexicon with a society thousands of years behind them, technologically speaking. If there had been a Prime Directive, she would have failed that class!

"Do you think your Armageddon has triggered ours?" It was an intellectual consideration probed by Ykstherin as he stroked his mustache, but a terrifying one as they deliberated the implications. "We have a legendary adventurer here goes by the name of Royvan Miral. My sources say he's found the Scroll of Carnac. That's supposed to be the First Seal, opened by the One, that starts our 'Armageddon.'"

"I think we're missing something. Something big." Radin was on to something, and he wasn't letting go. "Damon isn't interested in bringing about the End Times. I can promise you that. He wouldn't personally meddle with that."

"You've had one conversation with this man," Gareth had been quiet and just observing 'til now but he didn't understand how the young man could possibly know someone so complex and so ancient as Radin had described from just one conversation.

Using his natural *Telekinesis*, Radin stirred his tea with the small spoon Michelle had provided, causing everyone in the room to watch the spoon autonomously stir the liquid, occasionally tinging against the side of the fine teacup. Gareth especially continued to watch the spoon move via unseen forces as the conversation continued.

"I'm telling you, this man is no man," Radin emphasized. "He came across as a demigod. I think if he wanted to bring about the End Times, he could do it all by himself."

"Then I'm lost on next steps. I think the next step is to break the seal and talk to Damon again—carefully," Michelle proclaimed, while still watching Radin use his burgeoning *Telekinetic* powers, wondering what else he'd soon be capable of.

Radin nodded flatly. "So be it." Rising, he asked Michelle, "Can I use your bed?" Elise glared at him. "When I break the seal. I'm not sure if it's going to knock me out again or not. Last time my body stayed behind, and I have no idea what to expect."

"I didn't say anything," Elise feigned, but Radin knew better.

"Oh, but you did," Michelle retorted.

They really did behaved like sisters, Radin realized.

*   *   *   *

(South of Melshier, Perion, Present Day)

Nightfall had come to the quaint village of Mayel, several leagues south of Melshier—almost to the ancient lands of Saer—and no longer under the rule of Melshier's magistrate. She supposed she could have already been there by now, but it was so much more fun making Eldrac wait so he never quite knew where or when she might show herself. The cool night air felt blissfully naked and wondrous on her seductive, renewed flesh. *Strange*, she contemplated, *how she had taken to the simplest of pleasures since her freedom*. Whether the feel of the breeze caressing her silken thighs, the smell of the winter wheat fields that bent with the will of the wind or basking in the glow of the twin moons that set the stage for a night of games, she felt far more than just alive. When something—everything really—is taken from you so completely for so long and then returned in just as complete a fashion as was taken, there's really nothing to compare it to. She just had no frame of reference for the magnitude of her rebirth, but she knew it hadn't come without cost or expectation and that's what this night's games were about to unveil. Or at least, set in motion.

Xarn giggled like a giddy schoolgirl watching others pass by in their wagons and horses, looking back at her as if she were mad. She ran her fingers through her long, curly brown hair, savoring the sensations of the flesh. Her vibrant blue eyes and lush frame made her every man's dream, as did her soft red dress cut all the way up the outside of both legs. It would not have qualified as a dress for any decent woman—but that category did not befit her. *Just as well*, she thought. She was happy. And she was free.

No, Xarn found herself enjoying the smallest details in almost everything, from the horse dung that lined either side of the dirt road to the dew that bent each blade of grass this way or that. Mad? Perhaps. Free? Definitely. And this *Resha* would not change that if she had to put him to his death personally.

*   *   *   *

(Place of Defiling, Perion, Present Day)

Even as tall as it was, some twenty cubits in all, it blended into the sinister tree-line almost completely as its talons gripped the thousand-year-old tree to its right. With aged and weathered branch-like armor about its chest, head, and neck, its thick vine-like tail stabilized it for sitting comfortably as long as need be—and *that* could be a **very** long time. It had a job to do—

Charles W. McDonald Jr.

watching—observing the others prepare according to her instructions. She had been specific—both with the Six—and him, or *it,* depending on your point of view.

This place wasn't really on most maps, so to speak. But the locals—such as they were—knew never to enter this place in the Far Land of Golems where men came and never returned. Not ever the same as they went in anyway.

It was sure Anna knew she was being watched as she worked on accumulating her new comforts of the flesh, but that was to be expected so long as it didn't get in the way of her assignments. *Resha* may have been a big problem, but the Dark Knight of Magic was the far bigger one.

For certain, Anna would soon be about settling old scores, before she got to the long game she'd been explicitly ordered to deal with first. Her treachery had already been foreseen and prepared for.

Pensive, he, *it,* gripped the trunk of the ancient redwood harder, sinking its talons into the bark, into its flesh, like it would Anna if she failed her mission. A tuft of weathered moss against a backdrop of vine and branch moved ever so slightly—constituting a blink. It would observe Anna, and the others, as long as the great master required. Images of her scaled wings and venomous fangs fifty cubits tall permeated his, *its,* thoughts, causing another tuft of moss to move involuntarily.

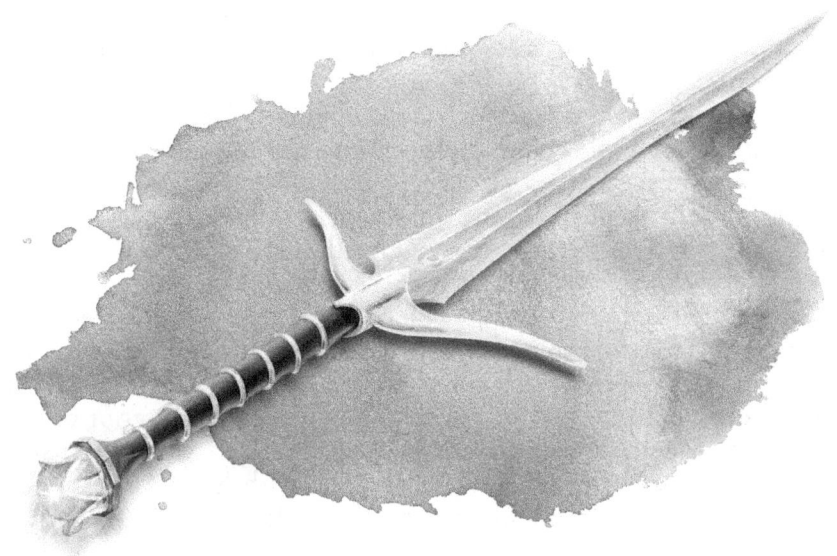

Chapter 32: The Right Question

(Damon's Manor, Kaleion, Present Day)

He found himself back in Damon's foyer. It appeared like there was a young maid up on a ladder, changing out something in the middle chandelier. As she came down off the ladder, approaching him, she was carrying something he didn't recognize—small, about one-fourth the size of her palm, white and clear with little crystal-like orbs inside it.

"Master Damon isn't here at the moment, but you're welcome to walk around until he arrives. Can I get you anything?" She was between cute and beautiful, maybe nineteen with red hair and forest green eyes. Her black and white serving outfit was not like anything he'd seen before, but it was evident to him that Damon had a weakness for women. He couldn't blame the man for that. Damon was a man—sort of.

"How many floors are there?"

"I'm not sure really. There are places I'm not allowed." She wanted to be helpful. He could see her struggling with not wanting to say anything that might cost her job or have an even worse penalty. "I've personally seen four levels up and two levels down, but I know there are more."

Charles W. McDonald Jr.

"I didn't get to see the fourth floor the first time I was here, so I'm going up there. Can you bring me some tea and something for Damon—whatever's his favorite?"

She beamed for him, curtsied as she appeared to admire either his face or his auburn hair or both before disappearing into the butler's kitchen to his immediate right, off the foyer.

Taking another look at the chandelier as he passed underneath on the way to the circular staircase, he wondered how the light was so smooth, bright, and steady. *And what was the purpose of the wire going up the middle of the chain into the center of the ceiling medallion?* He would have to ask Damon about that. Deciding to head straight to the fourth level, Radin ascended the circular main staircase where it terminated into a giant mural, which depicted a vast chamber carved out of what looked to be the interior of a mountain. In the mural, there were two man-sized niche's that had been shattered and some kind of center console made of stone with handprints—one larger looking to belong to a male and one smaller looking to belong to maybe a female or elf. There was even more detail, and he wanted to take it all in, but he wanted to see the rest of the floor first. Maybe by understanding where the man lived he could better understand the man himself. Left of the staircase was the largest indoor bathroom he'd ever seen and a double-door to a room that was closed. Carefully, he slid the pocket doors into their respective walls, revealing a huge, square room with a ceiling that tapered on the left where the roofline must have mandated. Large paintings on both the left and right walls, couldn't begin to take up even a small amount of the surface area still available. Strange silver spiders adorned the nightstands, dresser, and full-length wall mirror. There was something still very feminine about the room—it must have been the lavender and jasmine-based perfume in the air that gave it that feel. Nothing else gave away anything feminine. It was sparse, vast, and dark with a massive bed and only natural lighting. This was definitely *not* Damon's room.

Hands on the door pull, he noticed a subtle, naked room with no lighting opposite the huge bathroom. There were no doors inside, and it apparently went nowhere. *Hmmm*, he thought, making a mental note.

Closing the pocket doors, he went back the way he came passing the circular staircase, then passing another huge bedroom—this one long, rectangular, and very feminine. Live white roses, jasmine, lilies, and purple tulips populated many vases on the two nightstands and two dressers. There was a beautifully ornate staff of what looked to be dark-fired ash, twisted and gnarled, but elegant. Again, there was more of the smooth, bright, steady light, emanating from wall niches, trim, and ceiling fixtures. There was anoth-

Charles W. McDonald Jr.

er massive bed, but the décor, the sheets, the pillows, all screamed feminine. *Damon's weakness.*

A little further down the U-shaped hallway, as it started to make its first turn back toward what would have been the foyer below, brought another guest bedroom—this one much larger than most he'd seen on the floors below.

Moving ahead slowly, now right at the front of what would have been the foyer on the first floor, stood another set of pocket double-doors. Pulling them open, he took two steps back involuntarily. Huge black granite tile flooring laid on the diagonal with a symbol in the center of the floor that dominated the oval-shaped room—more like an oval with both its ends cut flat. The symbol an upright pentangle inside a pentagram, inside a pentagon, inside a circle. *Was this Damon's symbol? Or some ritualistic symbol?* Chalk marks with rune symbols inside Damon's symbol seemed almost ritualistic in nature. The walls looked much like the walls of the spell test room below—perhaps similar building materials and maybe it had to do with its proximity to the test room. He wasn't sure. An enormous balcony overseeing what must have been hundreds, if not thousands of acres of perfectly landscaped property beckoned through large sliding glass doors. A little fiddling with the strange collapsing lock, and he was able to push one sliding glass abreast the next, abreast the next, until the entire flat-side of the oval leading to the balcony was open to the outside—essentially making the oval room an indoor/outdoor experience.

Stepping out onto the balcony, leaning against cream-colored marble railing supported by ornately scrolled marble balusters, Radin just took a moment looking out across Damon's property, in awe. It appeared Damon's property was on a plateau or continental divide where the land had been pushed up for thousands of hectares in every direction as far as the eye could see. His eye was drawn above the horizon where only one of the twin moons was waxing. *Many worlds*, he contemplated, noting the difference in size and location of these twin moons versus those of his homeworld. A terrible racket came from just above and behind him where men were working on something on top of the roof. Perfectly uniform sheets of glossy, deep-blue material bordered by what looked like steel or some sort of silver, shiny metal sat atop the roof aimed at the apogee of the sun, while two men with some sort of tools in their hands worked. *More of those wires*, he pondered.

"I didn't expect to see you again so soon."

Radin tried not to flinch at Damon's interruption of his exploration... unsuccessfully so.

"Your tea, sir." The serving girl was standing beside Damon with two drinks—his tea and a tall glass with a lot of ice and what might have been a dark brown alcoholic drink from the smell.

Charles W. McDonald Jr.

Taking his tea so the very nervous girl could disappear, which she appeared all too anxious to do, Radin wondered how this conversation would go. He had to think on his feet around Damon and think very well! "So, the room with all the flowers in it, who was she?"

Damon nodded thoughtfully. Perhaps appreciating the curiosity. Perhaps enjoying the good memories that were...hard to come by these days. "That's Dallia's room."

"But Dallia's not with us anymore?" It was a hunch, but Damon was both sentimental and structured. He was sure of it. However ruthless and chaotic he appeared, there was a powerful logic at work with Damon.

"An Undead creature by the name of Chara killed her." Damon paused, remembering Dallia's beautiful features, her scent—her unconditional love for him. His brief time with Dallia, as short as it was in relation to his very long life since, flashed in front of his consciousness all too fast. And, in the wink of his mind's eye, it was gone, and all he could remember was her beautiful soul.

"And you took care of Chara." It wasn't a question. Though, the word *Undead* he'd have to come back to at some point.

"Oh, yes!" Damon smiled remembering even more fondly now how he'd exacted his revenge. "Completely!"

"Well then, Damon, you have *some* admirable qualities."

Almost coughing into his aged Kentucky bourbon, Damon wondered if Radin would feel the same way if he knew of Damon's testing of *Damnation*. Somehow, he doubted it.

"So, what are your thoughts on Armageddon?" It was the one question he had to ask Damon and ask in such a way so as not to invoke any mentor-student relationship. He knew they could never be equals, but he wanted to, as Michelle put it, just have an honest conversation. He believed Damon would appreciate that.

"Where did you hear that word?" Only somewhat surprised at his use of the word, Damon's mind was already working at top speed, wondering how many from Earth were interacting with the boy, and to what end. Would this disrupt, or aid, or accelerate his plans? He'd need to monitor this carefully.

"Oddly enough, they blamed their appearance on Perion on you."

Snorting, Damon was putting the pieces together already. This could work to his advantage. "Armageddon is supposedly the final battle between good and evil. Every world, where there's intelligent life, at least every one of them that I've been to, has a similar End Times prophecy—Earth included. It doesn't necessarily impact your world right now, but you never know. Prophecy has a funny way of forcing its way into our reality wherever we find ourselves. Perhaps that is more a reflection on us than on the prophecy itself....

Charles W. McDonald Jr.

Moreover, prophecy has a funny way of being both wrong and right in the most inconvenient ways imaginable."

"Agreed, and the Scroll of Carnac—the First Seal—**has** been found by Royvan Miral."

"It has." Damon nodded knowingly—neither challenging nor hiding, just a matter of fact. The boy had good advisors—good sources. He had a quick mind and would make a good student. For someone else....

"I know you're not the least bit interested in bringing about the End Times on my world." Just a matter of fact statement from Radin, but he was sure.

Nodding knowingly in admiration. This boy was impressive. "You're on the precipice of asking the right question."

"Very well then, here it goes," Radin paused, pivoting around Damon with his back now to the great ritual room. "Good and evil are far less relevant than agendas. And...I'm just trying to figure out if your agenda and mine are going to collide."

"THAT is the right question, Radin," Damon smiled, legitimately offering a level of pride for the young man.

"So, what is your agenda then?" There it was. As blunt as blunt gets. Damon *was* smiling until Radin asked that question.

"You're not powerful enough yet to keep that secret safe, and I don't know if you ever will be. If I could share that with you, I would. It would be helpful to know whether we overlap or not right now so I could act, but I don't think it's the right time. I'm not ready yet." Walking to the edge of marble railing, resting his left elbow as he looked out over his property, he looked back at Radin with respect. "I'm glad you came to visit. You don't disappoint."

Radin scratched his chin, not quite sure how to take that, or how to take Damon. How could he respect Damon in turn? He knew this man to be heinously evil—capable of vile things. But there was a legitimate appreciation for qualities they shared—integrity, transparency, loyalty, and a forthright nature. Not quite ready to be shown the door so to speak, Radin thought of more questions that might shine more light on Damon as a person. "So, tell me about the wires, the unusual candleless lighting, and whatever those things are," pointing at the men working on the panels atop the roof, Radin looked back to Damon walking back out onto the balcony with him as he sipped his tea.

"Well before I explain those, you need to understand electricity." Damon had promised not to teach, but there he was—teaching Radin about solar arrays, inverters, battery technology and the idiosyncrasies of AC/DC electrical current.

Charles W. McDonald Jr.

(Axum, Perion, Present Day)

The translucent, long, black negligée seductively moved about her long legs revealing a not so large, yet attractive, bosom here and there as she imperially sauntered around the stake. The silver-haired, silver-eyed old man watched as one of his ancient enemies pranced around him, gloating in the success of capturing him so quickly after her release. He had little will remaining with which to hang on. He knew she would kill him, and he just wanted her to get on with it. Anna was always the no-nonsense one of the bunch. That's what made her so much more dangerous than the others. She did not waste time with play, nor pleasantries. Anna, normally, got right to the killing. *So be it*, he thought as he looked up at the constellations overhead the Holy Grounds.

The tropical breeze coming off of the bay was welcome as it caressed Anna's long fiery-red hair. She never was one for the daytime, as evidenced by her milky white skin that sun never caressed. The night was always more her calling.

Anna had been very busy since being set free, and she already knew many more pieces to the puzzle than any of the others, if not all of them put together. She could see the board clearly and her role in it, as well as the role to be played by so many others. For that reason, the first of many impediments stood before her, tied to a stake on which he would soon burn.

Anna's smile was wicked, self-righteous, and oh-so arrogantly knowing as she picked up the unlit torch, kindling its brilliant fiery flame with her magic. "*Ahhh*," she exuded aloud. It felt so wonderful to cast again. It had been so very long for her since being condemned even before the others. The silver-haired man saw a cold fire dance in her ice blue eyes as she came ever nearer with the torch.

"Do you know why I've brought you here," she mocked quietly into his ear—her soft, full lips teasing his earlobe.

"Get on with it, Anna." The old man replied with finality, hoping for the end to come soon. For him, the games had already come to an end—an end he had not seen—but an end nonetheless.

Anna walked away from him, making one more lap around the stake as she panoramically viewed the landscape of the most sacred ground of Axum. Rolling brush and tall grass had long since overgrown the ring of the Nine, yet she knew precisely the location of the Rune Stones. It was a perfectly ironic site on which to take his life.

Charles W. McDonald Jr.

Even from here she could feel the power resonating from the Rune Stones. Anna turned back to the old man, tossing the torch at him. "So be it," she whispered to the coastal breeze.

The old man did not fear as the fire lit the dry brush at his feet, quickly spreading and lapping at his ankles. He could feel his clothes catch fire and knew his flesh would soon be next. Something inside told him to close his eyes and recall what it was that was in his heart—to forgive Anna. Opening his eyes with clarity of mind, the old man looked at his ancient enemy and smiled a smile of redemption, and of victory.

Anna marched closer to the stake, seeing the ropes and clothes burn while his flesh did not. She reeled backward in anger, pivoting away from his mocking smile. Anna concentrated, trying to maintain calm. Quickly she spun back towards the old man as she cast several of the most powerful spells in her deadly arsenal, even to the point of halting time so as to make several spells strike him at the same instant. Fire, acid, lightning, earth, and ice—enough to kill an army—all hurled toward the old man, striking in one instant. All for naught as the spells hit a wall of her own fire—buttressed by something she could not understand—surrounding him. The very flames that had threatened to take his life only moments before now shielded him from his ancient enemy.

Anna tilted her head, screaming at the night, and in a fit of rage rushed towards the old man, who did not even try to run now that his ropes were burned. Something, or someone, whispered to his inner thoughts telling him to stay, and stay he did. Even as Anna rushed toward him, picking up his sword—*Starfire*—along the way, it lit up the night sky as she screamed and swung it at him. Her face twisted with contempt as she ran him through, feeling the blade pierce his ribcage, then his heart, then cartilage as it struck the back of his ribcage before exiting out his back. In the instant she thought she had finally won, his mortal shell suddenly burst into seven white doves that quickly scattered to the crisp winds.

"NOOO," she screamed again at the constellations. Anna held *Starfire* high into the air and watched as *it* became too hot for her to hold. Letting it fall to the beach sand below where the tide would soon claim it, Anna stormed off and through the *Portal* she hastily invoked letting it violently twist and rip the air in her wake.

Charles W. McDonald Jr.

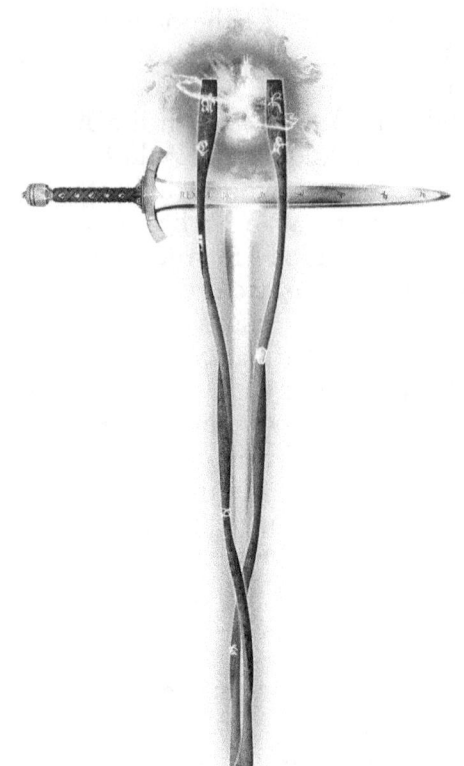

Chapter 33: The Long Game

(Holden, Perion, Present Day)

Breath leapt back into Radin's mortal coil as his immortal lifeforce crashed back down into his physical body, causing his chest to heave back to life. Moving back to his side, where she stroked his hair gently, Elise had wondered if she'd lost him. "Was this what it was like the last time?" Her question meant more for Ykstherin than for Radin.

"I'm afraid so. I suppose whenever he travels, via that method, his body goes into some sort of stasis while it waits for his lifeforce to return. This Damon is quite clever, and I've never seen magic quite like this before in my time. Nor have I ever read of such magic but that doesn't surprise me given his reputation."

Charles W. McDonald Jr.

"I'm fine, just help me up." Trying to get his legs to work and get himself to the edge of the bed where he could better sit up, Radin sought to recall as much detail as possible. "We should gather everyone so they can all hear this. Is everyone here at the house?"

"I set up some more comfortable chairs and a large sofa in the study," Michelle offered from her position standing in the doorway. "That should make for a more comfortable place to gather than the dining room. Why don't you bring him down there?" Pivoting away from Radin's room after visually examining Radin from the doorway, Michelle walked back downstairs to gather everyone.

*   *   *   *

The study had already proven more comfortable with its soft fabric akin to silk on large wing-back chairs atop beautiful large surface rugs and a warm fire. Radin wasn't sure how long he'd been out, and he hadn't asked, but it was mid-morning when he broke the seal, and it was well into the night now. Sleep would have to wait. It was imperative to get this all out of his head while it was fresh.

"So, as far as I can tell, I was right about the Armageddon thing. That's of little interest to him—at least our understanding of Armageddon intersecting with his plans. My view is that he sees that as an inevitability each on their own world at their own pace, but he didn't dismiss the idea outright that one may trigger another." Radin sipped his tea slowly. While apparently refreshing his body at Damon's manor had not done so for his real body here—he was both parched and famished. "I'm not sure if he means to use the chaos of such an event to aid him in his plans, or what his plans really even are at this point. He wouldn't tell me."

"You flat out asked him what his plans were? You were just supposed to have a friendly conversation, Radin." Michelle wasn't trying to berate him, but it came off that way.

"We did have a friendly conversation. We talked about Dallia, one of his loves. We talked about electricity, solar energy, physics, spacetime, magic, and a great many other things. We talked for hours, but yes, I was blunt with him about agendas, and the subject came up, so I asked him outright."

"What was his exact response to that question?" Lawna ever one for the minutia and the fine-grain details, but details mattered. The smallest mannerisms often shouted the loudest.

"I don't know if I recall the exact phrase he used, but it was something

like, 'You're not powerful enough yet, and you may never be, to keep that secret safe. I would love nothing more than to share that information with you
to understand where you stand, and then act upon that. However, I'm not
ready to commit yet.' That's not word for word, but you get the idea."

Looking to each other, apparently deep in thought, both Gareth and
Ykstherin got up almost simultaneously to have a private conversation just outside the study in the main foyer where old and familiar companionship could
dissect meaning in the light of like minds. Michelle, interjected right about
when they made it to the entrance, "You two both know there isn't a place
anywhere close by where Lawna or I couldn't hear every single word you're saying right?" It wasn't really a question, just a fact to save everyone some time.

Striding back into the study, Ykstherin cleared his throat, apparently
ready to speak for him and Gareth. "My concern, and Gareth's, is given everything he was willing to reveal, and the fact that he held back on that, leads
us only to guess at how broad the impact of his actions will be. I mean he's
apparently not the least bit concerned with the End Times." Ykstherin paused,
considering aloud, "Tell me, is he at all concerned about the End Times on his
homeworld or wherever he calls home now?"

"That's a fair question," Radin accepted. "…And I didn't ask, but my
guess would be no. I suppose he'd just build a new home somewhere else.
Damon is playing the long game, and I don't know exactly what that means
to him. I can tell you for right now, he's not our enemy, regardless of how vile
you may view him. But I would encourage you to look beyond his reputation
of ruthlessness. I feel Damon is a very misunderstood person. And that his
actions might be more just than you realize."

"That sounds a lot like you've come to like him." Elise only expressed
aloud what everyone else was thinking. Radin looked at each of them in turn
and could see in their eyes the very same concern.

"Damon is highly complicated. We share integrity, loyalty, and transparency, among other things, but I could never do many of the things he's already done without any compunction whatsoever. He's a monster, but not one
like any of us have ever seen before. He's unique. I'll give him that. Damon
cannot be painted in broad brush strokes of one color here and another color
there. He's nuanced. Textured."

"Do we have any better idea of what our next step might be? I mean
that was the whole purpose of the trip, right?" *Leave it to Michelle to facilitate
staying on point*, Lawna realized, smiling in appreciation.

"I know. I know," Radin chided then paused with his right hand raised
in recognition of what he hadn't done. He didn't have an answer, and that was
the entire point of the trip. "If it's safe for us to stay here overnight, I'd like to

Charles W. McDonald Jr.

get some food, some sleep, and just think about it."

"Don't think too long," *Okay, now Michelle was being crass*, Lawna kicked Michelle's shin as Michelle rose from the couch where she'd been sitting next to her.

The room dispersed. Kerrich, quiet throughout the entire meeting, just looked at his friend as if he no longer recognized him. Without saying a word, Kerrich turned to the foyer and walked straight out the front door in the middle of the night. Leaving only Elise to comfort Radin as she held him arm in arm while he tried to process his thoughts and his intense, wide-ranging conversation with Damon.

Part 6: Stones Cast into the Pond of Creation

Charles W. McDonald Jr.

Chapter 34: A Working Prototype

(Damon's Manor, Kaleion, Present Day)

amon worried about the structural integrity of the spell test room and its ability to withstand what he was about to attempt. This room, however thoughtfully architected, hadn't been designed for anything even close to this. If it were to structurally fail, during any of these tests, there might not be a manor anymore. *There might not be a planet anymore either.* His thoughts wandered to some of the scientists who worked on the Manhattan Project on Earth, where it was thought the chain reaction might not have a constraining end point and it had the potential to consume the entire planet in a runaway scenario. Not a comforting thought as he prepared the smallest possible test case. It needed to be a spell that didn't scale with his own power, that way he could isolate the incremental scale at-

tributable to the Zero-Point energy source field. Many combat spells scaled up with the mage's ability as they progressed in their profession and experience. He couldn't use a spell like that for this test case, otherwise, he wouldn't easily be able to tell what part of the scaling up came from his own power versus that of the Zero-Point field.

While Arcane derived its power from all living organisms, allowing one with the proper talent to channel Arcane into forms of matter or energy of one's choosing, it could not scale, or even operate, where there were no living organisms. That was going to become a very big problem he had to overcome for his Master Plan to work. Arcane was also limited where magic was dying, dead, forbidden, or obfuscated into the realms of disbelief. Many of the protective shields used to either keep magic out or keep someone from sourcing energy were dependent on solely the Arcane energy source. That produced many unfavorable possibilities and potential kinks in his Master Plan that must be properly addressed before the Master Plan could proceed much further. As a reliable, scalable energy source, Arcane just couldn't compare to Zero-Point or Dark Energy—especially in the possible ecosystems he might soon find himself. Future battlefields wouldn't lend themselves well to the limitations of the Arcane, living source field.

He needed a baseline—something small, something safe. Ensuring he closed the doors to the spell test room behind him with his *Telekinesis*, he produced a single glowing *Light Orb*, which exclusively used Arcane, about the size of his head. It slowly floated away from him, winking out of existence when it floated away to hit the far wall.

Rarely did Damon ever get nervous, but he was searching for the confidence now to continue this test. Thinking momentarily while he paused, *what other precautions should I take? Ah....* His black eyes sparkled, backlit in gold. Touching the closest test wall, he channeled *Damon's Improved Shield* into it, letting it scale normally with his immense power. An instant later, channeling, he put up the same protections upon himself.

Seemingly satisfied now, he focused on the task in front of him. With his left hand sourcing the Zero-Point field he could sense closest to him, he slowly allowed it to scale up to the area surrounding him, then this room, then his manor, and then the manor grounds, but not allowing to go *beyond that*. It was as if he could sense his energetic self almost inside the toroidal field of energy he now accumulated into his left hand. With his right hand, he attempted to use Arcane to describe, shape, and control the energy he wanted to form in front of him. Thinking only of the *Light Orb,* he opened his left hand and channeled the Zero-Point source field into his right.... *Blindness!*

Charles W. McDonald Jr.

*   *   *   *

(About a half-hour later....)

His eyelids felt stuck shut as something pecked at his face. *Was that a bird? Where am I?* It took way more effort than it should, but he managed to eke out a tiny bit of vision out of his left eye where he was barely able to separate his eyelid. *Why am I outside*, he wondered, looking at the big yellow ball in the sky that was the sun. A bit more effort and his left eye was fully open— his right not so much. Damon touched his right eye. It was caked with blood, so he forced it open. *Not good*, he judged, looking around, trying to get his bearings. *Man, it's hot.* He could see his manor way off in the distance. Rough guess, he might have been a mile to a mile-and-a-half away, and he saw what looked like trenches in his well-kept grass where he could only assume his body had been skidding to a stop.

Getting up wasn't easy. Painful was more like it. It felt like his left leg was broken, but he'd been injured much worse before. *Only, not from a Light Orb spell.* Starting the long walk back to the manor, he actually had to concentrate on putting one foot in front of the other as his physical body groaned at the difficulty of it, sending sharp shockwaves of pain throughout his nervous system each time his broken leg made contact with the Kaleion crust of his manor's grounds.

"Shit," walking on one good leg took a bit of time, but he could already see the damage to the front of his manor, and it was **extensive**. Examining the ten-foot by twelve-foot, rough-edged cavity right about where the third floor would be, he could see pieces of his robes, flesh, and blood, all over the opening he'd blown in his manor. Looking around the grounds, he found one of the double-doors, then the other about one hundred feet away blown in opposite directions from one another. He couldn't quite make out the condition of the spell test room, but it looked like his manor was now tilting. "Shit!"

Inside, it was worse. *No power*, he considered, looking at the dead chandeliers hanging askew from a ripped ceiling with jagged cracks that now ran from one corner to the next—their individual ceiling medallions partially hanging from the ceiling in broken plaster. *Can't be good.* The second-floor grand library had been blown downward into the foyer. Hundreds of books lay everywhere in thousands of pieces all over the floor, ceiling, stairway, butler's kitchen, and main kitchen. Pretty much everywhere he looked was wrecked!

He had to use the staircase railing to help himself up the circular staircase. At least it didn't appear blocked, so far. He bypassed the second floor, heading straight to the third and fourth where he had things he really ***did*** care about—things it had taken him many lifetimes to acquire. Stepping into the third-floor hallway, or what was left of it, it looked as if the walls, ceiling, and floor of the spell test room had swollen like the walls of a balloon bursting all the way through here and there. Interior construction materials of the spell test room could be found throughout the U-shaped hallway, and parts of the fourth floor were visible from where he now stood on the third floor, directly in between the great hole that he'd blown in the front of his manor and what used to be the entrance of the spell test room. He examined the gaping hole in the front of his manor first, nodding. *Impressive, Day. Good job!* He didn't need to examine his body to know the pieces of flesh on the wall were his. *Might need Kellen's help again*, he thought. Turning to the spell test room where it appeared the right side of the room had exploded downward with slightly more force than the left. *Hmmm, I was trying to control it with my right hand, and I was standing just right of center in the room.* That was telling.

Heading back to the staircase, "Let's go see what else you fucked up," cursing himself aloud as he headed up to the fourth floor.

"Wow!" That was really the only word for it. Dallia's room and Evanyil's room survived the blast pretty well, but his ritual room did not. From here he could see down into the spell test room, library, and even down into the foyer on the first floor. Black granite flooring from the ritual room had been blown outward through the ritual room ceiling, through the roof. "So much for the new solar panels." Damon just shook his head at his incompetence. But as he looked outside, through the hundred-foot-diameter hole he'd blown in his roof, something was off about the time of day. Then he remembered, it had just turned nightfall when he began his test. "No *fucking* way," he realized aloud as reality slammed home, looking up into the sky at the sun that was not a sun at all. He estimated his *Light Orb* to be about twenty miles up by now, bright enough to light up about a third of his homeworld when it should have been the dead of night. He wasn't sure if that qualified for a working prototype or not, but it was certainly going to draw some unwanted attention.

*   *   *   *

The odor from the burning entrails in his open brazier perfumed Kellen's robes in a most foul way; it was still discernible as he stepped through a hastily formed *Portal* to Damon's manor. Damon had lost his mind this time! He was going to get them both killed—or worse!

Kellen the Destroyer's *Portal* hissed to a close that whipped little shards

Charles W. McDonald Jr.

of electrical current all over the remnants of Damon's spell test room floor where they announced his mighty presence in their hot and sharded crackle of the *Light-Orb*-warmed air.

"Hey, Damon." That was bad…when Kellen used his full name. Kellen scratched the stubble on his face in deliberation as his eyes looked around while his torso turned more directly toward Damon. "So, I was working on finding out some information for us. You know burning the midnight oil and stuff—so to speak, and out of the corner of my eye, I notice the sunrise in the FUCKING MIDDLE OF THE NIGHT!" Placing—no, slapping really—his right hand on Damon's left collar bone where pieces of flesh had been sheared away enough to expose bloodied bone, causing Damon to wince, Kellen wanted—*no, Kellen deserved*—some answers. "So, what's up, Ra?"

Kellen's reference to the Egyptian Pantheon Sun God 'Ra' hadn't gone unnoticed, and in fact made Damon smile even though his body seared with pain.

"Part of my Master Plan," Damon quipped, seemingly impressed with his own feat of harnessing the seemingly impossible.

"THIS," Kellen pointed up through the hole in Damon's roof to the new star Damon had unintentionally created, while nearly hopping as his hand stretched outward to the sky, "THIS IS PART OF YOUR MASTER PLAN?!!" Looking around at the devastation Damon had wrought on his manor, Kellen nodded in satisfaction. "You need to *fire* your interior decorator by the way."

"Believe it or not, I **did** take precautions."

"Oh, THIS is YOU taking precautions?!!!" Motioning around to the rubble of what remained of Damon's manor, it took effort for Kellen not to jump up and down, he was so mad.

Just shaking his head in indignation, Damon didn't know what to say, but this was bad!

"I mean, WHAT?" Kellen paused, thinking about the power it must have taken to do all this, far beyond anything he'd ever channeled before and knowing how much more experienced he was than Damon, it made Kellen legitimately nervous, nearly terrified. "HOW?!"

"Let me get the bugs worked out, and then I'll show you. This was my first prototype."

"Geez, Day. I mean…." Thinking about the long game, Kellen was worried. "This is going to draw the WRONG kind of attention."

"Oh yes, I'm fully aware."

"So, what else is part of your Master Plan?"

"Well, beyond repairing my home, I need to build a new test facility designed to handle this kind of energy."

Charles W. McDonald Jr.

"Somewhere not on our homeworld!" It wasn't a request from Kellen.

"Somewhere not on our homeworld," Damon agreed.

Still shaking his head back and forth, Kellen was still in awe. Damon's Star had to be five miles across—at least! "I gotta tell you Day when you fail, you don't fuck around!"

Damon laughed, "Yeoooow...." Wincing again in horrific pain that shot from his head to his toes enough to make them curl.

"I mean THAT," Kellen pointing at what he would forever recall as 'Damon's Star,' "is the very definition of the phrase 'Epic Fail!'"

"Could you help me out a little please?" Trying to point to his wounds but stopping because it was too painful to point.

Damon didn't deserve *Healing*, but then again, Damon didn't deserve a lot of things. Placing both hands on his friend's shoulder, Kellen concentrated as bones began popping and wounds closing up before their eyes.

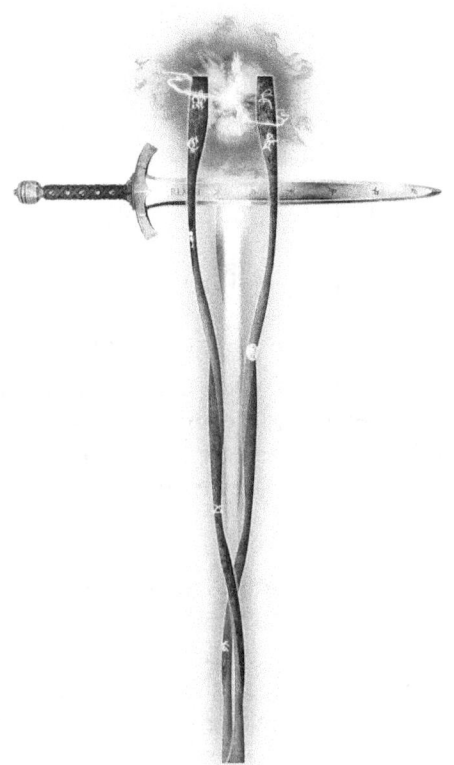

Chapter 35: Damon's Star

(Damon's Manor, Kaleion, Present Day)

It was going to cost a fortune to rebuild his manor, but Damon didn't care. It had extreme sentimental value, and as long as he lived, he wanted to live *here*. Everywhere, dozens of construction workers furiously worked day and day—since there was no longer a night anymore—still hauling off broken rubble and debris some thirty-six hours after "The Incident" as it was being called locally. Oddly enough, it was the electricity he missed the most. After having gone so much of his life without it, *who'd have thought*. Down in sub-level four, he was staring at the cavern ceiling Dallia had carved out with her magic so long ago, trying to assess the damage to the foundation. He knew it would take magic to repair a significant part of what he'd accidentally destroyed. The manor had many sections

Charles W. McDonald Jr.

that had been built with magic, and it would have to be rebuilt with magic. "At least I've got the ability to build it better than it was before," he considered aloud. It was true, but he still wished it hadn't happened.

"So, they've already taken to calling it 'Damon's Star.'" He never got used to the way Illirian could just slip in and out without getting noticed, but all of his warning systems were down right now. Practically anyone could sneak up on him. He would have to do something about that while his systems were being restored.

Pivoting to Illirian, Damon replied, smiling, "That has a proper ring to it."

"So, how long do you think it will…? Well, you know." She pointed only her right index finger skyward, even though they were nearly at the bottom of Dallia's subterranean expansion of his manor.

"Honestly, I don't know. I expected it to burn out by now."

"Why not just build a giant strobe light or a spotlight and shine it on your house?"

"Ha-ha."

"So, should I even ask how you managed to do that?"

"Oh, you can *ask*…." Damon's smile was as smug as he could manage through the pain. Kellen's *Healing* hadn't fixed everything—not even close really. The damage to his body was nearly as extensive as the damage to his manor. Apparently, there was internal bleeding, and he was still trying to fix it himself with what power he could manage but *Healing* just wasn't his specialty—especially self-*Healing*.

"You won't even share with me?" Illirian sauntered over to him, laying her right hand on his chest as she leaned into him, tenderly caressing his lips with hers as her sexy jasmine scent perfumed his nostrils. He could feel her *Healing* magic flowing through him, making his whole body hum from the tips of his toes to the edges of his black bangs.

"Thank you." Damon paused, looking into Illirian's beautiful eyes. "I'm legitimately afraid of this power. That's why I'm not sharing it yet. It's an order of magnitude more powerful than any of us could even imagine. So, you'll just have to forgive my secrecy for now. I mean look what I did by accident."

"Fair enough," she paused, putting some distance between them, pivoting away, "…but when you understand it better and can control it better, you'll come see me right?" *Was Damon afraid?* A terrifying consideration that took conscious control to keep her from shivering.

"Count on it."

In all her experience, Damon was always good for his word. If he gave you a promise, it was as good as done, so she accepted that. Still, Damon's

Star had made her very nervous, and she wasn't the only one.

While still an independent operator, she had responsibilities to the Council, both Councils she sat on, actually. And, both Councils wanted answers. What had Damon done? How did he do it? And, most important, what are his plans with this new power source? Illirian felt trapped between her adoration of Damon, her hopes for his future, and her assurances for her own. Those assurances came at a cost, and if spying on Damon served dual purposes, then so be it. She would spy and meddle in Damon's business with or without the Council's demands for intelligence, but she hated owing the Council. It was far better for everyone if they didn't know some of what Damon was doing.

"Damon?"

"Yes," he smiled for her beautiful red-gold hair that gleamed in the soft glow of his *Light Orbs* meant to help him see the foundation issues.

"How do I fit into your plans?" That was a bold, but inaccurate question and she knew it. "How do we…," she self-corrected her question.

Damon's mouth twisted, not in a bad way—more like in a thought-filled way. Punting that one back at her, he countered, "When you figure that out, will you tell me?"

"Count on it," she smiled, kissing him unlike before in the void where it was building towards sex. This kiss was more like a *don't forget about me* kiss.

Whatever Damon was doing, whatever his plan, she did trust that she fit into that plan. Somewhere. That made her reports to both Councils complicated at best, complicit at worst. She just hoped that if it leaned towards the worst, she'd have some level of plausible deniability to fall back on. It was dangerous, circling this close to Damon's Star—in all its meanings. Her personal stakes couldn't be any higher if his Master Plan did more damage than she planned or set expectations to accommodate across all timelines where she operated.

Breaking the kiss delicately, sensing his emotions and his thoughts of her, Illirian disappeared before him without a flash or sound or theatrics of any kind.

*   *   *   *

A few hours later and now back at ground level, Damon walked outside to check on Damon's Star. It was nightfall, or trying to be, but there it was, settled in around twenty-five miles high, captured in orbit by his home-world, unable to achieve escape velocity. It wasn't quite full daylight outside, but it was more than enough light to keep the construction workers busy non-stop round the clock. At least his manor would get repaired sooner. Just shaking his head, he tried to understand what had gone wrong during the channeling process.

Thinking about how he would control this new power, if it were possible, he wondered if it was even possible to safely test it again. He had to find a way to test it, or he could never use it for what he'd intended. *That would be insanity!* Thinking back to how he'd built the floors, walls, ceiling, and doors for the spell test room, he tried to think of a way to apply that process to create something suitable and nearly indestructible to control this immense toroidal field energy source that rose from just a seemingly small potential.

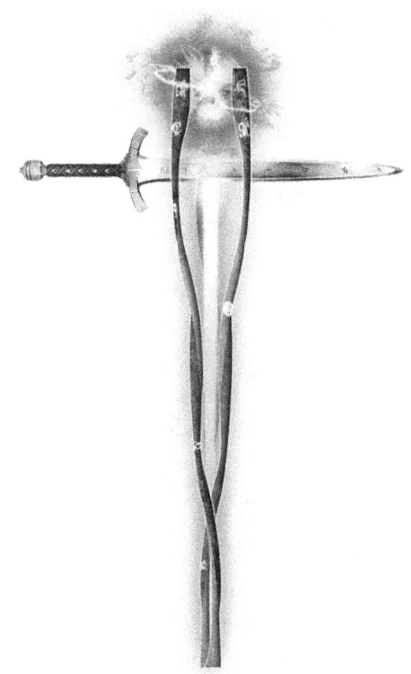

Chapter 36: Baby Steps

(Holden, Perion, Present Day)

Elise caressed Radin's face and forehead, kissing his neck. She wasn't trying to seduce him. They had just finished another round of sex. There was so much about him that reminded her of her husband, yet the more time she spent with him, the more convinced she became that she'd never see her Michael ever again. She didn't know if that was due to Damon's irreparable influence on him or not. Either way, she detested Damon and tried with all her charms to prevent Radin from being influenced by that man—*that thing*—any further.

"Talk to me," she whispered in his ear, laying her head on his chest while they lay in bed together.

"About what?"

"Anything. Surely, there's something going on in that head of yours. You never shut off your thoughts. Your mind is always churning for some reason. I just want to know what it's churning on."

Charles W. McDonald Jr.

Page 292 of A Kingdom Forgotten

"You, us, Damon, this impossible situation we find ourselves in.... Where do I begin?"

"With us, you dolt," she chided, playfully slapping his chest hair.

"Right...." *You should have known better.* "I think we communicate well with each other physically, emotionally, and intellectually. I miss you when I'm not with you, and it's hard not to think about you. But...."

"No. No buts.... You were doing perfect until the 'but.'" She sounded pouty, but she wasn't trying to be.

"Why did you come here, Elise? Where do you really belong?"

She hated his intellect at times. How quickly he'd flipped the emotional leverage back onto her.

Waiting on her response, Radin practiced controlling two of Lawna's borrowed daggers with his *Telekinesis*, making them spin on end, then throwing them against the door to his room, stopping them just shy of penetrating the wood. His smile indicated a level of satisfaction at the practice result. *You're going to have to get a lot better than that*, he thought, still waiting for Elise's reply. *Baby steps.*

He was really only beginning to understand where the power was coming from—both the Arcane and his natural abilities. Damon talked a lot about Arcane and the energy it flowed from, but it was going to take lots of time and practice. He wanted to practice his swordsmanship, but the room wasn't big enough for all that movement, and he didn't want the attention that came with leaving his room right now. Everyone would be asking for next steps. Since when did he become the leader of *this*...? Whatever *this* was. Practically all of them were far more experienced than he.

"That's it." A sudden epiphany hit him just as a knock at the door got him scrambling out of bed to put on pants as Lawna's blades dropped to the floor, sticking into the wood floorboards.

Flinging open the door, Radin noticed Kerrich just outside, standing watch.

"What's up," Kerrich asked, looking between Radin and Elise.

His timing always just a little bit off, Radin considered, wondering what unspoken and unresolved stuff was going on between Kerrich and Elise. "Let's let Elise sleep," Radin deflected. While not quite a lie, he wasn't ready to face the truth of Elise's answers anyway. "If Michelle and Ykstherin are awake, I'd like to talk to them."

"Okay...," Kerrich countered, not really understanding why he was being left out, but not really questioning either, he strode down the hall to Michelle's room.

Only a moment later, Michelle came out wearing a white bathrobe, which she was still wrapping around her nude body as she walked down the hall toward him. Radin didn't exactly look away but didn't gawk either. Michelle didn't appear to be the 'shy' type. More the smash-your-face-in-until-she-got-the-answers-she-wanted type.

"What's up," Michelle asked, still approaching with her bare feet stone cold silent on the floorboards.

"Next steps," Radin replied flatly, looking down the other hall to see Ykstherin now walking toward them and the staircase between them. "Let's go downstairs," he suggested with Michelle in tow.

*   *   *   *

Moments later, in the study, Radin offered, "I think our next step should be to get me to someone that can help mentor my skills." He paused, "I mean, if we're right, I barely understand this very powerful thing I'm wielding like a toy." Radin spun Lawna's dagger around on the tip of its blade in mid-air, using his thoughts to drive it into the executive desk on the far side of the study. "I mean, I'm seeing things in my sleep, and even while I'm awake. Things I don't understand."

"May I show you something?" Ykstherin made a motion in the air with his index finger, drawing a symbol similar to the one Damon showed him during his first visit. "Do you ever see any of these symbols?"

℘ℰℵℜℑ

"This one," he drew it alone in the air, leaving a burning gold symbol at eye level that looked like a snake that had crossed its tail and curled its head, almost making the letter P—as it appeared to Michelle. The symbol danced to and fro in mid-air right in front of Radin, causing his temple to throb as it had in Damon's spell test room. "This is the symbol to draw the energy you need to channel from a power source. It's also the initial step to form the energy into its intended final state." Sourcing was always such an important part of the whole process of magic, it really required more explanation than what he was giving Radin, regardless of how bright he felt the boy was. "Perhaps a little more explanation is required. When sourcing energy for transformation in magic, we pull from the energy of all living things—people, animal, plant life, etc."

"This," Ykstherin pulled the second symbol, resembling the letter E to

Michelle, from the group of symbols, putting it in front of Radin, now at eye level as it danced to and fro before him. "…is the symbol for aggregating and final intended form."

The pain was growing sharper and more acute in Radin's mind, so much so he visibly had to place his left hand over his temple, shielding his vision from looking directly at the two symbols now dancing in mid-air before him.

"I think we should stop," Michelle voiced her concern, placing her right hand on Radin's left shoulder supportively.

Straightening, trying to control the pain, Radin looked directly at the symbols. "Keep going."

"Very well then," Ykstherin had to admire Radin's courage, even if he didn't agree. He hadn't seen such a reaction like Radin's in his lifetime. Either it would sear him alive, or he'd be able to draw more than any he'd ever seen. He pulled the third symbol from the group upward, right in front of Radin, like he had the others, this one resembling the letter N to Michelle, "This is the symbol to create."

Keeping his eyes on Radin, waiting to see when it would be too much, Ykstherin noticed beads of sweat forming on Radin's brow, but Radin didn't shield his face nor look away. Pulling the fourth fundamental rune from the group of five before Radin, Ykstherin instructed, "This is the symbol to destroy."

Again, Radin winced in pain as his mind felt on fire, but he kept his hands at his side, looking directly into each symbol, in turn, allowing them to sear into his mind. Pulling the fifth rune from the group before Radin, Ykstherin explained, "And this is the symbol for defining and delivering to the target." Ykstherin paused, delivering the bad news, "These are but five of hundreds of known symbols. There are more specialties than one can count, and each specialty brings with it new symbols, new fundamentals, new techniques, and new consequences of misuse. What I've shown you are only the most basic building blocks—the first in a series of baby steps."

It was hard to smile through the intense pain coursing through his mind's eye right now, but a smile Radin managed nonetheless. "Funny you should use those words. That was a good start. Can you show me how to begin practicing with them safely, so I don't accidentally destroy something?"

"Yeah, let's be careful with *what* and *who* we destroy—that's a good plan," Michelle quipped with a smile, trying to mask her legitimate concern by what she'd seen already from the young man. *He was dangerous!*

"My boy, I'd love nothing more than to teach you, but I'm not the right choice."

Charles W. M\^cDonald Jr.

"Oh please, don't be the second person already to refuse to teach me. Am I really so bad that no one wants to mentor me?"

"It's not that, Radin, and I would be honored to teach you, but from what you've explained about Damon, we have to consider the possibilities of having to go into combat with him at one point or another."

"No, we can't…." Waving his hands, Radin vehemently protested. "He could destroy us all with barely a thought."

"Perhaps, but my point, my dear boy, is that I believe we need a teacher for you that is a specialist in combative use—a Forkettè. That's not me—not even close. It's probably my weakest capability. Better for you to learn the right way the first time, rather than having to unlearn poor technique." Smiling and facing Radin with both hands on his shoulders, Ykstherin looked him right in the eyes, seeing the reflection of the symbols he'd drawn in Radin's eyes, "Don't you think it's best we prepare for the worst?"

"Got anyone in mind," Michelle prodded, looking into Radin's eyes that now sparkled and blazed, backlit in gold.

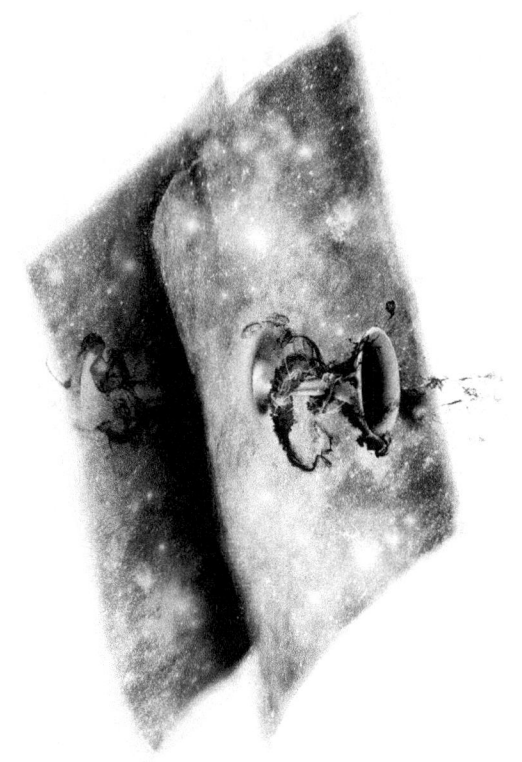

Chapter 37: A Suitable Test Site

(University of Texas at Austin, Robert Lee Memorial Hall, Earth, Mid-day, Present Day)

ed Zeppelin's Battle of Evermore blared through Damon's earbuds as he sang along, correcting the living legend—Robert Plant—along the way, "...with flames from the *Dragon of Darkness*, the sunlight blinds *her* eyes." Tapping away at his laptop with long fingers more dexterous for piano or casting but still nimble on the awkward little keypad nonetheless. He'd been researching results from the Kepler telescope for more than two days straight, hoping repairs on his manor were going to according to plan. He didn't have time to deal with that problem right now. He had to perform multiple large tasks asynchronously, hoping aces-in-their-places methodology would get each job done right. His attention had to be focused

Charles W. McDonald Jr.

on finding a suitable test site for the next phase of testing, though still in Phase I of his Master Plan. Ultimately, he wanted the remodeled spell test room to be robust enough to handle limited Zero-Point energy usage, but that would take too long. The longer he took to prepare, the more likely the details of his plans would become known—especially now with the attention from Damon's Star in orbit around his homeworld. It still hadn't burned out as of a couple of days ago, and he had no idea when it would eventually burn itself out. This power he was messing with was dangerous, unproven, and incredibly unpredictable. The toroidal field itself was more stable than that. It was his usage and method of access of it that was unstable, and he needed to understand why that was the case.

Looking through the Kepler findings, he'd already found several possibilities. He was looking for a planetary object that did not cause a wobble in the star and only passed once in the last five years causing light from the star to dim—the Transit Technique/Method. He was searching for a runaway planet—also known as a rogue planet, or Planet-X. A world that had time to develop a civilization, that had proven to be suitable for life at one time but had either been pulled from its orbit or blown from it, leaving the planetary object itself intact. Even though the Transit Technique was part of how he'd find his Planet-X, the way he was running his search patterns ran against the grain of Kepler's normal search parameters, but Kepler found many things not within its standard search parameters if you knew where to look—and how.

Tapping his Android to the next song in the playlist, it had already cycled through Alter Bridge, Black Sabbath, Elvis Presley, Seether, and Volbeat, but he required something more thought-provoking in a stellar manner now. *Rage Against the Machine's Renegades of Funk*, he appreciated, smiling. Dressed in Levi's® 501s and a solid cobalt-blue, button-down collared shirt—Damon was tapping his soft brown shoes as he tapped the keys on his laptop sifting through kepler.nasa.gov.

It was hard, very hard, not to notice the likely sophomore, busty brunette walking into the fifteenth-floor study hall where he now worked. One of the few students here that didn't wear that gawdawful burnt-orange. Working a tight, white miniskirt, with a hem that hit thigh high, and a tight, gold, button-down blouse complementing her cleavage and her bright sapphire eyes, she would have gleefully tormented any male classmates. She might have been 5'9" in her three-inch heels. *She's not here to study*, Damon surmised.

"Hi," extending his hand before she'd started the process of picking a place to sit. "I'm Damon." He rose from his chair to greet her, allowing his earbuds to fall out, as his nose caught a solid whiff of her sweet perfume that already followed her into the classroom.

Charles W. McDonald Jr.

"Mira," extending her hand to shake his, quite accustomed to the jaw drop he just gave her. *He's hot. You'd think he'd have more confidence than that,* she wondered.

Thrown completely off balance, Damon had to force his jaw shut. *Good job!* "Ummm, that's a beautiful name."

"Is it?" She flirted, lifting her right leg just a bit to twist her heel playfully, intentionally setting her books down in the row behind Damon as if to make a point.

"Sorry, that name just took me off guard a bit."

"Old girlfriend," Mira asked.

"Yeah, you could say that."

"Was it a bad breakup?" She was a little disappointed in herself for her haughty tone. It wasn't like her to come off like that, but she'd seen his kind of reaction before.

"No, she died." Involuntarily looking down at his shoes in remembrance, Damon tried not to let his past get in the way of his future.

There it was. Something in those black eyes of his. As beautiful and chiseled as he was, something was severely off. Maybe it was something in his hard features or cultureless accent and aura. A man of many places and of none. He was dangerous. *Was that how she died?* She considered leaving— immediately.

"Sorry, I was just about finished here...." he wanted to defuse the situation, but he didn't really want to leave her. "I can give you the room."

She paused, visibly. She thought he could tell that might be best—his leaving. "No, you're fine. Stay." Moving her books to his row, she moved to sit down beside him. "What are you listening to?"

"*Rage Against the Machine*, and a little bit of everything," pushing his Android over to her so she could flip through his playlist.

A couple of flips of the touchscreen, taking note of *Foreigner, Pink Floyd, AC/DC, Audioslave, Alter Bridge, Velvet Revolver, The Black Crowes....* Okay, she'd seen enough, pushing the phone back to him. "SAWEET JESUS! How **old** are you?"

Chuckling, Damon, recovered his phone with his left hand, "Ha-ha...." Giving her a playful wink, "Just because I appreciate the classics doesn't make me THAT old."

"Mhmm." She handed over her iPhone letting him flip through hers.

A couple of flips later, taking note of *Taylor Swift, Adelle, Zayn, Rihanna, P!nk, Carrie Underwood, Kelly Clarkson, Christina Aguilera*, and dozens of other artists he'd never heard of before. Oh well, he was kinda late to the game when it came to Earth music. "That's about what I expected."

Charles W. McDonald Jr.

"Hey!" *Asshole.* But he was gorgeous. *Why do all the hot ones have to be assholes?* "I've seen you around a couple of times, and don't tell me you're a sophomore."

"Hardly," smiling, he was trying not to let her name take him too off-guard. He could envision…. No, he didn't even want to think that. "Post-grad."

"Kepler—that's kind of cool. Looking for a new world compatible for colonization?"

Damon coughed into his right hand now balled up. *Damn, that was a pretty good guess.* Closing the lid of his laptop, "Not important."

Furrowing a brow at him and his secrecy. "Okay, Mr. Secret."

"Look, I've gotta run," punching in a number on his phone, causing her phone to ring, he winked at her with those black eyes of his that tended to intimidate, awe, and fascinate all simultaneously.

"Hey," she protested, "I didn't give you permission to take down my number. And how'd you do that without me noticing anyway?"

"Relax, you've got my number so you can call me." Cupping her beautiful face in his hands as he began to rise again, he kissed her. Taking his time as he worked her tongue softly with his, tenderly caressing her face with the backs of his fingertips as she began kissing him back almost involuntarily, feeling a coursing warmth quicky surging and rushing up her beautiful cheeks and neck.

And then, as suddenly as it had begun, he'd stopped—pulling away from her touch and her soft and sensual kiss to turn his body away as if he was seriously going to leave her. She could still smell and taste him on her lips, and it wasn't…. "HEY! You can't just leave me after that," Mira protested, incredulous at him actually leaving **her**.

Damon cleared the room for her, walking out without saying another word and without looking back at her. He had a suitable test site to check out.

*   *   *   *

The first bathroom had been far too busy—class had just let out. This was now his third—hoping to find enough seclusion and room to cast. Looking around, kicking open the stall doors just to be certain, Damon cast *Distorting Web* to encapsulate some environment to take with him, as he focused on the map coordinates from Kepler. Somewhat surprised that *Distorting Web* had even worked here, given how powerful a spell that was, Damon considered how dead magic really was here on this world. *Perhaps his being here and casting more and more frequently was having an impact on that.* Superheated air in front of him split in two, bordered by silvery-blue flashes of light licking outwardly, as Damon walked through the *Portal, Distorting Web* and all.

Now standing on a rogue world, about twice the size of Earth, he could immediately feel the gravitational difference, but it didn't bother him nearly as much as the view. Ruins of metal for as far as the eye could see—it had been a civilization at one time but with construction like nothing he'd ever seen before. His homeworld had a beautiful architecture that could best be described with sweeping gothic styles—not everywhere on his homeworld of course, but a good amount of the design could fit into that style. Perion had a wide range of styles mostly influenced by nature, muscular influences of horse and beast, airy influences of bird and dragon, earthly influences of mountain and reed, and oceanic influences of frothy sea caps and whirlpools. This was like unto none of that. Piercing sharp-edged metal buildings reaching to the sky, succumbing to some cataclysmic event that cast the planet from its stellar orbit. There were no windows he could discern, but diamond-shaped portions of the metal appeared almost translucent even now after the cataclysm had stricken. *Perhaps a civilization more advanced than Earth*, Damon considered, surveying the horizon. It literally had the appearance of standing on the edge of the world, with no atmosphere, no magnetic shield, no solar radiation to hinder his view into the abyss of space. Standing in the Void was the closest experience to this he could recall in all his travels.

Exploring a bit, having to use magic to move from one ancient city to the next, he searched for bones, or records, or anything that would describe the civilization that once thrived here. He needed to see what it had been to have a good idea of what it could become. Now on the other side of the world, he could see what might have been the rogue world's home star. Dim, and farther away than Jupiter was to Earth's star, he didn't know exactly how long ago this world had dislodged from its stellar orbit, but he estimated maybe a couple of years from Kepler's data.

Damon's specialty had always been much better suited for destruction than creation so he couldn't be certain what might come of his experiment— this part of his Master Plan. He needed to get back to the other side of the planet, away from the star-side where he currently stood. Taking his environment shell with him as he stepped through the *Portal*, Damon cast *Damon's Improved Foresight*, searching for the closest large celestial body objects that needed to be either moved or dealt with, to make the next part of his tests successful.

Making note of two planetoids that could interfere, Damon used $\wp$ and ξ to draw, aggregate, and direct. Touching the Zero-Point field of the planet itself from ground level up to about thirty miles, Damon attempted to aggregate enough power to move worlds. Suddenly, the *Distorting Web* cracked as his atmosphere started venting into the void of space. "Shit," dispelling the source, Damon quickly opened a *Portal* to his manor, throwing his body unceremoniously onto his front lawn now under the light of Damon's Star. Looking around identifying the moons, and not his homeworld's star, he figured it must have been close to midnight. *Why did Distorting Web fail?* Damon began running through some calculations in his mind as the construction workers gave him a very wide berth.

Ascending the main staircase, Damon made note of the progress while he'd been gone, the foyer ceiling, walls, and most of the first level had been repaired, as had the foundation. He headed straight for the fourth level, needing something he kept hidden in his private study.

"There you are. Master Damon, could I bother you for a moment to show you something?" Storming down from the fourth level to the third, his middle-aged chief of staff, Edgar Hastings, caught Damon mid-staircase.

"It will have to be quick. What is it?" Damon towered over his chief of staff, though barely a hand taller.

"The materials you asked for to rebuild the spell test room…. I'd like you to look at something I found…," He paused, scratching his graying designer stubble, "…erh, something Master Kellen put me on to." Being in charge of this massive remodeling effort would gray far more than just the stubble on his face. His short cropped brown hair was already beginning to gray at the edges and along the sideburns. Dressed in fine charcoal pants and matching button-down long-sleeve shirt, Edgar tried not to sweat, but Damon's Star hadn't allowed the ground to cool at night, and it was getting intolerably stuffy with the central air still not working.

"This should be good," Damon considered aloud, knowing Kellen rarely disappointed when it came to new materials or spells.

Edgar, now walking at his side, led Damon down the hall where he had some samples for Damon to examine, well outside the spell test room that was still in a state of demolition. Handing Damon a six-inch by six-inch square sample of what looked like steel, Edgar explained, "It's a high-aluminum-content, low-density steel, about two times stronger than the best titanium we could find, pound-for-pound. It's actually very porous under a microscope and should absorb enchantment as good or better than any stone we would have used in the past."

Taking the sample with him as he stepped over debris still in the process of being removed, Damon walked to the entrance of the spell test room. He could see all the way to the roof that had been fully repaired, obviously leaving the fourth floor untouched until they figured out what to do with the spell test room. Looking for a place to sit the sample down, there was no floor or walls, instead deciding to suspend the sample with his *Telekinesis* in front of him, Damon cast *Damon's Improved Shield v4*—his most powerful protection—along with *Damon's Absorption* into the sample before them.

"So far, so good," Edgar nodded in satisfaction, watching the metal turn from a burnished silver to a darker, glossier sheen as it accepted Damon's enchantments.

"Let's find out," Damon cast his most powerful selectively destructive spell—*Damon's Surprise*—not specific to living matter, causing a light amber stream of fire to erupt from Damon's right index finger as tiny lightning bolts rode the stream of fire all the way to the floating target before them. Hitting, engulfing, then wrapping around the floating metal before winking out of existence, the metal sample floated, silent and smoking before them—unscathed. Nodding, somewhat unsatisfied, Damon wasn't entirely pleased, but it was still a vast improvement over what he had. "I'll have to work on better absorption but go ahead and tell them to start building it with this. I think we can make it work." He dare not add Zero-Point here for another test—not yet. Not ready yet. "Get them to work faster. Bring in more help if you need, but we need to move faster."

"I'll get it done, Master Damon. You can count on me." Nodding with approval, Damon started heading back toward the staircase and the fourth floor. "We've already got the secret door materials in place for your private study, sir. It should be ready for you now."

"Good, that's why I'm here."

As they climbed the circular staircase approaching the fourth-floor U-Shaped hallway, making the left turn toward the tiny, square and barren innocuous room, Damon could see only by use of *Detect Everything* a suitable adamantine door blending into the bare wall. Focusing, Damon channeled into the door, creating the secret door that would allow only him passage into the private study on the other side of the wall. "Has anyone else been in here while this was being remodeled?"

Edgar's eyes shifted while he was momentarily in thought, "Yes, sir, and I executed him on the front lawn in front of all the construction workers. He took nothing. I checked...," pausing, Edgar wanted...no needed, Damon to be satisfied with his thoroughness of dealing with the unpleasant matter. "... Actually, I scaled him alive, checking every cavity and his clothes of course. I think it was just a matter of curiosity, but they had all been warned."

"I'll verify everything is untouched. Stay right here. Don't move," Damon commanded, walking toward the secret door he'd just finished, disappearing into the wall.

Now on the other side of the disguised entrance to his private study, which bordered the left curved wall of the ritual room, Damon checked around for missing or disturbed items. Fortunately, this room had mostly been spared, minus some cracks in the bookshelves that attached to this side of the curved wall of the ritual room, a few cracks in the wood flooring, and minor damage to both secret entrances. Walking to the far end of the curved study where the curved wall of the ritual room flattened out forming the recessed entrance to the ritual room on the other side, Damon noticed the second secret entrance, not yet enchanted from the remodel. Focusing, he took care of that, then turned his attention back to the contents of the study and what he'd specifically come back for in the first place.

Moving between his study bed and the study table with chairs for six, Damon walked to the flat wall that formed the main hallway of the fourth floor, running his fingers and eye line along the floor-to-ceiling bookcase that was the entire wall. "Ah…," he thought aloud as he came to the first bin of scrolls, "…There you are." Carefully opening the scroll, in search of a more robust self-containment environmental shell he could take with him to the test site, Damon nodded in satisfaction. *This should work. Damon's Improved Shell v3.*

A slower panoramic search of the study revealed nothing out of place. *The Staff of the Invoker* leaned against the wall between bed and bookcase wall; its three metal helixes coiled around one another in parallel, each with three complete revolutions—only held together by Dallia's enchantment, causing a permanent, ethereal charcoal-blue, evil aura to radiate from the staff in a seven-foot diameter hemisphere all around it. No footprints disturbed the light dust on the floor. No obvious missing or disturbed books—close to two thousand just in this room along with another ten thousand in the main library on the second floor. *The desk looks in place.* Walking over to it, checking the drawers he made note of the lambskin parchment, octopi black inkwells, luminous white inkwells, and gold flake inkwells. Nodding in satisfaction, he would be able to resume creation of new spells. A few paces from the desk, heading back toward the small decoy room, Damon kicked the hardwood floorboards revealing two secret compartments, each with their own small iron box. No lock nor lid apparently visible on either one, Damon waved his left hand over the first, causing the top of the box to wink out of existence, revealing ten rings he'd accumulated over many lifetimes. Many were important, but one in particular he picked up and examined carefully. It bore his symbol atop it like unto a signet, though he rarely wore it—only for special occasions. Pausing, recalling what had happened the last time he drew energy other than

Arcane, Damon placed the black signet ring on his right hand's third finger. Immediately, he could feel its power coursing through him, increasing the power he could draw—the power he could control. A motion of his left hand over the second box caused the top of that one to disappear similarly, revealing a couple of black velvet bags with silver glittering drawstrings as well as a couple of small rods about half the length of his forearm, each about the diameter of his index finger. One rod was made of burnished Sterling silver encrusted with twelve 2-carat diamonds, reflecting every bit of light in the room off of Damon's corneas. The other rod merely looked like a piece of satin steel with no markings or embellishments of any kind. Picking it up to examine it, its natural properties made it hotter and hotter the longer he held it. "Mhmm," he remembered aloud. "Good."

Another wave of his left hand and everything went back in place, down into the floorboard compartments with the hidden compartments closing on their own as he walked out of the study back into the decoy room where Edgar had literally not moved even an inch. Edgar's anxiety had made a few beads of sweat form on his brow, running down, into, and over his large brown eyes.

"Relax," Damon assured, "I didn't find anything missing."

"Oh, thank you," Edgar sighed in relief, though Damon wasn't sure who he was thanking.

Placing his right hand on Edgar's left shoulder as he faced him, "Relax," Damon reassured. It was increasingly hard to find people he could trust. He needed Edgar, and Edgar had proven that he had the mettle to be his chief of staff. *Must get things done asynchronously*, he thought to himself. "You did well, Edgar. Thank you."

Edgar beamed with pride, clearing this throat, "Thank you, sir. Kind of you to say." Noticing the ring on Damon's right hand and the soft black glow it emitted, Edgar tried not to miscalculate the man in front of him. Fewer words were always best with Damon—broad smiles and fewer words. Unconsciously, Edgar smiled again—his survival instinct at work most likely. "Will you be gone long again?"

"Things haven't been going as smooth as I'd hoped, so I can't say. Just keep doing the good job you've been doing and let me handle the rest." Ripping the air apart only inches from Edgar's face, Damon pivoted walking through the *Portal* to the other side.

Not recognizing the bustling metropolis on the other end of the *Portal*, but recognizing some things running on electricity like the red, yellow, and green streetlights, Edgar didn't want to know any more. Knowing too much was dangerous, as was asking too many questions. Unconsciously, Edgar's survival instincts made him smile again as Damon walked through to the streets of downtown Austin, Texas.

Charles W. McDonald Jr.

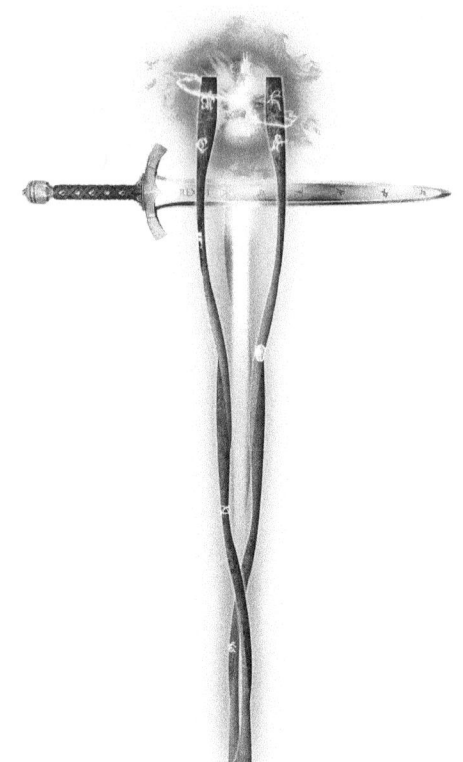

Chapter 38: The Valley of Power

(Isle of Breaking, Perion, Present Day)

omewhere south of the Valley of Power, on the far western edge of the Isle of Breaking, the air rent with the forming of a *Portal* as Ykstherin, Radin, Kerrich, Gareth, Michelle, Lawna, and Elise walked through, feeling the chilled winds of the Ocean of Faith batter their faces. Ykstherin warned them to dress warm, and they had—all wearing full-length thick coats, but the elements here still had to be experienced to be fully appreciated.

Exactly seven snow and ice-laden mountain peaks jutted out jaggedly in the far northern distance, providing a silent, yet ominous and chilling foreboding to the distant sound of the nearby ocean that wasn't entirely frozen on this end of the island.

Charles W. McDonald Jr.

"We dare not try any closer," Ykstherin warned, almost shouting against the elements as he worked his cane to move forward, though people began to question just how much his mobility was truly impacted by his apparent age. "Use of *Portals* close to the Valley of Power is incredibly dangerous. We'll have to walk and pay close attention…," Ykstherin paused, throwing the hood of his cloak over his face, "…to everything." They could have brought horses, of course, but they might have been more trouble than they were worth in the mountain passes and Ykstherin really didn't know how deep into the mountains they would need to go.

Walking right behind Ykstherin, then alongside him, so they could continue their discussion, "What can you tell me about him," Radin asked of his new-found friend.

"He's older than I, but he won't look like it, at least he might not. I'm not even sure what to expect. I've only met him once, a long time ago."

"And you're sure he's in the Valley of Power?"

"No…," Ykstherin paused, replying flatly. "I'm not."

"And how do you know he won't kill us on sight?" Lawna asked, moving up alongside them, her dirty-blonde hair stuffed under the hood of her plain snowy-white coat. She had wanted to appear as innocuous as possible, and it was a good color choice against the backdrop of where they now found themselves, if blending in was the intent.

"I don't."

Michelle moved up in between Lawna and Radin, dressed in a full-length cream-colored coat with gold trim matching her hair, wanting to hear more of the conversation over the howl of the chilled air. "We just got here, so we can't have all these dire predictions already." Darting her eyes between Radin and Ykstherin, Michelle tried to probe, "Are you at least going to tell us his name? I'm assuming it's a 'he.'"

"The man we're going to see is called, Talemar." Michelle, Radin, Elise, and Kerrich all stopped dead in their tracks. Ykstherin nodding in satisfaction—that *should* have been their response.

"What am I missing?" Lawna paused after a couple of more paces, not getting the historical reference. Apparently, her research hadn't been as thorough as Michelle's.

Ykstherin continued, "I'm not even sure if he's still alive. I'm not sure about anything, but if he lives…" he paused looking and pointing to Radin, "…then he's your mentor."

"Who are *they?*" Kerrich pointed off in the far distance, just at the edge of their visibility, they could start to make the outline of a group of men on horseback—maybe twenty or more, all making their way south as Radin's party traveled north toward the Valley of Power.

"Talemar isn't the kind of man to travel in large parties," Ykstherin noted aloud. Keeping his thoughts of the men in the distance to himself.

*   *   *   *

They hadn't seen a soul since they'd left the Isle of Fate days ago. Crossing the ice bridge between the Isle of Fate and the Cursed Capes, slowly making their way south to their expedition boats, they hoped would still be there a little further to the south. Royvan Miral heeled his Grey, pivoting himself around, looking back to the Valley of Power, wondering who the people were south of them, and what they'd be doing this far out on the edge of the world. He didn't like, nor believe in, coincidence. "Rake, Levi, Ham, you're on me. The rest of you stay here." Royvan Miral spurred his Grey forward, taking his best and most trusted fighters along with him while leaving behind the remainder of the expeditionary force.

*   *   *   *

"Well, I'd say they definitely noticed us," Lawna quipped, making sure her Glock® 22 was ready as she pulled back the slide, forcing a round into the chamber. Michelle preferred her M-4, *Bad Intentions*, currently slung over the back of her right shoulder under her coat, but the Glock was easier to hide from those who wouldn't understand. She instinctively settled her hand on the grip of her longsword sheathed on her left side.

"You won't need your weapons," Ykstherin proclaimed, holding his right hand up and open in recognition of the approaching party. "'Tis good to see you, Royvan Miral."

"Of all the places I expected to see you again, Ykstherin, this wouldn't have crossed my wildest thoughts." Royvan heeled his Grey, dismounting to shake Ykstherin's hand. His men remained mounted, swords drawn. Well, except for Ham, who always held a giant battle-axe in his right hand.

Taking in each of Ykstherin's party in turn as Royvan examined them, noticing their trepidation relaxing as soon as his name had been mentioned, Royvan assumed them of no ill intent. He had become accustomed to not being able to go anywhere without being recognized—or at least known by name if not by face. He motioned to each of his men in turn, "This," he offered pointing to the tallest and oldest of the men he brought with him, "…is Rake. This," he continued in turn, referring to his youngest, "is Levi. And this,"

Charles W. McDonald Jr.

pointing to the broadest, "…is Ham."

"Ham," Kerrich snorted, causing Radin to shake his head in disapproval.

"He likes ham," Levi quipped, dismounting, sheathing his sword.

"A lot!" Rake exclaimed deciding to remain mounted as he heeled back looking back to the Valley of Power, ensuring there was no trouble.

Ham grunted in acknowledgment, smiling as he shoved his battle-axe into its heavy leather holster.

"What are you doing out here on the edge of the world, Ykstherin?" Royvan Miral asked—his long, heavily weathered grey cloak bristling in the stiff, chilled oceanic breeze. Throwing back his hood, letting that chilled air rouse his face down to his hard, chiseled cheekbones, Royvan Miral had a hard and piercing look about him with those smoke-hued eyes and long curly locks of hair. "We've seen no one since the Isle of Fate."

"I doubt you would see this person. He's not much for company." Actually, Ykstherin had never known him to talk to more than one or two people since he met the man. Not much of a man for having friends around. He was aware that this was going to be a difficult ask, Talemar potentially taking on Radin as a protégé. It would take more than a little convincing. "I trust you'll treat that with the greatest of care," Ykstherin suggested, deftly pointing at the gold scroll case, etched in ancient runes, slung around Royvan's waist, only partially hidden under his weathered cloak. Royvan Miral noticed the eyes of Radin, Michelle, Lawna, and Elise all on him—on the scroll—causing him to involuntarily close his cloak, covering the sealed scroll casing.

"Is that the Scroll of Carnac?" It was the first thing Radin had asked of the famed adventurer, but he certainly had Royvan's attention now.

"Perhaps introductions are warranted, my boy." Royvan didn't mean his reply to be condescending, but it had been taken that way, nonetheless.

"I'm Radin d'Aguillon." Despite the previous remark, he extended his hand firmly, shaking the legend's hand. He was a hard man as was evident in Royvan's eyes.

"Michelle Blade," she tried not to crush Royvan's hand, but he winced slightly when she took his, regardless.

"Lawna." This time, Royvan really winced—noticeably—causing Radin to smile if ever so brief.

"Elise." Apparently the only 'normal' female by the way she shook Royvan's hand. He wasn't sure about the others, except they were no ordinary women. Then again, Ykstherin historically didn't keep average company, either.

"Kerrich." Kerrich chose not to offer his hand, instead remaining withdrawn, offering him a nod from the back of the party, to which Royvan offered him one of respect, in turn.

With a respectful nod shared between Gareth and Royvan Miral, it was obvious the two had met before.

"Good, now that we all know who we're talking to, even if we don't know what," briefly glancing to Michelle and Lawna, Royvan continued, "Yes, I have it. Yes, I intend on being very careful with it. And yes, it took a long time to find it. We've been on the road for years after finding some clues to its location half-way-round the world. It's the greatest discovery of my career, and I'm well aware of its power."

"Its real power is only available to the One," Radin stated the obvious. Perhaps there was more to this Radin boy than met the eye. He had clearly been in Ykstherin's company long enough to learn some things. Pausing, taking in Royvan's public examination of him, Radin seized the opportunity. "I know you've been traveling a great distance for a considerable time, but you know these lands better than any of us. Would you help us find Talemar?"

Royvan's eyes swelled with that name, as he visibly took two steps back. "*That* is who you seek," looking to Ykstherin then to Radin in turn. "You might as well seek a phantasm. He doesn't exist." Pausing for a moment before offering respect to the name at least, "Not anymore."

Ykstherin offered a hand on Royvan's shoulder calmingly, "You don't have to help us, Royvan Miral. We will seek him out regardless, but this boy needs a proper teacher, and if you'd like to come with us, I would explain more." If Royvan Miral hadn't looked snake-bit by Radin before, he certainly did now, as he now gave Radin a wide berth.

Mouth dry and drawn inward to a thin, hard-pressed line Royvan Miral paused and considered before answering. He had provisions still, but Talemar—that couldn't be. *And what if it was?* He was Royvan Miral, what if he were forever remembered as the man who found both the Scroll of Carnac and Talemar in the same adventure. His name would be immortal—though he might be physically dead. "Go back and gather up the men," Royvan pivoted to Rake—his second in command, "...tell him we'll be splitting up, and we'll need nearly seventy percent of the provisions with me. Levi will lead them back to the boats and back to their homes. You, Ham, and I are going with the boy to find Talemar...if he still exists."

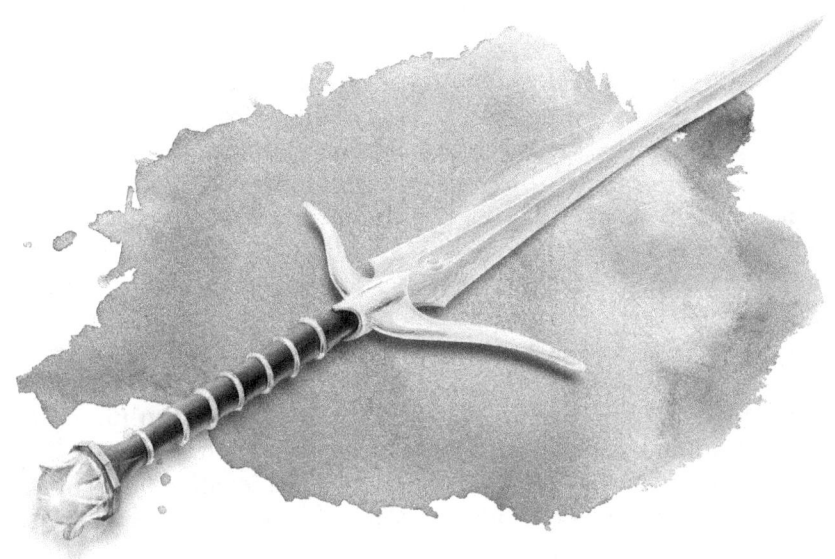

Chapter 39: Halls of Aaramus

(The Halls of Aaramus, Time Neutral)

Engaged in this search for a way out for what seemed to pass like days, Talemar really had no consciousness of time here. He could see the great halls behind a high gate off in the distance for days now, but he thought he would have been there long ago. Every day, he rested, he would wake up, and it would still be there with little-to-no progress from the day's journey before. He had to use magic just to keep himself from starving to death as his provisions ran out long ago. If time wasn't correlative here, maybe space wasn't either. Each time he slept, though, he dreamed. A brilliant sword like none he'd ever seen or heard of before, like unto a star, held high overhead by someone else amidst a lake of crystal bathed in absolute purity of light, and a booming voice commanding someone—if not him—to do something, though he couldn't say who or why.

Pinching himself on the forearm, ensuring he was indeed awake, then unrolling the sleeves of his charcoal-blue robes, Talemar gathered his things to continue. At least whatever had been keeping the great hall at a distance had stopped or lessened, so the structure was now seemingly a day's journey or less if all things held equal this day. And that was a big 'if' in this place.

Charles W. McDonald Jr.

*   *   *   *

Some hours later, Talemar found himself standing before a great gate five men high, with the walls going off in either direction as far as the eye could see, beyond the blackness of the horizon. Endless grounds upon which to build the greatest of halls. The walls made of large clay-fired bricks of about ten matching hues of variation, joined with buff grout with a great concrete lip at the top, sticking out over the edge just slightly with concrete pedestals about every hundred paces or so where the bricks elevated slightly for the pedestal to sit atop. The gates themselves were heavy iron with a great seal in the center; raised iron rivets bordered each of the great gates. The great center seal looked to be a depiction of the sun, orbited by a great sphere, which was orbited by an even smaller orb. Approaching the seal, he could see even more detail. It looked like another smaller sun, orbiting the sphere that was circling what looked to be another sun. "Strange," Talemar considered aloud as he gave the gate a heave, hearing its smooth oiled action yield to him. He hadn't heard the voices in days, but as he pushed open the unlocked gate, they made themselves known to him again—loudly. He wondered if others could hear them, or if they were just in his head.

Briefly, he paused his steps to gather himself before proceeding. "If you're going to kill me, then get on with it," he told the voices aloud as he forced one foot to land in front of the other—toward the great hall. It was arranged more horizontal in footprint than front to back. He wasn't sure of the front-to-back measurements, but side-to-side each wing went as far as the eye could see. There appeared to be three main floors of flying buttress cathedral architecture with magnificent stained-glass acorn-shaped windows of increasing size as you went up in levels, such that the first floor had the smallest windows, and the third-floor walls were almost all exposed glass. Great keystones, different in color but beautifully matching, marked the top of each window. The overall color scheme was aged burgundy stone against off-white accents. *Marble perhaps*, he thought to himself, taking in the awesome sight of the architecture up close. A pair of heavy, charred oak doors marked the main entrance.

Taking very cautious steps forward, Talemar pushed open the massive oak doors, which operated smoothly with almost no effort as if regularly maintained. Yet, he saw not a soul anywhere in sight. "I made it here. Either you wanted me here, or someone else did. So, I'm here nonetheless," Talemar declared to the ancient, aged air of the Halls of Aaramus. From the appearance outside, he had assumed to find three independent floors inside. That was not what lay before him. Instead, the Halls of Aaramus was one great chamber

Charles W. McDonald Jr.

end-to-end, floor-to-ceiling with books, artifacts, bins, trinkets, rings, and treasures of both knowledge and wealth. Great ladders leaned at a slight angle with wheels on tracks, allowing access to the upper bins and shelves.

"I don't have a clue why I'm here or what I'm looking for," he thought aloud. *Might as well start from the beginning.* Starting on his left and walking down the great hall, Talemar briefly examined each shelf and each bin. Pulling over one of the great track ladders, he climbed to the second-level containers after finding nothing of consequence on the first-floor shelves. The bins were organized, somewhat, by artifact type, but for many of these artifact types he had no frame of reference to describe or comprehend—like the one he held in his left hand. It was a shimmering silver disk with a hole in the center and thousands of perfect shimmering engraved concentric rings, each larger than the previous, all the way to the outer edges of the circle that were transparent. "I wonder if this was created with magic," he thought, admiring its perfection before putting it back into its transparent casing with little prongs that held the center of the disk affixed inside the case. There were hundreds of these, if not thousands. *Surely, he wasn't here for this, though. I don't even understand what these things are.*

Climbing to the third storey bins and shelves, he did see some books that he could actually read, that were written in his native tongue. One of the titles caught his attention: *A Game of Gods—A Historical Reference. Hmmm,* he considered, opening it. *This should be good.* Fumbling with it a bit, since he had to hold himself steady with his left hand on the ladder, the book fell open to page 16. *As good a place to start as any I guess,* he thought as he began to read. *My Sacrifice* was the chapter heading, just below a pictograph. *Had he seen that pictograph before?*

A clank of metal on the giant four-cubit by four-cubit marble tiles below caught his attention as he shut the book, making his way down the ladder to investigate. He thought he saw movement in his peripheral vision, but whoever it was, was already gone.

Another series of bins over he noticed tiny 'devices' which was the best word he could think of to describe the small metallic items sticking out of a material that was lightweight and multi-colored, unlike anything he'd ever seen before. The metallic ends were rectangular with more of that colored material inside along with tiny little linear beads of silver. "What the...," Talemar pondered aloud, wondering what else he was going to find and if any of it was going to make sense to him why he was brought, *or sent,* here. The entire device couldn't have been much bigger than half of his index finger, and there were hundreds of them organized into what he assumed were different categories he couldn't quite interpret.

Charles W. McDonald Jr.

Getting down from the slightly angled ladder, he hadn't noticed them before, but clearly, there was a group of swords all organized and stored together on the first floor leaning against the opposite wall of the wing he currently searched. Walking to them, careful to look thoroughly in both directions, he wondered what he'd find. Some were magnificent—he could tell from a distance. Some were clearly your typical longsword he might find a dozen of at any given blacksmith. Within the longsword group, one adorned in his native tongue with the words *Faith Precedes Hope* with runes and symbols of magic dancing and alive within the center of the fuller. It had coiled steel-rings about a grip of a textured material that was not leather with a full, flat guard that flared both toward the blade and back to the pommel at each end. The entire hilt appeared to be made of a bronze-influenced steel from the satin reflection peering back at him. Four beautiful metallic leaves opened up, revealing a magnificent star-sapphire in the center of what would be the pommel. The blade itself had wave upon wave upon wave hinting at the many different enchanted metal ingots from which it had been forged. Varying light streams of silver, white, and silvery-blue—like unto a *Portal*—danced off the metallic waves of the blade and fuller. It was a magnificent piece and it looked…familiar. *I wonder if this is Starfire*, he considered.

Putting the book he had brought with him from the third floor in his satchel, he sheathed the *Faith Precedes Hope* blade in his scabbard, contributing his blade in its place. It had served him well over the years, and he'd worked on it with Xaldran to enchant it over a period of days. He knew it to be an excellent defensive weapon, and maybe it would be an important contribution—maybe enough to let him walk out of here alive with a few things.

Examining the others, one sword stood out among all the others of all types for it appeared to hold a place of honor among them. It was amidst a group of what he might consider, or call, short swords. Each had a short but functional guard, if they had one at all, with a one-handed grip. However, the one that drew his eye, and would draw the eye of any really, had a hand-and-a-half grip, just slightly longer than the other short swords, but not long enough to qualify as a longsword. It had five runes down the fuller of one side and an inscription down the fuller of the other side. The inscription was of a language similar to his common tongue but not similar enough to read it coherently. Something about 'behind me' or something akin to that. *Perhaps, I can get that inscription translated*, he considered, taking it with him. Suddenly the image from his dreams and the booming voice flooded the front of his thoughts. The vision in his mind was strong enough to force him to shield his eyes. It was a vision of the sword he'd just been examining suspended in the air, shimmering like a star—that was *this* blade. As soon as he sat the five-rune blade back down, his waking vision fled, immediately, as did the commanding voice that it seemed to have invoked.

"That isn't meant for you," a scratchy and weathered voice declared from behind him.

Pivoting as fast as he could, channeling, and finding nothing. He could not cast. Panic!

"Your powers are useless here," the decrepit creature with decaying flesh declared whilst now staring right at him. Eye sockets filled with little red dots of life undead, but the rest of him was...*dead?* Red robes falling and flowing over decayed flesh and exposed bone; it threatened without movement or words.

Talemar pulled *Faith Precedes Hope—Starfire* as it glowed in his hands much like the sword he had put down—the sword this *thing* had warned was 'not for him.'

Laughing at Talemar's pathetic attempt to ward him off, Aaramus tsked at him with an index finger of exposed bone. "You cannot kill me, Talemar. Why don't you leave while you still can?"

"I don't even know why I'm here."

"Don't you?" The red little eye dots blazed in their lifeless sockets under the secrecy of his red-robed hood.

"No, I don't." It was hard to hide his frustration, but he was out of his depths here.

"I cannot do your thinking for you, Talemar," Aaramus chided, circling him slowly. "I think you should go now."

Pausing, looking into its pyre eyes, trying to discern a mouth or any other features he might remember, Talemar needed to be careful—thoughtful. "I'm gracious for your hospitality and your shelter. Thank you." Talemar sheathed *Starfire.* "By your leave," Talemar offered a half bow before the creature, though not enough to expose himself to attack, before pivoting to walk back towards the entrance he could only assume was also the exit from the Halls of Aaramus.

A knowing and very slow nod of approval, Aaramus let Talemar live, and for now, Aaramus would also allow him to leave.

(Valley of Power, Perion, Recent History)

Closing the door as Talemar walked back out the way he came, he did not recognize the mountain peaks in front of him—at least not at first. There were seven in all with one great one, twice the size of the second largest to the west. These mountain peaks formed the Valley of Power, where *Portal* movement was not allowed, and yet here he was right in their foothills in the dead of winter. Chilled ocean air raced over the Isle of Breaking, cutting through him in an instant, and he was shaking already. At least he was home—sort of.

Chapter 40: A Kingdom Forgotten

(Somewhere in the Cumberland Plateau, Earth, Christmas Eve, 11:45 p.m.

Eastern, Near Future)

Snow had come hard and heavy to the Ohio River Valley. It was, by far, the harshest winter on record, with temperatures rivaling Antarctica for the last ten days. All of which did not help quell the fears of nuclear winter, brought on by the limited nuclear exchange at the beginning of the war.

The whole Cumberland Plateau was quiet—too quiet. One could hear a squirrel trapsing through a thicket of brush among the silver maple, syca-more, cottonwood, birch, hickory, and black willow trees from two hundred yards away. No sounds of mechanized armor. No troops. No aircover. It was just damned eerie quiet. Like the whole world, as a living being, was holding its breath, about to gasp out its convictions of the justness of war upon its scarred and battered face.

On a snow-covered hillside just outside of Middlesboro, Kentucky sat a small makeshift building, hidden in between a thick growth of evergreens. One flag rippled in the cold, stiff breeze atop the aluminum structure. A banner kept in honor with a Celtic cross embroidered in pewter against diag-onally opposing white panel backgrounds while the Cup of Christ was em-broidered in burnished rust and gold against diagonally opposing patriot-blue and blood-red panel backgrounds. The crest of a fallen king and a kingdom in memoriam. It didn't matter that this wasn't Michael's kingdom. That crest flew everywhere around the world once the news of his death had spread like a deadly contagion of hate and despair.

Two hundred miles behind enemy lines meant they couldn't hear all the action, but they were perfectly positioned to bring the action to the foreign occupying armies of the New World Order. There had been almost no action taken by the Chinese in several days. One would think there would be at least

Charles W. McDonald Jr.

some maneuvering by the enemy but the bone-crushing hum of treaded armor had silenced days ago. Something big was brewing....

The hasty ribbed-aluminum construction of the makeshift CNC did almost nothing to stop the elements. It probably would have been just as warm in the Hummer just outside the front door, had it not been for the raging fire in the back of the building. It was all open-area inside, so that what little heat there was would not be blocked by walls. The whole building couldn't have been more than a thousand square feet. Dozens of men, most in Chinese BDUs made especially for the civilian collaborators, littered the dirt floor and cots strewn throughout the CNC. Most were asleep. A small particle board desk sat in one of the back corners of the room, close to the fire. There was no real reason for it. Their leader was not the kind of man who sat behind a desk.

Ron Stencowsky sat on the edge of his desk, trying to strike a match on its surface, but surrendered to letting one of the roaring flames from the fireplace take care of that job. The match was probably ruined, just like everything else in his non-issue collaborator Chinese BDUs, from when he had to cross the river a few days ago. They thought its surface was frozen solid enough to pass, but as with most things in war, nothing is for certain. The frostbite and pneumonia almost killed him, but he didn't care anymore. He had stared death in the face at least a dozen times since this war had begun. Stencowsky didn't give a flipping damn about himself anymore, not since the night he buried both the Major and his driver just south of Warwick. *Man, that was a bloody battle*, he recalled. His men were all he cared about now. It was the only reason he had to wake up in the morning. *If* he could sleep.

Poor fit or not, he was grateful for the collaborator Chinese BDUs they'd found some months back. His men weren't going to pass for Chinese, and they needed to blend in at times when they weren't skulking around causing trouble for the invading forces.

Ron limped back from the fireplace—lit match in tow—as he sat back on the edge of his desk, lighting another one of his worthless Chinese cigarettes. He hated them—truly, but they *did* have nicotine, and they were just about the only thing he could find behind enemy lines. His face was well known, and a bounty had been placed on his head. It wasn't as if he could just waltz into downtown Middlesboro, such as it was, and ask for a pack of Marlboro's®. They were having to move at least once a week now. The heat was getting pretty intense to find them. After all, they had wrought a lot of havoc on the occupying forces over the past few months. Nothing made him smile quite like blowing up this outpost or that armory of this enemy that had turned *his* country inside out. And over what...? Some incident in the South

Charles W. McDonald Jr.

China Sea…? *Hardly justification for all this death and suffering*, in his mind. But his instincts, and good intelligence on the ground, said there was a lot more to it than that.…

Here it was Christmas Day, and the only sign of it was a small pine they had pulled inside and stuck in the corner of the pre-fab. There were no presents under it, of course. They were lucky to have food and clothing, and even that had to be taken from the Chinese. Their attire had proven convenient on many occasions over the last few months while they had been on the run all the way from New York. They were within reach of Free America if only they could hold together a little while longer. Perhaps, they could have already been there had they not stopped to cause problems for the Chinese at every opportunity along the way. Stencowsky wouldn't have it any other way and neither would his men. But he did want his men to make it back to the green zones, if for nothing more than to rest from combat for a while. All of them had been fighting relentlessly since the Battle for New York, and fatigue had set in long ago.

You might say everything had gone to Hell since that fateful night, just outside of Warwick. The Allies had lost a lot of ground to the Chinese, who now had the help and support of the North Korean Army and others as well. Supplies just seemed to come out of nowhere for the occupying armies just in the nick of time to save their asses and that was a telling sign.… There were still some skirmishes at sea, but the Allies had pretty well wrapped up a total naval victory, which was just fine for the British but had not proven to be much help for the Americans on land. After Michael's death, their commitment waned. It's not like the Allies could simply bomb U.S. cities to purge the enemy, not with the vast civilian population living under occupation. And not with the threat of their unleashing a dirty bomb in a major city either. Too much collateral damage was on the table. The Allies needed a better hold on the situation and a firm understanding of what threats had been neutralized before the escalation towards freedom could begin.

No, the only way to find victory would be in purging the Chinese on the ground, and that would be an ugly situation any way you sliced it. Fortunate for them that the Chinese had been unable to take Washington, New York City, or Norfolk. All of the eastern seaboard, south of New York, was free territory, but they had taken so much of Canada and the inland east that it almost cut the country in half with this ovoid wedge of occupation running straight down the Ohio River Valley. What little bit of movement of goods that occurred had to do so south of Tennessee, and that was the reason for all the rumors about some big Chinese offensive scheduled in the next few weeks. If they could carve up Free America into totally separate zones, they could be

Charles W. McDonald Jr.

almost assured of a lasting occupation, and any thoughts of an Allied victory to this war would be placed on a very long-delayed timer.

It was hard to believe that all this destruction, all of this suffering, could come out of an incident with the Chinese and American navies. He supposed it was no more crazy than the reasons several other wars had started throughout history. But then he knew that many wars throughout history had been started by false flags, for war was profitable for the central bank who funded both sides. So there was that too.... This war, he hoped, would be a Vietnam-in-waiting for the Chinese. They were already facing a big problem with the Allied forces, but the thing they had not counted on was the uprising of the strongest resistance in history. They damn sure had not counted on so many Americans owning guns and rapidly learning how to use them with deadly proficiency, nor the sovereign citizen militias that gave them a good ass whipping throughout the 'moonshine territory' of the Appalachian Mountains.

All wars were usually said to be started over some grand purpose, but this one didn't need any explanation—not for their part anyway. This was a zero-sum game. Live or die. They were fighting for their home, and if they did not win, there would be nothing to go home to. The one thing that really pissed him off, even more, was all the damn propaganda being tossed around by the Chinese, making it sound like the U.S. had actually brought this upon itself. *Well,* he figured, *there might be some truth to that.* The U.S. did have a nasty habit of making everything that went on in the world their private business, whether it was or wasn't, but even that kind of arrogance didn't justify this, certainly not in the ways that the Chinese would have liked you to believe. *Hell,* he thought, *the Chinese were slinging around so many damn lies that you needed a DNA test just to find the truth.* Stencowsky laughed, puffing on his cigarette—cringing over its appalling flavor. Just one prevailing thought came to his mind as he watched his men sleep for the first time in days: *Will this damn war ever come to an end? And would there be freedom on the other side of it?*

*   *   *   *

(Dover Castle, England, Earth, Near Future)

A warm fire crackled inside the massive three-storey study. Books on dark stained oak shelves covered all four walls of the room; a walkway ran around the room at each storey level, leading out to the massive stairwell through secret doors hidden amongst the shelves. A dark walnut and maple executive desk stood on a large Persian rug that took up almost a third of the study's two thousand square feet of floor space. Four huge executive wingback burgundy leather chairs, sharing the Persian rug, stood a few feet from the fireplace, with a small, round, matching coffee table set in between them. With no obvious way in or out of the unique room, one had the feeling they were locked inside a tomb of knowledge—thousands of books within reach. This had always been the king's favorite room, and Christmas was the perfect time to bring them here. They had never been allowed in this room when Michael was alive, but it was Christmas, and Billings thought it best that they spend this time someplace dear to their father's heart. This Christmas would be far worse on them than any of them than any before. They had been told that mommy was okay and that she had gone in search of daddy, but they didn't know that mommy wouldn't be home for Christmas. He just hoped that wherever Elise was, that she was safe. The children could not survive the loss of another parent. The loss of their father would leave wounds on their soul in perpetuity. And, even now, Alexander had drawn inward as a way of protecting himself from further hurt and heartache. His silence had become a deafening reminder of Michael's absence.

Godspeed, my Queen, Billings had said to her just before she left. He knew she had to go, and she might need to be gone for quite some time, but he never imagined that she would be gone this long. He assumed that the problem here must be getting even worse for her not to come back for Christmas. Perhaps, she feared that she would not be able to leave again. *Yes*, he thought with the fading satisfaction of justification, *that must be it! My Queen must fear not being able to leave again if she came home.* The pleasure dissipated swiftly as Billings wondered where she could be and what she might find.

Walking past the fourteen-foot-tall Christmas tree, stocked with toys for the royal family, Billings walked hand-in-hand with the king's treasures to sit them down by the fire.

Wherever Elise was, he was confident that, as long as she still breathed, she cared, and that she must miss both her children greatly. *All this time and still no word*, he worried as he took a seat next to the fire, pulling both Elizabeth and Alexander into his lap. Elizabeth, not even two, with her mother's strawberry-blonde hair, was already beginning to look like the sweet princess that she was becoming. She seemed distant and uncertain as she reached up to pull at Billing's full, grey beard. Alexander wasn't yet three, but one could see the similarities between them and pictures of their parents. Alexander had his mother's blonde hair and sharp green eyes, but he already possessed some of the character of the king. Alexander seemed much more alert and perceptive than a child of that age should be, but he too seemed distant and guarded. He wondered if they knew the importance of this day and understood what had happened to their father. He hoped they would be too young to remember, but something told him, as Elizabeth continued to tug at his beard, that would not be the case.

Contemplating the future of the king's children, Billings watched the fire blaze, listening to its hypnotizing crackle. Reflections of the fire danced within his burdened eyes, but the shadows cast by the flickering light revealed the deep lines of his face. As he let his soul sink into the depths of the flames, seeking both warmth and refuge, his thoughts became focused on the memory of his king. He could never allow himself to forget Michael—certainly not after all the things Michael had done for him, for their country, and for the Allies—not after his great sacrifice. It was a small thing, but he could let his king live in his memory, and in doing so, maybe he could help the king live in the memory of his precious children. As long as he breathed, he would never forget Michael. It was a promise to himself, but a promise he had to keep.

"Would you like to hear a story," Billings proffered with an old and broken voice, a reflection of his own heart. To his great joy both of the children turned around, smiling. Standing on the very tips of her little toes, while in his lap, putting her almost face to face with him Elizabeth asked, "Tell us about, Daddy. *PLEASE....*" Sighing and managing a big smile, Billings told Michael's children, "It would be my *great* honor to tell you another story about your father—the King." Elizabeth and Alexander looked up at him anxiously with wide and attentive eyes awaiting his story—a story of *A Kingdom Forgotten.*

Charles W. McDonald Jr.

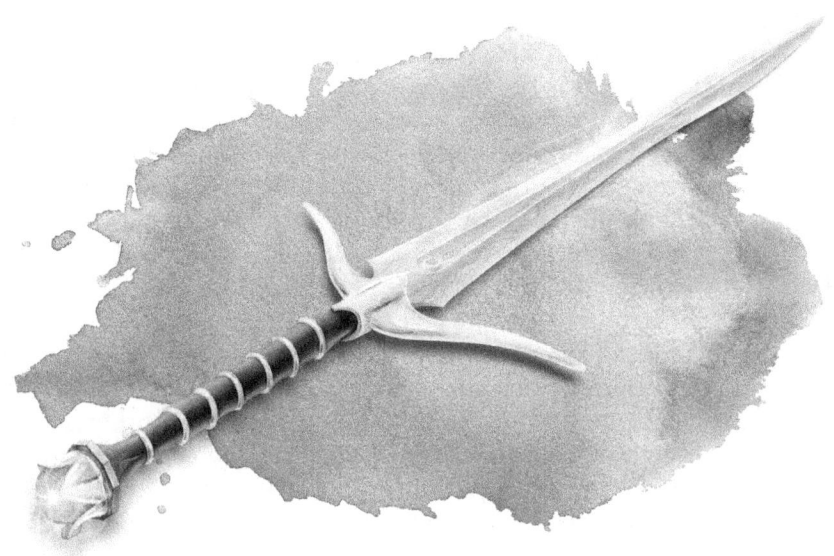

Chapter 41: Of Plans Most Secret

(Isle of Breaking, Perion, Present Day)

The largest of the seven peaks of The Valley of Power lay before them as they took the only mountain pass Royvan Miral knew would allow them access to the other side, beyond the Valley of Power, if need be. They needed to keep their options open for a fast escape. He wasn't sure how far outside the Valley of Power they needed to be for Ykstherin's *Portal* to work, but he didn't want to find out. The voices of the Scroll of Carnac played with his mind again, just the way they had before when he passed through the Valley of Power a few days back. *I'm going mad—that has to be it.*

Powerful snow-laden winds threatened to blow them all off the pass, down the jagged rocky mountainside to their deaths. Royvan Miral held point, as he had the whole way, leaning his body forward into the strong headwinds as they left footprints in snow soon to be blown clean by the mountain-pass winds. Pulling his hood down over his face to keep the frostbite at bay, Royvan shouted over the wind to his men, "Keep them in line and keep the horses calm. If we lose anyone down the side, they're dead, and if we lose provisions, we're all dead."

Charles W. McDonald Jr.

"I've got it, Boss," Rake shouted back in reply, keeping his horse on a tight leash close to him with his right hand as he braced himself against the side of the mountain with his left hand. Rake could be trusted with just about anything, and that's why Royvan never went anywhere without him. Ham, he kept just for fun; and for killing.

"Do we have any idea of what we're looking for?" It was a valid question Radin had brought up more than once already. He wouldn't keep bringing it up if he'd been given a reasonable answer, but none had been offered. Silence was Ykstherin's reply, though he offered a calming glance that wasn't entirely calming to Radin. More like a glare of appeasement.

Michelle adjusted *Bad Intentions* on her right shoulder to keep it hidden and more comfortably away from the jagged side of the mountain. The cold didn't bother her or Lawna, but she knew it would bother Elise. She wasn't appropriately dressed for this, even though she wore a full-length, heavy coat. The snow had found its way into her boots long ago, and she was sure her feet were frostbitten or not. They needed to find shelter. Soon.

Suddenly a cracking sound from above preambled snow and ice falling atop them in waves, forcing Royvan to immediately search for an answer. He remembered passing an opening only a moment ago, "Go back," he commanded, "look for an opening about a hundred paces back that way." Bringing up the rear, Kerrich searched for, and quickly found, the opening Royvan mentioned, ducking inside, out of the avalanche starting to rain down over them. Reaching out to grab Elise, Kerrich pulled her into the mouth of the cave. "Gotcha," he sat her down just as Gareth followed in brushing himself off. An instant later Radin hustled into the mouth of the cave alongside Ykstherin, bringing him in tow. Michelle and Lawna helped Royvan's men, choosing not to offer any advice to the legendary adventurer as they came into the mouth simultaneously alongside Royvan, just as a huge boulder rolled down right in front of the mouth of the cave.

"You found your way in. You can find your way out," the rich voice of an unknown man declared behind them, standing deeper in the cave, just in front of the union of three varying paths that tunneled their way deeper into the Valley of Power. Just standing there, ash staff in hand, a brilliant ball of light at the end of his staff revealed black and grey stubble on chiseled hard good looks and long hair between auburn and raven-black in charcoal-blue robes—a sword with a glowing pommel of budding metallic leaves revealing a massive and beautiful star-sapphire gem upon his left hip. Already turning back whence he came, Talemar offered neither counsel nor pleasantries before going back to *his* prison of *his own* making.

"Talemar, your work here is not done. The time for your rest is not yet at hand," Ykstherin chastised the gruff man from the mouth of the cave. Ykstherin had never spoken that way to anyone—not that Radin had seen; and that fact alone drew everyone's attention to him—and Talemar.

"I told you the last time I saw you, Ykstherin, you were to leave me alone!" Shimmering silver eyes burned in those handsome eye sockets creased and aged by the burden of so many deaths from so long ago.

"You think you do the world a favor, keeping yourself hidden while the Scroll of Carnac has just been found," pointing to Royvan Miral, Ykstherin continued to scold, "Whatever your past sins, you need to let them go! We have no time for them, and I will suffer your obliviousness not a moment longer!"

Michelle's mouth worked like she was about to say something, but instead chose to remain quiet while the pissing war reached a natural conclusion.

"Please hear us out just for a little while, then if you choose, we'll never bother you again." Radin's plea settling upon Talemar stirred old memories of those he'd failed.

"You don't want my help." Talemar knew it to be true whether they did or not.

"NO, I don't." There it was—totally brutal honesty—that one quality Radin shared with Damon. "I need your help, but I don't want it. If I'm right, we'll all need your help before it's done."

"Even if I help him, he cannot stop what is to come." Talemar seeing beyond as per usual for him, but his foresight hadn't saved his friends and it wouldn't save the people before him now either. He knew that.

"NO, I can't. I'm more worried about what's to come after **that**." Radin's seeing beyond as well, caused Talemar pause as he saw the young man with eyes anew. Trying to see past the youth. Past the boy, and into the man of many layers behind the eyes.

"I will listen to your proposal, young man. Come." A wave of Talemar's hand and the fork of three paths became a fork of four as a previously hidden trail revealed itself before them, heading down at a relatively steep angle, deep into the heart of the Valley of Power.

*　　*　　*　　*

"So, let's say the End Times are upon us, whether they be upon the other worlds or not. The Creator's plan is the Creator's plan, and we cannot change it. We can only follow our roles and be where we must when we must." Talemar's view of prophecy had a ring of fatalism to it, and it was clear

Charles W. McDonald Jr.

it would take more than a little convincing to have him see otherwise. Yet the young man was trying.

"I don't argue the Creator's plan. Who am I to argue such a thing? I just think there are far more things in motion that we're not entirely seeing, and if we fail to keep our eyes open to those possibilities, then we'll inevitably be limited to only the vision of the future Talemar describes."

"And how is just the Creator's plan, by itself, such a limited outcome?" Talemar's logic, however dated and tested, leaned on the inevitability of goodness of the Creator of all things. Of Love and Light of Creation, but that did not make it so....

"The End Times is more about good versus evil—the outcome we hope will be the Creator's vision." Radin paused, also drawing upon the assumption that the Creator's outcome was the rightful outcome for Mankind. Drawing Damon's symbol in the dirt of the cavern Talemar had called home the last thirty years, Radin offered, "I don't know his role, but I don't see it being about good versus evil.... I've come to know him at least a little, and his plans go far beyond good versus evil. I feel he's grown tired of that game."

"How often is too often for you to visit with him?" Elise had been mostly quiet, electing to listen instead, but it needed to be considered. She, of all people, didn't want him spending any more time with Damon than absolutely necessary. Already, Damon's influence on Radin was changing him in ways she didn't like, and it was tearing at the frayed seams of their relationship, but *this* was much bigger than their relationship and she knew it.

"You can visit with this…man," Talemar probed, not entirely incredulous, but certainly surprised at the magic at work between them. Now it was beginning to make sense—the young man was getting his information from somewhere, but the question was how trustworthy could the information be, coming from someone like who they described?

Showing Talemar the scroll he'd be using, Radin warned him of breaking the seal as he passed it over to him to examine. "Hmmm," Talemar contemplated aloud, examining the paper, the runes, and especially the seal—where the bulk of the enchantment lay. "This is a one-way trip and not a *Portal.*"

"No, it's not. My body stays, but it *feels* like my body is transported to his manor. It feels totally normal like I have all my senses as I walk around, talking to him. When we finish our conversation, I wake up a little disoriented, but much like I'd been asleep for a very long time."

Nodding knowingly, Talemar rubbed his stubbled face and brushed back his bangs, thinking. "Tell me about these conversations—every word you can remember." At least Radin fully held Talemar's interest now. The question was: would he help?

* * * *

A few hours of Radin recounting his interactions with Damon, and Talemar legitimately feared what may lie *beyond* the End Times. Would it be a great reset to be repeated in a thousand years or more? Would it be the end of all things? The end of Creation itself? Would good overcome evil or vice versa or was that—as Radin had so often mentioned—irrelevant to Damon's plans and possibly to the End Times...? Was it too simplistic a question as Radin also suggested with good and evil too blended to be categorized into this side or that? Where agendas mattered more as the war over the status quo finally forced sides? Most of all, would Damon's agenda be something he supported or something he must fight? The very thought of fighting Damon, from what he'd read in the book he took from the Halls of Aaramus, chilled him to the core. *How does one fight a demigod?* And these trips of Radin's to see Damon, the book hadn't mentioned them at all. For a historical reference, that was a big detail to omit. As were Damon's many trips to Earth Radin spoke of. He needed to keep *A Game of Gods* to himself for now. It might shed some much-needed light soon, but it was too incomplete a reference to be trustworthy in guiding their actions for the moment. And, even if they used it to guide their actions, the best outcome they could hope for would be to repeat the outcome it only hinted at. He didn't see how that could be helpful.

"I think Elise is right. You should talk to Damon." Never one to parse words, Michelle threw it out there to stir the pot. In the back of her mind, she still wondered why she wasn't sensing her girls. She'd lost the tether as soon as she'd arrived here and never regained it. It unnerved her to no end. Her instincts told her the answer to the problem before them was related to why she could no longer sense her babies. But Damon was the keystone at the center of this problem.

"I'm not looking to become Damon's best pal," Radin protested and rightfully so. *They* weren't the ones circling too close to the sun to get scorched. He was willing to accept the risk, but he needed to be sure he'd done enough research on his own to merit having a discussion where he could contribute rather than just take and be an ever-present pest to Damon. "We need to have something to contribute to these conversations I'm having with Damon. If all I do is ask about this or that, then what am I contributing? I know it sounds weird, but there needs to be some give to go along with the take—otherwise, I become a pest. What am I contributing to Damon if I go

Charles W. McDonald Jr.

see Damon right now?"

Michelle thought for a minute, offering. "You can tell him at least three people followed his wake from Earth to Perion." Radin nodded. *It was something, but not enough.*

It had been so long since Talemar had even opened *A Game of Gods*, let alone read it cover to cover, but he searched his memory for something useful. "Tell him Aaramus may know his plans."

Radin coughed into his bread, trying to warm himself by the fire, "Who's Aaramus, and what are you not telling us?"

Shoving Damon's scroll into Radin's hand, Talemar broke the seal for the young boy as Radin's body collapsed right there on the spot, causing Talemar to have to pull Radin's torso away from the fire as it fell to the cavern floor.

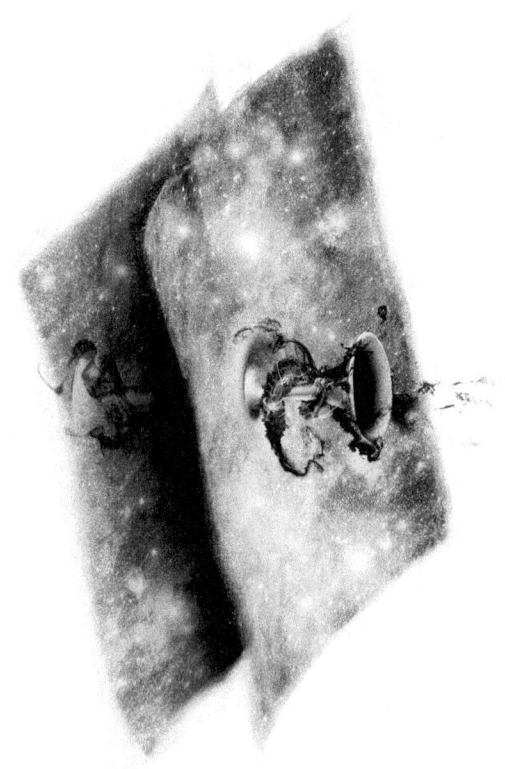

Chapter 42: Mira

(Downtown Austin, TX, Earth, 1:00 p.m. Central, Present Day)

Damon appeared on the park side of the Lamar and MLK Boulevard intersection—a dangerous move in broad daylight, but he didn't think anyone had directly seen him arrive. He had to better understand how he was sourcing Zero-Point, and why sourcing it in larger quantities was breaking magic he'd already tethered off. *That shouldn't be happening*, Damon surmised, crossing Lamar and heading towards the campus. His Android started buzzing almost as soon as he walked through the *Portal*—three text messages and a voice message. *Mira*, he thought to himself, reading her texts.

'How's it going?'
'Where are you?'

Charles W. McDonald Jr.

'Why aren't you replying?'

He thought about replying, but now wasn't the time for that.... Noticing Cain and Abel's on his way back, he hadn't eaten in what seemed like forever, he headed that way. He wasn't much for Earth food, but in fairness, he hadn't really tried all that much yet either. He needed a guide. Smiling, he thought of Mira again.

Cain and Abel's Sports Bar and Grill was wall-to-wall with students and the occasional faculty member trying to get something to eat. He started to re-read Mira's texts and the menu simultaneously.

"Busy day," the sexy female voice asked from behind him.

Pivoting, Mira was staring him down. Pissed. "Uhhh.... Just got your texts." Damon smiled for her—a bit too sarcastically for her taste.

"I call *bullshit* on that one." She was tapping her three-inch heels—same shoes, but very different clothes. Was it a different day already, he wondered, examining her beautiful long legs, tight waist, and voluptuous curves straining against her tight black minidress. He didn't know a lot about American women, but he was fairly sure heel tapping wasn't good, at least with the radiating waves of suspicion currently rolling off Mira at the moment.

Shrugging his shoulder, "Really, I'd never blow you off."

"Mhmm," Mira not buying it, "Sure...." Looking Damon up and down with more than a cursory glance, "Where have you been that you didn't even bother to change?"

"Let me make it up to you, Mira—please."

Damon didn't come off as the kind of guy to use the word 'please' very often and she didn't have a claim on him...yet. His obviously unfamiliar use of the word made Mira's mouth twist in deliberation. "What did you have in mind?" Heels still tapping, faster than before.

Did that mean she was still pissed? "I've got some research to do over the next few hours, but how about a date tonight?"

Mira's twisted mouth turned into a smile.

"I'll send you a picture of what I need you to wear for tonight. And details of where to meet."

Just like that, her smile vanished. "Excuse me?!" She wanted to strangle him, but she didn't think a physical confrontation with this guy would go over so well—in public or otherwise.

"Oh, you heard me," he paused, looking her directly in the eyes as his black irises flashed for her. "I'll send you a picture of what I expect you to wear tonight along with details of when and where to meet for our date. I'll show you a wonderful time. I promise! I'll make it **all** up to you!" Leaning forward and pulling her to him, Damon kissed Mira, not quite as lengthy as

Charles W. McDonald Jr.

their first, but *enough* to remind.

"Oh, if you think that's going to make everything alright...." She made this back-and-forth, side-to-side motion with her index finger.

He didn't quite get that reference. He'd have to ask someone about that. "Great then—I'll see you tonight." Turning, he placed his order for lunch, hearing something of a huff as she stormed—heels clapping on concrete—outside.

Asshole, she realized, slamming the door, stomping on the concrete streets of Austin hard enough to shatter her right heel. *FUCK!!!*

*   *   *   *

His cheeseburger with hot wings and chipotle dipping sauce might have filled his stomach, but they hadn't helped him with Mira, nor his understanding how to better access and control Zero-Point energy to use it for what he needed. Hours ago, he had texted Mira a picture of a white diaphanous micro dress with his home address in Austin, indicating a 7:00 p.m. meeting time for their date. She hadn't responded—not a word.

Well played, he thought, checking his phone again. He might have blown it with this one, but the Internet was an incredible tool, and he needed to make the most of it while he was here. Sex was important too—very important, but not more important than the long game of his Master Plan. He had network access at his place, so he decided to start walking from the campus. It was a bit of a trek, and he didn't feel like pushing his luck with drawing enough energy for a *Portal*, except when he was leaving—planetarily speaking. *Time to walk off that heavy lunch*, he thought, heading north on Duval towards his house.

A bit more than an hour-walk and now sweating like a stuck pig, Damon waved his right hand, causing the remote access security system to engage, popping the front door lock open for him. A typical single-family unit for campus corner, like a mix between what might have once passed for a frat house, now fully remodeled and suitable with all the modern features and options, this split-level brick and siding in neutral tones suited his purposes. He had to keep his time here limited anyway—*mustn't get trapped here*. Technology was well on its way to killing God here—killing all gods. *Magic would die that death with them*, he presumed.

Stripping while he walked to the master bath, Damon paid no attention to the wide-open window treatments. Jeans, shirt, socks and shoes landing on various pieces of furniture as he walked straight into the shower. It was now only moments from 7:00 p.m.

Moments later, right at 7:00 p.m., he'd managed to get re-dressed in Levi's® 501's with a blue and green tartan, button-down, short-sleeve untucked shirt, running his fingers through his still drying, shoulder-length black hair. He hadn't heard the bell, and it was now just after 7:00 p.m. Walking to the living room at the front of the house, he opened the door checking around looking for Mira. Nothing. Not a sign. Frowning, he checked his Android. Nothing. Not a single text since he'd sent her the pictures and date logistics. *Well played,* he thought.

At least I'll get some research done, he thought. Heading to his desk, he opened his laptop resuming his research—albeit his focus divided between physics and Mira.

*   *   *   *

(UT Dorms, Earth, Present Day, the Following Morning)

A rap upon Mira's dorm room door the following morning took Mira by surprise. Mira's roommate, Katherine, offered to get it from where she was getting ready in front of the bathroom vanity, but Mira was already dressed in a white summer dress—already up and about. *Who the fuck knocks on a dorm room door at 8:35 on a Saturday morning?* A push on the door lever from inside and she had her answer…. "Shit, Damon! What the fuck are you doing here?" All 6'4" of him in jeans and a Led Zeppelin Icarus t-shirt menacing her doorway and with a look of bad intentions that immediately chilled her to the core and caused her to interject her body into the doorframe as if to stop him from any thought of entering.

His unique black magic eyes devoured her from head to toe as his gaze projected sinful and invasive thoughts into her head, though his massive body didn't flinch an inch. He might as well have been an immovable piece of granite just staring back at her until his eyes landed upon her soft lips.

"Damon?!" She'd seen that look before in men and…

Pulling Mira to him, not asking, and resisting the temptation to seduce her with his magic, Damon kissed her with everything he physically had; and he had a lot. Draping his lips across hers from left to right as his right hand nestled in the small of her back where it traced little ringlets of love and lust against her warm and soft bare flesh, exposed by her backless summer dress, his tongue found hers in little explosions of electricity and fate…. Just an instant into the kiss, he felt Mira's resistance give way against him while his body hardened and swelled against her thigh.

Charles W. McDonald Jr.

Trying to resist, trying to hold her ground, Mira placed her right foot on the outside of the doorframe, attempting to resist Damon pushing his way in. It was a futile effort; her body wanted him, whether her mind did or not. Her heart was anybody's guess, including her own. Pushing her to the closest bed inside, he fell down on top of her, where his right hand ripped at the tiny little straps that barely made an attempt to cover her large, bare breasts and areola. Teasing her left nipple between teeth and tongue, Mira gasped at how her body was responding to him in much the way it had before on campus—completely on fire. "Mmmmnnnnnhhhh...."

His left hand searching the right side of Mira's body for that most tender spot between the bottom outside edge of her right breast and her ribcage up underneath her arm where he caressed in silky, milking motions as his hot lips found the perfect spot between her neck and clavicle as he captured her most tender flesh between his teeth and devoured Mira, feeling her thighs unconsciously dividing for him—her hands moving to unbutton him as another soft moan involuntarily escaped her wanton lips and tongue.

All the racket on the bed had brought Katherine hurrying out of the common bathroom they shared with their dorm neighbors. "Hey, what the fuck!" Katherine panicked, reaching for the 4-inch switchblade she kept for protection in her top right desk drawer.

Waiving Katherine off with her free right hand, Mira's eyes rolled back in her head with Damon already throbbing and twitching against the velvety hot caress of her hymen as he pushed his way inside her with her left hand guiding him to take her right there in front of Katherine with the door to their dorm still open and a smart-phone-wielding audience gathering outside the front door, recording everything.

Charles W. McDonald Jr.

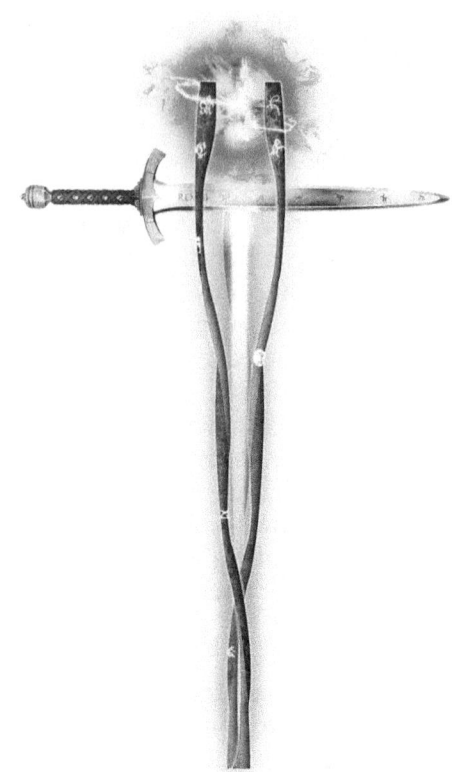

Chapter 43: A Valuable Contribution

(Damon's Manor, Kaleion, Present Day)

inding himself back in Damon's foyer, Radin had to avoid all the men with tools, bustling in and out of the front doors of Damon's manor. *Wow, lots of activity*, Radin noticed. Everyone was sweating profusely with all the bright sunlight beaming in from outside. *Hmmm*, he thought, *I wonder if I should wait to be recognized.* Just then, "Master Damon is away at the moment. Would you like something while you wait?" The beautiful maid, in her familiar black and white outfit, asked of him, trying to stay out of the way of all the construction—debris being hauled out—new materials being hauled in. "Um, sure. Can you tell me what happened here?" Looking around, Radin didn't see any obvious damage on the first floor, but all the activity was coming from the spiral staircase, where con-

struction workers furiously carried new building materials to and fro. *Something had definitely happened on one of the upper levels.*

"I'm not really sure what happened, but sometimes Master Damon's spells don't always work the way they're supposed to, and well...," glancing around with that last implication, she didn't dare say more.

"I'll take some tea if you have it. I'll be upstairs," as he started making his way to the circular staircase, she called after him, "Do be careful up there...." Her voice trailed off as they went in opposite directions.

Avoiding the construction workers proved increasingly challenging as he shared the staircase with what must have been dozens of them, everyone near a state of continuous running to and fro. *This can't be good,* he realized. Briefly taking a look around the second floor, everything looked normal, just like it did the last time he was here—except maybe newer, like a fresh coat of paint. Heading up to the third floor, everything was chaos. New and barren construction of the spell test room—*definitely don't remember it looking like that.* Burnished grey metallic surfaces on all the walls, floor, and ceiling of the test room appeared dull and lifeless, yet new and clean, with bustling activity all around the perimeter of the third floor going up to the fourth floor.

"May I help you, sir?" Edgar Hastings popped up behind Radin, only a few paces away, carrying something he recognized as an Earth weapon.

"I'm Radin, a guest of Damon. He's expecting me."

"My apologies, sir, but certain parts of the manor are still not fully functional again and securing those off-limits areas is my direct responsibility. I'm Edgar Hastings, Chief of Staff," he offered his hand to Radin, who shook it firmly and immediately.

"I'll stay out of any areas you say are off limits. In fact, I can wait in the foyer if you want."

"No, sir, you can walk around freely, but if you see any areas sealed off with yellow tape, please stay out of those. I've had to kill one worker already for violation of secured areas."

Nodding while taking a couple of steps back from the weaponized and lethal chief of staff, Radin opted to head up to the fourth-floor area to put some distance between him and the man.

Up here, the ritual room was still being pieced back together with more of the same burnished grey metal tiles being used to create a subfloor between the top of the spell test room and what he could only assume would be a stone flooring to match what was going onto the walls of the ritual room now. He wasn't sure if it was going to be granite, marble, or something else entirely—it really didn't look like either—it was mostly black, flaked and fissured with off-whites.

Charles W. McDonald Jr.

"Your timing *really sucks,* Radin." Damon was wearing similar Earth garb to what he wore last time, only a green and blue tartan pattern shirt with each of the buttons one level off from where they should have been joined. His hair looked disheveled too. "You're abusing the gift I gave you."

Waving his hands in protest, "It wasn't me this time. Talemar," he'd barely got the name out of his mouth.

"What about Talemar?" Damon hissed, appearing ready to pounce with those *black mirrors of the soul* now glowing before him only inches away.

He didn't like that look in Damon. It unnerved him. "I don't know who Aaramus even is, but Talemar said, 'he might know details about your plans.'"

Tightening his fists 'til they squeezed blood out of his hands onto the ritual room subfloor, Damon pivoted, walking out of the ritual room construction area. Radin didn't want Damon to think he had anything to do with letting out details of his plans—he didn't even have a clue as to what they are, "I don't know the details. Just as I asked Talemar to tell me more, he shoved your scroll into my hands and broke the seal, sending me here with that message for you. I didn't mean to bring you a raw problem—I'm sorry." Whatever their relationship was, or might become, Radin didn't like being a pest, and that was exactly how he felt.

Damon's lips tightened, thinking. "Was there anything else? Anything at all?"

"Multiple people followed you from Earth to Perion saying, 'they followed your wake to Perion.'"

"Mhmm," Damon nodded, but Radin couldn't tell if it was in satisfaction or just acknowledgment.

"So, who's Aaramus?"

"Not so much a *who* as a *what.*" It was almost involuntary, his pivoting into mentor mode with Radin, and very much against Damon's better judgment. "He created a place that is between what is, what was, and what could be. He's neither enemy nor friend. He is feared by anyone who has the intellect to visit his domain.... And he knows it."

"Same Aaramus as in the Halls of Aaramus you've mentioned to me before?"

"The very same."

Nodding, "We have Royvan Miral with us, and we have the Scroll of Carnac."

"Do you?" Trying to remain stone-faced, Damon gave nothing away. "I'm sure you had something important you wanted to ask me. What was it?"

Radin saw his opening and he took it, "I intend to open the Scroll of

Carnac and utter the words of the First Seal." He'd given it a lot of consideration, especially in light of his dreams and Damon's intervention into his life.

"Wow!" Damon didn't know quite what to think…. His black eyes measured Radin from head to toe and he could easily see his aura of magic growing from just the last time they'd met. "Do you now? Soooo certain you are the One, then?"

"If I weren't, you wouldn't have pulled me out of my life to wake me to this one. You're the reason I've come to believe I'm the One. You wouldn't waste your time with me otherwise." He still had his own doubts he chose not to voice, but logic had led him down this path. Now he just needed to do his best to read Damon's reactions to his plans. That would be more telling than any of his own private thoughts.

Nodding slowly, genuinely proud of the young man who'd just taken on the heaviest of burden and responsibilities upon his youthful shoulders. Damon wanted to probe the thought at the front of the boy's mind a bit, "So let's say you utter the words, then what?"

"I want to know if that puts us at immediate odds. Does that mean we're at war with one another?" His eyes observed Damon closely. His body language. His demeanor. His unique and mysterious, black eyes.

"Not necessarily. I'm still not entirely fated—not to the point where I'm acting under orders. Technically, I'm outside the sphere of influence of Perion. Your Seals only affect Perion, though they, and some scholars, might indicate otherwise." Internally Damon wondered if that was the truth, scratching the designer stubble he'd been growing to seduce Mira. His research indicated it was correct, but he had been wrong before. Damon's Star was a good example of that.

"Yet you've injected yourself into our sphere of influence by pulling me to you, by opening my eyes. By placing your transportation scroll where I could find it. Where I *would* find it…."

"Perhaps…, but if you're asking me if your opening the First Seal is going to bring down my wrath upon you or your friends, the answer is a flat 'no,' and you know I wouldn't lie to you."

"I know your word is good, Damon. I do know that about you." His own expression remained flat. Indeterminant. Though his eyes observed every little thing about Damon.

"I'd be more concerned about Eldrac and the rest of the Six that have been unleashed to deal with the One. If you're going to accept, or rather hostilely take, The Crystal Throne of your world, then you'd better have a plan to deal with the Six and right now you're not powerful enough to take on even the least of them let alone all of them."

Charles W. McDonald Jr.

"What do you think the Scroll of Carnac does? How bad will it get?" He wasn't sure of how robust Damon's knowledge was of the First Seal, but it would be reckless for him not to at least ask and measure his response.

"Beyond beginning the End, you mean...?" Damon's tone was non-chalant—as if they were discussing girls over afternoon tea. But his eyes said he was deadly serious.

Radin offered him only an affirming nod, but his lips and mouth went instantly dry with implications.

"If it were me.... If I had written them—the scrolls—and I...were the meddling sort.... I think I'd want to get Humanity's attention. To make sure they were listening. To make certain they knew just how serious I was." Damon could only guess at God the Creator's intentions and motives. Could only surmise at just how such a God had intervened in his Creation through-out time immemorial. And why....

Radin gulped, considering a myriad of possible outcomes in his dangerous and seemingly private thoughts. His mind raced as he knew or expected Damon to be reading his thoughts far better than he could read Damon. He was but a child and Damon was the grand master. "What if you sent me a little help?" *Yes*, he considered. *Good thinking*. Radin wasn't entirely sure what he was asking of Damon, but he thought Damon might be able to measure out a bit of something he could use without becoming *too* involved in Perion's affairs. Assuming the Scroll of Carnac only or mostly affected Perion. And that was a very big assumption.

Starting to walk away from Radin, towards Dallia's room, Damon paused his pace in thought, allowing Radin to quickly follow and catch up to him. Radin agreed with Damon that he needed a plan to deal with the Six and perhaps that was a plan he'd have to come up with on his own. But, as for having a plan for what came after opening the First Seal, that was a plan he'd have to forge in collaboration with Damon—at least as far as he saw it.

Entering Dallia's room, Damon walked to the far corner where her staff still leaned against the wall. Picking it up and tossing it to Radin to see him reach out and catch it mid-air with his right hand, Damon challenged him. "If you're going to cast, you're going to need an aid to channel, both to help you channel more energy and to be able to control it—at least at first. Take care of that, or I'll take it from your cold, dead hands myself."

Nodding in acceptance, Radin knew Damon meant what he said, word for word. Dallia's staff felt both heavy in its construction, yet light when wielding it. "I'll try to make Dallia proud with it."

"Just try not to die using it," Damon chaffed in response—obviously still irritated by the interruption. It was the first time Radin had noticed the smoke-hued ring on Damon's right hand and the soft, dark glow around the signet it produced while he wore it. *That's new*, Radin noted.

"The magic that brought me here won't let me take this back with me, will it?" It wasn't really a question as much an observation. Radin was beginning to understand more and more. It was coming to him fast.

Shaking his head Damon corrected, "No, it won't, but I've got that covered. Just don't freak out when you go back."

Opening a Portal to the busy night streets of Austin, Texas for him, Damon directed, "I'm going to be very busy for a while, so tell the others this was your last visit with me until I say otherwise." The floor opened up beneath Radin in Damon's manor, and suddenly Radin witnessed his own body vanish before him as Michelle and Lawna looked up at him, then over to where his body had been by the cavern fire only an instant before. Everyone else appeared asleep. He wasn't looking forward to explaining this one. He wasn't even sure he could, but he could feel the power of Dallia's staff come to life in his hands on his homeworld, where magic flowed like a powerful river.

*   *   *   *

(Valley of Power, Perion, Present Day)

Moments later, after explaining to Michelle and Lawna and waking up the rest of the group, Radin recounted the conversation to everyone, but it was the last that piqued their interest, "Yeah, it was nightfall wherever he was going, and I got the feeling from all the times he's met me in the attire he's been wearing, that he's been *very* busy off-world. In fact, he told me to tell all of you that this was the last meeting with him until he said otherwise—he's going to be *busy*."

"Radin, think back and be precise. Tell me everything you could see on the other side of the *Portal* Damon was about to use." Trying not to be too pushy but trying to put together something that didn't quite make sense to her either, Lawna needed more detail. So did Michelle and Elise. They were all on the same mental track together.

"Wherever it was, it was nightfall, lit up everywhere with those electric lights and lots of 'cars.'" The use of that last word was still so odd to him. Now Royvan Miral's team was trying to grapple with Earth terminology too. At least Michelle didn't have to hide her M-4 anymore. Expertly cleaning *Bad Intentions* in front of everyone, Michelle smiled as it went back together in seconds.

"You're certain you saw lots of cars. Were they all green or black or like this," Lawna showed off her camouflaged Glock®.

"Nope, I didn't see a single car that had colors anything like that. Most were white, silver, gold, red, and blue—lots of solid colors and decorative stripes."

Michelle, Lawna, and Elise all exchanged knowing glances. Definitely on the same mental track with one another. "Radin, the Earth you're describing doesn't exist anymore. Remember our world is in a global conflict. The only 'cars' you should have seen would have been military vehicles. That means you saw our past, which begs the question, what is Damon doing spending so much time 'busy,' in his own words, in Earth's history?"

*   *   *   *

(Valley of Power, Perion, A Short Time Ago)

Moments after Radin's conscience traveled to Damon's Manor, Talemar rose from the fire, keeping one eye on Radin's body resting breathless, his chest not moving. He had a mission, and he knew just the man for the job. By the entrance of the caverns, he found Gareth, honing his sword with a whetstone, "That's a mighty fine weapon." Talemar wasn't into false praise, and the weapon didn't fit the man—meaning it must have been passed down or taken. Either way, it was a start.

"What's going on in there? With the boy? I heard a commotion."

"He's resting. What do you know of this place?" Using the cave wall in front of Gareth to divine a window to Axum and the famed grounds of the Rune Stones, Talemar panned around 'til the South Sea lapping at the virgin white sand beaches of the Nine Towers was visible. Nine massive blue-grey granite sarsens, some broken into pieces, marched about a three-quarter staggered circle, flanked by massive white marble Humanoid statues, half buried by weather and time. The statues further flanked by nine quartz-like obelisks, shooting up out of the ground at a slight angle, as if leaning on their backs. Each ring marched three-quarters of the way around like unto a king's crown. The white-capped waves battering the solemn shores of the Nine Towers, accompanied by the wind whipping across the tall grassy fields of sarsen rubble Rune Stones, gave the entire site a feeling of ageless royalty like unto a forever king. *The most holy place in the world*, just as his grandfather had described. Recalling his grandfather's description vividly, Gareth felt humble even looking upon the sacred grounds—a lump forming in his throat.

"Only what my grandfather taught me, and what he mentioned in his journal." A forced swallow to get rid of the lump in his throat wasn't able to calm the hackles currently running up Gareth's spine.

"Tell me about this journal. Do you have it?"

Pulling Luke's journal from his pack, Gareth showed it to Talemar. Plain and straightforward, a possession of the poor or the meek, and very aged like his grandfather, the journal bore no outer markings. Flipping through the journal, Talemar looked for any reference to the Nine Towers. "There's a lot of detail in here. Your grandfather paid attention to such things." Noting all adventures throughout Luke's lifetime, Talemar was impressed with both his company and his travels. "I recognize many of these people. Your grandfather must have been a great man. I'm assuming he's no longer with us."

Gareth, shaking his head, confirming, "What's this about?"

Changing the view on the cavern wall to another single brown leather manuscript, darker and far more aged than Luke's journal, hidden in a secret wood floor panel, Talemar showed Gareth as much detail as he could recall. "I need you to find this for me, and I think this," handing Luke's journal back to Gareth, "…might have some clues as to where you can find it. If I send you to where it was last known to be, can you find it and bring it back to me? Getting off of Axum might prove to be a challenge, so take this with you and break it if you locate the manuscript." Talemar handing a small ivory tooth, or maybe it was a fang, to Gareth.

"What is this thing? This manuscript? What's in it?"

"Something you don't want to fall into the wrong hands. That's why I want you to look for it. Your judgment I trust. I accept your judgment of me, so after you read what's in it, if you think I'm still the right man to care for it, you can give it to me. I won't take it from you."

Gareth, nodding in acceptance of both the task and of Talemar himself, replied, "Fair enough. When do I go?"

Opening a *Gate* underneath Gareth, Talemar unceremoniously sent Gareth, without warning, to the coastline of the Holy Ground of Axum.

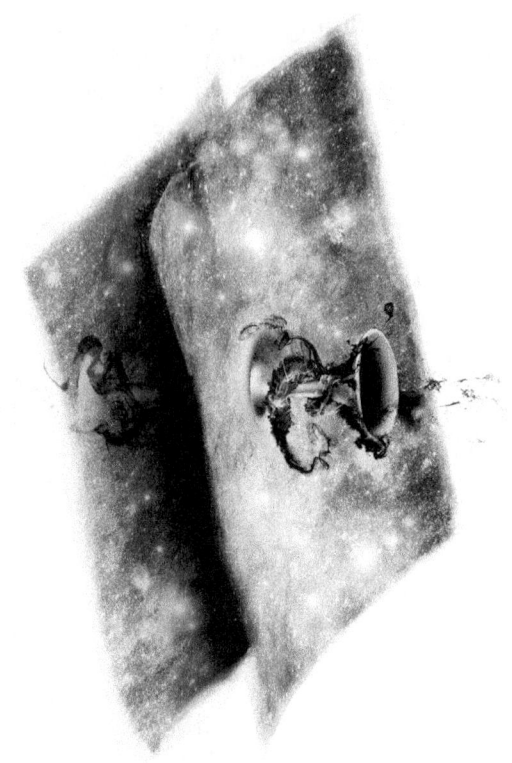

Chapter 44: A Valuable Lesson

(Austin, TX, Earth, Present Day)

Mira lay nude in Damon's bed, partially covered with the cream-colored bedding and duvet. She thought she heard his front door open, barely having time to gather her thoughts as Damon walked into the room. *God, he was tall*, she considered—still not quite used to it. She'd noticed his new ring but was afraid to even bring it up. Something about him was so dangerous it was becoming unsettling. A fertile ground for mistrust to grow in between them.

     "Sorry for the interruption. I'll try to keep the disruptions to a minimum," Damon posed, looking for something in a small desk he kept in the bedroom, then closing the drawer.

     "Wherever you went, you went with your shirt like *that* and with JBF hair?!" Pointing first to his shirt, then to his hair, Mira raised her eyebrows incredulously.

JBF, another phrase he'd have to Google® when he had time.

"Sorry, it was important. I wouldn't have left you otherwise."

"Yeah, well, Katherine called me while you were gone, checking on me. Apparently, everyone in the dorm was worried about me after your little display earlier today."

"Ha! It was hardly little," Damon mused with a wink from those beautifully wicked black eyes as his body turned to face Mira in bed.

"Oh, so true, Darling. So very true." She rubbed her thighs one against the other remembering their display fondly. "Still, we probably broke just about every on-prem housing rule there was with that one, and I'm probably going to get kicked out of the dorm, so we can't be doing that again."

"Let them kick you out. You've got a place to stay as long as you want."

"Damon, we just had sex. We're not married, and I'm not moving in with you. I don't even know if I want to date you or not."

"Mira Darling, your words contradict your body, your heart, and your mind. You can't fool me." Damon was arrogant and proud but not wrong. Mira's body language said everything that needed to be said. She was into him as much as he was into her. He watched the way her pretty eyes followed him everywhere, observing his every little movement. It was far more than just sex....

"Okay then, Damon Darling, how about this?" Shifting in the sheets, covering her exposed breasts up to the tops of her nipples, Mira tried talking from the heart for a moment. "You scare the ever living shit out of me, and I'm terrified of even being this close to you until you tell me more about who you really are and what you're really doing. My BS meter has been going off from the moment we met. You're no fucking grad student!"

BS Meter, furrowing his brow, he was going to have to spend some serious time on Google® looking up all these references being flung at him at a relentless pace. *Hmmm, how much could he show her before she freaked out?* Extending his hand toward Mira, palm up, Damon produced a small ball—roughly tennis ball size, with tiny lightning bolts encapsulated in a self-contained transparent sphere. Carefully examining Mira's reaction of wide eyes and dropped jaw, he decided this would be enough for now, tossing the ball of lightning toward the wall where it would have ripped an explosive hole in the wall had he not dispelled it before it hit. "I'm not...as you say, a 'fucking grad student.'"

"No, you're fucking *David Copperfield*." Pulling the sheets fully around her protectively, then realizing how futile and stupid her efforts must have looked before Damon, Mira wanted to crawl into a safe place and hide from him.

David Copperfield, he thought. *Another reference I'll have to Google®.* They were piling up rapidly in her presence. "I won't allow anyone to hurt you, Mira."

"Even you?" Her curled up body—nearly in a fetal position—spoke volumes her words needn't.

"If I wanted to hurt you, I would have done it already. You bring nothing but the fondest of memories to me."

"I'm not your Mira, Damon."

"You're probably right, but you *do* remind me of her." *Or of someone else?* He paused, thinking about her own identity over the Mira he once knew and loved, "Don't get me wrong, I'm not saying you're her reincarnation or anything. I'm just enamored with parts of you that are both alike the old Mira, and completely new and unique to you."

"I don't want to remind you of anyone except me, Damon."

Just sex my ass.... "Fair enough. The door's always open for you to come and go as you please. I'm not going to stop you."

"That didn't mean I want to go, Damon. It just meant I'm me, not your other Mira. It just means I want to know what the Hell is going on with you. What are you doing? Where are you going when you have these *emergencies?*"

"You would…" This was opening a huge can of worms for him that he really didn't want to deal with right now. "…Not understand."

"REALLY?!!" Now the sheets were off, and she was standing nude right in front of him. "I'm an honor student, majoring in Quantum Mechanics, at a Tier 1 University by the way. I'm no fucking dummy."

"Very well," opening a *Portal* just inches in front of her just so she could see the rogue Planet-X on the other side, Damon explained, "Here is where I was going to go next. To apply my research, that I've been doing here on Earth." There it was, 'On Earth.'

David Copperfield my ass, Mira corrected her own analogy of Damon internally. She took a step towards Planet-X, and Damon's *Portal*, only to feel Damon's hand grip her upper arm tightly. "No, you can't. You can't go without an atmosphere you can take with you, or you'll die." Dispelling the *Portal* that had been taking a great deal more energy than it should have required staying open this long, Damon didn't want to push his luck any further and not be able to leave.

Mira's high-IQ mind was running a thousand miles per hour with her processing of her old reality being shattered in an instant, only to be replaced with Damon's extraterrestrial reality and physics that only hinted at what she thought she knew. "What? How? Why?"

"Do you want to be with me?"

Her mouth worked about as well as her thoughts, still gyrating in a great tempest over her old reality in shards on the floor, but the answers did not come to her lips.

"I can selectively eliminate these memories and return you to your life as it was."

"Does that mean what I think it does, Damon?"

"It means I can't let you live knowing what you've seen unless you're with me—all the way with me. Otherwise, I'd have to wipe your memories and say goodbye." Contemplating his offer, Mira was trying to put together the bigger picture.

"Where are you from and why are you here? I mean I get the research here, led you to there," pointing to where the *Portal* had been, "What is your interest in that Planet?"

"I'm not going to show or tell you any more until you answer my question, Mira. Are you with me? Yes, or no?"

*   *   *   *

It had taken more than a little convincing to get Mira to let him leave for Planet-X for the next phase of testing without giving away too many more details. She had wanted to come with him, but Damon expressly forbade it. With Mira's understanding of astrophysics and unification theory, she'd be a valuable addition to his research if he could ensure she'd remain quiet. Women had a way of talking, on any planet.

Damon's Improved Shell v3 would hopefully do a better job of containing his oxygen-nitrogen atmosphere as he stood on the away side of Planet-X, casting *Damon's Improved Foresight*, regaining bearings on the two celestial objects that had to be moved before the next phase.

Using the fundamental rune to source, Damon cast, reaching out to the lattice framework of dark matter all around Planet-X, touching the toroidal field energy holding that dark matter in place all the way from ground level up to thirty miles above him. Just as Damon sourced Arcane to aggregate with his Zero-Point field energy, the ground spun as he collapsed inside his *Improved Shell*.

*   *   *   *

Charles W. McDonald Jr.

Waking up to the total blackness of space was far beyond unnerving, even for Damon. He wasn't sure how long he'd been out, but the atmosphere was thin. *At least you still have an atmosphere*, he thought, opening a *Portal* back to Earth and Mira—stepping through.

It was so odd, seeing the air rip open right in front of her, and seeing Damon walk through carrying this semi-transparent orb with him as he walked inside of it—it moving with him. She wondered how long he would continue to scare the ever living shit out of her. And when, or if, she'd ever become accustomed to his fantastic feats of magic. "I was getting worried. You left almost twelve hours ago."

"I'm really getting frustrated. Perhaps you can help." Just four words, but it caused her to beam. Her smile could have lit up a city, and those magnificent big sapphire eyes could bring any man to yield.

"How so," she asked, her heel tapping again.

He still couldn't tell with her—*was that a good tap or a bad tap?* "I think there's something flawed in my understanding of Dark Energy and the Zero-Point Field—the fabric of it and how it works in general."

"Oh, that's all?! Well, shit, that's easy," she mocked, rolling those pretty eyes. "Only the greatest astrophysicists on the planet have struggled with that for decades." Pouring him a bourbon on ice, she explained, "The reason we call it Dark Energy, in the first place, is because we simply don't understand it. We don't even really have a practical way of measuring it yet. I mean we have grants and experiments in place that 'should' be able to measure it, but if it were easy to understand, we wouldn't call it Dark Energy. The only reason we know it exists at all is because the math tells us there is simply no way the Universe, or multiverse, could exist or behave the way it is observed to behave without the presence of a lesser understood energy within the lattice or manifold of spacetime. Thus, Dark Energy. That doesn't preclude more than one category of Dark Energy, just that there is/are energy sources at play in the manifold of spacetime that is considered part of the vacuum." Seemingly satisfied with that summary, she paused, blinking at him.

He'd have to probe more on the 'multiverse' with her. He thought she'd understand more on that topic than he, but that knowledge wasn't the immediate need.

"So that's your big hush-hush experiment," she examined his eyes much the way she'd read a polygraph, continuing, "You're experimenting with exotic energy sources? Why? I mean you're already powerful enough to travel between worlds. What do you need this exotic energy source for all of a sudden?"

He didn't want to concern her with the fact that he wasn't the only one

Charles W. McDonald Jr.

capable of traveling between worlds. There would be time for that conversation later, but he struggled with how much he could safely reveal. "I want to create a fully functional inhabitable planet." There it was. Mira worked her mouth, but right now she was trying not to pass out, holding herself up against the granite island countertops in Damon's kitchen.

"May I ask why?"

"Call it my backup plan," Damon quipped, but something told her he wasn't kidding.

*   *   *   *

A considerable amount more convincing had been required before Mira would eventually help Damon with his research, but eventually, the two sat down together at his laptop, collaborating for the first time ever. For Mira, it was the love of her favorite subject mixed with her already powerful emotions for Damon, making her realize that this man might possibly be able to not only advance her studies in exotic energy, but he might also provide the experimental physics side of her theories. The only problem was: *how would she ever publish anything she discovered via Damon as a source?* She'd have to work on that problem later.

Mira started slow, but proceeded at a pretty good clip with Damon, knowing his practical experience with physics far exceeded her own, "In a vacuum state, the quantum field fluctuates just above zero due, at least in part, to wave-particle duality as described in Heisenberg's uncertainty principle. The difference between zero and this measurement represents Zero-Point energy or the so-called toroidal field energy. This potential in the toroidal field is very different from Dark Energy, and I think easier for you to perceive, measure, and access." Mira continued, knowing Damon would catch up fast if he was behind her at all, "That's the layperson explanation, but we can go deeper whenever you want." Her mental juices were flowing now, thinking in terms Damon might more easily grasp. "I know Dark Energy will provide a much bigger source for you, but I think you should start with Zero-Point for your experiments, and I think you'll be shocked at how much you can accomplish with just Zero-Point."

"I did that already, and I ran into some of the same control issues I'm having now. Either I pass out, suffer an uncontrolled explosion, or lose control of other elements I'm using and coordinating to keep myself alive long enough to cast and control it. Reaching the energy has never been a problem for me. Touching it is easy. Controlling it is not." Damon wondered, *how much of*

Dark Energy is Zero-Point responsible for? What was the gap between the two and how much more of a jump would it be from Zero-Point to what remained of Dark Energy?

"Wow! Touching it is easy? Can you measure how much you're touching?"

"Sort of, I start by limiting the scoped area of the toroidal source field," Damon paused, pivoting to stand up as he began to pace to and fro.

"Talk to me Damon. I see the wheels turning behind those big black eyes of yours."

The source field. That was it.

(Valley of Power, Perion, Present Day)

"You're focusing too much on the rune itself, rather than its intent. The rune only behaves like a doorway to the act or intent itself." Pulling the staff from Radin's hand—more like prying it away—Talemar sat it down against the cavern wall that he'd called home the last thirty years. "You need to learn to walk before you can run. I'll give this back to you when you're ready." He wasn't trying to be cruel to the boy, but he was dangerous enough without the artifact, let alone with it. Safety played a big part in tutoring someone in magic.

The jumbled mess of thoughts and emotions churning inside Radin made it all but impossible for him to think clearly, causing his instinct and intuition to rule. He needed Talemar, but he didn't trust him. Using only his natural abilities in *Telekinesis*, Radin easily snatched Dallia's staff back from Talemar. As soon it was back in his grip, he immediately sourced all the energy he could find, filling himself up entirely before using the form aggregate, along with destroy and channeling air with fire, blowing Talemar up against the cavern ceiling. Punching him in the gut with *Telekinesis* as Talemar's body fell to the cavern floor, Radin sent Talemar flying against the cavern wall. "You won't be giving back what *isn't yours* to give, Talemar."

Now bruised and bleeding about his face and arms, with his bangs now coated in his own blood, Talemar pushed himself up with his forearms. "Perhaps you need a valuable lesson beyond the teaching of magic...." Sending Radin and staff flailing up against the cavern wall alongside long iron pikes that chased and nailed his body to the wall by way of Radin's clothes, the Great Talemar meant to drive home his point. "You're growing powerful, and that has the potential of being a good thing, but don't forget your place, Radin."

Charles W. McDonald Jr.

Radin had to channel just to get himself down off the cavern wall, but they'd both made their respective points. "Nice to see you two getting along." Elise walked in, covered with fresh snow, having just returned from her journey with Royvan Miral to the site of where he'd found the Scroll of Carnac.

"The boy is insufferable and doesn't have the proper temperament to learn the craft. I'm wasting my time with him." Still cleaning himself off after the thrashing given to him by Radin, the Great Talemar was more interested in the girl's report of what they had seen. "What did you find?"

"Nothing more related to the Seals. Royvan Miral insists on heading to the Isle of Romney for Second Seal, and I saw nothing to indicate either the location of the second or any other of the Seals anywhere close to where the first was found."

"You saw nothing useful there?" Talemar paced to and fro about his cavern fire, eagerly consuming Elise's report while Radin brushed off his clothes...and his pride.

"Oh, I didn't say that...," Elise made a waving motion with her index finger. Talemar wasn't sure what that meant exactly. *Must be an Earth thing.* "Here, I found this," handing Talemar an aged bronze scroll case with no discernible markings inside or out, nor on either end-cap. "And this," she handed him another piece of paper, looking to have been recently inked, "I wrote this down from one of the camp tents Royvan's team had abandoned when they left, apparently in a hurry. Someone had scratched it into the dirt floor of the tent."

> And there shall be but seven trumpets, bearing seven messages,
> For all the worlds to hear, and all men therein.
> And each message shall be sealed up in itself.
> And woe unto the men of the worlds, for once the first is uttered,
> What will be will be swiftly, and nothing in creation shall hinder.

"Did Royvan say whose tent it had been in?" Talemar read the phrase, then handed it to Radin, who seemed to process it over and over in his private thoughts, considering its larger meaning in the framework of the Seals.

"He claimed not to know," Elise reported, obviously dubious of the claim in her tone.

Reading the phrase for himself, Radin began running through scenarios in his head about the End Times being coordinated—an idea he'd been the one to dismiss. "Where is the Scroll of Carnac right at this moment?" Radin had been keeping an eye on it, and an eye on Royvan Miral as well, but it was

Charles W. McDonald Jr.

now time he took command of the First Seal. As power grew and stakes rose, trust shrank.

"I haven't seen it leave Royvan Miral's side—ever," Elise pointed back to the entrance of the cavern; they could see Royvan Miral walking toward them.

Breaking the seal of the end caps of the bronze scroll case, Radin noticed Royvan Miral rushing up to stop him, waving his hands in protest, "What are you doing? That's probably been sealed for over a thousand years! You're being reckless!"

"Do you have the Scroll of Carnac, Royvan Miral?" Radin's tone foretelling of his intentions. It wasn't a tone in complete disregard for the legend of Royvan Miral, but it was ominous as his eyes lingered over the ancient scroll now in his hands.

Royvan Miral stepped back from Radin a few paces, placing his left hip guarded and away from Radin; it was a valuable body language tell. "You're not mad enough to open it as carelessly as you opened *that*, are you?" Pointing to the bronze scroll case as Radin now emptied the thousand-year-old parchment before them, unraveling it unceremoniously. Elise looked at Radin anew—this wasn't her Michael, nor was it the young man she met in Stirling. He'd grown...unsettlingly fast. Though she saw something in his eyes that burned with a knowledge beyond his years.

Reading aloud, Radin cleared his throat as his body sang with vivid energy and life:

> With the light of his heart,
> He looks down from on high,
> Piercing the darkness of a Creation on the brink of ruin,
> Searching to illuminate the One,
> And he remembers....
> Memories were simply not supposed to be...here,
> Where time and space hold no worth,
> Yet, memories did torment where there was no torment,
> Tears came where there should only be joy,
> And love, ages old, swept over him,
> Memory after tortured memory, as he wept for his beloved.
> A lone tear fell upon what was, what is, and what is yet to come,
> And behold:

A lone tear involuntarily streaked down Radin's left cheek, causing him to crush the ancient parchment to dust in his hands.

Charles W. McDonald Jr.

Royvan Miral, Talemar, and Elise all horrified before him at the utter destruction of both history and artifact alike.

"Give me the Scroll of Carnac, Royvan Miral." The command boomed from Radin's lips unnaturally so as if aided by magic not yet cast. He couldn't describe the epiphany and light/life-affirming vividness that surrounded his vision of reality now around him. It was like seeing with eyes that were not eyes at all. As if every visual sensation that had come before was dark and colorless. *They cannot understand....*

Backing away from them, Royvan Miral immediately pivoted, running for the mountain pass.

Charles W. McDonald Jr.

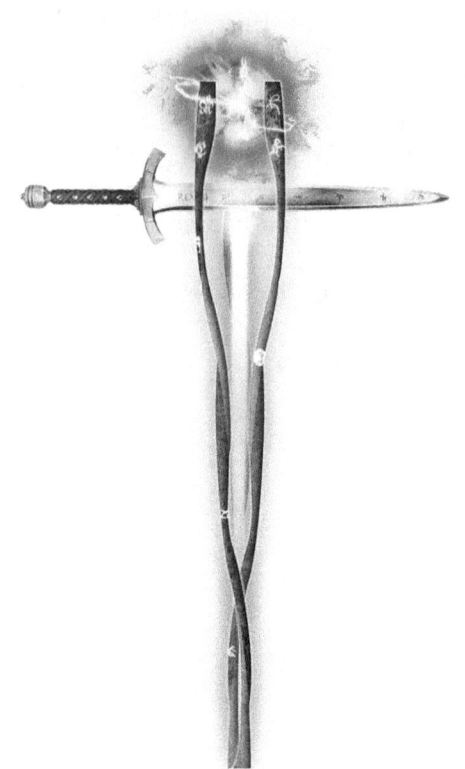

Chapter 45: A Valuable Clue

(Kingdom of Gawth, Perion, Present Day)

Grey-green storm clouds gathered darkly over Almeron Castle, where Eldrac now called home. It was going to storm—ferociously so. Eldrac sipped his tea, growing ever more tired, waiting for a report from his man in the field. Asamel had failed him, and yet taught him a valuable lesson: *surrogates couldn't be used anymore*. Too little margin for error. The boy was growing more powerful by the moment, and he could feel it from here. A valuable clue had been left behind with Asamel's last contact. Vosh was likely in the north of the Valley of Xal, and he needed Vosh to control the actions of *Resha*. Her footsteps were not as soft as she hoped. "Anna, you're late," Eldrac breathed, seethingly, accusingly at her.

"I came nearly as soon as I got your message, and you don't have the authority to summon me, Eldrac."

"We have work to do. My man says Vosh might be hiding in the Valley of Xal."

"Hardly new information." Anna moved about him seductively, but she was not dressed in an apparent attempt to seduce him.

Just the same—she couldn't be trusted, and he had no time for such things. He had work to do to secure his station and his future.

*   *   *   *

(Xal, Perion, Present Day)

Etched into the side of a mountain, with man-sized stones of the same rock as the mountainside, Vosh's estate hid in plain sight, completely blending into the mountain. It was on the backside of the north mountain range, on the north side, so not as to be visible at all from the Valley of Xal, but Rowarc wasn't sure how she'd been left alone all this time, nor how she'd been so hard to find for Asamel. Walking through the small turret gate, the house offered a level of protection, but not like a great castle or manor. Iain guessed maybe three or four guards at most, probably doing double duty for chores and services, presumably not even real fighting men. Vosh didn't seem the trusting sort, nor the sociable type either.

Entering the small, enclosed courtyard that would have made for a medium-size foyer, Vosh greeted her security, "Ector. Gawrin. Please find some food and drink for our guests. They won't be staying long, and we want to be sure they have food for their journey," she'd made her implied desire of 'get out and be on your way' quite clear—nearing on the opaque.

Both Ector and Gawrin, just slightly shorter than Rowarc and not as muscular as Iain, held the appearance of being more than capable of using their swords. Ector carried a shortbow slung over his shoulder as well, looking to be a good decade younger than Gawrin. Both had varying shades of blond hair. Gawrin's was short with light green eyes; Ector's was long and wavy with smoke blue eyes. Ector looked to be the more muscular and warlike of the two; perhaps a seasoned mercenary Vosh picked up along the way.

Walking toward the stone fireplace, which looked to have been carved out of the mountain, Vosh removed her full-length coat, placing it on a man-sized oak coat spindle to the right of the fireplace, revealing her dark-grey and silver dress that reminded Rowarc of storm clouds. He hoped it wasn't a foretelling, as he eyed every visible corridor for trouble.

"Listening to your account of Asamel during our walk didn't make me

Charles W. McDonald Jr.

any more inclined to go with you Rowarc. I know I'm safe here.... Well...,
safer at least. What reason do I have to go with you?"

Cutting off Rowarc abruptly, though not harshly, Iain interjected. "I
think we all agree Asamel, and whoever's pulling his strings, isn't to be trusted.
What if we just made camp close by and just stayed around long enough until
we all felt like the danger to you had passed?"

Initially, upset at the interruption of his friend, but then nodding in
agreement, Rowarc added, "You wouldn't have to pay us. We just don't want
to see any harm come to you."

"I hear the right intentions in your voice—both of you. However,
just your being here has brought unnecessary risk to me. Your presence brings
more trouble than your help. You have no idea for how long I went unnoticed
before your arrival."

"Can we look at this a little differently," Rowarc, suggesting another angle, "Why is it you think Asamel, and whoever we agree is pulling his
strings, is trying to gain direct access to you?"

*   *   *   *

The *Portal* to the north of the Valley of Xal was the closest and safest
bet for Eldrac and Anna, crushing wildflowers and underbrush as they trekked
through the fresh layer of snow. Chilled, water-laden air gust down from
where the North Sea met the Bay of Winter, caused Eldrac to raise the hood of
his black and brown robes. Anna, normally one for seductive attire, opting for
warmer wear for this trip, wore thigh high boots that her black pants slipped
into with a charcoal-grey, button-down, long-sleeve shirt. Her long red curls,
long slender legs, and ice blue eyes made her stunning in anything—yet she
cursed the thought of how she must have looked, trudging through the fresh
snow and this forsaken cold, damp air.

Only a matter of hours later, still not yet dusk and Eldrac's intelligence
had proven accurate. The stone mountain fortress, such as it was, lay a few
thousand paces in front of them, well within the horizon. That had to be
Vosh.

*   *   *   *

Rowarc's suggestion, however innocuous its intent may have been,
wasn't welcome in her home. She'd been as far removed from the game as one
could have been ever since she'd left Damon nearly two decades before. "I un-

Charles W. McDonald Jr.

derstand your point Rowarc, and it's not lost on me, but I don't have an om-nipotent view into everyone's intentions."

Her front door blasting to shards before them with long thick splinters embedding themselves into both Ector and Gawrin, Eldrac and Anna casually and confidently strode through what remained of the entryway, knocking both Ector and Gawrin to the ground in writhing agony. Vosh always kept some degree of protection up at all times, but she had to act fast, casting *Damon's Improved Shell v2*, invoking a protective shell around Rowarc, Iain, and herself.

Intense fire, hot enough to melt stone and metal alike, bounced off Vosh's protective shell, super-heating the air inside the shell enough to force beads of sweat to cascade down the brow of both Iain and Rowarc. Directing *Damon's Contained Blast* at Eldrac, Vosh attempted to eliminate the biggest threat first, causing a white-hot blast radius about ten cubits wide, complete-ly engulfing Eldrac and his protective shell. Poison-tipped arrows from Iain's shortbow that had been bouncing off Eldrac's shell, finally pierced home, caus-ing Eldrac to collapse where he stood.

Not having a ranged weapon of his own, Rowarc rushed Anna, sword in hand, feeling unseen hands fling his body like a child into the burning fire-place. Vosh seized the opportunity, sending spheres of intense lightning that grew from source to target, eventually man-sized each when hitting Anna, causing her to flail backward as each chipped away at her protections.

Suddenly the floor opened up beneath Vosh, and in but an instant, collapsed shut on itself. Vosh was gone. "Enough," Eldrac commanded, still picking himself up off the floor, using something Iain didn't recognize as a *Portal* to get himself and Anna out of harm's way where they stood. He was gone, leaving only Iain to pull his friend Rowarc from the burning fireplace in a singed heap. Ector and Gawrin were still alive, but the massive oak splinters that pinned their bodies to the stone walls didn't give them much chance of survival as their blood trailed down the pale stone onto the floor of the en-closed stone courtyard.

Groans from Rowarc said he was still alive, but the burns engulfing his forearms said he'd never be the same. *Should have stayed retired;* Rowarc's last thought before passing out.

*   *   *   *

(Valley of Power, Perion, Present Day)

Unseen hands grabbed Royvan Miral before he could make it to the cavern exit leading to the mountain pass, throwing him up against the cave wall as Radin approached, fire blazing in his new eyes as fresh mountain head-winds blew at his long auburn bangs. "Give me the Scroll of Carnac. Now!"

An abrupt upheaval of the ground underneath Radin, and he found himself flung out the cavern exit cascading down the snowy mountainside from Talemar's magic. "Go! Meet me at the Rune Stones in five days!" Knowing he couldn't use a *Portal* here, in the Valley of Power, and knowing he had to get the scroll as far away from Radin as possible, Talemar used a *Gate* to open up the cavern floor beneath Royvan Miral, and, in an instant, it slammed shut as if never opened. Royvan Miral was gone and with him the First Seal.

Radin's eyes were all-consuming fire, rising in midair from where Talemar had thrown him over the edge of the cliff. Dallia's staff still in his grip as he rose over the cavern entrance, Radin flooded his body with surging Arcane, enough to obliterate an entire mountain if necessary, with Talemar as his sole target. His anger and emotions now ruling the young boy-become-man. He wanted to make them see what he saw, but there was no longer time for that. Talemar was standing in the way of what must be....

Charles W. M\ :sup:`c`Donald Jr.

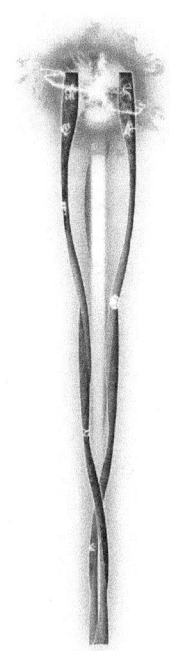

Chapter 46: Plagues of Locusts

(Austin, TX, Earth, Present Day)

The desk from Damon's private study looked an anachronism hundreds of years out of time in the same room with the seventy-inch, wall-mounted, flat screen TV in Damon's Earth-based living room. However, creativity often required the familiar with Damon. He was more a creature of habit than he'd ever care to admit. He'd been working at the desk for hours, all through the night and into the early hours of the morning. Mira watched him from the couch, keeping the volume down while binge watching the first six seasons of *The X-Files* on Netflix®. Between the intense sex and the even more intense research with Damon, she was spent, and she had no idea where he got his energy from. She hadn't been as flippant with the 'old man' ribbing lately, given how she could barely walk.

Suddenly what she'd come to know as a *Portal* split open only about four feet from her and behind Damon while he worked. "Uh, Darling...." Pointing, Mira urged Damon to do something.

"Relax but keep quiet." Damon cautioned, stepping away from the desk, casually covering his work. "Kellen." A simple acknowledgment—nothing more.

"Hey Ra, what's up?" Clearly, Mira didn't understand the reference from her furrowing brow as she covered herself on the couch. "Oh sorry, do I need to take care of that," pointing to Mira—apparently an implied reference to neutralize the problem on Damon's sofa.

Waiving off Kellen in protest, Damon moved between Kellen and Mira to make sure nothing 'bad' happened to her. Kellen couldn't be trusted around women—ANY women.

Frowning, Kellen continued, "Hey, so we've got a problem."

"Oh…?" It wasn't quite flippant, but apparently, Damon was trying to get across to Kellen that he was definitely interrupting something important.

"Yeah, OH. We've got crops failing over more than half the planet now. Dogs molesting cats. Cats molesting rats. Plagues of Locusts. End of the world shit!" Damon made a mental note of the last, giving nothing away—not even to Kellen. "So, when's this fucking Damon's Star going to burn out before it burns the planet to a crisp?"

"I keep telling you, Kellen, it should have burned out already. I still haven't learned how to control this yet, or I'd already be talking to you about how we can use it."

"Yeah, well *I* tried to destroy it. *ME!*" The 'and I couldn't' was implied, but not explicit in front of the mixed company.

"I'm close. Really close to being able to control this. Give me another week."

"Hey Day, you know I don't give a shit. I'll just go build another place on another world—not this one," definite disdain in his tone towards Earth, causing Mira to frown, "I just need to know what's going on so I can make plans. There's a lot of stuff I need to save. Or relocate."

"I promise I'm going to fix this."

"Okay, are you sure I don't need to take care of this?" Again, pointing to Mira on the couch, who appeared sufficiently insulted now.

"I've got it, Kellen. Trust me."

The air superheated directly in front of Kellen as he walked through to an apparently very bright landscape where the grass was scorched and brittle on the other side of Kellen's *Portal* as little lightning shards upon Damon's flooring chased Kellen the Destroyer's exit.

"Damon's Star?" Mira chaffed to a sufficiently guarded Damon…, "You failed to mention that."

"I might have neglected to mention that. It was my first attempt to access Zero-Point in a room specially built to absorb magic, and it blew the room—along with most of my manor—apart at the seams, creating a new small star that now orbits my homeworld." *Let's see how much of the truth she can handle.*

Eyes wide, not exactly knowing how to have these world-ending conversations with this incredibly dangerous man, Mira asked, "Um, you're not planning on doing any of this exotic energy testing here on Earth, or directed at Earth, are you?" She paused, licking her lips that had suddenly gone dry at the thought of the perilous, "…because I kind of like my homeworld the way it is now. You know, fully functional, no plagues of locusts and shit."

He didn't have the heart to tell her, that her world was on the brink of destroying itself with, or without, his influence. *We'll hold off on telling her about that.*

*   *   *   *

Eyes opening to the kicking on of the AC/DC alarm he'd set for himself on his Android, Damon looked around the master suite, reorienting himself until his eyes fell upon the magnificently gorgeous 5'6" red-gold haired female sitting at the foot of his king-size bed atop the linen storage bench in her usual off-white and gold dress with the crest of her flower upon her breast. Damon, giving her a WTF look, pointed to the naked brunette under the sheets with him. Recognizing the distinct feature of many of their conversations as Illirian Starfire seized time, causing Damon to immediately notice music from his alarm had stopped, as Mira's hair, previously moving with the current of cool HVAC airflow, now held captive to the will of Illirian.

Casting *Distorting Web* around them, Damon ensured the encryption of their conversation. "You obviously wanted to talk," Damon tried to hide his irritation, but just looking at Illirian, he could never be upset with her coming into his presence. "What did you need?"

"So, Damon's Star, talk to me about it…."

"What do you want me to say? You already know it was the result of an experiment that went horribly wrong. I mean it nearly destroyed my manor."

"Yes, and well it hasn't been too kind to our homeworld either. Maybe you've been spending so much time here, you haven't noticed it's killing your world slowly but steadily as the crops are dying all over the planet."

"Kellen was just here talking to me about it, still trying to get me to give him the details of how I made it."

"Oh, Damon…. Surely you're smarter than that."

Charles W. McDonald Jr.

"You know me better than that. I'd sooner give you that information before I gave it to him."

"That seemed a political response. You're not a politician, Damon."

"Hardly, but you know I trust your judgment far better than his."

"Yes, but he's your friend."

"And what are we?" Raised eyebrows from Damon as he actively probed the unspoken between them.

"Well, Damon Dear, you're not the monogamous type," Illirian looking over to Mira, then back to him. "So, we could never be what it is you wish. And there's that little matter of *Damnation*."

Damon, giving a dismissive wave with a smile as he tried to push out of his consciousness all the wickedness he'd done; but he knew what she meant.

"I'll try to answer your question—truthfully." She meant it, but it's not like she could make promises she couldn't keep. Damon could, at any moment, do something or start something that could make any relationship between them untenable. "We're far more than Allies. Our interests align more than they should. I care for you far more than I should. I miss you far more than I should. And you are uniquely special to me. There will never be another Damon—anywhere—in any timeline."

Hand to his heart, getting out of bed to walk to her without bothering to put on even a shred of clothing. "I'm touched beyond words, and yet not surprised by anything you just said, because I felt the same, probably longer ago than you. I know the risks to you, to your future, and to your status you take every time you see me. It hasn't gone unnoticed or without appreciation, I assure you." Now standing directly in front of Illirian, she tried not to let the obvious get in her way, nor start something she didn't want to happen—at least not with Mira in front of them.

"Just tell me you're going to do something about Damon's Star and that you're going to be more careful going forward with whatever or however you did that." Her tender caress of Damon with her delicate fingertips and backs of her gold fingernails excited him to the point of not being able to concentrate.

"I promise," was all he could manage, pulling Illirian Starfire into his naked lap while they sat on the bench at the foot of his bed. His *black mirrors of the soul* drank in his oldest of frenemies as the peach gloss of her lips picked up hints of sunlight trickling in through plantation shutter window treatments that played off the golden fire in her eyes.

A bite of her lower lip at the corner of her mouth as she contemplated the kiss she knew neither of them could resist.

Charles W. M\cDonald Jr.

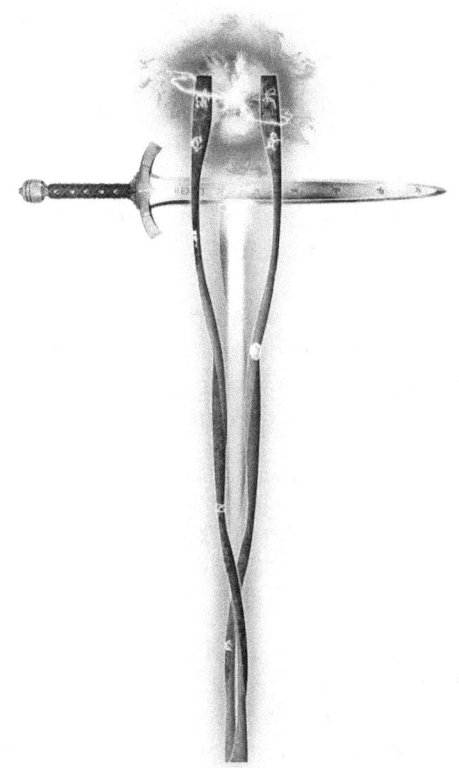

Chapter 47: A New Fundamental

(Austin, TX, Earth, Present Day)

reating spells was one thing, creating a new language was yet another, but creating a new fundamental.... Well, that was game-changing. Damon crafted the new symbol slowly, not out of reverence but out of necessity, as he bonded it to the Zero-Point field all around him, creating an in-perpetuity doorway to it that could be opened or shut at will for those few who would have knowledge of this new fundamental. Even though this fundamental was being bonded to a doorway, to a tiny fraction of what Zero-Point energy was out there, he was making an assumption that it would work with the same energy type that existed everywhere in nature. Everywhere the toroidal field existed around every atom, in every timeline, on every spacetime manifold, he presumed it would work.

Charles W. McDonald Jr.

Observing Damon from the sofa while watching Netflix® and multi-tasking more research on Planet-X, Mira noted the sweat forming all over Damon's body, cascading off him in waves as if he'd just completed the Boston Marathon.

This fundamental had to be something completely new and unlike anything he'd seen in all his experience, in all the specialties on every world he'd ever known, something highly complex and not something easily teachable, discernible, or intuitive. He didn't want others stumbling upon something this dangerous.

Scrolling carefully into the parchment while he shaped the bond that would become an entirely new source fundamental for magic, Damon focused all his being as the entirely new symbol gated out of his fingertips into existence for the first time ever onto his parchment.

If this worked, he'd need to do the same for Dark Energy, and again for Dark Matter. If Dark Matter existed, and the propaganda of mainstream science around Dark Matter certainly led him to doubt that it did. Or at least to doubt that it did in the quantities mainstream science claimed. He knew science to be corrupted on Earth by the system at play, so he couldn't take everything he read at face value. If there was a concerted effort to hide the true nature of Creation from the public, it would have to be done at a fundamental level, so he had to take that into consideration with everything he read from Earth.

Focus on the plan at hand, he thought, admiring his completed work.

Suddenly, the tether between himself and Vosh snapped, coiling back toward him like a snapped rubber band. Turning to Mira, "I have to go. Now! I'll be back." Not used to the manner in which he disappeared before her this time, Mira examined the floor that just opened and shut before her directly under where Damon had just stood as Damon just disappeared—violently swallowed whole with his *Gate*.

(Valley of Power, Perion, Present Day)

Charles W. McDonald Jr.

"I doubt Talemar will ever be convinced to teach again," Ykstherin examined the remains of Talemar's cavern home, now utterly destroyed by the second battle between Radin and Talemar only moments before. He had tried to intervene, but that only got him knocked out. Michelle, Lawna, and Elise had smartly stayed out of it, and Kerrich hadn't been seen since Royvan Miral's party went back to the Isle of Fate.

"Just as well. If you can't follow, or contribute, I don't need you," Radin breathed aloud, looking around at the devastation he'd wrought.

"Talemar could have contributed." Not trying to argue, more trying to reason with the boy rapidly becoming a man, Ykstherin wanted Radin to see more completely the pieces before him and how he could best use those individual parts in a symphony of warfare against a common foe.

It wasn't a sharp rebuke of a look from Radin, but it wasn't far from it either, "Why did he have to fight me? Why couldn't he just have helped me get the scroll?"

"Probably because he thinks *he's the One*." The last came from behind him, standing in the cavern entrance was Damon. "Talemar's always had an inflated opinion of himself since he survived the Halls of Aaramus, but he's no match for you. Nor is he the One."

Ykstherin, Michelle, Lawna, and Elise all fixated on Damon as he walked in, wearing Earth garb, but like unto no mortal they'd ever seen. Instead looking more like a demigod as his black eyes pierced each of their souls as he examined them deeply in the most cursory of glances. Passing Michelle, running his fingers across *Bad Intentions*, Damon noted aloud, "Nice."

"Something important must have happened for you to come here as urgently as you did, especially given what you told me about meeting too often and you having a lot of work." Radin turned to face Damon, his auburn hair shifting upon his shoulders as he glared at Damon through those straight, red bangs of his.

"You are correct," Damon countered with a half-smile for the young boy-become-man as he passed Radin. "Someone vital to me has disappeared, and I would like you to make a priority of finding her and saving her if saving is required. My guess would be that it is."

"I want *you* to teach me." It wasn't a request from Radin, but Damon wouldn't have respected a request either.

Sighing, looking at the horrified faces of the others, especially that of the old man, Damon considered it, "I know that there are many cases where teachers and students have chosen very different paths, and I suppose this could be like that. What I cannot have is you following my path." That found nods of approval all the way around. "I can show you the way to use magic as

Charles W. McDonald Jr.

a tool. What you do with this tool is entirely yours to decide. Understood?"

A solitary nod from Radin caused those long, auburn bangs about his face to shift as his glare upon Damon became more of an accepting expression. Possibly accepting that his future was his own to decide.... "What about the Scroll of Carnac? And where would I find this friend of yours?"

"My guess is that you'll find Vosh somewhere in the possession of Eldrac. He would be the only one capable of taking her alive or dead, and the only one with motive. And, as far as the First Seal goes, it would be best if you didn't have it in your possession when you went to Eldrac. If anything became compromised, the First Seal would be more valuable to him than Vosh. Deal with the Scroll of Carnac after you deal with Eldrac—after you get Vosh back safely." Pulling a small pebble from his jeans pocket, Damon handed it to Radin, "Throw this in any calm body of fresh water whenever you have Vosh in your possession; even if she appears mortally wounded."

"What are you?" Michelle, never mixing words as she stared Damon down.

"That's an interesting question coming from the *Undead*." Damon barely affording her the most cursory of a glance while preparing a spell he made just for such a beast. Foul thing, the Undead, his stomach curdled just from the memories that word stirred in his thoughts.

All eyes, minus those of Lawna, were now on Michelle, perhaps that didn't go over the way Michelle had planned.

"I see you still have the staff," Damon pointed to Dallia's staff ever clutched in Radin's right hand. "Don't let that fall into Eldrac's hands. He'll want that as soon as he sees it."

"Aren't you and Eldrac on the same team?" Damon wasn't the only one raising his guard, as Michelle did the same, before calling him out.

"As I told the boy." Damon paused, twisting his mouth at the last word he'd accidentally used. He corrected himself, continuing, "As I told *Radin*, my agenda and his are not necessarily at odds. One could deduce from that statement, my plan and Eldrac's do not overlap as much as one might think. I operate independently. Eldrac does not. He's following orders, and he's motivated to succeed in following those orders. Failure to him means his own destruction. My failure...." Damon wasn't about to finish that sentence. *Let them guess at what he meant.* He'd made his point, but not before giving Michelle a knowing wink, making her shiver and Lawna snort in derision.

*   *   *   *

Charles W. McDonald Jr.

(Valley of Power, Perion, A Few Moments later….)

"I don't get why Damon is helping you now, and I surely don't get why you're taking his help, or even helping him. He's using you, and by his own admission, his agenda can't be good." Elise had been mostly quiet, but her relationship to Radin was suffering, her thoughts of who he was inside all on the precipice of doubt. There had been so many confirmations to verify her hopes, but so many actions and words from Radin that said otherwise. She was turning into a basket case, and it was torture for her to be around him.

"He never said anything about his agenda, to you or me or anyone as far as I can tell. That's a secret he protects very carefully." Pausing, giving serious consideration to his foundational thoughts, "Suppose I am the One, why must I break the Seals at all?"

"To bring about the clash between the Creator and the Dragon." Ykstherin quoted prophecy, but he wasn't free-thinking like Radin and his thought experiment that went far outside the lines of words written on scrolls thousands of years ago by Men who may or may not have had hidden agendas.

"That clash will happen throughout time whether on this world or not. Why must it happen at all on this world?" It was a good question from Radin, and one currently being pondered by the rest of the group as he could see in their eyes.

"The Dragon has already set loose upon us those who will come to destroy you, broken Seals or not." Ykstherin, still not on the same wavelength as Radin, who was several steps ahead in his mind.

"Are you trying to short circuit the End Times, Radin?" Michelle was following Radin, but not quite caught up to him yet, then realizing he might not get the 'short circuit' reference.

"I'm not sure about the 'short circuit,' but before I go and do something that cannot be undone and will supposedly set in motion the End Times, I want to fully understand all the driving forces behind it, and what might come after." Pausing, the light came on in Radin's mind, "I can leverage my study time with Damon to probe these questions because I know he has those answers. He has to."

"So, when do we go kick some ass and see how badass this Eldrac really is?" Lawna always radiated action, but her camo Glock® was burning a hole in its holster as she slipped it back into place after cleaning it and loading a round in the chamber—testing the laser targeting optics on the cavern wall. Michelle snorted a laugh, shaking her head at Lawna, *God I love her*, Michelle thought.

"I think carrying out this request from Damon is a given. We don't want to even consider not doing it, and I'm not even considering who or what

Vosh may be. I'm just saying the downside of not fulfilling that request is so big, we're not likely to recover from it." Ever to the point, Michelle was just like Lawna's laser target finder.

Radin nodded knowingly in agreement, as did Ykstherin and Elise. The path was set.

Chapter 48: Help

(Florè, Perion, Present Day)

here were many places throughout Tannanvar, around Florè Castle, where mercenaries and honorable swordsmen alike could be found. Radin hadn't counted on how valuable that information would become until now, but Eldrac was an unknown to him. Unknowns required caution, surprise, and overwhelming force. Walking the city streets leading up to Florè Castle, Radin brought more than enough coin, which he'd taken from Talemar's cave, to find and acquire the services of the best he could find. "Keep that thing hidden, I don't want to have to explain more than absolutely necessary," Radin warned Michelle, eyeing the M-4 slung over her shoulder under her gold, grey, and white cloak.

"I think that staff of yours will raise more eyebrows here." Michelle maneuvered her cloak more tightly around her buxom frame as her soft leather boots avoided pools in the cobblestone from a recent rainfall.

She isn't wrong, Radin agreed internally, trying not to slide around too much on the muddy streets.

"I've only been here one time before, but I saw the kind of folks we might need at the pub just inside the castle walls, next to the blacksmith," Elise proposed as they walked inside the gates, pointing to the right. Each nodding to the gatehouse guardsmen, who eyed each of them with suspicion as they passed by—especially Radin. One looked to challenge them, but oddly enough he opted not to when he noticed Michelle. Noticing Lawna's fierce gaze and lithe but muscular frame might've added to his better thinking as well.

Ykstherin separated from them only saying that he had an idea of someone who might help if they gave him some time and would meet him outside Stirling in but a day. 'Twas a day's ride from Florè to Stirling and he figured they could purchase of *Portal* if necessary, so Radin agreed. Radin wasn't in the habit of questioning Ykstherin—nor his intent—though he wondered why it was necessary to separate from them to get aid from the source he discussed. Walking towards the Crooked Leg Pub, just inside the gates, Radin was grateful for the cobblestone paving. There'd been so much rain lately; it made the dirt streets barely passable. The door was open wide with a large white—well its fur was *originally* white, though it was filthy—dog guarding the front entrance. It looked more akin to a wild wolf with its long coat and long, sharp teeth, though it seemed as if someone had domesticated it. At least a little.... Radin leaned down to let the wolf smell the back of his hand as the wolf rose, licking him and following Radin's party into the Crooked Leg.

Inside all manner of sordid debauchery could be found, causing both Radin and Michelle to smile at one another, probably sharing similar thoughts. Elise kept her head down under the hood of her cloak, while Lawna threw back her hood, walking to the bar for a drink. "It's not every day a handsome young man is accompanied by three beautiful women," Michelle quipped, slapping Radin on the back of his right shoulder taking a seat at the only open table left—dead center of the room. She preferred having her back to the wall, as did he.

Sell-swordsmen, whores, off-duty guardsmen, trackers, along with all manner of farmers and merchants filled their bellies with ale, bread, cured meats and good times. Standing out in the crowd of filth was a table of four hard, weathered men, all clean-kept in bright colored leather and ringlet armor, one—the enormous one with the full beard—with chainmail. The way they were talking, huddled around him, he must have been their leader. Nodding in the direction of the muscular hulk of a man, Radin whispered in Michelle's ear, "What do your instincts tell you about him?" Something about the man triggered a memory for Radin, but he couldn't place it other than the man's obvious hulking size. *Where have I seen him before?*

"I noticed him as soon as we walked in, and he noticed us too, but he never gave us more than a passing glance. He's careful, measured, and experienced. He could be our guy. We don't want to approach him as a group. We don't want to present a threat or provoke him in any way."

Nodding in agreement, Radin put a comforting hand on Elise, walking over to the bar to grab a drink before walking over to their table against the back wall.

Drink in hand, Radin noticed their eyes on him instantly as he approached. All of their hands moving to the grips of their weapons, he didn't want to make any sudden moves, "Afternoon," Radin offered in common tongue, giving them each of them an acknowledging and respectful nod.

Radin had no idea how much of a hulk he was dealing with until he now stood before Radin, towering over him. Taller than either Damon or himself by at least a full hand, the man must have been twice Radin's girth. "A young man traveling with three girls…. If I didn't know better, I'd say you were begging for trouble to find you."

Intentionally making his eyes burn with fire, Radin's right hand index fingernail suddenly turned a liquefied gold as it gripped Dallia's staff tight—though that had not been intentional. "No trouble intended here, but I am planning on bringing trouble to someone who deserves it."

The whole table burst into laughter, except the hulk in chainmail who was stone-faced. "I'm not sure where you mean to bring your trouble, but you can take it away from *my* table."

He didn't want to use magic to persuade the man, but he needed an opening. He had to learn persuasion without the use of magic. "You're clearly a great man, and I need great men. And, if you give a few moments of your time, this is yours. You don't have to do anything but listen, and it's yours." Setting a large gold coin on the table next to the hulk's left hand, Radin backed up a step giving the other man a little more space.

The hulking man grunted, motioning for Radin to sit beside him, "My name is Brigance Fireheart. This is Ethan Marshall," pointing to his immediate left, "…the best blacksmith in these parts." Most blacksmiths were fat and hefty men. This Ethan was leaner than himself, and not quite as tall, though he looked to have the biceps of a blacksmith. Radin nodded in acknowledgment, receiving a nod in return from Ethan. *Probably the only blacksmith I've ever seen wearing a leather jerkin*, Radin considered, carefully examining the rest of Brigance's crew. "This," pointing to his left on the opposite side of the table, "…is Hugon, one of the best trackers since Rowarc d'Aguillon." The last causing a broad smile on Radin's face, with an accepting raise of his right hand, acknowledging Hugon, who gave only the slightest twist of a smile in return. Hugon wasn't the only man of color Radin had seen in Tannanvar, but they were far from common. With his shaggy black hair and dark brown eyes, he was about as muscular as Ethan and just a hair shorter. Hugon carried some rugged good looks and didn't appear to be the type to refuse hard work for good pay.

"This," Brigance pointing to Hugon's immediate left, "…is Gouen." Gouen was definitely the largest and most intimidating in looks, next to Brigance; he offered no flourishing reputation with that name in introducing the dirty blond haired, brown-eyed man. Radin chose to leave that alone, instead offering his best smile in acknowledgment. Gouen apparently not knowing how to accept that, providing a blank look in return. "I'm Radin," he paused, knowing his family name might be risky, "Radin d'Aguillon. And yes, Rowarc is my father."

All of Brigance's crew looked to be in their prime. These were the kind of people Radin needed on his side.

"I knew your father, and he didn't have a son when I knew him," Brigance gruffly replied, eyeing him with more suspicion than before.

"My father doesn't talk much about his past. In fact, since mother died, he hasn't mentioned hardly any of his past. The only time I hear of his work is from people like you."

An affirming nod from Brigance with a relaxing look about the hulk's frame told Radin he might be making some ground with Brigance, but he was a hard man. Of that, there was no doubt.

"How is that old shit," Brigance asked with a managed smile.

"Fine, but I haven't seen him in a couple of weeks, since he was hired to find someone. He never said who."

"That old shit's still working? I thought he retired."

"I'll grant you, he's past his prime," Radin agreed, but his hope for his father's wellbeing was now becoming prescient in his foremost thoughts. "... But he's still in good shape for a man his age."

"Mhmm," it was a gruff acknowledgment from Brigance, his glare turning hard again at the boy as he carefully measured, "So how did his boy become a lamean?" With that word, others turned around looking at Radin. The dull roar of the place calming, yielding the room to their previously private conversation.

Opting not to answer, because that conversation would not serve any useful purpose here, Radin considered how he might both gain the man's trust and his undivided attention. "I mean to start a war with a great lamean. A lamean that kills women and children. A lamean that captures young women, using them for leverage for an agenda one can only assume is dire and threatens us all."

Laughter bursting out again, this time beyond just their own table— Brigance remaining stone-faced, measuring the boy's resolve to do as he so boastfully claimed. "I like your tenacity, but you need skill *and power* for what you claim. I don't see that in you." Picking up the coin, putting it in his purse as if the conversation was over, Brigance dismissed, "I don't see anything but a very young lamean with some stolen coin."

Suddenly Michelle sat in between Brigance and Ethan. He hadn't even seen her move to cover the distance of the three tables between them, but she had his undivided attention now. "I don't think you want to say *no* to this,

Charles W. McDonald Jr.

Brigance." It wasn't a request from Michelle; and how had she heard his name from way over there?

Brigance made a sound between a groan and a mournful acknowledgment, facing Michelle, "Okay, maybe more than just a little boy with some stolen coin he might be. You propose taking on a powerful lamean with just us and that small gang you walked in here with?" Brigance wasn't fazed, but he wasn't relaxed either. Michelle had definitely unnerved him—given away by his fidgeting on his hefty broadsword's grip. She could tell he wanted to be standing with some distance, not sitting next to her like this.

"Brigance," Radin offered another three gold coins, one for each of his men, "...we need you. We need your crew. Do you have a pressing and paying engagement, or can you spare some time to come with us?" Watching the natural daylight gleam off Radin's gold, Brigance pondered. "How far, for how long?"

Radin wasn't going to start off this relationship with a lie, "I don't know, but I will tell you this: If I knew, I would tell you. Any information I get along the way, I'll share it with you immediately. You can count on me to be straight with you as much as you could rely on my father."

It was against Brigance's better judgment, but it wouldn't be the first time he'd taken on a great lamean and lived to tell the tale. If the boy was anything like his father, Brigance could deal with him, "We would each require two silver coins per day, three squares a day each, equal shares to you for spoils, and another gold coin each at the end."

A hard bargain, Ethan Marshall thought, nodding in approval with a smile as he was yet again impressed with his boss.

Getting up, they all started walking out of the Crooked Leg together, Lawna falling in behind them bringing up the rear, scanning for trouble. As they reached the doorway, Radin looked down, noticing the white wolf about to follow them out the doorway, "You can come too." White wolf in tow, they hadn't got five steps out of the doorway when Radin turned to Brigance, "We're taking on Eldrac." Brigance Fireheart stopped in his tracks so fast his hulking frame almost skid on the wet cobblestone.

Now he knew what they knew! Something in the way Brigance was standing there looking at him; Brigance Fireheart *was* the man from Radin's dreams that included Damon, Evanyil, and Elise. The man trying to take others off him so Radin could escape to higher ground. That was Brigance! Now he was certain, he'd found the right help, assuming his dreams were prophetic. And that was a big assumption.

*   *   *   *

It had taken more convincing, more coin, and more rations, but Brigance and crew held company with Radin as they approached the western city gates of Stirling, looking for Ykstherin. They were drawing more attention now with the giant Brigance Fireheart and team in tow. The city guard never took their eyes off them as they stood fifty paces from the city gates, waiting for Ykstherin, who promised to meet them before sunset. City gates closed each night at sunset for security reasons, and Ykstherin didn't have much time left, not that closed gates would present a problem for him. It was the timing that bothered Radin. Ykstherin had impeccable timing as if his internal clock was flawless.

"There he is," Michelle pointed, causing Radin to look. He couldn't see anything in the mass of people moving about. Neither could Brigance.

"I don't...," Radin started just as Ykstherin emerged far in the distance, stopping Radin from correcting her. The only problem was that he was alone. *He's supposed to be bringing help,* Radin chastised internally.

Moments later as they all began moving away from the gates, allowing the city guard to finally relax, Radin looked to Ykstherin expecting a helpful answer. "You were supposed to bring help," Radin chastised aloud this time.

"I did." Ykstherin just smiled as if his help were obvious.

Radin, motioning around them, "Where? Who? How?"

Placing a comforting hand on Radin's shoulder, Ykstherin coached the young boy-become-man, "Sometimes help isn't obvious."

"I don't like how this is starting off," Brigance retorted, looking around not seeing the promised help that was supposed to accompany them to face Eldrac.

"You don't have to like it; you just have to fight," Michelle corrected, looking back at them as she took point, giving them some distance before they could use a *Portal.* "By the way, you're going to need your ranged weapons for this one." She didn't expose *Bad Intentions this* time, but she wouldn't let reserved thinking prevent its use if their lives depended on it.

"Do we even know where we're going," Elise asked, looking to Ykstherin.

"That was part of what I was researching in Stirling. Castle Almeron is about two hours' walk," Ykstherin offered, deliberatively.

"We don't have time for that," Radin proclaimed, extending Dallia's staff before him, casting, causing the air before them to superheat with silvery-blue flashes of light that tore the fabric of space in front of them, creating his first ever *Portal.* "Yes well...," from Ykstherin. The young man was learning—fast! The only question was would his wisdom grow at the same pace as his abilities?

* * * *

Almeron Castle lay quiet, yet brooding, against the tapestry of four huge majestic rectangular arboretum gardens that framed the lattice of the ground's boundaries. Watching the sunset from the vantage point of the master bedroom balcony overlooking the gardens below, Eldrac pondered his next line of questioning. He hadn't really expected to get any real information out of her, of course. Torture wasn't a reliable means of getting trustworthy information—he knew that. Sometimes torture for torture's sake was more than enough reasoning for him. He'd been abused in the arms of the Dragon for as long as he could remember. He needed to share the experience. *Where's that useless bitch*, Eldrac considered, thinking of Anna.

She hadn't acknowledged his summons, and even if she had, she would have waited longer to come to him just because she could. Even now, her long legs gliding across the marble tile that spanned from the master suite out into the hallway made Eldrac uncomfortable in ways he couldn't describe or entertain. *Mustn't.* She'd be upset with him, for allowing distractions to get in the way. "Must you?" Eldrac eyeing her scant diaphanous blood-red dress precisely matching the long red locks of hair that flowed down the exposed small of her back.

"Must I what?" She loved toying with men. Eldrac especially so. She would never allow him to have her but teasing him was too much fun to be denied.

"We need answers—not distractions. You *could* help with this interrogation!"

"Is that what you call this? Darling, you're never going to get anything out of her with torture. Even now she's downstairs steeling herself for your next assault."

"Oh, I know. That's what makes it so fun—the knowing that I'm going to break her at her strongest."

"How very powerful you are to beat a captured and restrained woman." That earned her a blistering slap across her right cheek from unseen hands with but a thought from Eldrac, hard enough to loosen her teeth.

"You'll find my power has grown since we last tested one another, Anna. I wouldn't encourage testing me again." He couldn't allow Anna's antics to get in the way of his promised rewards. Not when he was this close....

Charles W. McDonald Jr.

Rubbing her jaw and feeling the molars he loosened with a thought, Anna reconsidered who and *what* she was working with.

* * * *

Chained to a chair inside an iron cage in the middle of the marble floor of the foyer, Vosh tried to reach the source of her power, which she'd been trying to reach every waking minute since she'd been captured. Anna had cut off her source to Arcane as soon as she'd been gated here into their elaborate trap. They would be back to torture her again soon, but her cuts and broken bones would heal. Her fingernails would grow back—eventually. She wasn't sure she would recover if they began dismembering her, and she was certain that was the next step in her torture. She was preparing herself for it, hoping they would start with digits she didn't require to cast—assuming she ever got away alive and would ever be able cast again.

* * * *

Almeron Castle was now on the horizon. Vosh could wait no longer. They would have to *Portal* inside in mere moments so as not to be seen approaching. Elise had been quiet, traveling in the back of the pack with Lawna, exchanging glances that qualified more as glares with the tall and muscular dirty-blonde. She needed a moment of privacy or a distraction. Or she needed to just tell the truth. *What use is it trying to hide this in front of everyone? We're about to go into combat, and we need all the help we can get.*

Abruptly Elise halted in her tracks, not really trying to hide, but not announcing it either, as she pulled a small crystal sphere suspended in between silver talons on a silver chain from her belongings. Inside the crystal sphere, a blue light glowed suspended in mid-air, not enough to radiate beyond the walls of its crystal confinement, but sufficiently enough for Lawna to identify it as a magical artifact.

Peering deeply into the blue light of the prison that voluntarily held her powers, Elise hoped with this she would be able to contribute more to the cause. Lawna halted her forward progress, drawing attention from the rest of the group as the sapphire blue light from the crystal prison of Elise's powers engulfed Elise, causing the silver talons to open and release the blue sphere prison, which floated to the height of Brigance's head before shattering and sending shards of crystal exploding in all directions.

At the front of the now-halted group, looking back at an Elise bathed

Charles W. McDonald Jr.

in a blue light that would now reveal only some of her true identity, Radin began to wonder if he knew Elise at all—if he had ever known her. *Not everyone values honesty the way you do*, Radin considered as that thought made him think of Damon. Looking into the now blazing green eyes of Elise as all of her fingernails turned liquefied gold before him, Radin nodded in acceptance of her secret now revealed. In her cloud-grey and full-length silver cloak, Elise now not only looked the part of a lamean but a deadly one at that. *What else is she hiding*, Radin's internal rebuke stroked the back of his thoughts as he quietly accepted her help—if not her lies.

Charles W. McDonald Jr.

Chapter 49: Retribution

(Almeron Castle, Perion, Present Day)

"reator as my witness, he will heal my soul, Eldrac, and even you can't destroy that."

"Are you certain of that, Witch?" Moving about Vosh, Eldrac began gating Arcane through his right index finger, ripping flesh from the most tender and sensitive parts of her upper thighs and her breasts. Vosh's clothes ripped, alongside her flesh, landing in the foyer with even more spurts of her own blood. Vosh's screams and howls could be heard more than a hundred spans away through multiple walls as tears streaked down her agonized face.

The scent of sweat, tears and blood perfumed the chambers and corridors of Almeron Castle as the dismemberment of Vosh began.

"I know a way to destroy your soul—your very lifeforce," Eldrac seethed before her, continuing to gate and tear pieces of Vosh away wherever he pleased.

Vosh knew of what he spoke; she'd seen Damon use it before, though he had promised to stop for her. "You can't use that spell," Vosh was losing strength, and he could hear it in the meekness of her reply. Struggling against her restraints and trying to stay conscious took everything she had. Summoning her strength, she hoped she could convince, but Eldrac wasn't the convincing type, "It draws attention—changes the balance of power. That spell has far reaching consequences you can't possibly imagine!"

"Oh, but I can, and I have." Eldrac spoke with authority as if in his eyes Vosh had seen his own witnessing of *Damon's Damnation* at work.

Anna laughed; Eldrac thought so highly of his abilities—both now and before. Still, she didn't want to test him. Something in his eyes spoke to her as well. Eldrac had seen something; something firsthand.

She'd get to see Eldrac's full powers soon enough as hundreds of fiery, finger-sized blasts streaked into the foyer from both sides hitting her and Eldrac simultaneously, causing her fire-red dress to set ablaze. The flames of her dress licked aimlessly at her flesh that refused to burn as she smartly had a level of her protections up—Anna already casting yet again to strengthen them. *We're flanked*, Anna realized, disappearing into the marble floor with red and amber flashes of still-charged lightning chasing her exit, leaving Eldrac to fight them off himself.

Pivoting from where he'd faced Vosh's cage, in the center-right of the foyer, now facing the kitchen, Eldrac witnessed Ykstherin already casting again. Dozens of black vipers struck at Eldrac's shins, the vast majority of them breaking their fangs on an invisible shield of protection all around him. Eldrac's volley of dozens of lightning balls barely had time to leave his hand before he was slammed violently against, then through, the three walls between him and the exterior of Almeron Castle. He only had an instant to see the young auburn-haired boy before violently hitting the first wall of the foyer.

The scent of turmeric, sulfur, ash, and earth perfumed the air all around Eldrac—the familiar smells of combat. *They've come in force.* Eldrac had to move fast, focusing first on protection spells as he tried to right himself from skidding along the garden grounds outside. Even before he got the first protection spell off, something clawed him through his mortal shell so fast he couldn't even see it approach, nor leave. He was bleeding—a lot. A pool of blood forming at his feet, and he found himself flying through the air again, at a violent velocity, as he was unceremoniously blasted against the keep exterior walls, hard enough to leave an imprint of his body in the stones. Again, never seeing the attacker come nor go, and barely even seeing a blur flash across the garden. Eldrac had seen enough. *Gate* opening beneath him, Eldrac escaped with his life still intact. Barely....

Pouting from the spot in the garden where she'd just tossed Eldrac against the brick of the keep, Lawna scanned around, looking for Anna, "That's no fun. I thought he was supposed to be a badass."

Walking through the outwardly-blown double doors to the foyer, Brigance Fireheart looked around at Michelle, Lawna, and Elise, "The idea was that you would be outside so WE would be the ones to engage him first."

Ethan followed Brigance through the blown-out doors and wrecked keep, smiling from ear to ear, "That's the easiest money I've made in years." Looking around nervously, he didn't want to push his luck, "Still we should get the woman and leave."

"We just got lucky.... We took him by surprise," Radin pointed out, walking outside just far enough to see the destruction wrought by Michelle and Lawna, seemingly impressed as he nodded in satisfaction. "Now, let's get out of here before he does the same to us!"

Walking back into the broken foyer of the now-ablaze Almeron Keep, Radin cleared his way to the cage, housing a very injured Vosh, who looked at him with swollen, teary eyes. "You have to leave," she urged. "He'll come back stronger than ever. They both will."

"Ykstherin, help me get her out. Everyone else, form a circle facing outward from the cage. Keep an eye out—assume they'll be back." Radin's instructions had barely fallen on the room, and he was reaching out to the Arcane through Dallia's staff, bending the iron bars of the cage until they snapped at the bottom, giving them access to pull Vosh out. "I can't leave," she protested. "I've been cut off from the source of Arcane, and if I *Portal*, still cut off, I might never be able to cast again."

Looking to Ykstherin for guidance, Radin questioned with his eyes, asking for suggestions, "How does one cut off another from the source? More importantly, how do we restore it?"

"I don't know if what she says is correct, but it could destroy her ability to channel permanently. It's possible." Ykstherin tried every detection spell he could think of, one after another, trying to see the mechanism for her being cut off from the source of all the energy surrounding them. "I believe we need Elise to look at this. Here," Ykstherin offered, pointing to a spot just over Vosh's head. At first, Elise saw nothing abnormal, but the more energy she drew looking, the less faint the ethereal threads were, appearing to create a barrier between Vosh and the source of magic. "I've never seen anything like this before, and I wouldn't know where to even begin." Now outside the cage, Vosh wept as Elise tried to comfort her, holding her upright as Vosh wilted against Elise.

Trying to see what Ykstherin and Elise had seen, Radin thought about using the stone in his pocket to summon Damon, but that idea was quickly vanquished as the front of the keep was blown to bits, producing a new jagged opening some forty cubits high by fifty cubits wide, exposing Eldrac and Anna standing side by side. Anna, still practically nude from her tattered red dress having been burned off her body, worked a spell, sending dozens of small iron spikes from her hands that grew as they each raced to their targets all around the cage while fireballs the size of boulders danced about her body searching for a target to strike.

"Shields," Brigance barely had time to command before the iron spikes drove into his shield, knocking him and his crew backward, some as many as twenty cubits further into the keep near the end of the foyer, where it met the staircase.

Dozens of lightning balls, one after the other, shot from Ykstherin's hands, growing as they raced to Eldrac where they managed to hit his transparent shield, fizzling into nothingness and causing Lawna and Michelle to disappear in violent gusts of wind.

Dark grey-green storm clouds gathered over the now fully-exposed foyer, causing intense lightning to strike here and there upon Eldrac's index-fingered direction. A direct hit on Ykstherin sent him flying, clothes on fire, now skidding across the broken marble of the foyer. Another direct hit on Radin, absorbed by Dallia's staff, allowed Radin to redirect the heavily charged bolt directly at Eldrac where it pierced his protections, striking him square in the abdomen, knocking him down and backward, scarring him through his robes.

Anna worked another spell, but not before Ethan, Hugon, and Brigance loosed their nocked crossbow bolts, striking three direct hits into her chest and legs, sending her backward upon broken marble tiles. A bloodied and bruised Eldrac was already getting back on his feet, moving his hands furiously, trying to cast as fast as possible against all the threats Radin had brought against him. *Take out the crossbows*, Eldrac estimated, but before the bolts of fire and acid could reach them, a powerful shield shimmered to life—he couldn't tell from where—probably the Witch!

Again, powerful claws pierced his shell, attacking from nowhere and everywhere with but a gust of wind, and he was bleeding profusely again all over the garden flowers. This time, he saw her, as she skidded to a halt in front of him, aiming something long, black, and metallic at his body. *What is th...?* Eldrac didn't even have time to finish the thought as the ancient Golden-Brown Dragon swooped down at an attack angle, talons fully extended, preparing to breathe fire. *That's it.* Another *Gate* formed instantly underneath Eldrac, and he was gone. A golden burst of fire, burning everything to a cinder in the place Eldrac once stood only an instant before, caused Michelle to sling *Bad Intentions* back over her shoulder, without ever firing a shot. *Where the Hell is Lawna*, she wondered, as the gold dragon swooped back into the air in a climbing spiral back into the clouds.

As if to answer Michelle's unvoiced concerns, Anna's neck suddenly jerked backward with two sharp piercing wounds, sending spurts of blood uncontrollably shooting out over the garden. Another *Gate* beneath Anna and she was gone, never having seen *who* or *what* had mortally wounded her.

The ground shook violently as Toblain the Gold landed outside, creating large craters in the garden where his man-sized feet gripped the lush and verdant spring turf.

Kneeling down beside Ykstherin, pulling him to his feet, Radin stated the obvious, "So that's your help outside?"

Ykstherin merely nodded, managing a small, if brief, smile. "I told you, help isn't always so obvious." Ykstherin coughed blood, laughing a short laugh, "I doubt Eldrac will be back today. I think he's had enough. All the same, we should get Vosh out of here now, even if it permanently risks breaking her ability to cast."

A molten, fiery snort from Toblain started a grass fire that was now beginning to consume the grounds.

Walking back to Vosh, Radin resumed his thoughts of freeing her and of how to break this unusual thread above Vosh's head, that he presumed cut her off from the source.

"What if we looked at this a little differently?" Elise asked, walking around Vosh again, looking at the tethered and severed link above her head. "I'm not sure I believe it's possible to truly cut one off from Arcane since it's in every living thing around us. However, it might be possible to make someone so resistant to magic, that anything they attempt to form breaks as soon as it begins to form. Think of it like an advanced protection spell only reversed and centered on a given person." Extending her hand out to Radin, Elise pleaded, "May I borrow that," pointing to Dallia's staff. "Please, Darling. I'll give it right back to you."

"I'm more worried about Damon having an issue with it than anything else. He was very explicit." Handing over Dallia's staff, half expecting to be killed on the spot, Radin hoped for the best.

Taking Dallia's ash staff, Elise focused on her best protection magic, attempting to dispel the protection energy around Vosh. Dallia's staff began glowing amber as wispy and ethereal amber tendrils extended out from the staff over Vosh, interacting with an untangling, the wispy white tendrils above Vosh only visible to Elise and Radin. Vosh exhaled a heavy sigh of relief through tears of torment, feeling the source of all living things fill her soul and her energetic life once again. "Thank you, my Dear. Thank you. Thank you." Vosh planted a grateful kiss on Elise's cheek, looking to Radin through eyes that beckoned forgiveness and emanated pride.

"Let's go," Radin rallied, opening a *Portal* to a place where he'd grown up fishing with his father some miles north of Florè.

Moments later, standing before the Melshier Throne Lake, outside Florè, Radin reached into his pocket for Damon's summoning stone, casting it into the placid, ice-blue lake water.

"Where did you get that," Vosh asked, recognizing the signature of the magic at work. Recognizing a totem of Damon of Basrat—The Dark Knight of Magic. In Radin's hands....

Charles W. McDonald Jr.

Part 7: The Guile of Mortals

Charles W. M\^cDonald Jr.

A piece is stirred.
A sword drawn.
A life rent.
And, a soul bartered.
Dare they not look with their own eyes,
Beyond the shores of their own ambitions,
To see the guile of mortals....

Charles W. McDonald Jr.

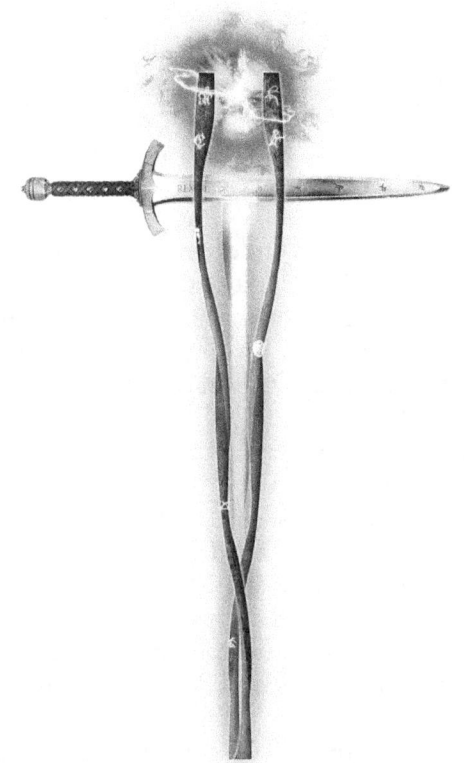

Chapter 50: Zero Day Minus Four

(Florè, Perion, Present Day)

Even though the *Distorting Web* obscured his view, Brigance Fireheart never took his eyes off Damon, Radin, and Vosh as they spoke privately inside Damon's protections. Rubbing his two-week-old, gruff stubble, standing some two hundred spans away under a shade tree overlooking Melshier Throne Lake, Brigance seriously questioned his decision to follow Radin. Damon was not the sort he wanted any affiliation with; it went against everything he'd stood for all his life. Money or not, he had standards. The problem was figuring out who was the bigger threat: Eldrac or Damon.

"You know *Healing* isn't my forte, but I'll try." Laying both hands on

Charles W. McDonald Jr.

Vosh, Damon sourced only living Arcane energy—no experimenting with Zero-Point here—casting the most powerful *Healing* spell he knew as new flesh began to form on Vosh, where it had been rent from bone and muscle moments before. Gold fingernails grew back where they'd been ripped away as bruises healed before their eyes. Her body wilting as her knees suddenly lost strength, Vosh reached out to Radin so as not to collapse before Damon—or against him.

"Thank you." No terms of endearment for Radin, nor recognition of his name, though that wasn't from a lack of respect or appreciation—more a result of awkwardness. This wasn't how she wanted to meet her only son.

"I did what you asked," Radin didn't want to bring up the teaching thing again just yet but reminding Damon of his contributions seemed reasonable. Though the horrified look from Vosh made him rethink that strategy.

"Radin, you can't possibly be.... You have *no idea* what this man is capable of. Are you working for Damon?"

Offering his help to hold up Vosh only to see her fight him off in protest, Damon wanted to remove the awkwardness, but it wasn't going to be easy convincing her, considering the way she'd left. "If I didn't think Radin could pull it off, I would have gone myself to get you, but either way I wasn't going to leave you in Eldrac's hands. However, I think you should know Radin and I have been talking for some time now. We have...an understanding of one another."

"An UNDERSTANDING," Vosh protested fervently with hands angrily waving between the two of them. "Do tell!"

"Am I the One," Radin asked. There it was—a simple question really. An honest question in search of a candid answer. Only four words posed to Vosh, but it was enough to turn a vehemently protesting look into one of profound sadness.

"I believe it's possible," the only words Vosh could manage in reply as tears formed in her eyes backlit in gold. She knew the burden he'd have to carry if he was. Moreover, she knew she'd done nothing to prepare him for it.

Nodding in acceptance, Radin continued his line of thinking, "Then I have to grow my powers at an incredible rate to have any chance of survival, let alone achieving the things I am meant to—assuming prophecy has any level of accuracy and I'm certainly not convinced of that. Talemar has abandoned me. I'm left with few choices for a teacher that could help me accomplish the impossible."

"I could help you," Vosh wanted to call him 'my son,' but refrained from using any terms of endearment. Anything that might lay claim to him as hers.

Charles W. McDonald Jr.

"I will accept all the help I can get, but I still want Damon to teach me."

Horrified, Vosh placed her face in her hands, nearly collapsing now into Damon's towering body as he held her up with some aid from Radin.

"He knows my path is set. He knows he's not to follow it—no matter what. I've done what I can to separate actions and choices from the substance of material, and I don't believe that Arcane is inherently evil. If he chooses to use it in a malevolent way, that's his choice. I will only teach him the Arcane, the runes, and how to use his natural abilities. His judgment and conscience will have to be the difference in how he uses it."

Tears streaked down Vosh's beautiful, high cheekbones as she resigned herself to the idea of her only son learning from the man she hated and reviled more than anyone. She knew things about Damon she hoped Radin would never discover…. It was difficult gathering enough strength to walk so soon after the Healing she'd received, but Vosh had to put some space between her and Damon. Mustering more will than physical constitution, she walked in less-than-straight lines toward the large shade elm where the others stood watching them, the *Distorting Web* sealing up around her form as she walked through.

"I'm going to measure your strength by spell. Meaning, I'm going to give you a stretch goal that is well beyond your reach right now, but by the time you can successfully cast and control it, you'll be ready to deal with Eldrac one-on-one. He's grown stronger since I last met him, but he's no match for me, so if you can cast and control the spell I'm thinking of, you'll be well on your way."

Nodding in acceptance, Radin only briefly looked down at the second of his fingernails now turning like unto living, liquefied gold dust. "You're going to have to learn to hide that unless you want to advertise your power and experience," Damon, showing off his normal fingernails with the one black aura signet ring on his right-hand ring finger.

"What is the name of this stretch-goal spell, and what does it do?"

"Oh, I think you're going to like it…." Damon smiled, still questioning his better judgment about this whole idea and the fact he might have to kill Radin if things didn't go as planned. The thought of his own spells being used against him wasn't at all a foreign one; he had taught so many over the years, 'twas inevitable. "It's called Damon's Big Boom."

"I love it already…." Radin smiled with a brief chuckle—not knowing how to react around Damon; it was a tenuous and awkward relationship at the start, but he'd have to see how it developed over time. If it were to get better, would that be a good thing?

Charles W. McDonald Jr.

Radin leaned in, carefully listening to Damon's instructions. Damon began describing Big Boom to Radin in terms he could understand as the *Distorting Web* encrypted and protected their private session. Damon's warning not to use the stretch-goal spell in a 'confined space' seared into his memory.

*   *   *   *

(Damon's Manor, Kaleion, Present Day)

The remodeling of Damon's manor still held a furious pace despite the barren drought conditions outside that left the grounds' normally verdant gardens looking like burned dirt. Pretty much everything outside was dead, but the inside of the manor was looking better as Damon began ascending the circular main staircase, heading to the spell test room. Damon's chief of staff stood in the entrance of the spell test room, coordinating the hanging of the new metallic doors that must have been over two inches thick, hanging them on sturdy titanium hinges only barely visible from the room's interior.

"Ah, sir, glad to see you. I assumed you'd want these hinges visible only from the inside. Is this okay? We can hide them even more if you prefer."

"Yeah, let's do that, but not now. If the room is substantially complete and usable, I'd like to test it."

A horrifying thought to Edgar Hastings, remembering the destruction from the last 'test.' It was enough to cause even more sweat to run down his brow as his lips tightened at the prospect, wondering if he could slip away—far away. "Of course, sir. The room is yours." Pointing to the top hinge on the left door—the only one not yet complete—Chief ordered, "Don't just stand there, get that last hinge in place, get the door hung on it, and get out! Now!" The short-haired middle-aged construction worker furiously slammed the pin home as if his life depended on it—because it did.

"Very good, sir. It's all yours." Edgar didn't waste any time, nor wait for approval, before putting some serious distance between himself and the third floor as his body hustled down the main circular staircase and quickly out of Damon's line of sight.

Recalling his enchantment from the test material days ago and facing the front of the room, Damon touched the right wall of the newly-constructed spell test room with his left hand and one of the double-door set with his other, concentrating as he focused on his new Zero-Point fundamental and reaching out to everything he could sense for miles around. A glossy, charcoal-grey finish raced across the burnished, light-grey, fissured finish, consuming it in its place as it raced forth from Damon's hands as a point of origin, engulfing the entire room in mere seconds. Carefully examining every millimeter of the ceiling, floor, walls, doors and crevices, Damon ensured only the glossy charcoal-grey finish was visible. "Okay, here goes everything," he breathed aloud to himself, and perhaps to Dallia's living presence that seemed to permeate every part of his manor—both new and old. Touching only the Zero-Point source again via his new fundamental, Damon formed the massive amounts of energy into the smallest, most densely formed *Light Orb* he could make. It was nearly large enough to touch both ceiling and floor simultaneously, with barely an inch of buffer space at either side. There was barely enough room for Damon to stand in the spell test room with the massive *Light Orb* without touching it as he waved his right hand, tossing the massive *Light Orb* against the far-right wall of the spell test room, watching it wink out of existence as soon as it hit. A heavy sigh of relief from Damon expelled his foremost concerns on pillowy waves of his exhaled breath as he finally allowed himself the freedom to think of next steps.

Walking out of the spell test room upstairs to the fourth floor, Damon thought the best place to reach Damon's Star, from its current position overhead, would be from his balcony, assuming the balcony was even complete. Rounding the corner of Dallia's room, he began to see the substantially complete ritual room, allowing another heavy sigh when he saw the freshly finished balcony with glossy new coats of paint. Looking up as he cleared the roofline just overhead, he spotted Damon's Star, roughly twenty-five miles up in geosynchronous orbit. He'd need two spells to accomplish this task. Concentrating, reaching out as far and wide as he could with Zero-Point source, he cast Damon's Far Reaching, allowing him to source, cast, and target further than normal. Rolling and aggregating that massive amount of energy, more than he'd ever used before, Damon cast Dispel, watching a massive cobalt-blue beam of energy, with a diameter of two humans, race forth from him up to Damon's Star. A great thunderclap accompanied the beam's breaking of the sound barrier as it shattered windows all around Damon's Manor and beyond. Even though it moved beyond the speed of sound, it still took some time to reach Damon's Star, but the working prototype winked out of existence as soon as the beam just barely clipped its right side. Cheers rose around the grounds outside as natural nightfall finally took its normal place in what was now a blighted wasteland as far as the eye could see.

Clapping from behind caused Damon to pivot, though he wanted to continue admiring his work.

"Nice work, Ra," Kellen announced, striding through the newly refurbished ritual room toward his oldest friend and ally.

Charles W. McDonald Jr.

"I said I'd take care of it, didn't I," Damon chaffed at Kellen's seemingly lack of appreciation.

"Oh, you took care of it, alright. Probably millions of people dead from starvation already, and millions more yet to die while the planet recovers." Kellen the Destroyer couldn't judge. He'd killed at least as many as Damon, but that was intentional, and they deserved it. Damon did so out of his own incompetence. The situations were very different.

A shrug from Damon as he considered Kellen's words. *Had it really caused so much damage?* He'd kept himself so busy off-world with other aspects of the Master Plan, there was no way of knowing. Only time would tell, and he was sure he'd be held accountable one way or the other. Still, there was really no pleasing the man before him. "Big plans call for big risks," Damon offered, knowing it was barely an excuse.

"Yeah, about that, Ra…." Kellen apparently determined to make that nickname stick. "How about clueing me in on your big plans, since I was obviously not in the loop on this…." Kellen, pointing up to where Damon's Star previously dominated the skyline of their homeworld.

Casting Distorting Web, forming a shell around them to encrypt their conversation, Damon's calculus fought with his friendship and trust of Kellen as he struggled with how much he could reveal, even to him, "I'm *creating* an inhabitable world."

"Why?" Just one word from Kellen the Destroyer, but it was the right one. If Damon wanted an inhabitable world, he could easily go find one already in existence. *Why create one?*

"Because the manifestation of the consequences of my actions will soon reach me, and I need to be ready for that moment."

"Not really the answer I was looking for, Ra," Kellen, scratching his head then his overgrown beard, though Damon's flat expression said he was done explaining.

"Look, we both know she knows more than we can afford. Every word we utter about this puts us at greater risk. You're just going to have to trust me," Damon's reasoning was understandable given what Kellen already knew, but Kellen wasn't the trusting sort—even when it came to Damon. Especially when it came to Damon!

"Oh sure, I've just gotta trust you—*Maker and Destroyer of Worlds*. What's not to trust?" Kellen disappeared in a huff, leaving little lightning shards chasing his exit on the floor attempting to mar his new floor and utterly failing.

Charles W. McDonald Jr.

*   *   *   *

Now carrying the Staff of the Invoker with him, holding it by one of its three metal helix rods, Damon left his concealed study. It was a prized and immensely powerful artifact, almost never used by Damon anymore, but he would soon need its power more and more as the Master Plan manifested its own reality. Overlooking his fourth-floor balcony again, thinking, he contemplated using Earth as a waypoint to Planet-X—only due to his unfamiliarity with its location in relation to Kaleion—but then thought better of it. He had to limit his risk and exposure there, even though he missed Mira. Focusing on the away-side of Planet-X, Damon opened a Portal. "Shit," realizing his mistake immediately; he hadn't calculated for orbit travel of his homeworld in relation—Planet-X wasn't even there. Dispel as he tried again, opening another Portal, this time seeing his intended location about its distant home star it had escaped. That looks like the away side, he estimated, casting Damon's Improved Shell v3 to carry his atmosphere with him, Damon walked through to the barren crust Planet-X.

Now standing what he estimated was a couple of hundred miles away from where he last tried this experiment, he cast Damon's Far Reaching, immediately followed by Damon's Improved Foresight, as he gathered stellar locational data on the objects in his way. Making note of their location, he reached out the Zero-Point source, opening his stable doorway, using Damon's Far Reaching to gather all the Zero-Point energy he could find planet-wide and beyond—as far as he could see, and beyond. Aggregating Zero-Point with Arcane, he began the desired form in his mind. Holding up the Staff of the Invoker, basking in its terrifying charcoal-blue hemispherical aura, he channeled exponentially more energy through it than ever before, focusing as two white-gold beams, each larger than twenty men in diameter, shot forth from his staff piercing the darkness of space from Planet-X's surface. He wanted to keep one eye on his atmosphere shell, but he needed to focus as the beams shot forth to their distant targets, not visible to the naked eye. He couldn't see the beams strike their target, but his Improved Foresight told them they had struck home as they both now had escape momentum—enough to get out of his way at least.

"Here goes everything," he thought aloud, aggregating all the Zero-Point he could find with all the Arcane he could find, Damon's Far Reaching still in effect as he began forming the new star in the creativity and imagination of his mind. Imagineering the new electric star into its rightful place within the cosmic web. Calculating the 'Goldilocks Zone' for Planet-X, again he held the Staff of the Invoker high above him. No beam shot forth this

Charles W. McDonald Jr.

time. Looking almost like it had failed, Damon watched as the stellar nursery gasses began forming from nothing, under multiple compression forces he'd put in place around the forming gas cloud that would create both the negative pole and the positive. Realizing even under the intense compression he'd created, it would still take far too long for him to sit here and observe the results of his work—he'd run out of atmosphere if he waited—Damon hastily formed a Portal to Mira and Earth, walking through and taking his environmental shell with him.

*   *   *   *

(Austin, TX, Earth, Present Day)

"Damon," Mira jumped up from the sofa smiling as she threw herself at him in a big Texas-sized hug, "you were gone longer than I expected. What happened?" Trying to get a peek through the other side of his Portal before it winked out, she saw a celestial nursery forming beyond the horizon of Planet-X. Observing Damon now basked in the charcoal-blue hemisphere aura emanating from the Staff of the Invoker, she felt both terrified and excited in its presence. Cautiously glaring at the staff, she positioned herself to his other side—away from it and its aura.

"I'll have to go back later to see how it's going."

"What did you do?"

"My backup plan…." Damon's *Telekinesis* floated his mighty *Staff of the Invoker* over to the far corner of his open-concept living room as he sensed the discomfort it brought to Mira. Pulling Mira into his arms, Damon kissed her like he missed her as she felt him start to grow against her caress and the taste of her lips on his.

Mira's body wilted against his will—his power—but her mind couldn't help drift to the realization she was circling too close to a star; destined to burn up in its orbit.

Planet X Becoming Eden — Spatial View

Charles W. McDonald Jr.

Chapter 51: Zero Day Minus Three

(Austin, TX, Earth, Present Day)

Simply gorgeous with radiant and almost translucent black skin, the 5'7" female—perfection incarnate—in a diaphanous white wrap dress with a deeply plunging V-neck, sat at the foot of Damon's bed, not more than inches away from where Illirian had come to see him only a short time before. Her long platinum hair and violet eyes glowed against her beautiful black elven skin giving her lush feminine curves a surreal appearance. Beads of moisture—not sweat—caused her diaphanous dress to cling to her iridescent skin giving her almost a hazy aura of sensuality Damon could not describe in words. There was no one who could ever compare to her. She was entirely…unique. Evanyil almost never visited him anymore; this couldn't be good.

Trying to force his eyes open from the exhaustion of channeling so much energy, Damon looked to his left to see if Mira was awake. The vibrating crackle of her hideous snoring made him cringe, even if answering his concern. "To what do I owe this honor, My Dear?" He managed a tense smile, trying to ignore the giant, venomous spiders that always accompanied her presence; one of them crawling over the bedding now just above Mira's feet. He supposed the definition of 'familiars' would be appropriate in describing her spiders, though Evanyil was no mage. He used to use crows for his familiars, though he hadn't had much need of them in a long time.

"Well, I thought you could explain this…?" Extending out her right hand, causing the air to ripple before them, the disturbance formed into a peering window allowing them to see his celestial nursery doing its job and a bright new star forming in the middle of the gas cloud. It wasn't quite a divination spell she'd used, more a natural 'ability' accompanying her station.

"Oh that…," pointing to Evanyil's window with his right index finger nonchalantly, "…it's nothing really—just a test."

A dubious nod from Evanyil, followed by, "Mhmm." Closing the view to Damon's new star—or test rather—Evanyil pivoted to start crawling on the bed over Damon; she moved up toward him 'til her lips were inches away from his. She recalled, "I don't remember THAT being part of our plan."

"I might have forgotten to mention it." *Did he?* Being in bed with her this close to him made him feel…uniquely vulnerable to her. His retort was met with a slowly accepting nod from Evanyil as Damon continued. "Kellen was furious about the tests at my manor, and the spell test room wasn't actually designed for this scale of a test, so I had to move to a bigger, safer test site. It's really nothing to concern yourself over." His reassurances—however just—fell duly dubious upon his oldest of traveling companion's reservations.

"Sweetie, you're creating stars now. Trust me, it's a big deal! Oh, and your signature is all over this. It's not like those who would have the power to notice such things, couldn't trace it straight to you." Her lips now precariously close to tasting his as she breathed her words straight into his essence as if they'd just shared the most intimate of kisses. The seemingly delicate feminine fingertips of her left hand creeped and crawled in a caressing fashion over his right cheek all the way to the corner of his mouth and lips as she warned, "… and then they'll trace it all the way back to *me*." Her magnificent violet eyes flashed in a glossy glow with an aura that seemingly burst forth off her cornea straight into his *black mirrors of the soul.*

He felt her spell, if he could call it that, try to pierce him, but Evanyil always played dangerous games with him. The more lethal, the more she got off on it. Even now he could feel and sense her getting wet with his knee now in her center above him, through his bedding. "We always knew there was potential for getting noticed earlier than we wanted, but we have also taken all necessary precautions. And to think we're going to be taking anyone by surprise is pure folly. She already knows."

Drawing back from Damon while getting up to pace, Evanyil displayed…uncharacteristic tension, "How much?"

Part of him wanted her back on top of him, and already he missed her scent no longer filling her nostrils as she paced alongside his bed. "Enough."

"Well, we're certainly committed then."

"We were committed long before now. At least *I* was." He wasn't questioning her commitment, but he was right.

"Does that move up the timing?" Spiders followed Evanyil around the room as she paced, increasing the already rising level of tension in the room.

"I honestly don't know. I hope not because a great deal of what I've already set in motion is time-sensitive."

"Do I need to modify any of my plans?" Evanyil placed her index finger seductively in her mouth—just the tip. He wasn't sure if it was a pondering look or a 'sexy messing with him' look.

"Just show up like we planned. Don't leave me hanging."

"Oh Sweetie, I'll be there. Have I ever let you down?"

He could see the offense on her face when he began looking up at the ceiling, pondering—remembering. He was pretty certain her of commitment, but he still loved toying with her just as much as she loved toying with him. The spider that had been crawling over Mira began moving in his direction with some pace.

"No Darling, you haven't," he relented, causing the spider to retreat as Evanyil disappeared—her minions along with her. The dawn of the new day waited for Evanyil's exit before casting its burnt-ocher rays into Damon's master suite.

(Edinaiel, Perion, Present Day)

Nine massive quartz-like pillars formed the back of the Crystal Throne Adena had stolen from the Nine Towers of Axum—home of the Rune Stones. Platinum Dragon Scales, from a species no longer in existence, formed the sides, seat, and the back of The Crystal Throne, providing something hard and permanent to fix the quartz-like pillars to and ensure overall rigidity to the artifact, which held no real power with Adena in its seat. She would argue that fact and had many times, overturning even sovereign Kings in massive land disputes 'til she ruled nearly everything from the Needles to Xal; from the Bay of Winter to Corning and the Broken Towers—her first throne.

The Crystal Throne held no real power unless it was occupied by the One—then it would rule all of the Nine Kingdoms of Perion—if not beyond. Slowly striding, almost gliding across the ivory dais to the diamond-crystal transparent seeing tiles, Adena needed to see her treasures again. Ever since the theft some days back, she'd made an effort to make daily trips to the vault each morning. It wasn't a terribly long walk, and the views were always nothing less than breathtaking—well, breathtaking for others—nearing on boredom for

Adena's fragile and warped mind. Making her way to the treasury, she allowed herself the luxury of looking through the diamond-shaped divination tiles, making up the causeway, watching the boy's powers grow with each scene she viewed. She'd even seen the great Gold, Toblain, coming to his aid. She had suspected Toblain, from the very beginning, for the treasury theft a few days' past. He hadn't bothered to cover his tracks that closely. Besides, she had her little spies *everywhere*....

Making the final right turn into the far side spire of the crown, where the treasury was housed, guardsmen quickly moved out of her way—dozens of them in all. Fine breastplate designs, all adorned with a silver background and a foreground of a golden upside-down V with rounded edges, provided a place for her seal to be broken into three parts. The lower right side of the upside-down V held an embossed crest of The Crown of Spires. The lower left side of the upside-down V held an embossed crest of a platinum Dragon. The upper center of the upside-down V held an embossed crest of the Crystal Throne.

"No sign of trouble," her best field colonel reported. Galfrid, with his brown hair, brown eyes, and tall, thick, muscular frame, would have looked commanding without the added flourish to his uniform. Some just had the look of a leader—as did Galfrid. Leader or not, he'd be worse than dead if anything happened in the treasury going forward—beyond his control or not. He just had to find ways to ensure nothing else that happened was outside his control. A hard thing to do housed amidst so many dangerous and capable witches and backdropped against so many backstabbing royals and would-be kings.

"That's a good thing for you Galfrid, now unlock it for me, please." It had taken a while for her to create an impenetrable lock with only two keys in existence, one around her neck, the other around Galfrid's, but it was the only way he'd even consider accepting this post. Adena tried not to cast anymore, not for small things anyway. It took far too much of her abilities to keep herself young, beautiful and well..., lucid.

Slipping the glass key—as big as his hands—into the lock, Galfrid watched as the lock shone prismatic rays through the glass, illuminating the handle of the key. Taking a step back as the ten-cubit by four-cubit thick onyx cream and gold fissured door, clicked in acceptance, sliding into the wall cavity allowing passage, Galfrid began an immediate inventory of all Adena's most prized possessions.

Inside the alcove among hidden corridors, where even the brilliant hues of dawn could not penetrate, vertically positioned in dozens of man-sized nooks magnificently carved out of whole slabs of blue-grey granite, Adena's secret army lay motionless. Appearing androgynous, yet mostly large and masculine, with very long, straight brown hair, slender arms, and fingertips appearing to belong to something other than a human, their eyes lay closed to the world outside—asleep; save the one Titan-sized niche that now lay empty with shards of broken granite laying atop the crystal seeing tiles. Walking past the broken and stolen object, Adena's heels caused shards of granite to ting on the seeing tiles as she passed. Adena checked on her most precious possession, breathing a soft sigh at the sight of it sitting atop its quartz-like pedestal—a place of honor. Her sigh wasn't one of relief, more one of a realization of a frail reality of doldrum. She was quite mad in her desire for the end of all things—but on her terms—not the terms of others.

Tracing her beautiful delicate fingers on the Crystal Crown, Adena noted its circular frame, made from enchanted, powdered platinum dragon scales, was far too big to fit her small head. Twigs, formed from the same enchanted metal as the frame, gave the crown its traditional forward leaning triangular appearance with two opposing stallions holding up the center quartz-like pillar with their hooves blending into the ornamental twig cylinder that housed the center quartz pillar itself. Nine quartz-like pillars in all, marched around the crown's perimeter, each held similarly with the ornate twig-decorated cylinders. It too, had been taken from Axum so long ago that she no longer could isolate those memories as her own. It was nothing short of magnificent! It was incredibly powerful, and the key to using the true power of the Crystal Throne, which she also possessed, but only the One could wield them both as One. 'Twas the source of nearly all her joy and frustrations, and holding it daily was beginning to test her fragile sanity buttressed only by her power and ambition from so long ago.

Placing the Crystal Crown over her head ceremoniously as she hovered it just over her beautiful hair, its magic refused to allow her to lower it any further onto her head, even if it had fit. Paying no attention to the alarmed look about Galfrid as she spun back to the pedestal, Adena put the Crystal Crown back in its designated place of honor. Looking down into the seeing tiles, she tried to locate the strange, black-haired, black-eyed, tall man in the odd clothes. It was another source of frustration, not being able to locate or observe him from the seeing tiles. *Who was he, and what was he doing with the boy?* In a rare moment of heavy casting, Adena summoned, causing all the man-sized granite nooks to shatter before them as Galfrid took several steps back out into the causeway to yield some space. Shards of granite were tinging on the seeing tiles below as the androgynous large forms, with decaying flesh, stepped forward, answering Adena's summons. Now twelve in all, minus the stolen one, they obeyed Adena, observing the seeing tiles as she recounted the only image she had captured of the black-haired, black-eyed man in the strange clothes, showing it to them. Their eyes glowing hot like an amber fire in acknowledgment, "You will find and destroy him, bringing everything he has on him to me." She paused, thinking for a moment. "You may bring me his corpse as well. I will allow it." All twelve bowed deeply in acceptance of their orders before a crude flourish for Adena's station.

*   *   *   *

(The Valley of Power, Perion, Present Day)

"Embrace the Arcane." It was a simple coaching from Damon really, but it wasn't coming to Radin as easily as he'd hoped. "Think of it as nothing more than a doorway you already know how to walk through, and really you don't even need to walk through it. It merely needs to be open, allowing the energy to flow. Think of the doorway as a floating void of pleasure where your memories are given as an offering in order to accept the energy of the Arcane. An exchange of imagination for power. That energy you borrow making your own memories more vivid than life itself. Everything becomes sharper, more clear, more defined, and more *alive.* Why?" Damon paused at the last question, knowing he'd have to provide the answer, "…Because you're channeling life itself. You are manifesting your own reality every time you cast…."

Inside the *Distorting Web* in Talemar's cavern on the Isle of Breaking, Damon and Radin continued their sessions, Damon giving stretch goals each and every time they met. "It's older than the oldest living things. The Arcane source energy wants to return to its natural form, so you need to coax it into temporary obedience. Don't command. Ask. Show." Damon paused, circling Radin in only his jeans and a Led Zeppelin Icarus T-shirt, allowing the chilled elements of the Valley of Power to roll off his body through sheer will. Damon felt no elements unless he chose to do so. He had become immeasurably disciplined to go along with his immeasurable power. "Focus on what I told you. You can't open a *Portal* here, but other means are available to you at your discretion."

The cavern wall, all of it all the way to the entrance, became a window observing the actions of Gareth, who'd been sent by Talemar to find something he hadn't shared with Radin. "I know this place," Radin stated matter-of-factly. Damon nodded, adding, "Axum, close to the Rune Stones. Known by the other name: The Monuments of Creation."

"What do you think Talemar sent him there for?" Observing, while trying to hold together the threads and forms of the divination spell, Radin

Charles W. McDonald Jr.

wondered if he could still trust Gareth. He had been sent by Talemar before Talemar's betrayal had manifested so obviously as it had.

"Everything there is sacred and old. Very old. No villages or real population to speak of, so whatever he was sent for has been there a very long time." Damon's tutoring and rational seemed genuine in tone and intent. Whatever Radin thought of him, he felt no deception from Damon. Ever.

Observing Gareth digging in a field for what seemed like it must have been hours, if not days, going by the piles of dirt already accumulated around him, Radin's calculus began evolving, "Whatever it is, I'm going to let him find it first before I take it."

Nodding, Damon was on the same wavelength with Radin, but that bothered him greatly to the point that he was frowning as he watched Radin carefully. "Talemar will be observing him too, so you'll have to act fast. *Gate* is your best option from here since *Portals* have been blocked. Do you remember how I told you to make one? Watch me one more time while I demonstrate." Damon didn't move; only a mere thought sent him traveling through the cave floor that rapidly sealed up in an instant for him to land right back where he had stood the moment before, arriving through a tear in the cavern ceiling.

"Love it," Radin quipped, with a slight smile, watching the threads Damon used for sourcing the energy required and that of forming the matter that both opened and closed the *Gate* as well as the location references used in the casting.

"I need you to trust me for a minute." It wasn't a request from Damon, but it wasn't a command either as he approached close enough to physically lay hands on Radin. Carefully he moved his hands up toward Radin's temples, grabbing his head gently as he showed Radin—in his mind's eye—how he had formed the *Gate*.

"Now," backing away from Radin as he removed his hands from Radin's temples, Damon continued, "why don't you try to make one over there," pointing to where the fire had been a few nights before. "Send some of those stones to a location you're most familiar with."

Radin couldn't maintain the divination spell and create the *Gate* as well. So, releasing the observation window, Radin focused on the dining hall of his father's inn, causing the cavern floor to open up beneath the entire campfire and all the belongings around it, sucking them down into the *Gate*.

"Well, that was about ten times bigger than you needed to make it, but I'd say that worked," Damon coached with an approving and affirmative nod.

Radin sighed, realizing he'd only missed *Gating* Dallia's staff by a couple of paces. Still, his satchel with his change of clothes had been an unintended traveler through his first *Gate*.

Charles W. McDonald Jr.

*   *   *   *

(Stirling, Perion, Present Day)

Iain Longbow and Rowarc sat facing one another, sharing old stories over another pint. Rowarc had been quiet since letting Vosh slip through his hands into that *thing*. He'd seen his wife make one once before, but that was so long ago. It had taken an obscene amount of coin to make it back home, and nearly as much for the *Healing*, but he was retired this time, and he meant it*! Just run your damn inn and stay out of things that are none of your business*, he scolded himself internally, but he had to work hard to suppress the urge to search for Vosh. He'd have to at least begin searching for his son soon, since no one had seen or heard from them while they'd been away.

Stones falling from directly above crashed into their table, smashing it to pieces, sending Iain and Rowarc scattering across the floor to get away from all the debris coming through the *Gate* in the ceiling above. Campfire ash and burned pieces of wood along with some belongings, both male and female, littered the dining area of his inn. *What the....*

"I'll say this, Rowarc," Iain began, picking himself up off the floor, "Your retirement has got some excitement to it."

Looking at the male satchel between him and Iain, Rowarc had an answer to the only question more pressing to him than that of what happened to Vosh: *Where was his son?* Picking it up, opening it, he instantly recognized the shirts, the size, the pants, the gloves he'd given Radin for his birthday, "So much for retirement." He paused looking to Iain, "We need a lamean to tell us where these came from. If it's to the ends of the world, we're going there to get my boy! Right now!"

"Oh, I already have someone in mind," Iain offered, giving a hand to help up his old friend as they immediately headed for the door. Besides, retirement would have killed Rowarc of boredom anyway.

*   *   *   *

North of Exeter, Darthen, Toblain soared overhead, searching based on the requirements Radin had provided. 'Large Manor with at least a thousand acres of land, shielded by thick forest on one side, one or more sides to the Darthen Straight, on a hill with at least twenty leagues of unobstructed visibility on a clear day.' They needed a place for Radin to begin gathering his forces, close enough to resources for building supplies and close enough to a substantial population of experienced soldiers he could pull from surrounding

Charles W. McDonald Jr.

kingdoms and countryside.

The wind coursing over Toblain's wingspan made him grateful for the assignment, though he knew he'd soon need to return to the source of his powers, the Fear Spires on Dragon Isle, in the southern part of The Dracon Sea.

A glimpse out of the corner of his eye caused him to directionally kick his massive tail to the right, flipping his body down and to the left as he began spiraling down to lose some altitude for a closer look. Radin had said not to worry about being seen—good thing, a densely populated area like this would make going unseen impossible. People were already pointing up at him, some screaming and running, others mouth agape, just watching as he cruised overhead, heading straight for a hillside rising some four hundred cubits from the surrounding grounds. It was well-manicured and well-built with high-walled, heavy construction. *This might be just the place,* he thought, careening his massive body for another pass.

A fast flyby confirmed his thoughts. He'd need to get the others.

*   *   *   *

The high-walled Exeter proper was filled with every kind imaginable: whores, sell-swordsmen, mercenaries of all kinds, king's guard, king's infantry, king's navy, farmers, fishermen, pirates, and just about every kind of merchant one could ever need. Michelle had kept *Bad Intentions* well hidden under layers even though she was sweltering, not allowing even the sling to be visible. The white wolf that Radin had renamed Smoke for his smoky ice-colored piercing eyes rarely left Michelle's side unless Radin was around. Following Michelle down the main merchant street of Exeter, Smoke pushed forward in front of Michelle, clearing a path for her and the others in the congested, sweaty streets.

"Aye, watch that thing," a passing king's guard kicked at Smoke, causing him to snarl and growl—bearing his fangs.

"Pardon us, sir," Michelle gave a half bow, directing Smoke with right hand, as she turned to let Smoke get behind her while encouraging Smoke to heel. "We," motioning to the all-female crew of herself, Lawna and Elise, "… would feel more comfortable around lots of big strong men. Where would the King's finest men be found?"

The middle-aged man smiled, "I just came from there. That great big hall across the courtyard from the main keep. That's where you'll find my mates and me late in the day if you're needing some company." His two missing front teeth didn't help his smile much, neither did the warts or scars about his face. He surely didn't represent the king's finest, but the place he pointed to was logical enough for recruiting the best available people. Wherever Brigance and his crew were right now, he hoped they were making faster progress. Wherever Toblain and Ykstherin were, they'd surely be causing a stir any minute now. News like that traveled fast, and she'd already seen a significant number of carrier pigeons flying overhead in the direction of the king's keep.

"Thank you so much, sir. I think we'll be okay," Michelle offered with her hands pressed together in a prayer-like position as she looked down at Smoke, now right at her heels, teeth bared for the creepy guard, with a guttural snarl for the man. Petting Smoke and pivoting in the direction of the great hall, Michelle began walking away from the man, with Elise and Lawna in tow.

Not quite out of earshot of the creepy guard, Lawna couldn't resist, "I think he's in love with you."

"Does he make you jealous?" Michelle offered Lawna a wink with her tongue satisfactorily hanging out of her sweet lips.

Raised eyebrows from Elise as an earlier suspicion of hers appeared to now be confirmed.

Charles W. McDonald Jr.

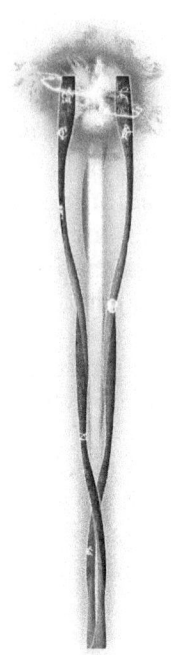

Chapter 52: Zero Day Minus Two

(Planet-X, Present Day)

Even through his atmospheric protection shell, he could feel the warmth from his new rapidly evolving protostar, but it wasn't nearly as warm as it should have been. Either his math was severely off, or Zero-Point was the wrong tool for this job. Now on the near side of Planet-X to his new star, Damon measured the size of the star based on the horizon and the shadow it cast. He'd missed the 'Goldilocks Zone' because his new star wasn't as big as it should have been. "That's going to change the dynamic of its lifecycle," he thought aloud. "Shit." Taking a few pictures with his Android for reference, he considered his options. Opening a *Portal* to Mira and Austin, Damon stepped through, taking his shell with him, dispelling it as soon as his right foot landed inside his living room.

The whoosh of the *Portal* closing caused Mira to walk out of the master bath, wrapped in a towel. "I thought that was you." Running to his embrace, Mira kissed him as his fingers ran through her wet hair.

Damon, obviously troubled and lost in deliberation, did kiss her back,

Charles W. McDonald Jr.

but he didn't wrap his arms around her and pull her to him like he normally would.

"Talk to me," she offered, "What happened?"

"So, take a look," handing Mira his phone, showing her the pictures he took from the surface of Planet-X with his Android.

"That doesn't look right. It's either too far away or too small."

"Both," he countered in a resigned tone. Not a defeated expression from Damon, but one in search of what to do next. *Do I need to start over?*

"Well, shit, that's not going to work."

"I need to think about some options. Maybe Zero-Point doesn't give me access to enough energy to do what I'm trying to accomplish. I might have to destroy it and start over."

"Well, Love," it was the first time she'd called him that, and it hadn't gone unnoticed, "...there's another option."

"I'm listening."

"Could you move something as big as Planet-X to bring it closer to the protostar so it could capture the planet in a closer, but stable, orbit? You wouldn't want to push it directly at the star head-on, but at an angle, so you just barely clip the closer orbital perimeter of the new star but still on the ecliptic plane of its equatorial axis. We would need to get some better measurements of the star's density to figure out where the boundary of its orbit might be, given what we know about the mass of Planet-X, but it's doable if you could directionally move the planet at a controllable and steady velocity. *And* slow it down enough to be captured.... Actually, we would probably want the velocity to decelerate right at the moment it's clipping the perimeter of the star's orbital pattern. Again, it might be doable." She began moving over to Damon's homeworld desk he'd brought to work in the living room, taking a seat at it like it had been hers all her life. "We just need to do some math."

It was there again, that moment where commonality of purpose and thought meshed with a beautiful woman who was far more than just a woman; and it made Damon question how he'd found another Mira so very similar to the one he had before. Or did she remind him of someone else? She couldn't cast, and she wasn't powerful like him, in her own right, but her mind worked in similar circles to his, and it was even more attractive than her magnificent physical features. His thoughts on reincarnation were uncertain, but it was almost as if someone was giving him a second chance with someone he once knew. His exponentially increasing attachment, combined with her Human and mortal fragility, terrified him. She could be a dangerous impediment to his plans, but right now she was a far too valuable asset to even consider losing. His body ached for her. His mind loved her. His heart still longed for Dallia,

Mira of old, and Victoria, while Banthis loomed large for whatever immortality followed this life. But there was a normality to this Mira that beckoned him the most. Though normalcy had been antithetical to Damon all his life....

"I can see your mind running a million miles an hour over there, Love. What's on your mind?" She beamed for him as she watched his mind work behind those beautiful and dark gems of his. At first, they were fearsome and awesome to behold. Now they were becoming a unique attribute that anchored her to him.

That smile and that look from her was just...all-consuming for him.

"Just working the problem in my head," Damon deflected, smiling back while giving her a wink.

"Darling, when it comes to problem-solving, you're like a ten-pound tick on a two-pound dog," Mira bantered sarcastically with a pretty smile.

Okay, more time Googling phrases was going to have to become a priority sooner or later.... *Fuck it*, he thought, sitting down before his laptop, he began typing 'ten-pound tick on a two-pound dog,' and after clicking through a few of his first search results he started laughing.

Mira loved his laugh. It was throaty, hearty, and honest—though sometimes a little too *dastardly* for her taste. The way his chest moved in concert with his hands when he laughed.... It was just wrong enough to be right. "It wasn't *that* funny."

Okay, maybe she was her very own instantiation of the Mira he once knew, or maybe he was just lucky enough to find two similar enough, and both very unique in their own right, but the original Mira never had this one's sense of humor.

"I can go back and get some more accurate dimension and mass measurements. I'll be back," refocusing on the problem at hand, sucking it dry like the ten-pound tick he was proudly compared to only a moment before. With a whoosh, the *Portal* closed around him, as a new atmospheric shell kept pace with Damon back to Planet-X.

Anna hadn't been able to stop shaking since she'd been bitten on the neck by that *thing* parading around as a woman. Her body violently swinging from icy to smoldering hot; back and forth all night long her body fought mortal fever. Dreams of her life before flashing through her mind's eye— the little girl in bright, golden curls and cream pleats of her father's fancy just short enough to please her father in the ways he always sought. The way father 'played' with her until she grew powerful enough to 'play' with him in the ways he so richly deserved.

Now the morning after, the amber rays of dawn upon her fiery-red hair forced her to retreat from all her windows and doorways. Even now, as she finger curled her red locks to place the ends in a shaft of light, peeking around the doorjamb from the Perion star, only to see them singe and smoke and burn her fingertip enough to force her to retract into the shadows, remembering the golden curls she once bore. She had put up every protection spell she had to keep Eldrac—and others—out. Now in her secret home on the far side of the world, in the Land of Golems, Anna couldn't look at herself in the mirror, because she no longer bore any reflection. Of this life nor the past one.

*   *   *   *

Royvan Miral walked confidently among the crowded seaport streets of Yknyr, casually shaking hands of local admirers half a world away from where he'd been only a couple of days before. He only had a couple more days to gather supplies and men to meet Talemar. His fame, and with it, his legacy, had grown since the Great Talemar had sent him half a world away to what Talemar must have known was one of the oldest and largest cities in the world. The Hag's Head of the continent separated The Sea of Portean and The Aedrinon Sea facing the Ocean of Mohers. Yknyr proper itself had grown to consume almost half of the sea-facing real estate of the Hag's Head.

Not everyone recognized his face, of course, but most smiled knowingly, some stopping him to hear tales of his exploits. The sea breeze blowing his shoulder-length brown locks back away from his weathered but handsome face, Royvan Miral sought to secure Iamean passage to Axum—and maybe a bit more help than just that. He'd been there many times in the past, of course. Before finding both Talemar and the Scroll of Carnac in the same adventure, he'd cut his teeth as a ranger in Axum. His adventures there had built his legacy and reputation as the greatest ranger of all time. That place, as holy as it was, had been picked over thoroughly. He wasn't sure what Talemar was thinking by meeting him there of all places, but if the Great Talemar wanted to meet him on holy ground, he'd be there. *Maybe he thinks he's the One*; that consideration he chased from his mind as soon as it entered. Royvan Miral only put as much stock in religion and prophecy as the pay and legacy provided, but that didn't mean he would turn over the Scroll of Carnac to just anyone. He wasn't a fool, and the boy, however capable, didn't strike him as the type. Something about his features reminded him of someone.... Running

Charles W. McDonald Jr.

a finger across the First Seal in his leather jerkin pocket, Royvan tried not to stumble as the blinding white light consumed his vision from within his own thoughts, only allowing it to return to normal when taking his finger off the Scroll of Carnac. Visibly gathering himself in the middle of the street, he proceeded to his intended destination. If this Wraith Silverstring lived up to his reputation, he would take him along with his party. Assuming he could afford the man.

He could use regular access to a great lamean; besides travel by boat took forever. He still had quite the legacy he intended to build, and those lofty goals didn't allow for time to travel by boat.

The massive gated and walled-off house—an estate really—on prime real estate overlooking the Ocean of Mohers from its elevated mesa position, stood out among the surrounding area. *That had to be him*, he estimated as his soft and worn leather boots conformed to the cobblestone path that led up to Wraith's estate. It was a 150-cubit sheer drop of limestone rock from the top of the estate foundation, with green-treed hillside rising in the background of the property. The estate itself was built from limestone bricks, most likely quarried on site to form the plateau for the foundation. Half-ellipse alcoves marched along the façade at what appeared to be a third-storey level where copper-bifurcated cathedral windows paired up with lower-level simplistic slender archery windows. Two square archer towers flanked each wing of the estate, having access to the cliff-side, the hillside, and the surrounding cityscape. Pops of color, mostly crimson and cream with gold, fluttered on banners held stiff in the salt-laden sea breeze.

Limestone rampart lions marched along both sides of the pathway leading up to the main gatehouse. Thick oak double doors came together in an acorn shape at the top, hung on black, heavy iron hinges. Royvan's approach hadn't gone unnoticed, as he could see four archers had tracked him all the way up to the gatehouse where he was challenged at the left gate door: a guardsman opening a peephole. "State your business," the tone was harsh for a moment, but then recognition in the guard's face might have bought Royvan some goodwill.

"Royvan Miral to see the Master Wraith Silverstring," Royvan offered with a proper flourish as his nostrils took in the familiar scent of open water and gulls on the cool and welcome sea breeze.

"Give us a moment while we check." A series of white and green flags flashed from the gatehouse to the keep—visible to Royvan through the top of the gate, which looked to have been left intentionally open to drop rocks or hot tar on a would-be attacking force.

Moments later, he saw another series of flags flashing from the keep, causing the left gate to sweep open for him.

"My apologies for the wait, Master Miral. We have to be careful. Walk with me, and I'll show you to Master Silverstring." Closing the gate after Royvan Miral walked through, the guardsman engaged a series of heavy locks behind them before pivoting to escort Royvan through the courtyard and covered walkway leading to the west entrance to the keep. Following a series of turns and staircases, Royvan tried to keep track of them all, and they found themselves in a twenty-cubit-high, ocean-side walkway leading to a wing seemingly dedicated to Wraith's operations. Everywhere he looked he saw artifacts, some he recognized dating back hundreds of years, maybe even a thousand or more. He'd surely be interested in hearing about his stories of interacting with Talemar, but Royvan didn't want to start with that. He'd save that until it suited him.

Finally, leading Royvan to a large octagon War Room flanked by four arched open doorways containing more of the same banners from outside—crimson and cream, piped in gold—along with dozens of weapons of every kind mounted upon the walls. The guardsman motioned to a very slight young man, shorter than Royvan with long blond hair—a silver lock flowing over his left ear—and dark emerald eyes. "Master Royvan Miral of Darthen seeks your audience, sir."

He was known here. *Good*, Royvan considered, examining the impressive array of armory mounted on all eight walls. This wasn't a traditional receiving room. There was no throne, seat, or dais of any kind. It surely wasn't a bedroom either—no bed in sight. It had more of a purpose-built War Room look about it. A table about six cubits long by three cubits broad sat at one end of the room. Atop the table were open maps with icons resembling symbols of the famed houses, placed strategically about the map. "My apologies for not sending word before my arrival, Master Silverstring."

Walking to the map on the table, Wraith never turned his back to Royvan as he paced to and fro mapside, "It's okay. I wasn't terribly busy. What can I do for you?" Wraith's hand gestures were minimalistic as he spoke. And his tone was…careful. Regarded. And soft.

His voice wasn't that of a young man, more middle-aged, with a well-traveled accent. Though he must have used his magic to maintain his youthful appearance, as was often the case with lameans. *Always superficial in one way or another. Always.* "I can tell a man who enjoys his adventure when I see one," Royvan offered—if carefully so. "I might have something of interest for you."

"You have quite the reputation, Royvan Miral. The streets are humming with how you were sent here, and by whom."

Charles W. McDonald Jr.

He had hoped to save that, but it was out, so he might as well lead with that angle instead, "Yes, Talemar lives. I found him in the Valley of Power when returning from my trip discovering the Scroll of Carnac."

"Yes, yes," Wraith waving dismissively as if tired of hearing about it already—all of his golden fingernails prominently visible, "finding both the First Seal and Talemar in the same trip within days of one another. Congratulations." That hadn't sounded sincere, nor impressed either.

Royvan Miral, frowning slightly, "I have need of a great lamean."

"But you have the Great Talemar at your services." It was a quick and terse response—nearly mocking. One made on the pivot of a quick mind.

He needed a different approach or better communication skills. He barely had time to gather his thoughts before a magnificent girl, or rather a very young *lady*, walked in on them. Shorter than Wraith, with long brunette hair and the same silver lock flowing down over her right ear as well as those same dark emerald eyes, she smoothed her simple forest green dress which had a deep V-cut that exposed about a third of her breasts as she walked through one of the open archways. *His sister...twin maybe,* he wondered, just before Wraith introduced her, "Ah, Royvan Miral, meet my wife, Silura."

Wow! That was really the only word for it, and he had to once again gather his thoughts so he could continue. "True, I do have access to the Great Talemar, and he's asked me to meet him at the holy grounds of the Rune Stones two-and-a-half days from now. Naturally, your help in getting me there, and back, would be greatly rewarded."

"Why him?" Silura pointed to her twin brother and husband—all of her fingernails golden just like Wraith. "You could find *much* cheaper means of travel to get you there safely in time."

"I'm looking for the best available lamean I can find. I now carry the Scroll of Carnac on my person," pulling it out to show them, "...and I'm trusting you with my very life just by showing it to you." Royvan Miral pausing, *Yes, this was the right approach,* he thought. He had their attention—both of them were transfixed on him *and the scroll.* "I need protection to ensure this doesn't fall into the wrong hands. I need the smartest, most powerful lamean with excellent judgment and experience to help me. I believe we could partner and help one another a great deal." Royvan, paused to move toward the map, Silura following him closely. "I know these houses intimately. I know their strengths and weaknesses, and I recognize a man of ambition. I can help you."

Silura stood right beside him; Royvan Miral found her perfume sweet and intoxicating, wishing her to stand even closer. "May I hold it?" Silura asked, eyeing the First Seal. It was testing his trust a great deal, but he needed their help. They were definitely the right choice to join his party. Contemplating only a moment before handing it to Silura, Royvan recounted, "I haven't told you about the boy, Radin, who insisted I give the Scroll to him. That's how I found myself here." He paused, looking between them, trying not to take his eye off the Scroll for even an instant. "There was a huge scuffle between Talemar and Radin that tore Talemar's place, such as it was, completely apart, before Talemar sent me here, telling me to meet him at the Rune Stones in five days. And that was two days ago."

Knowing glances rapidly exchanged between Silura and her twin brother and husband. Wraith adding, "Well you've certainly piqued our interest. We will go if we're equal partners to anything found. Any one thing of significance that cannot be split goes to Silura and myself, no questions asked. But we will pay you for it handsomely. We will always be fair."

"And I with you, Master Silverstring."

"When do you wish to leave for the Rune Stones?" Silura asked, handing the Scroll back to him unmolested—though he examined it thoroughly before putting it back in his jerkin pocket.

"Would leaving from here tomorrow be okay," Royvan Miral suggested, now leaning forward on the map table with his hands against the edge. "I'd like time to set up camp and defenses at the Rune Stones since I haven't been there in a very long time, and I have no idea how much the place has changed or what to expect Talemar will bring with him. Or who."

"Reasonable," Wraith replied again in his minimalist ways, looking to his sister for approval which she provided with a knowing nod and the briefest of smiles for their new traveling companion. "If that concludes our business, I'll have you seen out."

Stepping forward to shake Wraith's hand, Royvan Miral gave Wraith a firm contract handshake. A bow or flourish wasn't the right approach with this man. This Wraith appeared a more direct and transactional type. Seeing the tight but approving smile and the flash in Wraith's eyes told him he had his man. Turning to follow the guardsman out the way he'd come, Royvan Miral was pleased with himself—his senses and instincts were still sharp. He still had it.

*　　*　　*　　*

Lazily kicking his right leg as he sat on the edge of the bar stool, sipping ale to help force down the best butter bread he'd had since home, Kerrich listened attentively to the stories Levi shared of him and Royvan Miral and their following of clues to the Scroll of Carnac. He was a much better storyteller than most, but he would have loved to have been there in person, if only he had been old enough. Well, he was old enough now, and he was now part of Royvan Miral's crew—for what it was worth.

"Royvan thinks the scrolls are meant to fit into those shafts in the Rune Stones, but *I* disagree with him," Levi boasted as if he knew better.

"We've all heard this before," Ham protested, waving his big leg of ham in the air, "You think you've got **all** the answers."

"I just know there are *three* holes, one on each of those center Rune Stones, and there are *seven* seals, so you do the math." Levi paused, looking at Ham as he sheared another huge chunk of meat off the bone, "Look who I'm talking to about doing the math. Phoagh!" Levi snorting at Ham in disgust just as he offered a knowing wink for their new traveling companion and Royvan Miral acolyte.

"So, what do you think goes in those shafts then?" Kerrich was more than curious, and these men had literally traveled the entire world. He no longer recognized the man Radin was becoming, but if he was the One, he wanted to understand exactly what that meant. And, if Radin *wasn't* the One.... The implications of Radin's actions were literally life and death. For everyone....

"One of them is much larger than the other two, and I'm talking about the one in the center Rune Stone. The alter stone. Big enough for a grapefruit to get stuck down in there," he paused again illustrating the size with his hands for Kerrich. "The other two on the stones flanking the center are roughly half the size, and they're all really worn.... You know, from the weathering of time and all."

"So, what do you think the purpose of those shafts are," Kerrich queried, genuinely engaged in the conversation as his wide eyes and leaned-in body language would suggest.

"I don't know, really. Royvan and I have talked about the prophecies so many times, and there is just no mention of why those shafts were built into the Rune Stones. Most everything that was ever written about the Rune Stones is lost to time—and who knows if you could even trust it if it were in writing anyway. Prophecy was a fool's game any way you looked at it. We don't even really know why they were built, except that they're part of the power of the Crystal Crown and the Crystal Throne. Allegedly."

"Who made them?" Kerrich now sitting up straight, attentively listening to Levi's stories.

"The Creator," Ham blurted out, spitting shards of ham into the air between them.

"Ugh," Levi blurted in disgust, wiping the shards of meat from Ham's mouth off his face, lips, and pants. "We don't know that."

Ham just nodded knowingly, as if he wasn't going to be convinced otherwise.

It was a lot to think about, *the Creator walking amongst mortals. Why, and for what purpose?* This stuff about Michelle, Elise and many worlds, it was all a lot to take in for a kid becoming a man. Kerrich had no idea whether they should be helping Talemar, or Radin, or neither. Bringing about the end of the world, or possibly many worlds, didn't sound like the best idea, but what could he do to stop it?

Planet X Becoming Eden

Charles W. McDonald Jr.

Chapter 53: Zero Day Minus One

(Western Bouschè, Perion, Present Day)

Brigance Fireheart tried not to coerce through intimidation tactics, but his orders were clear, and he was beginning to believe in them the more time he spent with Radin. He had his doubts about Damon's influence—they all did—but it was clear they needed more capable fighting forces. The strife between Talemar and Radin was palpable and real. And while both seemed good men, his bets had fallen on Radin despite the rashness that came with his youth and inexperience. Something about his aura spoke to Brigance and his own experience with other leaders around the world he'd dealt with in the past. Radin had the mettle to make big decisions and the heart to care that they were the right decisions. If he could only learn to temper that with the patience to wait for the right moment. Such were the struggles he was dealing with as he began constructing this army for what was to come....

His fist slamming down on the heavy poplar dining table of House Palomides, Steward of Bouschè and the Throne of Knor, Brigance caused a new crack to form where his fist struck. "You're involved whether you want to be or not. This fight will come to your front door in a matter of days, and you don't want to find yourself on the wrong side of it." Brigance leaning in to emphasize his point with Sir Palomides. This wasn't his first encounter with the man, of course. He'd led a campaign for him taking twelve thousand acres back from a competing Lord, who Brigance had to kill with his bare hands.

Charles W. McDonald Jr.

Some people were entirely too stubborn, including the man before him now.

"Do not think me ungrateful, Lord Fireheart," Sir Palomides protested with a reference to a title Brigance long since left behind. "There are still competing interests here, and I have but ten thousand fighting men; perhaps only one in ten good enough to meet your standards, and such a vacancy of security will not go unnoticed by my enemies."

"I believe you...," Brigance began with a deliberate pause to look the man in the eyes. "What you're not hearing is that your enemies will soon be the least of your concerns."

Sir Palomides, stroking his lengthy graying beard, which nearly touched his breastplate in thoughtful contemplation. His smoke-grey eyes and a Y-shaped scar under his right eye marked him a hard and seasoned man of battle. Nearly as tall as Brigance, his broad shoulders and gruff build marked him a rule-by-force sort, though his temperament said his people loved him. Brigance understood the power vacuum he was about to create and its consequences, but what had to be done had to be done right now. *Patience was for yesterday.*

"Tell me more about this boy you think is the One."

"He's growing stronger by the day. He has the most powerful lamean I've ever met, or heard of for that matter, for a teacher. He has followers the likes of which we've never seen before—downright lethal people, and none too afraid to do what requires doing. I trust Radin's judgment," he offered with an involuntary pause as he wondered whether or not he really did trust the boy's judgment. "...But I do concern myself with certain people around him. Still, I believe Radin would do the right thing when pressed. Especially if we surround him with sound advisors..." The last an afterthought, but a valid one.

"And what do you believe is the right thing?"

"I think he means to open the First Seal," Brigance offered flatly.

"Do you agree with that?"

"It's prophecy, so it doesn't matter what I believe."

"That's not like you. Tell me what you really think, Lord Fireheart. Is it time to open the First Seal?"

"That's not for me to judge. I don't know." He paused, wanting to give a complete answer to the just question, "What I do know is that when that Seal is opened, we'll need an army to battle what comes forth, and ten thousand men will only be the start of it."

"What else are you not telling me, Lord Fireheart?" The experience of a leader shining through the hard, partial smile Sir Palomides offered for his old acquaintance.

"The lamean teaching Radin is more than just dangerous. I worry he

Charles W. McDonald Jr.

could kill us all if he wanted, with but a thought."

Raised eyebrows from Sir Palomides, "...And what are the odds we're going to cause his wrath?"

"I can't say. He's a tough man to read, but he does exactly what he says, so I guess that's something. And Radin has a rapport with him that appears genuine if more than a bit odd. Reading that man's intentions is pretty much impossible, though. So that's what's bothering me every night when I go to sleep. That uncertainty."

"That's a huge blind spot you're asking me to expose myself to."

"Aye," Brigance returning a thoughtful look with his eyes, "...It is."

"Very well," Sir Palomides, scratching his facial scar in consideration. "You'll have my men."

A smile of relief from Brigance Fireheart quickly interrupted as Sir Palomides completed his thought, "On one condition."

"I'm listening."

"We're going to need everyone we can get our hands on, which will leave my lands unguarded. So, I'm thinking, I will offer the Stewardship of these lands to House Aegon in return for eight thousand of his best fighting men to fight under my command for the next two years." *Wow*, Brigance thought, but the Palomides he remembered was an ingenious man. He was going somewhere with this. "And in return, when all this is over, I want Radin, and his teacher, to commit to me they'll ensure I'm made King of the Throne of Knor, even if it means they have to kill Sir Aegon—*and every last one of his heirs.*"

Brigance nodded, genuinely impressed at the bold political move his old acquaintance just made, if a bit apprehensive at the idea of getting Radin to make such a lethal commitment when other solutions might avail themselves. He was assuming Sir Palomides would lead with other alternatives first, but the Palomides he remembered was pretty impatient—and ambitious. "I'll see to it myself," Brigance promised, offering his hand to Sir Palomides as they sealed the deal for all the lands of Knor in a single handshake.

*　　*　　*　　*

(Yknyr, Perion, Present Day)

He hadn't slept well last night, but today was another day, a glorious day, as Royvan Miral headed back to Wraith Silverstring's estate. *Perhaps I'll get to see Silura again*, he hoped. She was magnificent. The thought of Silura was only a brief distraction, but the distraction proved more than enough to

Charles W. McDonald Jr.

find himself suspended in mid-air, floating a couple of cubits off the ground as Eldrac slowly rotated him upside down like a roasted piece of meat about a spit, causing all of Royvan Miral's belongings to fall onto the rust-colored cobblestones of the path leading up to Wraith's estate.

A clank of the rough-hewn gold scroll case as it struck the cobblestone path caused Royvan Miral to cringe, hoping it didn't break open, or worse, hoping Eldrac didn't open it. He immediately recognized the man from his exploits around the world. There wasn't a major tome on the planet that didn't have his face, or tales of his destruction, in it.

Unseen hands picking up the First Seal with only a thought, Eldrac read the inscription as the Scroll of Carnac floated before him, 'Herein lay the first breath of God. Woe unto he that is unworthy.'

"Congratulations," Eldrac mocked, "I'm feeling generous today. You get to live." Dropping Royvan Miral unceremoniously to the cobblestone path, nearly breaking Royvan's bones in the process, Eldrac disappeared in the brief swallowing flash of a *Gate*, taking the Scroll of Carnac with him.

The consequences of Royvan's arrogance slammed home as he lay on his back on the stone pathway, people passing by in the mid-morning light, observing him weeping over his stupidity. His fame and recognition weren't very helpful in this case as he heard some muttering, *Isn't that Royvan Miral?*

*   *   *   *

It hadn't been easy to clean up in what little distance there was left between where Eldrac had robbed him and the main gate to Wraith's estate. The guardsman recognizing him, "Sir, I was told to expect you. Everything okay?"

Royvan Miral, smoothing his leather vest jerkin, holding himself back from wiping his eyes which he hoped he'd adequately dried on the way up, "Just show me the way if you could. Thanks." A few flashes of flags back and forth between the gatehouse and the keep and the left gate swung open for Royvan Miral as he was escorted back to the octagon War Room.

*   *   *   *

"Royvan Miral to see you again, sir." The guard offered with Wraith standing over the maps in his War Room, studying them again before he pivoted to Royvan to greet the legendary ranger. Wearing leather armor, with a solid red-wrap robe, Wraith closed the distance with Royvan Miral to shake hands.

Charles W. McDonald Jr.

"You look rough," Wraith observed, letting his eyes take in Royvan's defeated demeanor and disheveled appearance.

"Ummm," Royvan paused, this was going to be difficult, "I don't know quite where to start, but...."

"Silura, could you come, Dearheart?" Wraith called out to the hallway that must have led to their marital chambers.

Only a brief moment later and Silura walked out in a diaphanous white nightgown that came down to mid-thigh. Royvan didn't really need to see *that* right now. His lips were already pressed into a hard, thin line as he worked his lips dryly trying to explain. "I...the Scroll of Carnac..." Royvan began briefly, only pausing to lick his lips, "...I failed."

"Well, that must have been hard for you," Silura stroked Royvan's left arm, comforting him as she stood beside him so closely her body pressed against his. Her pressed lips and thoughtful expression didn't really give anything away, but Royvan's senses were either way off or seriously messed up. He was getting readings all over the place from this beautiful young woman. "We took precautions when you were last here," Silura announced, leaving the room and still talking as she walked out, "You asked us for our protection, so that's what we provided you."

A brief moment and she was back, Scroll of Carnac in hand. Royvan Miral dropped to his knees where he stood, kissing the floor. "Oh Creator, Thank you!"

"Really, as much as you couldn't keep your eyes off me or the Scroll, a little sleight-of-hand was all it took." Silura coached in a tone careful not to mock the living legend, but definitely enough to get him to think better and use all his faculties going forward. "Still, consider our services rendered. We'll keep the First Seal safe until we meet both Radin *and* Talemar."

"That wasn't the deal," Royvan Miral protested.

"I hardly think we can trust your judgment to tell us who we should, or should not, give the Scroll of Carnac to. We will meet them both and decide for ourselves. Until then it stays in our hands." Silura proclaimed, looking to Wraith, who held up his hands as if to say, *You got this.*

"You did ask for our protection, and you now have it. You should be happy," Wraith concurred with his beautiful wife and twin sister, offering her an affirming nod.

"Well, now that all that unpleasant business is settled, shall we go?" Wraith hastily opened a *Portal* to the holy ground of the Nine Towers of Axum.

This day had already gone very far off course for Royvan Miral. Maybe he didn't still have it after all.

Charles W. McDonald Jr.

(Damon's Manor, Kaleion, Present Day)

Having cast now on both Damon's homeworld and Perion, Radin was beginning to be able to tell the difference in the strength of the energy between the two worlds. Perion was slightly stronger than Damon's homeworld; even Damon would agree. Damon claimed part of that was the unintended consequences of his Master Plan gone awry, killing thousands—if not millions—accidentally. The loss of all that lifeforce energy severely impacted what was available to draw from on Kaleion.

Now in Damon's remodeled spell test room, Damon gave him more stretch-goal spells—some exceptionally destructive. Thus, the reason for using the spell test room for today's lesson. *Damon's Inundation, Damon's Improved Shield, Damon's Ball of Lightning,* and *Damon's Stone Showering* all came relatively quickly, one of them causing a third fingernail on Radin to turn like unto living liquid gold dust. *Damon's Tentacles of Lightning* was the stretch-goal spell of the moment, and it was taking everything Radin had to control the amount of energy it took just to get the spell to form, let alone aggregate any real energy to put anything into it. It was supposed to invoke tentacles of lightning to erupt from the floor, dozens of them, spreading outward from the epicenter about forty or more paces, but theoretically he could limit the scope area and intensify it. Unfortunately, it was fighting him enough to make his forehead sweat profusely as he tried to control it.

"Relax...." Damon coached, providing another example as Radin watched the room explode with hundreds of tentacles of lightning, stopping just shy of where they stood in a highly controlled manner. "You're never going to control the Arcane. You're going to have to convince it. You're just the conduit," Damon explained. "When you think you're in control, that's when you're really screwed." Smiling a little, recognizing the awkwardness of their relationship, "And that's when you'll get a very real and very rude surprise." Recognizing the frustration that brought back memories, though Damon was mostly self-taught and had the scars to prove it. "Maybe we need to take a break."

"Let's try again. I'm ready to try again.... I think." Palms turned up toward the ceiling just as Damon had shown, smooth and straightforward, not even thinking about it, this time, just doing, asking... A burst of thirty tentacles of lightning shot up through the bottom of the spell test room floor, only for a brief couple of moments while he coaxed them to expand outward, then

Charles W. McDonald Jr.

side-to-side, before they dispelled on their own.

"Better…," Damon encouraged, "…much better." Smiling, opening the double doors to exit the spell test room, Damon led them away, "I think we can take a break now." Radin in tow and now following, Damon was already out in the third-floor hallway continuing, "Destroying stuff is relatively easy. Creating, Healing, and Divining…now those are not so easy. If you're going to go into combat, you *have* to know how to protect yourself, and you *have* to know how to *Heal*. We'll work on those next before we call it a day."

Radin thinking for a moment about *Healing*, "How do you propose we test *Healing*?"

Damon smiled, "Relax, I'm not going to cut up a human being or anything. I figured we could start with some mice and work our way up." A measured and tense smile from Radin showed awkward agreement. It was a tough relationship between them, for certain.

(Planet-X, Hours Later)

Damon had the stellar coordinates from Mira for proper orbit capture as well as the clip rate velocity. Now he just needed to move this beast of a rock. *Easier said than done*, he estimated inside his atmospheric shell on the side of Planet-X nearest the protostar that barely qualified as a yellow dwarf. Still, it was a significant step in the right direction if he could pull this off and not have to start over. *No time for that.* Concentrating as he held the *Staff of the Invoker* high overhead, pointing it in the direction he wanted to move Planet-X, Damon cast his latest version of *Damon's Far Reaching*. Reaching out to touch the Zero-Point all around the entire crust of the planet, high up into the sky, thirty, then fifty, then two-hundred miles outward, then nearly all the way to the protostar, Damon's signet ring plus the *Staff of the Invoker* allowed him to conduit more energy than ever before. Carefully, he coaxed, controlled, and formed the energy, now moving Planet-X along the calculated trajectory. It took everything Damon had, and he was weak from the extra gravity, as the *Staff of the Invoker* felt heavier and heavier over his head as he held the energy form in place until the desired velocity was achieved.

A sudden tap on his right shoulder from behind nearly made him jump out of his skin as Damon dropped the *Staff of the Invoker* outside his protective shell—the staff skidding on the planet's still barren and hard crust. A magnificent brunette with large breasts, slender waist, legs, and frame, just more than a hand shorter than he, wearing those familiar, extremely revealing

Charles W. McDonald Jr.

Roman robes and high heels seemingly part of her own feet, walked about him without a protective atmosphere. In her elements in the nakedness of the vacuum. Damon knew when he was being measured up, and she'd never looked at him in such a way before. He wanted his staff. With a thought, his natural *Telekinesis* yanked the *Staff of the Invoker* off the planet's crust, pulling it firmly into the grip of his right hand—its power palpable now in the presence of the Dragon of Darkness.

"You wouldn't have bothered coming all the way out here if it wasn't important. I'm listening," Damon offered with careful measure in his tone. Not combative. Not frustrated. But not subservient or malleable either. Rigid and matter of fact was the way he looked at her along body language that said so very much more than the spoken word. *Especially with her.*

"I'm wondering why all of this is necessary…?" The Dragon motioning to the yellow dwarf protostar in the distance as the space between it and Planet-X closed quickly behind Damon. "You're thinking the manifestation of your own consequences warrants all of this…?" A flourish of her beautiful, delicate and seemingly feminine hand toward what was taking place behind Damon made him want to look, if not for the fact he didn't trust her. At all….

He didn't have *Distorting Web* up. She could *read* him! *Careful*, he realized. It would only take one careless slip, and….

"Yes," he replied flatly and honestly needing to defuse and deflect. "You've always known where we stand."

"True. I HAVE ALWAYS known." She pronounced, circling about him, probing his naked thoughts, emphasizing her own omnipotence. So careful this one. It was a big slip for Damon, and she needed to seize this rare moment. "I just wanted to see just how far you were willing to go."

No reply. Damon stared her down cold, never taking his eyes off her. Taking the measure of her in kind, his *Black Mirrors of the Soul* called her bluff, as the Zero-Point plus all the Arcane he could muster going out thousands of miles, coursed through him. More than he'd ever held before. *The Staff of the Invoker* resonated with all the energy coursing through it and its master, as its normally seven-foot hemispherical aura, now stretched out for miles—encompassing Damon and the Dragon of Darkness and so very much more.

"Very well then…. Damon, it's always a pleasure. You might want to watch your experiment, or you'll ruin your *little* world." With the patronizing retort, she was gone. Dissolved and disintegrated in a gust of wind that didn't yet exist on Planet-X.

Pivoting around, Damon's eyes nearly popped out of their sockets at the sight closing in on him. "SHIT! Brakes," he thought aloud watching the distance to the protostar closing on him entirely too fast. Holding up the

Charles W. McDonald Jr.

Staff of the Invoker high overhead, he channeled everything he'd been holding for the Dragon of Darkness to slow Planet-X to a capture velocity rate as it clipped the apex of the perimeter orbit he had wanted for the planet's steady-state. Right along the ecliptic plane of his yellow dwarf star. It would develop other orbital bodies, no doubt. But for now....

"That was your last big mistake, Day," he scolded himself aloud. *Another one like that and it's all over. If it isn't already.*

Focusing, Damon felt through the planet's mantle for the planet's core, sensing the incredibly dense deposit of cold metal, now already beginning to warm. He redirected all his energy to warming it more, causing its mantle to move about its solid core, creating the electric circuit that would mate this world to its new protostar and to the cosmic web. Concentrating more, he tilted the vertical axis, along with its poles, to lean on its back, away from the yellow dwarf, as he slowly felt the crust obeying his will to start turning. Slowly, the planet began rotating about its axis, accepting Damon's new closer orbit to the new protostar.

One last thing to do, he needed to get rid of the excess matter and local interstellar medium around the protostar to reduce the probability of it coalescing into a planetary-sized object that could collide with his new world. Or from causing the star to cyclically gain and shed material through micro-novas that could destabilize his new world. Planet-X still needed a moon for stabilization of its oceans and of its axial rotation—that would be the perfect use of this excess material from the creation of the yellow dwarf. As he coaxed Arcane to work with his Zero-Point, trying not to pass out from channeling all this energy, Damon couldn't help but think, *what am I going to call this thing?* Thinking of his favorite bands, *Volbeat, Tristania, Led Zeppelin, Black Sabbath, and Alter Bridge. No. None of those.* He was giving this place another chance, another life. *Phoenix?* No. All his life he'd excelled at destroying—now he excelled at creation itself. *Eden—the garden of creation itself. Yes,* he accepted. *Eden.*

(Northwest Exeter, Helios Manor, Perion, Present Day)

Brigance Fireheart continued explaining the arrangement to Radin, brokering the meeting he hoped would seal the deal for all the forces Radin would need to capture the Crystal Throne. "The thing you need to understand about a force this size, Radin, is that it can rapidly, within a couple of days, collapse under its own weight. The logistics, supply lines, money, food...."

Charles W. McDonald Jr.

Even where to take a crap can become a lethal issue of dysentery if not handled properly." Brigance was his usual stone-faced while explaining the literal minutia of large-scale fighting forces.

"I don't mean any disrespect to your youth or inexperience, lad," Sir Palomides began, resting his gauntlet-protected hand on the map-strewn table, helping him stand in his full armor. *Creator, it was heavy hulking this thing around.* "My men are yours by our arrangement, but I would feel far more comfortable with Brigance in direct responsibility of leading them. He knows the details. He knows siege tactics, battle maneuvers, and he has a mind for both military strategy and tactics. You've found a great man," resting his other gauntlet-protected hand on Brigance's shoulder, Sir Palomides continued, "May I recommend you make Lord Fireheart your General in direct control over all your military assets and resources?"

"That's a reasonable recommendation, which I accept, Sir Palomides. I'll listen to his counsel on military strategy and tactics, but there may come a time when traditional thinking doesn't serve us well, and that's where I may override." Radin had given them both a lot of latitude in sharing their opinions, but at some point, he'd have to take command. The End Times would come whether he set them in motion, or someone else did. Of that, he was certain. Better to have a controlled instantiation of chaos, than an uncontrolled one. At least that was his thinking into opening the Scroll of Carnac now, but all plans had a tendency to go off kilter as soon as the first arrow was loosed.

The mere thought of controlling any outcomes once he opened the First Seal seemed utterly ludicrous to him. Still, he would do what he could. Thoughts of opening the Scroll of Carnac always led him to wonder about Talemar, and how things had gone so quickly askew between them. Could he have handled that differently? *More maturely,* he wondered. He was still but a child really—certainly not qualified for all the responsibilities now thrust upon his shoulders.

Yanking himself mentally back to the conversation at hand, Radin pressed for answers, "Can I get some suggestions on what kind of resources we need to start gathering to support these forces? How much money per day are we talking about?"

Scratching his gruff stubble in deliberation, Brigance ran some quick numbers in his head. This was by far the largest fighting force he'd ever assembled or led, so some of this was new to even him. "Let's see, just in payroll, you're looking at well over ten thousand silver coins per day, add food, armor, uniform maintenance, weaponry support, and general other items, I'd say you're north of forty thousand silver coins per day."

Charles W. McDonald Jr.

"Well then, General Fireheart," Radin seemed to enjoy the title he'd given, "I'd say your first order of business is to appoint a suitable and highly trustworthy Treasurer. Have him report to me before sunset. I have an idea to raise some revenue, and we have enough treasure for a couple of days but taking the Crystal Throne will take far longer than that. And who knows what lay behind the Crystal Throne once I have it."

Radin's confidence radiated from him in waves—perhaps a product of being in Damon's presence so frequently these days. Still, Brigance Fireheart and Sir Palomides glanced at each other sidelong, not really knowing what to make of their burgeoning leader.

*   *   *   *

(Land of Golems, Perion, Present Day)

Dusk still a few tense moments away, Anna still didn't have full freedom of movement, but she had at least managed to feed when one of her staff came to check on her condition. She'd been convulsing on the floor much of the day, wanting neither food nor water, yet languishing in utter hunger for an insatiable thirst she could no longer control.

"I barely recognized you, My Dear," Eldrac announced, slithering about her estate, but freely walking in the light of dusk still pouring through the windows. "May I?" Pulling the drapes closed for her, Eldrac pointed to the food he'd brought for her in the form of a man in tattered clothes beaten more than half to death, laying on the floor and bleeding out where he'd come through Eldrac's *Portal*. In less than the blink of an eye, Anna had her fangs buried deep in the man's neck, snapping it cleanly as she hadn't yet realized her new-found *physical* strength.

"How did you know," she asked, pulling her blood-soaked fangs from the man's withered and dry husk of a neck, his crimson lifeforce streaking down her chin.

"Oh, your place was easy to find my Dear, but you've always underestimated me."

"No, how did you know about this?" Anna motioned to the blood on her chin as she watched Eldrac strut about like a peacock.

"Ah that," he paced from the now-draped window to her, kneeling down at her level as he extended his hand to her chin to better examine her eyes, fangs, and disposition of her Undead state. "I've seen this before but never *here*. You have an affliction that has been brought here from another world."

Charles W. McDonald Jr.

The possibilities rang true, though she'd never seen this curse before. She knew these kinds of afflictions existed but never thought to be so completely transformed like this. *Better to be dead.* "Can this be undone," she asked—in her heart, knowing otherwise. She hadn't even become accustomed to her *new* body yet and already it had been taken from her.

"Not to my knowledge, but I will look further into it for you." Still getting the measure of her as he walked about her, "Are you sure…? I mean, do you still have your abilities?"

She hadn't even thought to cast. All her instincts revolved around her new physical transformation. To kill and to feed. Getting to her feet, still nude, her kill's blood now flowing from her chin down her chest and over her left breast, Anna made a *Portal* to the place she recognized above all others— the white beaches of Axum.

"Good," Eldrac surmised as he continued, "You're many times more lethal now than ever before. Are you sure you want me to try to undo this?" His senses told him to do whatever convincing was necessary since they needed every advantage they could get, and an element of surprise never hurt either. Yet, he wondered if he could still take her in her current form. Before, it wouldn't have been a contest, but now…with this….

"No," she smiled looking back at the corpse she'd drained so completely as to shrivel up his now dead grey husk of a shell. She really only had one request in mind she truly did want, "If you could tell me *who* did this to me, that would be more than enough."

"Good. Then I can count on you."

A blood-stained smile, with fangs bare, gave Eldrac all the acknowledgment he required.

*   *   *   *

(Further South, Near Golem's Point, Perion, Present Day)

In a giant mountain pass, formed by the southernmost edge of the mountain range and the mountain of Golem's Point itself, Eldrac formed his army in ranks by the hundreds, performing combat drills.

In the valley of the pass itself, King Aaron, Keeper of the Wind, sat on his royal mount—a beautiful white stallion—watching archery drills being coordinated with surging infantry. With nearly twelve thousand of his most elite fighting forces, combined with nearly six thousand mercenaries and sell-swordsmen, it was the largest fighting force he'd ever seen assembled in person. Whoever this impostor was, masquerading around as the One, he'd

Charles W. McDonald Jr.

soon be dead. These were not the End Times, and it wasn't this boy's place to bring about such chaos when so many of his own plans had yet to be fulfilled. No, better to be on the right side of history as he saw it.

"Impressive, isn't it?" He still wasn't used to Eldrac appearing out of nowhere, so light-footed it startled him each time.

"Indeed," spinning his stallion about to face Eldrac head on. "My generals have been whipping your sell-swordsmen into shape, integrating one hundred of your men per regiment into our infantry. They're beginning to fight as a unit now. The boy won't know what hit him."

"Yes, well, about that…" Eldrac, pausing, trying to think of the best way to play off of Aaron's maniacal ego, "I fully expect Talemar to be there as well."

"*The* Talemar," King Aaron questioned.

"The very same."

"Well, we'll certainly be writing our victory into the pages of history for all times then."

So easy, Eldrac plotted. What Eldrac couldn't foresee was Talemar's involvement. He knew the boy would invoke the Scroll. Damnable Royvan Miral for fooling him. *I will kill that man slowly*, he thought. But, Eldrac had no visibility into Talemar's intentions. Talemar was the unknown variable in this equation, and it bothered him immensely as he watched the combat drills from his high-ground vantage.

* * * *

The amber hues of dusk, amidst the backdrop of a partly cloudy sky, still provided enough daylight to see days of Gareth's hard labor in his search for Xaldran's Tome of Power as he'd come to find out its meaning over the last few hours of reading. He hadn't broken the ivory tooth yet, though he'd held it in his hands for hours while he read. Some he understood. Some were in a language he didn't know, but he understood Talemar's caution in who possessed it. Sitting on one of the many massive piles of dirt where he'd been led to believe it would be, from the brief and cryptic passages in his grandfather's journal, he pondered no further…. Setting the tooth down on a nearby rock, he shattered the tooth with the edge of his blade as he brought his sword down upon it to summon the Great Talemar.

A moment later, a *Portal* opened up by the grassy field, just in front of the massive Rune Stones where he hadn't been forced to dig. *Thankfully*. Most of his digging had happened away from the beach and to the south of the

Rune Stones, away from the Nine Towers and the statues. Though the Tome had actually been found very close to the white sands of the beach; a bit longer and it would have uncovered itself through the act of beach erosion from the South Sea.

Looking very different from the last time they'd met, Talemar stepped through the *Portal*. Nightfall had already set on the other side of the *Portal* from whence he came. Dressed in fresh light-greys and reds with what his grandfather's journal described as *Starfire* at his side. At least the hilt matched the description of *Starfire*. No robes for the most famous of all lamean, just a fine vest with charcoal wool pants and a dark-green cape clasped in golden anchors about his neck and clavicle.

"I see you found it." Talemar confidently strode towards Gareth, smiling.

"Perhaps we should put it back," Gareth suggested, closing the Tome, seriously considering whether or not he was the right judge of who should possess such a thing.

"I learned from that book as a child. I know its contents."

"Then why do you need it so?" A fair question no doubt, though the tense line it drew across Talemar's lips said it wasn't a question he cared to answer at this very moment. At least not to him.

A *Portal* suddenly opening between the two, caused Talemar to draw *Starfire*, holding it at the ready as it glowed white-hot in his hands, ready to aid him in his channeling. Two men and one beautiful woman walked through the *Portal*—one of the men he recognized as Royvan Miral—though that didn't look like the Royvan Miral of old. This one was different, his body language carrying his frame very differently, as if a defeated man.

Not thirty paces from Talemar, Royvan Miral waved down *Starfire*—he recognized it instantly, though no one had seen it in hundreds of years to his recollection. He supposed it made sense to him that it would have found its way to Talemar. "We came early, but I see we're not alone," Royvan Miral began, looking between Talemar, Gareth, Wraith and Silura. "My apologies," Royvan motioned to Wraith, "This is Wraith Silverstring and his wife, Silura. This," he continued, motioning to Talemar, "I suppose you already know is Talemar, and this…," he finished motioning to Gareth, "…is Gareth Armstead."

Talemar hadn't sheathed *Starfire* yet, and he really didn't have plans to do so until he was more certain about the two Royvan had brought. He began contemplating Royvan's posture. He was hiding something—something big. "I assume the First Seal is still safe," he probed, watching Royvan's eyes carefully and noting how they deferred to Wraith and Silura. Not a good sign.

Charles W. McDonald Jr.

Royvan Miral's mouth worked, but nothing came out.

"Your friend asked us to protect it. We have it." Silura offering her hand to Talemar, though Talemar made no motion to accept it, or her. Silura halted her advance toward Talemar in her tracks, pulling the Scroll of Carnac, unmolested, from a small light brown satchel she carried slung about her slender hips. "You can examine it if you wish, Great Talemar...."

Through long bangs between black and auburn did Talemar reach out to accept the scroll and examine it as his eyes slowly walked over ever part of it.

These two were very accomplished at working together—that he could tell from just a cursory glance, just by observing how one laid back while the other advanced. "I think a man should stand beside his wife. Don't you," Talemar reasonably asked of Wraith to an affirming nod from the seemingly young lamean. Talemar's eyes made obvious his mistrust of Wraith exceeded that of his wife, though Silura seemed to him the more dangerous threat of the two. *Starfire* never pointing away from Silura confirmed that much as Talemar's hackles stood on end from all the energy he held at the ready.

"Darling," Silura suggested, turning back towards her twin brother, "Perhaps we should meet with Radin."

Talemar instantly felt his lips run dry as he struggled with his trust of these two. His eyes now darting between Wraith and Silura, trying to read their aura and the soul that lay behind those pretty eyes these twins shared.

"Would you be a Dear and go get Radin while I stay here with the Great Talemar," Silura asked of her husband, knowing Talemar wanted the Scroll of Carnac for himself—and the Tome Gareth currently clutched to for all he was worth.

They hadn't physically gone there yet to verify his presence but had gathered enough details from Royvan Miral to know the boy they sought was near Exeter, and they knew the specific manor he'd acquired, having been there before.

Silent this entire time, just watching his sister work the 'Great' Talemar with the precision of a master craftsman building a simple bassinet, Wraith winked in reply, opening another *Portal* west of Exeter, where it was at least midnight, walking through to go fetch the boy called, Radin.

* * * *

(Northwest Exeter, Helios Manor, Perion, Present Day)

Hours of meeting with his newly appointed Treasurer had given Radin even more burden to shoulder, and it was only going to get worse with each success, and with each failure. He had been discussing forms of government with Damon to get perspectives beyond just a typical monarchy. If he were successful, he'd have to stand up a government-in-waiting, but that was getting ahead of himself. For now, it was enough to 'feed the beast' as Brigance often said.

Sipping evening tea in his makeshift war room, what had been the receiving room before he bought the entire estate with funds he'd found in Talemar's cave, Radin listened to the breeze coming through the two open windows, considering options for funding his army. Looking at the map table, he studied the individual icons for Adena, Talemar, King Aaron's Army, Eldrac, Anna, and the list went on and on. The problem with facing so many forces wasn't having the number of troops to match, it was understanding each of the forces and their motivations on both sides; for surely there would be some on both sides that didn't follow the plan. They had their own plan, as Damon had coached him. Understanding who would fall into what camp was essential. Talemar and Adena jumped to mind as he sipped again, noticing a flash of silvery-blue light just outside his window.

A moment later, one of his guardsmen he recognized from Brigance's introduction hours before—Jac Haden, one of Sir Palomides captains—stormed into his war room. "Sir, you have a young male visitor, dressed like a lamean, calls himself Wraith Silverstring. Seeking an urgent audience, sir," Jac finished with a flourish, his brown eyes darting back to where he'd left Wraith in waiting. Jac was fidgety for such a big man, indicating Wraith a greater potential threat than accustomed.

Reaching for Dallia's staff, never far away from his side these days, Radin considered waking Elise, Lawna, or Michelle, but thought better. "Show him in Jac but keep four of your best men trained on him with heavy ranged weapons at all times." Radin's eyes flared in consideration of what this Wraith Silverstring might want in this impromptu audience, but he didn't want his mind always racing to negative intent. That was a characteristic he'd assumed of Damon, but assumptions were just as dangerous as unvetted threats he supposed. *Still, give the man the benefit of the doubt*, he considered.

"SIR!" Jac acknowledged the command in firm agreement, pivoting back to the hallway to get Wraith.

A moment later, the young lamean, slight and lithe, though walking brimmed with confidence, strode through the main hall and through the large archway opening up into Radin's war room. "Wraith Silverstring to see you, sir." Jac offering another flourish, accompanied by four other guardsmen, each with heavy crossbows trained on the seemingly young visitor. Though Wraith,

Charles W. McDonald Jr.

however masked by magic, appeared at least a few years older than Radin. The magic-smoothed but meandering creases in Wraith's frown lines notably the difference between the two.

A light sigh from Wraith, though not from fatigue, "Sorry to bother you so late, Radin. May I shake your hand?" Wraith slowly extended his open hand as his feet slowly closed the distance between them.

Wraith didn't come across as threatening, but all ten gold fingernails warned otherwise. Still, Radin switched Dallia's staff to his left, offering his dominant right hand to shake Wraith's. "Whatever brings you in the middle of the night must be urgent." Radin, getting the measure of the man as he shook hands. His red robes, carrying almost no accouterments save a wooden staff—slight and lithe, just like its master.

"I came from the Rune Stones where we just met Talemar for the first time."

Radin coughing into his fist as he pulled his hand back, "And how is Talemar?"

"Nervous." Wraith made no sudden motions, just standing there with a sidelong stance to Radin, keeping right side away from Radin.

Radin couldn't help but chuckle at that. "Sounds about right."

"I don't want to waste your time, Radin. We have the Scroll of Carnac, and it clearly is meant for one of you. I can't say who just yet, but we have no intention of keeping such a thing for ourselves."

Another cough into his fist; *this just kept getting better.* "Where is Roy-van Miral?"

"He sought out our protections and was wise to do so. Eldrac made an attempt to take the Scroll of Carnac, that we foiled."

"Well…," Radin responded, offering Wraith a chair, making a downward motion with his right hand to train the weapons down off of Wraith. "…Then, you have my thanks." He motioned to his tea, offering with his eyes.

"Oh no, I'm fine," Wraith protested, waving off the idea.

"What is it you're proposing exactly?"

"Would you allow myself and my wife to probe your thoughts?" Wraith offered nonchalantly, "…and Talemar's too, of course."

"I'm afraid I can't allow that," Radin thinking of not just his plans, but plans of others that could be put in jeopardy if they became known. "Is there another way you could feel comfortable with your decision?"

Wraith pausing, thinking, "If I knew your origin it might help."

"My origin…. How would that help you?"

"I think prophecies are highly glorified in their flourishing embellishments and exaggerated in their accounts. Frankly, I think Talemar's legend

Charles W. McDonald Jr.

precedes him."

"Oh, he's powerful; I can say firsthand," Radin protested.

"Power doesn't determine the One," Wraith postulated as a matter-of-fact statement, likely indicative of years of research into the subject. But Wraith's body language oozed confidence on the matter.

"What does?" Radin knew the answer, but he wanted to see if Wraith did.

"The Crystal Crown," Wraith affirmed with certainty, his eyes now deadlocked with Radin's.

"But we don't have that to make the determination. So, we're left to your judgment."

"What if I told you I knew where the Crystal Crown is?"

"Then I'd say you have two things to barter, and I have none."

Wraith chuckled, enjoying the intellectual banter. Radin was certainly easier to work with than Talemar, but that didn't make him the One either. "Adena has it in her vault. She's had it a very long time and *will not* give it up easily."

"Are you proposing you and I simply go take the Crown from Adena, right now in the middle of the night, so we can figure out who to give the First Seal to," Radin asked, shaking his head, incredulous.

"No," Wraith protested, instead offering, "…I'm suggesting you, I, my wife, and Talemar ALL go steal the Crystal Crown so we will know for certain." Wraith rising to walk to Radin's map table, "You can't just march into Edinaiel with twenty thousand strong. Logistically, it won't work. You need a small, potent raiding party."

"Small is a relative term," Radin began, letting his fingers walk over the map of Edinaiel. "Would one or two more make it that much more challenging?" On the one hand, he'd love nothing more than to prove his leadership by going and taking the Crystal Crown on his own, or with this small group, but he didn't know any of these people except Royvan Miral and Talemar, and they hadn't proven to be entirely committed to him yet. He needed at least someone that was committed to him on this raid. He had to have someone with him that he knew had his back. It was the minimum level of safety he could request, and Wraith would simply have to deal with it.

"Everyone we add makes it more likely we'll be discovered sooner than later, but I think one more might be workable."

"Jac, please go wake up Michelle and tell her to bring *all* her combat gear with her."

"SIR!" And he was off to go fetch Michelle, though he'd never seen her sleep. Not yet.

Charles W. McDonald Jr.

*   *   *   *

"No Ma'am," Jac explained to an already dressed Michelle, who apparently was never asleep, now dressed in not-so-flattering forest green and brown pants, matching elbow guards and a bustier. The bustier was tight and low across her breasts, more than making up for the unflattering and neutral color choices. Reaching down, she slung a shortbow and quiver over her back, along with a strange black metallic thing with a long barrel that had some inscription on it Jac couldn't discern: *Bad Intentions*. "You're the only one invited to come. They were very clear on that," Jac continued, explaining to her.

"Take me to them," Michelle acknowledged, picking up two extra clips for her M-4 she stuck in her belt, where they hung across her butt.

*   *   *   *

Wraith and Radin looked over the map together, discussing where best to *Portal* into Adena's stronghold. There were always pros and cons, of course. Come in too close without knowing, and you've just set off enough traps to kill everyone. Come in too far away, and the element of surprise is lost, causing just as many, if not more, casualties or deaths. Consensus was building around a patch of high ground just outside the Crystal Spires where they could understand the landscape, and the threats.

Michelle, walking into the war room, immediately garnered the attention of Wraith, who eyed her with obvious lust. "You're already making decisions without me," she asked.

"Just looking over where best to *Portal* in with a subtle but potent raiding party," Radin informed, showing her with his right index finger on the map where they intended for point of entry.

"Three questions: what, or who, are we going after, why now, and who's Slim over there?"

"My apologies," Wraith offered, extending his hand to Michelle. She immediately noticed the fingernails, but still offered her hand to him in return, if carefully so, never breaking eye contact with him. "I'm Wraith Silverstring. We are trying to assess just who is who in all of this," he motioned around at all the icons on the map illustrating Talemar, Adena, King Aaron, etc. "The Crystal Crown should help us make sense of at least some details, and the sooner we know, the better for everyone."

"Got it," she offered, now up to speed enough to continue planning while retracting her hand slowly from Wraith, though she wasn't sure what to offer in return for his wink. They didn't know each other well enough for that

Charles W. McDonald Jr.

yet.

Wraith's eyes had taken notice of Michelle's M-4 though he made no comment on it—only casting a few curious glances as he continued offering more details about the raid at the map table.

"I think ranged weapons should form the perimeter around Talemar, Radin, and myself while my...," he paused to clear his throat, "...wife," he murmured, "stays well behind us, clearing and protecting our flank as we move toward Adena's treasury here...." Wraith pointed with his index finger upon the blown-up map of Adena's Crown of Spires.

"Wait, Talemar," Michelle looking to Radin for clarification, "I thought you two hated each other."

"Hate is a strong word," Radin replied, half-smiling, "We don't even know if Talemar will join us, but he has a vested interest in having access to the Crystal Crown as much as I do, so we'll see what he says."

*   *   *   *

(Axum, Perion, Present Day)

The sun just now setting on the horizon in night-chased and fading amber hues, Talemar sat on one of the Rune Stones with Gareth, looking over Xaldran's Tome—remembering. It hadn't been so long since the Halls of Aaramus had thrust him so far forward in time, but his memories seemed to be tethered to time whether his body was or not. As if the great chasm of linear time had spread his frame of memories far enough apart from one another to match the canyon betwixt now and then. Silura had been in and out of the giant obelisks, observing every little detail as she ran her delicate hands over the stone's time and weathered surface.

Suddenly, a *Portal* opened from a pitch-black part of the world not far from where the grassy field gave way to white sand beaches, both Wraith and a striking blonde archer in neutral tones walking through. Only a moment later, the boy she presumed Radin strode through looking in all directions as he noticed Talemar immediately. Carrying a staff, she could see the boy channeling to hold onto as much source as he could as he confidently closed the distance between them.

Talemar rose from his seated position on the Rune Stone rubble laying amidst the grassy field, casting precautionary measures as he walked to meet Radin at the southeastern tip of the Nine Towers. Gareth following close behind, Talemar looked back to see Silura still touring each obelisk in turn, apparently in no hurry to join the meeting.

Charles W. McDonald Jr.

"I see you're well," Talemar offered Radin, noticing now four gold fingernails dancing with life on his fingertips. "...And learning," he surmised with a matter-of-fact look, neither threatening nor giving anything away.

"Things didn't have to go the way they did, Talemar," Radin offered, "I'm not your enemy, and you're not mine."

"Lovely start," Wraith concurred in a seemingly facilitating capacity, "...I can see this is going to go smashingly." Wraith looked between the two hotheads, but never actually took an eye off Michelle, who carefully observed from a distance, never taking her hands off that black metallic barrel object she had partially slung about her shoulders. *What was that thing*, he contemplated in deep curiosity. Very briefly, he looked around for his sister, only catching a glimpse of her walking out of one of the far obelisks but losing her when she reached the large statues half-buried by passage of time.

"We have an idea we'd like to share with you," Radin began, gesturing with his hands at the map of Adena's complex that he'd brought with him. "Wraith believes the Crystal Crown is here," he offered, pointing, "...if so, we can take a small, but potent, raiding party to here," Radin now pointing to a small, elevated position just beyond The Crown of Spires. "Wraith suggested Silura would hold back guarding our flank while we advance to the treasury over here," Radin moved his index finger to the far side spire of The Crown of Spires, down the divination causeways.

"So, whoever can wear the Crown gets the Scroll of Carnac. Is that the deal?" Talemar followed quickly, but his nervousness around Radin was only eclipsed by his trepidation of Silura and Wraith. His last expeditions into combat hadn't gone well, and it weighed on his confidence as well as his abilities.

"We will honor that," Wraith promised flatly, but Radin and Talemar wondered how far their promise would travel.

Royvan Miral stood quietly beside Michelle and Gareth as they observed the tense negotiations between lameans. Nightfall consumed the horizon now, causing Michelle to pace about them in expanding circles spiraling outward in a threat watch, *Bad Intentions* now drawn with her laser targeting sight-finder painting a red-dot laser of lethality out into the void of the night.

A movement out of the corner of her eye and her finger was beginning to apply pressure on the trigger. Silura made sudden and direct eye contact with her, coming at her from the large statues. "I don't know what that is, but I'm going to assume it's a weapon." Silura was beautiful, even next to Michelle, but the way she moved—with utter confidence and chaos of pattern—she was not like anyone Michelle had encountered before.

"Shouldn't you be over there with them," Michelle motioned with her

M-4, back to the southeastern tip of the Nine Towers grounds.

"I wanted to give the boys time to piss out their aggressions before I showed up," Silura's disarming smile was deceptive as if a great secret precariously hung on the edges of her pretty little lips.

"Come on, I'll walk you back over there. I think they're done pissing out their aggressions," Michelle offered with a smile—sort of. Silura was as much a mystery to Michelle as Michelle was to Silura. Walking together side-by-side, they measured each other cautiously all the way back to the boy's meeting.

"This one," Silura motioning to Michelle at her side as they approached the group, "...said you boys were done playing around and suggested we come join you."

"So, what do we have for ranged weapons to protect you except what I brought to the party," Michelle slung *Bad Intentions* back over her shoulder, pulling out her shortbow, which she offered to Royvan Miral along with her quiver.

"I've got a bow myself...," Gareth offered, "...and throwing daggers."

"That's not much firepower to protect you at that distance," Michelle analyzed the map Radin brought to the meeting. "How far is this," she motioned from the point of ingress to the treasury wing itself.

"At least three hundred paces would be my guess," Wraith surmised looking at the map while still sizing up Michelle in many more ways than one, that caught the attention of his wife.

"Geez," Michelle looked worried, running the numbers in her head. "Besides Adena herself, what kind of firepower would she have close around her?"

While not entirely familiar with the word 'firepower,' Radin gathered her meaning, suggesting, "From what Toblain and Ykstherin have been teaching me, you're looking at close to three hundred people who can cast in this facility. Figure one to three percent on guard at this time of night spread out all across this ridgeline, with another one to three percent spread out across this breezeway, and I'm going to assume about equal numbers equipped with ranged weapons in the same relative positions."

"You're not making this sound like a better idea," Michelle wisecracked, looking to Wraith for suggestions.

"Look, a quiet entrance is ten times better than bringing ten times the force." Wraith was no stranger to this kind of risky maneuver, but he had no history or chemistry working with this group. Yes, they were all powerful in their own right, but could they all tactically work well together as a unit? Michelle wondered exactly the same thought; the two of them sharing knowing sidelong glances at one another.

"Don't worry about my being quiet. I think everyone here can operate relatively quietly, but when, not if, we get noticed, I just don't see us having enough firepower to get out of there alive," Talemar still struggled with his confidence both individually, and as a team, but internally he was calculating whether or not the Crown was worth all this. Especially now. Everything felt…rushed. He, better than anyone here, knew its capabilities and what lay before them—prophecy or not. Trying to discern whether the risk outweighed the reward was the question.

"Suggestions?" Wraith asked. "I know you have some ideas you're not voicing," looking to Michelle.

"Let me take point. Silura take flank, a hundred paces behind us at least as you suggested," Michelle pointing to the map running her index finger in a practice run to the treasury, "My guess is we'll probably get noticed somewhere along here when we get onto the breezeway in clear view. When that happens, I'll lay down suppression fire, then I need Gareth to swing around to my left and Royvan my right, in an echelon spear formation. At that point, our flank will be more exposed, so we'll need Talemar to protect our flank from an advancing position, while Silura protects the far rear from a trailing position."

"That's a good plan," Radin complimented his new and beautiful friend, offering a friendly hand on her shoulder, "…and I can focus on taking out guardsmen and traps as we get close to the treasury if Wraith can get us into the treasury room itself."

"I used to know the best thief ever to live and he taught me well," Talemar suggested, "I can help get us in the treasury, if needed."

"I think that's a good enough approach for now, and we'll stick with it unless conditions on the ground dictate a change of plans. Let's go see what we're facing." Michelle pivoting back to where she came in by *Portal*, assumed one of the lameans would address the travel.

Michelle hadn't taken two steps before Wraith opened a *Portal* to Ediniael. Michelle, turning her back to the *Portal*, *Bad Intentions* drawn as she faced away, motioned everyone through the *Portal* in a command position. Old habits died hard for Michelle. Her SEAL Operator training would serve her well tonight. She just wished her fellow Operators—Lawna especially— were coming with them. They needed more help. This was not the best of ideas—taking on this gigantic task with such a small force and so little planning. SEAL raids typically required weeks of practice, not minutes of deliberation between highly disparate forces.

Royvan Miral was first through the *Portal*, then Gareth, taking fan-

ning positions with their ranged weapons as they took kneeling positions in
the dark of the night on the ingress elevated grassy position overlooking The
Crown of Spires.

Radin strode through, Dallia's staff in hand, holding everything he
could muster, recalling his training with both Talemar and Damon. Talemar
and Wraith quickly followed in the pre-dawn hours.

Still on the Axum side of the *Portal* and sauntering up to Michelle
nonchalantly, Silura offered, "My husband loves blondes if you couldn't tell."
A very bold offer from a wife offering up her husband, but very little surprised
Michelle. For only being twenty-five, and her aging frozen at twenty-two,
she'd seen and heard pretty much everything.

"Your brother's not my type," Michelle firmly slammed the door shut
on Silura's sexual offering of her husband with a cute smile and a knowing
wink.

"What about me...," Silura offered again, "...am *I* your type?" Silura
batted her eyelashes at Michelle with a more than suggestive stance, baring one
of her legs with a slit that ran all the way up her shimmering and translucent,
forest-green dress.

"Just stay the Hell behind me and watch our flank," Michelle countered with furrowed brow, as the two walked last through the *Portal* to the
Crown of Spires and Adena.

*   *   *   *

(Edinaiel, Perion, Present Day)

The weight and reality of being here immediately hit Radin like a hammer to his consciousness as he stood on the grassy knoll overlooking the magnificent crystal tiled divination causeways, which seemed to shift with imagery
associated to each person who walked them. He estimated ten or so robed
personnel walking sparsely about four hundred paces apart from one another.
He couldn't see any guardsmen, and that bothered him. *Had they foreseen this
assault on the very divination tiles he now observed?*

"So, which one of us is taking responsibility for Adena," Radin asked,
looking between the lamean.

"Better leave that to me," Talemar offered, "I've dealt with her before.
She can be very clever in combat."

"If you need help...," Radin didn't have to finish as the Great Talemar
nodded knowingly. At least for the moment, they were trying to work as a
unit, and he was grateful for the knowledge and experience of Talemar—if he

could be trusted.… He still wasn't sure of the size of the gap between the Talemar of legend and the Talemar before him. Tales had a way of growing much larger and grandiose than real life.

Radin estimated less than an hour remaining before dawn; they had to move fast.

*   *   *   *

Colonel Galfrid woke at his usual time, long before the crack of dawn, running through his usual, but detailed, routine of putting on his armor. Sliding his white long-sleeve undershirt on, he paid no attention to the mass of scars across his chest and abdomen; they never bothered him anymore. No incidents since his watch had begun a few days back. *So far, so good*, he reasoned, slapping on his elbow padding and breastplate. Dawn was threatening outside. Time to start his watch.

*   *   *   *

Not really resuming his mentoring position with Radin, but supposing it might help them all get out of here alive, Talemar showed Radin how to cast his *Web of Mirrors* shell so they could make it deeper into the treasury without being noticed. "As you're forming, think of standing on the inside of a mirror. The shell is really nothing more than a big mirror that redirects light around it, and a mirror without edges or borders looks invisible to its surrounding." Talemar illustrated on a smaller scale to Radin, forming a tiny transparent *Web of Mirrors* hemisphere in the palm of his right hand. Radin, in turn, nodded knowingly, realizing most of his tutorial sessions had been on destructive combat spells. Still, it was more than useful, given the goal ahead of them.

Scaling the cloak to cover the advancing party that excluded Silura, Talemar gave the go-ahead, "I think we're ready. I'll keep an eye out for Adena if you want to start advancing," Talemar offered, looking to Michelle, who ran point with *Bad Intentions* drawn.

Carefully, and slowly at first, Michelle led feather-footed with utter silence as she advanced. Her naturally enhanced night-vision found many targets though her laser target-finder which was turned off for the moment. No sense painting targets with a red laser and drawing attention to them when they were invisible.

Making his way down the crystal divination diamond-tiled causeway, Radin was struck by visions Damon had taught him were the window into the possible. He assumed the divination images were tailored to each individual, considering what that meant, given what he was now being shown. For a moment, he lost track of where he was, consumed by the visions before him. *Were they leading him to a specific outcome or the other way around?* The divination tiles showed him making the final turn into the treasury, finally seeing the guardsmen for the first time, acutely aware of their presence—in waiting. Then he saw it—the Crystal Crown—atop Talemar, causing a hard gulp from him as his feet involuntarily stopped his movement down the divination causeways.

The mechanical and explosive sounds of three-round burst gunfire coming from Michelle's M-4 immediately snapped Radin back to reality. Fully armored infantry now rushing down the causeway toward a fiery hail of bullets, only to be mercilessly mowed down by Michelle, seemed like utter suicide to Radin as he resumed his assault toward the treasury. Shards of steel and fire, leaping from Talemar's hands, shredded robed females coming from everywhere, running down the divination causeway toward them. Gareth and Royvan laid down ranged fire with crossbow and shortbow from their advancing echelon positions on either side of Michelle, while Wraith rushed forward to where Radin had just seen the turn into the treasury, yelling, "WAIT, Wraith! HOLD ON!" His hand outstretched as Radin shouted as loud as he could to be heard over Michelle's gunfire.

"Lay down fire over there," Radin directed Michelle's three-round suppression bursts with a beam of fire from his right index finger, highlighting where the causeway of divination tiles made the right turn into the far tower of the treasury, just in front of where Wraith had halted. Dark pools of blood poured out of the darkened archway, blotting out the divination visions on the diamond-shaped crystal tiles. In the blink of an eye, Michelle already had a fresh clip from the back of her duty belt, slamming it home as she laid down more suppression fire from a temporary knelt position along the causeway. Even with her extraordinary vision, she could barely see what she was hitting, but the blood spurts told her to keep shooting.

Suddenly, Michelle, along with her M-4, went skidding across the crystalline tiles with her breath knocked out of her. She was fully visible to everyone now. Apparently, the *Web of Mirrors* had been shielding them from the vision of some of the guards, but not everyone. Now she was out there for everyone to see—and the primary target. Now facing the way she'd just come, she could see a magnificent nude young woman of slight and lithe build, but large breasts, gracefully walking the causeways up to them as if she owned them. Her long black hair was caught in a rush of hot air from Talemar's *Blistering Iron*—cast by Silura, protecting their rear. Exploding metal and fire,

Charles W. McDonald Jr.

right beside the magnificent nude brunette, didn't even phase her, as she calmly advanced toward them down the divining causeway. *Adena*, Michelle realized. *SHIT!*

"Talemar, behind you to your right, to your 7 o' clock," Michelle shouted, not even thinking the clock position would mean absolutely nothing to him. In a blurring wake, Michelle had her M-4 and back on her feet, rushing into the treasury, leaving Adena to Talemar.

Pivoting while holding his ground, Talemar tossed a shield of energy out two cubits in front of him, ten cubits high by twenty cubits wide, watching it immediately wrap all the way around him, protecting him from 360 degrees of ranged weapon fire. He immediately followed that with palms turned up, watching as balled lightning erupted from the divination tiles all around Adena, striking at her shapely legs, but never harming her through her protections.

A disappointed look quickly crossed Adena's beautiful face before she made a downward stroke of her right hand, forcing a massive bolt of lightning to collapse from a cloudless sky. It struck with a reverberating thunderclap, easily piercing and destroying Talemar's protective shell in one stroke, hurling his body off of the causeway down to the grassy fields below the Crown of Spires. Suddenly, a massive ball of fiery light-blue flashes of lightning, completely engulfing Adena, shot her straight backward, skidding backward across the divination tiles.

Extending Dallia's staff out before him, Radin watched as his *Damon's Ball of Lightning* hit home on Adena as he prepared himself to unleash everything he had. Either it was going to work, or it wasn't. *Do or Die!* Left palm turned up, then immediately down, he unleashed, for the first time in real combat, *Damon's Big Boom*, causing mostly overlapping hemispheres—one of lightning, the other of fire and acid—to land dead center on where he'd last seen Adena's body come to a stop on the tiles. Utterly destroying the structural integrity of the causeway, *Damon's Big Boom* sent Adena, along with a huge chunk of the causeway and its supporting structure, crashing to the grassy field beneath the Crown of Spires. Radin waited briefly for the smoke to clear, with no sign of Adena below. Though he did see Silura looking in all directions, as she carefully advanced behind them.

"Watch for her," Radin ordered, briefly pondering Talemar's location, seeking out Michelle as he rushed to Wraith, Gareth, and Royvan, just in front of the darkened and bloody archway leading to the treasury with blood still oozing out onto the tiles from the darkened corridors just beyond. "Anyone see her?" Radin asked; he couldn't see Michelle either.

A disapproving nod from Wraith, "And I thought *I* was careless. We need to advance together." Wraith didn't see anything living as he took point. Inside, his eyes adjusted, making out lots of dead bodies slumped over, full of holes, bleeding from dozens of animalistic wounds he'd never seen the likes of before. Something in between the wounds from a black bear and a great wolf.

"CLEAR," Michelle shouted. Radin and Wraith continued to see horror after horror as they advanced further toward the treasury—dismembered body parts, heads that looked as if they'd been torn—rather than cut—off. Stepping over a guard's body that looked to have been torn apart at the waist, Gareth looked at Michelle anew, and with horror.

"I'm going to get Talemar," Royvan Miral offered, quickly disappearing back out into the connecting causeways. The treasury was important, and the central objective, but his instincts told him to find Talemar and do it now.

Moving past the ten-cubit-tall by four-cubit-broad, thick onyx cream and gold fissured door, now cleaved in two—each piece now sitting on either side of the treasury's wall—Michelle showed them into the treasury. "I found this," Michelle pointed to the shards of granite before the man-sized niches in the wall, "and this," motioning to the Crystal Crown sitting atop a quartz-like pedestal all to itself, surrounded both low and high by other objects of great wealth. The Crystal Crown was not the only Crown in the treasury but was the only one of their interest. "Do we need Talemar to authenticate it?" It was a fair question from Michelle, and not one they'd actively considered before undertaking all this work—the authentication of the artifact itself.

"No, but it would be good to get his thoughts and confirmation," Wraith countered. "...and I don't know how much time we're going to have here. Silura can guard our backs momentarily, but...."

As if to complete his thought, he could hear a great commotion at the entrance of the treasury as he saw Silura being pressed backward into the treasury entryway and corridor by what looked like a highly decorated field soldier—not a typical guard. His sword ablaze as Galfrid struck home on Silura several times, causing her to backpedal, throwing everything she had at him. Casting *Wraith's Chain Blaster*, hand-sized bolts of fiery acid leapt from her fingertips, rushing the tall, brown haired, brown eyed, middle-aged Galfrid; bouncing off his armor with but glancing blows from what looked sure to have been direct hits. Silura bled from six large open wounds where Galfrid had slashed her through her forest green robes, cutting her red sash and leaving only a burned nub left about her waist. Galfrid continued advancing, thrust by thrust, his blade just barely missing if it missed at all, hastily pushing Silura further inside the treasury.

Charles W. McDonald Jr.

Trying to help, Michelle brought *Bad Intentions* to bear on Galfrid, lasing his forehead through the target finder, suddenly finding herself blown up against the far wall of the treasury—only a few feet from the Crystal Crown. Advancing through the archway, Adena was the last thing Michelle saw before she passed out though she was vaguely aware of the massive amount of blood flowing from her mid-section.

Radin had but an instant, seeing Michelle nearly cut in half by the crystalline tile debris Adena had hurled into her, pinning her now lifeless body up against the far wall of the treasury, the wound going from her navel all the way to her flank. With Michelle's body now pinned to the far wall of the treasury, Radin began to drive Adena deeper inside from his position just outside the treasury with *Damon's Contained Blast*. A brute-force, white-hot explosion, erupting out of nothing, directly in front of Adena, sent her body flailing through the gunpowder-perfumed air as Radin cast *Gate* just behind her, swallowing Adena into nothingness.

Gareth was now holding off several advancing guardsmen with his shortbow, while Wraith used Radin's idea to *Gate* Galfrid just before the soldier's blazing sword struck his wife again.

"Where'd you send him?" Radin asked, forcing a tense smile.

"Where'd you send her?" Wraith countered, reaching back behind him snatching the Crystal Crown off the obelisk. No time for authentication. "Did you see Royvan or Talemar," Wraith asked both Radin and Gareth, who knocked another arrow, firing it immediately at another advancing guard.

"I saw them disappear into one of those *Portals* a moment ago," Gareth, pointing downward to where Talemar's body had been blown, "down there in the grassy field below the structure."

Radin's silence toward the question hadn't gone unnoticed by Wraith nor Gareth. Gareth himself had seen Radin not forty paces from Talemar when they had left by *Portal*, so surely Radin had seen what he'd seen himself.

Shaking his head in disgust, Radin offered, "Clearly they're not worried about us, so let's not bother worrying about them. Let's go." They needed to save Michelle's body. He wasn't sure if she was dead or not, but he knew she was special, and he wasn't leaving her behind. Focusing his natural *Telekinesis* on the tile splitting her body open, it flew across the treasury room and out the entry-way, releasing Michelle's body from the granite treasury wall.

A wave of his hand and Radin opened a *Portal* to his Exeter Estate, immediately walking through with Wraith, a very injured Silura, Gareth, Michelle's lifeless body, and The Crystal Crown.

Charles W. McDonald Jr.

*   *   *   *

(Mirac, Perion, Present Day)

A frozen tundra at the northern-most icecap of the planet wasn't the place to be in the nude, as Adena took a moment to soak in the surroundings of her location and evaluate the blood pouring from her wounds. She would need *Healing*, and she would need to leave immediately, before she froze to death, if she even could still channel enough for a *Portal*. She was bleeding profusely. The boy had become *very* powerful, *very* fast, and not on his own. Many of his arsenal she'd never seen before as visions of the dark-haired, black-eyed tall man began making more sense to her. Adena wouldn't be taken off guard like that again. She took a deep breath, focusing with all she had left to open a *Portal* back home, just in time to see her treasury robbed. *Again!*

*   *   *   *

(The Sea of Needles, Perion, Present Day)

Pillowy-crested waves of ocean came rushing fast at the rate Colonel Galfrid was falling in his heavy armor. He briefly recognized the shoreline of the Needles before the belly flop crushed his armor into his mid-section, knocking him unconscious, causing his grip to let go of his still-gleaming sword. *Better to die than to fail Adena and live*, was Galfrid's last thought as the ocean consumed him.

*   *   *   *

(Northwest Exeter, Helios Manor, Perion, Present Day)

Silura couldn't move for a while after Wraith's *Healing*, but her *Healing* wasn't the only pressing business, as morning arrived in gleaming purple and amber rays across the Exeter horizon. Holding the Crystal Crown over Radin's head, Wraith slowly lowered it, not sure if it would resist or not—really not even sure if it was authentic. Feeling no resistance as it fell upon Radin's head, Wraith offered a slight bow, "I think we have our answer."

The moment wasn't lost on Radin as he felt a massive resonant background energy humming just at the edge of his consciousness like a peripheral vision of the source field. He had so many thoughts of what this moment might be like, and none of them matched the vision before him, nor the feeling. But seeing Talemar *Portal* in right before him wasn't fully unexpected. It was hard focusing on Talemar advancing towards him as the bright flashes of a still crystal-blue lake, surrounded by perfect pure-white light and a booming voice of Creation, smashed all reality in his mind. The images, however brief, caused him an ever-so-slight side-step before he regained his balance, now directly in front of Talemar.

"It *is* the Crystal Crown," Talemar proclaimed flatly, halting his advance upon Radin at some ten paces away.

"So, what happened to you? Why did you abandon us?" Radin questioned with more than just words as the look in his eyes prosecuted Talemar from a scant distance. Talemar's focus was entirely on a crowned Radin, so he didn't notice Wraith flooding his entire body with Arcane in preparation for what he saw as the inevitable.

"I saw this moment on the causeway," Talemar offered truthfully. "That's why."

Radin appreciated the honesty, and thinking back, Talemar had risked his life after seeing that moment, so he supposed that was something. Another bright flash in his mind—that booming voice ringing in his head—this time causing his entire body to shift, as Radin collapsed to his left side. The Crystal Crown slipped from Radin's head onto the hardwood floor of the War Room in a dulled tinging sound, as it began rolling across the floor. Just then, Elise walked out of Radin's suite in her white nightgown, vaguely aware as Talemar began picking up the Crystal Crown before him.

A calling, like none before, sang to the Great Talemar in his thoughts, resonating through the powdered dragon metal of the Crystal Crown he now held in his hands. The quartz-like shaped stones pricked at his fingertips, sending his whole body into a state of shock; a shock of life like none before. He stopped asking himself whether or not he deserved it, holding it over his hair he let it fall about his head without the futility of resistance.

"NO!" Elise fell to the floor where she stood just a few steps away, weeping inconsolably. "It can't be," she wept into the palms of her hands, falling to her knees.

Bringing himself upright, standing before a crowned Talemar, Radin's eyes burned with pyre as his body flooded with everything he could channel. He was running entirely on instinct and his instinct said not that Talemar was the enemy, but that *he* was the One. The waking visions that had caused him to collapse to the floor a more-than-compelling sign that he was the conduit of the voice of Creation as that voice still boomed throughout his Arcane-flooded consciousness.

"Maybe this wasn't a good idea," Wraith reflected aloud.

Charles W. McDonald Jr.

A crowned Talemar wrestled with memories not his own; a study and fireplace with a young boy and girl, a great mechanized battlefield somewhere else with a sword he knew firsthand but could *not* possess—memories of *A Kingdom Forgotten*.

"NO!" Lawna howled in a blood-curdling scream, seeing Michelle's bleeding, lifeless body laying between a seething, fire-aura enshrouded Radin and a crowned Talemar.

Chapter 54: Zero Day

(Exeter, Perion, Present Day)

The Scroll of Carnac shot forth from a concealed pocket within Wraith's robes, snatched by unseen hands, launching towards Radin's glowing, Arcane-filled body. Immediately breaking the First Seal to a thunderclap that cracked the walls of his War Room, Radin began to speak the ancient words written by the hand of the Creator himself—every righteous word *boomed* from Radin in a voice not his own:

> Behold, ye scoffers,
> For in the final days,
> I will rent Kingdoms from Kings
> And Kings from Kingdoms.
> The seas will burn,
> And the sky will bleed.
> Your crops will fail,
> And your land will perish,
> For it will sleep with the Dragon of Despair.
> Those who would stand and believe:

Charles W. McDonald Jr.

Prepare, Wait, and Behold,
For I will come like the Thunder
And blister the moonless night on trumpets of amber light.
The righteous shall be delivered,
And the **unholy** shall be **destroyed**!

Every witness, including the crowned Talemar, began shaking uncontrollably in utter terror at the voice of the Creator shouting like a storm through Radin.

"What have you done?!" Wraith yelled what everyone else was thinking. They all knew this moment was coming but living through it was nothing like any had expected. Beyond terrifying, the hairs on their bodies stood on end, electrified by the moment of a Creation undone.

Glorious amber rays of dawn immediately turned red from their vantage of the War Room windows as a blood rain began to fall on the grounds of Radin's estate for as far as the eye could see. The Blood Night had been summoned. The End of Creation had been summoned.

*   *   *   *

(Golem's Point, Perion, Present Day)

On the far side of the world, Eldrac sat atop his Grey, alongside King Aaron as they advanced toward a truly massive *Portal* for his infantry, cavalry, archers, and all manner of weapons of war. Here, on the other side of the *Portal*, dawn had broken in trumpets of amber light a little more than an hour ago. Looking skyward, Eldrac heard a voice like none he had heard before utter the blasphemy of the First Seal, causing every man and king alike to quake at the booming voice of Creation brought down upon Man. A giant thunderclap followed lightning from a cloudless sky that suddenly turned blood-red as it began to rain on the holy ground of the Nine Towers before them. Eldrac remained calm. This was all part of the plan from his perspective. "General Tomain," Eldrac commanded, looking to his left for his field General.

"Sir!" A man of decades of experience under King Aaron, but Aaron's men had never been in a massive battle like this before. His graying beard, against his gold-crested silver-burnished breastplate, marked him on the field of battle, as did the red-corded sash hanging from each of his shoulders. Tomain had seen far more combat than most of his men combined because he was a hired man from the land of Xal, where he'd seen gaming between the houses tear the land, and the men, apart in one battle after another for power. At least King Aaron saw the wisdom in searching out the best people; he was not stuck to the people of his own lands that had seen decades of stability in uninterrupted transition by lineage.

"Set your men up like we discussed, there, there, and there," Eldrac pointed to the high ground positions on the north away-side of the quartz-like obelisks that made up the Holy Ground's Nine Towers.

"Already on it, sir," the general replied flatly, pivoting to the ever-present field colonel at his left side. "Colonel Phet, pass along to the men: I want those pikes we brought with us up in defensive positions within the hour."

"Sir!" The clean-cut middle-aged Colonel Phet passing on his General's command without never leaving his side. His armor was silver without the red-corded sash hanging from each shoulder but shined brighter than anyone else on the field. Colonel Phet was both the organization and the oil in this machine, seeing to the mechanics of death Eldrac had brought with him.

*   *   *   *

(The Valley of Power, Perion, Present Day)

Still putting together the pieces, Rowarc looked to Iain, examining where the *Gate* consumed the campfire debris in Talemar's cavern in the Valley of Power. "A massive fight broke out here. *Lameans*," Rowarc thought aloud. "Powerful ones."

"I see *Gate* signatures to several different places, quite a few I don't recognize," the stocky Quin proclaimed, smoothing his reddish-brown robes as he shuffled about the cavern, trying not to freeze. He didn't see how the blizzard outside wasn't getting to Iain, but he'd known him to be a hard man all his life. Rowarc he only knew by reputation, but he found nothing objectionable about the man. His light blue eyes flashed, looking at the most recent *Gate* signature, "The Nine Towers," Quin announced breathlessly. "Why would they go there?"

"Where else did they go?" Iain asked his old friend, who'd helped him find and get to Rowarc in the first place. Quin was as useful as a bloodhound when it came to tracking, and very helpful when it came to *Healing*. He'd saved Iain from certain death many times. Excellent *Healers* were hard to come by, and the most respected of the lameans. That allowed him the courtesy of operating more freely than others.

"Exeter, Bouschè, and *beyond*," Quin trailed off with the last, his fingertips stroking the cavern floor, close to the campfire, where the *Gate* had unceremoniously dumped Radin from Damon's manor on Kaleion.

"Beyond where?" Rowarc asked, trying to understand where his young man of a boy could be, and what trouble he could have found. Or what troubles may have already found him.

"Bey…." Quin's explanation, interrupted by the booming voice of Creation from above, that immediately ceased the white blowing snow in favor of blood rain falling from a cloudless red sky just outside the cavern entrance.

Quin, Iain, and Rowarc walked to the cavern entrance, watching all living manner of flying animal fall dead from the red sky above, crashing down into the Valley of Power on the aptly named Isle of Breaking—for surely this was the breaking of all things. Prophecy had come in its own way, and the Scroll of Carnac found here. Now opened, the End was upon them all.

"Was that what I thought it was?" Iain looked to Quin.

"I wish it weren't," Quinn countered while pausing to scratch his chin in deliberation of the most horrific as he looked between the two older men. "I think the Nine Towers may have answers for us…for all of this," Quin motioned to the birds falling dead out of the sky.

"If you can send us there," Rowarc conditioned, "I'd like to see my boy again before it all ends." He paused, thinking of the others, "If you have somewhere you need to be, to say goodbye to your loved ones, I will understand."

"My life of solitude doesn't afford a wife and children," Quin muttered, watching the beginning of the end of all things before him. "I'll go where you go," he offered.

"If it's not too much to ask," Iain offered, scratching his stubble, "I really need my horse. Especially if there's a possibility of heavy combat, and looking at this," he motioned outside the cave entrance, "I'm going to say that's a good possibility."

Quin smiled, *Gating* them all to the grassy field, where he'd opened the *Portal* for Iain to find Rowarc many days back.

*   *   *   *

(Northwest Exeter, Helios Manor, Perion, Present Day)

Brigance Fireheart looked through the viewing window Radin offered of the holy grounds of Axum, watching Eldrac's army taking up defensive positions upon the high grounds of the quartz-like obelisks that formed the Nine Towers. "He's going to take up his primary defensive positions here, here, and here," Brigance motioned his index finger to the three center tallest obelisks forming the heart of the Crystal Throne—a scaled variant of the Crystal

Crown upon Talemar's head. "Attacking from the southern grassy field below is both suicide and will most likely result in the destruction of the Crystal Throne—and I know you don't want that," Brigance thinking aloud, while Radin and Wraith nodded, concurring while looking between the war map and the viewing window. Brigance continued, "Attacking from behind the Nine Towers would cause the least amount of collateral damage, but it's still going to be tough, and the longer we sit here talking about it, the tougher it's going to get as their defenses strengthen." Combat tactics were nothing new to Brigance, but Eldrac was a totally different animal, and this was a totally different kind of battle plan he needed to come up with. Anything traditional wasn't going to work. He needed something....

"We've got an advantage with our lameans," Brigance suggested, thinking aloud. "What if we present a traditional front with formations attacking from here, here, and here," Brigance offered, pointing to locations behind the three, center quartz-like obelisks where Eldrac was already taking up defensive positions. "He would expect a lamean behind each of these formations lobbing combat spells at his dug-in positions, so let's give him that," Brigance continuing to his unconventional plans, "How far can your combat spells work and still be effective," he asked of both Wraith and Radin.

"Maybe as far out as here," Radin offered, pointing to the beachhead.

"Farther out than that. I'd say three times as far away with a little ingenuity," Wraith suggested.

"You read my mind." Brigance pointed each of them in turn. "I was thinking about having one of you attack from the southern beachhead, using your divination spells to see what's happening on the far side, and dropping combat spells through *Portals* on defensive positions. That way you're far enough away that it would take time for Eldrac to respond, yet still close enough to advance rapidly to positions where and when they're needed." Brigance scanned the war map briefly, "I'd like another one of you over here at the northeastern beachhead on the far side of the Towers, and another here in this western field position with no line-of-sight to Eldrac's primary formations."

"I like it," Michelle's soft, parched voice came as a shock even though most had become accustomed to her silently skulking about.

"You're as hard to kill as I had hoped," Radin hugged the beautiful blonde who slowly and carefully withdrew after his embrace.

"Still not one hundred percent," she offered, motioning to her still-healing mid-section that looked heavily scabbed-over to him.

"I don't think you're quite combat ready," Radin smiled at Michelle, knowing there was no way she wasn't going to take part in this fight. *She's tougher than nails.*

Charles W. McDonald Jr.

"You're not going to talk her out of it," Lawna informed, walking up to the group, carrying more of what he learned were varying types of machine guns. "She's more stubborn than any of you."

"Only in a loving way," Michelle countered with a half-smile as she tried to ignore the pain radiating from her flank.

Wraith, Radin, and Brigance exchanging confused looks as Brigance continued, "Can your weapons set things on fire?"

"Can they?!" Michelle smiled broadly this time, making her side hurt.

"Good, I want you to start a fire in the middle of his regiments here, here, and here. Then I want fires here, here, here, and here," Brigance, pointing to the three distant lamean locations along with a new location he had not mentioned 'til now—a far southern position just in range of line-of-sight to the horizon from Eldrac's primary positions.

"Why there?" Wraith asked, moving his finger along the map.

"Can you take care of it?" Brigance asked flatly.

"Consider it done," Wraith assured, looking to Michelle. "I'll wait for Michelle to start the other fires if that timing works for you."

Brigance, nodding in acceptance, continued his strategy, "Where is the best spot for you," he asked of Michelle, deferring to her combat training.

"I'll be all over this field, but if I understand your end game, I think *here* is the best default position for me," Michelle pointing to a hillside west of the advancing traditional forces on the battlefield.

"Good, that's what I was thinking too. I would like Lawna and Silura to move with you. Staying with you at all times. You're going to become a pretty big target for Eldrac, very fast. Silura can offer protection for you and Lawna while you assault his primary forces."

Michelle and Lawna nodding in acceptance as Silura approached at the sound of hearing her name called.

"Now, I'd like Sir Palomides, Radin, Talemar, and Ykstherin to stay behind for the rest of what I have to say. The rest of you," Brigance motioned to his crew, and the rest of the leadership, "The troops were supposed to assemble an hour ago, so if you could assemble everyone else in ranks six-wide for the *Portal*, we'll join you momentarily at the assembly grounds out front."

The leadership yielded them the room as Lord Fireheart put the finishing touches on what he hoped would be a plan unconventional enough to send Eldrac back whence he came, "Eldrac is going to offer up something we haven't seen before. It's a guarantee, and you can count on it." Everyone nodding in agreement around the war map, listening to Brigance. "I can promise it's going to make part of this plan useless, and we'll just have to adapt when it happens, but I want to offer him something just as shocking that *he'll* have to deal with. So, here's what I was thinking...."

Radin and Brigance bounced ideas between the group for a few more minutes, coming out together where twenty thousand men lay in ranks six-wide, awaiting their orders. A still-crowned Talemar summoned more power than he'd ever held before, opening dozens of *Portals* around the assembly grounds, massive enough for the six-wide ranks to march through to Axum, along with one suspended in the air large enough for the Great Gold Toblain to fly through, laying down suppressing fire on Eldrac's men below.

*   *   *   *

(Axum, Perion, Present Day)

Toblain flying and screeching through the red skies above proved a bit of a surprise for Eldrac. "They have a Dragon," Eldrac realized aloud, sitting beside King Aaron, watching his men dig in—some panic over the fire raining down from above where blood had been raining some hours before. The fertile grassy ground still stained with blood without a casualty in sight.

Terrorizing from the air, Toblain laid downburst streams of sticky fire on now-forming ranks of King Aaron's troops who threw up their shields in futility as his fiery breath stuck to surfaces, continuing to burn.

A look down from his lofty position saw thousands of arrows suddenly loosed from Eldrac's high ground positions upon the ranks streaming through the dozens of Talemar's *Portals* forming all around them.

Toblain, staying out of the range of their weapons, levied tolls in the dozens with each lethal pass before his fire hit a transparent dome shell around Eldrac's men. *That didn't take long*, he thought, knowing Eldrac would quickly protect his men. Lightning from the Blood Night sky above, struck at Toblain's right wing sending him spiraling to the ground, trying to regain his aerodynamics, but the ground was rushing up at him fast.

"Too easy," Eldrac commented to King Aaron, striking the great gold from the sky with one massive lightning bolt while watching Radin's forces forming in traditional ranks before him. *Too easy.*

Michelle still had some speed in her movement, enough to slip through the *Portal* unseen, but the stealth was broken as soon as she started laying

Charles W. McDonald Jr.

down incendiary tracer rounds with her M-4 at Eldrac's two closest regiments, totaling some twelve thousand men of the eighteen thousand they estimated to be here. Red streaks formed by the tracer rounds drew a direct line back to Michelle, Lawna, and Silura. Lawna came up behind both of them laying down 7.62mm tracer-round fire with her M134 Minigun at a rate of four-thousand-rounds-per-minute—mowing down Eldrac's men at a rate of dozens per second. Throwing up protection shields around the both of them and herself, Silura immediately began searching for Eldrac, her shields shimmering in the red light from the tracer rounds and the Blood Night sky.

Ykstherin stepped through the *Portal* to the west of Eldrac's forces, just out of their line-of-sight like Brigance designed, immediately opening a *Portal* above Eldrac's farthest eastern positions as he began sending massive granite stones above the *Portal* sourced from the quarry that produced the Sarsen Rune Stones before them. The huge loose rocks fell through the *Portal* in the red sky above, onto Eldrac's men, piercing through their shields and crushing them by the dozens.

To the northeast, Wraith stepped through a *Portal*, walking onto the white sand beaches of Axum, letting the South Sea lap at his feet. Immediately locating Eldrac with his divination window—directly north of the center-most quartz-like obelisk—Wraith exposed Eldrac's location with a bright and contrasting white X in the Blood Night sky over Eldrac. There, Wraith summoned a volley of acid rain, dropping through the *Portal* he made just below the white X in the sky.

Wraith's marker for Eldrac's position helped as Radin stepped through the *Portal* to the southeast, now walking on the white sand beaches of Axum, just to the south of Wraith. He could see Wraith in the distance, summoning acid rain, dropping through a *Portal* directly onto Eldrac. *Smart*, he thought. Casting *Lady of the Guillotine* above a *Portal*, Radin brought into existence falling scimitar blades, some as big as a Dragon, striking a horrific blow to Eldrac's easternmost defensive positions.

Arrows suddenly loosed from behind Brigance's main advancing echelon infantry positions in support of their direct confrontation of Eldrac's westernmost defensive formations. Brigance was going to give Eldrac an unbalanced and staggered look: from the west, unbalanced heavy physical; from the east and south, unbalanced heavy magic. More than seventy percent of their twenty thousand men were going to crush his westernmost positions head-on. "LOOSE," Lord Fireheart commanded, driving his mount forward at a pace his archers could keep, then kneel and nock, then loose again, then advance. Looking to the east, Brigance could see his best friend, Ethan Marshall, commanding a four-thousand-man force, flanking Eldrac's easternmost positions. Brigance's infantry would be within hand-to-hand range in mere moments. Then all plans would inevitably disintegrate. He could see Vosh's balls of lightning streaking overhead from behind his main force, nearly forty at a time, growing as they flew to their target—the middle of Eldrac's westernmost forces. A transparent shield ceiling two-hundred-cubits by two-hundred-cubits formed overhead of the main battlegroup as they continued advancing to engage Eldrac's westernmost position. Ethan Marshall's forces were naked out there, having no lamean support, but Brigance had asked Vosh and Wraith to provide support from their positions when possible. "LOOSE," Brigance shouted again, sending the archers to their kneeling position as he watched Toblain get struck out of the sky by Eldrac's lightning bolt that sent him spiraling to the ground where he crash-landed less than gracefully, looking at the huge hole in his right wing. *So much for their air support*, Brigance judged, knowing the plan would be forced to change as soon as they walked through the *Portal*. It had.

Michelle and Lawna's incendiary rounds streaked overhead from their hillside position immediately behind his main advancing force, piercing Eldrac's shield and mowing down his men by the hundreds. What wasn't killed, was terrified, demoralized, and burning. At least that part of the plan was still working.

Another rank of General Tomain's men fell before him, cut to bits and set aflame by whatever that thing was shooting at them from the hillside. "I want a signal arrow shot up that hill NOW," the General commanded, causing Colonel Phet to make a hand signal to his Vedette, where the colonel's hands pulled apart from one another at the fingertips. That signal, in turn, causing the Vedette to nock an arrow with the shaft coated with little dots of grey matter trailing backward from the arrowhead. The archer hastily lit the tip of his arrow off of a dead and burning body before him, immediately letting the arrow fly high into the air up the hillside. Streaking through the air, the arrow popped with brilliant sparks while it sailed aflame, causing a hail of arrows to rain down on Michelle's position.

General Tomain hoped it would be enough to get Eldrac's attention, but he knew he was very busy with all the Iamean support they had brought to the fight. They had the higher ground, and he was grateful for that, but he knew they were at least three-quarters surrounded, and their opponent's battle plan was looking more and more unconventional by the moment. He wondered if he'd live to meet the brilliant general behind this highly unconventional battle plan unfolding before them.

It was still quite some time before the sun would set enough for the rest of his plan to take place, but with the sun now largely blotted out by the Blood Night sky, he wondered if Anna could operate in what passed for daylight now that the Scroll of Carnac had been opened. *A chance I'll have to take*, Eldrac thought, summoning while simultaneously tossing his most powerful protection shield overhead to protect him and King Aaron. Reaching his right hand out to the king, Eldrac commanded, "Give me the Keeper of the Wind." King Aaron had already pulled out the small white figurine, matching the larger scale beautiful woman reaching out to the sky thousands of leagues away. Handing it to Eldrac, he watched with intense curiosity, wondering what he would be able to do with it. He had held the title Keeper of the Winds without truly ever knowing the power behind that title. He bristled with anticipation at the prospect of now knowing at least some of its powers.

Focusing thousands of leagues away on the massive statue, standing in the center of the grand old city of Stirling, Eldrac recalled the magic that had gone into its creation, summoning the Keeper of the Winds with the small scaled-down figurine of the woman of crystal and gold.

(Center of Stirling, The Kingdom of Gawth, Perion, Present Day)

Soaring three hundred cubits into the air, before arching outward to sea like half of a great crystal rainbow, the watch tower held only one occupant for nearly a thousand years, a beautiful womanly figure of crystal and gold with her sword pointed out to sea—The Keeper of the Wind. Standing four times the size of a human female, her great crystal sword proportionate to her form, it was a very remarkable feat of architecture—especially now as her eyes came to life with dancing flames. A yellow glow of life came to the Keeper's face, cascading from the licking flames of her irises to her cheeks, to her neck, shoulders, down her arms to the great crystal sword in her right hand extended out toward the ocean. There, inside the sword, the yellow glow grew hotter, more intense until it shone white-hot, bursting from its tip a pure-white prismatic ray racing out to the horizon—to the southwest.

Charles W. McDonald Jr.

The increase in the intensity of the waves crashing and lapping at Radin's feet preceded the great white streak of a beam suddenly appearing out of the eastern sky, crashing into the South Sea just to the right of Radin's peripheral vision. *What was that?* Radin tried not to panic, looking behind him.

From her overwatch view just outside Exeter, Elise could see the Keeper's beam flash outside Radin's War Room window moments before she saw it strike into the South Sea from the vantage of her viewing *Portal*. Brigance Fireheart wasn't into taking unnecessary risks with valuable people, especially not one who was now with child. He ordered Elise to stay behind, monitoring for Eldrac's big surprise he knew would come sooner than later. She'd say the bright white flash of a beam outside qualified, so Elise cast her strongest protections over Wraith and Radin through the *Portal* before her, lifting them both skyward out of harm's way of the ever-rising and raging tide of the now angered South Sea.

"Give me the amulet," Damon's voice startled Elise so much she nearly jumped out of her skin.

"What are you doing here? I thought you were staying out of this. You said you were too busy to help us." She wasn't used to seeing Damon in his full mage regalia. He looked…menacing, god-like, and radiated power.

"Elise, I don't have time for this argument. I'll give it back to you, but right now, I need it. I'm not asking."

Given her condition and the fact she was practically alone, it was an easy decision to hand over the *Amulet of the Five Gates* to him. Reaching to unclasp it from around her neck, she handed the amulet to Damon.

"Thank you," he bowed and was gone before she could even think of what to say or do next. There was no *Portal*, no *Gate*, no means of transportation she recognized. Damon was just gone, as silently as he had come.

Brigance Fireheart saw the flash of the great white beam out of the corner of his eye, probably striking ten leagues off the coastline, he estimated. Now he'd have to divide his attention between signaling his leadership, commanding the main battlegroup, and watching for the effects of whatever had just struck the South Sea. Signaling Michelle with a flaming arrow shot in the direction of where the beam had struck the South Sea, Brigance needed extra eyes on this developing problem. Michelle immediately responding with three distinct tracer rounds fired off in the air in the same direction as his arrow.

Charles W. McDonald Jr.

Michelle had a better vantage point than Brigance, though they weren't separated by more than four hundred yards. Michelle could both see and hear the waters rising up through the grassy fields of the Rune Stones not more than two thousand feet beyond their forward positions. The flood waters would soon engulf all of their forces leaving Eldrac's men, on higher ground, untouched.

"We've got to drive up that hill now," Michelle was at Brigance Fireheart's side before he even realized it. It was impossible not to be startled, even when knowing her abilities.

"What did you see?"

"We've got the ocean pounding us from the south and east, and it's already flooding the shoreline, moving inland fast. I don't know if that hill is going to be high enough to prevent drowning our forces, but they stand a better chance against those defenses, than they do against an advancing ocean."

"Right," Brigance agreed, giving the command, "Show the advance signal," he ordered his Vedette. Two archers, roughly one hundred cubits apart, clipped their bows with the arrows in their hands, holding their bows high overhead so each other could see. Lit arrows shot forth from each of their distant positions crossing overhead; creating a streaking amber X in the sky, signaling the forward ranks to rush the hillside and clash with Eldrac's main body of men.

"Can you...." Brigance didn't get to finish his question—Michelle was already gone. He'd never get used to that! Brigance, scanning ahead, saw her halfway up the hill in a kneeling position, laying down automatic fire, changing clips furiously as Eldrac's men fell dead by the dozens before her. Tracer rounds from Lawna's different—and far more lethal—weapon continued streaking over their heads from her hillside position behind them, setting ablaze the middle ranks of Eldrac's westernmost forces.

Waves of the angered South Sea now raced over the berms between them and the white beachheads to the east—heading their way.

Swinging his massive tail around, knocking ten of Eldrac's men off their feet so he could crush them with his right front foot, Toblain had been kept busy with the archers, crossbowmen, and infantry King Aaron had sent his way. With crossbolts and arrows sticking out of his chest and side, he was bleeding, but he still had his primary weapon. After crushing five men with one stomp of his right foot, Toblain inhaled, feeling the air leaking out of his punctured lungs. Streaks of fire expanding from his mouth, doubling in size every ten cubits in distance, stuck to armor, men, and equipment alike, setting them ablaze. *Can't escape*, Toblain realized, looking at the giant hole Eldrac had made in his right wing, *but I can stay and fight.* Toblain inhaled again, preparing another burst of fire to battle his ancient enemy.

No escaping Eldrac's attention now. Floating a hundred cubits in the air, Radin reached out toward Eldrac with Dallia's Staff, casting *Damon's Far Reaching*, followed immediately by *Damon's Big Boom.* Overlapping hemispheres of fire, acid, and lightning engulfing King Aaron and Eldrac, most of the damage deflected by Eldrac's shield, which winked out of existence after being exhausted by the force of Radin's blast. Though King Aaron's white robes ablaze with his flesh burning was a good sign he was getting through. He now had Eldrac's undivided attention, seeing his right index finger pointed straight at him, Radin felt his consciousness fading fast, falling from the sky, but not before seeing flashes of what he could only describe as visions of the underworld in his mind. His father had shared stories of real evil with him as a child, but they couldn't compare to the hellish landscape he confronted in his mind, with the *beast* coming to devour him. Blackness as he hit the flooded ground with a splashing thud, sending Dallia's Staff afloat on the advancing tide of the South Sea.

"ADVANCE," Ethan Marshall shouted to his men, seeing the glowing amber X in the sky, his sword held straight upward to the heavens as he pressed his black Friesian horse forward. The South Sea's waves were coming up on them fast from the lower lying grounds behind them. They had to get up that hill—fast! "Let's MOVE," he shouted, engaging in close combat with Eldrac's easternmost forces. He didn't have the men to take them on, but taking them on was his job, and he was going to do his job no matter what. The scores of ball-lightning streaking overhead from behind them were welcome, whoever they were coming from. He had been told he'd have no lamean support. *Praise the Creator*, he was told wrong. *Maybe he'd live, after all*, he estimated as his longsword crashed into the leather armored left shoulder of one of Eldrac's infantrymen.

"Holy Creator," Quin swore, stepping through the *Portal* onto the rapidly flooding grounds to the northeast of a massive battle like unto a scale he'd only read about in history books. It was hard to even identify who was who, and with the ocean rushing in all around them, he had to think fast. Identifying the unthinkable ahead, he couldn't believe his eyes, seeing Eldrac in the

Charles W. McDonald Jr.

living flesh. Quin immediately began hurling ball-lightning that expanded as they shot overhead, the attacking force now climbing the hill before them to clash with Eldrac's army.

Taking direction from his friend, Iain Longbow, atop his faithful Grey, rushed into the fray, high stepping through the rushing water, as he immediately began to nock and loose arrows on the run as he charged Eldrac's forces from behind the attacking force now making the bloody uphill ascent. Arrows struck home one after the other, but there were not enough arrows in the world for this fight. A storm of arrows streaked overhead from Eldrac's forces right at them. "SHIELDS," Iain shouted.

Last through the *Portal*, Rowarc immediately began looking for his son, paying no attention to the ocean water now nearly hip deep, threatening to drown them all in moments. So many people he didn't recognize; he was struggling to identify who was who. He'd never seen a battle like this in all his life. "RADIN," he cried out for his son. "RADIN, WHERE ARE YOU?" Sword drawn, he headed south where he'd just seen a young man fall out of the sky crashing into the waves.

Tracer rounds spent, Lawna was on her last belt of ammunition for her M134. This thing chewed through ammunition like there was no tomorrow, and they hadn't brought an unlimited supply of ammo with them from Earth. *If you're going to use it, this is the place*, she thought, mowing down hundreds of Eldrac's men until the Gatling barrels spun empty. "Shit," she thought aloud, only vaguely aware of the bleeding from her back.

Anna streaked to a stop, skidding on the hillside soil and grass as she tried to keep her balance after striking what she hoped would have been a lethal blow to the source of her affliction. Looking at her nails, seeing Lawna's flesh and blood dripping from her fingertips, she doubted it was a fatal wound, as she began to cast.

The two locked eyes with one another, Lawna ignoring the throbbing in her back as she rushed Anna in a blur with only her bare hands as her weapon.

Anna's writhing, squid-like, poisonous tentacles erupted from the ground where Lawna had been. *Spells will be useless with this one....*

A rushing blur striking Anna dead center mass in her chest sent her body flailing one hundred feet backward down the hillside where she was unceremoniously dumped into the now hip-deep ocean water gathering at the base of the once grassy field below. Anna barely had time to right herself in the water when she felt Lawna's hands on her neck from behind immediately

Charles W. McDonald Jr.

after a splash behind her. Without thinking, she shot out of the water, hundreds of cubits into the sky, taking Lawna with her as she began violent rolls in the air, trying to shake her off, causing Lawna's nails to grow and dig into her neck. The searing pain of Lawna's venomous bite into her clavicle told her she wasn't going to get rid of her that easy. She had to think fast, or she was going to die at the hands of this beast.

Following Brigance's plan to the letter, Talemar kept his presence completely silent, stepping through his *Portal* into the center of the Rune Stones. He was out of Eldrac's line-of-sight, though knew Eldrac's exact position.

Summoning massive bolts of lightning from a cloudless red sky where he still floated in midair, Wraith directed his fire at what remained of Eldrac's protections. Radin had already wiped out his shell that had encompassed both him and the king, but his individual protections remained 'til his bolt struck home, blasting Eldrac up against the side of the center obelisk. He couldn't use his most lethal combat spells, lest he'd destroy the Nine Towers. This required precision. He had an idea. The transparent web-like curtain began falling down upon Eldrac's position from above, but it was suspended on violent currents of air from the Blood Night. It would take time to reach him.

Rowarc sloshed through the water, getting to the young man he saw floating like a dead fish in the currents that threatened to carry him out to the open sea. He didn't recognize the clothes, but he quickly identified the body. "Radin, come back to me, my boy," turning his son's body over, he could only hope for the best—his chest wasn't moving. Rowarc pinched his son's mouth and massaged his airway as he began breathing life into his son's body, striking his chest with everything he had.

The violent clash with the quartz-like obelisk left him woozy—his confidence shaken. They had brought more to the fight than he had, and it was obvious he had to start prioritizing these threats. Fortunately, Anna had one of the biggest threats occupied, leaving the red-robed lamean to the northeast, and Vosh as the greatest remaining threats on the battlefield. Best to deal with the one you know, Eldrac thought, casting the spell he'd just used to kill the boy, though it hadn't worked exactly as it should have—he'd have to investigate why later. He gave Vosh *Damon's Damnation.*

Charles W. McDonald Jr.

Taking the hill had been a challenge, but the rising waters proved adequate motivation for Brigance's men, who drove forward like all the evil beasts of the underworld were behind them. Cutting another of Eldrac's men in half with a horse-propelled swipe of his broadsword, Brigance pivoted around just in time to see Vosh disappear in a cloud of black ash just as she sent another volley of ball-lightning into Eldrac's men. Nothing remained of her save the dust on the side of the hill where she once stood. Tears from his heavy eyes began streaking down his soot-laden jawline as he pivoted again, giving the signal with his battle-axe crossing his broadsword. Two Vedettes that had been laying back from the primary fight lit their arrows, loosing them simultaneously, forming two parallel, straight lines in the red sky.

The signal he'd expected, but never wanted to see, came, and Talemar knew. They needed more than they'd brought. Reaching out with all of the authority and power of the Crystal Crown, he summoned, cracking the red sky open with a blinding bright white light that seared the blood-red sky like unto looking into the heart of a blacksmith's forge.

Radin's breath shocked his father at first, but the water pouring out of Radin's mouth was a good sign.

Two parallel amber arrow streaks in the sky were the first thing Radin saw illuminating his father's face as he felt himself floating in the water. Uprighting himself immediately in the water, finding it had receded enough for him to stand just more than hip-deep, Radin quickly identified Eldrac, knowing the meaning of the distress signal above, casting *Damon's Contained Blast* with everything he had. Reaching out to the Arcane, he requested, at the behest of his memories, everything he could hold without Dallia's Staff; his memories becoming more vibrant as the summoned Arcane answered. A vision of what he knew to be himself in the womb and a voice talking to him from outside the womb—a voice he recognized. Just as Eldrac was beginning to point his right index finger upward at Wraith's position, the *Contained Blast* explosion blew Eldrac back up against the obelisk with a bone-crushing thud.

Eldrac knew his left leg was now broken. He'd heard and felt it snap this time when the white explosive burst just in front of him blew him back into the sidewalls of the obelisk. The boy wasn't dead after all. So be it. He still had plenty left. Extending his right index finger back towards the young man, he cast *Damon's Damnation* at the boy once again just as a translucent web fell upon him from above. Blackness. Eldrac was gone; there was nothing but black ash left where he once stood beside the obelisk. The shock and horror on King Aaron's face seemed as immeasurable as the memory would prove inerasable. Eldrac had held the Keeper of the Wind's figurine at the time he'd managed to destroy himself, and now it was gone along with Eldrac. His seat of authority for a thousand years was lost.

He hadn't seen it happen, but from the arrows sticking out of Ethan Marshall's chest as he slumped over his horse, Brigance Fireheart knew the king's archers had done their job. Pulling his friend from his mount, Lord Fireheart carried Ethan over his shoulder to higher ground where he could lay him with the rest of the dead. Carrying Ethan past Michelle, more tears fell from both of them, for they were not yet done counting the dead. This battle wasn't over.

Lawna's venom had proven to be more than that of what had transformed her, causing her to become flush, ill, and to the point of vomiting as they spiraled out of control through the air overhead. Losing consciousness, her powers fading, they began plummeting out of the red sky toward the grassy field where the water was now receding to the Rune Stones. A giant splashing thud and Lawna was finally thrown off Anna, but not without taking large chunks of her clavicle and neck with her. A dirty-blonde blur moving through the watery grassy field, and Lawna was back on her again.

"ENOUGH," Lawna shouted, ripping Anna's body in half with her bare hands, throwing her pelvis and legs a hundred feet to the south as she picked up her torso, separating Anna's head from her chest as she let the chest fall to the watery ground below. The sky opening up before them simultaneously to the ground beneath them.

Acrid black sulfur, ash, and soot escaped from the massive crack forming to the southwest of Radin's position causing him and Rowarc to lose his balance, as the water around them followed the forces of gravity, rushing to fill in the fiery void now forming on holy ground. A great and beastly roar proclaimed its arrival; part dragon, part man, with the head of a great wolf with dead white eyes and squared jaw, it clawed at the edges of the fissure in the ground, pulling itself from the rift it had created as its ribbed wings spread wider than forty paces.

Charles W. McDonald Jr.

Radin tried to maintain balance, but the pulsating whip of fire wrapping itself around his waist had other plans for him as his body was yanked through the air towards the black-winged Balak, now fully erect in the midst of the fissure. "I'VE COME TO CLAIM WHAT WAS PROMISED!" The booming voice came from lips that did not move upon a creature at least twenty times the size of a full-grown man.

A brilliant translucent white and gold winged being now falling from the sky over the center of the Rune Stones, answered Talemar's summons. Looking down, the archangel Uriel spotted the Balak, extending his Sword of Creation, sending a great beam of white-hot fire at the beast, striking it at the top of its right wing where the ribbed joints became a great talon, just as Uriel touched down on the ground beside Talemar's feet.

The white-hot blast came out of nowhere as the Balak roared in pain, disappearing in a great whirling motion that collapsed the fissure in on itself after the Balak's spear-like tail chased its body down into the pit from whence it came. Radin and the Balak were simply gone, leaving a smoking staggered line in the ground where the fissure to the underworld had just been.

(Eden, Present Day)

The atmosphere still needed some help, but the weight and balance of the rotation upon its axis looked good to produce a productive day that proved a balance from the varying worlds of Man. It was generating the desired magnetic field required to protect life. Full-blown photosynthesis had not taken root just yet, but he had a solution for that, and it was already in the works. The heat was melting the polar ice at a good rate, creating a thick and humid climate on the surface. It was very rich in oxygen, but he needed to help the nitrogen levels. Reaching out with the *Staff of the Invoker*, Damon focused on the delicate balance he was trying to help along at an expedited rate.

(Damon's Manor, Kaleion, Present Day)

Moments later, after advancing the terraforming on Eden, Damon sat

Charles W. McDonald Jr.

alone in his hidden study, witnessing the events at Axum through his *viewing window*, postulating the temerity of a God capable of bringing about such arbitrary destruction on people he so claimed to love. The audacity of such a meddling God had to be challenged, and he knew, deep within his heart, he could do better.

Angrily clinching Vosh's amulet in his left hand, he started to focus on the task at hand, but stopped himself. He considered the options before him. *Would this be the first truly altruistic moment of his life?* Since he was a child, since earning the permanency of his scars about his shoulders, neck, and chest, he had never done something so truly 'noble' as what he was about to attempt, except the love he gave so freely to Mira, Illirian, and Dallia. The motives may have been driven almost entirely by his Master Plan but clutching the amulet and seeing into the future—to the when and where of all those people who most needed him now—Damon found himself unrestrained by the hate that bound him to his scars, and his scars to his soul.

He knew his scars and knew them well. He knew their source. He knew the unresolved matters of the spirit manifested in the mind and unresolved matters of the mind manifested in the physical body. The correlation to spirit, consciousness and body never made more clear than that. His scars were evidence of the same relationship.

Was it only the motives behind his Master Plan at work, or was there something more, he considered as he recalled the source of his permanent wounds. The strike of the whip. Was he really so far gone this act couldn't be coming, at least in part, from within him? His mouth worked as he struggled with his own internal thoughts and emotions and their effect on the shared nature of reality. Those *black mirrors of the soul* burned with a cool, smoky hue enough to challenge the ominous aura of the *Staff of the Invoker* nearby as he struggled internally between singling out those mortals most needed for his plans and his new society, versus saving as many as he could. Slamming his right fist down onto his desk hard enough to mar its surface, Damon made a decision most profound.

If he was going to do this truly good thing, he'd need proper inspiration. Flip, flip, flip through his Android to the top of his artist's list, Damon smiled coming upon the most inspirational song he'd ever heard—*My Champion by Alter Bridge*. Putting his earbuds in his ears and cranking up the volume, Damon pressed the play button, focusing on all those who needed a champion before they perished along timelines both near and far.

Letting the music flood his soul, *The Amulet of the Five Gates* still clutched in his left hand, Damon focused on the 'when' he needed to target along with the 'where,' and with his right hand began opening *Portal* upon

Charles W. McDonald Jr.

Portal upon *Portal* on all the worlds of Man he had scouted over the last several years. Reaching out with his *Telekinesis* to snatch the mighty *Staff of the Invoker* with unseen hands, it flew across his secreted study into the grip of his right hand as he clutched one of its thrice helical rods. Drawing more energy than ever before, Damon flooded himself perilously close to the edge with the Zero-Point field as he stretched himself as hard as he could. *Portals* by the hundreds, by the thousands, opened as far as his advanced mind's eye could see, as he tried with everything he had to save all he could.

He needed a message that would be small enough to transcend upstream the timeline—just enough to get them to believe—to give them *hope*. "Jump now," he breathed aloud as if speaking to the winds of time, hoping it would be enough.

Phase One of the Master Plan now complete—a plan so very many years in the making, Damon wondered if time itself would break due to his actions. He didn't smile all that often anymore, but a thin smile pressed his lips with his *black mirrors of the soul* closed to focus on the next group of families he would save on distant worlds away.

In his peripheral vision, Damon couldn't help but notice something new in the terrifying charcoal-blue aura of the *Staff of the Invoker*. *Was that a man hung upside-down on the left side of the hemispherical aura?*

(The North American Midwest, Earth, Near Future)

Mushroom clouds in the distance, maybe thirty miles to the northwest, told Ron Stencowsky everything he needed to know. He had to find a way to get his men underground—fast! He had hundreds of men he had to save.

Suddenly, to his immediate southwest, the air shimmered before him, superheating up to about head-height level with silvery-blue fissures of electricity ripping the air open in the shape of an ovoid massive doorway, wide enough for twenty men at a time to get through. He didn't recognize the place on other side of the doorway, but there weren't nukes going off there, nor blast waves coming to shred his men apart. He thought he heard the words 'jump now' on the leading edge of the blast wave coming to rip them apart, and that was all the confirmation he required. "MOVE!" Ron shouted, did his best to limp and then jump through to the other side of the doorway; his men following right on his heels.

*   *   *   *

Charles W. M{c}Donald Jr.

(The North Central Texas Plains, Earth, Near Future)

Mira sweated over fixing her Jeep® Renegade. It hadn't run in forever, but she knew she was getting close, and if she could get herself farther south-west, she might have a chance at survival with the heart of the resistance. A mushrooming fireball, as bright as the Sun, erupted to the north, right about where Dallas–Fort Worth would have been, immediately followed by another, then another. The shockwave was coming fast; she had to get down.

Suddenly, what she knew to be a *Portal* opened up beside her as she heard a familiar voice on the leading edge of the blast wave telling her to 'jump now.' *Damon*, she knew, *where have you been? We've needed you!* Just then the heat blast from the nuclear explosion blew Mira through the silvery-blue open-ing mid-air, closing behind her with a sudden whoosh of the collapsing *Portal*.

*   *   *   *

(Dover Castle, England, Earth, Near Future)

The explosions came with such voracity outside the keep, there was barely enough time to grab the children, let alone possessions. The most valuable possession Elise had taken with her, so Billings never questioned nor looked back. Hearing the whisper 'jump now' rattle inside the old stone and mortar of Dover Castle eliminated his last shred of doubt of what must be done. Billings held onto Michael's children for dear life as he started running for the *Portal*, appearing amidst the four-inch thick walls of the bunkered safe room, landing unceremoniously on the alien landscape of *hope* before him, now unsure of what the future held for them. *But, at least now they had a fu-ture*, he acknowledged as the *Portal* whooshed to a close behind them.

Charles W. McDonald Jr.

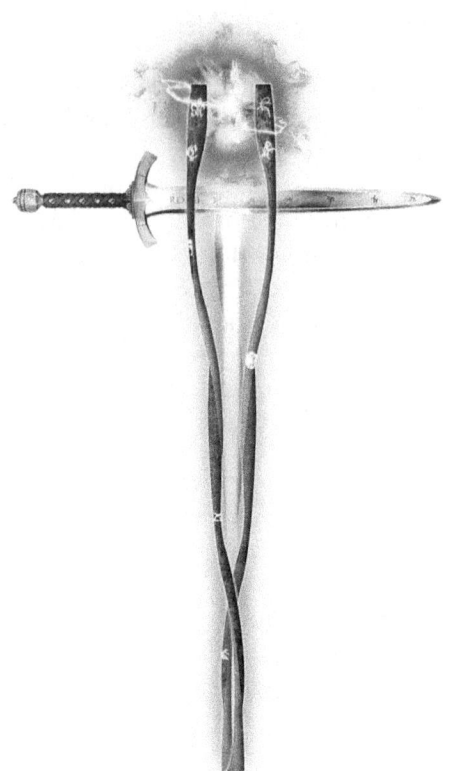

Epilogue: A Mortal Toll

(Eden, Present Day)

ortals suddenly burst open all the way to the horizon, some one-hundred-and-fifty-feet-wide by fifty-feet-tall as all manner of living things made their way to their new home, fleeing the barren lands of Kaleion, Earth, Perion, Graelon and other worlds of Man Damon had been scouting. The clash of Humanoid cultures and varying beasts, as well as diverse levels of technology, met one another on an entirely alien landscape. Humanoids of every size and shape began taking the measure of their new home and their fellow...*Man*.

A young family of children walking with their mother, taking in the alien landscape, noticed the construction building supplies, equipment, and power tools stretched out as far as the eye could see. "Mommy, where are we,"

Charles W. McDonald Jr.

the adorable five-year-old daughter asked her mother in a soft Georgian accent as the mother tried her cell service. Not a single bar. *Where is this place?* The moon didn't look right at all. It was huge in the sky. The sun looked…different. The mother, turning to face the opposite horizon in the fading twilight, jumped back several steps in shock before realizing *it* was just a statue. A massive black granite statue of a tall, young man with flowing hair and a strong jawline, wearing flowing herringbone robes and carrying a massive triple helix staff pointed skyward standing on a five-sided pedestal. An inscription adorned each of the five sides in what she could only assume were distinct languages, but only one side she recognized as "English:"

I brought you here to save you, your families, and your civilizations. Your worlds and your kingdoms are dying; no longer capable of bearing fruit for you or your children. There are rules you must follow here on this world I have made just for you. Some of the most important rules are listed here. A Constitution, along with a manual of governing laws and covenants can be found throughout the provided construction equipment, tools, and building supplies. I will enforce these laws personally, and everyone will be held to account for adhering to them, without exception.

The primary laws are as follows:
I am Damon of Basrat—your God. I require your weekly worship and your obedience.
Maintain the population of this new world, Eden, below five hundred million Humanoids.
Do not burn any fossil fuels.
Do not kill any animal life except in the protection of Human life, or for food.
Do not steal from one another.
Do not kill other Humanoids except in enforcement of my laws.
Do not take my name in vain.
Do not bear false witness.

The petite, 5'4", blonde Georgia native, Mellissa, walked around the statue, looking at what she assumed were other languages of the same message, but she did not recognize any of them, and she had been a linguist at the University of Georgia for the last ten years. She wanted to spend time deciphering these other languages—some looking similar to a root of Latin—others more symbol-driven. Interesting, she considered, and he had left out a few of the big commandments about 'coveting thy neighbor's wife' and 'committing adultery.' She wondered what that said about this *Damon of Basrat*, and what to do about the crucifix she wore around her neck. They had been spared, and that was more than just something. Removing her crucifix to lay it at the feet of his statue, Mellissa took the hand of her daughter and son, walking off to

Charles W. McDonald Jr.

explore their new home.

(Damon's Manor, Kaleion, Two Days Ago)

   Damon's coaching echoed in Radin's thoughts as he felt the tranquil state of the flow of Arcane all around him, filling the chalice of his essence with the vivid colors of reality as he worked on something of his own making…. Damon spoke often of the rarity of custom spells and the unique abilities required to create something so tangible from nothingness. To be able to connect to the doorways of time/space and space/time and to touch that underlayment manifold of reality and pull from it whatever one wished into being. That was pure genius as Damon described. He was certain there was bluster in it that was most certainly self-serving as most of Damon's spells that he regularly used were custom made by him for him—only poached by his leaking of them to friends and allies who later proved less reliable than himself at keeping his secrets.

   Still…. Now, as he worked his imagineering to manifest from nothingness, he asked and shaped and coaxed and formed that from his visions of the great fluid of time cascading before him in a technical marvel, like a waterfall of potential outcomes, down into a nest of wires and a wellspring of white light, shimmering and reflecting all possibilities and none. 'Twas not the waking dream of a great lake of blue crystal placid waters in the presence of a booming voice of Creation and blinding white light all around. This was something else entirely. The room itself was dark in contrast to the waterfall of a rainbow of light, bursting forth a powerful white center, from the wired nest it dipped into, from a technical oculus above. These metal things—neither creatures nor man—floated to and fro panels making adjustments and noticing his presence until he reached forth his closed right fist, opening it sharply and abruptly causing them to explode from within to tiny metal shards. That, he knew, to be a spell of his own making. And, as he channeled his natural abilities in *Telekinesis* into the power he sourced from all living things, he did open his right hand abruptly in the same way he'd envisioned, causing the handle of the shovel floating in Damon's spell test room to separate from its shaft and metal spade and cleaved the spade itself in half, causing the wooden shaft itself to blister all the way down its length. Not quite the impressive outcomes he'd envisioned in his dreams, but it was a start.

   Something to work on and improve over time, he thought…. If only he understood the dream and what it was he was facing. It felt important. Like

Charles W. McDonald Jr.

his very life depended on it. Like countless lives depended on it. And the weight of it terrified him....

Damon had taught him to listen to his dreams, for that was where the imagination of his spirit would speak to him. That was where he could tap into all knowledge across all time/space and space/time and it would speak to him in ways he might never fully understand. He didn't yet know how to tap into that source on demand, but it was freely flowing to him nearly every night in his sleep. Like an avalanche of data he didn't yet have the experience to funnel or focus. *But experience would come*, he hoped. *And then answers....*

(Exeter, Perion, Present Day)

Sorrow filled the sparse room of the Marshalls. All of Ethan's belongings had been packed away or given to trusted friends who had been so good and faithful to the family over the years. All that was left now were bittersweet memories, a few trinkets of her own, a few of the children's toys, and their marital bed. Lynn Marshall sat on the edge of that bed now, her face racked with the torment of knowing—hearing the tales of their battle with this ancient enemy made new again. Hearing the tales of that *thing* that took Radin.... And the Blood Night that sang songs of death and chaos for their world outside....

Aaron straddled her lap with a blank expression that reflected the emptiness of Daddy being gone. *Could he understand this young*, she wondered. *Is it better if he does?* She did not feel qualified to answer her own question, but she would have to answer Aaron's.

Now clutching Mommy's dress, Aaron ruffled her lace in his tiny hands. "Mommy, what happened to Daddy," he asked with wide eyes, tugging at the white buttons of his Lynn's deep-blue dress. She could not bear to wear black. Ethan loved this dress on her.

"Sweetheart, Daddy had to go to sleep." Her eyes welled on the brink of tears she couldn't allow. She wanted to weep. She wanted to scream. She wanted to kill. She fought that last feeling with everything that she had left inside of her, but there was nothing left inside her with which to fight. Everything in her heart that had been Ethan's love was now obliterated.

A small boy beginning to understand asked solemnly, "Is Daddy going to wake up?"

And, a broken heart responded, "No, Sweetheart, he's not."

Aaron wept inconsolably in Lynn's arms—his tiny little body hysterically shaking against her embrace. Trying to hold her son as tight as a mother's love could, Lynn knew no matter how close she held him, she could not give her son enough reason to *hope*.

End Book 1

of

A Throne of Souls

Charles W. McDonald Jr.

A Throne of Souls

Book 1: A Kingdom Forgotten Published September 2016
Book 2: Black Mirrors of the Soul Published April 2017
Book 3: The Fall of Hate Published June 2018
Book 4: The Rise of Hope Published December 2020

Look for *The Veil of White* ©2017
The Mind-Blowing Conclusion of
A Throne of Souls ®2016
Anticipated Late 2022

Charles W. McDonald Jr.

Thank you for reading *A Kingdom Forgotten*. I hope you enjoyed it immensely, and I would be greatly honored for you to leave a review of your thoughts and impressions on either the channel of purchase and/or Goodreads. Self-published authors live and die by reviews. So, I would strongly encourage you to take a moment to leave an honest review and would greatly appreciate your time in doing so. I welcome any and all constructive, positive-intent feedback and would love to hear from you.

Please feel free to contact me at:
http://www.facebook.com/throneofsouls
https://www.facebook.com/royvanmiral/
https://www.athroneofsouls.com
Parler @CharlesMcDonald
Twitter @athroneofsouls
https://pilled.net/#/profile/2818 (@AThroneofSouls)
Email: royvanmiral@hotmail.com
Goodreads Author Page:
https://www.goodreads.com/author/show/16002346.Charles_W_McDonald_Jr_
Amazon Author Page:
https://www.amazon.com/-/e/B01MDPEUAW
https://itunes.apple.com/us/author/charles-w-mcdonald-jr/id1198345238?mt=11

Sincerely,

Charles W. McDonald Jr.

Charles W. McDonald Jr.

About the Author:

Charles W. McDonald Jr. was born in Oklahoma City, raised in Norman, Oklahoma, and is a graduate of the University of Oklahoma with a BBA in Management Information Systems and a Minor in Economics. He also has a background in Aerospace Engineering, High Availability Systems Engineering, Disaster Recovery, Cloud Architecture (Azure, AWS, and GCP), and DevOps. Honorably discharged from the United States Air Force Reserves, he also has a background in the armed forces and is a full member of both the AFIO (Association of Former Intelligence Officers) and NDIA (National Defense Industry Association) organizations. He lives in Roanoke, TX.

In the summer of 1995, Charles read every available book on the Wheel of Time by Robert Jordan in a couple of weeks, and later that same July awoke in the middle of the night from an incredibly immersive dream. Charles began writing, by hand, everything he could remember from that dream which became the outline for the story of A Throne of Souls. Very shortly afterwards, Charles wrote Robert Jordan directly, looking for advice and inspiration for his own work, and Robert Jordan personally responded in a three-page letter, encouraging Charles to tell his story in his way, in his voice, and in his time. The completion of A Throne of Souls is a deeply personal mission for Charles to thank the spirit of Robert Jordan.

Charles W. McDonald Jr.

Glossary of Terms

†¤‡- ͵Æ‡:ˇŒ – Earth, Graelon, Kaleion, Perion, Setinon, in that order precisely. Two icons per world.

Actual – Word used to describe the person with the actual call sign. Team members are associated with a call sign, but an individual specifically assigned that call sign is referred to as call-sign actual. This is typically, though not always, the team lead of that given unit.

APEX – 25mm high explosive round designed specifically for the J-35 Joint Strike Fighter.

ARV – Alien Reproduction Vehicle. As opposed to ETV (extraterrestrial vehicle).

AWR – Allah's Waiting Room. Squirters fleeing from a contact situation will typically gather in another structure to regroup. When an airstrike is called in on said location, it's typically referred to as AWR.

Balak – Typically a mid-to-high level demon, appearing part dragon, part man, with the head of a great wolf with a squared jaw.

BFT – Blue Force Tracker, a vitally important piece of electronic field equipment identifying friendlies (via IFF – Identify Friend or Foe) and hostiles on a battlefield.

Bigot List – A Military Industrial Complex term used to describe those who are authorized to be read into an Unacknowledged Special Access Program. Usually curated by what is called "The Watch Committee." What religious order has a periodical called "The Watch Tower?" In the Book of Enoch, what were the fallen 200 angels called? Coincidence…? Something for you to think about….

BUD/S – Basic Underwater Demolition/SEAL training.

CCP – Chinese Communist Party.

Contact – Usually a directional reference to making gunfire and/or explosive contact with hostiles.

Codenames of Presidents:

> **Eagle** – William Jefferson Clinton
> **Deacon** – Jimmy Carter
> **Lancer** – John F. Kennedy
> **Mogul** – 45
> **Passkey** – Gerald R. Ford
> **Rawhide** – Ronald W. Reagan
> **Renegade** – Barak H. Obama
> **Searchlight** – Richard M. Nixon
> **Scorecard** – General Dwight D. Eisenhower
> **Supervise** – Harry S. Truman
> **Timberwolf** – George H. W. Bush (former DCI and VP)
> **Trailblazer** – George W. Bush

Death Blossom – When a mujahid blindly sprays automatic gunfire in a contact situation.

DNA vs RNA – AGCU = RNA (adenine, guanine, cytosine, and uracil) while AGCT (adenine, guanine, cytosine, thymine) = DNA.

Durial's Eye – See the Starlight of Immortality for one of its two definitions. The other definition refers to a scaled-up model of the first definition of Durial's Eye using the crater lake atop a dormant volcano on Eden as the eye of the scaled-up divination tool itself. Illirian Starfire was the Guardian of *Durial's Eye* until she gave it to Damon in *The Fall of Hate*. She described it to Damon in this manner, "You, of all people, are the one most like Durial, Damon. You work closely with both magic and technology, and Durial's Eye requires equal talent in both. Magic sees the future while technology refines the vision like a great and polished lens to a telescope."

EBEN – Extraterrestrial Biological Entities. EBEN. This is not a reference to ALL extraterrestrials, but of a particular race of extraterrestrials thought to be generally benevolent to, and establishing a working relationship with, Earth Humans.

Elian – A mostly diaphanous exotic textile material manufactured only by cave elves in the World Below and Between. Its exact composition is unknown, though it is often sought after by witches for reasons not known to the general public.

Entropy – An element of the Second Law of Thermodynamics describing the linearity of time as it relates to irreversible processes and their increasing levels of entropy versus reversible processes and their constant entropy (aka isentropic processes).

https://www.grc.nasa.gov/www/k-12/airplane/thermo2.html

ETV – Extraterrestrial Vehicle.

EXFIL – Exfiltrate, to leave or exit/egress a hostile zone of action.

Ferian – A dead language on Perion derived from Aramaic and Latin.

Forkettè – A Perion equivalent of an invocation/elemental specialist on Kaleion.

GCP – Global Consciousness Project (http://noosphere.princeton.edu/). Research data leveraged in the chapter 'Presentiment.'

Goat Trail – A fucked-up road, usually dirt, gravel, or mostly rubble from being bombed to dust.

Intelligence Categories and Terms:

    COMINT – Communications Intelligence

    DCI – Director of Central Intelligence. Usually, but not always synonymous with MJ-1.

    ELINT – Electronics Intelligence

    FISINT – Foreign Instrumentation Signals Intelligence; FISINT is intelligence from the interception of foreign electromagnetic emissions.

    GEOINT – Geospatial Intelligence

    HUMINT – Human Intelligence

    IMINT – Image(s) Intelligence; often inclusive of GEOINT.

    INTSUM – Intelligence Summary

    SIGINT – Signals Intelligence; often inclusive of COMINT and FISINT.

    MASSINT – Measurement and Signatures Intelligence; often inclusive of TELINT, SIGINT, and IMINT.

    OSINT – Open-Source Intelligence

    TELINT – Telemetry Intelligence

Goyim – A term of derision used by the Jesuits Watchtower (the Elite of the Jesuits) and Khazarian Mafia (The New World Order / Illuminati / Luciferian Cabal) to refer to the 99+% of the population, whom they do not consider worthy of having progeny or owning property of any kind.

The Haedron – See map of Kaleion. This is a sacred place with a great stone in an immense crater, presumed to have fallen from the stars and yet did not shatter or explode upon impact, suggesting its structure is incredibly dense. Perhaps more so than even iron.

Lamean – A mage on Kaleion, Graelon, or Terran system. This word is commonly associated with the general ability to cast Arcane on Perion.

Looking Glass – The US Airborne Command and Control System in place 24-7-365, intended to provide a real-time, national backup to the NCA and NMCC should those ground-based systems be destroyed or rendered inoperable. In the event those ground-based systems are destroyed or rendered inoperable, the NCA would transition to the Looking Glass in real time and provide options for an immediate tactical or strategic response at the discretion of US Government Civilian Command and Control (POTUS and the National Security Team). There are actually several Looking Glass aircraft, but one is airborne at all times of the day and night protecting the United States of America and its interests around the world.

LZ – Landing Zone.

M-249/SAW – Fully-automatic-tactical-weapon-carrying member of the Teams.

MCCC - The MCCC is comprised of High-Altitude Electronic Pulse (HEMP) hardened tractor trailers enclosing a secure Command and Control (C2) network operations and communications center. The MCCC platform must be sustained to provide survivable and endurable C2 of strategic and space forces for situation monitoring, tactical warning, force management, force direction, and decision support. In addition, this contract will provide for internal integration among platform network and communication systems, as well as for external integration of these systems with other C2 systems (e.g., MILSATCOM, GCCS, and the like). (Sourced: https://www.fbo.gov/index?s=opportunity&mode=form&id=562422c06e7019192f-be943ad51ecaf7&tab=core&_cview=1)

National Command Authority (NCA) – Within the US Government, the NCA represents the lawful and final source for any and all use of military orders, especially as they relate to the US nuclear arsenal.

National Institute of Discovery Sciences (NIDS) – A Robert Bigalow investigative unit (Est. 1994) of scientists and subject matter experts engaged in analyzing paranormal events and deriving hard, applied sciences from them. This unit dispenses with the minutiae of whether or not extraterrestrials exist. They know they do…. Their (NIDS) focus is on gaining access to metamaterials and Close Encounters of the Second Kind artifacts from which to conduct real, applied sciences to them and gain a working knowledge of how these things work in the larger whole. They have produced real, tangible scientific data results, which have been purchased by the DIA and shared on the official, secured DIA file share system for internal use and further diagnosis.

National Military Command Center (NMCC) – Within the US Military, the NMCC has three primary missions: 1) generate Emergency Action Messages directed to the battlefield; 2) provide solution/response options to the Joint Chiefs of Staff in response to attacks on Americans/American interests/assets around the world; 3) provide a strategic watch component monitoring nuclear weaponized activity around the world in real time.

Nuclear Command and Control Systems (NCCS) – The collective infrastructure of assets, systems, resources, and agencies that supports the President of the United States and his military chain of command with the ability to accurately direct the nation's nuclear forces in real time. The NCCS includes within its infrastructure other components and systems (ground-based, sea-based, and air-based), which include, but are not limited to, the Looking Glass/NAOC, MCCC, NMCC, NCA, and USSSTRATCOM among others.

OGA – Other Government Agency (i.e. CIA).

Operator – An honored term for a special operations team member in the field.

OPORD – Operational Orders.

OSCAR MIKE – On the Move.

PCC – Pre-Combat Check.

PKM – A soviet-era general-purpose machine gun.

PLF – Programed Life Form. Typically, neutral in alignment (neither good nor evil), these semi-sentient, autonomous life forms operate similar to a cyborg but are more organic in nature.

PLUGGER – GPS Unit.

POTUS – President of the United States of America.

Raphael – Often depicted holding a staff, Raphael is considered by the three great Terran religions to be the archangel of healing but is also known to bring comfort to the dying and help transition their souls to the afterlife.

Resha – Old Tongue Ferian for The Breaker of Seals, The Destroyer of Men, and thought to be, by some, the Son of God the Creator.

Resident Identity Code Checksum – This site is designed to provide valid checksum resident identity codes for Chinese male and females. https://code-complete.com/chinaid/validids.php

Retrocausality – The concept of influencing the past from the future through communication mechanisms that cut across timelines, usually by nonlocality principles or to explain nonlocality behaviors. https://phys.org/news/2017-07-physicists-retrocausal-quantum-theory-future.html

Rose Silk – On Perion, some silkworms feed only on the nectar of roses. Their silk is often referred to as rose silk.

RPG – Rocket Propelled Grenade.

Sandbox – Operating in a theater of war associated with the Middle East or Persian Empire lands.

Shofar – A ram's-horn trumpet used by ancient Jews in religious ceremonies and in combat.

Sorians – A malevolent race of extraterrestrials, originating from the Orion star cluster and having a great empire of conquest made up of several different races from many worlds. Considered possibly synonymous with Draco and Anunnaki.

Squirter – A hostile leaving the contact zone expeditiously to avoid certain death at the hands of an Operator.

SRR – British Special Reconnaissance Regiment.

Stasis Stone – A physical gemstone imbued with the abilities to capture and maintain the immortal soul of a mortal being and to house said soul for an indefinite period of time (for safe keeping).

Staff of the Invoker – This staff was about three's—three acid-etched metal triangular helical rods, twisted in exactly three revolutions each, in a triple helix masterpiece with a massive iolite gem at its tip where the helical assembly flowered open suspending the gem in mid-air. The metallic, triple helix framework was forged in Black-Dragon fire and shaped by a great

Titan, then enchanted and imbued with great powers by Dallia (Kaleion arcmage of enchantment) over the period of several days roughly a thousand years ago as a wedding present for her husband, the infamous Damon of Basrat. Specifically, its powers greatly increase the amount of energy Damon, and only Damon, can channel. The types of energy it can augment is universal. If anyone, other than Damon attempts to use it, the staff will obliterate them. It is a central artifact in this story and the story could not be told without it.

Starlight of Immortality – Small blue-green star sapphire made of supersolids materials, roughly the size of a human palm. Neither solid nor gas nor liquid, it holds many secrets, not the least of which is to incredible longevity.

Supersolids – Wikipedia defines supersolids as: "In condensed matter physics, a supersolid is a spatially ordered material with superfluid properties. In the case of helium-4, it has been conjectured since the 1960s that it might be possible to create a supersolid.[1] Starting from 2017, a definitive proof for the existence of this state was provided by several experiments using atomic Bose-Einstein condensates.[2] The general conditions required for supersolidity to emerge in a certain substance are a topic of ongoing research."

Telomere – A telomere is a region of repetitive nucleotide sequences at each end of a chromosome, which protects the end of the chromosome from deterioration or from fusion with neighboring chromosomes. Its name is derived from the Greek nouns telos (τέλος) 'end' and merOs (μέρος, root: μερ-) 'part.' (Sourced: from www.wikipedia.org). Unsourced: The telomere essentially shrinks with age, thus providing a mechanism by which we can determine biological age. For more information, go to www.teloyears.com.

The Halls of Aaramus – Created by an immeasurably powerful lich known as Aaramus. This plane of existence is time neutral, and the normal laws of physics are suspended here, as it is created out of space that does not exist in the normal/known universe; it is extra-dimensional. As such, travel here is incredibly dangerous, as one is held hostage to the rules of physics, magic, and technology allowed by Aaramus, which are dynamic to his will. *Portal / Gate* entry into the Halls of Aaramus is allowed, but *Portal / Gate* exit typically is not, at least not without the expressed permission of Aaramus himself.

The Seeds of Humanity:

Kaleion – The homeworld of Damon, Kellen, Illirian, Goldenbow, and several other characters. This world is one of the Seeds of Humanity, with twin moons, developed into an agrarian and magical society.

Perion – The homeworld of Talemar, Radin, Brigance Fireheart, and several other characters. This world is one of the seeds of Humanity, with twin moons, developed into an agrarian and magical society.

The Terran System – Also known as Earth. This is the homeworld to Michelle, Lawna, Michael, and several other characters. This world developed into a mostly technological society, though some belief in magic and witchcraft still exists, allowing some operational and effective use of same.

Graelon – One of the five homeworlds of the seeds of Humanity, Graelon is a mostly technical society where magic and witchcraft still work to a limited degree. It is the homeworld most closely associated and comparable with the Terran system. Their technology allowed them to colonize outposts where magic was more freely accepted, to disastrous outcomes in some cases.

Setinon – Possibly the oldest home of Humanity and the original seed of the

Human race, Setinon is an entirely technical and highly advanced society capable of controlling planetary weather, FTL travel, and using energy directly from a star—also known as Helium 3.

Pleiadian – Introduced as a possible source world for Man pre-dating even Setinon. This is a series of seven extraordinarily bright stars arranged in a unique constellation that folds back in on itself. It is not one given solar system but a great series of solar systems 444.2 light years from the Terran solar system (Sol). https://www.gaia.com/article/who-are-the-pleiadians

UNFPA – *United Nations Population Fund.* You will not believe the evil and disgusting things this organization is involved with and responsible for until you do your own research. And just remember that any time they talk about 'voluntary' *sterilization* and/or *termination/abortion* programs, they really mean 'compulsory.'

The Void – Also known as the Nether, no one knows who, when, or why the Void was created, but it is a highly dangerous place home to souls lost between death and destiny. Large asteroids perilously collide with one another on a regular basis, making the entire Void an unstable place to visit. *Portal/Gate* entry and exit is allowed, but strongly ill-advised.

The World Below and Between – Created by unknown entities, this gateway between worlds that house the seeds of Humanity allows those who understand its navigational systems to traverse great distances in a very short period of time. Those who do not understand are permanently lost. *Portal/Gate* entry into the World Below and Between is permitted, but *Portal/Gate* exit is not. This plane of existence is time neutral.

Throne of Souls – The first Throne of Souls was made by Damon of Basrat for his wife (Banthis). There have since been others made for other entities given the travel of Damon's first spell that made such an abomination (*Damnation*). Since that time, Damon has made a highly modified version of *Damnation*, called *A Throne of Souls* that allows the caster to grant the *Throne of Souls* to himself/herself. Literally speaking, it combines some characteristics of a *Stasis Stone* in that it can capture and hold inside itself the living immortal soul of a mortal being. However, unlike a *Stasis Stone*, it affords the holder of the *Throne of Souls* the living energy given off by that soul or a collection/aggregation of souls within the *Throne of Souls* itself. In other words, there is no theoretical limit to how many souls could be captured in a given Throne of Souls, so the energy output of such a device could become unfathomable. Soul energy is electromagnetic, so if one has a way to use such an energy type as a source/input, then the output of such a source could be fantastic in scale and scope.

Timeline – The timeline and location markers provided throughout the novel are intended to help the reader navigate the story. Here is a rough guideline to follow when reading these markers:

    A Very Long Time Ago – More than a thousand years in the past.

    A Long Time Ago – Up to one thousand years in the past.

    Present Day – Within a few months, weeks, and hours of the "now" in the timeline.

    Near Future – Within the next two to five years of the "now" in the timeline.

Uriel – The Book of Enoch declares the archangel Uriel is 'the Light of God.' Some traditions recognize Uriel as Patron Saint of the Sacrament of Confirmation. Some believe he guards the consciousness of Jesus Christ.

U.S. Strategic Command (USSTRATCOM) - USSTRATCOM combines the synergy of the U.S. legacy nuclear command and control mission with responsibility for space operations; global strike; global missile defense; and global command, control, communications, computers, intelligence, surveillance and reconnaissance (C4ISR), and combating weapons of mass destruction. This dynamic command gives national leadership a unified resource for greater understanding of specific threats around the world and the means to respond to those threats rapidly. (Sourced: http://www.stratcom.mil/About/)

Washington's Driver – A pseudo-derogatory and somewhat friendly term for a very senior Operator (i.e. He's old enough to be George Washington's driver).

Wave-Particle Duality – In experimental physics, and as evidenced by the two-slit experiment, the observation that photons behave as a wave when not observed and as a particle when observed. In other words, photon particles can behave both as a fermion and as a boson.

This is the essence of the Uncertainty Principle.

Charles W. McDonald Jr.

Glossary of Characters

This is a 5+1-world story and as such has a plethora of characters. This glossary is my attempt to help you keep them all straight. Within this glossary, I'll show you a glimpse of the character development behind them. For example, I possess some seventy pages describing Damon of Basrat, but here you'll see a robust paragraph.

Aaramus – A lich of profound power, wealth, knowledge, and agenda. A Tier A character central to all things. Founder of The Halls of Aaramus and creator of new planes of existence that operate outside the limitations of spacetime and linear time. Allegiances unknown.

President Abel – A Tier B character and elected President of Eden's government. Has a rather extensive history with Damon and understands him better than most. He knows Damon's history—at least, as Damon has shared it with him—and is someone Damon would call a friend and ally. Whether Damon has befriended Abel because of the name and his likeness to the friend he accidentally killed so long ago is unknown, but it wasn't lost on Damon when Abel ran for and then won the presidency without his aid. Now, they work together as best they can with compartmentalized sharing of information more than occasionally getting in their way.

Armstead:

    Pern – Left Bouschè years ago for places and purposes unknown to his brother (Gareth). A Tier B character who finds himself in the middle of a maelstrom, raising the hidden grandson of Damon the Banished.

    Leah – Tier B character; wife of Pern. Adopted mother of baby Ryker.

    Gareth – A Tier B character whose purpose alludes him, but his belief in his grandfather's words and deeds carries the day for him, and it is in the simplicity of his guiding principles that he hopes to find the hour of his brother's greatest need and then the hour of his own.

    Luke – A Tier B character and a beautiful soul carried away by the archangel Raphael. His role was to teach and prepare both Pern and Gareth and to hold true the most important truths: that Humanity is not the work of the random and that both science and history will prove that so.

Arturus Ambrosius Aurelianus – Welsh: Emrys Wledig or Romano-British: Riothamus/Supreme Leader. What fable pronounced as King Arthur.

Asamel – Tier B character. Agent of Eldrac.

Banthis – Once a modest succubus of unlimited ambition and intellect and now heir-apparent to the Dragon of Darkness. The holder of the oldest and original Throne of Souls with powers only rivaled by the Dragon of Darkness and Lilith. Current wife to Damon of Basrat. A Tier A character whose master-level manipulation is central to many parts of the storylines. The key thing to understand about Banthis is how greatly she has suffered and the lengths to which she would go to unleash and redirect that suffering upon others. The only thing or person she could ever claim she truly loved (via her own warped view of love) is Damon and, because of her love for Damon, their daughters.

Brigance Fireheart – A Tier A character of no real power save the one he makes through his sheer will. A brute of a man both broad and tall—more akin to a bear than a man

Charles W. McDonald Jr.

in stature. Brigance is a pragmatic general of generals. Ever more scrutinizing of both Radin and especially Damon, Brigance only affords the light of realism to shine and show the way for him and his men as the Banner of Hope hangs on but a thread.

Chara – Both vampire and mage, Chara was one of the most powerful and lethal forces of Kaleion until obliterated by Damon of Basrat. Her seed and bloodline extend across multiple worlds and is considered to be the source of bloodlust across both Terran and Perion. She is the seed and fire of Damon's hate, though not the root cause.

Daedrin – Brother of Seren. Stripped Keirill of all his great powers. Allegiances unknown.

Dallia – A Tier A character of more consequence than any might understand, Dallia—The Enchantress of Winds—is the first wife and first love of Damon. His unconditional adoration of her broke his then-healing soul irreparably so. In a very short time, she wove her existence and her presence into every fiber of Damon's being. Whether a selfless act or a selfish one, she knew her time short and her love for him immortal. Her magic still lives and works itself upon Damon each and every day he draws breath. Her light and her promise are the most beautiful of all characters in the story, and her time is not yet done.

Damon of Basrat – Only child of the famed Keirill and Seren. Grandchild to Emry and Ersila, as well as Grant and Sala. Great-grandchild of Durial and Fara. Once known as Kaylan until the age of thirteen when he murdered his father. Also goes by the titles: Dark Knight of Magic, Wielder of the Staff of the Invoker, Author of Damnation, Maker and Destroyer of Worlds, and Damon the Banished. Likely the most central Tier A character in the story. A profound and prolific womanizer who has a monstrous past and has killed more than can be counted. He has an ethical compass that rarely allows him to lie and a heart tormented by being abandoned to the hate of his father as a child. For much of Damon's life, he has been wronged by others, and now he seeks to unmake his greatest mistakes afforded by his blind ambition of avenging the death of his first wife and most precious gift of love: Dallia.

Duron of Erden – Placeholder for this character.

Dylan – Placeholder for this character.

Elise Day – Tier A character born Farelise Camden on Graelon—mage registration number: 07874376Alpha221321. Elise has been manipulated and led to the point she finds herself by the Dark Knight of Magic for purposes she's only now beginning to understand. She knows she wasn't recruited for her powers, which are significant, yet nothing compared to those of Damon. Her assumption is Damon needed a fully registered mage to help execute some part of his Master Plan, but every time she solidifies the justification of her doubt of Damon, he puts forth actions that bring her squarely back into his fold. She considers Damon a complete enigma and keeps him at arm's distance, expecting the day will come when she will be forced to pick sides—permanently so. Wife to Michael Anthony Day and lover to Radin, she left Graelon to pursue Michael Anthony Day on Earth and then left Earth to pursue the reincarnation of Michael on Perion only to find herself intimately involved with Radin, whom she considered Michael's possible kindred soul.

Emrys Wledig – Arturus Ambrosius AurElianus – Welsh: Emrys Wledig or Romano-British: Riothamus/Supreme Leader. What fable pronounced as King Arthur.

Evanyil – A dark/cave elf that is supremely capable at thievery, death, and deceit. This darkest of all pure dark elves, Evanyil is the personification of self-sustaining, self-interest. Her ever-present poisoned dagger about her right hip is one of her few constants in life, else she is as chaotic as the quantum particles Mira studies in college. Her compass is always and forever pointed in her own best interest, yet how she gets there is anything but a straight line. Straddling the fine line betwixt genius and insanity, Evanyil is just lucid enough to bring brilliant unconventional thinking to Damon's structure—making their partnership uniquely dangerous for any of their most unfortunate targets. At their peak, they pulled off some of the most legendary and atrocious acts in the history of Kaleion. Their adventures are the source of many biographical texts on Kaleion. Evanyil and Damon share a rich, passionate, and lethal history with one another and with Evanyil's sister, Lorianus. A living god now, Evanyil's ask of Damon some years back in the current continuum is the source of Damon's Master Plan and his need to grow his powers.

The Four Brothers:

   Durial – Settled Kaleion with Fara. The leader of the Four Brothers. Maker and Wielder of The Starlight of Immortality, Father of Dragons, The Great Life-Bringer, and The Wellspring of Humanity.

   Pierio – Settled Graelon with Ceres. The technologist and scientist of the Four Brothers, Pierio sought to recreate the conditions of Setinon where magic and technology collided, experimenting with how best to integrate and isolate the two where applicable. His foremost desire was to understand what conditions led Setinon down its path to create a more durable path for Graelon and Humanity as a whole, as well as to afford them the best opportunities to defeat the *Eye*.

   Alexelio – Settled Perion with Elsa. Only second to Durial in his powers, Alexelio was the artist, the sculptor, and the creator of the Four Brothers. His bloodline created great and sweeping architectural elements inspired of wind, ocean, and starlight. He sought to keep magic, in its most powerful forms, alive at all costs—even if it meant the loss of the knowledge of science and technology. Is considered the most likely candidate for the architect of The World Below and Between.

   Adamian – Settled Terran (Earth).

Goldenbow – Lineage unknown. Origin unknown. Kindred brother to Damon and long-time associate to Kellen the Destroyer. Tier A character whose compass and kinship closely aligns with Damon of Basrat. Professional assassin and living legend on Kaleion, Goldenbow holds a special and central place in the story, which—in time—will be revealed. He is often the source of special counsel to Damon and is Damon's most-trusted ally in all things.

Hadley Mason – Former SRI master Remote Viewer trained, like his father, by Military Intelligence before breaking away from the government's grip upon him and working alongside Ron Stencowsky after the Battle of Warwick. It should be noted Hadley is 6'1." His father, also in this story, in "The Looking Glass," is 6'2," so when you see that delta, I'm referring to the difference between father and son. These are not the same character.

Harrison – An alien hybrid son of one of the very first Men in Black and a deep black operative within one of the Secret Space Program(s).

Hersila – Placeholder for this character.

Herot – Placeholder for this character.

Iain Longbow – A Tier B character and a legendary archer on Perion and companion to Rowarc.

Illirian Starfire – Only child of Jorah and Hannah, grandchild of Grant and Sala, and great-grandchild of Durial and Fara. Born the daughter of a mariner, she often uses maritime idioms and analogies, even when not entirely appropriate. Illirian and Damon's history goes back a millennia or more as her affinity for Damon became far more dangerous over the centuries. Illirian holds many titles: 'Ruler of the Rod of the Nine,' 'Watcher of the Runes of Fate,' 'Guardian of *Durial's Eye*.' The Starlight of Immortality is synonymous with *Durial's Eye* (the original version used by the Great Durial himself), but also affords its master unlimited lifespan without the need for magic. Damon and Illirian's relationship is the definition of the word, 'complicated.' How they sort through that relationship is fundamental to the unmaking of *A Throne of Souls*. From none-too-far a distance, she both meddles and guides Damon's actions by manipulating and controlling his psyche. Some would say she keeps it on the frayed edges of sanity to keep Damon cold, calculated, and ruthless. Illirian's seal is that of a pale-pink rose with white leaves on a tan clay-cast circle. Illirian Starfire also sits on what used to be called Kaleion's Council of Mages.

Joran of Erden – A Tier B character and Royvan Miral's counterpart on Kaleion. A legend in his own right, he has a great, in-depth knowledge of both ancient and modern languages, history, lore, and relics. His power and influences come from his travels and the unearthing of secrets most profound affecting every major seat of power on Kaleion.

Keirill – One of the greatest and most powerful of all mages in history—second only to the Great Durial—Keirill tested the boundaries of what was safe and authorized to risk becoming the greatest of all. His heart was relatively pure and his compass modestly true until his greed and lust for power led him to a path of hate that would result in his hating of his own existence more than anything else. A Tier A character, Keirill's infection of the *Instrument of Humanity's Hate* both drives and vexes Damon into being. Kaylan may have been his physical progeny, but Damon was his most significant achievement for Man or Man's undoing—depending on your perspective.

Kellen the Destroyer – Child of Hersila and Herot, grandchild of Castlier and Freya, great grandchild of Durial and Fara, Kellen is a bane to all things female. There is no fouler misogynist that Kellen the Destroyer. His legendary hatred of women the only forerunner to his infamy. His actions are not entirely self-serving—at least, not on the surface—and his agenda is entirely veiled in mystery. If past is prologue, it won't be good. Like Damon, or because of Damon, he pays his debts and holds his word high in merit. Unlike Damon, he's incapable of seeing women as anything other than something to be used—usually as little more than his personal sex slaves. He has a tense but working relationship with Illirian Starfire only because of Damon's intermediary status between them. Before Damon they found themselves in combat with one another on more than one occasion but have dialed back the hostilities toward one another to see where the Master Plan is going and where they will fall on opposing sides of it. They may very well need each other, and Damon may very well need them both to work together to unmake *A Throne of Souls*. Kellen also sits on what was formerly called Kaleion's Council of Mages. A Tier A character, Kellen is one of Damon's oldest friends and Allies, but the circle of his trust with Damon has found its limits on a few occasions. He is only afforded what information Damon must provide for him to serve his function within Damon's Master Plan, and that level of trust/distrust extends in both directions, as Kellen has a great secret of his own that greatly impacts Damon and the central storylines. Kellen the Destroyer holds many titles and monikers, 'The Hate of Mankind,' 'The Midnight Morning,' and 'The Flame of Hate.'

Lis – The Genesis input of *A Throne of Souls*, though the Genesis motive stems from Dallia's death. The theft and unjust condemnation of this beautiful soul forever altered the balance of power and became the first stone cast into the pond of Creation that would present and precipitate its unmaking.

Marshall:

> **Ethan** – A Tier B character murdered in the first great battle for Man. Ethan's contributions to that war have yet to be fulfilled.

> **Lynn** – A Tier B character, wife to the murdered Ethan Marshall, and now love of Talemar, Lynn has advanced and grown but has stumbled along the way in her love of a baby not her own. Now the balance of her life belongs to that baby boy. Her hopes and dreams now become his.

Michael Anthony Day – Tier A character and the first love of Elise. Michael is central to many—if not all—threads of the storyline. A great many characters in *A Throne of Souls* fall into categories that are very fluid between the spectrum of good and evil. Many characters in this story are quite far from either end of that spectrum, but Michael Anthony Day is an exception. He is the most extreme example of pure goodness available in this story. He is not without flaw and certainly not without internal conflict, but his compass is the truest (morally speaking) of any character in this story. There is no moral ambiguity in the character of his soul—whatsoever. And, quite possibly, the reincarnation of Emrys Wledig.

Mira Castille – Daughter of Charles and Elizabeth Castille. Dean's list sophomore physicist at the University of Texas at Austin. Intimately close to Damon of Basrat. Mira is a foul-mouthed, mouthy preacher's daughter of a Christian parentage, naughty by nature and rebellious by necessity of survival. Her far-reaching understanding of nature described through mathematics and the laws of physics are her most trusted guide to the new realities exposed to her through Damon and his Master Plan.

Mira (Original) – Long ago, after Dallia's death, he went through many loves and lovers, but the original Mira was special. She held the same passion and mage talents as Damon—though not holding all of his natural abilities. She specialized in the same categories of magic as Damon and was nearly his equal in all things and intellect. She was murdered shortly after her visit to the Graelon Colonial Outpost, as were many of Damon's loves whose orbit was too close for their own survival. Damon and this Mira never married, but they were as close as a couple could be, and her loss took Damon centuries to fully mourn.

Mora – A significantly powerful mage and member of the former Kaleion Council of Mages, this Tier B character held ties with Eldrac, though not by choice. More of a trophy to Eldrac, she once ran in circles close to Damon and now (via Talemar's great magic) finds herself in ever tighter circles with Radin. Mora longs to chart a path for herself of her own making, but fate may have other plans for her—as may *The Eye of Time*.

Morden – A Tier B character and arch nemesis to Damon the Banished. He served as court arcmage to many kings and stewards and had more than one run-in with Damon that didn't fare him well. But, Morden is a powerful sorcerer, home to Kaleion, and one who has never found himself on the same side as Damon—until the latter stages of Damon's Master Plan, where Radin mended old fences of hate between the two and proposed their working together towards a common enemy. Or, enemies common to the Master Plan....

Miss X – A Tier B character high up in the directorship chain of command for Continuity of Government and COG planning.

Quincy Arthur Billings – Once the head of Whitehall and formerly the superior of Michael Anthony Day, Billings was asked by Michael to be his Senior Advisor when elevated to the throne. Since that time and Michael's death, Billings has looked after his children as Elise went in search of Michael's soul.

Quinn – A Tier B character and companion of Iain Longbow and Rowarc. A generic mage of modest-but-growing abilities and a good heart.

Radin d'Aguillon – Biological child of Damon of Basrat and Vosh. Raised by Rowarc (famed retired ranger) and Arella d'Aguillon. A Tier A character central to many threads of the storylines. Has rapidly developing powers and immeasurable potential with morals deeply conflicted by personal experiences and his proximity to Damon. The threads connecting him to his past with Rowarc fade on almost an hourly basis as he grows under Damon's wing but are more persistent than even he understands.

Rathemeer – Placeholder for this character.

Rena Rectovich – A Tier A character, born Carastovich Catarena Rectovich, she is one of a very select few surviving witnesses (other than Damon) to Dallia's death. She heads a massive corporate empire amassed over a thousand years of experience and investments. She has extensive reach—politically, influentially, and otherwise—into every major government on Earth and maintains an Immortal Army that can now operate in daylight, thanks to gene therapy of the genetic code belonging to three young babes (the Blade daughters). Catarena's agenda and Damon's may overlap at times and may conflict at others, but she has long sought out the man she saw robbed a life she thought might make him a totally different person than the man he is today.

Rena's Immortal Army:

Michelle Alexandra Blade – A Tier A character born in Denver, CO to Chase and Marie Blade, Michelle began a successful investigative firm that partnered closely with state and federal government officials. Discovered by and finding herself in reach of Rena's radar, Michelle was offered the opportunity to have something she'd only dreamed of before—but at an immortal price. Michelle's motives and drivers are relatively simple. She loves and adores her daughters, and that drives nearly all of her decisions. She has a healthy distrust for Rena and an even more robust distrust of Damon, but her gut and palpable instincts connect her to both and tell her to hold fast.

Lawna Blade – A Tier B character and wife to Michelle, Lawna's mistrust of Rena is almost legendary. Like Michelle, her driving force is the daughters they share, but her love for Michelle is paramount and affords with it a lethal amount of jealousy. As far as capabilities go, Lawna is likely one of the most dangerous characters in the story.

Ryker – The only child of Elise and Radin, hidden from existence for sake of his own survival. Grandson of Damon the Banished.

Ron Stencowsky – Tier B character, former M1A2 Abrams tank personnel, and now master builder and security director on Eden. Runs in circles close to Damon and is extremely limited in his trust of Damon.

Rowarc d'Aguillon – A Tier B character, he raised Radin from a baby but was and is still conflicted over his absence in Radin's life and the absence of his wife—Arella d'Aguillon. Rowarc carries a great burden of guilt extending from his wife's death and what he now knows to be the death of his biological child lost some twenty years past.

Royvan Miral – Tier A character, legendary adventurer on Perion, and crucial to the Seals thread of the storylines. Many biographical novels have been written of his adventures and his findings. He has a mind for academia, languages, and cultures. He considers himself agnostic but cannot ignore what he has seen and experienced. He's trying—greatly so—to keep an open mind in operating this close to Radin and Damon, but his reservations of Damon's Master Plan run deep.

Royvan Miral's Crew:

Kerrich – Tier B character who grew up with Radin—a man he no longer recognizes due to his close proximity to Damon and Damon's agenda. Kerrich doesn't make pretense of an agenda that he doesn't understand, but in Royvan Miral, he found a man he believes he can trust and has ascribed himself to protégé to Royvan Miral as best he can. The End is upon them regardless, and the only way through this is through it. That much he agrees upon, but how we most safely get from here to the other side is a matter of the most urgent and delicate judgment, and that's where his mistrust of Damon leads him to defer to Royvan Miral—for now.

Levi – Tier B character and member of Royvan Miral's crew. Generally considered Royvan Miral's right-hand man and trusted advisor.

Ham – Tier B character and member of Royvan Miral's crew. A good and hearty soul, more in tune with the big picture than most afford him credit.

Seren – A beautiful soul compromised by hate's reach into her own life and the life of her progeny. A Tier A character whose role in this story changed everything. If not for her, there would be no Unmaking.

Silverstring:

Wraith – A Tier A mage of somewhat compromised values and mysterious background wed to his fraternal twin sister. Like many characters in the story, Wraith is neither good nor evil and wouldn't even fit solidly anywhere on that spectrum. His behaviors are more fluidly fitting to the dynamics of the situations before him. He's very much an agenda-driven character, but his agenda is shut to all but his sister and wife.

Silura – A Tier A very promiscuous character who is a mage and wife to her fraternal twin brother, Wraith. Even more complicated than her twin brother and husband, Silura shrouds herself in mystery and frivolity, masking intentions known only to her. With all the tact of a machine gun, Silura's brutal honesty is generally off-putting to others. As shut as Wraith is to the outside world, Silura is even more so and holds secrets, even from her husband—sometimes especially so. Both Silura and Wraith have silver locks of hair on opposing sides.

Sophia – Dean of the College of Invocation (Basrat, Kaleion). Potentially one of the incarnations of Mira Castille. One who imparted some vital information to Damon when he was but fifteen years of age and not yet a mage.

The Chairman – The right hand of God the Creator. From time immemorial, it was the Prince of Egypt until his immortal shell was slain in combat by Damon of Basrat. Now held by Illirian Starfire.

The Six:

Anna – One of the Six. A Tier B character converted by Lawna Blade into an immortal creature, Anna's history is one of a lust for both power and flesh, but her driving force now is the revenge of her affliction and it threatens to compromise her task that affords her newfound existence. As one of the Six, she has been given a mission that is expected to be carried out, and she knows herself not indispensable in that role.

Asmodeus – Prince of the Abyss. One of the Six.

Castlin – One of the Six. A Tier B character, careful and methodical and not entirely on-board or married to the role to which he was assigned. He has a long history with both Talemar and Eldrac and with Damon by reputation. His allegiances are his own, but which side he falls on may change the balance of power just enough.

Eldrac – One of the Six. Murdered by Damon the Banished.

Lilith – The Great Princess of the Abyss. One of the Six. A Tier A character, Lilith is known for an appearance so perfect and so abhorrent as to make those who look upon her physically ill. With a serpentine tail and flesh that is acidic to all living things, Lilith is a being most vile and with a contempt for Man only surpassed by her need to keep the status quo.

Xarn – One of the Six. A Tier B character, Xarn's lust for sex (with both men and women) is as legendary as her frivolity and volatility. She is quite mad and dangerously powerful with a unique gift for working massive-scale objects that will become apparent in later parts of the story. Her role is one pivotal in relation to the Monuments of Creation.

The Great Talemar – Once married with family, stranded and left behind to a fate unknown and only barely chronicled by books, half-buried by fiction, quarter-buried by time, Talemar is seeking new meaning to his life in a timeline not his own as he tries to leverage the best parts of his past to make better decisions in the future and tries to use the worst parts of his past as fuel to destroy those standing in his path. He knows himself *the One* yet is mystified by how Radin can wear his crown. He secretly seeks the answers to this question, but for now Radin has proven both powerful and useful, and he'll continue to leverage that situation for as long as need be—to buy time—as well as to understand Damon's role and Damon's Master Plan. Talemar has a great deal on his plate as he does all these things, while holding together Humanity on Perion, knowing that role will soon expand as the scrolls expound their reach throughout all the *Seeds of Humanity*. The time for his greatness may have to wait, but it *is* coming.

Terry Goodwin – A Tier B character and leader of Michael Anthony Day's SRR unit on Earth.

Toblain – A Tier B character and living gold dragon.

Voltor – Once a lesser demon, Voltor ascended to great power when allying with Eldrac (and others), who afforded Voltor souls he wouldn't have otherwise held claim over. Voltor's Throne of Souls was obliterated when his immortal shell was destroyed by Damon of Basrat. Voltor is most known for his capture and torment of Radin.

Vosh – Perion arcmage and lover to Damon of Basrat (Kaleion), who together are the biological parents of Radin.

Witches:

Adena – A Tier A character, Adena is the Mother and High Seat of witches for over a thousand years. Adena ruled with the antithesis of her seemingly fragile and delicate frame. Feared by all who knew her, Adena is a formidable foe who demands utter loyalty, and one not to be taken lightly.

Desindra – A Tier B character, Desindra is a legitimate threat to Adena, Desindra's burgeoning guile finds new life in the most unlikely of sources and newfound friendships.

Silvaran – Character definitions forthcoming. As the witch thread becomes more

Charles W. McDonald Jr.

integral in the story, you'll see many more of these characters and their development become front-and-center.

Minna – Character definitions forthcoming. As the witch thread becomes more integral in the story, you'll see many more of these characters and their development become front-and-center.

Sabine – Character definitions forthcoming. As the witch thread becomes more integral in the story, you'll see many more of these characters and their development become front and center.

Xaldran – A Tier B character and living legend of a mage on Perion though his true origins and fate were and still are unknown. Author to a great Tome of Power that articulates the history of Humanity as well as hinting to its fate, Xaldran's true purpose has yet to be fulfilled, but may yet come by that which (and who) have survived him.

Ykstherin – A Tier A character, counsel to both Radin and Talemar, whose history and future is veiled in mystery. This character hints at greatness yet yields the limelight, for it is fleeting, and he is not. Precisely who and what Ykstherin is will become known in time. Don't underestimate this character and his potential in the story.

www.ingramcontent.com/pod-product-compliance
Lightning Source LLC
Chambersburg PA
CBHW051937020726
47501CB00001B/161